PHOENIX
IN THE MIDDLE OF THE ROAD

J.R. BALE

J.R. BALE

Books by J.R. Bale

Phoenix in the Middle of the Road
Cognition Chronicles: The Redstone Legacy

Learn more about the author at www.jrbale.com

Published by CopperKnight Publishing.
www.CopperKnightPublishing.com

This is a work of fiction. Any resemblance of characters to real people is purely coincidental.

The author is a member of the Page Bound Success cooperative marketing group, which can be found at www.PageBoundSuccess.com.

Cover design by Balefire Communications LLC.
No flags were harmed in the creation of this image.

ISBN-10: 0-9967610-2-0
ISBN-13: 978-0-9967610-2-4

ACKNOWLEDGEMENTS

The idea for this book crept up on me slowly. The genesis was my frustration with the sad state of American politics. At first, writing it was a way for me to vent and stay awake while waiting up for my teenage son to get home. Then a very dear friend and colleague, Vivian Fransen, suggested I join her writing group, the Watchung Writers. There, Vivian introduced me to a group of writers, who each week provided excellent critique and encouragement. Special thanks to Gordon McLenithan, Bob Mayers, Pat Rydberg, David Kaplan, Phil Lear, Alan Wohl and most especially Vivian, who is the best proofreader in the Western Hemisphere. This dedication would not be complete if I did not mention the support of my wife and my two sons, including the one who stayed out so late.

This story takes place in the near future.
How far depends upon when you read it.
But that day grows closer every minute.

J.R. BALE

CHAPTER 1

Eight sat around the polished oak table, completely exhausted and numb by the events of the last few hours.

"Is what I've been told about Mr. Hingecliff true?" Justice Sisk asked.

"Yes, Madame Justice," answered the man at the other end of the table. "And that is why we need your guidance."

"My guidance?"

"As to what to do next."

"Look," the most junior senator interrupted, "we've been through constitutional crises before. The country survived. I mean, we survived Watergate."

"Senator," Justice Sisk countered, "Despite the insistence of some *commentators*, Watergate was not a constitutional crisis. Neither was the recent election, despite some irregularities. Sometimes certain politicians have failed to follow the Constitution. However, the failing was not in the Constitution. Tonight is different. Nothing in that revered document, or in any other law, covers this situation."

"Isn't there something in the Constitution to guide us?" the man at the other end of the table asked.

"Only its spirit. The Presidency, the Congress and the Supreme Court, for the moment, are completely paralyzed. We are in a legal oblivion."

The word *oblivion* echoed uncomfortably in the psyche of everyone present, and probably beyond.

How had they come to what many would describe as the country's darkest hour? This was a crisis years in the making.

ॐ ॐ ৎ ৎ

"So the deed is done?" David Grant inquired, knowing full well the answer.

"Yup," Arturo Fuentes confirmed. "Calibrent signed the papers with great flourish. You should've seen the grin on ol' Egan's face. I know it's a bit late, but I still think you could have gotten more."

David was tempted. "No," he said firmly, tired of Fuentes's well-meaning nagging. "The cost of getting more was just too high. I have no interest in that kind of greed."

"I still say you're a soft touch," Fuentes said, getting in his last taunt.

"I doubt Darren would say that," David, sighing.

"Well, that's another matter altogether. He deserved what he got, and you shouldn't feel guilty about it."

David nodded, and then pulled himself together. "Anyway, it's time to inform the troops."

"I hope the troops appreciate what you did for them."

"Well Art, if they don't, you can explain it through the grapevine."

"There's going to be a lot of anxiety," Fuentes warned.

"I know," David agreed, as he opened the door to see who was in the main cubicle area, or "cube farm" as some called it. Diana Gennaro was just leaving her cubicle.

"Excuse me, Diana. Could you gather everyone together?"

"In the conference room?"

"Yeah."

"What's up?"

"I'd rather save it for the announcement."

Diana heard the word "announcement" as if it had been from a loudspeaker. David Grant didn't make formal announcements. The atmosphere of Simplexia Software had always been casual, ever since David Grant founded the company seven years earlier.

"Is 20 minutes soon enough?" Diana asked.

"Sure."

Within 15 minutes, about two dozen Simplexia employees were stuffed into the conference room.

"Okay," David started nervously. "I have three announcements. First, we got the LFX contract." This was a small contract, but in light of a difficult economy, any new business was good news. *Best to start with good news.*

"Second, as a couple of you know," David added. "I had to let Darren Sagamore go."

"It's about time," mumbled one of the women in the back. While few knew of Sagamore's dismissal, it was a surprise to no one.

The last announcement was the proverbial other shoe waiting to drop. *Now, the hard part.*

"As you know, our attorney Art Fuentes and I have been talking to Calibrent Systems about a strategic alliance or joint venture. However, the result of those talks has brought about a different opportunity." David felt he had delayed the bombshell long enough. "We've just made a deal with Calibrent for them to purchase Simplexia."

This was followed by murmurs of shock. David had been in a merger before, when he worked for a large corporation. Fear and apprehension among employees in a merger was never an easy thing to manage.

"Listen, I worked for Calibrent for years. They're good people. More importantly, they have an intensive distribution network that could really benefit our products. One of my conditions for the deal was that no one gets laid off, which wasn't a problem for them, since they really value our products and the employees who create them. Now, I'm sure you all have a lot of questions."

ᛞ ᛞ ᚳ ᚳ

Sara Grant was running late. Her boss, Matt Cartwright, had wanted some last minute revisions to the roof plans of the city center they were designing. As a senior architect at Gunther & Cartwright, Sara could have delegated this simple task to one of her staff, but she wanted an excuse to be late. She also told herself it was important to maintain her AutoCAD skills.

David had not returned any of her text messages all day. She knew he had a big deal brewing, but was annoyed he hadn't taken time to text her. *Men!* She decided her husband's punishment would be leftovers. He was not fond of leftovers.

ᛞ ᛞ ᚳ ᚳ

Robert Hingecliff had been waiting in the White House lobby for almost forty minutes. He noted with some amusement the faces of the new administration. They were young faces, a bit unsure of themselves, yet beaming at their incredible fortune of actually working in the White House. Of course, it was different for Hingecliff, now a seasoned veteran of Washington politics. It was his sixty-third birthday. Yet, instead of having a birthday dinner with his children and grandchildren as originally planned, he was spending it waiting for a job interview. Of course, no one would be so crass as to call it that. It was a "consultation." However, it was not just any job he reminded himself.

A young beaming face arrived to usher him in.

"Mr. Hingecliff, I'm Amy Greene. The President is ready for you now," Amy said respectfully. Yet, she almost bubbled over at being able to say the words. "Have you ever been to the White House before?" she asked as they headed toward the Oval Office.

"Yes, I used to work here."

She nodded, seeming deflated by his response.

"Yet, it never gets old, does it?" he added kindly.

"No, it doesn't," she said with a broad smile. Amy walked up to the peephole in the Oval Office door to make sure the President was ready. Then, she entered.

"Mr. President, Mr. Hingecliff is here to see you."

"Great. Robert, come on in," said Gregory Farnum, the newly inaugurated President of the United States.

3

Another bright and energetic president, thought Hingecliff, as he walked into the Oval Office.

Farnum had won in a landslide over the incumbent Republican, campaigning on "New Ideas for Old Problems." During the campaign, Hingecliff observed that people were drawn to Gregory Farnum. He enjoyed handsome good looks, yet not so much that he would be accused of being a pretty boy. He could muster the personal warmth of Bill Clinton, but had also acquired the cool self-discipline of Barack Obama.

"I haven't had an opportunity to congratulate you, Mr. President," Hingecliff said, "on such a well-run campaign."

"Thank you, Robert," the President responded cordially. "I'm sorry we haven't had a chance to sit down before this. After Election Day, everything became a hyperactive blur. I'm still getting used to the title, and just about everything else around this place."

Hingecliff was sure Farnum had endured similar conversations several times a day for the past two weeks since Inauguration Day. Farnum thanked him for his support in the campaign and was quite specific with the details. Hingecliff was sure a presidential aide supplied him with particulars too tedious for a candidate to retain. Farnum executed this ritual with the same discipline he had applied to his campaign.

This part of the conversation ended with Hingecliff's pledge to do anything in his power to support Farnum's presidency and agenda. Of course, Farnum wouldn't say anything to directly suggest an offer of a cabinet position.

"Robert," he began, "I'd like to pick your brain on how you think the Department of Commerce should be run."

This caught Hingecliff off-guard. He felt his background was more appropriate for Treasury. But he wouldn't flinch. Seasoned Washingtonians didn't flinch.

"I thought you were bringing in Sean Castleton to head Commerce," commented Hingecliff. Of course, he knew the truth. The vetting process had discovered Castleton's mistress. Castleton's indiscretions were already known to Hingecliff. Many had known. Hingecliff had marveled at the stupidity of those who expected their status to isolate them from scandal when it did just the opposite.

"No decision has been made on Commerce yet," Farnum replied. "But I'd like your opinion on the department's role in economic policy."

And so, the interview began in earnest.

Sara Grant arrived home at 6:45. The Grant home was their sanctuary. Sara had designed it herself, contained many traditional elements providing a warm and cozy environment. It was quite spacious without appearing ostentatious.

"You're late," David called out from the bedroom.

"Don't worry. We have plenty of leftovers in the frig, ready to go," she assured him.

"Well, Wendy's having her overnight at Nancy Garthwell's. And Chris is hanging out with his friends. So, I made a reservation at Fortella's."

So much for punishment, Sara thought.

"Are we celebrating something?"

"Maybe."

"So, did you make a distribution deal with Calibrent or not?"

"Kind of."

"Kind of? What does that mean?"

David sighed. "I'm selling them the company."

"What?" she cried out in shock.

"For ten million dollars."

Sara was stunned. "Ten million?" It took a moment for the figure to sink in. "You sold Simplexia, the company you spent years building, for only ten million dollars?" Sara wasn't a financial expert, but she knew the company was worth more.

"Well," David said, "that and five million Calibrent stock options."

Sara realized this might be far more reasonable. Like most people, Sarah had heard the term, but didn't actually know how a stock option worked. David had received some options many years before when he worked for Calibrent and his previous company before that. However, in each case they were small bonuses, so she didn't pay attention.

"Remind me exactly how a stock option works," she said.

"It's the right to buy a share of stock at a predetermined price."

"What price?"

"Actually today's price, $27.80."

"Couldn't we buy the stock at that price anyway?"

"Today, yes. But when the price goes up in a two years, I'll still be able to buy it at $27.80."

"And if the price goes down?"

"Then, I don't buy. Upside, with no downside."

"Except you no longer have your company. Why on Earth did you do this?"

"Did I mention ten million dollars and the stock options?" David said, smiling a self-satisfied grin.

His wife gave him a withering look. David realized he miscalculated the impact of this news.

"Sara," he began in a more serious tone. "As you know, we've been getting fierce competition. A lot of people have been trying to copy our products, both legally and illegally, especially overseas. Especially in China. We had to do something. We needed Calibrent's distribution power to expand and combat the pirating. And the only way to do that was to sell them the company."

"Why didn't you tell me you were contemplating this?"

"Well, I wasn't completely sure it would come to this. Art and I tried to negotiate an alternative. But in the end, it was the most logical choice. The only reason not to go ahead would have been my own ego. I suppose I didn't tell you because I hoped it wouldn't come to that." He sighed. "Plus, you're friendly with Pam and Randy from the office. How would you feel not telling them this was coming?"

"What will happen to them?"

"They'll be fine. Part of the agreement was that no one can be laid off for at least two years. That's why I had to terminate Darren Sagamore."

"Was he harassing women again?"

"No, but he was stealing competitors' code. That, on top of the harassment, meant he had to go. In all good conscience, I couldn't saddle the others or Calibrent with him."

"So, what about you?"

"I was planning on becoming a couch potato, specializing in soap operas and reality TV," he smirked. Sara grabbed the nearest sofa pillow and hit him with it. She wasn't quite as mad now that she knew the entire situation.

"I mean, are you going to return to Calibrent?"

"No. I don't think so. It would feel weird going back. It would feel like taking a step backward. Actually, I'll be phased out slowly," David explained. "First, I'll continue to manage the company, while training a Calibrent manager. Then, I'll be a consultant."

"That's going to be very difficult for you, becoming less relevant at the company you built from the ground up."

"Yeah," he sighed. "But honestly, I didn't see any other way."

"So, now what?"

"I'm sure something will come up."

CHAPTER 2

Now, over a month since the sale of Simplexia, Sara Grant had become accustomed to finding David already home when she arrived from work. He was usually watching CNBC. She suspected he was looking for his next business opportunity. Although more recently, he could be found watching CNN, or MSNBC and FOX in a split-screen.

"Can you believe it?" David called out. "Farnum's appointed Robert Hingecliff as Secretary of Commerce. In this economy? The man's never run a business in his life! Never created a single job! I really hope I don't regret voting for Farnum."

Sara couldn't have cared less. Until there was a Secretary of Architecture, politics didn't really matter to her that much. "And hello to you, too."

"Sorry," David said, turning off the television. "How was your day?"

"Actually, not bad," Sara answered. "Gunther & Cartwright has been asked to bid on a new courthouse in Yardley. If we win the bid, I'll be the project manager."

"That's great."

"Well, we haven't won the bid yet. How was your day?"

"Boring, but I've made a decision."

"You didn't sell our house, did you?" Sara asked. Even though it had been over a month since David sold the company, she was still slightly annoyed over his unilateral decision. Both Sara and David were confident and independent professionals. They shared their successes and frustrations, as any couple did. However, as long as it didn't impact their family, they didn't feel the need to consult each other on every professional decision. However, David selling his company clearly tested the frontiers of their mutual independence.

"No, no, I didn't sell anything. I'm going to teach some classes over at Winton College."

"Hmm. Is this going to be a full-time gig?"

"No, I'll just be an adjunct. The head of the business department appreciated my background. But since I didn't have any teaching experience, he only offered me a couple of courses. Who knows? If I don't screw it up, maybe he'll offer me more. We'll see."

"Good, I've been worried about you," Sara said. "You need something to do. You know, Tom Burke asked me if you'd like to run for Embler Town Council again."

"No thanks. I did my time on the council, hearing people complain about everything from leaf pickup to how high their taxes were. Besides, the current council is doing just fine."

"Can't blame a girl for trying."

"What? You don't like having me around the house?"

"One word, couch potato."

"Actually, that's two words."

"Shut up and kiss me, *Professor*."

ᘇ ᘆ ᘅ ᘄ

During the following months, David Grant transitioned from CEO to adjunct business professor. Winton College was a small four-year college nestled in the southern Pocono Mountains, just north of Philadelphia.

David enjoyed teaching more than he had expected. The broad mix of students challenged and energized him. Some struggled because they came from poor school systems or bad neighborhoods. He found particular satisfaction helping students who were struggling.

Once in a business ethics class, Latisha, a young student from Philadelphia, proclaimed, "Professor Grant, I know you have to teach us this stuff, but I know that's not how business is really done. You're say'n that successful people are all ethical-like, but that's all crap."

"Really?" he replied. The class waited to see how their instructor handled this challenge.

"Yeah, folks do whatever they can get away with."

"Like Madoff? Or Enron?"

"I don't know who Madoff and Enron are."

"Well, Bernie Madoff, and some of the people who worked *at* Enron went to prison."

Some of the students laughed.

"But there are others out there," she insisted. "Right?"

"That's probably true, but most successful people are ethical. I don't say they're perfect. And people will admittedly differ about the gray areas. But let me ask you this, would you rather do business with someone who has a track record of ethical behavior? Or someone who is known to pull a fast one from time to time?"

The students all agreed they rather work with ethical people.

"No offense, Professor, but you're just not in the real world," she insisted.

"You mean like running a real company?"

"Yeah!"

"I ran my own company for seven years. Before that, I worked for two Fortune 500 companies. And in that time, I never bribed anyone or misrepresented my product. And I always kept my word, even if there wasn't a contract."

"When you say you owned your own company, you mean like Professor Harringer who's a consultant?" she said in a mocking tone, especially when she pronounced "consultant."

"No, I had two dozen employees when I sold the company last year."

"See, you betrayed your own employees!" Latisha yelped in triumph.

"Not at all," he said with a smile to show he wasn't worried. "I sold it to a company that promised to retain my employees. In fact, since taking over, they've added employees."

"Did they get their pay cut?"

"No, in fact they now have a better healthcare plan than I could offer."

David enjoyed this type of exchange, and never minded students challenging with him. He found it usually made for a better exploration of a topic. But today time was running out. Some of the students were already packing their bags.

"OK, don't forget to read Chapter 5 on corporate governance for next class." Most of the student rushed out of the classroom.

"Professor, how much did you sell your company for?" asked one of the remaining students.

"I'm sorry, that's confidential." Actually, Calibrent wouldn't have minded, but he didn't want students thinking of him as the "rich" professor.

While David enjoyed the classroom, he was more intrigued by the academic culture outside the classroom. Most striking was that beyond the business department, many faculty members harbored distinctly anti-business attitudes.

One English professor, who discovered David had sold his company, referred to him as an "evil capitalist." David had never really thought of himself as a capitalist, merely an entrepreneur. That instructor didn't want to hear about how David had secured a good future for his former employees. He was surprised how some supposedly thoughtful academics could be so closed-minded.

One exception was Fred Arkin, an adjunct professor who taught history. In fact, they had developed a friendship. To support himself, Arkin taught at three different colleges, two in New Jersey where he lived. Twice a week, he crossed the Delaware River to teach courses at Winton.

Breaks in their schedules coincided. They'd often talk in the adjunct office, which served as a home base for the part-time instructors to prepare lessons, grade papers and tests, and meet with students. The dingy room in the basement of one of the older buildings had empty staplers, a copier that constantly jammed, and an odd collection of mismatched chairs and tables. The computers usually worked despite using antiquated operating systems. David had offered to upgrade them, but was told of union restrictions on who could perform maintenance and upgrades. David quickly discovered the primary use of the room was extended coffee clutches and academic debates. So David and Fred Arkin did likewise. Their conversations often turned to politics.

"The problem is that only extremists are motivated to make a difference," Arkin explained. "Moderates are generally apathetic because from their perspective, the world isn't that far from their worldview. But if you're a liberal or conservative, the world is just too far from your ideal."

"Well, I think few like the world the way it is these days."

"True, but the extremes are always more motivated. Look how Henderson's right-wing agenda motivated the Left. And we're already seeing the Right ratcheting up the rhetoric against Farnum."

"But you do have moderates in both parties," David countered.

"Yes, but they're an endangered species. And the political bases and leadership are anything but moderate. On the Right, you've got a bunch of Bible-thumping zealots trying to dictate *everyone's* values, and turn America into a Christian theocracy. They're joined by a bunch of *laissez-faire* capitalists who think even the slightest business regulation is an abomination to free enterprise. Oh, and I'm sorry, I forgot the gun nuts who think every kindergartener should have an AK-47."

"I think they prefer the M-16. Higher quality," David quipped. "Plus, it's American-made."

"Then on the Left," Arkin continued undeterred. "You've got the trial lawyers who want more regulation only so they can generate infinite litigation with all the associated legal fees. Add to that, social engineers who want the government to create a nanny-state to dole out money we don't have at the drop of a hat, with no concern for economic reality."

David laughed. He was becoming accustomed to Fred's rants.

"Okay, okay, I know I'm a little over the top, but these assholes drive me nuts," Arkin admitted. "Look at Farnum's campaign, 'New Ideas for Old Problems.' Has he brought a single new idea in yet? They're all recycled entitlement programs. And the pork train goes on forever. My state university in Jersey was just awarded another million dollars for cranberry and blueberry research! I love blueberries, but they're not exactly a national priority."

"I agree both sides spend more than we have. No business could be run this way."

"No household either."

"It's all these campaign contributions," David added. "In the *Citizens United* case, the Supreme Court ruled money is free speech, but in reality, it's bribery."

"Exactly!" Arkin cried out, finally finding someone on campus who understood his viewpoint.

David and Fred were becoming fast friends, something that would change both their lives.

ᘓ ᘓ ᘕ ᘕ

Erin Korelev, VP at Kadler Steele, sat nervously in the U.S. Attorney's office. She had quit smoking months ago, but now desperately craved a cigarette. Unfortunately, smoking was prohibited in federal buildings. What she was about to do would be considered treason if her firm were a country. From now on, she would forever be known as the "Kadler Steele Whistleblower." And in a few moments, there would be no turning back. It was far easier to be brave over the telephone. The heavy mahogany office door opened, revealing Kevin O'Hara, the heavyset U.S. Attorney for the Southern District of New York.

"Ms. Korelev?"

CHAPTER 3

Amy Greene was always at her desk outside the Oval Office by 6:00 a.m., although President Farnum rarely arrived before 6:30. Her start time was dictated by the White House Chief of Staff, Harris Carver. If the White House had a train, Harris Carver would make it run on time.

"Good morning, Amy," Carver said in a flat tone, while inspecting the President's morning briefs laid out on the credenza.

"Good morning, Mr. Carver." Carver didn't seem to hear Amy as he thoughtfully rearranged the folders.

"OK, we're good to go here," he said. Amy quickly moved the briefs to the President's desk in the order Carver had determined.

Just then, Amy's phone rang. Darius Jackson, the Residence Manager, was giving her the morning signal. President Farnum was walking over from the Residence.

"Mr. Carver, the President's on his way."

Carver nodded. Within a minute the President walked in.

"Good morning, everyone," Farnum called out.

"Good morning, Mr. President," they said in unison.

"This morning's briefs are on your desk, sir," Amy informed him.

"Thank you, Amy. By the way, how is your brother doing?"

"The doctor said his femur was broken in two spots," she answered, referring to her brother's recent skiing accident. Carver gave Amy the look to cut it short. "But he's on the mend. Thank you for asking."

"Good. Tell him I was asking about him."

"Thank you, Mr. President. I will."

Carver followed the President into the Oval Office. Farnum glanced at the brief on his desk. "I see the North Koreans are being bad boys again."

"Yes, they attempted another major cyber attack last night. No damage, but General Harcroft from Cyber Command is ready to brief you."

"This seems to be the only thing the North Koreans know how to do with the Internet."

"Yes, sir. Also, Senator Carstairs wants to meet with you about the education bill. He might be useful if we need bipartisan support. He believes—"

Farnum held up his hand. "I spoke with the Attorney General at last night's dinner. Warrenburg says there may be something serious stirring at Kadler Steele. Apparently, they have a high-level whistleblower."

"Really? I'll keep an eye on it, Mr. President."

"Good, I don't want whatever this is blowing up on us, or at least at the wrong time."

As soon as Carver's morning briefing with the President concluded, Carver double-timed it back to his office. "Karen, get me that S.O.B. Warrenburg on the line."

Carver closed his door and sat down at his desk. Karen dutifully made the call.

"Mr. Attorney General, I understand you had a conversation with the President last night....Uh huh...No, I mean Kadler Steele....Well, let me tell you something. We have a process. Like anyone, the President only has so much bandwidth. Information has to be prioritized. That's why we have goddamn channels. So far, this Kadler Steele thing is nothing, especially compared with this North Korean incident and the education bill. But now, you've cluttered the President's radar unnecessarily. Do you read me?...Good... Next time you want to have small talk with the President, make it sports or the weather. Now, since you've already stuck your foot in it, tell me what you have on Kadler so far."

80 80 03 03

One Thursday afternoon, Fred Arkin and David were in the "cave" as they had started calling the adjunct office. "So, what are you doing next Saturday afternoon?" Fred asked.

"Nothing planned." David answered, as he made copies of a quiz for his management class. "Why?"

"There's someone I'd like you to meet. He's going to be speaking in Philadelphia on Saturday. He thinks like we do, politically I mean. What do you say?"

"I don't think so. Sara's going to be away at an architecture conference. I have to watch Wendy."

"He's only going to be in Philadelphia over the weekend."

"I'd need a sitter for Wendy."

"Bring her along."

"Uh, she's only nine."

"Come on, I'll buy dinner."

"You're a starving adjunct. You need to save your money."

"It'll be worth it, I promise."

"All right, maybe. I can see if Wendy can stay with the Garthwells. So, what's this guy's name?"

"Jason Kennerly."

80 80 03 03

After graduating as a political science major at Northwestern University, Jason Kennerly had taken the unusual step of starting his own political party, the Centrist Patriots Party. Many of his college friends thought he was crazy to start such a venture. Like many of his generation, he

13

was quite adept at creating websites, blogging, making Internet videos, and leveraging various forms of social media.

Through party donations, he was almost able to support himself as the only party staff member. Whenever there were sufficient funds, he would travel to meet members and promote the centrist cause. Tonight, he was giving a talk at a library in Philadelphia.

David and Fred were late arriving. Kennerly had already begun. Despite his youthful and slightly nerdy appearance, Kennerly had the cadence and vocabulary of someone older.

"In any population, regardless of what is being measured, most people will fall in the middle." Kennerly pointed to a normal distribution or bell curve on the screen. "It applies to almost any population attribute you can think of, height, weight, or shoe size. It also can be applied to political views in a left-right construct. Most people are politically moderate, as represented in the middle bump. In fact, the more intellectually honest they are, the more centrist they are. The liberals are represented by the small tail to the left. And, the conservatives by the right tail."

"Yet, in almost a paradox, the extreme power structures have always wielded the most power. The tails are literally wagging the dog."

"Someone should explain to him what the word 'literally' literally means." David whispered.

"Shhh," Fred whispered.

"The reason is simple," Kennerly continued. "People in the extremes are usually the most discontented. They are, by virtue of their extremeness, the most motivated to change things. A friend of mine put it quite simply: 'Whoever cares the most, wins.'"

However as the polarity of the parties increase, each represents the majority less and less. We are forced to choose the lesser of two evils. What holds most Americans back is the lack of a vibrant centrist organization. The Centrist Patriot's Party can provide that organization."

Kennerly proceeded to lay out the Centrist Patriots Party state-by-state national strategy, finally ending with a call to join the CPP.

"So what do you think?" Fred asked as the audience's applause began to subside.

"Interesting guy."

"You're not impressed?"

"I agree with his ideas, but he's a little on the young side. Can he even shave?"

"Don't be nasty," Fred insisted. "Let's go talk to him,"

"Why?"

"Humor me."

After a number of questioners departed, Fred dragged David up to meet Kennerly.

"Fred!" Kennerly exclaimed. "I didn't think you were going to make it."

"Good to see you, Jason. I'd like you to meet a friend of mind, David Grant. He teaches at Winton with me."

"Nice to meet you, David."

"Same here." David replied politely.

"Jason has built up quite a following," Fred said. "How many CPP members now? Forty thousand?"

"Forty six thousand," Kennerly corrected him.

"Ever expanding," Fred exclaimed. "See David, we are not alone. There is a centrist third party on the rise."

"Perhaps."

"Ah, the polite skeptic," Kennerly said.

"Jason, I mean no offense, but you're never going to get anywhere with your current strategy," David warned.

"I've grown accustomed to naysayers to the centrist cause."

"You misunderstand me. I like your ideas and your passion, but you're going about it the wrong way. You're spreading yourself and your people too thin. You've got people across the country trying to win races that are too little and too big."

"Go on," Jason said. "I'm all ears."

"I look at market opportunities. If you're small, you can't sell into every market. Your competition is too powerful. You need to find a niche market. Running a candidate for president is a waste. Farnum's campaign alone spent nearly three billion. Henderson spent even more. There's no way to compete with that."

"Yeah, but just running a candidate gives us a platform to get our ideas heard."

"Running and losing so big makes people take you even less seriously."

"We're also running in smaller elections at the local level: mayors, councils, etc."

"I was a councilman for four years. No one cared about my political philosophy. They just wanted their garbage picked up and the fire engines to arrive quickly. These town council and county supervisor races are too small to be noticed nationally and only deal with local issues anyway. As for getting heard, nothing succeeds like success."

"Alright Mr. Grant, what do you suggest?"

"Congress."

"We had eight people run last election."

"That's your problem right there. You need to focus on a single Senate or House race. Come to think of it, the House would probably be best. Less expense. More local geography for mobilizing your sales force."

"Sales force?"

"I mean your campaign workers," David explained. "Find the district that's most vulnerable, one where the voters aren't too liberal or conservative, one that hasn't been gerrymandered into a safe seat. If you can find a district where there's no incumbent running, so much the better. Then, focus all your forces there."

"Isn't that putting all the eggs in one basket?"

"Let's be honest," David said, "you don't have that many eggs to begin with."

"What do you think, Jason?" Fred asked.

"I'm not sure," Kennerly mumbled, feeling a little uncomfortable with the overwhelming logic.

"I told you, David was a smart guy," Fred continued. "Let's get him on our side."

"What do you mean?" David asked.

"We need state chairs," Kennerly said.

"I chair the New Jersey state party," Fred explained. "You could be the Pennsylvania chair."

"So that's what this is all about," David realized out loud.

CHAPTER 4

The following week, David was in the adjunct cave, reviewing a lesson plan when Fred Arkin came bouncing in.

"Hey, David, I'm glad I caught you. I was thinking about what you said last week."

"About what?" David said, with a wary expression.

"The Centrist Patriot Party. I spent the weekend looking at all the House races last election," Fred said, as he sat down at one of the more dilapidated tables. "Following your suggestion, I found 17 districts where the winner won by less than one percent."

"Have you told Jason Kennedy?"

"Kennerly," Fred corrected him. "And yes, I did. I ranked them in order. See." Fred handed him a spreadsheet. "Unfortunately, the five closest races were in states where the CPP has no real presence. But then I noticed that Congressman Sheldon Lannier won by less than 800 votes."

"Sheldon Lannier is my congressman."

"Yes, he is," Fred said, beaming.

David looked up at him, realizing what was being implied. Fred's grin grew bigger.

"No," David said.

"It was your strategy," Fred insisted.

"Yeah, but..."

"Listen, I spoke with Jason. He said if you agree to run, he'll have the entire party back you."

"This is insane," David protested.

"Why? You told Jason it was our best shot."

"But sometimes best shots aren't good enough."

"David, let me be indelicate. Most people can't afford to run for office unless they're career politicians, or if they don't need to worry about job security. You're one of the few people who has enough money to put it where your mouth is."

David sighed. "That's great, but I don't know anything about running for Congress."

"Well, I do. I know all the campaign requirements and rules, well for New Jersey. But I'll learn all the Pennsylvania ones, I promise."

"I still don't know," David said, rubbing his forehead.

"While you're thinking about it, let's go talk to a real-life congressman."

"What? You think Sheldon Lannier will give me advice on how to beat him?"

"Actually, I had someone else in mind: Marcus Finn."

"The name rings a bell, but—"

"He was a congressman from Wisconsin. He retired four years ago."

"Another friend of yours?" David asked guardedly.

"No, actually I've never met the man," Fred said.

"Well, I'm not flying to Wisconsin."

"Good, because he's not there right now."

"Where is he?" David asked, fearing the answer.

"New Jersey."

"Is this a Jersey joke?"

"I'm from New Jersey. I don't make Jersey jokes."

"Sorry," David mumbled.

"Marcus Finn is giving a series of lectures at the Leeson School of Government. He's lecturing tomorrow night on 'The Failure of Bipartisanship'."

"Another centrist?"

"Not exactly. He's a Republican, but he chaired the Republicans for Farnum committee."

ဆ ဆ ﭺ ﭺ

Marcus Finn looked every inch an elder statesman, from his silver gray hair combed back majestically to his kindly smile. Yet, there was also a steely-eyed look he could turn on or off as needed. But he rarely needed it anymore. Finn was enjoying his retirement on the lecture circuit. The Palmer School brought him the type of audience he liked best—intelligent, but not particularly partisan. No longer did he have to deliver barn-burner speeches to pander to voters. He could say what he meant, and have a little fun with doing so.

"Good evening. Before I begin, I'd like to thank the University and the Leeson School for having me here tonight. It's important that we nurture political discourse that is honest and frank, but also civil. Before I talk about bi-partisanship, we must examine what it actually is. Partisanship is a natural process hardwired into our very DNA, as naturally selected for as the opposable thumb. Any creature that will cooperate with another will have a greater chance of survival. Ask any biologist. That's why fish swim in schools, birds fly in flocks, and land mammals run in herds. To create alliances is a survival instinct. But these alliances are only formed with one's own kind. The trout does not swim with the pike. The goose does not fly with the hawk. And so the Republican does not caucus with the Democrat." This was met with mild laughter.

"Bipartisanship, if real, is an anomaly of human nature. To be honest, bipartisanship is not a value that most politicians hold dear. Outside of those rare occasions of mutual threat, it usually just serves as a fig leaf for one's own legislation. It's a word invoked to make oneself seem more cooperative, when usually the opposite is true."

Finn proceeded to share various anecdotes of his time in Congress. Most were humorous, but also quite telling of how dysfunctional government had become.

"One time I went into the Democratic cloakroom, looking for Congressman Mike Chilton. With the looks I got, one would have thought I was a Jap Zero flying into Pearl Harbor. To break the ice, I asked if Chilton could come out and play. All of a sudden, he was the Zero."

Again, many laughed, although David noticed an Asian man with a rather grim look on his face, clearly displeased with Finn's analogy.

"Our problems, the economy and the environment among others, are approaching critical mass. Real bipartisanship is needed. To honestly address these matters will require a lot of pain, one way or another, sooner or later. Unfortunately, public pain makes each side vulnerable to attack from their opposition. However, we need cooperation between the two sides like never before, or a miraculous change in human nature. I hope the next generation will find the strength and courage to make it happen. Thank you for your kind attention this evening, and God bless."

There was a small reception after Finn's speech. One of the student volunteers brought their honored speaker a tumbler of scotch.

"Glenfiddich?" he asked.

"No, my name is Steve. I don't know any Glen."

Finn just laughed. "Thank you, Steve," he said, accepting the glass from the confused intern.

Fred Arkin moved determinedly through the throngs of attendees toward Finn. "Good evening, Congressman Finn. I'm Fred Arkin. I really enjoyed your talk,"

"Thank you, Mr. Arkin."

"I have a friend who is planning on running for the House as an Independent."

Finn raised his eyebrows and smiled. "That's quite an undertaking. You realize few Independents have ever made it into the House or Senate."

"I know Congressman, but that doesn't mean it's impossible."

"True, very true. Is your quixotic candidate here tonight?"

"He's right over there." Arkin signaled to David. "David, over here. The Congressman wants to meet you."

"Well, I didn't exactly say that," Finn murmured, slightly amused.

"Congressman, I enjoyed your talk very much," David said.

"Thank you. Mr...uh?"

"Grant, David Grant."

"Anyway, Mr. Arkin here tells me you're running for Congress as an Independent."

"I'm considering it."

"Considering it, eh? And why would you consider such a foolhardy venture?"

"I suppose I'm tired of seeing both parties ignoring the majority of the citizens to put forth their own partisan agendas. No offense."

"None taken. But politics is a fickle and unforgiving profession. I had been a loyal Republican for decades, representing my constituents fairly well I believed. But then, I was targeted as a RINO," Finn said, taking another swig of his single-malt.

"Republican In Name Only," Fred confirmed.

"Exactly. In my day, it was an honor and a privilege to serve in Congress. Now, Congress has the lowest approval rating ever, and deservedly so. It's degenerated into tribal warfare, even within the tribes. Mr. Grant, if you're serious, understand that running for Congress requires a serious commitment of time, resources, and sanity."

"Although I did a stint on my town council, I am concerned about not having enough political experience, in both running and governing. Perhaps I'm a fool."

"Oh, you probably are. No offense," Finn said.

David smiled at the returned barb. "So what would you recommend?" he asked.

"In all good conscience, not running," Finn chortled, taking another sip of his scotch. "But if you insist, you'll need to find an issue that can magically separate you from both parties. Of course, all the good issues have been taken, triangulated, and polarized."

"What about the ever-increasing national debt?"

"Ah, a deficit hawk, a truly endangered species, despite all that Tea Party business years ago. True, it meets the criteria. Unfortunately, the deficit is the infinite chasm from which all federal politicians draw their power. It is the ability to buy votes by creating jobs in one's district. Or, pay off one's true constituents, the contributors."

"But eventually it will cause an economic catastrophe."

"The key word is *eventually*. It's like playing catch with a time bomb. The thing is to not be around when it goes off. Why do you think I retired?"

"The trouble is that everyone else in the country will be around when it goes off."

"I'm afraid so," Finn said

"Excuse me, Congressman," interrupted a young woman from the school. "The president of the university is leaving soon, and we still need a photograph of you two together."

"Of course," he said. He turned back to David. "Mr. Grant, for whatever it's worth, I wish you luck."

"Thank you, Congressman" David said, as Finn headed away for the photo opportunity. David smiled at Fred.

"I guess," Fred said. "Congressman Finn wasn't as encouraging as I hoped."

৪০ ৪০ ৫৫ ৫৪

The phone rang on Harris Carver's desk. He was expecting Peter Warrenburg's call. "Mr. Attorney General."

"Good evening, Harris. Please note I am going through channels," Warrenburg said pointedly. "The Kadler Steele whistleblower has painted a pretty grim picture. I firmly believe it now deserves a place on the President's radar."

"I understand. I'll set up a meeting when the President gets back from California. In the meantime, tell me what you have so far."

ஐ ஐ ௧ ௧

The following Monday, David checked his e-mail. There were the usual excuse messages from students, requests from Calibrent people for information, and the ubiquitous spam. However, he was surprised to find a message from Marcus Finn:

Dear Mr. Grant,

Sorry if I was a little flippant the other night at the Leeson School. The extra glass of scotch gets me every time. Running for public office is a challenge for anyone, but it is an undertaking worthy of those of honorable spirit. I hope my glibness did not discourage you. If you are serious about running for Congress, I suggest you call Ellen Langford. She's a savvy political operative with plenty of campaign experience. And I happen to know she's available at the moment. Her contact information is attached.

Kindest regards,
Marcus Finn

David pondered this and all he had heard in the last week.

CHAPTER 5

A Brooks Brothers-clad Robert Hingecliff arrived at the White House early to reconcile some industrial figures with a staffer before the cabinet meeting. The bright faces from months before were now more serious. It was the natural progression, a cycle repeated through every administration. He had gone through it himself, working in an earlier administration years before.

First came the euphoria of working at the center of governmental power. Then, the anxiety of such great responsibility developed, the stage Hingecliff was now observing. If they didn't fail, their confidence would grow, perhaps even into cockiness.

But later, when the true scope and intricacies of governing the nation had sunk in, there would be the astonishment that they hadn't completely screwed up the delicate machinery of government. Few ever talked about that. Most moved to the private sector afterward, whether as lobbyists, media analysts, or private attorneys, depending on their particular skills.

However, if they hadn't lost their nerve or sanity, and still remained inside the Beltway, they became part of an unnamed, yet elite, group. This corps of "go-to" professionals constituted the expertise and the institutional memory of government, no secret handshakes, just service to the country. Administrations came and went, but Washingtonians like Hingecliff would out-serve them all.

"Good morning, Robert," the President said as he dashed by. "See you at the Cabinet Meeting."

"Good morning, Mr. President," Hingecliff said, but wasn't sure if he was heard, as the President headed to the Oval Office.

Farnum found Carver waiting in the Oval Office.

"Good morning, Mr. President. How was the California trip?" Carver asked.

"I'm sure you already know," Farnum said, smiling. "Does Leems have the figures on how much we raised?"

"Not exactly, but he estimates almost three million."

"Really?" Farnum said in a disappointed tone. "I guess I'll have to go back." He sighed. "Anyway, are we set for the Cabinet Meeting?"

"Yes, sir. But before the meeting, I've scheduled a briefing by the Attorney General."

"Kadler Steele?"

"Yes, sir."

"Is the Treasury Secretary back yet?"

"No, sir. Garrett Llewellyn is still in Brussels with the EU ministers."

"OK." Farnum said, as he looked down at the day's schedule, but then he looked up. "You know, I saw Robert Hingecliff in the hallway. Have Amy invite him to join us."

"But, he's Commerce."

"Yeah, but he has the background. He'll give us some perspective."

"Yes, sir. Thank you, Mr. President."

A few minutes later, Robert Hingecliff entered the Oval Office. "Mr. President. Your assistant said you wanted to see me about a steel company?"

Farnum chuckled. "Peter Warrenburg is going to brief us about some developments at Kadler Steele." They both grinned at Amy's lack of understanding. Harris Carver entered with the Attorney General along with another man.

"Good to see you, Peter," Farnum said.

"Thank you, Mr. President," said Warrenburg, whose smile made his eyes seem like slits behind his square glasses. "I'd like to introduce Kevin O'Hara, the U.S. Attorney for the Southern District of New York."

"It's a pleasure, Mr. President," said O'Hara,

"This is Commerce Secretary Hingecliff. I've asked him to sit in."

"A pleasure," O'Hara said as he shook Hingecliff's hand. O'Hara's hand was slightly clammy. Hingecliff suspected he never expected to be in the Oval Office, but yet he seemed solid enough.

"Please, everyone have a seat," the President said, as everyone awkwardly arranged themselves among the two parallel sofas. "So tell us, what's going on at Kadler Steele?"

"Several weeks ago," Warrenburg began. "Kevin's office was contacted by Erin Korelev, a VP at Kadler. She brought some very disturbing revelations about their trading department. Given that Kadler Steele is one of the biggest firms on Wall Street, we paid close attention to what she said." At that point, Warrenburg turned it over to O'Hara.

"Ms. Korelev discovered a second computer network within Kadler's trading operations. She calls it the 'Black Box.' Almost none of the employees know about it. It's used for, among other things, high frequency trading."

"That's not illegal," Hingecliff said.

"No, it's not," said O'Hara. "But the secrecy of the system piqued her curiosity. Apparently, the system is an invisible interface between Kadler traders and the various securities markets. The traders themselves don't seem to know about it. We believe within this system, there's an extremely fast supercomputer. It may even be fast enough to trigger a flash crash at will."

"There hasn't been a flash crash since 2010," Carver said.

"Korelev detected what may be a series of micro-crashes in the last year, usually confined to individual stocks or sectors," said Warrenburg. "It was what originally aroused her suspicions. However, we don't believe that is the primary purpose of the system."

"If not to create flash crashes, what purpose does it serve?" Farnum asked.

"Besides the obvious advantage higher speed provides in high frequency trading, the Black Box skims a little off each trade," O'Hara explained.

"Isn't that called a commission?" Carver suggested.

"No, the commissions come out of their regular trading systems. These are not being reported," O'Hara said. "So at the very least, it's tax evasion, with possible charges of stock manipulation."

Hingecliff wondered why this case was being briefed at the presidential level. "Excuse me," he interrupted. "But why did Ms. Korelev go to the Justice Department? I mean, why not to the SEC?"

"Apparently, Ronald Benton, the head of the SEC's Enforcement Division, is a former Kadler Steele employee."

"Has he been implicated?" Farnum asked.

"No, but it was enough for her to come to my office instead."

"Where does the investigation stand now?" the President asked.

"We've been discreetly investigating. But mostly, we're interviewing and working with Ms. Korelev."

"That's it?" asked Carver.

"Ms. Korelev is providing us with a fair amount of high-quality intelligence. As of now, Kadler doesn't suspect they're being investigated," O'Hara said. "I'd rather gather as much as I can before tipping them off. Erin Korelev still goes to work every day and is supplying us with even more evidence. If we raise any flags, Kadler's shields will go up, and it'll be much harder to obtain proof."

"If all that wasn't enough," Warrenburg continued. "We also believe Kadler Steele has been forming subsidiaries to flush their debt and camouflage their risk."

"Like Enron?" Farnum asked.

"Only more subtly and on a larger scale. And some of these subsidiaries are joint ventures with other financial institutions."

"Damn," Farnum said under his breath.

"This interconnection of major financial institutions could bring an economic meltdown," Hingecliff observed, now understanding why the President was being briefed.

"Yes sir," O'Hara said, turning back to the President. "Kadler Steele's operations are extraordinarily sophisticated. When the time comes, we're going to need an army of forensic accountants, as well as top computer specialists."

"Any chance this Korelev is wrong?" Carver asked.

"I wouldn't bet on it." O'Hara said. "Everything she's given us so far has checked out. And when this comes out, she'll be losing a pretty sweet paycheck."

"So what's in it for her?"

"Nothing, as far as I can see. She's a rare bird in the financial jungle. She has a conscience."

"In your ongoing investigation," Hingecliff interjected, "may I suggest you look into the bond side of the business."

"Why is that?" Warrenburg asked.

"The equities markets are fairly transparent, therefore easier to detect fraud. However, certain debt markets are quite opaque and serpentine. Don't forget the crash of 2009 had its roots in bonds." O'Hara made a quick notation.

"Mr. O'Hara, you'll receive whatever support you need," Farnum said as he stood up. "Coordinate with the Attorney General."

"Thank you, Mr. President." Warrenburg and O'Hara were escorted out by Carver, leaving Hingecliff with the President.

"Well Robert, what do you think?" Farnum asked.

"If Kadler Steele has interwoven their subsidiaries with other Wall Street firms, the result could be something akin to 2009 all over again. I don't mean to be negative, but I sense some falling dominoes in our future."

"What can we do to avoid it?"

"Not knowing the exact scope of this thing, it's hard to say. But staying on top of it is the only thing you can do right now, Mr. President. Sooner or later, the SEC will need to be involved. Before that happens, I would strongly suggest transferring the head of the SEC's Enforcement Division."

"Even if he's innocent?"

"Especially if he's innocent. When this becomes public, the media will dig up that coincidence. If Benton's guilty of something, you can hang him out to dry. But if he's innocent, it'll look like a cover up. It'll taint your administration, and he'll never be able to recover his reputation."

The President nodded in agreement. "Thank you, Robert. I'll see you shortly in the Cabinet Meeting."

"Thank you, Mr. President."

⁝ ⁝ ℭ ℭ

That night, David and Sara were celebrating at Fortella's. Sara's firm had just won the bid to build Harrisburg's newest courthouse. "Here's to Pennsylvania's greatest architect," he said, holding up his glass.

"Thank you," she said. "Have to admit I'm pretty happy about this one."

"Harrisburg is lucky to have your architectural influence."

"So, what's your news?" Sara asked.

"I don't have any news. We're celebrating your accomplishment."

"David, I know that look. You've had it on your face all evening. What's up?"

David felt annoyed at being so transparent. "I'm...I'm mulling over...the idea of running for Congress," he admitted.

Sara smiled. "Hmm, Senator Grant. That has a nice ring to it."

"No, I'm thinking about the House of Representatives. A statewide campaign would cost too much."

"You're serious?"

25

He nodded that he was.

"So, that's what you and this Arkin character have been up to."

"Well yes, Fred Arkin has been encouraging me. But, I thought I'd run it by you first."

"But, you didn't."

"I haven't made any decisions. And tonight, I didn't want to overshadow your real news with my hypothetical news."

"As a Democrat or Republican?"

"Excuse me?"

"Are you going to run as a Democrat or Republican?"

"In case you haven't noticed, I don't belong to either party. I'd run as a centrist Independent. However, I wanted to discuss it with you first." David knew there was still some annoyance lurking from selling Simplexia.

"I don't mean to rain on your parade," she said. "But you're not going to win."

"I'm not so sure. I've looked at the voting patterns, or rather Fred has. In our district, Sheldon Lannier won re-election by less than one percent. Two years before that, by just under two percent. The trend just might be in my favor."

"You're not going to win," Sara repeated.

"Perhaps not, but I feel the major parties are just slinging mud and spinning the truth into crap. Look, I'm in a position to run. We're financially secure. There's less and less for me to do at the company as Calibrent takes over. Winton doesn't require my services fulltime. Besides, not being from a political machine, I think I have something important to say."

"Is this some type of mid-life crisis?" Sara asked, frowning.

"Maybe. You know, I keep thinking about that Linda Ellis poem, *The Dash*. It's about the inscription on a tombstone. There's the name, the birth date, and the death date. But between the two dates is a dash. The poem talks about what that dash represents, the limited time we have on this Earth, and what we do with it. I suppose I'm looking for something where I might be able to make a difference."

"You've already made a difference. You have a family, including two wonderful children. You've built a company, for goodness sakes."

"But I sold that company, and I still have the rest of my dash left."

"Alright," Sara said, with a patient smile. "What if you win?"

"I thought you said I'm not going to win," David smirked.

"Dear, I know you're not going to win, but you don't. So given that you are a very capable and determined man, and don't believe you're going to lose, you might win."

"That's the most convoluted logic I've ever heard."

"My dear, that's nothing compared to what you'd find in Washington."

Just then, the waiter arrived with their entrees. "*Tortellini Bolognese* for the lady," the waiter announced in a cultured Italian accent. "And *Gamberi Alla Scampi* for the gentleman. May I bring you anything else?"

"No, we're fine. Thank you," David said.

Sara turned back to David. "Are you asking my permission?"

"I suppose since the subject has come up, I am asking your wise counsel."

"So, what will running for Congress entail?"

"Lots of speeches. So the weekends will be full. Probably lots of evenings too."

"And if you win?" Sara asked. "Hypothetically, I mean."

"Members of Congress spend four to five days a week in Washington, but there are occasional weekends. However, Washington is only a few hours by train."

"And what about the kids?"

"Chris will be headed off to college soon. So he won't even be around. Wendy's getting to the age when she's embarrassed by her parents. I can be back for anything important. I think congressmen can ignore the I-95 speed limit. I'm sure that's in the Constitution."

They laughed.

"And, what will I have to do in this campaign of yours?"

"I expect have some pictures taken with your ugly husband. I mean, you are pretty hot."

"Flattering me like that, you're already in campaign mode, aren't you? I won't have to make any speeches, will I?"

"Only if you want to."

"I'm not wearing one of those dowdy political wives' ensembles," she warned.

"Not so much as a pillbox hat."

"Okay."

"Okay?"

"Go play politician."

"Do you mean it?"

"Get it out of your system," she said, with a loving smile.

ᏮᏳᏳᏳ

It was late. The President had returned to the Residence. Harris Carver was in his office. Karen had left for the day. He dialed the number for the Democratic National Committee. Ed Leems, the DNC Chair, had also left for the day. Carver quickly dialed Leems's cell phone.

"Hello."

"Hi, Ed. It's Harris Carver."

"What can I do for you, Harris?"

"Are you anywhere near the White House?"

"I just went over the 14th Street Bridge, but I can turn around."

"How about the Filibuster in 20 minutes?"

"The Filibuster? Okay, see you in twenty."

The Filibuster was a bar a few blocks from the White House. It was not ordinarily patronized by political types, despite its name. The décor was designed more for tourists than locals. It could have been an Applebee's with a political history theme. But more importantly, it had private booths. Its selection told Leems that discretion was needed. Clearly, Carver didn't want a recorded visit to the White House. He was already seated when Leems arrived.

"So, what's up?" Leems asked, as he slid into the booth.

"Ed, I have a sensitive matter."

"I suspected as much," Leems said, glancing up at a photo of Harry Truman holding up the "Dewey Defeats Truman" headlined newspaper.

"I need you to find out which members of Congress have received donations from Kadler Steele."

"What's going on?"

"I can't tell you, but you must be discreet."

Leems shifted uncomfortably. "Harris, the DNC can't do anything illegal."

"I'm not asking you to. Use only public sources. This is more about number crunching than digging."

"If so, why can't the White House handle this?"

"It just can't. Besides, it's closer to an activity the DNC might undertake as part of its normal operations. Ed, I can't stress enough how quiet this has to be kept."

"Yeah, I got that. But, I'll have to tell my researchers something."

"Bury it in a broader search…say…all congressional campaign contributions from the financial sector, but break it out by donors and recipients."

"That's going to be a very intensive search, especially when the Wall Street crowd is involved. You know they give big and use lots of intermediaries."

"I don't need every dollar, just a sense of proportion and where the money is flowing. You can start with members of the finance and banking committees."

"I assume we're hunting Republicans?"

"No, either party. I need to know the lay of the land."

"This Kadler Steele thing, there's a storm coming, isn't there?"

Carver remained stone-faced. Leems understood.

CHAPTER 6

After a few weeks, it became clear that obtaining enough signatures would not be a problem. It was time for David to start building his organization. Fred Arkin would chair the Grant for Congress Committee. Art Fuentes would serve as treasurer and handle the state filings with Fred. David also had some preliminary discussions with a small local advertising agency.

He found several Pennsylvania-based CPP members, courtesy of Jason Kennerly, who were willing to donate time to his campaign. While they were enthusiastic, none impressed him as being particularly savvy in the area of politics. David quickly realized he needed some higher caliber talent. He finally called the woman Marcus Finn had recommended, Ellen Langford. David researched her online, and she seemed to have the right credentials.

They agreed to meet at a restaurant called Byron's on Market Street in Philadelphia. Langford drove up from Washington through a pouring rain. When David arrived, the raven-haired Langford was already seated at the table, wearing a well-tailored, dark maroon suit. After introductions and comments about the awful weather, Langford got down to business.

"So, have you obtained enough signatures to get on the ballot yet?" she asked.

"Not yet, but we're within striking distance. Pennsylvania law requires enough signatures equal to two percent of the vote for the winner in the last election. Lannier received just over 103,000 votes last time, so we need…"

"2087 signatures."

"Yes," David said, impressed. "Luckily, the last election was close and turnout was low, making the threshold easier. But our goal is 2500, just in case any are challenged."

"Good, you just saved me a lecture. So Mr. Grant, why are you running for Congress?" she asked.

"Please call me David. And I'm running because I'm tired of the Republican and Democrat B.S. in Washington."

"I'm afraid you'll need a sharper answer for the campaign trail. And yes, everybody's frustrated with Washington, from the President on down. But yet, you think you can go down to DC and clean things up?" she asked in a skeptical voice.

"I'm not that naïve. I'm just tired of the extremes controlling our political discourse. I want to be a voice for the forgotten center. Each of the last several presidents campaigned on undoing what their predecessor did, all to satisfy the political bases; the same with Congress. This never-ending cycle is wasted motion, a pendulum that takes us nowhere, except deeper in debt.

"Ah, a Born Again Tea Partier."

"No," David insisted. "I understand everything is a balance. Cutting the wrong way can be worse than not cutting at all."

"Be warned, the majority of voters don't give a damn about the national debt. It just doesn't tug at the heartstrings."

"Well, it should."

"Hey, I don't live in the land of should. I'm a jaded…no…make that a *very* jaded political operative, probably the sort of person you hate. But, I get serious people elected, provided they let me."

"You don't consider me serious?"

"I'm sure you think you're serious. But serious people join the parties."

"I did join a party, the Centrist Patriots Party." David sensed Langford was trying to not roll her eyes.

"Actually, you have to run as an Independent. The Centrist Patriots have no state party in Pennsylvania, maybe a chapter, but no legal party." She took a sip of her martini. "Look, let me be honest—and I always am with my clients—your odds on winning the election are extremely long. You're either egotistical enough to believe your money, good looks, and force of personality will win the day. Or, you're idealistic enough to believe bringing up issues in a campaign will force the other candidates to address them."

David smiled, suspecting Langford was testing the thickness of his skin. He wasn't going to take the bait.

"As Marcus told you," she continued. "I'm available right now, but I can't really further my career running an Independent congressional campaign."

"Then why did you agree to meet me?" David asked. "The martinis?"

Langford smiled. "No, two reasons. I'm available right now, even if it's only a short-term job. And Marcus Finn told me I should talk to you. I listen to Marcus."

David realized she was setting up for a negotiation.

"Normally," she continued. "I charge $200,000 for the duration of a campaign. Anyone worth their salt will charge at least that."

"What makes you think I can afford that?"

"The Internet. You sold your company to Calibrent for an undisclosed amount of money. 'Undisclosed' is never a euphemism for small. Besides, if you're seriously going up against Sheldon Lannier, you need to have a war chest."

"But there are campaign finance limits," David responded. Langford's expression indicated what she thought of that statement.

"You can loan your campaign the money," she said. "It's done all the time. I'll be honest. I've had some offers from K-Street, but I'm a creature of the election cycle. I can work with you for $4,000 a week, plus expenses, with the understanding that if I receive a better offer during the campaign, I'm out."

"You haven't been hired yet, and you already have an exit strategy? If this is your sales pitch…"

"Look, I'm a proven resource," she interrupted. "I understand polling, messaging, fundraising, voter turnout tactics—the whole nine yards. I won't be your official campaign manager, but I'll make the person who is look good. I got Marcus Finn reelected five times. When Marcus retired, I went out and got the late Sandra Hawthorne elected to the Senate after starting 38 points down. When she passed away, I found myself unemployed. So, I'm temporarily available."

"Despite your credentials, why should I hire an unmotivated worker, who is already looking to leave before she's been hired?"

"Because I'm the best you can get your hands on. Good political operatives only work for the major parties. They're where the money and power are. I'm in an unusual stage in my career, so I'm available. But don't think I'm unmotivated. When I'm on your team, I'm on it all the way."

The waiter arrived to take their order, giving David a moment to consider a counteroffer.

"Here's what I'll do. I'll pay you $2000 a week, plus your *legitimate* expenses, plus a bonus for performance." Langford appeared unimpressed with the offer. However, David wouldn't have expected anything else.

"How do you rate performance?" she asked.

"A thousand dollars for every percentage point I get at the polls in November. Another $10,000 if I win, provided you're still on board then. Also if I win, you can have a position on my congressional staff. During the campaign, you can quit anytime, with two weeks notice, but you can't go to work for my opponents." David could see Langford was doing the math and probabilities in her head.

"Three thousand a week, plus your performance bonus," she countered.

"Twenty-five hundred," he countered.

She nodded. "Anything else?" she finally asked.

"Yes, the issue we've danced around. If you're such a high-power political operative, why would you lower yourself to work for a lowly Independent like me?"

"I took a bullet for someone." Langford gave a taut smile. "The bullet hurt more than I expected."

"Could you be more specific?"

"No."

"Listen, if I'm going to hire you, I need to know your baggage."

"Mr. Grant, I'll accept your offer, but my baggage is my own. I have one very rare and important quality. I am discreet. And I guarantee my baggage will not interfere with your campaign in the least."

"I'll need to think about it."

"Fair enough."

ಐ ಐ ಣ ಞ

Several days later, outside the adjunct office, Fred ran to catch up with David.

"Congratulations, sir," Fred said, holding up a large envelope emblazoned with the Commonwealth of Pennsylvania Seal. "You are officially a candidate for the U.S. House of Representatives."

"Wow," David said, looking at the envelope. "I guess I'm really doing this."

"Yes, you are, my friend," Fred said, as they walked into the deserted adjunct office. "So how was your meeting with that Langford lady? Am I going to be replaced as your campaign manager?"

"Of course not," David answered, as he checked his mailbox. "Besides, she clearly has no enthusiasm for our chances."

"You can't expect her to. She hasn't drunk the Kool-Aid like you and me," Fred said. "Don't expect her or those like her to share our vision, at least right off the bat. If she's good, use her. Channel a little Machiavelli."

"Well, she also has some skeleton in her closet that she's not sharing," David said, as he opened an interoffice envelope.

"Would you share your skeletons in a job interview?" Fred asked. "If it's toxic, you can always dump her later and show your decisive leadership skills."

"Always the glass half full with you," David said, as he frowned at the memo in his hand. "By the way, can you give this a positive spin?" he asked, waving the memo in his hand.

"What is it?"

David handed Fred the letter from the Campus Activities Office. They had denied David's request for a rally on campus.

"That's not right," Fred said. "We should go see President Vander Waal about this."

"No, I'll go." He didn't want Fred caught up in this. If he had crossed some invisible line, he would take full responsibility. Fred couldn't afford to lose his job. Much to his surprise, David was able to make an appointment with Dr. Vander Waal that afternoon.

"It is Winton policy not to endorse any political candidates, overtly or otherwise," President Marta Vander Waal explained, sitting behind her large mahogany desk.

"I didn't ask for an endorsement, merely an opportunity to give a speech. You've allowed candidates from both major parties to speak on campus. I believe Sheldon Lannier has spoken on campus many times."

"Professor Grant, it is appropriate for Congressman Lannier to speak here. We are in his district. Many of our students are his constituents. Winton College, like other institutions, benefits from government grants and other aid programs. And in this economy, we can ill afford to antagonize either political party."

"Do you honestly think allowing an Independent to have a rally would really endanger those public grants?"

"In addition, we have a very full campus schedule."

"I checked with the activities office. Outside of an origami exhibit opening and a volleyball game, there are no events on campus that day.

Neither is going to overload the campus. I would hope there would be some deference for a faculty member. You know, during our orientation, you gave a short talk about trying to stimulate the minds and hearts of the students, giving them alternate points of view. That's part of what I am trying to do."

"That's why we provide a forum for both parties."

"However, there are often more than two points of view."

"I am sorry, Professor Grant." Vander Waal said in a tone that indicated that they were done. Leaving her office, David was livid. He pulled out his cell phone and punched in a number. Unfortunately, he only reached voice mail.

"Hello, Ellen. This is David Grant. Damn your baggage. You're hired."

CHAPTER 7

It was Saturday, the first official day of the Grant campaign. Instead of formally announcing his candidacy at Winton College as hoped, David was launching his campaign in front of the colonial-style Embler Town Hall. Fred Arkin had arranged for some local media, as well as a squad of cheerleaders from Embler High School. David was gratified by the support he was receiving from his neighbors. Even members of the town council who were Democrats and Republicans were supportive.

Jason Kennerly had driven up to Embler with some CPP representatives from other states, as well as his video camera for the party's video blog webpage. Ellen Langford had also driven up.

"So the big day is here," Langford commented, observing the activity on the town square.

"Yeah," David said, wincing at the cheerleaders rehearsing their 'Gimme a G-R-A-N-T' routine. "I'm sorry you couldn't make the planning meeting." David was not thrilled with Fred's local surprise.

"Since I'm going to be living in the Keystone State for the immediate future, I had to arrange some of my affairs down in D.C.," Langford said, as she watched one of the cheerleaders accidentally threw a pom-pom. Sara who was standing nearby retrieved it for her.

"What do you think so far?" David asked.

"It's very Mayberry," she said.

"You're not some kind of urban snob, are you?"

"No, it's just everybody rallying around their favorite son. Very Americana. All we need is a Barney—"

"Hi," Fred interrupted. "You must be Ellen Langford."

"Yes. I'm guessing you must be Fred Arkin."

"Yeah, it's great to finally meet you." He turned to David. "Mayor Burke is ready whenever you are."

"Thanks. See you all on the other side," David said, as he and Sara walked up to the platform that had been set up in front of the town hall. A "Grant for Congress" banner tied to the front columns, sagged high above them. The mayor, sporting an out-of-style suit with a red carnation, got up to speak first. He pulled in his stomach as he approached the rickety podium with the town seal on it.

"Good morning, everyone. Welcome to a special day. As you all know, Embler is a small town, but a good town, with lots of good things in it. One of those good things is the good man I'm about to introduce. David Grant served us as councilman for four years. And he did a real good job. And now he's running for Congress. Good citizens of Embler, I give you David Grant!"

David kissed Sara before standing up. "Break a leg," she whispered.

Mayor Burke intercepted David on his way to the podium. He grabbed David's hand awkwardly and turned to the audience with big grin. A pre-placed photographer quickly snapped their picture. Finally making it to the podium, David began.

"Good morning, everybody. I appreciate you all coming out and supporting me today. I particularly want to thank Tom Burke for his kind words this morning." There was polite applause. "As Mayor Burke told you, I'm running for Congress. And, I'm doing it as an Independent, which is appropriate. American Independence was forged right here in Pennsylvania, just down the road in Philadelphia."

"For too long we have been limited by the binary fallacy of the two-party system. Here in Embler, Democrats, Republicans and Independents work together. Shouldn't we expect the same of the Federal Government? Instead, they have tribal warfare between the two parties, ripping each other apart. The politicians in Washington are more fixated on defeating each other rather than serving the interests of the American people. And the American people are not happy." David went on to lay out his positions on the national debt, tax policy and ferreting out corruption.

"We have a Congress that has no self-control when it comes to pork barrel spending. And there is no motivation in government circles to be efficient. It's time for some adult supervision down in Washington. I ask that in November you send an adult to Congress. Thank you all for your support."

ಬ ಬ ಇ ೞ

After the rally, the campaign team gathered in a community room reserved at the Embler Public Library. Everybody gave David a standing ovation.

"Thank you all. I really appreciate everyone's support. I'm hoping we can really do something important here. I won't make you endure a second speech in the same morning. By now, I think you all know our campaign manager, Fred Arkin. So I'm going to have Fred run this meeting."

Fred gave him a salute and turned to the group. "Since this is the first time we have everyone in the same room, let's go around the table and introduce everyone. Immediately to my right is Zach McCarthy, who is going to run the campaign storefront on Maple Street, once we clean out the remnants of the old shoe shop." The gray-bearded McCarthy stood up and nodded to everyone.

"If anyone wants a deal on old loafers. Let me know." McCarthy quipped. Everyone laughed.

Fred continued. "Gary Jensen, Lynn Danielson, and Ken Lefevre are local CPP members here in Pennsylvania. They are going to be our ears on the ground, and be leading our ground team. Next, we have Jason Kennerly, National Chair of the Centrist Patriot Party. Jason is going try to rally national support and help us with social media."

"Excuse me, no offense to Mr. Kennerly," Zach McCarthy interrupted. "But I don't understand this 'national support' thing. I mean, only people in this district can vote for David. Right?"

"National support includes national media," Jason explained. "If the national media covers David Grant, then so will the local media. In addition, we can encourage financial donations from out-of-state."

"But my understanding is that David is financing his own campaign," Zach countered.

"Excuse me," Langford interrupted. "No one should ever say David Grant is financing his own campaign. It'll make him seem like a rich kid trying to buy a congressional seat. He has simply *loaned* his campaign some funds to get it started. Campaign donations from others are a sign of a candidate's credibility. It'll demonstrate voters are taking David Grant seriously as a candidate."

"I'm sorry, I didn't catch your name," McCarthy said.

"My name's Ellen Langford. I'm a professional political consultant. While Mr. Arkin is the manager of this team, you can think of me as the coach."

"I'm not sure what makes you the coach," McCarthy said. "I've worked on several campaigns, including David's Town Council campaign."

"All local campaigns, right?"

"Yeah," McCarthy admitted. "Aren't all politics local?"

"I've helped win six congressional races, including an Ohio Senate campaign. You'll be a great team, but you need a coach who's already been to the Super Bowl."

David smiled at the sports analogy.

"Anyway, let's continue with the introductions," Fred said. "Next, we have Art Fuentes, our treasurer and legal counsel. Ellen Langford has already introduced herself. And that's the team."

"Excuse me, Fred," Langford said. "Can we briefly review this morning's campaign launch?"

"I suppose," Fred said, not quite sure.

"Mr. Kennerly, you took video of today's event. Could we see that footage?"

"Sure." Kennerly was flattered by the interest. He quickly connected his camera to the digital projector suspended from the ceiling.

"First, let's watch the Mayor's introduction." They watched the replay of Tom Burke's remarks. "Does this man know any other adjective besides 'good'?" Everyone laughed. "But to be fair, we can't expect eloquent rhetoric from a man whose day job is running the local hardware store. Somebody should have written a better introduction for him."

"Well, Tom Burke may not be a fancy orator," McCarthy snarled. "But he's one hell of a mayor. When we got flooded a few years ago, Tom Burke was in a boat, checking on everyone's house in the flood plain."

"I'm in no way impugning the Mayor's good character," Ellen said. "It's just our candidate should always be put in the best light. And that means giving him the best introduction we can."

"What if there isn't anyone there to introduce him?" Danielson asked.

"Then, someone from the campaign should introduce him, touting the candidate's accomplishments. Everyone in this room should be prepared to introduce David Grant to an audience. Over the course of the campaign, the message, and therefore the introduction, will change. I'll be sending updates to everyone, once changes are approved by our candidate and his campaign manager."

"Jason, would you please play the rest of the footage?" David's speech played out and then the tape ended. "Did anyone notice what was missing?" No one wanted to venture a guess. "Where was the 'Grant for Congress' banner?"

"It was there," Danielson called out.

"That's probably my fault," Jason said. "I should have shot at a wider angle."

"No, there's no problem with your camerawork. Besides, we have no control over the media's cameras anyway. That sagging banner was just too high."

"That was so everyone could see it," Fred said.

"We barely had a hundred people. Even if we had two or three hundred, it could have been ten feet lower. Everyone would have still seen it. And, it would have easily been within camera frame."

"Come on, this is a load of piddley shit!" McCarthy said.

"Success is in the details, Mr. McCarthy," Langford explained. "Let's be honest. This is an independent campaign. The media and the voters are not going to pay a lot of attention to us, unless this campaign looks and sounds serious and professional in every way. I guarantee at Sheldon Lannier events, the banners will be perfect, no sagging. Whoever introduces him will be following a carefully crafted script. And sure as hell, there won't be any high school cheerleaders. Stagecraft may seem superficial, but getting the optics right is essential."

"Okay," Fred said, trying to regain control of the meeting. "Let's do a rundown of the schedule for the next few weeks." The meeting continued without any additional tension. After which, everyone went their separate ways for the day, leaving only David, Fred and Langford behind.

"What the hell was that?" Fred said, glaring at Langford.

"What was what?"

"Ripping everyone apart."

"I didn't rip anyone apart. I simply critiqued the event."

"Yeah, after you wouldn't even deign to show up for the planning meeting. Pretty passive-aggressive, if you ask me."

"Look. Every campaign I've ever worked on was manned by professionals. An all-volunteer organization is new to me. I needed to see what they would do on their own. A good chef needs to assess the ingredients in their raw state."

"This was the launch of the campaign," Fred snapped. "We needed all hands on deck!"

"This isn't a presidential campaign. Nobody will remember today's announcement. The only media was a public access channel and the Embler Dispatch with its 3000 readers."

"So, all this was a waste to you?"

"No, not at all. It was a live rehearsal. And I think everyone learned something from the post-mortem."

"Post-mortem?" Fred said, indignantly. "Excuse me, I have to go see Jason off before he leaves." Fred marched off.

"Day One, and you've already pissed off half my staff," David said. "You know, Fred's right. That was a fairly passive-aggressive move you made."

"Then, perhaps we're both guilty."

"How so?"

"I noticed you weren't very talkative in the meeting."

"I believe in delegating."

"Not that much," Langford said. "You were accessing your team too. I saw how you were watching everyone."

"But I didn't rip apart the job they did."

"That's why you hired me. Every good cop needs a bad cop."

"Hmm," David said, considering Langford's words. "I was waiting for you to skewer my speech next."

"Your people have to believe in the candidate, or there's really no campaign. So, I don't criticize the candidate in front of others. It's bad for morale."

"Now, you're concerned about morale?" David asked with a smirk.

"You know," Langford said, "my father was a Marine. He explained how in basic training, the drill sergeants broke the recruits' spirit, drove them right into the ground. And then, built them up. Some recruits washed out. But those who remained had their abilities and self-confidence grow even stronger. They became a cohesive unit."

"But these people aren't Marines. They're volunteers."

"The concept is the same. This McCarthy guy is a blowhard who may wash out, but the others will become stronger. And to your earlier question, yes, your speech does need a little work. You have the confidence and presence, but the content itself just needs a little fine tuning. For instance, very few people actually know what a binary fallacy is. You're not speaking in a boardroom or a classroom. But there was nothing we can't rework for your stump speech." Langford turned around as if searching for someone.

"By the way, what happened to your wife?"

"Sara had things to do."

"Will she be working on the campaign with us?"

"No, not very much."

"That's a shame. Sara's very attractive, and comes across well."

"But the voters aren't voting for her."

"You used to work in marketing, right?"

"Among other areas, yes."

"So, you know the packaging is often why people buy the product? An attractive and supportive spouse is always a plus in any campaign."

"I know exactly what you're saying. Sara has agreed to be available for some photo opportunities. Beyond that, she has her own career to attend to."

"You're going to need every edge you can muster. That's why I did what I did today. See if you can persuade her to change her mind."

"Anything else?"

"Oh, I have a whole list."

৪০ ৪৩ ୦୨ ୦୫

Fred caught up to Jason Kennerly as he finished loading video gear into his slightly battered station wagon. "Sorry about all that in there," Fred said, as Jason slammed his tailgate shut.

"Sorry about what?" Jason replied.

"That bitch, Langford."

Jason laughed. "Hey Fred, she's alright."

"She's arrogant, really arrogant."

"She has something to be arrogant about. She *actually* gets people elected. I'm going to do my best to come up here as often as I can. I can learn a lot from our Ms. Langford. We all can."

Fred just sighed in frustration.

৪০ ৪৩ ୦୨ ୦୫

It was one of those rare evenings Harris Carver arrived home at what civilized people called a reasonable hour. The President was spending the weekend at Camp David with the First Lady. As pre-arranged, a package had arrived at his home that evening by special courier. No signature was required. The donor report from Ed Leems was finally complete, all 1283 pages.

Carver eyed the black bottle of Courvoisier in his liquor cabinet, but then thought better of it. He opened a bottle of ginger ale instead. He laid the behemoth report down on the desk in his study, and cracked it open. Despite the cloak-and-dagger, the report was sufficiently large that no one would be able to discover its specific purpose even by reading through it, even if they had the stamina. Luckily, the DNC chair had placed sticky notes on the relevant pages. Carver read and reread the columns on those pages several times. Then, he read other pages not tagged by Leems. As he went, he scribbled a total of sixteen names on a pad of paper.

Carver pulled a folder out of his briefcase marked "Senate." After referring back to the heavy report on his desk, he crossed out seven of the

39

names. He pulled out another folder labeled "House," cross-checked it against the columns, and then scratched out another five names.

Now, he decided to open the black bottle. After rereading the four remaining names, Carver smiled. He sat back in his leather desk chair, took a sip of the cognac, and savored its flavor.

ಬ ಬ ಞ ಞ

The next morning, Carl Stavros, the White House Communications Director, walked towards the Press Secretary's office. He stopped just outside her door, and watched her for a second. The light hit Dana Seagram's blonde hair at just the right angle to make her look like an angel. Stavros fantasized about being less than angelic with her, but he knew Seagram was too professional for such a liaison.

"Hey Dana, I just got a heads-up that Glendenning was spitting fire at the President last night."

"So, what else is new?" she asked.

"Well, I think you're gonna get questions on it at the one o'clock briefing."

"What did the little darling say?"

"I don't exactly know, but Harlan at the *Post* asked me what I thought of Glendenning's comments last night. I feigned not caring. But I guarantee someone will ask you at the next briefing."

Seagram picked up the remote control and tapped in the time and channel. Installed only weeks after the inauguration, the video wall in her office could produce any program from any public program transmitted within the past week.

Ben Glendenning's show was on CPN, the new cable channel, where a third of the sponsors were conservative super-PACs. The bombastic Glendenning was starting to garner serious ratings. Finally, Seagram found his program, ironically titled *The Truth Report*.

"You know," Glendenning began with a sneer. "We have a Communist in the White House. The current generation doesn't know what a communist really is. To them, it's a quaint historical phrase, like Confederate or Whig. They probably only heard the term when they were taught about McCarthyism in school. But Communists were, and are, real! Oh, they don't call themselves that anymore. They call themselves Progressives."

"Well, Farnum is our Communist-in-Chief. He's already trying to capture the next generation with this takeover of education. Get'em while they're young. That's why ole Adolf had the Hitler Youth. Farnum wants to kill babies, control the youth, and silence opposition…"

"Why are people like Glendenning not sued for slander?" Seagram complained. "Killing babies? Hitler?"

"Technically, he's not lying," Robert Hingecliff commented from outside the door. He smiled at the naiveté of these staffers.

"Mr. Secretary, we didn't see you there," Stavros blurted out nervously. Both of the staffers began to rise, but Hingecliff waved them down to relax.

"Obviously, 'killing babies' refers to the President's pro-choice position," Hingecliff continued. "Controlling the youth refers to the education bill. And deep down, wouldn't everyone like to silence their opposition? Glendenning speaks nominal truths, twisting them into a mosaic of inflammatory lies. He's a reprehensible hate monger and a disgrace to humanity. But he's really nothing new, just magnified by cable and the Internet."

"But anyone who invokes Hitler as a political comparison...," Stavros snarled.

"Yes, the propagandists jump to that analogy far too quickly."

"I just don't know how people can watch him," Seagram sighed.

"To the Right, he's exciting," Hingecliff said. "And he boils complex issues down into easy-to-digest sound bites."

"No," insisted Stavros, "'boiling down' implies there's some honest analysis going on."

"True. But how is that any different than what you did in the campaign, Mr. Stavros?"

"What...what are you talking about?"

"I seem to recall that during the campaign, you had your agents accuse President Henderson of being a racist."

"He wanted to end Affirmative Action," Stavros countered.

"And I disagreed with Henderson's position. But eventually, if we get to an ideal point in race relations in this country, affirmative action should go away. I don't think we're there yet. Make no mistake, I am thrilled that Ted Henderson no longer occupies the Oval Office, but he was no racist. That didn't prevent you from weaving nominal truths into the mosaic of an implied inflammatory lie. Don't worry; you're no Ben Glendenning. But maybe someday."

"Is there something we can do for you, Mr. Secretary?" Seagram asked, trying to diffuse the tension.

"I'm scheduled for *Meet the Press* this Sunday. I'd like to review next week's talking points for this weekend."

"I was about to send them out, but I have a copy right here," Seagram pulled open a file folder. "Here you go."

"Thank you, Ms. Seagram," Hingecliff said, nodded to Stavros, and he headed down the hall.

"Pompous old windbag," Stavros muttered.

"Be careful, Carl. I hear he's becoming one of Farnum's favorites," Seagram warned.

ᛒᏉ ᏚᎾ ᏣᏒ ᏓᎶ

Down the hall and past the Oval Office, Harris Carver contemplated the list in front of him. In war, whether military or political, one had to choose the most appropriate weapon. Would the precision of a high-power rifle be the best approach? Or would it be better to go nuclear? This time, Carver chose to go with the loose cannon.

"Mr. Carver," Karen said from the door. "Congressman Barnes is holding for you."

"Thank you, Karen." She nodded and closed the door behind her. He picked up the receiver. "Good morning, Congressman."

"Not sure what's so good about it," Barnes's gravelly voice snapped. "I received the donor data you sent me. You want to explain what the hell this is all about?"

Porter Barnes represented a heavily Democratic district—gerrymandered to electoral perfection—which enabled him to win every election by excessive margins. Often the Republicans didn't even bother to put up a candidate. Electorally, he was invulnerable, which reduced the need for a tactful demeanor.

"Well Porter, within the next few days, the Justice Department is going to issue an announcement that will make that information I sent you very relevant and could make life hell for those on the list. I trust you don't have any particular affection for any of them?"

"As far as I'm concerned, they can all go suck farts out of a dead seagull."

Carver winced at the congressman's colorful language. *Loose cannon.* "Well, then watch for the announcement, and I'll leave you to your own devices."

"Yeah, whatever," he said, before hanging up. Despite Barnes's surliness and seeming indifference, Carver knew the Congressman would be chomping at the bit to use the information he had provided.

CHAPTER 8

Garrett Llewellyn had been a Wall Street wunderkind, possessing the youth and energy Greg Farnum had wanted on his team. He was square jawed and had just enough gray in the temples to suggest experience without contradicting his boyish good looks. This was part of the reason he had been tapped for Treasury Secretary over the more patrician Robert Hingecliff. Unfortunately, Llewellyn had developed an unexpected Achilles heel.

He has just arrived home from the Finance Ministers Conference in Brussels. Llewellyn didn't cross time zones particularly well, especially flying westward across the Atlantic. He was exhausted and felt he'd need the rest of the weekend to recover from the jetlag. When the telephone rang, he was tempted to ignore it. However, the caller ID indicated the White House was calling. He acquiesced.

"Hello."

"Good evening, Mr. Secretary." Llewellyn recognized Harris Carver's voice.

"Good evening, Harris. Is this something that can wait? I'm bushed."

"You've seen the Justice Department briefing on Kadler Steele?"

"Yes, I read it on the plane coming back. It's unbelievable. Back in 2008, we...uh...Kadler was one of the few firms to turn down Hank Paulsen's TARP funds. They ran a tight ship."

"You mean when you were there?"

"Yes. If there's anything I can do to help Warrenburg's people."

"There is something we need from you."

"Just name it."

"Your resignation."

"What?" Llewellyn wasn't sure he heard correctly, but then realized he had. "Harris, come on, I was never part of whatever's going on at Kadler now. Not even close."

"You were a Senior VP."

"In a completely separate division!"

"The public doesn't make those kinds of distinctions."

"They will, if it's explained correctly."

"That will take time away from the President's agenda and distract from his message."

"So, you're just going to hang me out to dry? Firing me will just make me look guilty."

"That's why he's not going to fire you. You're going to resign, citing personal reasons, health or family, whatever you prefer."

"Oh, thank you very much!" Llewellyn spat.

"Calm down. Believe me, it's better for you to leave before Kadler Steele becomes a story. Being in the administration just makes you a juicy target for the press. As a private citizen, your name may never come up." Of course, Carver knew otherwise, but that truth didn't help the immediate task of disposing of Llewellyn.

"I'd like to speak to the President about this," Llewellyn said in a determined tone.

"I already have. His mind is made up. Call me in the morning. If you depart gracefully, the President will say wonderful things about you. And calls will be made to the right people on your behalf. We're not trying to hurt you. We're trying to protect you."

"Bullshit!" Llewellyn slammed the receiver. Now, Llewellyn realized, there was no hope of any sleep.

಩ ಩ ಞ ಞ

The following Thursday, David was exhausted after making seven campaign stops across the district. Campaigning for town council had been much easier. He had to admit to himself the campaign grind was wearing on him a little. It would have been a lot easier if he could address larger crowds, but an Independent just didn't rate the big venues.

He slumped back on the couch. Sara was working late that night. He had arrived home too late to catch the 6 o'clock local news. He would watch the 6:30 network news and wait for the local news to come back on. Normally it wouldn't, but it was primary night in Pennsylvania. Of course, the incumbent Lannier was unchallenged within his own party. So, it was a Democratic night, with Linda Jansing being the favorite.

"And now the Evening News with Bob Summers," a deep-voiced narrator announced.

"Good Evening," Summers began. "At 2:47 today, the Los Angeles County Sheriff's office announced that film star Damian Cox died of what appears to be a drug overdose. Cox had been in and out of drug rehabilitation for years—"

David wasn't surprised. Cox had been a self-indulgent bad boy for as long as he could remember. Money from his earlier films insulated him from anyone ever saying no to him. David's daughter Wendy would be devastated. She had a poster of him on her bedroom wall from his earlier clean-cut days.

"In Washington, the Justice Department announced they were opening an investigation into Kadler Steele's trading practices—"

The telephone rang. It was Fred Arkin.

"Hi, Fred. Anyone call a winner for the primary yet?"

"No, but it's going to be Jansing. Everyone knows it. All the local pundits are leaning that way. But that's not why I called. Remember your favorite college president?"

"Marta Vander Waal? Yeah."

"Well, the board of trustees just gave her the boot."

"You're kidding. I mean I'll shed no tears for her, but why?"

"Apparently, Winton isn't in the financial shape they wanted."

"Really? When I spoke to her, funding was all she cared about."

"Maybe that's why."

David and Fred talked for a while about the campaign, including the Saturday barbeque in the next county. They finished talking after another twenty minutes. The network news continued, finishing with the quirky story of how a cat dialed 911 when its owner was having a heart attack.

Finally, the local Philadelphia news returned. David watched for Jansing's acceptance speech. When she finally spoke, David was unimpressed. Apparently, with a long-term incumbent like Lannier, few serious Democrats wanted to waste their time running against him. Jansing was the best Democrat willing to take on the challenge.

ഇ ഇ ൚ ൚

In the following weeks, the Kadler Steele scandal exploded across the media. The deals that interconnected Kadler Steele with other financial institutions were the focus of several exposés. The Dow Jones Index dropped 665 points on fears of revisiting the economic crisis of 2007. Everyone was blaming everyone else for the problem. Phrases such as "too big to fail" and "bailout" returned to the national lexicon. Comedians, critics and others were quick to use the inevitable shallow wit of "Kadler Steals." While the Justice Department and the Securities & Exchange Commission continued to investigate, members of Congress were quick to propose new legislation.

ഇ ഇ ൚ ൚

Debates in the U.S. House of Representatives are very structured and carefully timed. The rules of order are complex and specific, making it easy to confuse new members. For instance, representatives must address the Speaker or Speaker pro tempore of the day, not the opposing side. The Speaker of the House rarely presides over the day-to-day affairs of the Floor. Every day the House is in session, a Speaker pro tempore is designated, providing a good mechanism for newer members to get Floor experience. Aides stand by in case the acting Speaker needs help or advice.

The Majority and Minority Leaders each designate a debate manager who is assigned a certain amount of time for their respective sides. Each manager usually makes opening remarks, then yields part of his or her time to fellow party members in a predetermined sequence. Each party alternates speakers. On this day, Sheldon Lannier would manage the debate for the Republicans. Michelle McNair of Oregon would handle that duty for the Democrats. Representing the majority party, Lannier began first, stepping forward with his white mane and narrow eyes. Despite his elegantly coiffed hair, Lannier had a toughness in his face.

"Mr. Speaker, our party sets forth the Financial Stability Act for consideration, a piece of legislation which will curb abuses in the financial

45

sector, while not overreacting and causing excess damage to our economic institutions and the overall economy. I ask that my colleagues on both sides of the aisle join me in support and vote this into law."

McNair stepped up to the podium dressed in her red business suit.

"Mr. Speaker, in the midst of this Kadler Steele affair, we are witnesses to financial greed on steroids," McNair announced in a nasal voice. "The Kadler Steel situation is just another example of the Wall Street juggernaut once again trampling the economic well-being of ordinary Americans. We must act quickly to prevent any further economic turmoil. However, this so-called Financial Stability Act is nothing more than a fig leaf for doing nothing. In response, we offered the Jimenez-Eaton Act, which would truly demonstrate to the American people that their government is acting swiftly and decisively to protect their interests. And I invite my colleagues across the aisle to eschew the smoke-and-mirrors of this faux-legislation before us. Instead, I urge them to join us in bipartisan unity to defend our country from economic chaos by demanding the Speaker bring the Jimenez-Eaton Act up for consideration." McNair stepped back, signaling for the other side to speak.

"Hard Shell" Lannier had been the veteran of many legislative battles. He looked across at Michelle McNair, a woman young enough to be his daughter. He could easily humiliate her, but that wouldn't look very statesmanlike. "Beating up on a girl" never went over well. If McNair were older or a man, he might wield the rhetorical battle axe. But with Michelle McNair, he would need to play it differently.

"I applaud my colleague's desire to avoid chaos, yet chaos is exactly what her bill offers. Although well-intended, her bill is a hastily concocted jumble of rules and regulations. The SEC and the Justice Department haven't even come close to concluding their investigation. Many of my colleagues on this side of the aisle blame the Farnum Administration's failure to enforce current regulations that might have prevented this situation. But I won't take this opportunity to take cheap shots at the President. To be fair, it's difficult to navigate, much less enforce, the spaghetti-code regulations that the financial industry has had to endure. Why make a difficult job harder?"

"So before we start panicking, let's slow down and soberly consider the nature of our economic system. Free-market capitalism is a natural process that rewards good behavior and punishes bad behavior. When we recklessly interfere with that process, things go awry, like Dr. Frankenstein tinkering with unnatural forces. The Financial Stability Act, on the other hand, is a measured and intelligent adjustment to current law that will assure a stable economy."

As he spoke, Lannier spied in his peripheral vision a new oncoming storm. Despite public perception, there are actually few people on the floor during a debate. So it was easy for Lannier, even as he was speaking, to spot Porter Barnes striding onto the floor. His large frame pushed purposefully toward McNair like a lumbering locomotive. He whispered something into

Michelle McNair's ear. She didn't look happy. Lannier finally concluded his remarks.

"Mr. Speaker," McNair announced. "I would like to yield three minutes of my time to Mr. Barnes of California."

"Proceed," said the Speaker pro tempore.

Barnes stepped up to the Democratic podium. "Thank you, Mr. Speaker. I would like to know if the good Congressman Lannier is such an expert on the financial industry, why didn't he forewarn all the clients, investors, and innocent bystanders that such a thing was coming, especially given his intimate knowledge of Kadler Steele."

"Mr. Speaker, I object to the Congressman's insinuation," Lannier interrupted.

"Didn't you have drinks with their CEO, Corbin Beaumont, only a month ago? Haven't you used their private jet? Haven't you—"

The Speaker's gavel came down in a loud crack. "Order!" the Speaker pro tempore demanded. "Representatives will address the Speaker, and not each other!"

"My apologies, Mr. Speaker. But I would still like to know why Congressman Lannier's intimate relationship with Kadler Steele did not yield any warnings. I think it would be instructive for all of us if he addressed this burning issue."

"Mr. Speaker, again I object to Congressman Barnes's slander that I had an intimate relationship with any brokerage firm. As a member of the Financial Services Committee, it is appropriate to meet and discuss financial issues with major players in the market. I know Congressman Barnes does the same."

"Consulting with and taking large campaign contributions from Kadler Steele are two different things." Of course, Barnes had taken far more contributions from Wall Street firms, just not from Kadler Steele. Sometimes one was lucky.

"Mr. Speaker," Lannier pleaded. "We are here to discuss the bill before us, not to play cheap political theater, which is what Congressman Barnes seems to be fixated on. If he is not willing to even pretend to discuss the bill, he is out of order."

"Mr. Speaker." Barnes said. "I came here to ask a question. Since the gentleman from Pennsylvania refuses to answer, I yield the balance of my time back to Congresswoman McNair." Barnes quickly left the podium.

Lannier clenched his teeth, forcing himself to resume the task at hand. "Mr. Speaker, I now yield three minutes of my time to Congresswoman Marquette of Colorado."

Once out of range of the cameras, Barnes gave Lannier an impolite gesture and then smirked as he headed toward the press gallery. Every reporter there would have seen this exchange on the C-SPAN feed and would have plenty of questions. And Barnes would have plenty of answers.

Lannier, on the other hand, was managing the Republican half of the debate, keeping him stuck on the Floor for at least the next hour.

CHAPTER 9

Once out of the House chamber, Porter Barnes suppressed his smirk, adopting the practiced countenance of a grim patriot, as he walked down the marble corridor toward the press gallery. However, the competitive nature of TV journalism drove a flock of reporters with the requisite video cameras on an intercept course.

"Congressman Barnes," a reporter called out. "What exactly are you charging Congressman Lannier with?"

"I haven't charged him with anything," Barnes said in his gravelly voice. "I've merely gathered some facts and asked a question."

"What facts have you uncovered?" another reporter blurted out.

"I really should save the particulars for a discussion with the Ethics Committee. Of course, campaign contributions are publicly available information."

"In your remarks, you mentioned Congressman Lannier flying on a private Kadler Steele jet?"

"Yes, I did mention that."

"What proof do you have?"

"I didn't say I had proof. I have reports," Barnes said, lighting their journalistic fuses. "It's important to make that distinction. We should not condemn anyone on reports alone. Excuse me, I have a committee meeting," he added as he headed down the marble corridor and into a legislators-only elevator.

Barnes never made it to the press gallery. He didn't need to.

෨ ෨ ෬ ෬

That night, the scene from the House Floor and the Barnes hallway interview were played all across the network news. Newsrooms were in a frenzied scramble to find out more about the relationship between Lannier and Kadler Steele. Every news editor and producer knew that every big scandal story needed a face. Sheldon Lannier was now that face.

෨ ෨ ෬ ෬

Harris Carver watched the news reports from home that night, drinking a private Courvoisier toast to the "loose cannon." Carver had to hand it to Barnes. All he gave him was the donor information. The corporate jet information was all from Barnes. Carver wondered how he had obtained it. But it didn't matter. *Mission accomplished.*

෨ ෨ ෬ ෬

Ben Glendenning thought it was going to be a slow news day. He thought he was going to have to resort to a "rant rerun" to fill time. But luck had smiled on him. His first segment had already been recorded by the time they made sense of what had happened on the Floor of the House. But it was perfect for the second segment. Glendenning waited for the red light on the camera to flash. Flash. *Showtime.*

"Did you happen to see that miserable excuse for a congressman, Porter Barnes, cowardly ambush Sheldon Lannier?" Glendenning said with self-righteous indignation. "He disrupted a scheduled House debate. He disrupted democracy in action. Why? Because Democrats hate honest debate. But as one of Farnum's commissars, I'm sure he was just following orders."

"My fellow patriots, it was a hit-and-run. Barnes should know about hit and run. Before coming to Washington, he was an ambulance chaser. He didn't even have the courage to stay and debate Lannier. He ran away. Hit-and-run. Cut-and-run. Typical Democrat!"

Glendenning continued his attack on Porter Barnes and other Democrats, but never mentioned Kadler Steele or any related facts or issues.

೫ ೫ ೧ ೮

The next day, David Grant, Fred Arkin and Ellen Langford gathered for their first meeting since the "Great Ambush." By now, the Maple Street storefront in Embler had been completely purged of its former shoe shop identity. It was not fancy, but clearly a campaign office. They sat around an old wooden desk in the back on hard metal folding chairs.

"You are the luckiest Independent I know," Ellen said to David. "As you remember, I didn't give you much of a chance on winning this thing. But the electoral gods have smiled on you. Your prospects have now been officially elevated to slim chance."

"Thanks. You might have a future in motivational speaking," David joked. "Although, you might want to keep your day job."

"Maybe, we should send Porter Barnes some flowers," Fred mused, as he sat down.

"I don't know," David said, smiling. "He might get the wrong idea,"

"OK, cigars. But seriously, Sheldon Lannier is wounded now," Fred continued enthusiastically. "We've got to take advantage of this, run TV, radio…you know, a media full court press."

"That's fine, but let's not burn too much cash on it," Ellen warned. "Linda Jansing is going to come out swinging, and I expect the DNC will funnel money to her, now that Lannier is vulnerable. In addition, the national media will probably beat him up quite a bit."

"Luckily," Fred added, "this plays to your 'Washington is broken' message perfectly. I want to bring Jason Kennerly up here to do a video interview with you on Lannier."

"That's a good idea, Fred," Ellen said. "Let's do that quickly. It'll be good practice. This Lannier mess gives us an opening to get David booked on as many talk and news shows as possible, although admittedly most will want to talk to Jansing."

"Great, but if that's the case, I also want to do some serious media training," David insisted.

Fred looked a little puzzled.

"When I was in the corporate world I did some media training, you know eye contact, voice projection, nothing that extraordinary," David explained. "But I remember the trainer warned us to be ready for the sucker punch question. I want you two to come up with the nastiest below-the-belt questions you can think to ask me."

Ellen nodded approvingly. "No problem. But besides doing more media, you need to keep pounding your message on the stump."

"I certainly intend to. If Lannier was on the take, he deserves whatever he gets. And that's well and good, but I'm still only speaking to small groups. I need to get in front of bigger crowds."

"That's easier said than done," Ellen said. "It's summer. Everyone just wants to be on vacation. But, shaking hands with every voter you can gives you an advantage in a world where everyone's relationships are online."

"But I still want bigger audiences."

"Let me work on that," Fred suggested.

"Great," Ellen responded, not expecting anything to come from it. "In the meantime, I need to figure out Jansing's weak spot."

ಹಿ ಹಿ ಚ ಚ

At five foot eleven, Jessica Dandridge had been a strong athlete in school, intimidating both on and off the basketball court. Yet, she still had to endure all the Amazon jokes and taunts. After graduating from USC with a degree in journalism, she found work as a sportscaster on a local California television station.

When a competing station was pressured to put more women on the air, a savvy producer saw Dandridge as a diamond in the rough, and hired her. She was tall, blonde and had a hard beauty.

Over the years, as she gained experience and confidence, she had moved up. After a while though, it became clear she would never quite make the anchor track. She suspected her height was an issue. She knew certain male anchors didn't want to sit next to her at the anchor desk, much less stand next to her.

As the number of cable news channels increased, Dandridge eventually saw her path. She always had an acerbic sense of humor, hewn from the taunts of her teenage years. So making the move from roving correspondent to partisan pundit was a no-brainer. She found it quite liberating to cast aside the constraining journalistic mantra of "just-the-facts." The more barbed her opinions, the more success she garnered.

Eventually she caught Ellis Cornwall's eye. Cornwall, a liberal media mogul, started up a cable network to counter the conservative CPN network and the likes of Ben Glendenning. The new cable channel was called "Liberty!" complete with the exclamation point. The network's name irked conservatives to no end. How can you be against Liberty? Opponents had to be careful to always use the word "channel" when slamming the network. Dandridge started with the midnight show, but within a few months moved into prime time.

In addition to broadcasting, she wrote a bi-weekly column that was quite popular among progressives. Dandridge's books had done well. Her first book, *Heil Henderson!* sold over a 500,000 copies. She had followed that up two years later with *102 Uses for a Dead Republican.* That one had sold over three million copies. She was currently arguing with her publisher over her upcoming book. Dandridge wanted to call it either *Castrating Conservatives* or *Neutering NeoCons.* The publisher objected, probably more over the visual she wanted to use, which involved a large scissors and a cardboard cutout of Ben Glendenning.

One conservative senator once called her the "Queen Bitch of the Snark Squad" when he didn't realize a live microphone was nearby. Dandridge always smiled at that. It was a badge of honor. Sometimes she even used it on the air.

Like everyone else, she had caught the Barnes ambush of "Hardshell" Lannier on the C-SPAN reruns. Unfortunately, her show aired earlier than Glendenning's, and she wasn't able to comment on it, much less arrange for any guests. But as soon as she learned of the incident, she and her staff were immediately on the phone to get a hold of Porter Barnes. After a day of calling every contact, she was finally able to connect with him.

"Congressman, nice job cracking Shelly Lannier yesterday."

"Thanks, Jess. What can I do for you?" Barnes answered in less than his usual gruff manner.

"You know full well I want you with me tonight," she said in mock seductive tone.

"With you? Or just on your show?" he laughed.

"If you're really going after Shelly Lannier, we can set it up wherever you want."

"Sorry Jess. I need to let this percolate another day or so. Otherwise the story is Barnes versus Lannier. It's got to be Lannier in bed with Wall Street."

"You know, I'm willing to help make that happen."

"I know you are, honey. Don't worry, we'll have our time. Gotta go."

"You're breaking my heart."

"I'll make it up to you. I've still got Act Two to finish writing. Maybe I'll write you in. Like I said, gotta go."

Dandridge frowned as she hung up the telephone.

ଓ ଓ ଓଷ ଓଷ

Ed Leems poured himself a third cup of coffee, and it was only 10 AM. Heading toward the midterm elections, the primaries in most of the states were now over. Now they had to determine which candidates would receive DNC funding. His counterpart at the RNC would be doing the same.

Incumbents from every state sent funding requests months ago. Their surrogates also button-holed him at every turn to remind him of how imperative it was to keep Senator X or Representative Y in Congress. Now that the primaries were over, requests from the challengers were coming in. The whole process was triage.

Incumbents in solid Democratic districts got just enough so they wouldn't feel they were being ignored. Challengers who were foolish enough to take on strong Republican incumbents in effectively gerrymandered districts received nothing. There was no point in wasting the money. That left the battleground districts.

He waved Sonia and Cal into his newly remodeled office. Sonia Neilson and Calvin Sarno were his best political number crunchers. They sat down quickly at the polished oak conference table, and started laying out their files.

Sonia had arranged for the donor data that eventually made its way to Porter Barnes, although Leems didn't know if she suspected that connection. If she did, she didn't say anything. Perhaps she was distracted by the upcoming midterm elections like everyone else.

Leems had asked them to evaluate the incumbents, the challengers, the demographics, polls, and anything else that might be relevant, state by state, district by district. The whole process gave Leems a headache. The Senate side was so much easier; 33 or 34 races, tops. With 435 seats in the House, it was a nightmare repeated every two years.

"Cal, Sonia, can you make my life easy?" he pleaded.

"Easy? Not this time around," Cal laughed.

"So, which states are we looking at today?"

"Ohio and Pennsylvania," Sonia said. They could only do two states at a time, unless they were small-population states like Delaware, Vermont or Montana.

"Great." Leems mentally calculated that Ohio and Pennsylvania came to just under 40 seats. Half were probably battlegrounds. *Damn.* "Who's up first?"

"We think Vic Orsoni has a good chance of taking Ohio's 3rd," Cal announced.

"Against Naomi Corker?" Leems laughed. "Unless you find her in bed with a lesbian hooker, that's a pipe dream. Guys, this is a midterm with our guy in the White House. The pendulum always swings the other way. We are going to lose seats. It almost always happens when you're holding the White House, especially with this Kadler Steele mess. We need to think defensively."

"Ed, I've got to be honest," Sonia said. "We're getting a little worried about all the third parties and Independents entering races, more than ever before. Over 80 percent of the districts across the country have at least one Independent in the race,"

"It makes sense," Cal added. "Congress only has a six percent approval rating. It's never been so low. The country is really getting pissed."

"The country's been pissed for the last decade," Ed said dismissively. "But Independents don't get elected."

"What about Bernie Sanders?" Sonia asked.

"Okay, once every 80 years or so. Can we get serious now?"

"All right, but Independents can still siphon off votes," she countered.

Leems had to admit the truth of that.

"What about Pennsylvania's 20th?" Sonia asked. "You know, Sheldon Lannier's seat."

"Yeah, I think Porter Barnes pretty much stuck a fork in him the other day," Cal crowed.

"Don't count ol' Shelly Lannier out yet," Leems said, remembering the donor list he gave Harris Carver. "Who do we have running against him?"

"Linda Jansing, former Assemblywoman. She lost re-election for Assembly a year ago, but just barely. So, she decided on a Hail Mary with Lannier's seat. Boy, did she luck out."

"Great, a lucky dud," Leems mumbled, rubbing his eyes. "Any polling data?"

"Well, it doesn't account for yesterday's revelations, but...Lannier 41%, Jansing 33%, Grant 4%, Lurtz 1%. The other 21% undecided.

"Who the hell are Grant and Lurtz?"

"Independents. Remember?" said Sonia in an exasperated tone.

"They're both McQuacks," Cal said dismissively.

The few staffers at the DNC that paid attention to Independents divided them into three general categories: Professor McQuacks, Schlubs and Pirouettes. Professor McQuack had been a character in a low-brow comedy, starring the late Damian Cox. McQuack was shorthand for an academic candidate, usually a professor running on some narrow principle, often using his or her students as campaign staff for extra credit.

"Schlubs," with its Yiddish origins, referred to average citizens who were sincere, yet lacked financing, public speaking ability, or any political sophistication.

"Pirouettes" were usually businessmen running on money and ego. The label had nothing to do with ballet, but rather a reference to Ross Perot. Such a candidate's business connections and money could admittedly complicate a race.

"McQuacks?"

"Yeah, Grant is a college professor. Lurtz is a high school teacher."

"Okay, nothing to worry about there," Leems agreed.

"Still, Independents are on the rise," Sonia added. "We ignore them at our peril."

"Almost every district is infested with them," Cal said. "We may need an exterminator."

"Enough," Leems said wearily. He was tired of all this talk of Independents, mostly because he had all of Ohio and Pennsylvania to get through still. "Well, Ms. Jansing lucked out. Let's allocate thirty grand for her now. If she doesn't piss herself, we can revisit giving her more later on. Okay, who's next?"

CHAPTER 10

The Roosevelt Room at the White House was filled with a dozen officials waiting for the President. The portraits of Theodore and Franklin Roosevelt watched over them from opposite ends of the meeting room. During a Democratic administration, FDR held the more prestigious position above the fireplace mantle. When the Republicans controlled the White House, TR held that spot.

Peter Warrenburg stood admiring TR's portrait, before he turned around to find Robert Hingecliff standing behind him. "Good morning, Robert."

"How are you, Peter?" he said, shaking Warrenburg's hand.

"Fine."

"So today we learn more about Kadler Steele? The ticking time bomb?"

The Attorney General nodded, while waving someone over. "Yes," Warrenburg said. "I'm surprised Gordon LaSalle isn't here."

"I'm afraid the Fed Chairman is a bit under the weather," Hingecliff said.

"He must be at death's door if he's missing this." At that moment, an attractive Indian woman with sharp features stepped up to them. Warrenburg shepherded her closer.

"Robert, I don't know if you've met Niyathi Bachali, the new head of the SEC's enforcement division."

"No, I haven't. It's a pleasure, Ms. Bachali."

"Likewise, Mr. Secretary," she said with a slight British accent acquired while attending the London School of Economics.

"Niyathi has been terrific in wading through the complexities of Kadler Steele. In a moment, you're going to see how convoluted they are."

Just at that moment, the President entered with Harris Carver in tow.

"Sorry for the delay everybody," the President said. "Governor Yarrow's photo op turned into lobbying for harbor dredging."

Everyone laughed.

"So Peter, where do we stand on this Kadler Steele affair?"

For the benefit of the others, Warrenburg very briefly recapped Kevin O'Hara's investigation. "Of course, we had to bring in the SEC. And I have to say rarely has there been such smooth cooperation. I attribute that to the new head of the SEC's enforcement division, Niyathi Bachali, who really had to hit the ground running." He motioned to Bachali who promptly stood up.

"Good morning, Mr. President. During the last two months, we have had a team of forensic accountants examining Kadler Steele's books. To be honest, I've never seen a worst case of financial malfeasance."

"But they were clean back in 2008," Farnum said. "Weren't they considered the role model when compared to AIG and the others?"

"If they were a role model, it was only by comparison. Unlike so many Wall Street firms, Kadler Steele remained solvent. So no one was looking at them too closely. In 2006, they began shorting the mortgage bond market through carefully constructed credit default swaps. They saw the whole mortgage bond collapse coming. In fact, they bet on it."

"There were a number of hedge funds that did that," Hingecliff interrupted. "And that in itself is not a crime. However, I don't recall Kadler Steele ever being on that list."

"That is true Mr. Secretary. We've come to call it the 'invisible short,' because they did it through a series of elaborate subsidiaries, hedge funds, and joint ventures. At first glance, Kadler Steele's organization chart looks like a plate of spaghetti. One almost needs three or four dimensions to view it. In addition, they have been very creative with the valuation of their assets. I suspect their success in avoiding the crash made them arrogant. They've built themselves a giant house of cards, and here's how they did it..."

Using a PowerPoint presentation, Bachali proceeded to explain how Kadler Steele had created complicated financial instruments that interwove equity funds, currency exchange, mortgage rates, and a host of other economic factors and how they were interlinked with one another. Her presentation was filled with specialized jargon such as CDOs, tranches, bilateral counterparties, dark pool trading, and synthetic derivatives. Even someone schooled in finance might have found themselves a little lost. The one phrase everyone understood was "probable bankruptcy."

"To what extent could this affect the larger economy?" Farnum asked.

"Well Mr. President, the global credit derivatives market is estimated at 2.1 quadrillion US dollars.

"Did you say *quadrillion*?" Carver asked.

"Yes, that's a thousand trillion or a million billion."

"Holy shit!" someone murmured at the far end of the room. Everyone else was silent. The air had been sucked out of the room. Bachali looked nervously over at the President. But Farnum was stone-faced while processing this information. Everyone needed a moment to take in this new word, this new scope. What was a $27 trillion National Debt compared to this unreal quadrillion dollar amount?

"Obviously, Kadler Steele isn't liable for that entire amount, is it?" Hingecliff asked, trying to bring everyone back from the shockwave.

"No, of course not," Bachali answered.

"What portion of that is Kadler Steele exposed to?"

"Due to the lack of transparency in their books, I can't say for sure."

"Give us a range," Hingcliff insisted.

"I have to say their exposure is 400 billion at a minimum, but probably no higher than a trillion. However, the joint ventures and subsidiaries extend that exposure to others, thus magnifying it, depending on how those parties have managed their risk."

"How can any one company have that much liability? Are they stupid?" Carver asked.

"Worse than stupid, they were clever," she answered. "The irony is that much of this was created through risk management."

"How does this connect to the stock trading issues that Kevin O'Hara, the U.S. Attorney, brought to our attention?" Farnum asked.

"It doesn't, at least not directly. It's like a casino running a series of rigged, but independent, games. Mr. President, Kadler Steele is a lit fuse tied in a giant knot. There's no knowing exactly how it will ignite, but there's no doubt that it will."

ဆ ဆ ଔ ଔ

After the meeting, everyone looked shell-shocked. Most of the participants had departed. However, Hingecliff hung back catching Bachali as she exited the Roosevelt Room.

"Excuse me Ms. Bachali, could I have a word?" Hingecliff asked.

"Certainly, Mr. Secretary," she responded, seeming pleased at the attention.

"I have to compliment you of the depth and detail of your investigation."

"Thank you, but there's still much more to do."

"Understandably. Just a word to the wise. Throwing out that quadrillion dollar figure was a little off the mark, and inappropriate. You gave the impression that we had a two quadrillion dollar problem on our hands. And that is not so."

"Mr. Secretary, with all due respect, our economic system is quite vulnerable, not just because of Kadler Steele. Kadler Steele is a symptom of a reckless financial culture. Our trade deficit. The National Debt. The ripple effects of Kadler Steele could be enormous. I don't know if you appreciate the depth of the problem."

"I most definitely do," he said sternly. "It was I who suggested that the US Attorney take a look at the bond side of Kadler. You're not the only one who studied finance and macroeconomics. I don't dispute your facts. But the crux of the matter is, we don't spook the President. We need to give him the facts and advice without excess drama. A president must make cool, calm, well-thought-out decisions. Fear can drive even presidents to make mistakes."

"Point taken," Bachali said, probably to end the conversation. "If you'll excuse me."

Hingecliff turned to see Harris Carver watching him.

"Thank you for that," Carver said, nodding toward the departing Bachali. "You saved me a lecture."

"No problem."

"Should we replace her?"

Hingecliff was caught off-guard by Carver's suggestion. "No, I think she's very competent and motivated. It was just her first time briefing the President. She'll do better next time." Carver nodded in agreement.

57

"Robert, the President would like a private word with you in the Oval."

"Certainly."

~ ~ ~ ~

Hingecliff entered the Oval Office.

"Come on in Robert. Ms. Bachali really paints a grim picture," Farnum said as he sat on the edge of his desk.

"Yes, she did."

Farnum leaned forward. "Is it going to be as bad as 2008?" he asked, trying to conceal any panic in his voice.

"It's hard to tell the exact extent, but I don't believe so. There will be those who declare the sky is falling. However, more important than the size of the numbers is to examine carefully the way they are connected."

"Wise advice," Farnum breathed, and stood up abruptly. "Anyway, that's not why I asked you here. I wanted to start off with an apology."

"An apology?" Hingcliff asked. "I can't imagine what for, Mr. President."

The President smiled. "I know you wanted Treasury, but I gave you Commerce."

"I serve in whatever capacity the President deems appropriate."

"Still, after the midterm elections, I plan to name you as the nominee to replace Garrett Llewellyn as Treasury Secretary."

"Mr. President, I'm honored. However, I'm not sure that position can remain unoccupied until then?

"To be honest, I don't want your nomination to become a partisan issue for the Republicans. This Kadler thing has them smelling blood."

"If my nomination would be difficult, perhaps you should nominate someone else."

"Robert, you're an ideal nominee. But anyone I nominate could become a campaign issue. In the meantime, I'd like you to run Treasury unofficially."

"Sir, there are several legal issues that might make that inadvisable." Farnum waved him off.

"Do you know Van Stephens at Treasury?" the President asked.

"Yes, the Deputy Secretary, a good man."

"I'll have him function as Acting Secretary. I want you to advise him. And I guarantee he will take your advice. Robert, by this time next year, your signature will be in everyone's wallet."

"Thank you, Mr. President." Hingecliff permitted himself a smile, but not too wide.

~ ~ ~ ~

Thanks to the Lannier controversy, David was able to raise his public profile. Jason Kennerly had helped generate considerable online buzz with blogging, online videos and social media. Kennerly had also mobilized CPP members from across the country, who in turn blogged, tweeted and, more importantly, started to donate larger amounts of money. David had to admit his improved chances energized him.

This weekend, the campaign had reserved a booth at a street fair several towns west of Embler. David was shaking hands and talking to voters one-on-one. The late August sun beat down on everyone. The motto, "Never let them see you sweat," was clearly not going to apply today.

David's daughter Wendy joined the day's effort. Few could resist the cute 10-year old asking "Would you vote for my daddy?" David felt funny about using his daughter this way, but Wendy seemed to be enjoying herself. Perhaps she was the more natural politician. Wendy's participation had the added benefit of allowing David to discreetly slip away and change into a dry shirt.

At one point, a Tae Kwon Do school, whose booth was diagonally across the street, began a martial arts demonstration that bordered on acrobatics. It drew the entire crowd's attention. Even Wendy Grant was willing to abandon her father to watch the spectacle. It gave David and the others a moment to drink some water and talk. Ellen had finished up talking to someone on her mobile phone.

"Just got the word," she announced. "Congratulations, the latest poll has you at 12%."

"Great."

"The bad news is that Jansing has pulled ahead. She's viewed as the primary alternative to Lannier."

"So now, we need to focus on Jansing. Fred, did you call the Pennsylvania Democracy Institute?" David asked.

"Yes, unfortunately the PDI still insists they're only inviting Lannier and Jansing to the debate."

"Damn it, I declared before Jansing," David said, staring down at a forsaken ice cream cone surrendering to the hot asphalt. "Don't they have to include me? They're supposed to be non-partisan." He was feeling as helpless as the liquefying soft serve.

"The PDI is a privately funded organization," Ellen explained. "As the sponsors, they can invite, or not invite, whomever they want."

"I need to be in that debate."

"Are you a good debater?" Ellen asked.

"I don't know. But it doesn't matter."

"It could."

"There has to be another way," David mused. "Something creative."

"Maybe our friends at Winton might be able to help offer an alternate debate," Fred suggested.

"Great idea, but our 'friends' don't seem to include President Vander Waal. She wouldn't even let me have a rally on campus. Remember?"

"A debate is more neutral than a rally," Fred said. "And you forget, Vander Waal's gone. And, polling at 12% might make a difference."

"I don't know," Ellen said. "Neither Lannier or Jansing will want to come onto what they will consider your home turf. Although, I suppose Lurtz would come."

"Who's Lurtz?" David asked.

"Why do I do opposition research if you won't read it?" she said, slightly exasperated.

"I didn't even know there was another independent in the race."

"He's not a serious candidate," she said, opening a file folder. "Paul Lurtz is a middle school biology teacher promoting nutrition. He's running as the 'fruit and vegetable' candidate. Let's skip the obvious jokes. He acquired enough signatures to get on the ballot. So, he's part of the race."

"Well, he's clearly a joke," David said. "He can't have any expectations of winning."

David was waiting for a sarcastic 'and you do?' type of wisecrack from Ellen, but it never came.

"It's something he's doing to show students the importance of good nutrition. His wife is a social studies teacher, so this is sort of a family-slash-school project."

"So, what if Lurtz is the only one who wants to be in the debate?" David asked.

"I don't know," Ellen answered as she held up an 8x10 photo of Lurtz. "Do you really want to debate a man in a tomato suit?"

CHAPTER 11

David had made an appointment the following week with the new president of Winton College, Charles Danzig. Instead of being shown into the President's office, Danzig came out to greet him.

"President Danzig, thank you for taking the time to meet with me."

"Please, call me Chuck," Danzig said, shaking David's hand enthusiastically. "Do you mind if we take a walk outside while we talk?" he asked. "I've been stuck in this office with paperwork ever since I took over. Accreditation renewal, union contracts, you name it."

"No problem," David chuckled.

"So are you scheduled to teach during the upcoming semester?" Danzig asked, as they walked out the door toward the quad.

"No, I want to focus on my campaign this fall. And my department head has been quite accommodating. Whether he accommodates me with courses in the spring is another matter."

"Don't worry; he will. You're a valued member of the Winton community. And I hope you return to us soon. Well…I mean…only if you're…unsuccessful. The country's loss would be our gain."

David smiled at Danzig's awkward but quick recovery.

"Professor Arkin," he continued, "was quite exuberant in trying to sell me on the idea of Winton hosting the debate."

"Yes, his enthusiasm was what got me running in the first place."

"Well, I have to admit…" Suddenly they both had to duck to avoid being hit by a fluorescent orange Frisbee.

"Sorry!" the Frisbee-throwing student called out sheepishly. Danzig promptly picked up the orange disk and flipped it back in a perfect trajectory.

"Thanks." The student waved the Frisbee appreciatively.

"Where was I? Oh. I have to admit I like the idea of hosting a political debate. It would be great publicity for the college."

"A win-win for everyone," David said. "I thought the theater in Franklin Hall would be perfect."

"We're more than willing to rent out Franklin for the night."

"Rent?" David asked. "I thought you'd be hosting the debate. You know, with all the publicity."

Danzig stopped walking. "I'd love to. But confidentially, the college is in a tight financial position. Otherwise, I would just expense the costs to the public relations budget."

"What kinds of costs are we talking about?"

"Security, electricity, podium rental, paying students to act as ushers. I also assume you want this debate televised. Franklin has video capability, but there's the cost of camera operators. Perhaps the three campaigns could split the cost."

David realized some of these were imaginary costs. No college had any shortage of podiums or students who would volunteer to usher an event. This was a negotiation.

"Let me be honest," David said. "The other two campaigns don't really want me in the debate. They're not going to pay a dime to debate here, especially on what they might consider my home turf. Besides, the Pennsylvania Democracy Institute is already hosting a debate at no cost to the campaigns."

"So then, why do you need Winton to host a debate?"

"Because the PDI refuses to invite me."

"Ah." Danzig nodded and smiled. "Could *you* cover the cost?"

"I don't know if I want to be seen paying the costs. It might seem like a conflict of interest."

"You *could* make a donation to Winton's endowment fund instead."

"Well, if this is going to be such a public relations coup for Winton, how about if I donate a portion of the cost to the endowment fund?"

Danzig grinned. "Let's see what we can work out."

ဢ ဢ ଔ ଔ

Securing a debate venue was only half the battle, the easier half. The greater challenge was to convince the other candidates to participate. Ellen had made an appointment with Alan Traeger of the Lannier campaign, which was headquartered in a shopping mall, much more impressive than the recycled shoe store they had in Embler. As she entered the office area, she saw that Traeger looked haggard. He perked up, seeing her.

"Well, as I live and breathe, Ellen Langford, the prodigal Republican," Traeger crowed mockingly.

"Hello Alan, it's been a long time," she answered flatly, ignoring his obnoxious tone.

"Yeah, the last time I saw you was when Shelly and Marcus Finn collaborated on that banking bill. How the mighty have fallen. What, you couldn't find a real Republican to work for?"

"Don't be an ass when I'm bringing you a gift."

"Really? What gift?" he asked, pantomiming looking around her as if she were holding a gift box behind her.

"Lannier is getting his ass kicked in the polls."

"Yeah, tell me something I don't know," Traeger responded, slumping back in his chair, taking a gulp of his coffee.

"I'm offering you a wingman."

"Grant?" he asked incredulously.

"David Grant wants in on the debate."

"Grant is never going to win."

"Now, *you* tell me something I don't know. But, he still wants in on the debates. We're setting one up at Winton College."

"And you want Shelly to give Grant a seat at the adult table?"

"Exactly."

"I'm sorry, I still don't see the 'gift' in all this."

"I'll have David Grant pull his punches in Lannier's direction. Oh, he'll make general statements about how corruption is bad, *et cetera*, but he won't go in for the kill."

Traeger smiled knowingly. "And what if at the podium, Grant *forgets* to pull his punches?"

"Simple. Lannier punches back. I'm sure Sheldon Lannier is ten times the debater that David Grant is. But honestly, your guy is already bloodied. It's Jansing we want to hit. She's an inferior candidate, and never would have won the primary if the Democrats had any idea your boss would be vulnerable. Lannier's perceived invulnerability kept the challengers limited to the politically naïve or desperate like Jansing. But now, your guy has lost some credibility, he needs someone else to take her down."

"And Grant's that guy?"

"Yeah, he's the guy. He'll help Lannier make a fool out of Jansing. Not enough people are going to take a chance and vote for an Independent. So, they'll have to come back to the tried and true Sheldon Lannier. And it doesn't hurt my professional reputation that I helped a crippled Republican candidate get re-elected."

"So, you're betraying your own candidate?"

"Strangely, no. That's the beauty of it. From day one, I told David Grant, he was going to lose. I've been completely honest with him. He just wants to be heard in the debate."

"Let me talk to my boss," Traeger said, taking another gulp of his coffee. "I'll get back to you."

ಬ ಬ ಚಿ ಚ

Corbin Beaumont's chauffeur and bodyguard had driven around the block twice. It was their routine check for suspicious characters, or worse, reporters. "The sweep," as Craig called it, always made Beaumont impatient. This precaution stole minutes a day from his life, all because of meddling regulators and a hysterical media.

Summit, New Jersey, was one of those municipalities that attracted many in the financial community. It had convenient access to Manhattan's financial district, as well as fashionable amenities and a strong upscale suburban culture. The local police department regularly patrolled the neighborhood, but one couldn't be too careful.

Since the public announcement of the Kadler Steele investigation, their CEO's personal routine had changed, not just downgrading from limo to the less ostentatious sedan and the nightly circling of the block. He and his wife Amanda rarely ate out anymore. Too public. Beaumont had also cut back on playing golf at Baltusrol and completely stopped going to the Beacon Hill Club. The last time he was at the club, someone actually had the audacity and bad taste to ask how low he thought Kadler Steele stock would go. Admittedly, the stock had already dropped 23%.

After Craig made an unusually cautious third sweep of the neighborhood, he finally pulled into the deep cobblestone crescent driveway of the Beaumont residence. Craig scurried around to open the door for Beaumont.

"Thank you, Craig. See you tomorrow morning at the usual time."

"Very good, sir."

Craig didn't leave the driveway until Beaumont was safely inside his spacious home. The turn-of-the-century house had been completely gutted and rebuilt with the finest materials, as orchestrated by a very expensive local designer—all paid for by Kadler Steele. The board approved the expense, as Beaumont occasionally entertained clients there. It was a rationale no one on the board believed, but all approved.

Amanda, his much younger second wife, uncharacteristically greeted him at the door. "Corbin, there was a man here," she said, with concern in her voice. Her Texas twang, which she had worked years to suppress, still came out when she was upset.

"Did he hurt you?" he asked in a concerned voice.

"No, no, nothing like that."

"A reporter?"

"No, his suit was too fine for a reporter, Brookes Brothers I think." As a former fashion model, Amanda knew about such things. "He gave me this envelope, and said it was important you read it as soon as you got home." She handed her husband the small white linen envelope. It wasn't a subpoena. He opened it. The handwritten note was on high-quality paper, but had no official printing.

Dear Mr. Beaumont,

I am staying at the Summer Hills Hotel this evening in Room 507. I would appreciate it if you would join me for a drink. No lawyers or spin doctors, just a frank conversation between men.

Sincerely,
Robert Hingecliff

Who the hell is Robert Hingecliff? The name seemed familiar, but he couldn't recall where he had heard it. Was he an analyst? Or part of the government investigation? Why was this man leaving a note at his home? Beaumont pulled out his smart phone and typed in the name. He was surprised by the search result. *What was the Secretary of Commerce doing in Summit?*

CHAPTER 12

Sheldon Lannier's campaign finally agreed to the debate at Winton. Jansing's campaign followed suit, fearing it would send the wrong signal if she declined.

David stood in an empty Franklin Hall, staring solemnly at the three podiums on stage, pondering the next night's event.

"Hey," Fred called out from behind him.

"What are you doing here?" David asked in surprise.

"I called your house. Sara said you were here."

"Yeah, I always check out a venue before speaking if I can—an old habit from my corporate days."

"Penny for your thoughts," Fred said.

"My thoughts? Um, how the hell did I ever get here?"

"The same way those guys down in Independence Hall did. You gave a damn. You showed up."

"I don't know if showing up will be enough."

"That's why I brought these," Fred said, offering a large, white gift box.

"What's this?"

"Open it."

David opened the box to find a pair of boxing gloves. He laughed.

"Try 'em on," Fred said.

David pulled them on, punched them together like a boxer, and began to parody various boxing maneuverings. "Float like a butterfly; sting like a bee!" he said, allowing himself a moment of silliness.

"Okay, Mohammed, don't quit your day job." They both laughed, relieving the tension.

"Fred, regardless of how this goes," he said, gesturing to the stage, "thank you for all you've done."

"No, you have it backwards. Thank *you*. You know, a lot of Independents would like to run for office. Hell, a lot have. There are dozens of centrist parties across this country, and most of their candidates never seem quite ready for prime time. You're the first I could actually see as a congressman. Even if you don't win, you'll have shown the country that serious people are unhappy with the way things are going in this country and the major parties have failed us. Thank you for putting them on notice in a way that Jason or I never could."

ဆဝ ၄၀ ၄၃ ၄၃

Corbin Beaumont quickly called up the Commerce Department website and navigated to the page that showed a photograph of the Secretary. His wife confirmed that the man who delivered the note was indeed the authentic

Robert Hingecliff. Beaumont called the Summer Hills Hotel and confirmed that Hingecliff had indeed checked in. In addition, the Secretary had left a message for him to come over anytime. *How odd.*

Beaumont's chauffeur had already left. He had been very cautious about his personal security in the last month. Craig had driven him everywhere. He tried to reach the off-duty chauffeur on the telephone, but he wasn't answering. He decided to chance going to the hotel on his own. It was against his better judgment, but how often did a cabinet secretary literally show up on one's doorstep?

Beaumont gunned his BMW out of the driveway, and subsequently pulled onto Springfield Avenue, Summit's main road toward the Summer Hills Hotel. It had been built in 1868 as a rural resort, but suburbia had eventually caught up with it. He had been to this hotel dozens of times for local charity events, even a wedding once.

What concerned Beaumont was the prospect of someone recognizing and buttonholing him. With so many in the financial industry living in Summit, the probabilities were higher than he was comfortable with. He cautiously pulled into the back parking lot and avoided people as much as possible. Once in the door, Beaumont strode swiftly through the lobby. He was grateful when he reached the elevator. And thankfully, the young couple he shared the ride with seemed infinitely more interested in each other. He finally arrived at Room 507. He knocked. The door opened.

"Ah, Mr. Beaumont," Robert Hingecliff greeted him. "I'm so happy you could stop by. Do come in."

Beaumont walked into the nicely appointed suite.

"May I offer you a drink?"

"No, thank you."

"Please, have a seat. Relax."

Beaumont sat down in a red leather wingback chair in a completely unrelaxed manner. "So Mr. Secretary, what brings you to New Jersey?"

"You do, Mr. Beaumont," Hingecliff answered, smiling.

"Really?"

"I've been reading quite a lot about Kadler Steele."

"You and every other reader of *The Wall Street Journal*," Beaumont answered with a dark smirk.

"Oh, I have been reading very different reports—from people like Niyathi Bachali and Kevin O'Hara. So has my colleague, Peter Warrenburg."

Beaumont's smirk evaporated. "What makes you people think you can take away what I've built?" he snapped.

"Please understand. I'm not with the Justice Department or the Treasury. I myself used to work on Wall Street, in my distant youth."

"Your note said 'frank conversation.' What is it you want?"

Hingecliff sat down in the chair opposite Beaumont's. "I'm an economist. I want economic stability."

"Well, Farnum's goons have certainly created economic *instability*." Beaumont leaned forward. "Their alarmism has destroyed million of dollars in wealth."

"You refer to the drop in stock prices. I expect you're quite correct in that," Hingecliff admitted. "Perhaps certain members of the administration have been a bit ham-fisted."

"Finally, someone in government who gets it."

Hingecliff leaned forward, pressing his fingertips together. "In the spirit of frankness, your organization has constructed a labyrinth of extraordinarily complex securities."

"Admittedly, some are not suitable for the unsophisticated investor."

"And some are not suitable for any investor. It will take quite a bit to untangle them. If the financial structure of Kadler were simpler, any investigation would be brief. And the outcome, whatever it might be, would be less dramatic. I'm wondering if there is some way to bring the investigation, and the associated financial turmoil, to a close quickly."

"You mean before election day?" Beaumont asked, sensing a point of leverage.

"Oh no, I'm not concerned with the midterm elections," Hingecliff answered, dashing Beaumont's hopes. "Besides, having Wall Street as a straw man works well for Democrats. Many political operatives relish the prospect of running against the 'evil Wall Street.' You may have seen Congressman Barnes's performance on the House Floor a few weeks ago." Hingecliff leaned forward again. "But none of this is in the best interest of the economy or the country."

"So you're here to cut some sort of deal?"

"We're just having in informal discussion."

"Then, *informally*, what would you suggest?"

"That depends on the shape of things inside Kadler Steele. What has your internal investigation turned up?"

"I'm afraid my lawyer would have a fit if I discussed such things with a governmental official, at least without him present. Why don't you tell me what Mr. Warrenburg has read?"

"I'm afraid sharing that is not within my purview. Nevertheless, we both know Kadler's problems are systemic. However, I *imagine* a public investigation could confine itself to an isolated portion of Kadler's operations."

"That might be helpful," Beaumont answered cautiously.

"Although, in my imagined scenario, there would still be a need to address all the issues, perhaps through an internal audit and reorganization. This would signal to the market that the company had stumbled, but is stable and addressing discrepancies responsibly."

"It's funny you should mention that, as I've been considering just such a plan."

"Hmm, that's good to hear. Of course, I would envision that in exchange for an isolated investigation, there would need to be some supervision on how such a plan is implemented."

Beaumont shifted uncomfortably. "How would such supervision occur?"

"Full disclosure to the government of all details to start. All activities. All transactions.

"Disclosure to the government, not the public?"

"Possibly," Hingecliff conceded.

"Immunity might be required."

"That might be appropriate in your role as liaison between Kadler and the SEC."

A puzzled expression crossed Beaumont's face. "Liaison?"

"Yes, after you step down as Chairman and CEO."

"What?"

"Well, the government would need to know that you were acting in the best interest of the country, avoiding any conflict of interest, past, present or future."

Beaumont's face became flush with anger. "You have no right! Pushing me aside like that! While everybody else screwed the pooch, we thrived. I didn't take one red cent of TARP money."

"Yes, and you have my respect for that," Hingecliff said in a calming voice. "But your good fortune in that case has made you overconfident since, which has led to some overreaching. The serpentine nature of your deals was not revealed in the required financial statements. You know as well as I, Section 302 of the Sarbanes-Oxley Act requires principal officers to certify and approve the integrity of their company financial reports quarterly."

"You're threatening me with Sarbanes-Oxley? You've got to be kidding. No CEO or CFO has ever been convicted using Sox. I mean, there's no way any CEO could know every detail about every transaction in a firm of Kadler's size."

"Mr. Beaumont, relax. I have no prosecutorial power whatsoever. I am in no position to threaten you with anything. I'm merely exploring amicable solutions. It's just that to discern the truth, we need you out on the sidelines, for your own protection. You see, if you are absent from the situation, you can't be accused of any obstruction. As liaison, you would be aiding the government in decoding Kadler's finances. Do you think you can do that?"

"I can do that as Chairman and CEO."

"Truth be told, the liaison position I'm proposing is more honorary than functional—a mechanism for saving face. Bachali and O'Hara have an army of forensic accountants. They just need you to get out of the way."

Beaumont snorted a laugh. "Those second-rate government bookkeepers will never be able to comprehend the beauty or decode the complexity of Kadler's finances without me."

"That is a legitimate concern, one I suppose that will need to be addressed. I should confer with others." Hingecliff stood up. "We'll be in touch."

Beaumont stood up.

"Good evening, Mr. Beaumont."

"Good evening, Mr. Secretary," Beaumont replied, as he eyed Hingecliff suspiciously.

After Beaumont left, Hingecliff picked up the telephone to make a call. Before he could punch in the number, there was a knock at the door. He opened it to find Kevin O'Hara standing there.

"What are you doing here?" Hingecliff asked.

"Ham-fisted? Really?"

CHAPTER 13

Hingecliff smiled with a tinge of embarrassment, even though he knew O'Hara was teasing him. "Sorry about the 'ham-fisted' comment. I needed to suggest a certain sympathy."

"Are you sympathetic?"

"Certainly not. Beaumont is a crook, possibly a self-deluded one, but a crook nonetheless." He realized he had replied a bit more self-defensively than he intended. "I have to say I've never been part of a 'sting operation' before. It's actually quite exciting. Do you do this often?"

"No, I'm a prosecutor, not an investigator," O'Hara answered.

"Yes, I was wondering why you were here."

"Well Mr. Secretary, I have to admit I was very curious about what Beaumont would say. I'm surprised he came at all. I guess you were the perfect bait."

At that moment, a woman came into the room.

"Good evening, Agent Simms. Did you get everything on tape you needed?" Hingecliff asked.

"Actually, it's all digital now. And yes, I think we got exactly what we needed," she said, handing O'Hara a set of papers.

"A transcript so quickly?" O'Hara asked, amazed.

"Voice transcription software," she replied, pointing to a particular section.

O'Hara read Beaumont's words aloud, "Those second-rate government bookkeepers will never be able to comprehend the beauty or decode the complexity of Kadler's finances without me."

"It's not exactly a confession," Simms admitted. "But he won't be able to claim being an out-of-the-loop CEO."

"I have to admit, between this and what Erin Korelev has given us, we may be on the way to the first Sarbanes-Oxley conviction."

"Bait? Hmm, that'll be interesting to add to my résumé," he chuckled.

ဆ ဆ ർ ຕ

The following evening, Franklin Hall was filled. The oval-shaped auditorium had just over 800 seats. Each campaign had been allotted 200 tickets for their respective supporters. The balance was to be used by the college, which included board members, faculty, administration, and students.

Each candidate was given a nearby classroom to use as a "green room" or preparation area. Everyone from David's campaign staff was there, much to Ellen's annoyance. However, Fred and Sara were quick to clear them out.

"Do you have a watch on?" Ellen asked.

"Right here," David said, holding his wrist up to display the watch.

"Give it to me."

"Why?"

"Do you remember the Bush-Clinton debate, where George H.W. Bush checked the time in the middle of the debate, as if he had somewhere else he'd rather be. It was a very natural instinct, but it signaled his discomfort. So, hand it over."

David unfastened his watch reluctantly and placed it in his pocket.

"I promise I won't take it out."

"Okay," Ellen said. "You have three things to accomplish here tonight. First, don't screw up. On the issues or technicalities, I mean. Second, give the media some good sound bites. And third, land some punches on these guys. Show you're as tough as they are, without being out of control."

David wondered if Ellen knew about the boxing gloves Fred gave him the night before. "Thanks, coach. I'll see what I can do."

"Also, be on guard toward the end. That's when people get tired and make mistakes, usually around the 50-minute mark. That's when Gerald Ford mistakenly said, 'There was no Soviet domination of Czechoslovakia.' So, also be prepared for the sucker-punch question near the end."

"If I can't look at my watch, how will I know when it's 50 minutes?" he asked teasingly.

₧₧ ₧ ₧

A few minutes later, David walked onto the stage and shook hands with Lannier and Jansing. The candidates walked to their predetermined podiums. David was pleased to be positioned in the middle.

"Good evening, ladies and gentlemen," announced President Danzig, addressing the audience. "Welcome to Winton College. We are very proud to host the debate for the three candidates for the 20th District for the US House of Representatives. Even though I'm new to Winton, I was already aware of the College's strong participation in civil affairs. Tonight's panelists include Laura Gonnelli of PA-TV, Karl Montel, political reporter for the Philadelphia Post, and Professor Armand Nistle, professor of political science here at Winton College." Danzig proceeded to brag about the history and mission of Winton College. He wasn't going to miss the opportunity to promote the college during a televised event.

While Danzig was extolling the virtues of the college, David stared at Professor Nistle. He suddenly recognized him as the professor who had called him an "evil capitalist" when he first arrived at Winton College. He wondered how Nistle wangled a seat on this panel, and why.

Danzig continued. "I am told one of the requirements of a good debate is for the audience to remain silent, withholding their applause until the end. Therefore, anyone applauding before the end will be given detention." Everyone laughed. "However, laughing at my jokes is an exception. But seriously, the less we interrupt them, the more we can learn about the candidates. Thank you. Ms. Gonnelli, the debate is yours."

"Thank you, President Danzig. We will begin with the first question, for Linda Jansing," Gonnelli announced. "Assemblywoman, for years, there has been a lot of angst and debate over the rising cost of healthcare. What would your approach be to tackling the ongoing healthcare situation in this country?"

Jansing smiled widely. "America has a sacred responsibility to keep its citizens healthy. It's as simple as that. The only surefire method is universal healthcare. It's the only viable way to deliver healthcare services to everyone, regardless of economic status. The people want it, but the insurance companies fight it. Of course, Republicans like Sheldon Lannier will always side with greedy and heartless big business against the American people. They're just hurting working Americans."

"Congressman Lannier," Gonnelli said. Lannier straightened his back to bring himself to his full height.

"First, I don't accept Ms. Jansing's ridiculous assertion that the people are demanding universal healthcare, at least beyond an extreme left-wing faction. This only seems to come up when we have a Democratic administration, whether it's Clinton, Obama or Farnum, looking to pander to the entitlement crowd. Of course, the insurance companies don't want it, because it will put them out of business, and send their employees to the unemployment office. But that's an uncomfortable detail that Ms. Jansing conveniently overlooks. Universal healthcare is socialism, pure and simple. It's just part of the Left's agenda to make the American people completely dependent on Washington for essential services. The Democrats want a nanny state of sheep. But unlike Linda Jansing, I know the people of my district are not sheep."

"Mr. Grant?" David didn't seem to hear or respond. "Mr. Grant?" she repeated.

"I'm sorry," he said, then paused. Everyone was uncomfortable. Ellen inhaled, waiting for David to start.

"Healthcare is too complicated an issue to be fit into sound bites. However, let me address two important aspects. We can point to a host of effective government programs. But I challenge you to find an *efficient* one. People want more services for less money. Healthcare coverage is about efficiency. While not always perfect, private enterprise has always been much better at doing things efficiently. So no, I'm not in favor of creating another inefficient entitlement plan. That being said, we find ourselves in an economic environment where more and more citizens are working for themselves or small companies that can't afford very much in the way of healthcare coverage. There needs to be an equitable restructuring of the laws and regulations, so smaller groups and individuals can obtain affordable coverage. We need to look seriously at insurance portability, and things along those lines. It's not as sexy as universal healthcare, but it'll be a more efficient solution, easier to pass, and be less likely to be struck down when the opposing party gets into office."

Ellen looked at the audience. She wasn't sure how this was playing. "David needs quotable sound bites. He sounds too intellectual, like a college professor." Fred bristled at the professor comment, but held his tongue.

Karl Montel asked the next question. "Congressman Lannier, you've been accused of being too much under the influence of Wall Street, particularly in the light of the Kadler Steele scandal. What do you say to those who accuse you of ignoring the illegal acts of your campaign contributor?" This was the question everyone was waiting to be asked.

"First off, no one's illegal acts are being ignored," Lannier stated. "Many people have made financial contributions to my campaign. I don't keep track of them all in my head. No member of Congress can. I vote my conscience. If people believe in my values and my actions, they contribute to my campaign. And they have. I believe in maintaining America's strong economic future. So I don't condone illegal activities regardless of who commits them. But at the same time we shouldn't overreact."

"Congressman Lannier thinks we're naïve, or worse, stupid," Jansing blurted out without being cued. "He accepted contributions from Wall Street, and it clearly affected his voting record. Can we afford to allow this to continue? I, for one am determined to stop the Republicans from fleecing our country of its future. Well, apparently Ol' Hard-Shell Lannier is determined to go soft on the Robber Barons."

"I'll bet she's been waiting all evening to use that one," Ellen chuckled.

"Mr. Grant," Gonnelli prompted.

"I know this a great political opportunity for anyone running against Congressman Lannier to slam him," David admitted. "But the fact is we don't know exactly how such donations affected the Congressman's voting in Congress. Lobbyists should make their case on the merits, not the size of their campaign contributions. The only way to fix the problem is to eliminate PAC and Super-PAC contributions. The only way to achieve honest government is to remove the moral hazard of special interest money."

Ellen and Alan Traeger looked at each other from across the stage. He nodded to acknowledge that Ellen and David had indeed kept their word about not attacking Lannier directly.

It was Professor Nistle's turn. "Mr. Grant, you just indicated that members of Congress should be free of financial conflicts of interest. Yet in your financial disclosure, you failed to reveal that you are expecting to receive approximately ten million Calibrent stock options. Doesn't that create a conflict of interest for you? Aren't you just as susceptible to corruption?"

Ellen turned to Fred. "Crap. He has stock options?" she asked incredulously. "Did you know about this?" Fred just shrugged.

"My financial disclosure correctly covers current assets and revenues. Those options represent a possible gain in the future. Unfortunately, thanks to the recent drop in the stock market, those options have very little if any future value. I may actually lose money." David stopped himself, realizing an explanation of stock options was not going to win him any points. "Besides, did anyone tell Arnold Schwarzenegger he couldn't receive royalties from his films while serving as governor of California? Of course not."

"But given your business background and connections," Nistle interrupted, "aren't you just as corrupt as the likes of Sheldon Lannier and Corbin Beaumont?" Montel and Gonnelli looked at Nistle in shock.

"Excuse me?" David cried out. "Listen, I started a company. I grew a business. I *created jobs* and valued products, like thousands of other businesspeople across this country. Don't confuse free enterprise with the freewheeling chicanery of Wall Street. Don't confuse the entrepreneurial spirit with the corruption of Washington politics."

Nistle was going to respond, but Gonnelli grabbed his arm.

"Congressman Lannier," she began. "You've made several foreign policy speeches citing—"

Suddenly a blaring alarm sounded. Everyone looked around in confusion.

President Danzig walked briskly onto the stage. "I'm sorry, ladies and gentlemen. It's a fire alarm. We must evacuate the building." People seemed reluctant to move. "Local fire regulations require we evacuate," Danzig insisted, as he motioned the audience toward the back exits. Finally, people slowly started to file out.

Ellen and Fred walked outside with David. It was still light out. The heavy overcast was too much for the setting sun. "You've got to be kidding. A fire alarm?" David exclaimed, while craning his neck to find Sara.

Suddenly, Charles Danzig came up from behind him. "David," he called out. David and the others turned around. "I'm really sorry about this."

"It's a fire alarm. There's nothing you can do about that."

"No, I mean about Nistle. When he lobbied me to be on the panel, I had no idea he was going to attack you. He said it would be good for Winton to be represented by faculty on the panel. Unfortunately, I bought into it."

In the excitement of the fire alarm, David had forgotten about Nistle. "These things happen," David said, not wanting Danzig to feel worse than he already did. Just then, fire engines began entering the parking lot.

"Excuse me, I need to speak to the Fire Chief," Danzig said, as he headed through the chaotic crowd.

"Gee, I wonder if I can get my money back," David joked darkly.

"Let me talk to the other campaigns about rescheduling if this doesn't resolve itself quickly," Ellen said, walking off into the twilight.

"Fred, have you seen Sara?"

"No," he answered, looking around. They began searching. Then suddenly, Fred stopped and tapped David's shoulder. Fred pointed to a spot about a hundred feet away, where Jansing and Nistle were talking.

"Look at those two," he said. "They seem pretty chummy."

David turned and saw the two chatting like old friends, even laughing. He started walking toward them in a slow burn. Jansing turned and started to amble away. But Nistle still had his back to David.

"Should we have gotten you a podium, too?" he called out.

Nistle swung around. "What do you mean?"

"Well, you seem more interested in throwing mud than asking honest questions. You're an intellectually dishonest fraud."

"And how am I dishonest?" Nistle asked defiantly.

"You implied anyone in business is dishonest. That's not even guilt by association. It's guilt by profession. I would expect better of a college professor than to stoop to that kind of logical fallacy."

Suddenly, Danzig showed up, intentionally ignoring the conflict.

"Ladies and gentlemen, we have the 'all clear' from the fire department," he called out. "Somebody was smoking in the restroom, and threw a lit cigarette butt into the trash. Let's all head back in, and resume the debate."

The crowd started to migrate back toward Franklin Hall. Danzig grabbed Nistle's arm. "Professor, may I have a word?"

ಬಿ ಜಿ ಚ ಚಿ

Once everyone was back inside Franklin Hall, the rounds of questioning continued. Nistle restricted his questions primarily to Jansing and Lannier, although it was clear that he was biased against Lannier. Finally, they were nearing the end of the evening.

"Candidates," Gonnelli addressed them. "It's now time for final remarks. As agreed ahead of time, we will begin with Congressman Lannier."

"Thank you," Lannier said. "There's been a lot of 'gotcha' being played these days," he said, staring down at Nistle. "As some of you saw, a certain Congressman ambushed me several weeks ago on the floor of the House, which admittedly has made things somewhat difficult for me. It might even cost me my job. Oh, it's made for great chatter in the media, but serves no useful purpose in serious governing. It's hurt me personally. Yes. But I persevere. I persevere because I was entrusted with the faith and hope of the citizens of this district, whom I have served faithfully for 12 years. And I hope to continue to serve them."

"My god, I think he's just given up," Fred whispered, noting the flat tone in Lannier's voice.

Ellen nodded in agreement, glancing down at her watch. "Fifty-seven minutes. It's late, and he's tired."

Jansing moved the microphone closer to her mouth. "Sheldon Lannier and the Republicans have a funny idea about service, allying themselves with the Wall Street Robber Barons. Then, we have Mr. Grant, who claims to be a centrist, but is really just a conservative in moderate clothing. In addition, he has almost no experience and no judgment. While on the Embler Town

Council, he advocated shutting down the vital EMS Ambulance Service and other essential services to save money. It may have been fiscally conservative, but it was also morally reprehensible."

Ellen turned to Fred. "Do you know what she's talking about?"

Fred shook his head. "No, but it feels like an ambush."

"The number-one requirement for serving in Congress," Jansing continued, "is compassion, something that neither of these men has. Send me to Congress, and I will help enact legislation that will protect lives *and* our way of life."

It was finally David's turn. "I did have a final statement prepared," he said. "But instead, I now have to address Ms. Jansing's outrageous charge. Typical for a politician, Ms. Jansing has only given you part of the picture. In Embler, we have three state-of-the-art ambulances with a host of dedicated and well-trained volunteers. Good people, all of them. What I objected to was the county government trying to replace those volunteers with the paid services of a county pay-to-play contractor, whose ambulances would be farther away and take much longer to reach our citizens when needed. It was both safer and less expensive to maintain our own EMS, rather than depending on the County bureaucracy. But the County had other ideas, so I and others on the Embler Council fought the County plan."

"Not true according to my information," Jansing interrupted desperately.

"Then, your information is wrong," David snapped back. "It seems to me if you want to be a member of Congress, you should endeavor to get your facts straight!"

"Fred," Ellen said with a grin. "I think our little boy has just grown up."

"Please!" Gonnelli called out. "As per the agreed upon rules, candidates should address the audience, not each other."

"Very well," David continued. "It's interesting how Assemblywoman Jansing dismisses me. Of course, I'm not part of the politician class. She says I don't have any experience. Well, I don't. I don't have experience taking legalized bribes or compromising my principles. I've built a business, created jobs, and looked out for my employees. I think those are the skills needed in Washington."

David glanced down at his notes. "Albert Einstein once said 'the definition of insanity is doing the same thing over and over again and expecting different results.' Congress's approval rating is around 4%. If we don't approve of the job Congress is doing, why would anyone think sending yet another Democrat or Republican to Washington would bring us anything different? If we want a different result, isn't it time to send somebody *different*?"

CHAPTER 14

David had spent the day after the debate in back-to-back events and media interviews. That night, he and Sara took a night off to be with the family. The couple were cuddling on the couch, while Chris and Wendy were making pizzas in the kitchen, one with balsamic chicken, the other with goat cheese and Portobello mushrooms. David and Sara weren't sure about this meal, but Chris was insisting. Meanwhile, David had turned on the local news just to see if there was any coverage of the debate.

When he turned on the television, the local anchor, Laura Gonnelli, was in the middle of her evening broadcast.

In her earpiece, Gonnelli heard the director putting aside the story lineup for an unexpected live feed. The director fed her the opening during the brief commercial break.

"This just in, Federal Reserve Chairman Gordon LaSalle has died. Apparently, he had been secretly battling pancreatic cancer. I'm told we now have a live feed from the White House."

The station cut to the live feed, where Dana Seagram was stepping up to the podium in the Press Room.

"Good evening, ladies and gentlemen. I have a late announcement. At approximately 4:30 this afternoon, Federal Reserve Chairman Gordon LaSalle died at his home of pancreatic cancer. I am told he died peacefully with his family around him. President Farnum expressed his condolences to the LaSalle family shortly after receiving the news. The President went on further to say that 'Chairman LaSalle was an untiring advocate for responsible monetary policy, and he will be missed.' Now, I'll take any questions you may have."

The reporter from the *Washington Post* went first. "How long has the administration known about the Chairman's cancer?"

"We only learned of his cancer recently, just a few days ago."

"Isn't it incumbent on the administration to keep abreast of the health of key officials in the Federal government?" the new CPN reporter interrupted.

"Since the late Chairman didn't share that information, we would have had to violate his privacy to do that."

"But the President is required to have a physical examination. Isn't it irresponsible to ignore the health of other key officials in the executive branch?"

"First off, the President is not required by law to have a physical examination. It's just a good idea, and he does it. And second, as you'll discover in any political science textbook, the Federal Reserve Board operates independently of the executive branch." Having sufficiently spanked the CPN reporter in front of his peers, Seagram moved on to *The Wall Street Journal* reporter. "Yes, Gary."

"Some critics have said that the President has been too slow to replace Garrett Llewellyn. Now, with both the Treasury Secretary and the Federal Reserve Chair positions vacant, is the administration worried about being able to handle the Kadler Steele affair as well as other economic matters?"

"To your first statement, the President has been carefully vetting those who might replace Secretary Llewellyn. Given the importance of the position, it is a decision that should not be made hastily. As to the Kadler Steele matter, the Justice Department and the SEC are running their investigations, which will be unaffected by any changes at the Cabinet level. Thank you, everybody." With that, Seagram closed her briefing binder. "Have a good evening."

"That was Press Secretary Dana Seagram," Gonnelli, stated, "live from the White House, announcing the passing of Gordon LaSalle, Chairman of the Federal Reserve. To learn more about this developing story, stay tuned for the Evening News with Bob Summers."

Gonnelli then returned to the previously planned lineup. "In local political news, we had a lively debate last night between three candidates for Pennsylvania's 20th District on the campus of Winton College. The incumbent Republican Sheldon Lannier and Democrat Linda Jansing candidates thoroughly brutalized each other. As expected, Jansing took quite a few jabs at Lannier over his connection to the Kalder Steele scandal. But the real surprise was the Independent candidate, David Grant, who came across as both thoughtful, yet quite feisty. Shortly into the debate, it was interrupted by a fire alarm. But even that didn't shutdown the action. We have some cellphone video of a confrontation in the parking lot between David Grant and one of the panelists."

Grant: "You seem more interested in throwing mud than asking honest questions. You're an intellectually dishonest fraud."

Nistle: "And how am I dishonest?"

Grant: "You implied anyone in business is dishonest. That's not even guilt by association. It's guilt by profession. I would expect better of a college professor than to stoop to that kind of logical fallacy."

"As it turns out, Professor Armand Nistle, the panelist seen in this video, may have been actually working for the Jansing campaign. The Jansing camp denies this, but some eyewitnesses say they had seen Professor Nistle visiting the Jansing headquarters at least twice before the debate. It's certainly turning into an interesting election. And now, here's Kyle with the weather...."

"Yikes, I didn't realize anyone was recording us. I'm glad I didn't say anything worse."

"You were quite a tiger out there, Mr. Grant," Sara teased. "But I don't think Winton will be giving you the Professor Congeniality Award."

"Professor Congeniality?"

"You know...like Miss Congeniality...except you're a professor."

"Okay," David laughed. "I suppose not."

"By the way, what is a logical fallacy anyway? Shouldn't it be illogical fallacy?"

"No, a 'logical fallacy' is where the logic of an argument is flawed, yet that reasoning is often used."

"Such as guilt by association?"

"Exactly, but there are much more insidious ones," David explained. "For instance, there's the bandwagon effect. That's where somebody says, 'as everyone knows,' whether they do or not."

"But what if everyone does know?" Sara asked, sensing a flaw in the argument.

"Hmm, well everyone knew the Earth was flat. Didn't make it so. There's a whole bunch of others too: post hoc fallacy, ad hominem attacks, binary fallacy—"

"Binary fallacy, that must be a computer error," she teased.

"No, that's when someone insists there are two choices, such as 'vote for the school budget or our children will be uneducated.' Just make the alternative unacceptable, and people are likely to agree with you."

"Okay, but where is the fallacy in that?"

"In reality, there are almost always more than two alternatives."

"Hmm, that's pretty smart. Did your Ms. Langford teach you that?"

"No, I took a critical thinking course in college. I remember the professor saying 'logical fallacies make sense as long as you don't think about them too hard.'"

"I'm impressed. After all these years of marriage, I'm still learning things about you." Sara glanced back at the television. Then, a thought occurred to her. "Not to change the subject, but how did they figure out Nistle was in the Jansing camp so quickly?" Sara asked.

"Oh, we can thank our Ms. Langford for that. On a hunch, she hired a college student to go into Jansing's campaign office and simply ask for Nistle. The campaign staff let it slip he hadn't been around for several days, thus confirming his connection. So then, Ellen contacted the media, and I guess PA-TV did the rest."

"You were really pissed off at Nistle."

"Yeah, I was," David admitted. "You know, I don't mind someone disagreeing with me, but don't pretend to be neutral when you're not. Still, I wasn't thrilled about being seen losing my temper on TV."

"I don't think it was that bad," Sara said, trying to comfort him. "Besides, Laura Gonnelli called you 'fiesty.' Isn't that a good thing?"

"I suppose."

"So, are you *feisty*?" she asked, giving him a suggestive look.

He smiled back. "No, I think the word you're looking for is *frisky*."

Just then, Wendy came in and blurted out, "Dinner is being served."

80 80 03 03

The next morning, Karen transferred Porter Barnes's call to Harris Carver's office.

"Good morning, Congressman," Carver answered.

"How are you, Harris?" Barnes asked in an unusually cheery tone.

"Fine. I haven't spoken to you in a while, but you've been doing great work, Congressman."

"Thank you. You may have been wondering why I haven't revealed the other three names on the list you sent me."

"Not at all. You made quite a splash with just one. I couldn't have asked for more." Carver wondered what happened to Barnes's usual brusque manner. Then, he realized the Congressman wanted something.

"Well, the first name was free," Barnes said. "But...I want something for the next three."

"Actually, you did such a good job on Lannier, I thought we'd just quietly leak the other names through other sources."

"Oh, I wouldn't hear of it, Harris. I'll be revealing those names this week on Jessica Dandridge's show, regardless of the outcome of this conversation."

"Then, I'm not sure I'm following you."

"The question is whether I reveal my source or not," Barnes said, revealing his extortion point. There was nothing illegal about what Carver, Ed Leems or the DNC had done, but revealing it would generate a news narrative about partisanship, not Republican malfeasance. It was important to stay on message as the midterm election approached. *Damn the loose cannon*, thought Carver. "What are you looking for?" he asked flatly.

"Oh, don't worry. It's nothing you're not willing to do already. I just want the TK9 missile system approved. As you may know, part of it is going to be built in my district."

Carver felt relieved. "No need to be concerned. It's all clear sailing for the TK9 approval."

"No, Harris, I mean for *this* budget cycle."

"I'm sorry." Carver said. "No, that's impossible. The budget has already been locked down. It took us nearly eight months to work a deal with the Republicans. I'm sure you understand."

"Oh, I do understand. The total is locked down, but there's still wiggle room for some line item adjustments."

"Porter, we made a hard-fought deal with the Republicans. I don't want to give them any ammunition this close to the election."

"And just this once, I have no interest in upsetting our friends across the aisle. So, I have the solution. Just ditch the Cold Vulcan project. It's neither high profile nor critical to our national defense. More importantly, I don't know of any Republicans who were championing it. And cancelling Cold Vulcan will give you more than enough funds to cover starting the TK9 early. You can sell it to the Republicans as a bi-partisan effort to cut the budget, or some crap like that."

Suddenly, Carver realized what Barnes was up to. It had little to do with the TK9 itself. Cold Vulcan was an Ariskor defense contract. Ariskor was in the district of Wyatt Wickham, who had seniority on the Banking Committee. If the Democrats regained the House, Wickham would be Barnes's rival for the chairmanship.

"So, you're trying to stick it to Wyatt Wickham?"

"I wouldn't be upset," Barnes admitted, "if my gain is Wickham's loss."

ॐ ॐ ॐ ॐ

In the days following the debate, the local news media paid increasing attention to the Grant campaign. In three days, David did more media interviews than he had in all the time before the debate.

Toward the end of the week, Ellen called a meeting at the "shoe store" as they continued to call their headquarters. David and Fred were in good spirits, despite the rainy overcast. Fred was going through a stack of newspapers, reading the relevant bits.

"*The Philadelphia Inquirer* has the race as Jansing 34%, Lannier 31%, and Grant...drum roll please...27%." Fred quickly pulled another out of the stack. "Feinstein of the *Times* writes 'Of all the congressional races, Pennsylvania's 20th District is the one to watch. Not only does it feature the humiliated and limping incumbent Sheldon Lannier and the relentless Linda Jansing, but also a dynamic upstart Independent named David Grant.'"

"That's great," Ellen said, who just walked in. "But I'm not concerned with polls and editorials just now. David, I have something to show you. You won't like it, but at least it shows you're being taken seriously now."

She opened her laptop and pressed a few keystrokes, calling up an online video. The video began with an unflattering, grainy, black-and-white photo of David.

Narrator:	"Congressional candidate David Grant brags that he created jobs, but what do his former employees think of him?"
Employee #1:	"David made a lot of promises."
Employee #2:	"David Grant is an empty suit with nothing but greed in his heart"
Employee #1:	"We felt betrayed by David."
Employee #2:	"He just can't be trusted."
Employee #3:	"David said he'd be there for us."
Employee #4:	"I haven't heard from him in months."
Employee #2:	"David Grant in Congress? The idea just makes me sick."
Jansing:	"I'm Linda Jansing, and I approved this message."

"Who are these people, and why do they hate you so much, particularly that second guy?" Fred asked.

"The second guy is Darren Sagamore, I fired him for stealing code and harassing female employees just before I sold Simplexia."

"He actually stole code from you?"

"No, from a competitor. He was going to put it into our software." David sighed. "I can't believe this. The other three, Randy, Trish and Pam, are...were friends. When I sold Simplexia, I looked out for them, all of them. I secured their futures with Calibrent. You can ask Art Fuentes."

"Can we sue Jansing?" Fred asked.

"It's derogatory," Ellen admitted. "But there's no actual accusation of wrongdoing. It's just a string of people venting."

"When will this run?" Fred asked.

"It already has."

"I haven't seen it."

"Of course, you live in New Jersey." She turned to David. "It's been running only at the far end of the district for the past two days." Ellen explained. "You can do that with cable. I checked with the cable operators. It'll start running in this county tomorrow morning."

David felt sick to his stomach. "You know, I could have sold my company for more money, if only I hadn't made Calibrent guarantee they would keep all my employees. Maybe being a nice guy wasn't worth it." He picked up a glass and threw it against the far wall in frustration.

Everyone froze.

After a moment, Ellen was the first to speak. "I told you if you were successful, there would be an attack ad. You can't be thin-skinned."

"Lannier or Jansing can say whatever they want about me. This isn't about being attacked or being thin-skinned. It is about being betrayed by people I cared about, people I sacrificed for."

CHAPTER 15

David, Ellen and Fred were still discussing the Jansing attack ad.

"How did they even find Randy, Pam and Trish?" David wondered aloud.

"It's simple," Ellen said. "In the debate you mentioned protecting your employees. In the follow-up interviews, you were asked about how you did that. You told them how when you sold your business, you took less money in exchange for employment guarantees for your people. Protecting your employees is a fantastic narrative. So, Jansing's team needed to muddy that up a bit. So they went searching for the mud."

"That guy who hated you so much," Fred added, "What was his name? Sagamore? He might even have contacted them."

"That's quite possible," Ellen admitted.

Just then, David's cell phone rang. It was Sara. Still angry, David forced himself to speak in a calm tone. "Hi. What's up?"

"Randy Garber just called," she said.

David could feel his blood pressure rising. *That traitor had the audacity to call my wife.* "What did that Judas want?" he spat.

"Judas? Uh...well, he was rather upset. He said there was some commercial against you on the air. He said his words were twisted."

"Have you seen the ad?" he asked a bit too harshly.

"No, David, please calm down."

"I'm sorry...it was just...it was nastier than I could have imagined. Randy saying 'We felt betrayed by David' doesn't sound like twisted words. It sounds like a straightforward declarative statement."

"Well, Randy's pretty upset. Do me a favor. Hear him out."

"I'm not sure I can. He really stuck it to me."

"David, please hear him out. Do it for me."

"OK," he said, grudgingly. "Have him come over to the campaign office right away. Whatever this is, let's get this over with."

Within 20 minutes, Randy Garber walked into the campaign office, looking like a drowned rat with soaked clothing and hair matted down from the rain. David stared at Garber with his hands in his pockets, almost daring him to attempt a handshake.

"David, I feel sick about this," he blurted out as soon as he entered. "Some news people called us up and asked to interview us. We said a lot of really great things about you."

"Like 'we felt betrayed by David'?" David asked. If Randy could have looked more forlorn, he would have melted into the floor.

"What I said was something like, *at first* we felt betrayed, but once you explained the conditions of the sale to Calibrent, we knew you were looking out for us. I mean, they were news people."

"What station did they say they were from?" Ellen asked.

"They said they were from some syndicated news show, doing a human interest piece on independent candidates. David, we thought we were helping you. I swear we said a lot of really positive things."

"We still don't know who they were," Fred said.

"Wait, they made me sign something." Randy said, pulling a folded and wrinkled piece of paper out of his back pocket. He handed it to David.

"Hold on," said Ellen, with a suspicious look on her face. "People being interviewed for news don't have to sign releases."

Garber handed the paper to David, who tilted for Ellen and Fred to see.

"Haverhill Productions. I've never heard of them."

"That's not the production company Jansing's people are using. They use XLplus Multimedia.

"How do you know who Jansing uses?" David asked.

"Still not reading the opposition research I give you? Let me see that." Ellen took the release and read it while Randy kept explaining and apologizing.

"This is a standard talent release," Ellen finally said. "Legally, they treated Randy like an actor, and technically he released his statement and has given permission for them to use it 'in whole or in part.'"

"Clearly, they intended to use it in part," Fred added.

"I'm sorry. I didn't mean for this to happen," Randy insisted yet again.

"We understand," David said, comfortingly. "We'll figure this out."

"But obviously they're working for Jansing," Fred said. "We can sue her for slander."

"That will take too long," Ellen countered. "We wouldn't get them into court before election day."

"We could get a restraining order." Fred suggested.

"No," Ellen blurted out. "Not yet."

"Are you nuts?" Fred exclaimed.

"Give me a few hours. I have an idea."

"Why?" asked David.

"This may work for us. If I'm wrong, you can still get a restraining order." David pressed the speed dial button to call Art Fuentes. He was going to be ready one way or another.

೫ ೫ ೧ ೮

Carl Stavros, the Communications Director was the last to enter the Oval Office.

"Come on in, Carl," Carver said, "The President will be with us in a minute. He just received a call from the British Prime Minister." Stavros was surprised to see Hingecliff also standing there. Just then, the President entered.

"Cheerio, chaps," Farnum said in a mock English accent. They laughed.

"How's the Prime Minister?" Carver asked.

"He's 'chuffed to bits' about our meeting next week," he answered, continuing the accent.

"Is that a good or bad thing?" Carver asked.

"Good, I think." Farnum then gestured for everyone to have a seat, and start the meeting.

"Mr. President," Stavros began. "Obviously, the death of Gordon LaSalle comes at a very inconvenient time."

"Especially for Gordon LaSalle," Farnum countered.

"I'm sorry, Mr. President. I didn't mean to be insensitive. But with LaSalles's passing, we need to move quickly on nominating your new Treasury Secretary.

"Thank you, Carl. It had occurred to me," Farnum said. "But no need to worry. I'm nominating Robert here."

"Really?" Stavros looked awkwardly to Hingecliff. "Congratulations, Mr. Secretary."

"Thank you, Carl," Hingecliff answered softly.

"Robert," Farnum continued. "There's no way I can delay your appointment further. I'm afraid, this close to the election, the Republicans will use this as an opportunity to attack me through you. They're going to try to chew you up and spit you out."

"Don't worry about me, Mr. President." Hingecliff smiled. "It's not my first time to the dance."

"Sir, one thing that might make things easier," Stavros persisted, "is if you also nominated a new Fed Chair at the same time. Since you've been vetting people with similar backgrounds, financial and economic, selecting a Fed Chair should be quick and easy."

Farnum shifted uncomfortably. "Well, Robert was not simply at the top of my list; he was the list."

"Oh," Stavros said, "Dana has already told the press that multiple potential Treasury nominees were being vetted."

"Sorry, Carl. I played that one a little close to the vest," Farnum admitted.

"Sir, we can put together a list of potential nominees fairly quickly," Carver suggested, "but proper vetting will take some time."

"Mr. President," Hingecliff interrupted. "May I suggest Martha Addison? She's extremely qualified. She's worked on Wall Street, for the Federal Reserve, and served on the Council of Economic Advisors."

"I can add her to the list," Carver said, writing the name on a notepad.

"Beyond her resume, she had one additional asset, for the lack of a better term. She's African American."

Stavros eyes lit up. "That's great." Everyone looked at him, making him realize he had to explain his excitement. "Mr. President, we've had black Supreme Court Justices, Cabinet secretaries, even a President. But the one remaining bastion of old white men is the Federal Reserve. If you nominated her, you would be breaking another barrier. And, it wouldn't hurt your efforts come reelection time."

"Carl, I'm all for breaking barriers," the President responded. "But, I don't want to nominate someone just because she's African American. It's too important a position, especially now."

"Sir," Hingecliff interrupted. "I assure you, she's the real deal. Addison has a doctorate in economics. She even did her dissertation on monetary policy. I wouldn't suggest her if she weren't of the absolute highest caliber."

"Very well. Harris, let's check her out." Farnum stood up, signaling the end of the meeting.

"Thank you, Mr. President."

After Stavros and Hingecliff left, Carver approached Farnum. "Mr. President, I need to talk to you about the TK9 missile system."

℘ ℘ ℘ ℘

Ellen arrived at Haverhill Productions, about half an hour northwest of Embler. The production company was located in a well-landscaped light industrial park. She entered the small reception area, which had several plasma screens with looped reels of Haverhill's work. Their clients seem to consist of pharmaceutical companies, banks, and other corporate clients. The work seemed to be mostly corporate videos, with the occasional infomercial thrown in. Finally, the young receptionist got off the telephone.

"How may I help you?"

"Yes, I'm Ellen Langford. I'm looking for Mr. Haverhill."

"Hi, I'm Cindi. Do you have an appointment?" she said in a tone that could only be described as disgustingly perky.

"No, but it's very important."

"I'm afraid Danny is in post-production with a client."

"Linda Jansing's people?" The receptionist seemed to be thrown off by the mention of Jansing's name. "It's very important that I see Danny right away. There's a fair amount of money at stake."

"I'll see what I can do." Cindi stepped out of the reception area. A few minutes later, a heavyset man with a ruddy complexion and a full, red beard lumbered out into the reception area.

"Hi, I'm Danny Haverhill," he said as he extended a meaty hand. "How can I help you?"

"Ellen Langford. I was with Senator Hawthorne. I've heard your company was responsible for that brilliantly devastating Jansing spot against David Grant."

"Wow, news travels fast. That baby just started airing a couple days ago."

"Well, I have a special interest. I'm with the Grant for Congress campaign." Ellen enjoyed the expression of Haverhill's face. It was like teenager caught dead-to-rights in a lie.

"I thought you said Senator Hawthorne."

"I was with her office, at least up until she died. Now, I'm working for David Grant."

"Are you here to serve me with papers, or something?"

"That's a bit premature," Ellen said. "But don't worry your little head. There's plenty of time for that."

"Hey, there's nothing libelous in that TV spot," Haverhill insisted.

"That's true because libel is written; slander is spoken." Ellen chided him. "Actually, your spot is slanderous by omission, and it does impugn David Grant's character. Does your business insurance cover slander? I mean beyond the standard errors and omissions clause." Ellen looked around the small reception area. "You know, I think a lawsuit would bankrupt your little operation." She turned back to the receptionist. "Cindi, you just might want to have your résumé updated."

"Lawyers are expensive." Haverhill snapped. "And my understanding is your campaign doesn't have a very big war chest."

"Who told you that? Jansing's people?" Ellen smiled knowingly. "Even if there isn't enough in the war chest, David recently sold his company for a fair amount of money, as you well know. And he's pissed—threw a glass clear across the room when he saw the spot. Do you know why Jansing's people used you instead of their usual production company? Because XLplus would never have opened themselves up to this kind of legal exposure. So Jansing got a political novice to do her dirty work. By the way, did you ever actually meet Linda Jansing?"

"No."

"We call that *plausible deniability*."

"Excuse me, I guess I need to call my attorney."

"That's not really necessary, because I'm here to give you a get-out-of-jail-free card." Haverhill looked at her suspiciously.

"What do you want?"

"The footage."

"It's the client's footage," Haverhill shrugged, with what little defiance he could still muster.

"Did you shoot the footage?"

"What if I did?"

"Did you sign a work-for-hire agreement?"

"Hell, no."

"Then, you know very well you hold the copyright. The footage is yours to do with what you choose."

"If you provide me with the footage, and I mean *all* the footage, and give us permission to use it, I'll make sure David Grant never sues you."

"How can I be sure?

Ellen pulled a simple one-page release out of her briefcase. "Provide me with the footage and sign this release. As a condition, the release guarantees you won't be sued. Cindi can be a witness."

Haverhill scanned the release. "I better call my attorney."

"Ordinarily, I couldn't care less. But I'm on the clock. I have a studio and an edit suite on standby. So this is a limited-time offer. The alternative is that you get hung out to dry for fraud, slander, misrepresentation and defamation of character. So, this is a limited-time offer."

"I think you're overreaching," Haverhill spat back.

"Maybe. By the way, how would your corporate clients take to it if you were sued for slander?" Ellen asked, as she gestured to some video footage that appeared to be for a pharmaceutical company. "I hear those guys are very picky about who they work with. You know how those image-minded corporate types like to avoid any controversy. Oh, and by the way, Grant has a great PR firm on his side, too."

Haverhill's ruddy complexion went pale.

CHAPTER 16

"You got the footage?" Fred asked, as Ellen arrived in the video studio.

"Absolutely," she answered, waving a pair of DVDs bearing the Haverhill logo.

"Great. You know, we didn't need to rent an expensive studio," complained Fred. "This will really strain our budget. Jason Kennerly could have done this for next to nothing."

"This is too important for amateurs," snapped Langford. "He shoots and edits video for the Web, where production values are pretty low. Besides, broadcast television has very specific technical requirements."

Fred glared at her.

"Fred, Ellen's right," David said softly. "But we can use Jason for other things. Besides, there's not enough time for Jason to travel up here."

"You asked me to manage your campaign," Fred complained in a hushed tone, "but that seems to be in name only."

"Fred, I've managed a lot of people over the years. And one thing I've learned is to let people run with their passion. Ellen's in the zone right now. You were in the zone when you twisted my arm to run. And, you were instrumental in getting us the debate at Winton. I believe in tapping into people's passion. Let's allow Ellen's enthusiasm carry us for the next few hours. To be honest, this is the most passionate I've ever seen her."

"Okay," Fred nodded resentfully.

In the edit suite, they found the footage Jansing's campaign used. It was quickly evident how Jansing's people had truncated and juxtaposed positive statements to create the negative montage.

"We just play Jansing's original cuts, then show the clips in full. We've got her dead to rights."

"Hello?" Sara called out from the front room. David and Fred went out to meet her.

"Hi," David said, then kissed her. "Did you bring them?"

"Yeah, they're a bit upset."

"Where are they?"

"They're just parking. Pam and Trish are a little afraid of you right now. They feel you're angry at them for appearing in that commercial. I told them you weren't. But when you're portrayed on TV like that, I guess it's hard to get over it." Just then, Trish and Pam came through the door, looking quite uncomfortable.

"Hi guys." David walked up to the two apprehensive women. "I'm *really* sorry about this. I never imagined my running for Congress would put you in this position."

They both looked relieved.

"No, we're really sorry," Pam said.

"Stuff happens. But with your help," David said, "we're going to expose what Jansing did."

"Anything you need," Trish added. "Anything we can do."

Fred watched how David had put the two women at ease. It was clear he was upset by how his friends were used. "Brilliant," Fred muttered under his breath, as David escorted the others into the studio. He went back into the edit suite.

"I've got an idea," Fred said.

"Not now," Ellen said in an annoyed tone, as she scribbled various notes and then crossed them out.

"Dammit! I'm the manager of this campaign. So you'll at least listen to my idea!"

"Okay," Ellen answered skeptically.

"It's just an add-on to what you're already doing. Once Pam, Randy and Trish have their say, David enters the frame and says something like 'attacking him may be fair game, but manipulating the words of innocent friends is beyond the pale'. It makes Jansing seem even lower. David isn't simply defending himself, he's defending others."

"Good," she nodded receptively. "No, that's great. But, it pushes us past 60 seconds."

"So, we do a 90-second spot."

"Weren't you the one complaining about the budget?" she countered.

"Wait," interrupted David, who had just returned to the suite. "We can start running the 90-second spot. Then follow up with a 60-second version, or maybe even a 30-second one. It's done in product advertising all the time."

"No, even better," Fred said. "We do three 30-second spots, each highlighting one of them with an invitation to visit the website to view the others. We can just rotate them."

"Great idea," Ellen said.

"Let's do it," David said.

Over the next several hours, they worked with their director to write, shoot and edit the first spot. It began with the original footage from Jansing's spot in black and white.

Recorded Randy:	"We felt betrayed by David."
Live Randy:	"Yes, I said that, but that wasn't all I said"
Recorded Randy:	"At first, we felt betrayed by David, but he proved he was looking out for us."
Live Randy:	"Linda Jansing twisted my words, embarrassed me, and tried to hurt a good man, just to win an election. And this woman wants to represent me?"
David Grant:	"Humiliating innocent people and twisting the truth may be politics as usual. But that's not what our

country needs. We need integrity. I'm David Grant and I approved getting to the truth."

Narrator: "Learn more about the truth at grantforcongress.org."

By the end of the night, they finished editing all three spots along with additional material for the website. The next morning, the spots were distributed and scheduled to start playing on several local stations by the end of the next day.

Despite his exhaustion, David had a full day of campaigning scheduled. In between events, the three met for a status report

"I'm afraid Jason's a little perturbed," Fred explained. "He doesn't want to place the spots on the Centrist Patriot Party website. He says they're too much like attack ads. But truthfully, I think he was annoyed that he wasn't involved.

"NIH syndrome," Ellen muttered irritably.

"Excuse me?" Fred asked.

"N-I-H. Not-Invented-Here." David explained.

"He's picked a helluva time to get pissy," exclaimed Ellen. "What use is this guy?"

"Jason has helped us get donations," David insisted. "He's working on importing foot soldiers for the weekends just before Election Day. We need all the allies we can get." He turned to Fred. "Would you talk to Jason? You're closer to him. Please tell him we understand completely. Explain to him we had to move fast, and we don't want to undermine his efforts to build the party. Anything else?"

"Yes," Ellen said, looking at her smart phone. "We have requests from two of the Philadelphia stations. They're asking for copies of the footage, so they can verify our claims."

"Great. We can cut back on the paid media," Fred said. "Plus, I believe that'll mean more news interviews for you."

"Don't give them Danny Haverhill's name," Ellen warned.

"Why? Getting soft?" chided Fred.

"No, I don't want them to spin it as if Haverhill was a rogue operative. Keep the focus on Jansing. I don't want to give her a scapegoat."

৪০ ৪১ ෬ ෬

The executives at Liberty insisted on cross-promoting their new programs, just like other networks. Tonight, Jessica Dandridge had to promote the host of their new late night show. She had asked them to postpone his appearance, so she could give her real guest more attention, but the programming executives insisted it had to be tonight, because of scheduling.

In her opening segment, Dandridge began with her usual rundown of what she considered conservative atrocities, juxtaposing video clips to prove her points. She tried to present them not too far out of context. After the break, she began the interview portion of the program.

"Joining us at the roundtable is Joe Dreves, the host of *Dreves Peeves*, which premiered last week at 11:30 here on Liberty. So Joe, welcome to the program. Tell us about your show."

"Well, Jessica, thanks for having me on. I'm just trying to get the truth out, just like you. I try to blunt the lies and misrepresentations of reprehensible people like Ben Glendenning, but with a little humor. Hopefully, we'll also give the late night comedians a run for their money."

They chatted a little bit about some of the issues and guests who had appeared on Dreves' show in the past week. He was particularly proud of having the Democratic Governor of Maine as one of his first guests.

"You know, I think she could be President someday. Of course, only after a Farnum second term."

After the break, it was time to introduce her "real guest." Porter Barnes's large frame trudged to the semicircular table. He kissed Dandridge on the cheek and shook hands with Dreves. A sound technician quickly attached a microphone to Barnes's lapel. The stage manager cued them, and they were back on the air.

"Ladies and gentlemen, tonight, we have as our special guest, a crusader against right-wing corruption, and a true patriot, California Congressman Porter Barnes."

"Thanks for having me." Barnes said, automatically.

"So I have to ask, Congressman," Dandridge began. "Why aren't there congressional hearings over this Kadler Steele thing?"

"Right now, the House of Representatives is controlled by the Republicans. Let's face it, Republicans don't investigate Republicans. That's why it's so important for the voters to elect enough Democrats to Congress this November, so we can get to the bottom of this thing."

"No argument here," Dandridge agreed. "I mean there are so many of the GOP in the pocket of Wall Street, it isn't even funny."

"True, people think this scandal is just about Sheldon Lannier. But there are others."

"Like who?"

"There are three others in particular. Mel Dworsky of Colorado is a huge recipient of Kadler cash."

"Kadler Cash, I like that," Dreves blurted out. "It sounds like Kiddie Cash, you know like a type of Monopoly money."

Barnes tried to not show his annoyance on the air. Off the air, it would have been another story.

"No, Joe, the cash is very real, and there's a lot of it. Mel Dworsky accepted more campaign contributions than even Sheldon Lannier."

"Wow," Dandridge exclaimed. "Who are the others?"

"Clarissa Ragusa of Florida, and Jamie McCard of Arizona. The three of them, along with Sheldon Lannier, received millions." Barnes wasn't planning to mention the fact that many Democrats had also received Kadler contributions.

"Wow, with that kind of money, I need to talk to my agent about getting me a gig in Congress," Dreves joked. Dandridge wished Dreves would shut up. He was interfering with the predetermined narrative Dandridge and Barnes had agreed upon. She pondered kicking him under the table, but there was no knowing how he'd react.

"Joe, that's the trouble," Barnes said. "A lot of these Republicans think of it as a gig. But they're wrong; it's a calling. It's a sacred trust, a sacred trust they have violated."

"Well, then I guess we should be thankful that there are only four of them," Dandridge continued.

"But that's the problem. These four are simply the worst. No, wait, let me take that back. These four merely charged the *highest price*. Other Republicans took much less from Kadler. But I suppose they were satisfied with those lesser amounts to vote the way they were told."

"I guess some Republican souls can be bought cheaper than others," quipped Dreves.

ഇ ഇ രു രു

Dr. Daniel Narlstrom was sitting in his lab, reading the latest test results. He was enormously pleased. Three more degrees. A smile of deep satisfaction crossed his thin, frail-looking face, surrounded by unkempt gray hair. Three degrees wouldn't seem much to most people, but it was a major step forward.

Anson walked in, looking particularly grim. "Dan, they need us up in Human Resources."

"What for?"

"A staffing issue."

"Come on, I hate the administrative BS. Can't you handle it?"

"No, they need both of us."

"Is this about Boylan's prank? I did reprimand him. I told him pouring liquid nitrogen into Alonzo's aquarium wasn't funny."

Anson finally broke a smile, despite himself. This, in turn, caused Narlstrom to laugh.

"Okay, a little funny," Narlstrom admitted. "At least the fish thawed, well eventually."

"All right, seriously, I'll meet you up in Friedman's office in five minutes."

"Party pooper!"

Despite his protests, Narlstrom dutifully arrived at Friedman's door. Anson was already sitting in front of Friedman's large desk. It was always clear of any clutter, reminding him of the deck of an aircraft carrier. Was it compulsive neatness? Or maybe, the guy had nothing to do.

"So, what's up?"

"Please, have a seat, Dr. Narlstrom." Friedman was being uncharacteristically formal. Once Narlstrom sat down, Friedman continued. "Santos got a call from the Pentagon. Dan, they're killing the Cold Vulcan program."

"What?...No...No, Grisby was here last week, telling us how pleased he was with our progress. And, we just achieved another three degrees."

"Dan, it's a political thing," Friedman said. "Santos argued to the end, but the guillotine just came down anyway."

"Come on. The Pentagon doesn't kill projects like that," Narlstrom insisted. "Remember, we're Ariskor, you know, part of that big ol' military-industrial complex."

"Let's face it," Anson said. "Your project doesn't go boom. And the military really likes things that go boom."

"They also like stealth. That's why—" Narlstrom suddenly realized why they were meeting in Human Resources.

CHAPTER 17

It had been a week since the Grant campaign launched its "whole truth" ads, countering Jansing's ads. Everyone in the campaign was quite excited about the positive attention David had received. Randy, Pam and Trish volunteered to campaign for David. Of all the volunteers, they were the most enthusiastic. Despite his initial reluctance, Jason Kennerly posted all of the ads on the CPP website. The first "centrist reserves" had started to arrive from neighboring states during the weekends to campaign door-to-door. Most were from New Jersey, Maryland and Delaware. More were expected from Virginia and New York the following weekend.

Ellen coached the new volunteers who would campaign door-to-door. She explained how they shouldn't just blurt out the campaign talking points. They had to ask questions about the citizens' concerns and preferences first, and then react to those. They were also supposed to collect information, including their likelihood of voting for Grant, and whether they might have any difficulties traveling to the polling locations. Those individuals would be offered free transportation on Election Day.

According to the most recent polling, the candidates were locked in a close to three-way tie: Lannier 29.6%, Jansing 31.3%, Grant 30.1%, Lurtz 1.4%, with the balance undecided.

Ellen shared these polls with David and Fred in an early morning meeting in the shoe store.

"All the candidates are polling pretty tightly," she explained, "and with the margin of error, it's still anyone's race to win. Strangely enough, the biggest threat to you might be Paul Lurtz."

"The fruit and vegetable candidate? He has less than two percent. He can't win," David said.

"Of course not. But he could still receive a thousand votes or so. In a four way race, that could make the difference."

"Yeah, but only his friends, colleagues and nutrition nuts are going to vote for him."

"Yet strangely enough, their votes count as much as anyone else's."

"I know," David said. "What I mean is they're going to vote for Lurtz no matter what. He's promoting nutrition, not exactly a controversial issue. And he's not likely to alienate anyone."

"That's why we have to convince him to drop out of the race. We need those votes. But it's got to be right away, or his name will still appear on the ballot. I'll go talk to him."

"No, I'll do it," David insisted. "Weird or not, he's a candidate. So, we'll talk candidate to candidate."

ॐ ॐ ॐ ॐ

Daniel Narlstrom stood staring at all the papers spread out on his dining room table. Occasionally, he would break from his catatonic countenance to make a few scribbles on a notepad.

He tried not to wallow in the humiliation of being laid off after 23 years at Ariskor, but it was difficult. Explaining the whole experience to his wife was worse than the layoff itself. For years, he had been the breadwinner. And now, he felt discarded like an old crust.

Ariskor had given him a severance package, but it wasn't overly generous. He had requested a transfer to another project within the company, but he was told his background was too specialized. Besides, cuts were being made in other areas too.

He stared at the papers searching for a way out.

"So what's all this?" Jean asked, as she brought her husband a cup of apple cinnamon tea. He took it gratefully.

"My life's work."

"There's no point in reliving the past."

"Jeannie, I'm a realist. I've sent out fifty résumés. The only responses have been negative. No one wants a 58-year-old specialist in thermodynamics. No one wants a 58-year-old anything."

"What about teaching? You're a PhD for goodness sakes."

"I've called around. With the economy the way it is, there just don't seem to be any openings right now."

Jean Narlstrom gave her husband a hug. "Something will come up. In the meantime, why don't you throw out all these old papers?"

"No, these are my old patent applications. I'm trying to figure out some commercial application for my work. Maybe I could start a company or sell another company a product idea. I just can't figure out what."

Jean kissed him on the head. "I'm going to bed. Don't stay up too late."

ৡ ৡ ঙ ঙ

Earlier in the day, the White House announced the nominations of Robert Hingecliff and Martha Addison. This was the last topic of Ben Glendenning's pre-show meeting.

"Hingecliff and Addison, do we have any dirt of these two?" Glendenning asked. "Nothing so far," said Sergio, his head researcher. "I think they're actually pretty clean."

"Well, if they're not dirty, they must be stupid. So, that's how we'll play it,"

"Except, they both have PhDs."

"Piled higher and deeper, my friend," Glendenning scoffed, as he headed out for wardrobe and make-up. He had never finished college and held such high-and-mighty academics in low regard. He thought PhDs make them even more arrogant and detestable know-it-alls.

Less than an hour later, he stood before the cameras ready to do battle with the evil forces of liberalism. The red light went on. *Let the games begin.*

"Good evening, my fellow patriots," Glendenning bellowed at the camera. "Yes, it's another overcast day in America, and I don't mean the weather. As hard as we try to see the light, Commissar Farnum has done it again. Earlier today he nominated two of the worst left-wing liberals to fill the two most important positions relative to the economy, Robert Hingecliff and Martha Addison. Sort of a two-for-one sale on liberal lightweights. Mr. President—and I use the term loosely—we are facing a huge and complex financial situation, and you nominate these two jokers? You've got to be kidding!"

"Patriots, when is this man going to stop trying to undermine the American way of life? This is why it's so important to hold on to Congress this November. It's the only way to keep this socialist in check."

"Addison and Hingecliff? Honestly, these two are first-class public pickpockets. They will use both fiscal and monetary policies to make your money worthless. Everyone knows the Democrats want to destroy the financial system in this country. Why? Once they bankrupt your businesses, pensions and retirement accounts, the only alternative is for the government to take over and impose a socialist nanny state. That's the true Democratic Party nirvana."

"I know it's not *politically correct*, but capitalism, and therefore Wall Street, is the first defense against socialism, nay, communism. That's why they want to destroy it, and blame it on the Republicans at the same time. Then, they become the saviors of America. It's all part of their carefully concocted plan. It's a page right out of *Mein Kampf*."

ЯD ʃƆ ᢙ ᢗʒ

The next day, after calling ahead, David drove to James Smith Middle School. Once he checked in at the main office, he was directed to Paul Lurtz's classroom in the science wing. As he looked in, he saw a middle-age man with thinning hair, sitting at a science bench, correcting what David presumed were test papers.

"Excuse me, Paul Lurtz?"

The man looked up from his papers. "Ah, you must be Mr. Grant. Please come in." Lurtz stood up and approached David. "A pleasure to meet you."

"Please, call me David. I almost didn't recognize you without your tomato suit."

Lurtz chuckled. "Well, Mr. Grant...um...I mean, David, what can I do for you?"

"I wanted to talk to you about the campaign."

"If the publicity on TV is any indication, you're doing rather well. You made quite an impression at that debate."

"Well, I still have some rather stiff competition."

"Not in this room you don't. Somebody told me I'm polling less than one percent."

"I think you're up to almost two percent after the debate."

"Wow. Gee, maybe if I had participated, I could have gotten three percent. But seriously, what brings you out here?"

"I hate to say this, but I'd like you to drop out of the race. It's going to be close, very close. And, that one or two percent you would attract could make the difference. If you would endorse me, that would be even better."

Lurtz sighed. "To be honest, I'm not really that political. I'm just using my candidacy to promote better nutrition. It was my wife's idea. It may seem trivial to some, but we have a huge obesity problem in this country, and this school district is no exception. If I can save just one of our kids from diabetes or a heart attack down the line, it'll be worth it. Everywhere you look, you see the incessant promotion of high-calorie, fatty foods. If people adopted better diets and lifestyles, that would do a lot more to bring down healthcare costs than all those stupid healthcare bills."

"And yes," Lurtz continued, "if I have to wear a stupid tomato suit to grab their attention, then so be it. I don't want just better healthcare; I want better health."

"Now, you're giving me your stump speech."

"You're right. I'm sorry."

"No, I admire what you're doing. And I would never have thought to ask you to do anything else, until the race became so tight. I have my own cause, trying to help save this country from economic disaster and corruption. If this country goes bankrupt, people won't be focusing on a better diet. They'll be trying to find food. Period."

"I get what you're saying, but I'm trying to capture the imaginations of a whole bunch of kids, and maybe their parents too. And I'm up against the entire junk food industry."

"What if you had a congressman on your side? You know, to even the odds?"

"Let me ask you," Lurtz began, leaning back on his desk, "if I dropped out, would that make you a shoe-in? Honestly?"

"Honestly? I don't know."

"See, there's the dilemma. I may not be doing well in the polls, but I've got hundreds of young people making campaign pledges to eat better and exercise. How can I give that up and undercut what I'm doing for the kids?"

"A better question is how can you withdraw from the race without undercutting the progress you've made?" David mused. "What if I take on your quest? It is a serious healthcare...pardon me...health issue. I certainly have no problem supporting it."

"Ah, the proverbial campaign promise," chuckled Lurtz.

"Yeah, I know. Campaign promises are not very reliable currency. However, a moment ago you asked me if you dropped out would that make me a shoe-in. I could have lied, and said yes. Don't let this get around, but I *am* an honest person. I keep my promises."

Suddenly, a giant green, velvet pear waddled into the classroom.

"Hey, nice pear," Lurtz said suggestively.

"Why, thank you," said the woman in the pear suit. She then turned away. "Does this pear make my butt look big?"

"Oh, no, not at all," Lurtz said, with obvious insincerity. "By the way, this is David Grant."

The pear lady turned back quickly, slightly embarrassed. "Oh, sorry. I didn't see you there. This suit doesn't allow much in the way of peripheral vision."

"This is my wife and campaign manager, Donna. David Grant came to talk to me about the campaign."

"Oh, you're the other Independent running," she said excitedly. "I showed your TV spots in my class."

"In your class?"

"Yes, I'm a social studies teacher. We're studying the election process this semester."

"I don't know. Should children be exposed to something so unseemly as politics?" David joked.

"So Donna, apparently the election is so close, anyone—but me—could win. David is asking me to drop out in exchange for championing our cause."

"Interesting idea." Donna Lurtz turned to assess their visitor. "Honey, how do you think he'd look in a carrot suit?"

CHAPTER 18

The Healthy Living Rally was set for midday on Saturday in a park just half a mile from James Smith Middle School. The October day was cool, but still warm enough for an outdoor event. Officially, this was a political rally for Paul Lurtz. However, it had been enlarged, mostly paid for by the Grant campaign.

As with many outdoor events, the real draw was the food. Local vendors were donating some of their healthier fare for tastings in exchange for promotional consideration. The local farmers market was part of the event, but purveyors of less healthy snacks like cotton candy and funnel cakes were not invited. Fred made sure the food area had been roped off. Nothing can distract from a speech more than a food-driven stampede. David and Paul Lurtz did a quick tour of the various booths. Each one presented either healthy foods or a fun exercise activity. David was surprised to find his son manning the tofu hot dog booth.

"Chris, what are you doing here?" David asked.

"Mom said the campaign needed help. Mr. Arkin sent me here."

"Paul, this is my son, Chris."

"A pleasure to meet you, Chris," Lurtz said enthusiastically. "I appreciate all the support."

"Between last week with the homemade pizza and this...are you going all Julia Child on us?"

"Who?" Chris asked.

"Never mind."

"Hey Chris," Lurtz interrupted, "do you always cook healthy?"

"I guess."

"Tell you what, we have a healthy cookbook we're giving away. Go ask my wife for one before they're gone. She's the one over there in the pear suit. You can't miss her."

"Thanks, Mr. Lurtz."

"All right, Chef Chris," David said. "See you later."

They headed toward the platform, where Fred joined them. "We punched up the stump speech," he said.

David quickly reviewed the notes. "No, I can't use the 'adult supervision' line standing next to a giant tomato man. Besides, this is a different audience. I don't think I'm going to use the stump speech. I'll just wing it."

"You sure?"

They were interrupted by a large van that suddenly pulled up to the side of the platform. A young, sandy-haired teenager jumped out.

"Hey, you can't park here," David called out.

"Sorry, I'll move, but first I gotta deliver 80 pizzas, 30 cheese rolls, 20 bags of pork rinds and 40 two-liter bottles of soda," he called out, reading off his list. "Who do I see to get paid for these?"

"I don't know. Who ordered them?" David inquired.

"It says Grant for Congress."

"You ordered this junk food for today's event?" Lurtz asked, indignantly. "I thought you understood what we were trying to do here."

"I do," David insisted. "I didn't order this food," He turned back to the deliveryman. "Who ordered all this?"

"I told you, Grant for Congress."

"I'm Grant, and I didn't order any of that." Fred walked up. "Fred, did you order pizzas and pork rinds?"

"No," he answered.

David could see the steam coming out of Lurtz's ears.

"Typical politician," Lurtz murmured under his breath.

David tried to rest his hands on Lurtz's shoulders, but the padded tomato suit prevented him from finding them. "Paul, I'm being set up here."

"Yeah, looks like we're being screwed, Segretti-style," Ellen said, having just arrived.

"Who?"

"Donald Segretti. He did dirty tricks for Nixon. He'd send a load of pizzas to the opponent's rally, so they get distracted figuring out how who pays, just like you're doing now."

"Is this Segretti guy gonna pay for the pizzas?" the delivery kid asked.

"May I suggest that the candidates prepare for their speeches? Fred and I'll deal with Pizzaman here."

"I don't want that food distributed here," Lurtz insisted.

"Don't worry," she assured him.

Ellen watched David and Lurtz head up to the platform. "There's nothing like sending your candidate off with a walking tomato," Ellen murmured to herself. Then, she turned back to the task at hand. "OK, how much for the pizzas?"

"Twelve hundred dollars."

"Wait a minute," Fred said. "No pizza parlor is going to commit to delivering that much food without a credit card to guarantee payment."

"And it's also a surprisingly round number," Ellen observed. "Who put you up to this?"

"I'm just the delivery guy."

"Perhaps we need to speak to your boss," Fred suggested.

 භ ฿ ൫ ൲

David Grant appeared on the dais between the Lurtzes, both tomato and pear, and with some small children in berry costumes. He stepped up to the podium, looking quite drab, compared to his colorful companions.

"Good day, everybody. Beautiful day, isn't it? For those who don't know me, my name is David Grant. Like Paul Lurtz, I'm running for Congress." This seemed to catch everyone's attention, as they weren't expecting anyone other than Lurtz to speak. "I just lack Paul's colorful wardrobe."

This earned a laugh from the audience.

"Paul and I, each in our own way, want better things for America. There's a lot of misdirection and spin in today's politics. But people like Paul see through the smoke and mirrors."

"For instance, Paul said to me the other day, 'we don't have a healthcare problem, so much as a health problem.' Paul Lurtz understands that if people make better choices, they can obtain a better result, whether it's choosing better foods to eat, or voting for better candidates. Oh, it's easy to go along with the usual choices, hamburger and fries, or Democrats and Republicans. But in the long term, neither is very healthy for us. We need to make smarter, less expected choices."

"Both Paul and I are committed to improving America. Ladies and gentlemen, I give you one of the most dedicated teachers I know, Mr. Paul Lurtz." The two candidates embraced, or as best one could when one is wearing an overly padded costume.

"It's not too late for the carrot suit," Lurtz whispered. "I've got it in the car, all clean and pressed."

"I didn't promise that," David answered. "But I'll deliver what I promised."

"So will I," Lurtz said and smiled.

Lurtz stepped up to the podium. "Good morning, everyone." The Lurtz-friendly crowd cheered enthusiastically. "For months now, we've been talking about healthier living, healthier eating, and getting exercise. And yes, we've had some laughs. Some of us have lost some weight," he said, patting his tomato belly. The audience laughed. "But most of all, we've tried to get people to listen to our message. And guess what? We've gotten another candidate to hear and embrace our healthy living cause."

The crowd applauded.

"Not only is David Grant picking up the mantle of our message, he's willing to take it to Washington. While he may not wear a silly fruit-suit, he will carry our message to Congress. So as of today, I am withdrawing from the race for Congress."

"No," a number of people called out, disappointed.

"No, no, my friends; don't be sad. This is a good thing. It's been a lot of fun, but honestly, we all knew that I couldn't really win. But this is even better. We've gotten a serious and qualified candidate to take notice of our message. So, I hereby endorse our new health messenger to Congress, David Grant."

The crowd applauded, although not as enthusiastically as for Lurtz.

"Thank you again, Paul, not only for the endorsement, but also for bringing this important issue to our attention. Paul has made me think of health in a whole different way. Yes, we need doctors and hospitals and therapeutic drugs. But we also need to be smarter about maintaining our own health. Healthier habits will lower costs and lengthen lives. And that's something no politician can do for you. We need some common sense, which rarely makes it into Washington. For instance, we've all seen federally funded, anti-smoking campaigns. Yet, the government also subsidizes tobacco farming. Where is the common sense in that?"

"The government invests in research to prevent skin cancer, yet allows tanning parlors, despite the fact that tanning is a known cancer-inducing activity. Where is the common sense in that?"

David continued with a few more "common sense" points, and then encouraged everyone to visit the booths. After shaking hands and having pictures taken, he noticed Fred and Ellen had returned. They made their way over to him.

"I have to hand it to you," Ellen said. "I didn't think Lurtz would actually drop out of the race. Getting an opponent to drop is a rare thing, at least without blackmail."

"How would you know about the blackmail part?" David asked. "No, wait, I don't want to know. So, what happened with the pizza guy?"

"Fred and I went back to the pizzeria. Whoever paid for the food, used cash. However, when the kid was loading the truck, somebody pulled him aside and told him that he could keep any money he could get out of us."

"This has to be Jansing again," Fred spat.

"I'm not so sure," Ellen said. "It's very old school, Segretti-old school, Nixon-old school."

"Maybe Lannier-old school," David suggested.

"Maybe. I certainly hope not."

"Why not?" David asked.

"Forgive me for my Republican roots. Politics has been a dirty game since the beginning of time. And even the most honest Republican lives with the ghost of Watergate. I'm no saint, but I never pulled that kind of crap. I hate it when I see it. Listen, I know what you two think of me. You're the pure disciples of righteousness. And I'm the necessary evil. But I hope you both know there are lines I won't cross."

"I believe you," David said.

"By the way," Ellen added. "This also means we have a mole in the campaign."

"Why do you say that?" Fred asked.

"Because we weren't completely sure of Lurtz, we didn't announce his endorsement to the press ahead of time."

"So for them to try to disrupt this event, they needed a spy in our camp," David concluded.

"I doubt it's one of the centrist party imports." Fred insisted. "Jason vouched for them.

"How many new local volunteers have we had since the debate?"

103

"A bunch," he said. "Probably a dozen if we include Randy, Trish and Pam."

"I'm sure it's not one of them," David said, "but we need to check out the others."

"With the election so soon, does it really matter?"

"With everybody running neck and neck, somebody is getting desperate," Ellen explained. "Who knows what else they'll try? And we won't have much time to react to some October surprise."

"My money's still on Jansing," Fred insisted.

"You could be right. We need to whack that mole to find out. It would also be helpful to find out who paid the pizzeria. Do you know any local private detectives?" Ellen asked.

CHAPTER 19

The Lannier campaign office was buzzing with activity, as Ellen walked up to the young receptionist. "Yes, I'd like to see Alan Traeger. You can tell him it's Ellen Langford."

The reception's eyes widened. "You're from the Grant campaign. Are you even allowed to be here?" His naiveté reminded Ellen of Cindi from Haverhill's.

"Why don't you ask Alan? We're old friends."

The young Republican picked up the telephone and punched in Traeger's extension. After a confirmation, Ellen was escorted back to the campaign manager's office.

"So Alan, can I offer you some leftover pizza and pork rinds?" Ellen asked the head of the Lannier campaign.

"What the hell are you talking about?" Alan Traeger asked.

"They say 'you can't teach an old dog, new tricks,' but you know, sometimes those old dogs know those ancient tricks that no one else can remember. For instance, the old Segretti, pizza-delivery trick. It takes old political dogs like us to remember those."

"I was in grammar school when Segretti pulled dirty tricks for Nixon," Traeger said defensively.

"Oh come on, Alan, don't be that way. I'm paying you a compliment. Even though it was a classic, I have to admit I didn't see it coming."

"Listen, Shelly has enough image problems in the ethical department for us to pull that kind of stunt. I mean, so you get the endorsement of the one-percent tomato guy. Who cares?"

"Actually, you do, because those voters are not party loyalists, so they're more likely to vote for David Grant."

"I really don't care about this. So stop wasting our time."

"It's not been a waste of my time. You just confirmed you were behind the pizza delivery. You see, I never said the pizza delivery stunt had anything to do with the Lurtz rally."

"Get out." Traeger signaled the young Republican waiting at the door.

"Certainly. Thanks for the hospitality."

Ellen drove back to the shoe store. When she arrived, she found Fred had tacked photographs of various people on the wall in the back office.

"What's all this?"

"You mentioned hiring a private detective."

"But our candidate vetoed that."

"Yes, he did. But he didn't veto me looking into it myself. So, I staked out the Jansing's headquarters with a camera. I wanted to see if there was anyone our delivery boy could identify."

"So Philip Marlowe, find anything conclusive?"

"The kid thought it could be this guy," Fred said, pulling a photo off the wall, "but he can't be sure."

"I was just speaking to Alan Traeger at Lannier's office. He let it slip he knew about the Lurtz endorsement, which makes me believe he was behind the pizzas."

"But, that's not proof."

"True, but it gives us a direction to look."

Then they heard a cough coming from behind them. It was David standing there. "Alright, enough. You two just spent an entire day spinning your wheels. This pizza maneuver is still distracting us, which I suppose was the point. We need to get back on track."

"But if we can prove who did it," Fred insisted, "we can hit back like we did over Jansing's TV spot."

"Maybe, but we don't have any footage or other proof," David said. "With the election so close, I don't want to waste any more time on this."

"He's right," Ellen admitted. "But we may still have a mole. We have to protect ourselves."

"Do you have any suspects?" David asked.

"Through process of elimination," Fred reported, "I've got it down to four of the new local volunteers."

"Fine. Isolate those people, or tell them we don't need them."

"We also need to secure the computers and the stationery," Ellen warned. "Stealing campaign letterhead and sending out false statements is another dirty trick they can pull."

"Fine," David said. "But I don't want to waste any more time on this."

꣠ ꣠ ꣠ ꣠

Daniel Narlstrom sat in line at the unemployment office. He was number 168. Despite having an "appointment," he had already been waiting an hour and a half. A ceiling-mounted television in the large waiting area was tuned to one of the news channels. Commentators were discussing the election with some congressman named Barnes.

"It's important to restore integrity to Congress. But the Republicans..."

Narlstrom was only vaguely aware of what they were talking about. It was just noise.

"Hear dat?" said an older Jamaican man, sitting just ahead of him.

"What?" Narlstrom asked, coming out of his daze.

"Doze politicians. You know how you tell dey lyin'? You can see dere lips movin'. Ha."

Narlstrom smiled and nodded politely. Laughing would have encouraged his line mate too much.

"What choo, a banka?"

Narlstrom wondered why this man would guess such a thing. Then he realized he was the only man in this office wearing a jacket and tie. He loosened his tie self-consciously.

"Not a banka?" Clearly, this man wanted to talk.

"Me? No. I am…well, was…a scientist."

"Scientist? Hmm, it must really be bad out dere, if people like you in here."

Narlstrom shrugged.

"I blame de politicians, all doze smarty-pants gov-ment people in Wash'ton. Dey all promise dings, big dings. But dey forget us when dey get dere. Dey forget bout you an' me."

Narlstrom sighed. "I think you're right."

"One-six-five," a female voice called out. No one in the line of chairs responded.

Narlstrom reflexively looked at this ticket, even though he knew that wasn't his number. He looked up at the Jamaican man who was fixated on the television. "Is that you? One-six-five?" Narlstrom asked.

The man looked down at his ticket. "Ooh, yeah. Tank you. You look out fer me, better dan doze people," he said, gesturing to the television. "Maybe you should go to Wash'ton? Ha."

"Maybe," Narlstrom murmured to himself.

ಬ ಬ ಡ ಡ

TJ sat on the park bench, waiting, his sneakers twisting nervously on the pavement.

"Good afternoon, TJ."

TJ looked up anxiously. "Hi, Mr. Traeger."

"Good job on the pizza delivery," he said, sitting down next to TJ.

"Thanks. Things didn't go exactly as planned."

Traeger smiled. "Don't worry. These things rarely do. Chaos and distraction are the game."

"That Arkin guy," TJ added, "asked me to look at some pictures to see if I could identify someone."

"Any of our people?"

"No, I think they were all Ms. Jansing's people."

"Did you confirm anyone?"

"Only in a very fuzzy way. I told them I couldn't be sure."

Traeger nodded his approval. "Smart move. So, did you get any cash out of the deal?"

"No, Grant's people weren't buying it."

"Well TJ, keep a low profile for a couple weeks. Here's $500 for your troubles."

TJ looked at the unexpected bills being offered.

"Thanks, Mr. Traeger."

ಬ ಬ ಡ ಡ

107

After another twenty minutes, Daniel Narlstrom was finally able to speak with an unemployment representative named Carla.

"So, Mr. Narlstrom…"

"Actually, it's *Doctor* Narlstrom."

"Oh, sorry," she said in a mildly sarcastic way.

He could see she was about to say something, but decided against it.

"Pardon me, Doctor Narlstrom. Do you have your paperwork?"

"Yes." He handed her a manila folder with all his documents.

"My, I wish everyone was this organized." She quickly perused his papers and crossed checked them with the computer.

"OK, everything is in order. You'll have to file online every two weeks for your unemployment benefits. The website will ask you whether you've been looking for work. Also, it will ask if you've worked part time, how many hours, and how much you earned. Based on that, it will calculate your bi-weekly benefit. Your base benefit is $950. That's $1900 per month."

"$1900 per month? My mortgage is nearly twice that!"

"I'm sorry, but that's all you're eligible for. Actually, that's the maximum anyone would be eligible for. It used to be more, but ever since Henderson."

"How can I live on that?"

"If someone could live on it, everyone would quit their job."

"I didn't quit!" Narlstrom insisted loudly.

Carla's supervisor stepped forward, but she waved him off.

"I know, sir. I wasn't implying that you quit. Please calm down. I am trying to help you."

"I'm sorry," he said regretfully. "I know it's not your fault."

"Here's the information packet. Read it carefully. Here's one last form. It will allow us to deposit the money directly into your bank account. At the bottom, there's a toll-free number to call if you still have questions."

He stared at the packet in his hands. His eyes welled up.

"Mr.—I mean—Dr. Narlstrom, I see a lot of people in this office, people who are worse off than you. You have an education. You have a house. If things get too bad, you could sell it. That may not sound good, but it's something. I know you'll make it through this."

"Thank you for your encouraging words," he said. With that, he left.

Her supervisor came over. "Carla, is everything OK?"

"Yeah, just another lost soul. I think this one fell from an ivory tower."

CHAPTER 20

The opening graphics swirled in three dimensions, signaling the beginning of the network's election night reporting.

"Good evening. I'm Bob Summers. It's another election night across America, our annual rite of democracy. While not a presidential election year, the stakes are high with 435 House seats and 34 Senate seats up for grabs, not to mention 18 governorships and the usual gamut of local races. Joining us this evening is our chief political analyst, Dylan Reese. So Dylan, how would you characterize this off-year election?"

Reese wore glasses with circular lenses, which seemed a style from another era. His slight and owlish appearance made his deep authoritative voice almost shocking.

"Well Bob, it's a year of chaos and contradictions. Congressional approval is the lowest in history. People are anxious over the economy, especially since the Kadler Steele scandal broke, which is still playing out. And citizens are not completely sure who to blame. The Republicans are blaming President Farnum. The Democrats are blaming House Republicans, most famously Sheldon Lannier, who has become a poster boy for Wall Street-induced corruption."

"Which party's argument do you think will resonate most strongly with voters?" Summers asked.

"An excellent question, but it has no easy answer. It may come down to this: the President is not up for re-election. The congressional Republicans are. So, they're the only ones the electorate can take their anger out on."

"Of course, the big question inside the beltway is, will the Democrats regain the House of Representatives?"

"It's going to be very close." Reese proceeded to outline the complex election math and probabilities, the kind only political junkies could love. However, this early in the evening, that's exactly who would be watching.

"Has this political discontent led to any other developments?" Summers asked, knowing Reese's response.

"Yes, there has been a significant increase in the number of Independents running for office in this election cycle. Although very few, if any, will actually win. However, Independents may siphon off enough votes to seriously affect election results, particularly on the House side. It's a frustrated response to what is perceived as dire politics-as-usual."

"But, all of these Independents are nothing but spoilers?"

"In most cases, yes. There may be one possible exception," Reese said. "As you know, almost no one expects Sheldon Lannier to keep his seat in the House. Everyone assumed his seat would go to Democrat Linda Jansing.

However, an Independent named David Grant has made an unusually strong showing."

"Independents getting elected is pretty rare."

"Extraordinarily rare. One of the few in the House was self-proclaimed socialist, Bernie Sanders of Vermont, who served from 1991 to 2007, when he moved over to the Senate. However, unlike Sanders, who caucused with the Democrats, it's anyone's guess which side Grant would favor."

"An elected centrist completely contradicts the trend of increased political polarization. If Grant gets into office, it'll be interesting to see how he does. He'll be a completely unique life form in Congress."

80 80 03 03

For Election Night, David's campaign had rented out the Embler River Inn, located on the outskirts of town. Several widescreen televisions had been set up, so his guests could watch the election results. He invited all his volunteers, as well as anyone who had contributed or been in anyway supportive. Jason Kennerly was there with his video gear, hoping to record the first major electoral victory of his fledgling party. Although, he felt a little intimidated when PA-TV came in. Kennerly was suffering from a bit of camera envy.

In addition to the larger Oak Room, the campaign had reserved the adjacent Willow Room, a smaller room, off to the side. It would serve as their election night command center. It also had a television, several laptops, along with some whiteboards listing all the voting districts. The only one there when David entered was Ellen.

"So, what do you think?" David asked, holding out his two manila folders. "Victory speech? Concession speech?"

"Honestly," Ellen said, "I have no idea."

"Well, whatever the outcome, I couldn't have done it without you."

"Not so. If you win, you couldn't have done it without me. On the other hand, if you lose, that you could have definitely done on your own," she said toasting him with a ginger ale.

"Well, whatever the final result, I learned a lot from you."

"And I, you."

"Really? What did you learn from me?" David asked.

"That I can be wrong."

"You? Wrong?" He said with an amused grin. "About what?"

"About you. I didn't think you'd go the distance. I thought, like most Independents, you'd grow so frustrated, you'd fold. That's what most Independents do. Either that, or they just don't have it together."

"Hey you," a woman called out, interrupting the conversation.

"Hey, yourself." David and the woman hugged. He turned back to Ellen. "Ellen, this is Reverend Peggy Garthwell, our pastor. Also, our daughters are inseparable."

"Yes, two peas in a pod," Garthwell added.

"Peggy, this is Ellen Langford, my chief political strategist."

"A pleasure. Sara says you're a one-woman political juggernaut."

"I've never heard it put that way before, but thank you, Reverend."

"Please just call me Peggy." Garthwell turned back to David. "Is Sara here yet?"

"No, but she and the kids should be here shortly. In fact, I'm surprised they're not already."

"I want you to know I've been praying for you. If you win tonight, I'll be praying even harder."

"Good, I'll need it."

₧ ₧ ₥ ₧

The President had invited some key staffers and party favorites up to the Residence. Federal law took a dim view of fundraising on government property. While this wasn't a fundraiser, everyone invited knew that donations were expected for the next campaign cycle.

Harris Carver escorted Ellis Cornwall up to the Residence personally. Cornwall's suit was perfectly tailored to his slender frame. His gray hair was flawlessly coiffed. Besides being the owner of the Liberty network, Cornwall was also one of the biggest Democratic contributors. They ascended in the family elevator which opened onto the Main Hall, which was more like a long living room than hallway. Carver led Cornwall to the right toward the West Sitting Room. The large half-moon window showed the fading red dusk over the West Wing.

"I believe you know Ed Leems," Carver said.

"Everyone knows the DNC Chair," Cornwall said. "How are you, Ed?"

"Fine. A pleasure to see you again, Mr. Cornwall."

"So Ed, are we going to have a blowout tonight?" Cornwall asked.

"We'll see, but I'm cautiously optimistic."

"My prediction is that in January," Cornwall announced, "the President will indeed have a Democratic Congress to work with. There'll be no stopping him."

"From your mouth to God's ear," Leems said, holding his hands in mock prayer.

"God will have nothing to do with it. I spread enough money around to put those Republican bastards in their place."

"Good evening, Mr. President," many said in unison as Farnum entered the West Sitting Room. Cornwall turned to see the President walking toward them.

"Hello, Ellis. Thank you for joining us this evening," Farnum said, warmly shaking his hand.

"I'm honored to be here, Mr. President."

"I see nobody's offered you a drink yet." Farnum waved over a waiter. "What'll you have?"

"Just a club soda, thank you. I'm saving myself for the celebratory champagne later."

෴ ෴ ෴ ෴

Many of David's supporters had arrived, including Paul and Donna Lurtz. He was glad to see they left their costumes home. Sara and the children still had not made an appearance. He was getting anxious. Most people took it as being nervous about the election. He repeatedly called the house and Sara's mobile phone, but no answer.

"Any news?" David asked, popping his head into the Willow Room.

"There's only two things I can say for certain right now," Fred said. "While you won Embler Township by a landslide, it's close everywhere else. And second, Lannier is definitely out of the running. It's down to you and Jansing."

Fred's phone rang. He listened, and then turned to David. "It's Sheldon Lannier."

He accepted the telephone. "Hello."

"Good evening, Mr. Grant."

"How are you, Congressman?"

"I can't say I feel very good tonight." Lannier admitted. "I am calling to concede. You put on a remarkable campaign."

"Thank you. I just want you to know it wasn't anything personal."

"Oh, I appreciate that. You started your campaign before all of the shit hit the fan. I hope you have half the integrity governing as you did in running."

"Thank you, Congressman. I'll do my best."

"Good night." They hung up.

"Wow, he actually conceded." David said, feeling a little sad for Lannier.

"Yeah, but Jansing still has to concede," Ellen said, coming in.

"Does she actually need to concede?"

"No, the numbers are what count, which all seem to be in your favor. But it would make things easier."

"Damn," David said. "We could actually win this thing."

෴ ෴ ෴ ෴

After a half hour of small talk with Leems and some of the White House staff, Ellis Cornwall moved closer to Farnum. "Mr. President, may I speak to you privately for a moment?"

Farnum smiled. "Ellis, have you ever toured the Residence? Did you know it has a third floor?"

"Really? No, Mr. President, I didn't."

"Let me show you," Farnum said, guiding Cornwall out toward the Main Hall.

"Mr. President?" Harris Carver inquired.

"It's all right. I'm just going to give Ellis a private tour."

"Yes, sir," Carver said, but kept watching them like a hawk, until they ascended the stairs.

A Secret Service agent nearby whispered into his wrist microphone, "Eagle is ascending to the third floor with a guest, via the center stairway."

"The third floor isn't used that much. There are a few bedrooms, a workout room, a billiard room. But the prize up here is the Solarium," the President explained, as they crossed the third floor hall. They entered a room that was stylistically distinct from the rest of the White House. "The Solarium was originally added to the White House by Taft as a sleeping porch, in the days before air conditioning. A lot of history has happened here. This was where Nixon told his family he was resigning. Nancy Reagan was here when she found out her husband had been shot."

"Seems like a very tragic room. Although, since they were Republicans, maybe not," Cornwall said, with a not-so-guilty smile.

"It also served as a kindergarten classroom for Caroline Kennedy. Actually, during the daytime, this room is quite cheerful."

"Mr. President, I know you've been inhibited by a Republican Congress, especially when it's come to your education bill."

"Well, the whole Kadler Steele affair hasn't made working with a Republican Congress easy."

"Hopefully, with a Democratic Congress, you can finally push through your education bill."

'I certainly hope so."

"Mr. President, I'd like to make a *private* proposal." Cornwall paused dramatically. "Are you willing to hear my proposal?"

Farnum nodded.

℘ ℘ ℘ ℘

"...Thank you, Kate, for that report." Bob Summers turned back to Dylan Reese. "So, Dylan how do the congressional numbers line up?"

"Well, Bob, despite a handful of races too close to call, I think it's pretty safe to say that the next Congress will be a Democratic one."

Hearing this, Harris Carver smiled. He quickly checked the other networks. They confirmed the news. It was a perfect excuse to walk upstairs and find out what Ellis Cornwall was up to. He walked briskly to the stairs. Once on the third floor, he spied a Secret Service agent standing outside the Solarium. He knew the agent wouldn't stop him from walking in, but he also wouldn't tolerate eavesdropping. He walked up to the agent, pointed into the Solarium, and mouthed "the President?"

The agent nodded.

Carver pretended to be hesitant, but not too long, or the agent would become suspicious. He hesitated just enough to hear the President saying,

113

"not at least for four or five months." He has stayed on the threshold long enough. "Mr. President?" Carver called out, as he walked in.

Cornwall stiffened, as if embarrassed or guilty.

"Yes, Harris, what is it?"

"I just thought you'd like to know, the networks are all calling enough races to give us a Democratic Congress. It'll be thin, but a definite majority."

"Congratulations, Mr. President," Cornwall chortled enthusiastically. "Time for that celebratory champagne?"

"I'd say so. Oh Harris, Ellis here has made an interesting proposal."

"Mr. President, I don't think—"

"It's all right. It's nothing we can't share with Harris."

"Very well, Mr. President," Cornwall acquiesced.

దు దు యు యు

David was circulating in the Oak Room. Everyone's spirits were high from the encouraging news reports. Finally, Sara and the children arrived.

"Thank God, I was getting worried about you."

"Sorry, we're late. Our genius son insisted on mentioning we might be on TV. So then, Wendy started fretting over which dress she was going to wear. You know, it's her daddy's big night, so she just had to be perfect," Sara said, sarcastically. "Then, there was a detour, forcing me to go over Hillcrest Road."

"I'm just glad you're OK."

"So, how are things going?"

"Lannier has conceded. Jansing's holding out."

"Which means?"

"I may have won this thing."

"Wow," she whispered.

"David," Zach McCarthy called out. "PA-TV just called the race for you!"

"Woo-hoo!" someone else yelled out.

"Excuse me. I need to go see Fred and Ellen."

"Go," Sara said.

దు దు యు యు

"Just tell your candidate, she's lost...Yeah, I know it's close, but not that close. All the Philadelphia stations have called it, and *not* for Linda Jansing. Lannier conceded over an hour ago. At least, he's not a sore loser....No, but that's what the press will call her, if she doesn't concede very soon...We'll be waiting for your call, but not very long." With that, Fred hung up on the Jansing Campaign Chair.

"Go get 'em, tiger," Ellen teased.

"You want to give it a try?"

"No, I won't do any better," she admitted. "Jansing is in denial."

David walked in. "What's the word?"

"All the stations are calling it for you." Fred explained. "But Jansing still won't concede."

"We don't need her to concede."

"But it'll be a lot cleaner, if she does," Ellen said.

"I think they're screwing with us," Fred insisted. "It's the only thing they can do. If they delay enough, no one will be awake to see your acceptance speech."

"It is getting late," David admitted. "Give Jansing's people a call. They've got 10 minutes to concede, or I'm going out there without her concession."

"While Fred's doing that, let me get everyone lined up," Ellen said.

Ellen went out into the Oak Room and notified the PA-TV producer. She scanned the crowd for Sara, but could only find Chris and Wendy.

"Where's your mother?"

"She went to the bathroom," Wendy said.

"OK, your father is going to make his speech soon. So, head up to the stage. I'll find your mother." Ellen made her way through the excited crowd. She ducked into the restroom, only to find Sara Grant trying to dry her eyes.

"My god, what's the matter?" Ellen asked.

"I'm sorry," Sara said in a weepy voice. "Nothing, really. I'll be fine in a moment."

"Sara, David's about to give his acceptance speech. You can't go out there if you're falling apart. What can I do to help?"

"I don't know. Can you get my husband to concede?"

CHAPTER 21

Ellen couldn't believe what she was hearing.

"What's the matter, Sara? I thought you were fine with David running for office."

"I dismissed it as some mid-life crisis thing he had to get out of his system." Sara leaned back against the sink counter and looked up at the ceiling. "Why couldn't he just buy himself a damn Ferrari instead? Now, he'll spend every week down in Washington, away from his family, missing birthdays and school plays. I feel like I've just been widowed, except without the sympathy. As the race narrowed, I prayed one of those candidates would pull just one more dirty trick. But I can't complain, because I naively gave David my approval."

"Just not to win?"

Sara nodded.

"Sara, I'm not going to lie to you. Yes, Washington can be stressful on a marriage and a family. I've seen it firsthand, but the spouse can make all the difference. Please, consider me an ally. I can't guarantee I'll get him to every birthday party, but I'll try to reduce the strain as much as I can."

"No offense, but why would you care?" Sara closed her eyes in regret. "I'm sorry, I didn't mean—"

"It's alright. As much as everyone just thinks of me as a political bitch, I'm also a divorced woman. That would be no surprise to most people. But honestly, my ex-husband wasn't half the man David is. So, I envy your marriage. That kind of marriage is worth preserving. Besides, a stressed-out, distracted congressman isn't going to be much good to anyone. Will you let me help?"

"Well, I'm not sure what you can really do, but it's the best offer I've heard all evening. I'm sorry, I better pull myself together."

℘ ℘ ℃ ℃

The crowd was cheering as Fred and David pushed through the crowd, which seemed to have grown significantly in the last half-hour. As they approached the stage, David saw Chris and Wendy, but no Sara. He yelled to Fred, "Where's Sara? I need her here with me."

"I'm right behind you," Sara called out. She squeezed through and kissed him. "Sorry, I'm late."

"Sara, I couldn't have done this without your support."

She leaned in to him. "Let's be honest; I wasn't that supportive. But you did the impossible, even without me. I am so very, very proud of you," she whispered, with slightly moist eyes.

Fred walked up to the podium and addressed the crowd, "How's everyone doing tonight?" The crowd gave some alcohol-enhanced cheering. "Sounds like you've heard some news." He laughed along with the crowd. "Ladies and gentlemen, it is my honor to give you the next congressman for Pennsylvania's 20th District, David Grant!"

The crowd exploded with applause. David smiled and waved as the applause slowly died down.

"I am truly humbled. This isn't just a personal victory. You all put your hearts and souls, and a lot of hours into the idea of breaking the two-party monopoly. And I am very grateful. Of course, I couldn't have done this without the support of my wife Sara and my children, Chris and Wendy. But there are so many others. First, there's Fred Arkin, who worked very hard to convince me to undertake what for a long time felt like a quixotic journey. Thank you, Fred."

Fred was unexpectedly taken back by the enthusiastic applause.

"Ellen Langford has been invaluable with her sage council and unbridled tenacity. And I know without her, I would be giving a very different speech tonight."

The applause for Ellen was not quite as enthusiastic as for Fred.

"Of course, I'm grateful for the tireless efforts of my friends, Mayor Tom Burke, Zach McCarthy, and so many others, as well as my new friends from the Centrist Patriots Party, especially our national chairman, Jason Kennerly."

Kennerly waved, beaming from behind his video camera.

"I also want to thank Paul Lurtz, who put aside his own campaign for the greater good. Sacrificing for the greater good is something many Americans have forgotten. I'm sure I'm forgetting the names of so many who fought for this, but I thank you all for working so hard and being willing to take a chance on me."

The crowd applauded again.

"However, the struggle is not over. There will be other centrist candidates in the future. And they'll need your support, too. I am hoping we've started a movement here tonight, a movement that values sober discussion over shallow promises, practical solutions over special-interest wish lists, and personal sacrifice over personal enrichment. Thank you for your support, but also for your dedication to a better future."

৪০ ৪০ ଓ ଓ

Two days after the election, Niyathi Bachali and Kevin O'Hara presented the collective results of their Kadler Steele investigations. The President grimly thanked them for their thoroughness. Afterwards, Hingecliff, Warrenberg, Carver and Stavros joined the President in the Oval Office.

"So, Kadler seems to be circling the drain, as they say," Farnum began.

"Corbin Beaumont is claiming all the negative publicity from the government is causing the lack of confidence in their stock price," Stavros reported. "They're playing it like the SEC is Chicken Little."

"There's a small element of truth in that, but the fundamentals of Kadler's financial structure are quite flawed," Hingecliff explained. "They were too clever by half. It can all be fixed, but we'll need to prop the firm up to avoid a panic in the market."

"Prop them up?" Stravros called out. "You mean, you want to reward Beaumont for his dishonesty?"

"No, I've met Beaumont. He's a slippery character, who should be prosecuted to the fullest extent."

"And thanks to Robert," the Attorney General interjected, "we may get our first Sarbanes-Oxley conviction. As you've just heard, O'Hara and Bachali have a good case against Beaumont and his lieutenants."

"While Beaumont and his accomplices are prosecuted," Farnum said, "many others will be hurt if Kadler is allowed to default."

"Yes, sir," Hingecliff agreed.

"Sir, are we talking another TARP-like bailout?" Stavros asked.

"I'm sure you can find a better name for it," Hingecliff said.

"Sir, we're in very dangerous territory," Stavros insisted. "We just convinced voters that Kadler Steele was the Republicans' fault. There have even been crowds demonstrating near the Kadler Steele headquarters. One group calls itself 'Salvage And Liberate America' and another goes by 'Reoccupy Wall Street.' Nerves are still raw from the Great Recession. Right now, these people are on our side. But if we bail out Kadler, you might just be kissing a second term goodbye."

"Please don't forget the fallout that occurred when Bear Stearns was allowed to default," Hingecliff reminded them. "And Kadler is much bigger. If we do nothing, the economy will suffer for sure. That won't endear this administration to anyone."

"But another TARP, regardless of the name, would be a political disaster," Stavros insisted. "The Republicans won't miss the opportunity to make it a major issue in the presidential campaign."

"It seems to me the trick is to find a way to punish the guilty and assure stability without irritating the voters," Farnum said, then turned to his Chief-of-Staff, who seemed to be deep in thought. "Harris, you've been awfully quiet."

"Sir, what if the government assumed the Kadler liabilities into some sort of a limited trust or similar fund? Like the emergency funds used for 9-11 and the Katrina hurricane, we create a separate entity that pays out to those who deserve it on a merit basis."

"A merit basis?" Hingecliff inquired.

"By merit, I mean how culpable they were in Kadler's schemes. Remember what angered people about TARP? Executive bonuses and paying out funds to foreign creditors, among other things."

"What about the shareholders?" Farnum asked.

"Shareholders by their very nature are expected to bear the risks of ownership," Hingecliff countered.

"So, shareholders and guilty accomplices pay. And the good guys get saved and made whole."

"And what are the criteria for separating those two groups?" Warrenburg asked.

"I'm sure the SEC and Justice can provide us with that," Carver said.

"The data, yes. But that still doesn't give us the criteria," Hingecliff cautioned. "We'll be dealing with many shades of gray."

"We'll work it out," the President said.

୫୦ ୫୦ ଓଷ ଓଷ

The day after the election, David spent most of his time giving media interviews, and not only with local news. A couple of the networks also asked for interviews. They treated him almost as a man-bites-dog oddity to throw into the end of their broadcasts, but it was still welcome exposure.

By Thursday, the media mini-frenzy had died down. That afternoon, David was alone in the shoe store, sorting and throwing out trash, when Ellen came in.

"What are you doing here? Ellen asked. "I thought you were taking Sara and the kids away on a vacation."

"Not until the weekend. Sara has a regular work week. The kids have school," he said, as he bagged up shredded papers for recycling.

"You know, your staff could clean this stuff up."

"What staff? They volunteered for a campaign, not the clean-up afterward."

"Where's Fred?"

"He's teaching a course in Jersey this morning."

"Then, I guess that leaves me," Ellen said, as she started to tie up a full trash bag.

"I'm glad you stopped by. I have something for you." David pulled an envelope out of his brief case and handed it to her. "Your performance bonus. As agreed, ten thousand for winning, plus one thousand for each point."

"Wow, such a prompt payer. Thank you."

"Then there was the other part of the deal. I offered you a position on my staff, if you want it."

"Hmm, do I expected you to win, I would have negotiated a title."

"What title do you want?"

"How about Chief of Staff?"

"Done," he answered without hesitating.

"Really? What about Fred?"

"I owe Fred a lot. I wouldn't have gotten started on this path without him. Let me ask you, what is your assessment of Fred? Honestly."

"He's loyal."

119

"That's good, but a puppy's loyal."

"I know he and I have had some friction, but he's smart. He learns quickly. He doesn't have the killer instinct, but people respond well to him, and he handles them nicely. He stays on message when talking to the press. He doesn't let reporters pull him off message."

"That comes from teaching easily distractible college students," David said with a smile.

"He would be no worse than anyone else starting out on a congressional staff. But you have doubts?"

"Not in his abilities."

"Then, what?"

"You're a creature of Washington. He's a creature of local academia. If he goes with us, and I don't get re-elected, he'll have left behind three colleges that he may not be able to go back to."

"Professors take sabbaticals all the time."

"He's an adjunct. There's no such thing as a sabbatical for adjuncts. When an adjunct leaves, a college replaces him almost instantly. It's kind of a game of musical chairs. He'll lose his chairs."

"Why don't you let him make that decision?"

The telephone rang. David went to answer it.

"Excuse me, *Congressman*. Why don't you let your staff get that?" Ellen picked up the telephone. "Hello, Grant for Congress. How may I help you?"…"No, this is Ellen Langford."…"I'm going to be his Chief of Staff," she said, smiling at David. "Uh-huh." The expression on her face changed. "You're kidding?"…"I see."…"No. Thank you, we'll definitely be in touch."

"What is it?"

"Linda Jansing is challenging the signatures that put you on the ballot."

CHAPTER 22

Dana Seagram had just finished her morning White House press briefing when she decided to check in with Carl Stavros. He was pacing back and forth, staring at a large whiteboard with an array of handwritten words. Stavros had been working on a name for the Kadler-not-quite-a-bailout program since the night before.

"So, do you have an acronym for this new program yet?" Seagram asked.

Stavros sighed. "How about…Public Equity Asset Realignment?"

"PEAR. Hmm, sounds kinda fruity to me," she teased.

He smiled. "Okay. How about Public Asset Realignment Trust or PART?"

"Well, the Republicans will say it's 'part' of the problem. But it could be worse."

"Harris said he'd like 'Trust' to be in the name."

"That's okay, but I think I like the word Federal instead of Public."

"I don't know," Stavros said with a taught smile. "That would turn PEAR into FEAR, and PART into FART."

"Oops, I guess acronyms aren't as easy as I thought." Seagram eyed the word list more closely. "How about instead of Realignment, you use Restitution? Begins with the same letter."

"Hmm, that works," Stavros admitted. His eyes squinted in concentration. "I know, Capital Asset Restitution Trust, CART."

"You know there will be 'putting the CART before the horse' jokes."

"If that's the worst they can say, it's not so bad."

ଅ ଅ ର ଓ

Jean Narlstrom surveyed the dining room table, where her husband was poring over his patent paperwork. She was annoyed that even though they had a big house, he had insisted on using the dining room for whatever it was he was doing.

"Dan, I'm going to have to evict you from the dining room table. Thanksgiving's coming."

"Uh-huh," Narlstrom grunted.

"Dan, what are you still doing with this stuff?"

"I'm finishing my new patent applications."

"I thought they belonged to Ariskor."

"Ariskor never filed for most of the patents."

"I don't understand."

"Ariskor filled out patent applications," he explained, "but never actually filed them."

"Why would they not file them?" she asked, becoming more exasperated.

"It was a ploy," he said, leaning closer and lowering his voice as if they might be overheard. "If Ariskor mentioned that they were ready to file for a patent, the Pentagon would wave them off. It became a bargaining chip to negotiate for more money."

"I still don't understand," she said, beginning to regret the conversation."

"When someone files for a patent, complete plans and explanations need to be a part of the application, which then becomes a publicly available record. The Pentagon doesn't like 'public.' In exchange for not filing, the Pentagon paid Ariskor additional millions."

"OK, so now you file, but the Pentagon still doesn't want your technology."

"I'm not filing patents for weapon systems. Derivations of my work have all sorts of commercial applications: refrigeration, freezers, energy-efficient applications galore. Ariskor has never had any interest in non-defense applications."

"Are you sure this is legal?"

"Yes, I had a patent attorney review the applications, as well as my contract and termination agreement. There's no problem, no conflict."

"An attorney? How much did that cost?"

"About $1800."

"What?" Jean cried out. "We've been scrimping and saving since your layoff, and you spend $1800!"

"Jean, it's an investment, one that'll pay off," he insisted. "I've been talking to a bunch of my industry contacts. Remember Carson from MIT? He's one of the people I'm talking to. Anyway, I described my results, along with a vague description of the process. He and the others all saw a great deal of potential in it."

"Are you sure they weren't just being nice?" she asked.

"Don't worry. I was rigorous in my questioning. Once I file the patent applications, I can get down to some serious negotiations."

"Okay, but Thanksgiving it still coming. So in three days, the table is mine."

જી ઈ ભ ભ

David, Fred and Ellen met in Art Fuentes's law office.

"So the way I read the complaint," Fuentes began, "Jansing is claiming that you didn't obtain enough qualifying signatures to be on the ballot."

"We had over 400 extra signatures," David said.

"She contends many of the signers were not registered to vote, signed more than once, or were not even residents of the district," Fuentes explained. "And in some cases, she claims the names are of voters who were deceased."

"That's ridiculous," Fred blurted out. "Shouldn't she have challenged the signatures before the ballots were printed?"

"Yes, but I guess she didn't think she was going to lose way back then. Admittedly, there is a legal question whether she can even file a challenge at this late date. But she's still filing. However, as long as enough signatures qualify, she'll lose this, too."

"Then, what the hell is she up to?" Fred asked.

"Jansing's accusing David of old Chicago-style politics," Ellen said. "It's not quite stuffing the ballot box, but chances are she can produce a handful of legitimate examples. A few forgetful or overly helpful citizens may have signed more than one clipboard. Plus, half the people in this country don't know what congressional district they live in anyway, so mistakes are bound to happen."

"What about the deceased?" Fred asked. "How can she honestly get away with that?

"Out of the 2500 people who signed petitions, a few of them probably died," Fuentes explained, throwing the brief down in disgust.

"So David can be disqualified because a few people died in the interim?"

"As long as they died after signing, it should be no problem," Fuentes answered. "But verifying their signatures becomes more problematic." He leaned forward on his desk. "This is why Jansing didn't ask for a recount."

"That would just be a matter of numbers," David said. "The election authorities have a straightforward process for resolving it."

"Doesn't this woman know the election is over?" Fuentes asked. "Is she really that much of a sore loser?"

"This is not about losing the election. Ellen said, rising from her chair. "Jansing is trying to sully David's reputation for the future."

"Just for spite?" David asked.

"She's also trying to make you less effective in Washington. You can't attend any of the early congressional orientations until you're certified the winner. You'll be behind the curve in January when you're sworn in, assuming this is resolved by then."

"You think she's preparing for another run in two years?" Fred asked.

"Only if she is completely delusional," Ellen answered. "She's lost two elections in a row. She'll never survive the primary process next time around. Jansing is doing this for her party. It's even possible someone has promised her an appointment or something else, in exchange for tripping you up."

"There must be something we can do." David said, as he stood up and looked out the window. "I guess I'll have to cancel my vacation."

"David, don't," Ellen said. "You're going to be away from your family a lot over the next two years. Give them this time and attention now."

"I agree," Fuentes said. "The courts and the election board will have to sort this out."

"And while I'm on vacation, Jansing will being chipping away at my reputation."

"No, David has to be seen as being pro-active in fighting this," Fred insisted "Art, can't we verify the names ourselves?"

"I don't think so," Fuentes said. "That might be considered a conflict of interest."

"I've got to do something," David said, looking more and more restless by the minute.

"I say go on vacation," Ellen said. "We'll keep an eye on the situation. We'll call you if anything happens."

Fred looked very uncomfortable. "I'm the campaign manager, and I think David needs to be seen actively fighting this."

"The campaign's over," Ellen snapped.

"Guys, you're both right," David said, holding up his hands to halt the bickering. "So maybe…maybe, I should do both."

CHAPTER 23

The following morning was a rare day for the Farnum White House. The President was going to give a formal press conference. He preferred individual interviews with reporters. If they were informal and off the record, so much the better. This built relationships, created loyalties, and could make each reporter feel as if he or she was getting a scoop. Much more preparation was required for days like today, when he would have to face the press in full.

Dana Seagram walked into the Press Room and, joked with the reporters, warming them up for the main attraction. At 9:05, she announced, "Ladies and Gentlemen, the President of the United States."

The press corps all stood as the President walked up to the lectern.

"Good morning, ladies and gentlemen," he began, waving for them to sit. "As you know, over the last few months, the media has been saturated with the Kadler Steele affair. The SEC and the Justice Department have investigated the firm and will be proceeding with a number of prosecutions. However, the firm's solvency is also a major concern. Therefore, we are instituting a new program, the Capital Asset Restitution Trust, also known as CART."

"In lieu of a costly and time-consuming default and bankruptcy, the Board of Directors of Kadler Steele has agreed the newly established trust will take temporary control of Kadler Steele and its associated units, and manage those assets and liabilities until stability can be reestablished."

"It is our intention to restore Kadler Steele to full operations without the messiness of a bankruptcy, and without the devastating disruption to financial markets and the economy as a whole. This approach has never been tried before, but it allows us the flexibility to adapt to changing conditions. The board of Kadler Steele agreed. I campaigned on new ideas for old problems. Here's a perfect example. Now, I'll take some questions."

"Mr. President," the *Times* reporter called out. "Will the federal government be providing funds to assure Kadler Steele's solvency?"

"While we may make limited loans to stabilize the firm, this is not a TARP-like bailout. In fact, if financing is required, we hope to tap private capital sources."

"Who convinced the Kadler's board of directors to agree to this unusual arrangement?" asked one of the network reporters.

"Secretary Hingecliff and Attorney General Warrenburg met with the independent members of the board yesterday."

"What leverage was used to get them to sign on to this agreement? For instance, was any immunity from prosecution offered?"

"The Kadler board realized their situation, and agreed to this arrangement quite readily."

"Isn't the government really seizing private property here?" asked the reporter from the Conservative Patriot's Network.

"Not at all. Given the chaos of Kadler's financial structure, we're cleaning up their mess. And we plan to do it with a minimum of cost and disruption."

"Couldn't this be considered by some to be the first step in transforming America into a centrally controlled economy?"

Farnum smiled. "Right-wing alarmists will spin it that way. Certainly your colleagues at CPN will. However, thinking people of both parties will understand this is the least intrusive way of straightening out this situation."

"Mr. President—"

ॐ ॐ ॐ ॐ

Later that day, David Grant also called a press conference. Once again, he was standing in front of Embler Town Hall, which he thought appropriate since it was where his campaign began. Thankfully, no banners were sagging today.

"Good afternoon, ladies and gentlemen," he began. "As you all know, after I won the election for Representative for the 20th District, Linda Jansing filed a legal challenge, claiming that I had insufficient signatures to gain ballot access in the first place. Only after she lost, did she become so desperate. I find this rather sad, and not simply because it makes her look like a sore loser. It is a move designed to impede our democracy, to deprive our district of proper representation. If Ms. Jansing had honest concerns about my qualifying for ballot access, she would have done something months ago. It is nothing more than a petulant attempt to throw sand in the machinery of the democratic process. This is the same type of dirty politics that compelled me to run in the first place."

"My understanding is that first the court must rule on whether or not her challenge is legal. Then, if successful, the election board would proceed with a revalidation process. I have asked Linda Jansing to drop her challenge, but she has refused. I find it appalling that Ms. Jansing would insist on tying up these government institutions with her personal obsession. The government has enough important work to do. Therefore, to avoid wasting the court's time, I will join Ms. Jansing in her request to allow the challenge, thus relieving the court of any time-consuming responsibilities. And to avoid tying up the election board's time, I offer twelve volunteers who are willing, under the board's direct supervision, to assist in the revalidation process. These volunteers are led by Mayor Tom Burke, the *Democratic* Mayor of Embler. The other volunteers are members of a variety of parties. The diversity of these volunteers should allay any concerns of partisan bias."

"As for me, I will be departing on a previously planned vacation which I *promised* my family. And I keep my word regardless of the political situation. Besides, I already know what the outcome will be, unless of course, Ms. Jansing has another dirty trick up her sleeve. Now, I only have a few minutes for questions."

"Excuse me, Mr. Grant, what is your reaction to President Farnum's CART program?"

David was surprised at being asked a question unrelated to his own situation. Then, he realized it was a sign that the press saw through the Jansing charade and did consider him the true representative-elect after all.

"I'm intrigued by CART. Certainly, we all remember the pain and frustration under the TARP program. I think it's important for me to go to Washington with an open, yet somewhat skeptical, mind. As far as the CART program goes, the devil is in the details."

ಬಿ ಬಿ ಣ ಣ

That night, Ben Glendenning was ready to pounce. The camera light teased him like a scantily clad woman. And then, finally the tease was over. He was live.

"Good evening, patriots. Welcome to one of the last refuges of American sanity. So, did you hear what our Commissar-in-Chief is doing now? He is seizing an American company. Nationalizing the property of others like some third-world dictator. CART is an appropriate name for this program, because Farnum is *carting* away our property rights, and throwing them on the refuse heap, along with any sense of ethics or morality. This is yet another chapter of the Left's ongoing crusade to destroy free enterprise. Whose hard-built business will be next? Yours? Mine? Your children's?"

"Farnum's CART is really quite amazing. It carries both the smoke *and* the mirrors!" Glendenning seemed particularly proud of that statement. "But seriously, with property rights discarded so casually, and on such a large scale, and in the broad daylight, can suppressing freedom of speech be far behind?"

"I love America with my whole heart, my whole being. That's why the trampling of our civil rights is so…so…I can't even come up with a word to cover it. What word covers outrage? Cruelty? Unbelievability? Callousness? Tyranny? It's so extreme, we need another word for it. My friends, give me a moment."

The camera zoomed in on his teary eyes.

"I know. Perhaps, it's…it's…*Orwellian*. The truth no longer matters to Farnum. Four plus four can equal five as far as he is concerned. Actually, looking at his budget numbers, his atrocious math skills may actually allow him to believe it. But we don't have to. You and I see the truth."

ಬಿ ಬಿ ಣ ಣ

Russell Beacham, the RNC chairman arrived early at Le Chevalier to see that everything was ready for his dinner guests. More importantly, he wanted to make sure he could position the place cards on the table. He knew the personalities all too well to allow random seating.

The private wood-paneled room was just what he wanted. He had told the restaurant to prepare a table for ten, but he knew only nine were coming. The absent guest was the outgoing Speaker of the House, whom Beacham never really cared for. The dislike was mutual. The empty chair would make a statement.

Senator Howard Carstairs was the first to arrive. "Good evening, Russ. Thanks for the invite. Too many of our GOP colleagues are licking their wounds tonight. I'm glad to see at least our chairman isn't sucking his thumb."

Beacham laughed. "Thanks for coming, Howard. I was afraid you might have already left for Maine."

"I'm leaving for Bar Harbor in the morning. Emily and I are having all the children and grandkids for Thanksgiving."

"Sounds great."

A few minutes later, Congresswoman Cassandra Mirreau of Louisiana arrived. Many favored her to be the next Republican Minority Leader. However, she didn't look particularly happy tonight.

"Good evening, Cassie," Carstairs greeted her in an attempt to be cordial.

"Howard," Mirreau said flatly, making no such attempt.

"Ah, here's Dennis," Beacham said, hoping the arrival of Senator Dennis Ogden might provide a buffer between Carstairs and Mirreau.

"Good evening, everyone."

"Congratulations on your re-election, Dennis," Carstairs said. "Wisconsin is very lucky to have you for a second round. So are we."

"Thank you. You're very kind."

It was Ogden's first re-election to the Senate, the first sign that he would have staying power in Congress. In a few weeks, he would begin his second term and would not have to run again for six years. Time to breathe. Time to govern.

Other congressional Republicans arrived in short order, mostly members of the House. After everyone was assembled and had a drink in their hands, Beacham stood up to speak.

"Thank you all for coming tonight. I don't have to tell anyone here, it's not been a good season for the GOP. Two years ago, Ted Henderson lost re-election. And a week ago, we lost Congress. It would be easy to stay home and assume the fetal position." He subtly nodded at the Speaker's empty chair. "But we can't afford to do that. I have my own opinions about what must be done, but first I wanted to hear from you."

"It's real simple," said the Congressman from Tennessee. "We've got to kick Farnum's ass at every opportunity. I don't know what this CART crap is, but it can't be good."

"I think we need to take a very critical look at it," Ogden admitted. "But let's not shoot at it until we know exactly what kind of animal it is."

"Yes, Farnum won on an anti-Henderson platform," Mirreau interjected. "But he'll have to run on his own record next time."

"And we've got to make sure his record stinks to high heaven," someone else chimed in.

"Excuse me, but don't you think the voters will see that for what it is?" Carstairs asked. "Let's be honest. We had a majority, and we squandered it. We could have found some common ground with Farnum. We could have gotten something done. But no, we seem to be trapped in a reenactment of the Hatfields and the McCoys. Have any of you noticed that Congress's approval rating is at four percent? Four percent! Hell, Satan has a higher approval rating."

Carstairs noticed the congresswoman from South Carolina flinched at the mention of Satan.

"It's not about being popular; it's about being right," one of the others called out.

"Being right? Were we right about blocking Farnum's education bill? We could have helped shape it. Now, with a Democratic majority, he'll ram who knows what down our throat."

"Damn RINO" the South Carolinian Congresswoman muttered under her breath.

"Damn straight," the Tennessee Congressman whispered back.

Beacham gave them a withering stare. He then signaled for salads to be served. He hoped munching some greens would lower the temperature of the conversation.

"Well, there's little profit in lamenting the past," Beacham said. "Gregory Farnum is formidable, no doubt. But who can take him on?"

"I've been hearing that Buck Howell is putting together an exploratory committee." Mirreau offered.

"God help us," Carstairs muttered under his breath.

"What do you mean by that?" she demanded.

"When Governor Howell talks about 'One America,' he says it, looking in a mirror," Carstairs answered. "He's a fire-breathing, religious zealot who doesn't give a damn about anyone who isn't a Christian social conservative."

"I think that's unfair," the South Carolinian called out. "But, there does need to be a sharp division between the candidates,"

"And that's all we'll get, sharp division," Carstairs countered.

"There are rumors that Farnum is a closet atheist," she added.

"Rumors?" Carstairs asked. "Created by whom? Ben Glendenning?"

"What about Cory Johnson?" Ogden suggested, trying to redirect the conversation.

"Cory's a good legislator, a solid conservative." Mirreau said. "But, I just don't know if he's got the fire in his belly for a Presidential race."

"What about you, Dennis Ogden?" Beacham asked.

"Excuse me, no," Ogden said, blushing. "I feel I owe Wisconsin a few more years before I get too ambitious."

Over salad, other names were bandied about. Everyone speculated on their favorites. By the time the entrée arrived Beacham's guests had calmed down a bit.

"Cassie, how do things look in the House?" Beacham asked.

"I hear Porter Barnes is making some moves to become the next Speaker, but many Democrats hate him as much as we do," she reported.

"Really? With his sparkling personality?" Ogden asked.

Everyone laughed.

"Personally," Mirreau continued. "I'm betting on Everett Wilkers."

A few of them snorted or groaned their contempt.

"Barnes may get the Majority Whip position as a reward for knocking off Lannier and the others."

"That alone may convert a bunch to our side," someone blurted out.

A few of the others chuckled. Beacham was glad to see the evening winding down on a friendlier tone. After dessert, everyone departed, eager to begin their Thanksgiving break. The only ones left were Howard Carstairs and Beacham.

"You never did share your opinion," Carstairs observed, pulling out his pipe.

"You noticed. Can you ever remember a time when there was so much hatred within the party?"

"No, I can't," Carstairs said, absentmindedly scraping the last of the cake frosting from his plate.

"I ran into Ed Leems a while back, at some university panel discussion. Privately, he confided things were the same way on their side. Both sides are becoming so much more extreme and strident."

"This polarization is like a rubber band being stretched to its limit. Something's going to snap."

"I just wonder when the reckoning comes, what will it look like?"

"I suppose it'll be like nothing we can imagine," Carstairs said, contemplating his empty plate.

CHAPTER 24

By mid-December, the Board of Election for the Commonwealth of Pennsylvania reviewed the ballot petition signatures of the Grant for Congress campaign. Of the 2519 signatures, only 41 were disqualified. An additional 29 remained unconfirmed. The election board therefore certified David Grant, the next Congressman for Pennsylvania's 20th District.

On January 3rd, David Grant, along with 43 other new representatives, stood in the House Chamber to be sworn in by Everett Wilkers, who had himself just been sworn in as the new Speaker of the House. Wilkers's bald pate emphasized the heavy bags under his eyes. Conservative cartoonists had already caricatured him and labeled his bags "tax" and "spend". Wilkers made a terse speech, including a dig at the outgoing Speaker, who didn't even bother to show up. Wilkers picked up the heavy wooden gavel and pounded it. That put a wide grin on his face.

"As my first act as Speaker, it is my honor to swear in our newest members. Please raise your right hand."

Standing among his fellow freshmen, David proceeded to recite the oath for the office that he had worked so hard to attain. "*I, David Michael Grant, do solemnly swear that I will support and defend the Constitution of the United States against all enemies, foreign and domestic; that I will bear true faith and allegiance to the same; that I take this obligation freely, without any mental reservation or purpose of evasion, and that I will well and faithfully discharge the duties of the office on which I am about to enter. So help me God.*"

Then, out of the corner of his eye, he spotted Sara, Chris and Wendy up in the balcony gallery. When Wendy caught his eye, she waved enthusiastically, holding on to Chris with her other hand. Embarrassed, her brother tried to curtail her performance. David smiled at the sight. He then realized this was why he had endured all he had been through. It was quite simple: little Wendy Grant and her big brother.

"It is my great pleasure to welcome you to the U.S. House of Representatives," Wilkers began. "This democratic institution is the most representative body in the world. This is the People's House. And rarely have the people needed us more. Today, you will soon begin very important work, educating yourself further on the issues, performing committee work, and so forth. We need work horses, not show horses. I look forward to seeing what the House of Representatives will produce this session. I hope we make the most constructive and progressive advances for our great republic."

Once the swearing-in ceremony concluded, all the freshmen posed for a group photograph on the Capitol steps. Despite the cold, none of them wore overcoats. Afterwards, David met Sara and Wendy in Statuary Hall, just outside the House Chamber. Sara was looking up, admiring the neoclassical architecture, while Wendy's eyes were wide, gazing at all the statues. She suddenly saw her father approaching.

"Daddy!" she exclaimed, her voice echoing throughout Statuary Hall. David could easily understand how the acoustics forced the House to abandon this room as their meeting place in 1857.

"Hello pumpkin," he said in a lower voice. "So, how did you like the ceremony?"

"It was great. Are they going to make a statue of you now?" she asked, looking up at the statue of John Peter Gabriel Muhlenberg.

He laughed. "No, I don't think so." He looked around. "So, where's Chris?"

Sara pointed across the hall to where Chris was flirting with some young lady. "They were sitting next to each other in the gallery," Sara explained. "Her mother was sworn in with you. I think she's from out west."

"Yet, he's still taking the time to flirt with her," David mumbled to himself.

"Mommy, can we get some ice cream?" Wendy asked.

"On such a cold day?" Sara asked.

"But we're inside."

"Maybe on the way home, after you're off your sugar high."

"The way home?" David asked.

"After you went in, Matt Cartwright called me," Sara answered guiltily. "He says the client on the Thornton Library wants revisions. I have to be back for a meeting tomorrow morning. The kids and I have to drive back right away."

"I understand." David thought about suggesting some alternatives, but all of them would put the heavy lifting on Sara. He walked Sara, Chris and Wendy to the car. The children buckled themselves in, but Sara lingered outside for a moment, smiling.

"Just remember, Congressman, I'm your first constituent," Sara said, and kissed him. "And I expect special favors," she whispered suggestively in his ear.

As he watched his family drive off, David suddenly felt very alone. Refocusing himself, he headed briskly toward his new office. Because of the delay in certifying his election, David wasn't entered into the office lottery. As a result, he received what some considered the least desirable congressional real estate, the fifth floor of the Cannon House Office Building. Earlier, Sara explained how the Cannon building's elevations were divided into a rusticated base and a colonnade with an entablature and balustrade. He understood none of it. However, what stuck in David's mind was that his office was in the attic, which was converted to office space. The one advantage it had was its close proximity to the Metro train station, which would make commuting home easier.

As he approached his office, he saw that someone had finally finished putting his name plate next to the door. He found Ellen organizing the office suite.

"Nice. So where's Fred?"

"He should be here later this afternoon. I thought you would be having lunch with your family."

"No, they had to head home. Sara has a meeting early tomorrow."

"Not what you wanted?"

David nodded no.

"You often hear about someone in Washington claiming to resign so they can spend more time with their family. I'm usually a cynic about most things, but unless I have information to the contrary, I tend to believe it."

"That sounds uncharacteristically naïve."

"Listen, this town can take a heavy toll on family and friends. You're lucky that you're only a few hours from home."

"Well, I suppose I can't complain."

At that moment, there was a knock at the door.

"Hello," David said, greeting his first visitor as a congressman.

"Good Morning, Congressman. Congratulations. I'm William Lester, Architect of the Capitol. "

"Architect? I'm sorry, wouldn't the architect be dead for over a century?"

"No," the man said patiently. "There have been many Architects of the Capitol. But, I'm not actually an architect *per se*. The position has evolved. I manage the Capitol complex, which includes all the congressional buildings, the Supreme Court, and the Library of Congress, as well as the Botanical Gardens."

"Sorry, my mistake," David said with some embarrassment. "What can I do for you?"

"Actually, it's what I'm here to do for you. Normally, these sorts of things would be handled by party leadership. However, since you have no party, I'm taking it upon myself to attend to them."

"What sort of things?"

"First, I'd like to present you with your congressional pin. It will allow you access to secure areas, such as the Floor of the House, the congressional subway, and so forth. There's a map in the orientation handbook. You should always wear the pin, or have it on your person whenever you're within the complex. However, I don't recommend wearing it on the street. It might make you a target."

"I see." David accepted the pin, and looked at it carefully. "This is more than a pin; isn't it?"

"Yes, there's an RFID chip in it."

"Radio Frequency Identification? Is Big Brother trying to keep an eye on me?"

"It's so the Speaker can have an idea how many members are nearby when there's a call for a vote. It won't pinpoint your exact location; just indicate whether you're near the Floor, in your office, or somewhere in between."

"And now, something more important, your voting card. When a vote is called for, you simply swipe your card and vote yea or nay. There are five voting stations on the House Floor."

"Yes, I heard about that at the orientation."

"Anyway, congratulations again." He shook hands with David, and left.

"Well, it's official now," Ellen said. "You're part of the Washington power structure." She leaned back on her desk. "So, there's a question I need to ask."

"Go on."

"Which party do you plan to caucus with?"

"Can't I caucus with both?"

"No, not really. What was it Jim Hightower said? 'There's nothing in the middle of the road but a yellow stripe and dead armadillos.'"

David smiled at Ellen's dark humor. "Wait, what about Marcus Finn? Didn't he caucus with both sides?"

"Yes and no. He was a Republican. And believe me, no one put in more effort into reaching across the aisle, but his home base was the Republican Party. Honestly, you must be leaning one way or the other."

"On individual issues? Sure. But overall, why can't I be Switzerland?"

"They may need a neutral broker from time to time, but passionate people don't respect neutrality. And besides, I don't think you came all this way to be Switzerland."

"A lot of people worked very hard for me because I wasn't affiliated with either party."

"I'm not saying you have to join one of them, just get a Bernie Sanders-type deal, an informal agreement that you'll vote their way most of the time."

"I'm not prepared to do that, at least, not yet."

"Well unless you do, or pull some other rabbit out of your hat, we'll both be looking for jobs in two years."

"I'll start looking for hats," he said, looking at his watch. "Anyway, I have to head over to the White House for the reception. I'll see you later."

ಬ ಇ ಲ ಡ

David had taken the White House tour years before on a family vacation. It had been far less exciting than he had expected. The tour was only the first floor plus the basement. All he could remember was the China Room filled with antique dishes and that the East Room had been much smaller than he had expected. However, Sara enjoyed it immensely. She studied all the architectural details with great relish.

However, this visit had one extra feature: meeting the President of the United States. However, he cautiously kept his expectations low. He anticipated only a short speech with clichéd platitudes, nothing too meaningful. At least, he'd get a group picture with the President that he could hang on his wall.

"Ladies and Gentlemen, the President of the United States," said a disembodied voice over a loudspeaker. Everyone stood, as Gregory Farnum entered the room.

"Good afternoon, ladies and gentlemen. First, let me congratulate you all in winning your respective political campaigns, which these days seems to be the ultimate reality TV show."

Everyone laughed.

"You've all made a commitment to do your best to improve America. And for that, I salute you. Now usually, we take a group picture. But it's been suggested that we do some one-on-one pictures this afternoon…except for those who distanced themselves from me in the campaign. And yes, I know who you are," he joked.

Again, everyone laughed.

"All kidding aside, I hope during the next two years we can work together in good faith and rewarding synergy. Regardless of party, we are on the same team."

"Yeah, right," one of the freshman Republicans whispered sarcastically.

The White House photographer had a carefully lit setup, far more flattering to the subjects than a flat-lit, on-camera flash. Dana Seagram escorted each new member of Congress over to the President, one by one. The protocol secretary had advised all the freshman members of this in advance. This was to avoid an awkward and undignified lining up to have a picture with the President. David tried to ascertain the order. It wasn't alphabetical, although it seemed to alternate Democrat with Republican. He wondered if the electoral count had anything to do with it. As he couldn't remember who was who, much less what state they represented, David gave up trying to figure it out. Farnum would also spend a few minutes talking to each new member.

After about half an hour, the President thanked everyone and departed. Yet, David had never been escorted over for a picture. Farnum's departure was too quick for him to react. He wondered if the White House was intentionally slighted him for not being a member of a party. Once again, a visit to the White House had disappointed him.

Some of the freshman stayed for a few minutes, chatted, and then started to depart. David decided to do likewise.

"Excuse me, Congressman Grant," inquired a man whom David presumed was another member of Congress.

"Yes?"

"I'm Carl Stavros, White House Communications Director. President Farnum was wondering if you had a few minutes to join him in the Oval Office."

CHAPTER 25

The walk to the West Wing was remarkably short. In less than two minutes, David was standing outside the door of the President of the United States.

"Amy," Stavros said. "This is Congressman Grant to see the President."

"Certainly, the President is waiting," Amy informed them. "But it'll have to be fast. The President has an important meeting."

Stavros walked in first. Through the doorframe David saw Gregory Farnum, the most powerful man on planet Earth, talking quietly to another man. David recognized the other man but couldn't remember his name. He wondered what major issues they were talking about. *Defense? Kadler Steele? The budget?* Stavros waved him in.

"Mr. President," Stavros said. "May I introduce Congressman David Grant of Pennsylvania?"

Farnum quickly walked across the room. "Congressman, please forgive us. The congressional party leadership sent over the names of their new members. But you have no party leader, no one sent yours, an inexcusable oversight."

"Not at all, Mr. President. I understand completely," David answered. "You have far more important things on your plate than photo ops."

Stavros motioned for the photographer to come in. David and the President stood for the photograph in front of the Resolute Desk, the one known best for the photograph of JFK Jr. crawling underneath it. The flash fired several times. Then, the photographer relaxed.

"Thank you, Mr. President. That was very thoughtful. I won't take up any more of your time." David started to leave.

"Where are you going?" Farnum asked. "You have a hot date?"

"I was told you have an important meeting," David answered, slightly confused.

"Is that what Amy said?" Farnum asked, smiling. "She says that a lot. She is very protective of my time, and I love her for it. But please, let's sit for a moment," Farnum said, gesturing toward a very comfortable-looking chair. "The key to maintaining your sanity in this job is to know when to take a break. Besides, I'm curious about you. You've made a little history. You are the first Independent elected to the House since, uh…"

"Bernie Sanders in 1990?" suggested the other man.

"What about Virgil Goode? Farnum asked.

Goode started as a Democrat," Carver replied, "then became an Independent, then a Republican.

"I'm sorry. This is Harris Carver, my Chief of Staff and political encyclopedia."

"Pleasure to meet you, Congressman."

"Likewise, Mr. Carver."

"So," said Farnum. "You're the David that's taking on, not one, but two political Goliaths."

"Well, two severely wounded Goliaths, to be honest."

"Still, you're a formidable opponent."

"I'd prefer a more constructive approach, something more cooperative."

"I'm glad to hear you say that." Farnum said. "Our legislative office reviewed your positions just to get an idea where you stand on the issues."

"And what did you find?"

"A relatively refreshing set of attitudes. We were hoping you could help us with an education bill we are planning to send up to the Hill. What are your views on education?"

"Mr. President, I suspect you already know them."

"What someone says on the campaign trail isn't always what they believe."

"Yeah, I've noticed that, but I do believe what I said about education. I know, every president wants to be the Education President." He stopped himself from being too glib. "Listen, I won't stand before you and claim to be an education expert. To be honest, Mr. President, I only adjuncted at a college for less than two years."

"Hear that, Harris, a congressman claiming to not be an expert," Farnum said. "That's refreshing."

They all laughed. David couldn't believe this. He was sharing a laugh with the President of the United States, *in the Oval Office*.

"I'd still like to hear what you think," Farnum said.

"Certainly, Mr. President. Like many people, I believe education is better handled at the local and state levels. As for the role of the federal government in education, I'd limit it to looking for the successful schools, studying them, and touting them. Let those close to the problems make the decisions."

"But certainly poor urban schools need extra support."

"Sure, but we shouldn't be just throwing cash at school districts indiscriminately. For instance, there's a school in Philadelphia that does a fantastic job, top scores and everything. The kids get into great colleges and universities, and they don't even use computers. And I say that with some regret, since I used to sell educational software. I guess my point is there's no one-size-fits-all solution."

"David, you've made some very good points, and not that far from my own thinking. I suppose I'm more concerned with higher education, keeping our people competitive with relevant jobs skills.

"Well, it's no secret that factory jobs have been disappearing. New technologies are eliminating manufacturing jobs, which in turn is eroding our middle class. Educating people with advanced skills is essential. We should encourage promising young people to go into science and engineering, so they can create and develop unique technologies and other intellectual property, things China can't copy so easily. My son Chris, with my encouragement, is considering robotics engineering."

"That's great."

"Mr. President, I'm all for improving our education system, but the devil is in the details. If you really want to grab my attention, start talking about campaign finance reform and reducing the deficit."

"That's an uphill battle even for me."

Farnum stood up. David followed suit.

"Congressman, it was nice speaking with you. I hope we do it again."

"Thank you, Mr. President. I appreciate the talk." With that, David departed the Oval Office.

"What do you think, Harris?" Farnum asked. "Can we use him?"

"Maybe. He's not stupid. But the bit about campaign finance reform, he's still a touch naïve."

"We all were at first. Don't worry. In six months, he'll be pork-barreling with the best of them."

"Still, he's an Independent. Not exactly a dependable vote. Luckily, the margin in the House isn't that tight."

"Next time around, things may be tighter. Always think long term, even in the short term. By the way, Harris, 'forgetting' to take his picture was a nice move. Good work. Now, we just have to sweet-talk the other 43 freshmen."

"Thank you, Mr. President."

଼ ଼ ଼ ଼

David decided to walk back to Capitol Hill. He wanted to be alone to absorb what had just happened. As he made his way along Pennsylvania Avenue, his mind was racing. What had just happened? He was euphoric. Then, he started to think about all the things he should have said. Did he miss a once-in-a-lifetime opportunity? The President said he hoped to have David back. He'd have to be better prepared next time. Then, he remembered the meeting ended just after David mentioned campaign finance reform and the deficit. He wondered if he had put the President off in some way. Had he screwed up? No, David decided. He had been elected to speak his mind to power, even if that power was President Farnum. Still, he was fairly elated.

଼ ଼ ଼ ଼

Fred Arkin had arrived at the Cannon Building. It was his first day as a congressman's Communications Director. He took it all in, as Ellen showed him around the office suite.

"Not as big as I expected, but still nice. So, where do I sit?" he asked.

"I've saved the best for last," Ellen said, as she opened the door. "Your domain."

"Wow. Why do I get the biggest office?"

"Well, you'll be sharing it with others."

"Who?"

"A social media specialist, a constituent services representative, and a corresponding secretary. Sorry, there's not much privacy, but we can set up some cubicle dividers."

"Hey, it's still better than an adjunct cave. What are their names?" he asked, pointing to the empty desks.

"I don't know. You haven't interviewed them yet." Ellen handed him a stack of résumés. "Also, you need to obtain bids for the Congressman's website. First, you'll need to write an RFP."

"What's an RFP?"

"Request for proposal. Go to www.house.gov; take a look at other member sites. Write up what you think we need in our website. Follow these directions on government RFPs," she said, handing him a booklet. "The three of us will go over it. Then, you send out the RFP for multiple bids to the approved list of web developers."

"No problem. Who's in that office?" Fred asked, looking across the reception area.

"Me. But don't be too jealous. I'll be sharing it with our legislative assistant, whom I still need to hire. The only one who has his own office is the Congressman. And that's to receive visitors."

"Hey, here's the team," David called out enthusiastically, then gave Fred a bear hug.

"What's gotten into you?" Ellen asked, hoping to forestall a bear hug.

"I just had a very nice meeting with the President of the United States," David said with a certain satisfaction in his voice.

"The grip-and-grin photo op?"

"No, I was asked into the Oval Office for a *private* meeting."

"Congressman," Ellen said, smiling. "You need to save the BS for the press."

"Wow, I know I'm a politician now," David said. "But I didn't think my credibility would go down this fast."

"Hello? Messenger," called a voice from the reception area.

"We also need to get a receptionist." Ellen said to Fred.

"I'll take care of it," Fred said, heading out.

"So how are we settling in?"David asked.

Before Ellen could answer, Fred came back in with an opened package. "Holy cow. He *did* meet with the President. These just came from the White House Photography Office."

Ellen held out her hand, so Fred would pass the pictures.

"You really did have a private meeting with the President. I thought you were kidding," Ellen said. "These are great."

"What did you talk to him about?" Fred asked.

"An education bill he wants me to work on with him."

"With him?" Fred asked. "What does that mean?"

"I'm not sure. Ellen's the veteran of the Hill. What do you think?"

"I don't know, but he's after something," Ellen answered, looking at the photographs. "Regardless, this is a huge gift."

"How so?"

"Publicity. Do you know how many members of Congress would kill to have pictures like these *sitting down* with the President? Fred, you need to write a press release and send it with the picture to the local press back in the district."

"Really? It's just a posed, side-by-side shot. Nice for me. But it doesn't say much."

Ellen picked up one of the prints and showed it to David. "This one says plenty."

David hadn't remembered the White House photographer continuing to take pictures after he and Farnum sat down. The resulting images gave the impression of thoughtful consultation with the President.

"This candid shot is gold," Ellen said, grinning.

ဆ ဆ ca ca

Daniel Narlstrom had just gotten home from the supermarket, where he had been working part-time. Sometimes, he worked the register. At other times, he retrieved carts from the parking lot. He preferred the carts. That way, he could avoid people he knew. When on the register, he would have to explain that he had been laid off to neighbors and acquaintances stopping by for milk and bread. Sympathy was always given. The repeated offer of "If there's anything I can do…" became emptier with each utterance. The hollow offers required expressions of gratitude.

"Oh, thank you. You're very kind." It was a humiliating ritual, but the part-time work extended his unemployment benefits. And he couldn't find a job farther from home. Jobs were tight, and teenagers were preferred. Thankfully, his hours were over for the rest of the week.

Just then, the doorbell rang. Narlstrom opened it to find two people standing there, a woman in a suit and an Army major.

"Dr. Daniel Narlstrom?" the woman in the suit inquired.

"Yes."

"I'm Erica Belski with the National Security Agency. This is Major Nieves, US Air Force." Belski showed her identification. "May we speak privately?"

"Certainly." Narlstrom showed them in. "Can I offer you two something to drink?"

"No, thank you." Belski said. "Are we alone?"

"Yes, my wife is at work." Jean had reluctantly taken a part-time receptionist position. "What's this all about?"

"We're here to speak to you about your recent patent applications."

"Really?" he said, motioning for them to sit. "Why is the NSA interested in my commercial patents?"

"They are derived from the classified work you did for Ariskor on behalf of the Pentagon."

"No, that's not true," he said, shaking his head. "My recent patent applications are commercially oriented. My patents are based on the universal laws of thermodynamics."

"However, what you submitted to the Patent Office could be integrated into a weapon system."

"My patents are 'use' patents. They're not that detailed," he assured her. "I worked with a patent attorney to include enough detail to obtain the legal protection without providing too much detail."

"We assume you will attempt to sell or commercialize this technology. In which case, those products would be available on the open market and could be reverse engineered."

"But they would still be patent protected," Narlstrom countered.

"The enemies of the United States," said Major Nieves, speaking for the first time, "don't give a damn about patent protections."

"If you cared so much about this technology, why did the government cancel Cold Vulcan?"

"That was a political decision," the major said. "Our job is national security. Cold Vulcan and anything related to it is still classified."

"Are you making the laws of thermodynamics classified, too?" he asked. "If so, you may be a bit late."

"What you've done could be considered treason," Belski said.

"What?" Narlstrom snapped. "You're way out of line. I have been a loyal American since before either of you were born."

"We realize that. So as of now, no charges will be brought against you. But under no circumstances can you attempt to patent Ariskor-related technology."

"Does that mean anything to do with thermodynamics? Following your logic, any work I do in thermodynamics is automatically suspect because of my connection to Ariskor. If so, that's restraint of trade."

"Doctor, calm down. You're a physicist and an engineer. There are many other areas you can work in."

"I am a thermodynamics expert. That's my field. Meanwhile, you people wouldn't know a heat sink from a kitchen sink!"

"I'm sorry, Doctor," Belski said. "I'm not unsympathetic, but national security comes first."

"If I can't work in thermodynamics, you're condemning me to working in a supermarket. So I'm sorry, but I am not withdrawing my patent applications."

"You don't need to," Nieves said. "Any record of their existence has already been expunged."

"What? You bastards!"

"Doctor," Belski said. "This is your first, last and only warning. Do not pursue this."

CHAPTER 26

David, Ellen and Fred spent the next few days orienting themselves and interviewing potential staff members. The budget allowed for a staff of 20, with 16 people in Washington, and another four in the district office in Pennsylvania. However, there wasn't enough room in the "attic" office for a staff of 16 to fit comfortably. David decided to hold off hiring a full staff until the workload demanded it. They had filled all the positions they intended to for the time being, except for one.

"What's the issue with the legislative assistant?" David asked Ellen.

"Finding someone competent."

"Why is that a problem?"

"Most people who aspire to work in the Capitol choose a major party early on, and then network within that party. Don't get me wrong; we've received plenty of résumés. Let's see. We have the guy who looked great, until I discovered he failed the bar exam three times. We have a second-year law student who is on academic probation, and the lawyer who is on real probation. Oh, and the guy who earned his law degree in the Caribbean, some island I've never even heard of."

"So, I guess no one with legislative experience?"

"Not even close," Ellen replied.

"How about this one?" Fred asked, walking in and handing her a folder.

Ellen opened it and quickly scanned the résumé. "Where did you find this guy?"

"Tyler Benson's an old student of mine from Jersey. He's just earned his law degree, passed the bar, but can't find a job. It's a tough job market even for lawyers. So, he reached out to one of his old professors, hoping maybe for a teaching position."

"OK, let's get him in here."

"Meanwhile," David said. "I've finally been given an audience with the Speaker. See you later."

"Good luck," Ellen said.

&) &) C& C&

Carl Stavros came to Harris Carver's door. Carver was assembling some papers.

"Here's the latest polling data," he said, offering Carver a manila folder.

"Great. I'll read it later," Carver said, putting the folder into his brief case. "Just give me the takeaway."

"The President is getting high marks for the CART program. People don't understand it, but view it positively."

"I don't even know if I understand it," he said, as he pulled on his overcoat. "But that's the CART administrator's job. I'm going to meet with him now."

"Henry Stark?"

"Yeah. By the way, good job on selling CART."

"Thanks, but the President was the true salesman."

Carver nodded. "Carl, why don't you stop by the house tonight for a drink?"

"Um, sure," Stavros said.

In all the time Stavros had known Harris Carver, he had never invited anyone to his house. The professional distance and discipline Carver demanded didn't lend itself to happy-hour socializing.

"How about nine o'clock?"

"Sure," Stavros said, wondering what Carver had in mind.

ಔ ಔ ಞ ಞ

The photo incident at the White House made David realize no one in the congressional structure was going to look out for him. That included obtaining a committee assignment. It had taken several days to secure an appointment with the Speaker of the House.

When shown into the Speaker's office, David found Everett Wilkers was sitting behind his enormous desk, scanning some papers through his half-moon reading glasses. The glasses emphasized the "tax-and-spend" bags under his eyes. Wilkers did not look up.

After waiting a moment, David spoke up. "Good afternoon, Mr. Speaker."

Wilkers looked up as if he hadn't noticed David come in.

"Ah Congressman..." Wilkers looked down at a piece of paper. "...Grant. Oh yes, you're the Independent. What can I do for you?" he asked in his Midwestern twang.

"I want to contribute to the work of Congress. To do that, I need a committee assignment. My predecessor, Congressman Lannier, served on the Banking Committee, so...."

"I'm afraid committee positions aren't hereditary," Wilkers said. "I've already filled that slot with a more senior member."

"I understand. Perhaps there's an opening elsewhere?"

"As Speaker, I only assign representatives from my own party. Perhaps the Minority Leader could assign you a committee position."

"If that's your position, won't the Minority Leader take a similar one?"

"She might, but I would never presume to speak for Cassandra Mirreau," Wilkers said, looking back down at his papers.

"Mr. Speaker, I have significant business experience, yet I don't espouse a let-business-do-whatever-they-want philosophy. I believe I can bring great value to committee work."

"I don't doubt your qualifications or your enthusiasm," Wilkers said, standing up and navigating his way around the desk. "But here's the problem: You're only going to be here for two years."

"You don't think I'll run again? Or, you don't think I'll win?"

"Without a real party organization to back you, it doesn't matter. Both parties will be gunning for your seat. Lannier was doomed, and Jansing was reckless. You smartly rode the anti-incumbent wave and surprised everyone. And I give you full credit for your accomplishment. But it won't happen again. And it really takes two years to learn this job right. And, that's with party support. People scoff at seniority, but that's what preserves the intellectual capital of Congress.

"We'll see." David decided to try name dropping. "When I was speaking to the President in the Oval Office the other day, he seemed quite eager for me to work with him on his education bill."

Wilkers smiled. "Yes, I heard about your little tête-à-tête in the Oval Office," the Speaker said. "And I've even seen the picture. He wants your vote, if it comes cheap."

"Don't *you* want my vote?"

The Speaker leaned back on his desk, folding his arms.

"Would you be willing to formally join the Democratic Party?" Wilkers asked, thereby setting the price for a committee assignment.

"I'll be glad to work with you, but I ran as a centrist and an Independent."

"Congressman," Wilkers said, leaning forward. "I mean no offense to you personally. You seem like a nice guy. But your election will be a political footnote. In the future, people will say 'there hasn't been an Independent in the House of Representatives since David Grant.' As for the President, he works in a command-and-control environment. I herd cats for a living. I have to be careful how I spend my political capital. After the next election, you will be gone. Any committee slot you had would just need to be refilled. Win re-election. Then, maybe we'll talk."

"You can count on it."

David left the Speaker's office fuming. He wasn't asking for a chairmanship, just an opportunity to participate. As he chewed on his lip, David slowly realized he had been stupid. He had been in plenty of business negotiations. Yet in meeting with the Speaker, David had forgotten to bring anything of value to the table, a bargaining chip, something Everett Wilkers needed, wanted or feared.

When he returned to his office, he asked his new secretary to make an appointment with Cassandra Mirreau, the new House Minority Leader. Then, he asked Ellen to provide him with a list of all pending legislation.

80 80 03 03

That evening, Carl Stavros turned onto Carver's street. His house was in what certain local realtors called a four-year neighborhood. The houses tended to be resold every four years, maybe eight, depending on whether a president was re-elected. This neighborhood was filled with cabinet secretaries and senior administration officials. He passed a slow-moving car, which he suspected was an unmarked patrol car. While not a government facility, security in this area was high. All the houses were well-lit. If some burglar was stupid enough to break in within this neighborhood, it would be the sorriest day of his criminal life.

Stavros parked in front, walked up to the front door and rang the bell. Carver opened the door, still wearing his suit.

"Good evening, Carl. Right on time. Come on in."

Carver's cordial tone seemed surreal to Stavros.

"Did you have any trouble finding your way here?"

"No, none at all. Nice place you have here."

"Thanks, I take no credit. I had to hire a decorator. I just don't have time for the home stuff. I guess that's why I'm divorced."

Suddenly, Carver's mobile phone rang. He answered it. "Carver...hmm, hmm...okay, hold on." He turned back to Stavros. "I'm sorry, Carl. It's a classified issue."

"Anything, I can help with?"

"I hope not. Just go on in and fix yourself a drink. Make yourself comfortable. I'll be back out as soon as possible."

Stavros understood. Certain security and diplomatic issues required a tighter circle of confidence that would automatically exclude the "communications guy." He walked into another room, but saw no bottles or bar of any kind. Having walked into the wrong room, Stavros was about to reverse course when he was struck by the nearly two dozen pictures on the wall. Upon closer examination, he realized every picture was of Gregory Farnum and Harris Carver. Only a few of them had a third or fourth person. Everyone who worked in a presidential administration had a photograph or two of themselves with the President. However, he was surprised by the quantity here. He knew that Carver went back many years with Farnum, even back to the governor's mansion.

Stavros suddenly realized he needed to find a bathroom. He opened a promising door, only to discover access to the basement. He was about to close the door when he spied more pictures along the descending wall. He flipped on the light switch. The pictures were all of Farnum and Carver. He wondered if he'd find an altar to Gregory Farnum at the bottom of the steps. He was tempted to investigate, but thought better of it. Carver might return at any time. He quickly but quietly closed the door.

"You'll find the bar in the den," a voice behind him said, but it wasn't Carver's. He turned around to find Ellis Cornwall standing there.

"Mr. Cornwall," Stavros said. "I wasn't expecting you here tonight."

"That's the secret of my success, doing the unexpected. Let's head into the den. I think Harris has a nice single-malt we can share."

They moved into the next room. Ignoring his bladder, Stavros poured two glasses of scotch. They sat in wingback chairs across from the fireplace.

"I have to say your work on the President's campaign was quite impressive. You really walloped that bastard Henderson right where it hurt him the most."

"You're very kind, sir. And we certainly appreciate your support."

"Well, that's history. The next battle is brewing already. My sources tell me several Republicans have already started exploratory committees."

"Corey Johnson, John Sonner, Kate Fornoff, not to mention that Neanderthal Buck Howell. God help us if Howell ever makes it into the White House."

"Of all the Republicans, he's the one I'd want to go against."

"Really?"

"He's hard-right, and bombastic. He's bound to put three feet in his mouth."

"Hmm, interesting thought. Well, regardless of who they nominate, I'm planning to meet them head-on with a super-PAC to support the President."

"That's fantastic."

"It'll be 100 million dollars worth of fantastic," Cornwall boasted.

"Wow, that's extraordinarily generous."

"Of course, you know all about these idiotic campaign finance laws. No communicating or coordinating with the official campaign, and all that."

"Yes, I do."

"That means the man who runs it must have flawless political instincts," Cornwall said.

"I would trust your instincts completely," Stavros said, taking a sip of his single-malt.

"I'm afraid you're not catching my meaning. I have a communications empire to run. I can't be the face of a political action committee. I'm thinking someone like you."

"That's very flattering. However, I expect to be working on the campaign."

"Carl, there are many ways to serve the President. For instance, running a 100-million-dollar super-PAC. I need someone who can read the political tea leaves. Someone who can know what the President needs to win, without actually being in the White House. Harris tells me you are just such a person."

"I'll need to talk it over with him," Stavros answered.

"That might be considered violating one of those tedious campaign laws." Cornwall leaned forward. "You see, before doing anything, I always imagine myself testifying in front of Congress. So I, and many other people for that matter, avoid having conversations that we, or others, might have to testify about. The best lie is the truth. Don't worry, Harris Carver can also read tea leaves. In fact, you might say he's the one who poured our tea this evening."

CHAPTER 27

The next day, David had successfully scheduled a meeting with Cassandra Mirreau, the new Republican Minority Leader. Eloise, her secretary, had apologetically told him the Leader was on a conference call that had run over. She offered him tea and shortbread cookies as a consolation. David politely declined. The last thing he wanted were cookie crumbs on his jacket, or a bladder full of tea, when meeting Mirreau. After a half hour, he was finally admitted.

"Good afternoon, Leader Mirreau."

"Congressman Grant, good afternoon. I'm sorry, I don't have much time. I have another conference call in a few minutes."

David knew rushing was a negotiating tactic to throw an opponent off. "I can come back another time," he offered.

"Nonsense. We need to be productive every minute we can," Mirreau insisted. "What can I do for you?"

"I'm looking for a committee position, so I can 'be productive every minute' as you say."

Mirreau smiled at the turning of her words. "Then, you should approach the Speaker."

"I already have. Wilkers seems to feel that an Independent is unworthy of such responsibility, although he thought you might feel differently."

"Did he?" she said in a tone that revealed her disdain for Wilkers. "Let me speak plainly. You took Sheldon Lannier's seat, a Republican seat. Now, I can't be seen rewarding you with a Republican committee slot."

"That's one way of looking at it. But you know as well as anyone, Lannier wasn't coming back. The 20th District was going to pass to a Democrat. Think of it as me denying the Democrats that seat."

Mirreau nodded. "That is one way of looking at it. But most House Republicans won't."

"I understand. However, I also know Congress is a place for horse trading."

"And what horse have you brought today?"

"My vote against the upcoming commerce bill."

Mirreau curled up the corner of her lip, signaling her distain for the bill. "Unfortunately, we're going to lose that one anyway. The Dems have too many votes now that they hold the majority."

"Yes, but I can vote with you, and be very vocal about it, adding my voice to yours. And no one can accuse me of toting the party line, as I'm not a member of your party."

"Interesting idea. However, doesn't the commerce bill have many things you're for?"

"Yes, but there's plenty of pork in it for me to object to. I can say I like some of it, but the excessive spending is too much to secure my vote." David could tell Mirreau was considering it.

"Let me make a counter offer. Now that Lannier is gone, there's an opening on the banking committee. It's yours if you openly declare you're joining the Republican Party."

"I ran as an Independent."

"And you can still be independent in spirit. You can present the choice as picking the lesser of two evils."

"I don't think you'd appreciate my saying 'lesser of two evils' in a press conference."

"No," Mirreau laughed. "We can negotiate language."

"You do know I'm not a social conservative."

"We're not likely to see a social conservative from your district anyway. Lannier wasn't one either."

"I'm sorry, joining a major party is at odds with the position I campaigned on."

"There's a difference between campaigning and governing."

"That's the trouble. There shouldn't be that much of a difference."

"You're honestly not that naïve?"

"I said *shouldn't*, not *isn't*. I can vote with you on the commerce bill in exchange for a committee position. But I can't join the GOP."

"Which committee did you have in mind?"

"Way & Means, Banking, Appropriations?"

Mirreau laughed. "You know damn well those are the most sought after committees. You're the last one in the door. I've got well over a hundred representatives in line for those. There's no way *unless you join the party*." She paused looking at some papers on her desk. She sighed. Although, I might be able to offer you a slot on Agriculture."

"I'm afraid I don't know very much about agriculture."

"Aren't there a lot of dairy farms in Pennsylvania?" Mirreau asked.

"Yeah, but with my lack of knowledge, I won't be doing my farmer constituents any favors. How about Energy & Commerce?"

Mirreau smirked. "Let me get back to you."

ᏸ ᏸ ᏺ ᏺ

"Good evening, enlightened Americans," Jessica Dandridge said, welcoming her viewers. "It's been two weeks since the Farnum Administration announced the Capital Asset Restoration Trust program, also known as CART. As a result, we've seen the stock market rebound over 450 points. It's the result of something we don't witness very often, something called *decisive leadership*." It's something the Republicans should study and learn. I know, I know, I know. You really can't teach pigs to fly, and all that. But a girl can hope, can't she?"

148

"Our president has shown a stern resolve to fix the mess created by Wall Street greed and Republican malfeasance, without punishing the innocent. And, he's done it without hobbling the economy. Tonight, we'll be speaking with Carl Stavros, the White House Communications Director, in this very studio. After the break, he'll share with us what went into the creation of CART."

The camera's red recording light went out.

Dandridge saw Ellis Cornwall standing near the edge of the set well beyond camera range. She quickly detached herself from the various wires and made her way over.

"Mr. Cornwall, to what do we owe the pleasure?"

"I was curious to see Mr. Stavros in action."

"Don't worry. I'll treat him with kid gloves."

"No need for that. Just no mention of any Super-PACs."

"No problem," Dandridge said, as she saw Stavros walking into the TV studio.

"Mr. Cornwall," Stavros called out. "I didn't know you were joining us tonight."

"I'm not, at least not in front of the camera. But I do like to keep an eye on things."

"OK people, 45 seconds!" the stage manager called out. Dandridge and Stavros moved to their positions. "And five, four, three." The stage manager followed with the hand signals for two and one.

"We're back with White House Communications Director and Senior Advisor Carl Stavros. Welcome to the program."

"Thank you, Jessica. It's great to be here."

"So, who in the White House is the brains behind the whole CART program?"

"Well, there's this obscure man in the White House. Let me try to remember his name. Oh yes, Gregory Farnum."

Dandridge laughed. "But seriously?"

"Seriously? Greg Farnum. The President had a clear view of what he wanted to happen and not to happen. You nailed it on the head earlier when you said decisive leadership."

"So who will actually be working on the day-to-day details of figuring out how to clean up the mess?"

"To head the task force, the President has hand-picked Henry Stark, a highly qualified expert in these kinds of complex financial matters. In fact, Henry Stark had been considered for the Treasury Secretary position."

"But Robert Hingecliff won that position."

"The President is a very good judge of people. He seems to know instinctively how to best utilize people's strengths. Both men are very qualified. The President just attracts those types of quality people. For this sensitive job, the President chose Henry Stark."

"What's next on the President's agenda?" Dandridge prompted.

"As you know, the economy has been in the doldrums for well over a decade. The President realizes that to be more strategically competitive, education has to be our top priority."

In the corner of the studio, Ellis Cornwall smiled, liking what he was hearing.

છ છ ભ ભ

The last twilight rays were fading by the time David returned to his office. Carol, their new receptionist, handed him some messages.

"So, that was a long meeting. Any luck with the Minority Leader?" Ellen asked, as David walked into his private office.

"It was actually a short meeting with a long wait. And in the end, I received a definite maybe, which I interpret as congress-ese for *go to hell*."

"Sorry about that. I have Fred's protégé, Tyler Benson, in the other room. He's been waiting."

David had forgotten about interviewing Benson for the legislative aide position. "So, what do you think of this Benson?"

"A bit on the young side. Younger than I'd like. Inexperienced. But he seems bright for his age. Given our situation, we could do worse."

"Outside of you, Ellen, we're all inexperienced. So, let me talk to the young man."

Benson entered, looking a bit nervous.

"Good evening, Congressman."

"Thanks for waiting so long, Tyler. I apologize for keeping you so late."

"No problem, sir." He shook David's hand, holding on longer than was appropriate.

"Um, please have a seat."

Benson finally released David's hand and sat down.

"Your résumé looks good. And Fred Arkin seems to think you can help us. So, I have a question. What happens if we have a situation where you and I disagree on some issue?"

"I'm not sure I follow, sir."

"Let's say, hypothetically, you're for…um…hot-air balloon subsidies, and I'm against them. And I ask you to represent my position in a meeting with the Speaker."

"I will represent your position, just as if I were your attorney."

"Good answer. Just let me be clear. If you disagree with me, I want to know it. There's nothing worse than a 'yes man'. It's important for me to be challenged. Any idea or position worth a damn has to be able to hold up to scrutiny and challenge. But once my position is decided, you'll have to represent it with vigor. Understood?"

"Yes, sir."

"Have you ever written any legislation?"

Benson grimaced slightly. "No, sir."

"That's all right, I've only written a few local ordinances myself," David said with a smile. "What that means is we have to learn fast. You need to build relationships with other congressional staffers. Ellen tells me there can be great camaraderie between staffs. Use that. We're going to need you to network. Let me be honest. After the meetings I've had with the Speaker and Minority Leader, I realize we are outcasts. No, make that rebels. I'm going to need you to be my eyes and ears."

"Yes, sir."

"Welcome aboard."

૪૭ ૪૭ ૦૨ ૦૪

Daniel Narlstrom was cleaning his tools and reorganizing his basement workshop. He didn't really need to, but it helped him think, and gave him a rare sense of control these days. Looking down at the wooden bowl he had formed on his lathe weeks earlier, he realized it still needed sanding and staining. *Not now.* There was a time when he felt he could shape his world the way he shaped the wood. He sighed. Maybe next he'd make a bookshelf, maybe a chair. There was no urgency to decide, nor any real immediate desire. For now, he would just tidy the workshop for when the creative urge returned.

He hadn't told his wife about the visit from the government. Narlstrom had spoken with his attorney, but dealing with the Defense Department or the NSA was beyond his lawyer's experience. Besides, he didn't feel he could afford much more in legal fees. *There has to be a way around these damn people.*

"Dan?" Jean Narlstrom called out from upstairs, interrupting his train of thought. "Dan, can you hear me?"

"What?"

"Come up here!"

Jean didn't usually summon him without at least some explanation. He trudged upstairs to find out what was upsetting her.

"What's the matter?" he asked, with a slight annoyance in his voice.

"I was going to pay some bills online."

"So?"

"But the bank's website won't let me pay any bills."

"What? Don't be ridiculous."

"I am *not* being ridiculous," she snapped.

"Okay, okay, I'm sorry. But even if we bounced a check, there'd be a balance." He looked at the webpage, refreshed it, clicked on several other tabs. He finally found a notation, "Balance Locked."

"There has to be some glitch. Did you try calling them?"

"I did," she said, "but the menu didn't have an obvious option. So I pressed zero to speak to a representative. That was 45 minutes ago."

"Alright then, I'll go down to the bank first thing tomorrow and sort this out."

CHAPTER 28

The next morning, Narlstrom arrived early at the bank, which seemed more crowded than usual. After waiting in line, the teller directed him to a Mr. Bardini, who was visible inside a glass-walled office. Bardini was speaking to another customer. Neither he nor the customer looked happy. *Not a good sign*. Over an hour and seven unhappy customers later, he was finally able to obtain an audience with this man.

"Good morning," the branch officer said in a cheery tone, which seemed slightly forced and more for his own benefit. "How can I help you?"

Narlstrom looked outside the window to the line that formed behind him. "I think you know what's happened." He tossed the webpage printout on Bardini's desk.

Bardini's artificially cheery veneer evaporated as Narlstrom handed him the webpage printout.

"Why can't I get access to my own money?"

"Let me call up your account. Do you know your account number?"

"Isn't it on the page I just handed you?"

"No, but I can figure it out. Just a sec."

Bardini tapped in a few commands on his computer terminal. "It's as I suspected," he said. "You have a Command Gateway Account."

"Yeah, so?"

"It's an investment account."

"No, my wife and I have just a regular joint checking account. 'Command Gateway' is just one of those fancy marketing names you guys slap on it."

"Technically, it's an investment account with checking privileges."

"Alright, so?" Narlstrom said in exasperated tone.

"I'm sure you've heard about the CART program the President instituted."

"Yeah, yeah, that's the Kadler Steele thing."

"KS Community Bank is the banking arm of Kadler Steele. And the CART administrator has declared all investment funds are to be frozen."

"Shit." Narlstrom felt a deep, hollow feeling in his stomach. "I thought KS stood for Kansas. Wait a minute, wait a minute, aren't all our accounts FDIC insured?"

"That applies only to savings and regular checking accounts."

"We opened a checking account here 30 years ago, when this bank was called Eagleston Trust or something like that. This bank's had so many damn names over the years, I can't recall. But I do remember it was a plain-vanilla checking account."

"Well, it must have been converted to a Command Gateway Account when the bank was acquired by Kadler Steele."

"I didn't authorize that!"

"You must have." Bardini quickly held up his hand to forestall another outburst. "But let's double-check to make sure," he quickly added.

Bardini tapped another series of commands into his terminal.

"Here it is. Hold on, let me print it out."

"Apparently, you did authorize the change," Bardini said, handing Narlstrom a copy of the authorization. "Is this your signature?"

He nodded. "I guess so. Okay, so how do we get my money unfrozen?"

"I'm afraid that's up to the government. However, my colleagues and I believe it's a temporary measure to prevent big investors from manipulating their portfolios."

"Dammit, I don't even have my unemployment payments now."

"You're unemployed?"

"Yeah, and my payments are sent here through direct deposit."

"This CART program is so sudden. I don't know what would happen if a direct deposit from the state would come to this account."

"What do you mean?" Narlstorm demanded.

"Future payments might become frozen also. Or, it might be bounced back to the state. I don't know. Either way, we need to set up a separate savings or checking account for you, one that is FDIC-insured and unaffected by the freeze."

"How do I know you won't screw me over on this one, too?"

"Mr. Narlstrom," Bardini said, with an exhausted look on his face, "I don't like this anymore than you do. I want to make it right."

"Then, get me my money back!"

੭ ੭ ੧ ੧

Tyler Benson was reviewing some legislation when he heard someone walking into the reception area. He knew it was too soon for Carol to be back from the cafeteria. Besides, the footsteps sounded too heavy for the petite receptionist. He walked out to check.

"Good morning," said a tall man with a goatee.

"Good morning. How can I help you?"

"Yes, my name's Jack Kripke. I have an appointment with Congressman Grant."

Tyler walked over to Carol's desk to check the schedule. Kripke was indeed on the schedule, but not for another 15 minutes.

"The Congressman is in a meeting with his staff. Please have a seat."

"Thank you." Kripke said. "By the way, I didn't catch your name."

"Tyler Benson."

"You're the Congressman's new legislative aide, right?"

Tyler was surprised at being known by this stranger.

"It's only my first day on the job. How did you know?"

153

"It's my business to know these things. Legislative aides are the backbone of Congress. Politicians come and go, but legislative staffs give our government stability. For instance, your own Congressman not being in a major party means he's going to be at a disadvantage."

Tyler smiled tautly. "Yes, we're painfully aware of that."

"Don't get me wrong. I respect what you and the Congressman are trying to do. If there's ever anything I can do to help, don't hesitate to call," Kripke said, while handing him a business card.

"Thank you. You're very kind."

"Not at all. I'll just sit here and wait. I don't want to take you away from your work."

"Thank you. I'm sure the Congressman will be available in a few minutes."

Kripke sat down, as Benson returned to his office.

Within a few minutes, the inner office door opened. Fred and Ellen walked out.

Kripke stood immediately. "Well, well, well. If it isn't Ellen Langford," he called out. "The Prodigal Daughter has returned to Washington,"

"Well, well, well. If isn't Jack Kripke, the man who...."

"Now, now, be nice," he interrupted.

"I was going to say the man they call the Prince of K Street." Ellen said. "What brings you here?"

"I have an appointment with America's newest Congressman."

"Be careful of this one, Fred. He's a lobbyist's lobbyist."

"Very nice to meet you, Mr. Kripke. I apologize. I have some phone calls I have to make."

"No problem. Never let me hold up government business."

"Thanks." With that Fred ducked into the communications office.

"So Jack, what are you selling today?" Ellen asked.

"As always, American values, free enterprise and Mom's apple pie," Kripke said with a grin.

"Yeah, right. Be gentle. He's a K-Street virgin."

"That's the way I like 'em, all wide-eyed and innocent."

"Jack, be warned—he's not stupid, and he learns very quickly."

"Then, he deserves to learn from the best lobbyist in DC."

"Humble to the end."

"I know you're doing something very important with the Congressman. But when you're done—"

"Don't pull that stuff on me," Ellen said, holding up her finger. "Congressman Grant is on the phone with his wife right now. He'll be ready for you in a moment."

य़य़य़य़

"Hi, how's my favorite architect?" David asked.

"Fine," Sara answered, trying to pull together materials for work.

David could sense something in her voice. "What's the matter?"

"I just had a mother-daughter spat with Wendy."

"Sorry to hear that. Anything serious?"

"She wants pierced ears."

"Whoa, our little girl is growing up."

"She only wants them because Nancy Garthwell has them. She didn't like it when I said no."

"Well, if our pastor's daughter has them, they can't be too bad."

"I need you to support me on this. Be prepared for her to do an end-around maneuver this weekend. You are coming home this weekend?"

"Yes, I'm booked on the Friday afternoon train."

"While I'm warning you about things, I want to give you a heads-up on Chris. He's reconsidering engineering as a major."

"In favor of what?"

"Cooking."

"What?"

"He wants to go to some culinary school now."

"All right, I guess we have a lot to talk about this weekend. For now, I've got to go."

"Me, too."

"Sara, I love you."

"I love you, too. But it's only been two weeks, and I have to tell you I'm not loving this weekend-only version of you. See you Friday."

೮ ೮ ೞ ೞ

Within a few minutes, Ellen escorted Jack Kripke into David's office, but didn't stay.

"So Mr. Kripke, what can I do for you?" David asked.

"Please call me Jack. I just wanted to welcome you to Washington and introduce myself."

"Like a sort of Washington Welcome Wagon?"

Kripke chuckled. "You could say that."

"So, who do you represent?"

"Many people."

"Jack, I'm busy, and I'm playing catch-up. I assume you'd like me to vote for or against something. So why don't we get down to it."

"I like your directness, Congressman. It's refreshing. Are you familiar with orphan diseases?"

"Aren't orphans subject to diseases as the rest of us?"

Kripke smiled at that. "No, orphan diseases are those that afflict a smaller number of people, so few that it isn't profitable for pharmaceuticals companies to pursue developing drugs for them. Even if successful, they would never recover their costs."

"Go on."

155

"The Voraci-Peterson bill will incentivize biotech and pharmaceutical companies to pursue cures and treatments."

David thought about this for a moment. "While this sounds noble, I know the majority of biomedical research yields unusable results. That's the nature of research. This could easily turn into an open-ended drain that yields nothing much."

"That's a very thoughtful concern," Kripke observed.

David smiled at Kripke's attempt at flattery

"That's why," the lobbyist continued. "The bill only grants funding after a successful result has been achived. The government only pays for results."

David nodded his head. "Okay, sounds good."

"Can we count on you, when the bill comes up for a vote?"

"I haven't seen the bill yet. But, assuming there's nothing else in it, sure, I would certainly be open to voting for it."

"Fantastic."

ഇ ഇ ര ര

Returning from the bank, Narlstrom entered through the side door. He was surprised Jean wasn't rushing at him, demanding to know what had happened at the bank.

"Jean?" he called out. "Jean?" Perhaps she was visiting one of the neighbors, he thought. He was heading for the bedroom when he saw her. Her body was sprawled on the floor. The telephone was knocked off the end table.

"Jean?" he yelled again. He hastily knelt down and took her pulse. Nothing.

CHAPTER 29

"Congressman, a Mr. Arturo Fuentes is on the line," said Carol on the intercom. "He says he's your attorney."

"Yes, he is," David said.

Carol transferred the call.

"Hey, Art. How are things?"

"Fine." Fuentes said. "Just wanted to let you know, your campaign account has suddenly received a series of donations, totaling just over 12,000 dollars. Do you know anything about this?"

"No. Who are they from?"

"I'll send you the list, but I think they're mostly disease charities, mostly to relating to something called orphan diseases."

"Really?"

"Have you been campaigning for re-election already?"

"No. I've been too busy to even think that way. When did these donations start?"

"Last Friday."

"Interesting."

"Well, I just thought I'd let you know."

"Thanks, Art. I've got to go, but say hello to Maria for me."

"I will. Take care."

After hanging up, he walked into Ellen's office. She was talking to Tyler Benson.

"Congressman, what do you need?" she asked.

"A moment." He motioned her into his office. "Art Fuentes just called me. He said I just received a series of campaign donation totaling over $12,000."

"That's terrific," Ellen said.

"They began the day after I spoke with Jack Kripke about the Voraci-Peterson orphan disease bill. That can't be a coincidence."

"I'm sure it's not. I assume you didn't discuss any donations on government property."

"No, of course not."

"Then, what's the problem?"

"I'm not sure. It just feels weird."

"Jack Kripke is sending you a message that he's a powerful lobbyist who represents many interests. And, that he controls and influences a lot of purses. I assume you were agreeable to voting for the bill?"

"Yeah."

Ellen sat down and leaned forward. "He came in with an issue he knew you would support. So it was a softball issue for him. You said yes. And like magic, money appears in your campaign coffers."

"He wants me to salivate whenever I see him."

"Exactly."

"Wow, Pavlovian politics."

At that moment, Fred knocked at the door.

"Come on in, Fred. Have we heard back from Mirreau's office yet?"

"Yes, but just a repeat invitation to join the GOP."

"How about the White House?"

"You called the White House about this?" Ellen asked Fred incredulously.

"Yes, I asked him to," David said, and turned back to Fred. "Who did you speak to?"

"I spoke to various people in the Domestic Policy Office and Legislative Affairs. They gave me various versions of the same answer. The White House does not interfere with the internal affairs of other branches of government."

"That's bullshit I'm sure." David said. "But I guess a nice photograph is all I'm going to get out of the White House." He sighed. "It doesn't look like I'm going to get a committee slot."

"You still have your vote." Fred reminded him. "They can't take that away from you. At some point somebody's going to need it."

"With 435 representatives, I'm not going to hold my breath for a tie. Any ideas?"

"Mirreau did offer you a seat on the Agriculture Committee," Fred said.

"Yeah, but I don't know a chick pea from a garbanzo bean."

"Actually, they're the same thing." Ellen said.

"Really?" David said. "See what I mean? I wouldn't do it justice."

"I have to admit," Ellen said. "I'm not sure what to do. My advice is the same as before. Caucus with one of the parties."

"I'm not ready to do that."

"You are stubborn," Ellen declared.

"Somehow I need to apply some pressure," David said, almost to himself.

"Well, if you don't have something they want, perhaps you have something they don't want," Fred suggested.

"What's that?"

"Embarrassment. The public is pretty pissed off. Congress's approval rating is in the toilet. Right? What if you add to it?

"How do you mean?"

"Take your complaint to the Floor of the House," Fred suggested. "Go public. C-SPAN is unblinking. Make some waves. Show how dysfunctional government really is. It fits with how you campaigned."

"If I can't get a committee slot," David said, "they're certainly not going to let me debate. The debates are party controlled."

"I wasn't referring to a floor debate. Almost every morning session, the House has a series of one-minute speeches before the serious business of the day starts. They're rarely earth-shattering topics, but it's recorded, both in the Congressional Record and on C-SPAN." Fred turned to Ellen. "Isn't that so, Ellen?"

"Yes," she said.

"I forgot about the one-minute speeches," David said.

"Yes, but you have to be careful," Ellen said. "House Rules prohibit insulting people."

"But facts are facts," Fred insisted. "The leadership has denied David a committee position. All he has to do is tell the truth."

"OK, but do you really want your first speech on the Floor to sound like whining?" Ellen asked.

"Of course not. But they haven't left me much choice," David said.

"But if it doesn't work, you'll be giving your opponents in the next campaign their first TV spot against you."

"If I can't get a committee position, maybe I don't deserve to be reelected."

"Before you go ballistic on the Floor," Ellen insisted, "let me try to come up with something."

"Like what?"

"I don't know yet."

ༀ ༀ ༃ ༃

Jean Narlstrom's funeral service had concluded. Her husband received endless and awkward expressions of grief, "Dan, I'm sorry for your loss," "Jean was a wonderful woman," and the ever hollow, "If there's anything I can do...." In a way, Daniel Narlstrom felt sorry for the mourners. There were no words that truly comforted, yet they all tried anyway.

Everyone who attended the gravesite service was invited back to the Narlstrom house. The ladies from the church prepared sandwiches and beverages for the mourners. He had never been particularly devout, but Jean was active in the community. One unexpected mourner was George Anson from Ariskor.

"I'm so sorry, Dan. Jean was a wonderful woman."

"Thanks, George. I appreciate that."

"I just got in last night from Seattle. I didn't hear anything about her passing until this morning. How did she die?"

"Nothing very interesting, an old fashion heart attack, some valve thing that went undetected. If I had been here, I might have been able to save her, at the very least, call an ambulance."

"Don't blame yourself."

"I don't. I blame Washington."

"Washington?"

"No, not what you think. It's not about Ariskor," Narlstrom explained. "You know that CART program all those Washington weenies have been bragging about? They froze the assets in our checking account."

"What? How can they do that?"

"Apparently, Washington thinks we are, I mean, *were* big-shot investors. I was at the bank over two hours dealing with it. Instead, I should have been here."

"Wow, I'm so sorry."

"Anyway, how are things at Ariskor these days?" Narlstrom asked, trying to change the subject.

"Not great. There have been more layoffs. Another 260 people."

"Damn. How does your position look?" Narstrom asked as they walked away from the grave site.

"I'm not sure. Anson answered. "Nobody's sure. That's why I was up in Seattle. I had an interview."

"Sorry to hear that, George. I have what may seem an odd question. Has Ariskor ever explored consumer applications for Cold Vulcan technologies?"

"Not that I know of. You know we have no experience in that kind of market. Our people only seem to know how to pursue government contracts."

"And lose them."

Anson grimaced. "Yeah, I suppose so."

ᛞ ᛞ ᚳ ᚳ

Several days later, David was sitting in his office, writing drafts of a possible one-minute speech. Having yet to speak on the Floor, he decided to write one that was less controversial to test the process. He chose healthy eating as his topic. In this way, he would partially fulfill his campaign promise to Paul and Donna Lurtz. He heard a knock at the door. It was Ellen.

"Congressman, I have someone here who'd like to say hello. Do you remember Marcus Finn?"

"Of course. Congressman Finn, it's a pleasure to see you again. Please come in." David gestured him to the sofa.

"Please call me Marcus. I'm just a private citizen these days. So, how do you like Washington?"

"It's okay," David said unenthusiastically.

Finn chuckled. "My, my, disillusioned already?"

"Well, as I'm sure Ellen has already told you I've been having a bit of difficulty obtaining a committee assignment."

"Really?"

David looked at Ellen. "Yes. And I'm guessing your visit isn't a coincidence."

"Well," Finn said, "you have to build relationships."

"I've tried to meet as many House members as I can, but there are a lot of them."

"Yes, there are. Well, as I said, I'm just a private citizen now. But, I still have lots of old friendships on the Hill. However with security being so tight, I can't walk around the Capitol complex the way I used to. But if a current representative were to escort me, I might be able to introduce him to a few old acquaintances."

"Really?"

"I'd consider it a personal favor, I mean, if you have the time."

"Actually," Ellen interjected. "The Congressman's schedule is clear all afternoon."

David smiled knowingly at Ellen. "What a coincidence." He turned back to Finn. "Congressman, I mean Marcus, I'd be honored, and grateful."

ౡ ౡ ಞ ಞ

That afternoon, Marcus Finn introduced David to a number of representatives, Republicans and Democrats. The reception from these members was far warmer than from Wilkers or Mirreau. They all seemed eager to work with David on issues of mutual interest, and all agreed David should have a committee position. Some even promised to make some inquiries.

"David, there's one last person I'd like you to meet," Finn said. "But we're going to have to go north." By north, Finn meant the Senate. They walked downstairs to the subway which connected all the congressional office buildings.

"I'm not sure how a senator would have any pull on the House side."

"You have to think beyond simply securing a committee seat."

"Howard's a good man. You'll like him."

They soon found themselves in the office suite of Howard Carstairs, the senior senator from Maine. They asked if Senator Carstairs was available.

"I'm afraid the Senator is in a meeting, right now," said his receptionist.

Finn looked at his watch. "It's 3:18, which means his meeting with his pillow should be over in about two minutes. Could you then tell the Senator that Congressmen Finn and Grant are here? He'll want to see us."

The receptionist wrote a note and quietly slipped into the Senator's private office. "Howard," Finn explained, "takes 20 minutes for what used to be called a power nap, at least whenever the Senate is going into an evening session."

After a few minutes, Howard Carstairs came out.

"Marcus Finn, you old rascal!" He walked over and hugged Finn warmly. "How the hell are you?"

Finn smiled broadly "Living the high life on the lecture circuit. I'm hoping soon we could turn it into a two-act."

"Like Abbott and Costello?" Carstairs suggested.

Finn laughed, but then turned toward David. "I'd like you to meet Congressman David Grant."

"Yes, I've heard about you, Congressman." Carstairs shook David's hand warmly. "Please come on in."

The senator's office was filled with beautiful photographs of Maine and personal pictures of dignitaries. The walls told of long service and devotion.

"So Marcus, when the hell are you coming back to Washington?" Carstairs bellowed.

"I'm here now."

"You know what I mean. We need some statesmen with all these born-again hate-arati and unicorn chasers running around."

"I'm not sure I'm familiar with those terms," David said

Both Finn and Carstairs laughed.

"I'm sorry. The hate-arati are those intolerant members of the GOP who believe America should be a Christian theocracy, deporting non-Christians, gays, and most of Hollywood."

"The unicorn chasers," Finn added, "are those liberal Democrats who believe we should get in touch with our feelings, and love each other, and ignore all fiscal realities. As if compassion will make the national debt just melt away. And if you don't agree, then you should be deported."

"Extremists," David concluded.

"Yeah, it's amazing how visceral the hatred has become," Carstairs said. "But then, I'm just an embattled moderate."

"That's why I brought you Congressman Grant here." Finn explained. "He's a moderate Independent. He even has Ellen as his chief-of-staff."

"Ellen Langford?" Carstairs said. "My, my, who thought she'd ever come back to DC?"

"Yes, she's trying to help David to get on a committee."

"Yeah, I heard the leaders are giving you a hard time about that," Carstairs admitted.

"I've been thinking of complaining about it during the one-minute speeches. It's not the way I want to handle it, but my options are limited."

"Well, I would love to help you, but I'm in the wrong house, and Mirreau considers me too moderate to listen to. That's why I want Marcus back." He turned to Finn. "This old RINO is lonely."

"I thought RINO was a derogatory term," David said, "one that meant you weren't Republican enough."

"It is and does. But I've embraced the label because I've decided it now means Reasonably Intelligent National Optimist. If I'm going to be called it, I might as well make it mean something worthwhile."

"The Blue Dogs and RINOs are the most embattled members of Congress," Finn added.

"Remember Sarah Palin's website just before Gabby Giffords got shot?" Carstairs asked.

Finn sighed.

"I certainly do," David said, "the site had a cross-hair target on Giffords' district."

"Now despite all the TV jabber," Carstairs continued, "no one seriously believed Palin wanted Gabby Giffords shot. But the point is why were she and the other Blue Dogs targeted, and not the more liberal representatives like Barney Frank? The targets were moderate 'get-able' seats."

"Seems you have to be a militant fanatic to be elected these days," Finn said. "Howard is one of the few moderates left wandering around in no man's land, being shot at by both sides."

"What we need, gentlemen," David concluded, "is a centrist insurgency."

CHAPTER 30

David and Fred were sitting in the Congressman's office, waiting for Ellen to show up.

"Have you spoken to Jason Kennerly recently?" David asked, while squeezing a rubber ball in his hand.

"Yeah, a couple weeks ago. He's quite happy. His donation levels are up. But to be fair, they had little place to go but up."

"We should have Jason come up and visit us here at the Capitol. You know, give him the grand tour. As much as I hate to agree with Ellen, we've got to start thinking about the next election cycle."

"Isn't it a bit early?" Fred asked. "You know you'll have Jason's support no matter what."

"I know," David said, leaning forward on his desk. "But that's not what I want to talk to him about."

"Good morning," Ellen said, coming through the door. "Sorry I'm late. The President's motorcade shutdown traffic at the Arlington Memorial Bridge."

"No problem," David said, turning to Fred. "So what's on our agenda?"

"I have all the proposals back for your official website," Fred said, handing David and Ellen each a set of copies. "This one on the top by Constitution Web Design seems to be the best."

"Sounds like a very patriotic firm," David said. "With all the stress over a committee, I'd forgotten about the website. Let's see."

David scanned Constitution's proposal.

"The designs seem fine. They meet the specs," David said, frowning. "But the price is way out of line."

"Well, I'm not that familiar with website costs," Fred said, "but Constitution was the least expensive."

"Then the hell with all of them. Give Kim Mandalese at Pocono Interactive a call. She created a far more robust website for Simplexia at a third of this price."

"You can't," Ellen interrupted. "They're not a government-approved vendor. It would take months for Pocono to be cleared and approved. And that's if they get approved."

"Great, government bureaucracy at its best," David spat. "Okay, do you have list of approved vendors?"

Fred handed him a piece of paper out of his folder.

"Where are the others?"

"That's it," Fred answered.

"Only ten vendors?"

Fred nodded.

David shook his head in disgust. "That's an average of 53 congressional websites per design firm. No wonder the prices are so high. Between them, they've got a monopoly. Where the hell is the competition? And people wonder why the deficit keeps growing."

ઇ ઇ ୧ ୧

Henry Stark had just concluded the meeting with his chief investigators. As they filed out of his office, his secretary entered with a list of messages. He flipped through them quickly. Most he would ignore. Ever since Stark became the CART Administrator, members of Congress had been hounding him. Only Corbin Beaumont had been more persistent. Megan had circled one name in red, Porter Barnes, who was now Chair of the Banking Committee. Stark expected hearings at some point down the line, so this call he would return.

"Megan, would you call Congressman Barnes for me?"

She had already punched in the number, except for the last digit.

"Mr. Stark, how are you today?" Barnes asked.

"Quite busy, Congressman, as you can imagine."

"Yes. I can imagine. You have one of the most daunting and complex tasks in Washington."

"What can I do for you, Congressman?"

"I understand you've been freezing accounts."

"Yes, to prevent various investors from withdrawing funds, and thereby causing the collapse of Kadler Steele, which won't do anyone any good."

"Of course, I understand. However, some parties legitimately need to withdraw funds for operations."

"No savings or checking accounts have been frozen. Any person or organization can still withdraw those funds as they need or choose."

"I'm talking about certain organizations that keep their investment accounts liquid so they can use them in a manner similar to a checking account."

"Well, that was an unwise practice."

"Perhaps, but it was a practice Kadler was pushing. However, these organizations need help now, your help. We need to do some triage."

"Congressman, there are too many parties involved for that. We are proceeding in a systematic manner that will allow us to complete the entire process as quickly as possible. The type of triage you're talking about will only delay our progress."

"Let me be clear. These organizations warrant special attention," Barnes insisted. "There are only a few of them. I'm sure the administration will agree, if you know what I mean. I'll send over the list."

"Very well, Congressman," Stark conceded. "I'll take a look at the list."

ઇ ઇ ୧ ୧

It had been a few weeks since Marcus Finn had taken David on tour. Unfortunately, none of those efforts resulted in any movement toward receiving a committee position. David was finally able to give a one-minute speech on healthy eating. It required a special negotiation with the Clerk of the House over floor protocol. David assumed Everett Wilkers must have approved the adjustment to the House Rules. Denying a committee seat was one thing, but silencing a member of Congress was something else entirely. The adjustment allowed David to stand in the center of the well of the Floor. The acting speaker would recognize him after one Democrat and one Republican had spoken. The speech on healthy eating lulled them into, if not trusting him, at least not fearing him.

A few days later, he followed this up with a speech on how the limited number of approved web vendors was raising the costs of communicating with constituents. Both speeches had been respectful and not particularly threatening.

Today would be different.

"Why does the gentleman from Pennsylvania rise?" asked the acting Speaker.

"Mr. Speaker, I ask unanimous consent to address the House for one minute and to revise and extend my remarks," David said, following the House protocol.

"Without objection. So ordered."

"Mr. Speaker, I was elected to this House by my constituents in Pennsylvania without the benefit of a major political party. I did not come to make speeches. I came here to work. However, both the Speaker of the House and the Minority Leader have deprived me and my constituents of that opportunity through the denial of a committee assignment. Why do the two parties fear a lone congressman, simply because he was elected by the people, not a party machine? With a congressional approval rating of just four percent, that is a question we should all want an answer to. I look forward to receiving an answer on why the House leadership continues this discriminatory practice in a place so vital to our democracy. Thank you, Mr. Speaker."

ꙮ ꙮ ꙮ ꙮ

Fred Arkin walked into David's office. David was frowning as he read some piece of legislation.

"Tyler told me he heard through the grapevine that Everett Wilkers called a meeting after your speech this morning. Wilkers was heard to be yelling 'doesn't that idiot know we don't air our laundry in public?' Apparently, it was pretty hard not to overhear."

"The trouble is that the Speaker didn't want me to have any laundry at all," David said with a taut smile.

"I've received a bunch of calls from the media about this morning. They all want an interview."

"Not today. Just tell them I'm awaiting a response from the congressional leadership."

"But by tomorrow, the media may no longer be interested."

"Then, I'll give another speech," David said curtly. "I'm sorry," he said with regret. "I want to give the leadership just enough time to save face. They have a limited window before I really go ballistic. So, just tell anyone who asks, I'm awaiting a response. Besides, I have some legislation to review. There's a vote this afternoon on HR53, and I still don't completely understand it."

For the next few hours, David read the impending bill along with the sticky notes Tyler had attached for clarification. They made deciphering the bill only slightly easier. He wished bills were written in plain English. He wondered how many members of Congress voted for bills they didn't understand. *Probably too many to count.*

Carol knocked and came in. "Christa Lemmon is here—"

"What the hell is that, a soft drink?" he asked grumpily.

"No, I apologize," she said. "Congresswoman Christa Lemmon of Florida is here to see you, if you're available."

"Is that really her name?" he whispered, feeling embarrassed.

Carol nodded.

"Show her in," he said, as he pulled on his jacket.

"Congresswoman Lemmon, it's a pleasure."

"I can't believe you're actually here," she said, grinning.

"I'm not sure how to take that."

"Like everyone else, I heard that a David Grant had been elected from Pennsylvania. I just didn't know it was you, the same David Grant who spoke at the IP Conference three years ago."

"Oh yeah. Chicago, right?"

"Yes, I was particularly impressed with your passionate comments at the panel discussion on how intellectual property is America's greatest job creator."

"Well, I was particularly pissed off at a Chinese company that was pirating my software at the time."

"Yes, I remember you mentioning something about that," she said, "which is why I'm here. I'm the new chair of the Subcommittee on Intellectual Property. It's not the most high-profile subcommittee, but I could use someone with your knowledge and passion on IP issues."

"IP Subcommittee? That's under the Commerce and Energy Committee, isn't it?"

"Yes, so you'd be on the committee also. John Fontana is our new chair. He's a very decent guy."

"Is he decent enough to bump heads with Everett Wilkers?"

"I've already spoken to John. It won't be a problem."

"I can't help but think this opportunity came about because of my speech this morning."

"I'll admit you annoyed the hell out of the Democratic leadership. But again, the Speaker was an idiot for denying you a committee seat in the first place. True, your acceptance of the position would remove some of the egg from Wilkers' face. But I'm sincere when I say I want you on my team. I just wish I'd known you were here sooner. I could have saved you some of the stress."

CHAPTER 31

In the following weeks, David immersed himself in all the issues and processes of the committee system. He worked well with his subcommittee colleagues. He had met Chairman John Fontana, who he judged to be a fairly straightforward and likable man. David also discovered the committee staffs were very helpful and quick to respond to information requests. On most intellectual property issues he found surprisingly little partisan conflict.

David had also seen an increase in the number of lobbyists and other advocates knocking on his door since securing his committee position. However, this morning he had blocked out time for Jason Kennerly.

"Jason, glad you could come in," David greeted him.

"I'm thrilled to be here," Jason answered, beaming. "So, what's it like being a U.S. Congressman?"

"Not nearly as glamorous as you might think. I wanted to talk to you about the future of the Centrist Patriots Party," David said, gesturing him to the sofa.

"It's better than it's ever been, thanks to you. We've seen a jump in membership, and to a certain extent, donations."

"That's great. But here in Congress, I need reinforcements. I'm sure Fred has kept you up to date on the difficulties I've had so far. As an Independent, I'm alone and a target. Reelection is going to be tough."

"You know you'll have my support."

"I know, and I truly appreciate that. But it may not be enough. I won because of a fluke, a damaged incumbent and an incompetent challenger. Both the Democrats and the Republicans will be heavily targeting my district next election cycle. It's what they call a 'getable' seat. We need to find others willing to run for the House."

"I'm not sure how other people running will help you get reelected."

"Alone, it won't. But if the party is seen as more credible, then so am I."

"Don't worry. I've already heard from people who want to run under the CPP banner next time around. Two people want to run for Senate alone."

"That's great. But remember our strategy of focusing on the House of Representatives, smaller, concentrated electorates. Despite facing a tough reelection fight, I'm willing to assist serious people who want to run for the House. So, I'd appreciate it if you'd send me résumés of those who are interested."

"Résumés? Kennerly asked. "What's next, background checks?"

"Maybe. The major parties vet their candidates. We'll have to do the same. Come campaign season, I'll have a limited amount of time. I need to be sure of anyone I endorse. I can't have any surprises. It could hurt my own reelection. In that case, we'll lose all the gains we've made."

"Okay, I'll send you the list and résumés if I can get them."

"Great. I have a subcommittee meeting in a few minutes, but Fred's going to give you the inside tour of the Capitol."

"I appreciate that."

೮ ೮ ೮ ೮

As David returned from the subcommittee meeting a few hours later, Ellen beckoned him into her office.

"I've learned Congresswomen Santini is moving over to the Armed Services Committee."

"Good for her, I guess," David said, not quite seeing the point, nor really knowing Santini.

"That means," Ellen explained, "there's an opening on the Energy and Power Subcommittee."

"But I'm already on a subcommittee."

"Most representatives serve on more than one subcommittee."

"Provided they're with a party."

"I know you enjoy intellectual property issues, but the IP subcommittee is not particularly high-profile."

"True."

"So if you're interested, I've arranged for you to have a drink with Congressman Wickham, who chairs Energy and Power. But if you don't want to press your luck, I'll call and cancel it."

"No. Luck is where opportunity meets action. Time for action. When and where am I supposed to meet Wickham?"

"Today, 5:30 at the Hilton."

"Not today, I've got to make the 4:15 train home. Sara will kill me if I miss it."

"No, I won't," said a voice from the other room. Sara stepped through the door, while Ellen quietly stepped out.

"Sara, what are you doing here?"

"Well, since January, you've been commuting back to Embler every weekend. I thought this weekend I'd come to you."

"What about dinner with the Garthwells?"

"I postponed. But Wendy's still staying overnight."

"Of course. Wendy and Nancy, thick as thieves," David said, smiling.

"With the help of your chief-of-staff, I have procured tickets tonight to something called The Capitol Domes."

"What's that?"

"Ellen told me they're a musical-comedy troupe here in town. She said something about a Washington rite of passage."

"Ellen, huh? Hmm, I suspect the women in my life are conspiring."

"You better believe it," Sara said, giving him a kiss on the cheek.

೮ ೮ ೮ ೮

Congressman Wyatt Wickham sat at the bar at McClellan's inside the Hilton Hotel. He tossed back the last of his whiskey as he checked the score of the basketball game. His favorite team was going to lose.

"Good evening, Congressman Wickham," David said.

"Grant?"

"Yeah, sorry I'm running a little late. Traffic."

"Yeah, DuPont Circle can be a bitch this time of day, especially on a Friday. I have a dinner date in a few minutes," Wickham said, gesturing to the hotel's dining room. "So, I apologize if we have to cut this short."

"No problem, I have plans myself. My wife and I are seeing The Capitol Domes tonight."

"Love the Domes," Wickham said, as the bartender provided another glass. "So, what can I do for you?"

"I understand there's an opening on Energy and Power. Simply put, I'm interested."

"Well Congressman, I'm not so sure. Let me cut to the chase. Certain people feel, despite your independence, you have the smell of Republican about you, particularly on fiscal issues, being a former businessman and all. Plus, you've got a Republican chief-of-staff. And, you're from a coal state."

Before leaving, Ellen briefed David on the Chairman. So, David knew the litmus tests he would face with Wickham.

"Congressman, there's no coal in my district, and I don't buy the hype about so-called clean coal. However, half our energy comes from coal. As much as I'd like to change that, we can't just take all the coal plants off-line, at least not yet."

Wickham nodded in agreement. "What's your take on climate change?"

"With all the hurricanes and decimated barrier islands over the years, it's pretty hard to deny."

"Okay, but in your opinion, is it man-made or natural?" Wickham asked.

"I'm no scientist. But I guess I look at it this way: What's the cost of being wrong? If climate change is man-made, and we don't address it, we're screwed. If it's natural, but we act as if it's man-made, we'll have wasted some money, but cleaned up the environment."

Wickham nodded his approval.

"So what are the odds of me getting on the committee?" David asked.

"You know," Wickham began, "if you'd just join the Democratic Party, you wouldn't have to beg for assignments."

"Yeah, I get that a lot."

"Your odds? Well, Christa Lemmon likes you. Despite your one-minute rant a few weeks back, she says you're more workhorse than show horse. And I need workhorses. You're not a global warming denier. So, I say the odds aren't too bad."

David could see Wickham was still conflicted.

"I'll think it over and give you an answer by Monday."

"Fair enough, Congressman." David shook Wickham's hand. "Have a good night."

"You, too."

❦ ❦ ❦ ❦

"You know, Tyler, it wasn't necessary to take me out to dinner," Fred repeated, as they sat in the back of a cab making its way down Pennsylvania Avenue.

"Professor, I'm really grateful for the chance you gave me to work on the Congressman's staff. I just want to express my thanks."

"Tyler, I only submitted your name. You sold yourself to David, I mean, the Congressman."

"I know, but please allow me to show you my appreciation."

"Okay, on one condition. Stop calling me Professor. I don't teach anymore and we're colleagues now."

"Just seems a little weird."

"My name is Fred. Say it."

Tyler hesitated.

"Say it."

"Okay…Fred."

"See that. Didn't hurt a bit. The world didn't end. The planets are still orbiting the sun."

They both laughed.

"So, where are we headed again?"

"Le Chevalier."

"Whoa," Fred said. "Sounds pretty ritzy."

"We'll see."

Once Fred and Tyler had been seated at the restaurant, they perused the menu.

"Tyler, these are really expensive prices," Fred leaned forward. "Let's get out of here. There's a nice burger joint across the street. That'll do fine."

"Professor, I mean Fred, I got this. Really."

"Tyler, you don't make enough to afford these prices. Neither do I."

❦ ❦ ❦ ❦

David and Sara arrived at the Whitmore Dinner Theater around 7:00. The sign outside showed the cast wearing elongated beanies that resembled the dome of the Capitol building. One of the women in the group was dressed as the Statue of Liberty, while another was wearing two domes as a bra.

The menu was limited, but the food was acceptable. Clearly, the entertainment was the draw.

"So, how are the kids?" David asked.

"You saw them last weekend."

"It's not the same as seeing them every day."

172

"Oh, Wendy was very focused on the State of the Union."

"Really?"

"I think she was trying to see you in the crowd."

"Was she able to?"

"I don't think so."

"I'm not surprised. I didn't get a very good seat. Apparently, you have to get there many hours ahead to get a front or aisle seat. I was almost against the back wall. So, is Chris still determined to go to cooking school?" David asked.

"He's shown interest in CIA."

"The CIA?"

"Culinary Institute of America. It's in Hyde Park, New York."

"Oh," he said quietly.

"I know you disapprove."

"I don't disapprove, exactly. I just think the country needs engineers more than it needs chefs."

"Are you thinking about your son? Or about the country, Congressman?" Sara half-teased.

"It's just there will be a higher demand for engineers. And that means job security."

"He just wants to do something he loves."

"I thought he loved engineering."

ဢ ဢ ଔ ଔ

Dinner at Le Chevalier was superb. Despite ordering the least expensive items on the menu, Fred had rarely had such a fine meal.

"Can I interest anyone in dessert?" the waiter asked.

"Nothing for me. I'm full," Fred lied.

"OK, just the check please," Tyler said, handing the waiter a blue card.

"Don't you want to see the check before you hand them a credit card?"

"Oh that? That wasn't a credit card."

Fred frowned. "Then, what was it?"

"A promotional discount card," Tyler replied.

"This doesn't look like a place that discounts. Where did you get it?"

"Jack Kripke gave it to me."

"Are you kidding me?" Fred whispered. "You accepted a gift from a lobbyist?"

"No, I know better than that. It wasn't from him. He's friends with the owner. The owner tries to lure people from the Hill here. He asked Kripke to hand them out to as many people as possible."

The waiter returned with the check. Tyler promptly looked at the bill and gave him his credit card.

"See, I'm still paying for our dinner," he assured Fred.

"And Kripke didn't ask for anything in return?" Fred asked.

"Well."

173

"Yes?" Fred asked sternly.

"He asked that after our dinner, I write a review on their blog page. See, nothing whatsoever to do with government business."

"OK Tyler, but we have to be careful."

"I am. I made sure I read the ethics rules."

ॐ ॐ ॐ ॐ

As dinner moved on to dessert and coffee, the room lights dimmed. The Capitol Domes began their act with a skit mocking the President's recent social *faux pas* when meeting the British king on his recent European trip. Next was a song parody of Governor Buck Howell of Oklahoma, who had been mentioned as a presidential contender. The chorus went...

My name is Bucky
I'm sorta plucky
And just a little bit howl'n mad

David noticed even some of the Republicans in the room were rolling with laughter. Then, stage lights dimmed.

"Why does the gentleman from Pennsylvania rise?" bellowed an off-stage voice. The stage light brightened revealing one of the actors.

"Mr. Speaker, I ask unanimous consent to address the House for one minute and to revise and extend my remarks,"

"Without objection. So ordered," said the off-stage voice.

Then, the actor began to sing.

My name is David Grant
Forgive my little rant
Is it that I'm homely?
I'm just a bit lonely

David eyes went wide. Sara tried to stifle her laughing as she watched David's face turn bright pink.

Oh, I barely have a say
They just won't let me play
But I won't be a little mouse
I could be such a powerhouse

I can do loads, if only
But, I'm Mister Lonely
I may be without a crowd
But I'm righteous and proud

174

That Wilkers and Mirreau
Don't they now know?
They treat me like a pariah
Really, I'm a centrist messiah

"Excuse me, Congressman Grant" called an actress from off-stage.
David snapped his head.
"Yes?" answered the actor portraying David.
"Would you like to play with me on my committee?"
"Oh boy, would I!" the actor said excitedly, and skipped off stage.
Sara kissed David, while he tried to retain his composure. David wasn't
sure what he was feeling. Amused? Angry? Certainly embarrassed. During
the remaining songs and skits, David tried to absorb this surreal experience.
"Good evening, Congressman," said a familiar voice after the last skit.
David looked up to see Jack Kripke standing there.
"You know you've made it in Washington once the Domes have
lampooned you."
"Well, I have to admit I wasn't expecting it."
"Think of it as free publicity. May I join you for a moment?" Kripke
asked. "Just a second, I'm having dinner with Senator Schwartzman."
David nodded.
"And who is this lovely lady?"
"This is my wife, Sara."
"Jack Kripke, Kripke Associates. It's a pleasure, Mrs. Grant." Kripke
said, shaking Sara's hand. He turned back to David. "I was wondering where
you stood on the President's education bill."
"Outside of some broad strokes from the State of the Union," David
said, "I don't know much about the President's bill. Once I see specifics, I'll
be glad to render an opinion."
"Well, thank goodness you're more open-minded than some of your
Republican colleagues. But don't worry. I hear from my contacts, details
should be coming out soon."
"Well, I look forward to reading them."
"Great. I won't take up any more of your time. Have a good evening."

ဆဝ ဆဝ ૦૩ ૦૩

David and Sara returned to the modest apartment he was renting in
Washington. Sara was still laughing over the Domes parody. She kept trying
to recall the lyrics. All she could truly recall was "centrist messiah." David
was still blushing. He wished she would stop. At the same time, he was glad
she was enjoying Washington, even if it was at his expense.
He unlocked the apartment door and let Sara through. She turned around
suddenly, looking quite startled.
David looked past Sara into the apartment.
"Dammit, Fred! Put some clothes on!"

CHAPTER 32

Early Saturday morning, the halls of Congress seemed eerily vacant as Ellen came into the office to organize some reports for the following week. After she worked through a preliminary schedule and e-mailed it to David, she brought a hardcopy into his office and laid it on his desk. As she turned around, she gave a startled yell.

"Dammit, Fred! Put some clothes on!"

Fred, who had been lying on the sofa, pulled off his blanket, revealing he did indeed have clothes on from the waist down. She noted he was unexpectedly buff for a nerdy college professor type. He quickly pulled on an undershirt.

"No one told me Sara Grant was in town," Fred explained as he pulled the rest of his clothes on. "I thought David went back to Pennsylvania for the weekend."

"What has that to do you sleeping in the Congressman's office?"

"David and I share an apartment. Remember?"

"Yeah?"

"I thought he was out of town, so I was walking around the apartment in my underwear, not that I do that a lot. Then, all of a sudden, Sara Grant walks in, with David right behind her. After that, I felt a little uncomfortable staying in the apartment, at least until Sara heads back to Pennsylvania. It would have been a bit awkward at the breakfast table this morning."

Ellen laughed. Suddenly, they heard the outer door to the office suite open. She looked out the doorway. "Good morning, Congressman."

"Is Sara with him?" Fred whispered, as he finished fastening the last buttons on his shirt.

Ellen shook her head no, as David entered.

"Fred," David called out, "I'm sorry about last night. I shouldn't have reacted that way."

"Yeah," Fred said. "I think we have to initiate the old college roommate's signal code. You know, put a sock or tie on the doorknob if you've got a girl in."

"I didn't know Sara was coming down." David gave Ellen a sideways glance. "She surprised me."

"Surprised us both," Fred murmured. "You're lucky. If you had come in a few minutes earlier I, well, never mind."

"Thanks for putting that image in my head," Ellen groaned.

"I suppose timing really is everything," David said. "You know, Fred, you didn't have to leave."

"Is Sara coming in this morning?" Fred asked.

"No. She and I had a talk over breakfast. I think I'm going to move out. Don't worry; I'll cover my half of the rent until you can find a new roommate.

"Where are you going to move?"

"With the depressed housing market, Sara thinks there may be some bargains in the local area. Perhaps a townhouse in Georgetown. I don't know. Of the two of us, she's more real estate savvy. She's checking with a realtor this morning."

"By the way, how was your evening?" Ellen asked. "I mean before coming home. What did Congressman Wickham say about a seat on his subcommittee?"

"He said he'd decide by Monday. By the way, did you have any idea The Capitol Domes were going to make fun of me?"

"They parodied you?" she said with a chuckle.

"Yeah, they sang about my one-minute speech. A bit surreal. But then this morning, I started to think about it. In the overall scheme of things, how did I rate such attention? Since I didn't do any interviews after the speech, the media didn't make much of it. Why did the Domes?"

"Well, they're especially tuned into the activities of Congress. You see, every member of the Domes is a current or former Capitol Hill staffer. In fact, I used to be a member."

"You did musical comedy?" Fred asked.

"Yes, I used to do a dead-on impression of First Lady Chloe Henderson," she said with some pride.

"OK, let's hear it," Fred demanded.

"Oh, it was too long ago."

"Henderson has only been out of office two years. So it can't be that long ago. Let's hear it," David said, folding his arms and smiling. "Consider it a command performance."

Ellen rolled her eyes. "I can't. I don't have any music."

"Hmm, cop-out," David chuckled.

"Well in the meantime," Fred said, changing the subject, "we've been receiving a number of calls and e-mails from constituents about CART. Several constituents have had their assets frozen."

"Well, if they're Kadler Steele investors, what would they expect?"

"Well, here's the thing. They all claim to be depositors at local banks, not Kadler investors."

"That's strange. Pull together the specifics." He turned to Ellen. "Who's the new chair of the banking committee?"

"Porter Barnes."

ଔ ଔ ଔ ଔ

"Be very careful with that," Narlstrom demanded, as a couple of burly high school seniors moved his metal lathe onto the truck. "It may be heavy, but it's still a delicate precision instrument."

177

Moving his workshop out of the house was difficult enough without seeing these kids take less than perfect care with his equipment. If any of the equipment were damaged, it would outweigh the savings of hiring these kids through the local youth employment service. Their names were Hank and Jake, but he mentally labeled them Heckle and Jeckle.

Narlstrom's accounts were still frozen. Jean's meager life insurance provided a small financial buffer. However, that money would not last, especially after the funeral expenses.

A grief counselor had suggested he not make any serious life changes for at least six months. Narlstrom had only one session with the counselor. It didn't go well. He realized quickly he wasn't a feeling-sharing kind of guy.

Thanks to the decline in the stock market, his retirement accounts weren't worth very much. *So much for "balanced investing."* Besides, the withdrawal penalty was prohibitive.

"No, lift with your legs, not your back," he warned one of the teens.

"Don't worry, Mr. N. We got this," Jeckle shot back.

Stupid kid. Wait til he's forty with a slipped disk.

He had decided to sell the house. It would free up some equity. Besides, he could never keep the house as fastidiously clean as Jean had. He decided a change was needed. And he needed to do something to regain control of his life, grief counselors be damned.

His realtor had insisted he empty the basement, making it look more spacious, among other things. He really didn't understand this, but she persisted. *Doesn't this woman understand basic geometry? The dimensions of a room are unaffected by its contents.* Finally, he relented. He would have to move his equipment eventually.

The small rental truck was almost full, except for the last box of scrap wood. Heckle, the goofiest of the pair, threw the box into the truck. Pieces of wood bounced out of the box. Narlstrom was sure they both had bright futures as reality TV idiots.

"Okay, boys. I'll drive the truck. You can follow me in your car."

Narlstrom started the truck and headed for the new home of his workshop. He had originally planned to keep his equipment in a rental storage facility. But then, Saul, a friend of his, told him he had some extra room in the back of his warehouse. Saul's warehouse had the advantage of being both free and allowing him to plug the equipment in and operate it.

Ten minutes later, he pulled the truck up to the side entrance at Coburn Trucking & Storage. Saul Coburn was waving to him. Coburn hopped in the cab and directed him to the correct building entrance. Heckle and Jeckle unloaded the equipment and moved it into place in the back room.

"Even for a Saturday, this place seems pretty deserted, Saul. How's business?"

"Not great. That's why I can lend you the space. I had to lay off another two guys this week."

"You laid them off?"

"Hey, I didn't want to," Coburn said in a defensive tone. "I just can't afford to keep people on. All these politicians in Washington make me sick with all their grandiose plans. Oh yeah, now the President wants to do sump'n 'bout education. How's that gonna help me and my workers? Like, we need to be rocket scientists? Uh, I mean no offense. What we need is goods to ship. We need some good old-fashioned American manufacturing in this country, not all that airy-fairy digital crap."

There was an awkward silence.

"Sorry. Look at me, up on my soap box."

"No apologies, Saul. I've had a gut-full of Washington myself. Jean might still be alive, well, never mind."

"Anyway, I got to get back to what little work I have left," Coburn said. "Here's a key. Use the room anytime you want. It's locked off from the rest of the warehouse, so no one'll touch your stuff."

"Thanks, Saul. I really appreciate it. You're one of the few good guys left."

Coburn started to look uncomfortable. "We're not gonna hug or anything?"

Narlstorm smiled and shook his head no.

"Don't mention it. You did me a solid, tutoring my kid for the SATs. Friends help friends. And besides my wife still loves that walnut bowl you made her."

"Maybe I'll make her another one," Narlstrom said, looking at his new workshop.

ꙮ ꙮ ꙮ ꙮ

"So Henry, is this your first visit to the White House?" Harris Carver asked, greeting Henry Stark at the West Wing entrance.

"No," Stark answered. "I was here when the President announced my appointment as CART administrator."

"Oh, that's right. I forgot. Did you get the full tour of the White House while you were here?"

"No, I was just here for a quick press announcement."

"Well then, let me show you around," Carver said cheerfully, gesturing toward the left-hand exit from the lobby. They were heading up the corridor. "Just up ahead we have the Cabinet Room. This conference room is only for use by the President." Carver opened the heavy wooden door, beckoning Stark through. A very long oval conference table dominated the room.

"Each chair," Carver explained, "has a brass plate indicating the cabinet secretary who sits there."

Stark noted the chair in front of him had the name Peter F. Warrenburg, Attorney General, engraved on the plate.

"Perhaps someday you'll have your name of one of these chairs," Carver said.

"That's quite flattering," Stark answered, looking to the left, seeing alabaster busts of Jefferson and Hamilton set in opposition, just as they had been in life.

Carver walked along the conference table to the door at the far end. Stark followed closely. They entered a small outer office. Then, Carver opened a door into an office that needed no explanation. It was one of the most famous rooms in the world. His eyes immediately fell on the Resolute Desk. Stark could not help but be in awe of the history that had transpired in the Oval Office.

"Is it okay for us to be in here?" Stark asked. "I mean, where's the President?"

"He and the First Lady are spending the weekend at Camp David," Carver said, smiling. "My office is just down the hall, through this door." They cut across the room, over the Eagle-embroidered carpet. Once in Carver's office, they settled down to business.

"So Henry, how is CART proceeding?" Carver asked.

"Kadler Steele's finances are the equivalent of an Escher painting, disorienting and baffling. We are proceeding as meticulously as we can."

"Meticulous is not a description that polls well. 'Aggressive' and 'timely' sound much better."

"Be that as it may, Mr. Carver, meticulous is the best way to proceed. I have received numerous requests for special treatment from several dozen members of Congress. That would just add to the confusion."

"Were their requests reasonable?"

"Maybe. Maybe not. But if I cave to that pressure it will only create a flood of special requests, which in turn will create further chaos."

"I noticed you admiring the statues of Jefferson and Hamilton in the Cabinet Room."

Stark nodded.

"Two very interesting men. They were a counterbalance to one another. Hamilton wanted a strong central government, something that Jefferson opposed. Yet, when Jefferson became President, he expanded the power of the Presidency immeasurably. In fact, scholars believe the Louisiana Purchase, a move that doubled the size of the country and secured the country's future, was completely unconstitutional. How could Jefferson do that?"

"I'm not sure how this applies to our current situation."

"The point is that in addition to being a political philosopher, Jefferson was also a practical politician. Henry, I appreciate your sense of order and fairness, but we have to be practical too. There are those whose fate would impact more people. We, I mean you, need to prioritize for the greater good."

Stark shifted in his chair uncomfortably.

"I assume you watched the President's State of the Union address. He's making a push for his education bill. That's priority number one. And time is of the essence. Before you know it, we'll be up to our asses in the election cycle, which will prevent us from getting anything constructive done.

Complaints about how CART is being handled must be silenced. Give the squeaky wheels the oil they need."

"Are you suggesting I gloss over the culpability of less-than-honest investors?"

"Of course not. But there are honest, yet influential, parties that might make problems for the President, his education bill, and his reelection bid. All I'm saying is oil the squeaky wheels before they become a distraction."

"Do you have any suggestions on who should be focused on?" Stark asked, warily.

"I believe Porter Barnes made some suggestions. But you have to use your best judgment. Do a good job, and maybe you'll have a brass plate on one of those chairs in the next term."

CHAPTER 33

Wyatt Wickham had agreed to allow David on the Energy and Power subcommittee. This, in turn, led to even more lobbyists knocking on David's door. Despite being told they had limited time, most lobbyists would incessantly push for more. He realized fairly quickly he needed to have a way of limiting the amount of time lobbyists would consume.

David was determined not to be swayed by their implied donations. On the other hand, he preferred to avoid unnecessarily offending anyone, thus encouraging them to support a challenger in the next election. So instead of a direct confrontation, David devised a method of artificial interruption, where a member of his staff would interrupt a lobbyist meeting with a reason to cut it short. A typical example would be: "Excuse me, Congressman. Congresswoman so-and-so is holding an emergency caucus conference." That interruption five minutes into a meeting would give David an excuse to conclude without giving the lobbyist the impression he was uninterested.

The specifics of an interruption were always designed to be of little interest to the lobbyist at hand. For instance, a lobbyist pitching oil subsidies would be interrupted by an issue such as urban planning or veterans' benefits. The staff had a private competition for the most interesting interruption.

Today, David was meeting with Sam Hughes.

"Good morning, Congressman," Hughes said cheerfully.

David observed his ill-fitting suit. "Welcome. I'm sorry, Mr. Hughes, I don't recall which lobbying firm you're from?"

"I'm not a lobbyist. I'm a partner at Reflex Energy Systems. I wanted to talk to you about a new generation of smart grids we're developing," Hughes said with some nervousness in his voice.

"Well, I've certainly heard of smart grids."

"Since 1896, the US power grid has been a unidirectional system for electricity distribution." Hughes said, trying to rush through his memorized speech.

"I know," David interrupted, trying to speed up his presentation, "but now we have grids that allow electricity to flow both ways. So with solar panels or other devices, you can sell power back to the utility."

"Exactly," Hughes said, relieved at David's understanding. "But it's still about power generation."

"Well, what else would it be about?" David said, as he sat down behind his desk.

"We've developed a system for demand management, for example turning off air conditioners and water heaters during short-term spikes in electricity, instead of having full-blown blackouts. Honestly, does anyone's

182

water really need to be kept at maximum temperature throughout the entire night when they're asleep? Would anyone really be inconvenienced if it was turned off for twenty minutes?"

"What if I'm a night owl?"

"Then, our AI system will figure that out and adjust. Plus, every house or office would have a manual override."

"AI, as in artificial intelligence?"

"Yes, it will be able to analyze usage patterns, in the same way weather services use super computers to predict the weather. In addition, it would be able to make minor adjustments to demand that would have minimum impact."

David laughed. "Too bad the weather service can't make those kinds of adjustments. What is it you want from me?"

"We've demonstrated the viability of our technology, but we're at a point where we need a full-scale demonstration on a large community scale. That requires federal support. Power utilities won't buy it, until they see a full-scale pilot program."

"So, you want the Federal Government to finance the next step in your R&D?"

"We're at the point where there's no other way. We need to persuade a large utility and an entire community to integrate our system into their power systems. Once our system is operational, it can reduce power consumption by six percent."

"Only six percent?"

"Six percent is a lot when you apply it to the nation's power consumption. Six percent could prevent a blackout."

Carol knocked on the door and entered. "Excuse me Congressman. Congressman O'Mara called. He wanted to urgently speak with you. He's threatened to change his vote on Jai-Alai deregulation."

David rolled his eyes. "Tell 'Congressman O'Mara' to vote anyway he likes. I'll catch up with him another time," he said, ignoring the artificial interruption.

"Very good, sir." Carol withdrew, a little surprised.

"Mr. Hughes, why have you come to me with this?"

"I thought since you have a software background, you'd understand the concept more easily. Plus, like me, you're a visionary."

David laughed at the clumsy flattery. "Nice try. Who else have you approached?"

"Several people in the Department of Energy are interested. However, the few members of Congress who have actually been willing to meet with me have shown little enthusiasm."

"Who have you approached?"

Representatives Daniels, Ortiz and Hudge.

"Arlo Hudge? I haven't been here long, but I already know he's in the pocket of the oil and coal lobby."

"I know. But here's the thing: Our system is energy source neutral. It doesn't matter where the electricity comes from, oil, coal, nuclear, solar, hydro. It's all the same."

"Okay, you have me interested. I like the concept. But you do understand that Congress doesn't award contracts. And, it would be very difficult to write a law that would specifically designate your company to build such a smart grid. And I'm not sure I would want to."

"Congressman, if the parameters are specific enough, we're the only ones who can honestly fulfill such a contract. I have them right here, along with all the background information I think you'll need. If someone else can do it better, then I say Godspeed to them."

"Alright, I'll read over your materials, but I make no promises. You'll have to excuse me; I have my first committee hearing this afternoon. And I have to prepare."

David showed Hughes out, and then turned to Carol. "Jai alai deregulation? Really? Does anyone even play that anymore?"

ಬ ಬ ಞ ಞ

That afternoon, David walked into the hearing room and took his seat along the walnut-paneled dais, behind the black placard that read "Mr. Grant." He was surprised to see the C-SPAN cameras for what was supposed to be a fairly minor hearing. As he sat waiting for the other members, he reviewed the materials provided by the subcommittee staff. Finally, Wyatt Wickham strode in with his staff in tow, resulting in a quick fury of cameras clicking which just as quickly subsided. Wickham briefly chatted with various people, then made his way over to David.

"Good afternoon, Mr. Chairman."

"Good afternoon. So, ready for your first hearing?"

"Yes," David answered. "Looking forward to it."

"Good. What will happen is that first everyone gets to make two minutes of opening remarks. First, I'll recognize the ranking Democrat, then the ranking Republican, then alternate between the parties based on seniority. Questioning will follow the same order."

"When do I speak?"

"Well that's what I wanted to ask you. You can speak third, same as on the Floor, or since this is your first hearing, you can opt to go last. Your choice."

"I choose going third."

"Fair enough." Wickham slowly ambled over to his seat and banged his gavel. "The Subcommittee on Energy and Power is hereby called to order." He banged the gavel again for effect. After a moment of settling down, Wickham continued. "This afternoon, we are here to listen to testimony from Polaron Energy on the proposed dredging of Samu Bay in Alaska. Polaron is seeking support for dredging of the bay to facilitate tanker access. We will now hear opening remarks from members of the subcommittee. Congresswoman Parno, you are recognized for two minutes."

"Thank you, Mr. Chairman," responded Diane Parno, a narrow-faced woman with short reddish hair. "With the increased damage to our planet's climate and environment, I am deeply concerned about an oil company that once again wants to pillage our natural resources for profit. While I acknowledge the need for energy sources, cleaner sources have not been given an honest chance. Especially in the aftermath of the blatant disregard for the environment by the Henderson Administration, I believe it is past time to take a serious look into these reckless incursions by Polaron Energy and others into our pristine wildernesses, including Samu Bay. Thank you, Mr. Chairman."

"The Chair," Wickham announced, "recognizes Congressman Hudge for two minutes."

"Thank you, Mr. Chairman," Arlo Hudge said, in his Oklahoma drawl. "Well, I, for one, am pleased to see an American company working so hard to help our country achieve energy independence. And despite the worries of the environmentalist lobbies' scaredy-cats, I am gratified to read that Polaron has created an environmentally-responsible plan for dredging Samu Harbor..."

David thought it was interesting that the Democrats used the term "bay" while the Republicans used "harbor" to describe Samu, which did not even exist until receding ice created it.

"...and I look forward to hearing the details. Thank you, Mr. Chairman."

"The Chair recognizes Congressman Grant for two minutes."

"Thank you, Mr. Chairman," David said. "I would like to reserve my time, and apply it to the question and answer period with our witness."

Some of the other committee members looked at each other puzzled.

"That's not usually done," Wickham replied.

"I understand that. I just would like to use my time more efficiently."

"Are you implying this committee is inefficiently run?" Wickham asked.

"Not at all, Mr. Chairman. I meant no such sentiment. Since I'm new to the committee, I just thought it appropriate for me to focus more on questions than opening remarks."

"Very well. So ordered. The Chair recognizes..."

Fred, who was watching the hearing on C-SPAN, ran into Ellen's office. "David just declined to make an opening statement in the Polaron hearing. Is this some strategy thing? Do you know anything about this?"

"No," she said. "Declining to make an opening statement is almost unheard of."

"He asked the chairman to apply the minutes to his questioning period."

Opening statements continued, alternating between the Democrats and Republicans.

"Our witness today," Wickham announced, "is Mr. Victor Hasberg, CEO of Polaron Energy, the company that has petitioned the Energy and Interior Departments to dredge Samu Bay in Alaska to accommodate larger oil tankers. The chair recognizes Congresswoman Parno for five minutes.

"Thank you, Mr. Chairman. Mr. Hasberg, why have you not seen fit to pursue clean energy?"

Hasberg, an impeccably dressed man in his fifties, took his time before replying to Parno. "Quite to the contrary, Polaron continues to pursue balanced energy production, including solar, wind, and hydroelectric. However, for the time being, oil and gas still provide the most effective sources of—"

"Yes, yes, in other words you give lip service to green energy while forging ahead drilling like there's no tomorrow."

"I don't think—"

"Finally, one of you finally admits it. You don't think about the environment."

"That is not what I said," Hasberg spat. "If you're going to put words in my mouth instead of letting me answer your questions, Congresswoman, do I really need to be here?"

"Don't be disrespectful," Parno warned.

"Congresswoman, if you consult the record, it'll show it was you who interrupted me before I could finish my answer," Hasberg said calmly.

Parno scowled. Clearly, she had underestimated Hasberg. "Why has the search for oil in this region of Alaska suddenly grown, where as previously no one gave the Samu area a second look?"

"Large amounts of glacial ice previously prevented access to energy exploration in the Samu fields north of the harbor."

"But now the glaciers have receded?"

"Yes, Ma'am."

"So, in other words, global warming has benefitted Polaron Energy?" Parno spat.

"So-called climate change has had no significant effect of the demand for energy."

"I was referring to exploration."

"The receding glacier has provided somewhat easier access to the region."

"All I can say is what is good for Polaron is not good for the country. Or the world. Thank you, Mr. Chairman."

"The Chair recognizes Mr. Hudge of Oklahoma."

Hudge's gaunt face and intense eyes gave him the countenance of weathered political warrior. Yet when he smiled he almost looked kindly. "Thank you, Mr. Chairman. Mr. Hasberg, once the harbor is dredged and pumping operations are up and running, what effect would you expect it would have on the price of gasoline?"

"No one can predict all the factors that affect gas prices," Hasberg said, "but independent of all those other factors, we expect that because of increased supply, the price of gasoline will drop approximately three to four cents per gallon at the pump."

"Mr. Hasberg, aren't you being a bit conservative? I read a report that indicated that prices could drop as much as six or seven cents a gallon."

"I've also reviewed the Simmons report. And while I can find no fault with it, I prefer to be a bit cautious in such promises."

"While I compliment your caution and modesty—"

"Do we really have to watch this lovefest?" one of the congressmen behind David whispered. "Next thing, Arlo'll have his tongue down Hasberg's throat."

"Mr. Hasberg," Hudge continued, "just to allay the fears of some of my colleagues, what will the environmental impact of drilling and pumping be in the Samu fields?"

"Absolutely minimal. Since the glacier has recently receded, there is little in the way of wildlife there."

Hudge asked a few more softball questions, and then concluded.

"The Chair recognizes Mr. Grant of Pennsylvania."

"Thank you, Mr. Chairman," David said. "Mr. Hasberg, how much did Polaron Energy earn last year?"

"I can't recall the exact amount."

"An approximation then?"

"After income tax," Hasberg said, "I believe 43 billion dollars."

"And after oil is shipped through Samu, what do you project the effect on your bottom line will be?"

"We would expect it to increase, but I can't forecast the exact amount."

"With over 43 billion in profits," David pressed, "couldn't you easily cover the costs of dredging this bay or harbor?"

"Well, the government has traditionally assumed responsibility for improving port navigation," Hasberg explained. "For instance, several years ago, the government paid to have the harbor in Charleston, North Carolina, dredged."

"Very true, Mr. Hasberg. Although, the dredging of Charleston benefited a broad range of commercial interests. What other companies would benefit from the dredging in Samu? And by that, I mean other than Polaron contractors or vendors."

"I'm not really sure."

"The answer is none," David said. "Polaron and its operational partners will be the only ones to benefit financially."

"Not true, Congressman. There would be a reduction in gasoline prices as Congressman Hudge pointed out.

"Perhaps," David admitted, nodding his head. "What were Polaron's liabilities as of the last quarter?"

"I believe our current liabilities are at about 57 million dollars, with negligible long-term liabilities."

"But you expect to be able to cover those liabilities?"

"Yes, sir."

"Actually, as I look at your balance sheet, income sheet, and cash flow statement, I see a financially very well run company."

"Thank you, Congressman," Hasberg said, smiling at the compliment.

"Do you know what the financial liability of the United States government is?"

"Um, I'm..." Hasberg turned to his counsel, who didn't seem to know either.

"The answer is 31.9 trillion dollars. That's trillion with a T. That's our National Debt, which is nearly 600,000 times the liabilities of Polaron Energies. So let me ask this question: Why is a company that can easily cover the cost of dredging Samu asking the government, which is so deeply in debt, to foot the bill for a project that will only financially benefit them and their partners?"

"Well..." Hasberg sputtered, he looked to his counsel.

"Whoa, a knockout punch!" Fred yelled at the TV screen. "Go Davey boy, go!"

"Hopefully," Ellen said, "he'll stop there on a strong note."

Hasberg finally pulled himself together. "Congressman, this is not just about money. It's about energy independence, and therefore, national security. Consumers are demanding more and more energy every day."

"Congressman Grant, that concludes your time," Wickham announced.

"Actually, Mr. Chairman, I still have the time yielded from my opening statement."

"Um, yes, sorry, I forgot. You have another two minutes."

"Thank you, Mr. Chairman. Mr. Hasberg, you make part of your case based on the increasing demand for energy."

"Yes, if people would conserve and use less electricity, drive their cars less, and so on, we wouldn't have to work so hard to generate the massive amount of energy currently required. But our experience is that people don't like to conserve energy. They like their AC turned up in the summer. They like their SUVs and minivans. I visited a classroom several months back, and almost every student was taking notes on an electronic device, not pencil and paper, the way I grew up. Just the other day, I saw a man leave his truck idling while he went into the store to pick up some items. Not only that, the population is growing. So, to support these lifestyles, we need energy and lots of it."

"So an ideal solution would be to find a way to conserve energy without inconveniencing people?" David suggested.

"If you can find such a way," Hasberg said. "Then, God bless you."

"So you would support such a solution, if found?"

Hasberg's expression showed he was confused by the question. "I...I suppose so," he said slowly.

"Thank you, Mr. Hasberg. Mr. Chairman, I yield back any remaining time."

The hearing continued, alternating between the two parties. Almost all the questions were predictably along party lines. Once the hearing was adjourned, David returned to his office.

"So, how was your first hearing?" Ellen asked.

"I'm sure you watched it on C-SPAN, and you're ready to give me a critique," David said with a smile.

Ellen nodded. "You're right; I did see it. You did a great job smacking Hasberg around, which I assume was your intention."

"I have nothing against Hasberg. I just think it's ridiculous to subsidize Polaron's profits. Nobody subsidized Simplexia's profits."

"What was that business about conserving energy without inconveniencing people?" Ellen asked.

"Ah yes," he said, picking up a packet of reports. "This is the proposal from that guy Hughes, the one I met with this morning. I want someone to look at his system to see if it's viable."

"A way to conserve without inconvenience?" Ellen asked.

"Yes, I think it may be time to put forth my first piece of legislation."

CHAPTER 34

David looked around the conference table at his staff. "So the Reflex system checks out?"

"Absolutely," Fred answered. "Several people in the Department of Energy love it, and say it worked well in the preliminary demonstrations."

"My contacts," Ellen added, "tell me this kind of project will receive a lot of support from the Office of Energy Efficiency and Renewable Energy."

"Then why haven't they moved on it?"

"Distractions, I guess," Fred said. "They can't do everything. I guess this needed a champion."

"Good. Now we just have to deal with Congress." He turned to the other end of the table. "Tyler?"

Tyler was caught mid-bite of his bagel, which he quickly swallowed. "Um, well, the staffers on the Energy Subcommittee who know anything about it, don't see any technical problems."

"Any other kind of problems?"

"Not yet, as far as I can tell."

"Okay Tyler, you've got the brief. I want you to write up an initial draft of the bill. Are you up for it?"

"Yes, sir," he said with a smile.

"Any questions or concerns, ask Ellen."

Tyler nodded, grabbed the pile of specifications, put the remains of his bagel on top, and returned to his office to start working.

"You'll need cosponsors," Ellen advised, "You'll especially need someone in the Senate to be the ramrod on a parallel version of the bill."

"I think I know just the Senator."

ജ ജ ശ ശ

David was able to obtain an appointment with Howard Carstairs for the next morning. He walked over right after an early, but short, subcommittee meeting.

"Yo, Grant!" echoed in the corridor.

David turned around, puzzled at being addressed in such a way in the halls of Congress. He saw a shaggy-haired man lumbering toward him.

"Congressman Barnes, isn't it?"

"As if you didn't know," bellowed Barnes with a grin. "I understand you wanted to talk to me."

"Yes, I have reports from my constituents that their bank accounts have been frozen because of CART."

"Oh, this is about CART? Oh, I thought it was about something else."

"Like what?"

"Oh, maybe some gratitude for helping you get elected. It's been months since you got here. A little overdue."

"I'm not sure I follow."

"You know, for knocking off Shelly Lannier."

"That was over a year ago. Somehow I don't think you did it for me."

"Still, I little gratitude wouldn't go amiss."

"Well, thank you, I suppose. Anyway, back to CART. I've—"

"You tell your constituents, they should have invested better."

"But that's just the point. They weren't investing; they were saving."

"Listen, I got everybody whining at me. People want to play the market, but cry when their risk doesn't pay off."

"But—"

"I gotta go. Call me again when you get out of those short pants." With that, Barnes strode away.

David continued on his way to Carstairs' office, trying to forget the unpleasantness with Barnes. He was shown into the Senator's office immediately.

"Senator Carstairs, it's good to see you again. Thank you for taking the time to see me."

"No problem." Carstairs seemed a little distracted. "Ah," he said, remembering something. "Just a moment."

He walked over to the credenza and took an aspirin with a glass of water. He turned back to David.

"Sorry, headache. I'm sure your aspirin consumption has gone up since joining Congress. So, to what do I owe the pleasure?"

"I'll cut to the chase," David said. "I'm looking for a Senate cosponsor for a new bill I'd like to propose. I was wondering if you might be interested."

"Okay, tell me all about it." Carstairs gestured David to the couch.

David proceeded to explain the Reflex technology. Carstairs seemed to be listening intently. Either that or he was absorbed in a migraine. David couldn't tell. He paused, giving Carstairs a moment to react.

"I'm not an engineer, but this sounds kinda tricky."

"My staff has checked it out. It's all completely sound. I have more technical materials here. Perhaps they'll provide a better explanation than I've given," David said, placing the materials on the coffee table in front of the Senator.

"Won't this decrease the power company's revenues?"

"Yes, but it will be offset by an increase in their profit margin. And profit is what every company is most concerned about anyway."

"And, how much will this cost?"

"About 33 million."

"Hmm, and I take it you'd like me to take the lead on the Senate side?"

"Yes, as well as provide any advice you can offer."

"Okay, let me think about it," the Senator said, standing up. "I'll get back to you."

"Very well, Senator. Thank you for your time."

"My pleasure."

౭౦ ౭౦ ౪౨ ౪౨

The next day, Carol buzzed David on the intercom. "Congressman, Senator Carstairs is on line three for you."

"Thank you, Carol." David punched the button. "Good morning, Senator. I take it you've made a decision."

"I like what I've read. It makes sense."

"Fantastic."

"So you've got me as a cosponsor, but on one condition."

"And what would that be?" David asked cautiously.

"Join me this weekend at my house in Bar Harbor."

"That's very nice. But actually, I've committed to spend the weekend with my wife back in Pennsylvania."

"Well, bring her with you," Carstairs said. "My wife, Emily, is always looking to meet new people. We'll show you and your wife a great time, I promise. See ya Saturday." He hung up before David could respond.

౭౦ ౭౦ ౪౨ ౪౨

That following Saturday morning David and Sara flew into Bangor International Airport, rented a car, and drove south along Route 1A toward Acadia National Park, following the directions Carstair's office had sent.

"Explain to me why we're doing this again?" Sara asked.

"I need Carstairs' support for my energy management bill. Coming up here was the price for his support."

"Is he really that lonely?" she asked.

"No, but he is a bit of an eccentric. And I think he's testing me, to see how badly I want his support."

"Okay, you grovel and get your bill. What do I get out of this trek, Grant?" She always called him by his last name when she was teasing him.

"Time with your husband. And some lobster. It is Maine after all."

"I don't know, Grant. It seems a long way to go for some seafood."

David turned off Route 1A just before entering Bar Harbor. Within 15 minutes, they pulled up to Carstairs' home, a blue, rustic-looking, yet well-maintained, farmhouse with ornate Victorian trim. They walked up and rang the bell. Emily Carstairs opened the front door with a big smile on her face.

"You must be David and Sara. How was your trip?" she asked, waving them in.

"It was a very pleasant drive down from Bangor."

"It is beautiful, isn't it?" she said with pride.

David looked around. "Where's the Senator?"

"You'll find Howard in the back. He's playing with his wood."

"I beg your pardon?"

"He's chopping firewood. The man's in his seventies, but still likes to act like a macho Paul Bunyan. Go on out. Meanwhile, we girls'll just chat."

David walked out the back door.

Crack-Thunk. Carstairs split another log. *Crack-Thunk.*

"Hello, Senator," David called out.

"Senator? I think it's high time you call me Howard. So, how was your trip?"

"Just fine."

Carstairs picked up another log and placed it on the chopping block. *Crack-Thunk.* "You know the first time I met Ronald Reagan, he was chopping, just like this." *Crack-Thunk.* "People thought it was theater, but he genuinely enjoyed it."

"I have to admit," David said, "there is something therapeutic about chopping wood, that satisfying sound the wood makes."

"Ah, I suspected you might be a woodsman. Here, try your hand," Carstairs said, handing him the ax. Carstairs then placed a slightly thicker log on the block for David to chop.

David smiled at the challenge. He set his stance carefully, then swung. *Crack-Thunk.*

"Let me guess," Carstairs ventured. "An Eagle Scout?"

"No, I made Life Scout though. I was going to go on, but there was a girl I had my eye on."

"Ah, yes," Carstairs said, with a smile. "Teenage hormones. Even I remember the challenge of that age."

೮೦ ೮೦ ೧೪ ೧೪

The Carstairs took David and Sara on a tour of Bar Harbor and Acadia National Park. Sara did have her lobster at lunch in the form of a lobster roll. David particularly appreciated Thunder Hole, a coastal rock formation that concentrated the incoming waves into a geyser-like eruption. David thought Thunder Hole might make a good nickname for Porter Barnes. He tried not to laugh when Sara received a severe dose of Thunder Hole's ice-cold ocean spray. Luckily, Sara was a good sport.

After a while, they headed back to the Carstairs' home for dinner.

"Dinner's served," Emily Carstairs called out as she laid a succulent beef tenderloin with rosemary on the dinner table.

"What, no lobster?" David asked with a grin.

"I do enjoy a good lobster," Carstairs admitted, "but honestly we don't eat it all the time. You know, there was a time when lobster was mostly served in the Maine prison system."

"My, my, what swanky prisons you have," Sara joked.

"No, quite the opposite. Lobster was considered a cheap, low-quality protein from an underwater scavenger. But then, someone added a little butter, and all of a sudden it's a delicacy."

"Like so many things," David added, "it's a matter of marketing."

"Exactly. So anyway, I thought maybe tomorrow afternoon we might go whale watching. What do you think of that?"

"Uh," Sara said hesitantly. "I tend to get a little sea sick."

"Don't worry," Carstairs said, "I have some pills that'll take care of that. But we don't have to decide anything tonight."

The meal was delicious. There was some discussion of the energy bill, but it was kept to a minimum.

"So Sara, tell us about yourself," Carstairs insisted. "I understand you're an architect."

"Yes, ever since I was a little girl I loved architectural plans. I used to cut floor plans out of my mother's magazines and save them, often before she read them, much to my mother's annoyance."

Carstairs laughed. "So you design homes now?"

"It started that way. But now, I mostly design public buildings."

"Yes, Sara just finished a beautiful new library in Harrisburg," David said, with some pride in his voice. "In fact, I have some pictures." He pulled out his tablet and showed them.

"Very impressive, my dear."

"So David, were you always interested in computers?"

"No, I was originally going to be a firefighter, like my father."

"Really?"

"Yes, he was a firefighter down in Philly. During the summer, I used to hang out at the fire house. I even learned how to cook from one of my dad's buddies."

"Let me guess, Philly cheese steaks?"

"Sometimes," David said, nodding. "But like lobster, you don't want it every day."

"So, why didn't you become a fireman?"

"As I got older, I developed a keen interest in computers and writing my own software. Oddly, my father encouraged me to pursue that. He loved what he did, and I guess he wanted that for me, too. What about your parents?"

"My mother worked in a shop," Carstairs said. "My father was what must seem like a Maine stereotype. He was a lobsterman."

"Ah. Did you ever consider becoming one yourself?"

"Well, I might have," Carstairs said, "but he died when I was young. He went after a man who was poaching his lobster traps, a matter of great honor. You just don't touch another man's traps. Unfortunately, the poacher killed my father."

"I'm so sorry."

"Thank you, but it was a long time ago. Obviously, I followed the trial. The bastard got off on a technicality. In a strange way it helped me decide to become a lawyer. I was determined to prevent people from twisting the law again, a somewhat unrealistic goal admittedly. As I matured, I've come to realize the only true victories come in small bites."

"What about you, Emily?" Sara asked.

"Oh, I don't have anything as dramatic as you all. I did, however, get to marry the most handsome man in Maine," Emily said as she reached out for her husband's hand. "Hell, along the whole east coast. So now, who would like some blueberry cobbler?"

Like the tenderloin, it was delicious. It was still warm from the oven, and served a la mode.

"Now, David and I have to be up early. We have a little errand to run. We'll have to leave around 5:30."

"5:30 AM?" David asked. "What are we doing?"

"Oh, he's taking Mohammad to the mountain," Emily chuckled.

"Shush, Emily. An old man still needs his secrets," Carstairs said with a mischievous grin. "National security and all that."

Emily Carstairs just rolled her eyes with a smile.

ᛞ ᛞ ᛈ ᛈ

The next morning, David got up at 5:00 AM, trying not to wake Sara. He quickly dressed and padded his way downstairs, where Carstairs was already waiting for him.

"Punctuality in the wee hours—a good sign," he whispered.

They climbed into Carstairs' SUV and drove off into the moonless darkness. David suspected it was useless to further question him about their destination. After several turns, they climbed up a steep and winding road. David realized Emily's comment about a mountain wasn't quite a joke after all. He started to notice the odd vehicle ahead and behind, all traveling the same way, highly unusual for so early on a Sunday morning. David spied a sign that read "Cadillac Mountain."

"So Mohammed, what's at the top of this mountain?" he asked.

Carstairs smiled. "Something spectacular."

As they arrived at the top of the mountain, he was surprised to find a half-full parking lot and a small ranger office. They stepped out. Carstairs gestured the way ahead.

"There's a really good rock over there," he said, pointing into the semi-darkness. "I want to grab it before some tourist does."

As David's eyes adjusted, he could dimly see the Atlantic Ocean below them. The horizon had already made itself known by a dark purple band above it. The sight almost gave him the feeling he was sitting on the edge of the world.

He brought me here just to see a damn sunrise.

The rock Carstairs headed for was big enough for both to sit on and was luckily still vacant.

"Reagan used to talk about 'morning in America.' Well, this is where morning comes first. With the mountain's elevation, this is where the sun's rays first strike American soil."

The purple had lightened, diffusing into a muted pink sky.

"Don't those islands down there receive the light first?" David asked.

"They're too low. Curvature of the Earth and all that. Even so, those islands are Canadian, a reminder the US is not alone in the world."

I guess they should rename this Metaphor Mountain," David teased.

Carstairs smiled at that.

The light level rose, giving the surrounding white rocks a pleasant pink color. David had to admit this was a beautiful and calming sight. The sun finally peaked over the horizon. The pinks gave way to a golden ambience. With all the rushing around in the last several weeks, it was good to have this moment of peaceful beauty. David watched the older man next to him smile at the coming light as if it were giving him strength and happiness. He decided he would try to bring Sara back here someday to experience this, provided he could persuade her to wake up so early. Eventually, the golden light dissolved as the morning bloomed in full. The top of the mountain was still pretty, but not as magnificent as it had been for those few minutes.

"I guess this show's over," Carstairs said.

"It was beautiful. Thank you."

Carstairs nodded. "Time for breakfast."

David started to walk back to Carstairs' vehicle.

"No, David. Breakfast's this way," he said, pointing to a large white dining canopy that David hadn't noticed before.

As they walked over, David realized one of the people waiting under the canvas fly looked oddly like Robert Hingecliff, the Treasury Secretary.

CHAPTER 35

As he and Carstairs walked toward the dining canopy, David saw a number of men acknowledging him and the Senator, as they approached.

"David," Carstairs said, as they arrived, "I'd like you to meet a few people. This is Cal McCord."

David recognized the man. "Senior Democratic Senator from North Dakota, right?"

"South Dakota, actually. Glad to meet you, David," McCord said.

Carstairs turned and gestured to the man on McCord's right. "I don't know if you'd recognize Zeke Collier out of uniform."

The general's taut physique, gray buzz cut, and ramrod posture left no doubt this was a military man.

"Certainly." David said, "The former Chairman of the Joint Chiefs. I have to admit I never liked how Henderson treated you."

Collier smiled warmly. "Many serve at the pleasure of the President, but no one serves at his displeasure," the old soldier quipped.

"Still," David insisted, "I think his treatment of you may have contributed to his loss at the polls."

"I hope not. Ted Henderson committed far worse sins than firing me."

"And last, but not least," Carstairs continued, "Robert Hingecliff."

"Mr. Secretary, a pleasure."

"Same here, Congressman."

"So Robert," Carstairs said, looking around, "where's Martha?"

"Our new Fed Chair has a lot on her plate."

"And you don't?" Carstairs chuckled.

"Well, she has to testify before Porter Barnes's committee on Tuesday."

Old Thunder Hole himself, David thought.

Hingecliff looked around. "So what are we having this morning?"

"Omelets, made to order," called out a young man in crisp chef whites. "We have cheese, mushrooms, ham, sausage, and, of course, lobster."

"Where else would you be offered a lobster omelet?" Carstairs asked. "Only in Maine."

"You never stop promoting your state, do you?" David whispered to Carstairs.

"Senator, good-will ambassador, what's the difference?" he said with a grin.

Each put in their order. The young chef made two omelets at a time, serving them in record time. Carstairs gave him a nod, and the young man withdrew

"So let's commence our *summit* meeting," Carstairs announced, sitting down on one of the camping chairs set out for them.

"Is that why we had to meet here?" McCord asked. "So you could make that lame pun?"

The others laughed.

"Anyway," Carstairs continued, "David, here, has come to me with an idea for his first bill. And I've agreed to be a co-sponsor. So David, why don't you tell everyone about it?"

"Well, I wasn't expecting to make a mountaintop speech. If I knew I was going to make a presentation, I would have at least brought some sock puppets."

Again, they chuckled. David proceeded to take the group through the details of the Reflex system and the highlights of his proposed bill. Throughout it, he wondered why Carstairs had invited the Secretary of the Treasury and an ex-general to hear about his energy legislation. Once he completed his impromptu presentation, he opened the floor for questions.

"You could simply add it to another bill," McCord offered. "You know, as an amendment."

"I suppose I could."

"I think," Carstairs cut in, "David may be reluctant to do so because I suspect he wants to make a statement."

"And what would that statement be?" Hingecliff asked.

"Congress has a pretty dismal approval rating," David answered, "as I'm sure you all noticed. This would be a bill that is constructive, energy neutral, and shouldn't violate anyone's political ideology. It could demonstrate how Congress can actually work together."

"In other words, it would be bipartisan." McCord suggested.

"I'd prefer the term, non-partisan or tri-partisan."

A couple of the attendees chuckled.

"I stand corrected," McCord said. "But to be quite honest, Congress's low approval rating comes not from a lack of legislation, but from the endless tribal warfare between the parties."

"Poison pill amendments. Threats to close down the government. Sequesters. Public pissing matches of all sorts," Carstairs said. "Congress behaves worse than a Hollywood starlet on a cocaine binge." They all nodded in agreement.

"I'm no legislator," General Collier said, "and I'm less concerned about Congress's image. But I have a question about David's project: Is just one pilot project enough? There are different climates. A system that works well in California may not work so well in Minnesota, or vice versa. Shouldn't there be multiple pilot projects, in case one fails?"

"That's a very good point," David admitted.

"And how much will this pilot project cost?" McCord asked.

"About 33 million, assuming just one pilot."

"Pocket change," McCord said. "Maybe several pilot projects spread across the country in the right districts would facilitate getting some support."

"You mean turn it into pork barrel spending?" David asked.

"It's not really pork, if it benefits more than one state." McCord explained.

"No offense, but I think the definition needs to be expanded."

"Perhaps so," McCord said. "Anyway, if Howard is your cosponsor from the Senate, you'll also need a Democratic co-sponsor from the House."

"I've been thinking of some people who'll fit the bill." David then turned to Robert Hingecliff, who had been fairly silent throughout the conversation. "Mr. Secretary, do you think the President would support this legislation?"

Hingecliff leaned forward and paused before speaking. "I can't speak for the President on this issue, but I suspect he would sign it, if it came before him. But don't expect him to spend any political capital supporting it. He's been frustrated in getting his education plan through, first with a Republican Congress, and now with the Kadler-Steele distractions. But, the President's determined to get it passed before the campaign begins in earnest."

"I can appreciate that," David said.

"You know what David said to me during our first meeting?" Carstairs asked. "He told me what we need is a 'centrist insurgency.' Interesting term, don't you think?"

The others smiled as if they had a private joke between them.

Suddenly someone's cell phone started beeping.

"Sorry," Hingecliff said. "Who the hell is calling this early on a Sunday?" he mumbled as he fished the phone out of the pocket of his camping vest. He looked at it and walked away from the group before he answered, "Hingecliff here."

The others continued talking about the bill, until he returned. Hingecliff was stone-faced.

"So?" Carstairs asked. "What is it? World War Three?"

"No, but there is some breaking news. I need to head back to Washington immediately. You might check out the Sunday morning talk shows. I think *American Caucus* is the one."

"Is it military?" Collier asked.

"No, but I can't say any more. Sorry to leave the party so abruptly." He turned to David. "Good luck, Congressman." With that, Hingecliff walked to his car quickly and drove off.

"If you'd all like to come to my house," Carstairs offered, "we can see what the fuss is about."

⁝ ⁝    

"Good morning," Emily Carstairs called out, as Sara came down the stairs.

"Good morning," Sara answered, rubbing her eyes.

"Coffee?"

"Yes, thank you."

The morning rays filled the house with a golden hue.

"You have a beautiful home."

"Oh, thank you." Emily said. "You're so kind."

"I mean it. I really love the open design. And the Victorian trim on the outside is a very nice touch. I wanted to incorporate that into the design of our house, but David said he didn't want to feel like he was 'living in a girl's dollhouse.'"

Emily smiled. "Men have such fragile egos, whether it's worrying about Victorian trim or chopping wood like Paul Bunyan." She mimed wood chopping.

They both laughed.

"So how do you like being a congressional wife?" Emily asked.

"Is that what I am, a congressional wife?" Sara asked. "I never thought of it that way. I've always thought of myself as a professional woman, with an identity independent from my husband." Sara suddenly realized how that might sound to Emily Carstairs. "I mean no offense."

"None taken, dear." Emily said, handing Sara a coffee cup. "No matter what, it's not easy, for them or us, the time apart and all. I once read some psychology article about the difference between accomplishment and contribution. You're an accomplisher, an award-winning architect. I'm a contributor. And I believe my contributions have made Howard a better senator. I give him an outlet for his stress, and Washington is very stressful. I'm a sounding board, and I sometimes even throw some ideas his way. I've found it a very rewarding life."

"When David asked me what I thought about him running for Congress, I gave him my blessing. I gave it because I didn't expect he would win."

"Oh my," Emily said, taking a sip of her coffee. "And, I suppose you're feeling sort of trapped now."

"I'm not sure."

Suddenly the phone rang.

"Who the heck is calling at this hour?"

"Hello…oh, Howard…oh, my…okay, I'll let Sara know." She hung up the phone. The boys are coming back early, with company. Apparently something's happened. We better get presentable. We've got about thirty minutes before they all get here.

ᗖ ᗘ ሃ ሂ

Dylan Reese smiled as he reviewed his notes on the story they were about to break. As the network's chief political analyst and host of *American Caucus*, Reese had been expecting a story like this. In his mind, it was inevitable. Tara Nolan, the show's producer, and Skip Parker, the director, walked in.

"Okay, the segment with Interior Secretary runs 18:30," Parker announced. They had to prerecord the interview because the Secretary's travel plans.

200

"We have a change," Nolan said. "Reese has a breaking story."

"Yeah, I guessed that," Parker said grumpily. "You sent the roundtable home. I hope you can fill the time."

"Look, this program usually just reacts and analyzes the week's news. Today, we have a chance to actually break news." Reese briefly explained the story.

"Wow. Well, with this new material so late, we'll have to go live," Parker warned. "No time to tape and edit it in."

"Unfortunately, Cameron won't fill the time," Reese said. "He has the bombshell, but alone he's only worth 15 minutes, tops." He turned to Nolan. "Any luck getting hold of Stark?"

"Not going to happen." Nolan said. "If he knows anything, I expect he's in a bunker somewhere."

"We could have filled the balance with the roundtable," Parker reminded him.

"But our roundtable was all wrong. It was an energy and environmental panel to discuss Samu Bay," Reese explained. "Can we get Hingecliff?"

"No. Hingecliff is out of town," Nolan said

"Gee, that's convenient. What about Porter Barnes?"

"Same."

"Can't we get a feed from wherever he is? Barnes never lets time or space get in the way of an interview opportunity."

"We know he's in California, but can't find out where specifically."

"Anyone at the White House?"

"Dylan, my people have already called the White House, Treasury, the CART offices and any member of Congress who might be in town. Everyone's using the weekend as an excuse and keeping their head down until they know what we have."

"How can we fill the time then?" Dylan asked.

"It's alright. I called around. We have Jessica Dandridge and Ben Glendenning already on route for a new roundtable."

"Oh come on, Tara, not those two! We need people who actually know something."

"Well Dylan, the longer you can stretch out Cameron, the shorter the roundtable."

"Crap."

❦ ❦ ❧ ❧

Carstairs and David were driving down the curvy mountain road, followed by the others in another car.

"Howard, what was this?" David asked. "I mean, these particular people didn't just happen to come to Cadillac Mountain this morning by coincidence. And on top of that, Democrats and Republicans working together. Did I drop through the looking glass?"

201

"No. We're just a group of people in government who, like you, put the welfare of this country over party. Do you really think you're the first to realize the dangers of political polarization?"

"No, I suppose not," David mumbled. "Is there a secret handshake?"

That made Carstairs smile. "No."

"Does this group have a name?"

"No, but we sometimes refer to ourselves as The Circle, as in circle of friends. We're discreet. We don't always agree, but we always take one another's calls and listen."

"I have the feeling this was some sort of audition."

"You talked about a centrist insurgency. Well, you just met the centrist underground."

"Robert Hingecliff is a centrist? He works for a fairly liberal president."

"We live in a polarized world. We do what we can, where and when we can."

"If the Secretary is part of your group, why wouldn't he share whatever it is that's about to break?"

"I'm not completely sure. Robert is a very cautious man. I suspect it's because he doesn't know you yet."

Carstairs pulled into his driveway. They all went into the house, greeted Emily and Sara, and made introductions all around. After some socializing and more coffee, Carstairs turned on the television. They watched the morning news programs, but there was no hint of anything significant. Finally, *American Caucus* was about to come on.

Accompanied by rousing music, suggesting an urgent mission, the plasma screen swirled with a kinetic montage of political images, which in turn dissolved to an image of an earnest-looking, bespectacled Dylan Reese.

"Welcome. I'm Dylan Reese. This morning on *American Caucus*, we have Derek Cameron, Deputy Chief Auditor for Capital Asset Restoration Trust, also known as CART, who is here to share some disturbing developments in the handling of the task force."

He turned to Cameron who was a relatively young man with a narrow face and thinning hair. "Welcome to the program. It has been several months since CART was initiated to deal with the complex issues of the Kadler Steele's financial meltdown. How would you describe CART's performance?"

"Initially, Henry Stark, the CART Chief Administrator, brought a very deliberate and systematic approach to assessing and prioritizing creditors."

"But I take it that's no longer the case?"

"Lately, there has been significant deviation from the official protocols regarding Kadler Steele creditors and investors."

"What exactly does that mean?" Reese pushed.

"There seems to be a significant correlation between the speed of review and the likelihood of a favorable outcome for a particular party and whether that party was an administration contributor."

"Are you saying contributors to the Farnum campaign received preferential treatment from CART?"

"Well, they are definitely receiving a speedier review. But there also appears to be a higher likelihood of a more favorable judgment."

"Are these deviations coming from Henry Stark himself?"

"I can't say for sure, but the oversight has certainly loosened. And while this is very concerning, there's an even bigger problem. Many depositors in the Kadler commercial bank subsidiaries were convinced to move their deposits into so-called Command Gateway Accounts that were actually investment accounts. Unwitting depositors allowed Kadler to move their funds from FDIC-insured savings accounts into unprotected investment accounts. And because of that, they were frozen under CART rules."

"So in other words, many households who thought they had regular checking accounts are now unable to pay their bills through no fault of their own."

"Yes."

"This is the type of thing that would have been illegal under the Glass-Steagall Act from the 1930's, correct?" Reese knew the answer, but he was trying to stretch out the interview.

"Yes, but unfortunately, Glass-Steagall was repealed back in the '90s. This, in turn, contributed to the financial meltdown in 2009."

"And now, it's complicating the sorting out of Kadler Steele," Reese added.

"True, and many consumers are not aware or sophisticated enough to distinguish the legal and financial differences between saving and investing. The CART rules do not take that into consideration."

Reese continued with Cameron for several more minutes, and concluded when they started to repeat the same information.

"We'll be back in a moment with a roundtable discussion after this break."

"Well, the shit's really hitting the fan," Cal McCord blurted out in the Carstairs' living room.

"My constituents have complained about this exact thing," David snapped. "When I brought this to Porter Barnes' attention, he just blew me off, and quite rudely at that."

"Well, I guarantee Barnes will be paying attention now," Carstairs said.

The program returned after a series of commercials, the last one being for an anti-constipation product.

"And we're back," Reese announced. "To react to Derek Cameron's allegations against CART, we've put together an impromptu roundtable, including Jessica Dandridge from the Liberty Network, and Ben Glendenning from the Conservative Patriots Network. Welcome to the program."

They both nodded appreciatively.

"Let's start with you, Ben Glendenning," Reese began. "How do you think conservatives will react to these charges against CART?"

"Listen, it's quite obvious," Glendenning said. "This President tried to bamboozle the American people once again, just like every Democratic president before him."

Dandridge cut in. "This is not about the President. There's no suggestion the President had any knowledge of this, even if these allegations about CART are true. You're jumping to the typical right-wing, Farnum-bashing conclusions. If you want to find the cause of our troubles, go back to the Republican-controlled Congress. Remember Sheldon Lannier and his cronies took millions from Kadler Steele in campaign contributions. Kadler purchased a license to steal, and the Republicans gave it to them."

"To be fair," Reese cut in, "a survey of campaign contributions showed Democrats received roughly an equal amount of funding from the financial industry."

"Your earlier guest," Glendenning said, "Mr. Cameron, referred to the repeal of the Glass–Steagall Act, which I might point out was signed into law by Bill Clinton, a Democrat."

"Don't forget, it was served up by a Republican Congress," Dandridge countered.

"Sorry, Jessica. That won't stick. Even back in 1935, Senator Glass, a Democrat, attempted to repeal parts of his own legislation. Of course, that was before Democrats developed their hatred of a prosperous economy."

"And back then, Republicans didn't want to screw over the American people. What happened to you guys?"

This back and forth sniping continued. Reese tried to tamp down the increasingly vitriolic accusations. Once the program moved on to the taped interview with the Interior Secretary, Reese picked up the hotline to the control room.

"Tara, did you notice they didn't answer one question I asked? If we have people like Dandridge and Glendenning on again, I might as well quit. There's nothing close to honest analysis with them in the room."

ಬಿ ಬಿ ಛ ಛ

Carstairs shut off the television, and then turned to Sara, who was seated in the corner with Emily. "I'm sorry, Sara. I'm afraid whale watching is off. There's a storm coming."

CHAPTER 36

On Monday morning, President Farnum came down to the Oval Office earlier than usual. Harris Carver was still arranging the briefing folders with Amy Greene.

"Good morning, Mr. President," Amy greeted him, startled at his earlier-than-usual arrival.

"Good morning, Amy," Farnum said with none of his usual lightness. He signaled for Carver to come into the Oval Office. Carver complied, leaving the briefs in the outer office. The President closed the door behind them.

"Harris, what the hell is going on with CART?" Farnum demanded. "I thought Kadler was behind us."

"We're putting a briefing together for you now, Mr. President."

"CART was supposed to solve a problem, not create one. The media makes CART sound like Watergate. In fact, I heard someone on TV refer to it as CART-gate."

"Sir, it's not that bad."

"We need to act quickly, before this careens out of control."

"We are developing options, sir," Carver said calmly.

"Such as?"

"Among others, challenging the validity of Derek Cameron's claims. We may also need to reexamine Henry Stark's ability to manage CART."

"So in other words, we scapegoat someone." Farnum sighed. "Ah yes, the politics of personal destruction."

"Sir, the Republicans are chomping at the bit. They'll want somebody's head."

"Yes, but we both know whose head they really want. Do you really think Cameron or Stark will satisfy them? Scapegoating always looks exactly like what it is. We need to get ahead of this thing, be proactive, not reactive."

"We have already launched an internal investigation," Carver said.

"Internal? The Republicans will call it stonewalling."

"Well, I don't think a special prosecutor would be wise."

"Neither do I," Farnum agreed.

"Sir, the Republicans will call for hearings."

"But since we control Congress, I'm sure that's not going to happen."

"Perhaps we could change the conversation, *and* beat the GOP to the punch."

"Have us call for hearings on ourselves? Hearings rarely end well."

"If we simply say we are open to hearings, that'll steal the Republicans' thunder. That doesn't mean hearings actually have to happen."

"In other words, we stop any hearings through back channels."

"Yes, sir. But mentioning hearings before anyone else shows confidence and a lack of fear."

"That means both Steinberg in the Senate and Barnes in the House will need to hang tough on having no hearings."

"Steinberg's going to need us come next election, so she'll never allow hearings."

"Although that jackass Barnes just might."

"Well, say what you will about Barnes," Carver said, "he's a loyal Democrat. Even if he allows hearings, it's certainly better than a special prosecutor."

"Very well. Work up that briefing."

Farnum sat down and sighed. "Harris, has it occurred to you that this conversation has only been about political fallout?"

"Mr. President, to do all the great things, you first have to survive."

"You know, Harris, that's a very dangerous and sometimes self-deluding argument."

"Do you have an alternative, Mr. President?"

"No, that's why that argument is so dangerous."

� ৪০ ৫৪ ৫৪

In the early morning, David had taken to working out in the House gymnasium. He favored the treadmill over the stationary bike, primarily because of the better view of the television. The news had been mostly about CART and Derek Cameron's allegations. All the news channels were repeating the few details they had, over and over. However, the lack of detail didn't prevent Republicans from lambasting the President.

"Good morning."

David turned to find Arlo Hudge standing there, wearing a sweat shirt with suit pants and dress shoes.

"Sorry to keep you waiting," David said. "The treadmill is all yours."

"Actually, I was waiting for you, not the equipment."

"Really? What can I do for you, Congressman?"

"I wanted to talk to you 'bout Samu Harbor. It's comin' up for a subcommittee vote. And we'd like to know if we can count on you. We have all the Republican votes and even a few Democrats. Can I add your name to the list?"

"Do you mean my vote would break a tie?"

"I don't know about that. We haven't completed a vote count yet."

David suspected Hudge was lying about that. A subcommittee vote count was an easy thing to complete.

"Is the public funding still in it?" he asked, taking a towel and wiping his brow.

"Yes, but we still need your vote."

"Not if the taxpayers have to pay for it. Take out the public funding, and you have my vote."

"I got the impression you're not exactly a lefty, tree-huggin' type. I thought all that fuss at the hearing was for the cameras. You know this country needs energy, especially oil, don't you?"

"I know we need fossil fuels until renewable energy sources can be better developed. What's interesting is that you make speeches about how Americans need to be self-sufficient. You rail against any entitlement program that comes up, yet you want to subsidize multi-billion-dollar oil companies."

David could see Hudge was trying to contain his annoyance.

"This country built an interstate highway system for the sake of commerce," Hudge said.

"I thought Eisenhower pushed it for military purposes," David countered.

"Yeah, that's right," Hudge admitted, with increased annoyance showing. "But what got it passed was the potential for commerce. Dredging a harbor is no different."

"But it is different because there wasn't one single company benefitting from all the highway construction. Listen, I understand you're from Oklahoma, and the oil industry is a big contributor to your campaign."

"This isn't about campaign contributions," Hudge spat.

"Isn't it?"

"You say you don't want the people to foot the bill? All righty, fair enough. But let me be straight with you. One way or another, the people are going to pay, either via dredging now, or at the pump later."

"Polaron and every other oil company will charge whatever they can, regardless of dredging costs. I don't hold it against them. It's Economics 101. Oil is a commodity that sells at market-driven prices. We can't control that, unless you're suggesting price controls."

Hudge frowned at that last comment. "Grant, someday you're going to need my vote."

"And at that time, if I can't convince you on the merits of my bill, then I won't deserve your vote. If we have to buy each other's votes, then all we'll end up with is two bad bills."

"Are you really that naïve?" Hudge asked. "Or is that some liberal bill of goods your lesbo lieutenant sold you?"

"Excuse me? Who?"

"You know, Langford, that lipstick lesbian," Hudge said with utter disdain in his voice.

David glared at Hudge. "Excuse me, Congressman. I need to get showered before my first meeting."

ഇ ഇ ൚ ൚

All day, the news media were in full gear, discussing the CART scandal. Then, the White House announced an evening presidential press conference. On screens across the country "Special Report" animations swirled.

"Good evening. I'm Bob Summers with a special report. President Farnum has called a press conference, which will begin in a few minutes. No doubt, this is in response to the allegations made yesterday by Derek Cameron, the CART deputy chief auditor. We will be going to the White House Press Room any minute now. With us we have, Dylan Reese, our Chief Political Analyst and host of Reese's *American Caucus*, where he broke the news of the CART allegations." Summers turned to Reese. "Dylan, how serious do you feel Cameron's accusations are?"

"Well, very serious, especially if they've triggered the White House to call a press conference. The allegations—"

"Excuse me, Dylan," Summers said, holding his earpiece. "We have word that President Farnum is entering the press room now."

Farnum stepped up to the podium.

"Good evening. Yesterday, there was news that CART may not be completely operating according to its original design and intent. If this is true, it is unacceptable, regardless of whether any laws were violated or not. We have begun an informal investigation. If any processes need to be changed, we will do so."

"In addition, I have issued an executive order that any funds frozen in these quasi-savings accounts in Kadler-owned community banks be released to their rightful accountholders, so average Americans can pay their bills. In addition, there will be a thorough review of all judgments pertaining to Kadler Steele. Protecting the economic welfare of all Americans is a top priority of this administration."

"Furthermore, I welcome any hearings Congress may wish to hold. I hereby order all members of my administration to cooperate fully with any such hearings. This administration believes in full transparency, and will act accordingly. Now, I'll take some questions."

After the questions, the network cut back to Summers and Reese in the studio for some wrap-up commentary.

"So, that was President Farnum addressing charges that CART has been mismanaged." Summers turned to Reese. "Dylan, what strikes you most about tonight?"

"Well, first off, the speed in which the President moved out in front of this issue is quite remarkable. Our interview with Cameron was yesterday. And today the President vowed to clean up the mess before the specifics are even known. Past administrations have generally delayed bringing out the President. Even more significant is that the President brought up the idea of hearings before any outside critic. This means—"

Porter Barnes turned off the television and threw the remote control across his office, landing on the sofa. He picked up the phone and called Harris Carver at the White House. After a few minutes of waiting, he was connected.

"Good evening, Congressman."

"Harris, why the hell is the President talking about hearings?" Barnes demanded. "Do you honestly want hearings?"

"Of course not, Congressman," Carver answered.

"Then why?"

"Because we want you to say there's no need for hearings. Steinberg will say the same on the Senate side."

"I can't believe you're pulling this on me, you bastard. Well, what if I say I *want* hearings?"

"Then, you're free to call them, And, as the President stated, the administration will cooperate fully."

"Are you actually daring me to call for hearings to investigate a president of my own party?"

"It would be CART you'd investigate, not the President. Remember that. But yes, you're in the driver's seat on this one."

"Bastard!"

ꙮ ꙮ ꙮ ꙮ

Daniel Narlstrom had had a long day unpacking at his new apartment. Over the weekend, he dropped the first half of his belongings at his shop at Coburn Trucking, and the remainder here at the apartment. He wished he should have had a garage sale before he had sold the house. *Either way, a lifetime of stuff to sort through.*

The cable installer had arrived while he was unpacking. He was finishing up now.

"Okay, Mr. Narlson, you have TV, Internet and telephone," the installer said, handing him a tablet for an electronic signature.

Narlstrom didn't bother to correct him. He signed, not reading the half page of legal jargon. "Thank you," he said, handing back the clipboard. He wasn't sure whether he should tip the man or not. Jean always knew about tipping. The man didn't seem to be waiting for one, so he let it go.

After the installer left, Narlstrom went online and navigated to the unemployment website. He was slightly overdue for filing his biweekly claim. He couldn't remember the claim code. *Which box were those papers in?*

He rummaged through the boxes in search of his unemployment paperwork. Instead, he found his blueprints and patent applications. It made him mad just thinking about the day the government people came to his house and shut down his dream. He tossed the paperwork across the living room in frustration.

He was too exhausted to address the unemployment filing. He'd deal with it tomorrow. Instead, he dropped on the couch and turned on his newly connected television for a diversion. He channel-surfed for a while, but finally settled on some movie he hadn't seen before.

"You'll be through at this company!" an older actor yelled at a younger one.

"You think I care about your opinion?" the other actor snapped back.

"What are you going to do? Go over my head?"

"I'm not giving up. So if I have to leave a footprint on your fat forehead, so be it!"

Narlstrom hit the mute button and stared at the screen. The muted actors were still arguing. Over what, he still had no idea. Even without the sound, the younger actor's passion showed through. *I used to have that kind of fire in my belly.* He looked over his shoulder at the patent papers lying on the floor. *Why had I given up?* He glared at the papers. *What was it that Jamaican guy at Unemployment said? I should go to Washington?*

Hell, what do I have to lose?

CHAPTER 37

The CART media frenzy continued with little more than accusations and counter-accusations. Although David did do a few interviews for local Pennsylvania TV channels, he chose to stay out of the media crosshairs. Apparently, his rhetoric wasn't acidic enough to warrant national attention. Instead, he focused on generating support for his energy management bill, which had grown from a 33 million dollar project to over 230 million dollars. It had now ballooned to seven pilot projects, each one serving as an incentive for a key senator or representative.

David was about to head home for the weekend. But first, he wanted to review the progress with his staff.

"I think we have enough votes to clear the subcommittee," Ellen reported. "Wickham and Fontana are tentatively onboard. So are Lemmon, Parno and several others."

"We've steered clear of Arlo Hudge and his allies for the time being," Fred added.

"Good. He'd vote against it out of spite alone," David said. "When we're closer to a vote, I'll try to pitch it to him. Maybe he'll surprise us."

"How are Carstairs and McCord doing on the Senate side?" Fred asked.

"There shouldn't be any problems there," David said. "Carstairs and McCord are old pros."

"But they're not exactly popular with their respective parties," Fred said.

"Our job is to worry about the House version. Tyler, I want to see final revisions by Monday, or earlier if possible."

"Yes, sir."

"Okay, everybody, I'll see you all on Monday. Thanks."

Ellen stayed behind after the others left.

"Yes?" David said.

"This CART issue, I'm surprised you haven't jumped all over it, deriding dysfunctional government, *et cetera.*"

"I have no special insights. I'm not on the finance committee. Hey, I did do three local interviews."

"But you didn't really tear it up though."

"You mean I should make accusations without solid facts? No offense, but the Republicans are doing a fine job on that. They don't need me."

"You need to be heard and seen on this issue."

"I need to differentiate myself," David said.

"As the reasonable, thoughtful candidate?"

"Why not?"

"This isn't selling some nice commercial product. People want to see some outrage. Come election time, people will demand to know where you stood on this issue, and you want the video to prove it."

"I'll show my constituents some outrage tomorrow afternoon. I promise. In the meantime, could you send Fred in?"

Ellen nodded with a frustrated look on her face, but left quietly.

A few minutes later, Fred came in.

"Close the door," David mouthed.

Fred closed it.

"Fred," David began, speaking softly. "I've heard something—about Ellen."

"What kind of something?"

"Well, I don't want to spread a rumor, if it's not true."

"You mean that she might be a lesbian?"

David narrowed his eyes. "You knew?"

"Just a rumor," Fred said.

"Well, if it's true, it would explain a lot."

"Like what?" Fred asked, flopping on the sofa.

"Like why she came to work for the campaign in the first place. A known lesbian would be a pariah among the religious right."

"Do you feel she was dishonest in not disclosing this?"

"No, she said her personal baggage wouldn't interfere with my election. She was as good as her word."

"Do you want me to poke around? I could call Marcus Finn. He would know."

"No. Her personal life is just that, personal. But it does explain certain people's reaction when they realize she's my chief-of-staff."

David stood up, grabbed some folders and shoved them into his traveling bag. "Anyway, my train leaves in less than an hour. I better get going."

℘ ℘ ℘ ℘

It was a pleasantly warm day as David walked to the nearby Metro train station. Before heading to the platform, he went to buy a coffee and tried to pay the vendor with a twenty-dollar bill.

"Hey mister, come on," complained the rotund and sweaty coffee vendor. "Got anything smaller?"

David opened his wallet and tried to find a smaller bill. "Sorry, can you break a ten."

The vendor nodded, took it, and handed David a clammy wad of singles in return. He shoved them in his pocket and started walking to the platform. Looking at his watch, he realized it was later than he thought. He started to jog. David made the train with about a minute to spare. He quietly settled into a seat and took a sip of his coffee. *Damn, no sugar.*

He sat back and mentally reviewed his upcoming schedule. More and more, his weekends were being taken up with congressional business. In the morning, he had to meet with a handful of constituents at the local congressional office. Then, in the afternoon, he would participate in a political seminar at Winton College. He agreed to the seminar as a way of repaying Chuck Danzig for his support during the election. Also, it wouldn't hurt his reelection efforts down the line. He reminded himself to show some outrage to make Ellen happy.

After that, he and Sara planned to take Joe and Peggy Garthwell out for dinner. It was a small thank you for all the times they looked after Wendy. With David being in Washington and Sara often having to work late or go out of town, Peggy had become almost a second mother to Wendy.

David pulled the wrinkled bills from the coffee vendor out of his pocket, so he could air them out and put them in his wallet in an orderly fashion. It struck him oddly when he noticed a red stamp on one of the bills that read, "Track me at www.wheresgeorge.com." Curious, he pulled the tablet out of his bag and typed in the web address. David typed in the serial number of the bill in his hand. He was also required to type in a zip code.

The result was the travel history of this little piece of paper in his hand. The one-dollar bill was initially registered in Hood River, Oregon, a few years earlier. Several weeks later, it appeared in Seattle. Three months after that, it jumped all the way to Fulton, Missouri. Seven months later, Oakfield, New York. Then just over a year later, Watchung, New Jersey. Five months after that, Duluth, Georgia. And just one month before David bought his coffee, it returned north to Vienna, Virginia. And now, it had been registered in Washington, DC, heading to Embler, Pennsylvania. The site even included a map of the dollar's travels. David had never really thought about how far and wide currency traveled before.

David smiled in amusement. He wondered if Robert Hingecliff or anyone at the Treasury was aware of this website. Then, he had an idea. He turned the bill over to view the reverse side. It was a silly idea.

Just then, his cell phone rang.

"Hello."

"Hello, David? It's Jason Kennerly. I tried to call you at your office, but they said you'd already left for Embler. Is this a good time?"

"Sure, just hold on a second." David placed his tablet back in his bag, shoved the bills back in his pocket and moved to a vestibule to be considerate of the other passengers.

"So Jason, how have you been?" he asked in a low voice.

"Great. I've found nine people interested in running for the House, and two for the Senate."

"Now," David said, "we'll need to vet them, and see how electable they are."

"Sure. But better yet, I found, or rather, he found me—anyway, we have someone who wants to run for president."

David frowned. "Jason, don't forget our House strategy, you know, focusing our people and resources on smaller, more manageable electorates."

"But that's it, he's wealthy, I mean, really wealthy. Ever heard of Marshall Vreeland?"

"The name sounds vaguely familiar."

"He's made millions in construction and real estate. So, he can finance his own campaign."

"Yes, but he'll still lose, and that may hurt the credibility of the party."

"You don't know that," Kennerly insisted. "You won, and everybody told you you couldn't win."

"Ross Perot spent millions and didn't receive a single electoral vote. We need to stick to the strategy of focusing on congressional districts."

"Just meet him. Please."

"Let me think about it."

David hung up and sighed.

ဢ ဢ Ꮗ Ꮗ

Tyler looked up abruptly, reacting to the sound of footsteps. He found Jack Kripke standing outside the door.

"Good evening, Tyler."

"Mr. Kripke," Tyler said, surprised that anyone was here so late on a Friday. "I'm afraid the Congressman has already left for his home district."

"Not a problem. And please, call me Jack. So, how goes the Congressman's first piece of legislation?"

"What are you talking about?" Tyler asked.

"You know," Kripke began as he stepped into the small office, "the electrical management act, or whatever it's called."

"How did you know about that?" Tyler asked.

"Tyler, I know a lot of things. It's why I make the big bucks."

"No, I'm serious," Tyler insisted. "How did you specifically learn about this piece of legislation?"

"Very well. Your boss asked John Fontana to be a cosponsor. I'm friendly with his chief-of-staff. Don't worry, you haven't been compromised; I don't have any energy clients. I have no dog in that fight, scout's honor. I just like to know what's going on."

"So, will Fontana do it? Will he be a cosponsor?"

"That depends on you. I understand you're working on the first draft."

"*Final* draft, actually."

Kripke chuckled. "It'll be final, until it isn't. As it goes on, everyone will want to tweak it and make adjustments. How much has to be adjusted depends on how well you write it."

Tyler looked concerned.

"Would you like me to take a look?" Kripke offered.

"I don't think the Congressman would appreciate it if I shared this with anyone before he saw it."

"Good man. I would have lost respect for you if you had. Even if you can't share with me, I can still share some things with you."

"Like what?"

"My experience. Writing legislation is like creating a piece of artwork. It's not just about writing rules and parameters. It's about developing the right combination of nuances to get it past 535 of the most self-interested people in the world, the US Congress. The trick is to highlight the benefits, and obscure anything that might be perceived as objectionable. An old pro taught me that when I was a legislative assistant."

"How long were you a legislative assistant?"

"Four years with Senator Shannon Hawthorne."

"She's the one who died in a plane crash."

Kripke nodded. "She was a good senator, and a good person. I had moved on to greener pastures long before she died. Listen, I respect what you and Congressman Grant are trying to do. But when you've finished here with the Congressman, and gained a little more experience, I'd love for you to come work for me."

"Really?"

"Sure. The hours are a little better. The pay, *a lot* better. But most important, you can affect real change. People look down on lobbyists, but we can make a huge contribution to this country's laws. And, we don't have to run for reelection. Not a bad life. But I'm getting ahead of myself." Kripke pulled an envelope from his inside jacket pocket and offered it to Tyler.

"What's this?" he asked suspiciously.

"A series of general tips for writing your legislation. Use them. Don't use them. It's all up to you."

"Thank you."

"No problem. Have a good weekend, Tyler."

꿍 ꊓ ꆂ ꆆ

Sara picked up David at the train station

"Howdy, stranger," she said, as David moved into the passenger seat.

"Hi, gorgeous." He gave her a kiss on the cheek.

She started the car, and drove off.

"So how was the trip home?"

"Not bad, if you don't mind bad coffee."

"At least, it was some down time."

"No such luck. I received a call from Jason Kennerly along the way. Jason says he's found someone who wants to run for president under the Centrist banner. Some builder named Vreeland.

"Marshall Vreeland, who built the Zenith Center in Colorado?"

"You know him?"

"Not personally," Sara said. "But he puts up the most awful buildings. He maximizes floor space, but they are the ugliest things you'll ever lay your eyes on."

"I don't think he'll be running on the aesthetics of his buildings. If he runs. To be quite honest, I'm not thrilled with the idea of the party running a presidential candidate at all. Unfortunately, this Vreeland guy seems to have seduced Jason in some way. I've got a bad feeling about this."

CHAPTER 38

Once again, David found himself on the stage in Franklin Hall. The atmosphere was far more relaxed than the election debate the previous fall. Also on the panel were a local assemblyman and the head of the political science department. The audience contained a mix of students and local citizens.

President Danzig introduced the panel members as well as the moderator. For over an hour, David and the rest of the panel covered a broad range of current political topics. David did express some outrage at the Washington establishment, but kept his demeanor professional. The moderator finally opened the floor for questions. People lined up behind two microphones, one at the front of each aisle. Most of the questioners were students, but not all.

"I mean no disrespect, Congressman," said a young man, who David guessed was a freshman, barely older than his own son. "But why is the government trying to rip everyone off?"

"Although sometimes it may seem that way," David answered, "they're not really. However, there is a lot of narrow militant self interest in Washington. And, there's a lack of willingness to balance the interests of everyone. This has a lot to do with campaign finance. Whoever pays, gains access and influence, and pushes for their own desires above those of others. We really need comprehensive campaign finance reform. Unfortunately, there's a significant conflict of interest. The people who need to vote against the current system are the very same people who benefit from it."

"Why are you immune to this conflict of interest?" asked Armand Nistle from the opposing microphone.

David smiled. He wondered if Nistle would show up.

"That's a very good question. That's one people should be asking of all candidates and elected officials. Most members of Congress don't know any other life than working as an elected politician. But to answer your question, my self-worth and livelihood aren't tied to whether I'm a congressman or not. If any of you followed my election last year, it was far from a sure bet. I certainly didn't expect to win."

Nistle followed up. "If you didn't expect to win, why did you run?"

"I ran to make a statement that the majority is in the middle, not at the extremes."

Nistle seemed satisfied and sat down. David suspected President Danzig had warned him to "play nice."

An older man with a baseball cap stepped up to the other microphone. "What I'd like to know is why your pal, the President, is trying to fuck us all over with this CART thing?"

"Excuse me, sir." Danzig called out. "That language is…"

Suddenly, a tomato flew from the back corner of the auditorium. David just barely sidestepped the incoming vegetable. Unfortunately, the professor next to him was not so nimble. Her green jacket and blouse were saturated with red tomato, the juice dripping as she tried to wipe the pulp off with her hand.

"Screw you and everyone in Washington!" yelled someone from the back. A second tomato came flying. It fell just short of the stage, bursting as it hit an audience member in the back of the head.

An overweight security officer started to chase the perpetrator, but the wiry young man had too much of a head start.

"Really? Tomatoes? Isn't that a bit cliché?" David called out, trying to relieve the tension with some humor. He turned to see the tomato-stained professor was not amused.

The event wound down fairly quickly after that. Within minutes, the police had arrived. Apparently, campus security had called local law enforcement. The term "attack" had been misinterpreted as a shooting, bringing a response by a SWAT team. It made for a chaotic few moments. But eventually everything calmed down. Afterwards, Danzig pulled David aside.

"I'm really sorry about all this. There has been a lot student activism lately, but just meetings and small rallies, all peaceful stuff. I wouldn't have expected anything like this."

"I guess people are angrier than I realized. Unfortunately, poor Professor Mulrooney bore the brunt of it."

"But still, that tomato was aimed for you."

"Then, I guess I should pay for her dry cleaning."

"Don't worry; the college'll pick it up. Anyway, I know you have dinner plans, but there was something else I wanted to discuss with you," Danzig said, guiding David into the hallway. "My contacts tell me the President's education bill is coming up for a vote soon."

"You must have fantastic contacts," David said. "I've been asking the White House and Department of Education for a draft for months. The administration's been playing their cards pretty close to the chest."

"Well, I'm told it'll be good for colleges and students."

"The devil is in the details."

"The legislation will be very important to Winton."

"You have those kind of specifics?"

"Not too specific, but I consult with college presidents and others. So, I hear things. When I took over as President of Winton, I was charged with bringing the college up to snuff financially. We need that bill."

David frowned. "What do you know that I don't?"

"It's harder to sell high-cost education in this economic environment. While the bill provides no direct grants, my understanding is it will make it easier for students to get financial aid."

"The government already offers some generous financial aid grants."

"It's not just about the amount, but the ways it can be used."

"Obviously, I'm a big supporter of education. I'll see what I can do."

"Great. By the way, how's Fred Arkin doing these days?"

"He's good. I've been keeping him quite busy."

"Whenever you're finished in Washington, both of you will have a place back here at Winton, and I don't mean as adjuncts."

"Thank you, Chuck. That's very kind. Anyway, I better get going," David said looking at his watch. "Sara will be getting nervous."

ಬಂ ಬಂ ೞ ೞ

That night, the Grants took Joe and Peggy Garthwell to Fortella's, their favorite restaurant. David was recounting the tomato incident. "They're conducting forensics on the tomato to see which garden it came from," he joked.

"Can they really do that?" Peggy Garthwell asked.

"No, I'm just kidding," David admitted. "But whoever it was had a good arm. I told the police to look at pitchers and quarterbacks."

"David Grant," Peggy said in a stern tone a mother might use. "It's not nice to lie to your pastor."

David smiled. "Is my nose growing?"

"Hey, you are a politician now," Sara quipped, taking a sip of wine.

"Ouch," David said, feigning personal insult.

"Didn't you have trouble from a tomato guy before?" Joe Garthwell asked. "What was his name?"

"Paul Lurtz? No, he was fine. He wore tomatoes; but didn't throw them," David said. "I have to admit it's good to get out of Washington, and be with friends."

"Here, here," Joe Garthwell said, raising a glass. "To being with friends."

"To friends," they all toasted.

At that point, their entrees arrived.

"So David," Garthwell said. "I've been meaning to ask you, how does one go about getting government contracts?"

"Joe, you can't ask that sort of thing," Peggy said, mortified.

"I'm not asking him to do anything illegal."

"You're trying to take advantage of David's position," Peggy snapped.

"I'm just asking a question. It's not like I'm asking him to pull any strings."

"It's all right, Peggy," David interrupted. "I'd be glad to provide information. It's pretty standard stuff. I'll have someone from my office contact you."

"Thanks. The only reason I'm asking is that business is getting a little tight. Nobody knows what's going to happen with the economy. So clients are holding off making any business commitments. I'm just looking for new markets."

"Joe, it's alright. This Kadler Steele-CART mess isn't good for anyone, except maybe tomato farmers."

ဢ ဢ ಇ ಇ

Sunday morning was a lazy one at the Grant household. They had Belgian waffles in their pajamas. While waiting for Chris to finish his shower, David turned on the television to watch *American Caucus*. He had missed the opening.

"With us this morning," Dylan Reese announced, "we have Congressman Porter Barnes, chair of the House Finance committee."

David groaned.

"Last week on this show," Reese continued. "Derek Cameron, a member of the CART audit team, made some serious charges that there was corruption."

"Congressman, as chair of the House Finance Committee, what is your assessment of how CART is operating?"

"Like any bureaucracy, there have been mistakes, especially when dealing with such a complex entity as Kadler Steele. The freezing of these customer accounts, which Kadler mislabeled, is an example. And notice, once the administration learned of this problem, the President acted quickly with an executive order to unfreeze these accounts."

"What about Derek Cameron's charges about the inappropriate order in which cases are being handled?"

"Mr. Cameron is a bit young. What? Does he want the cases to be handled in alphabetical order? In size order? By age? Maybe young Derek should get out of short pants before he tells more experienced people how to drive the car."

David could feel his blood pressure rising as he listened to Barnes.

"But the question remains," Reese persisted, "shouldn't someone in the administration or Congress have known about these problems?"

"I only learned about the consumer account problem last weekend, thanks to the fine reporting on your show."

"That's a lie! I told you myself," David yelled at the screen. "And I know others did, too!"

"Honey, please calm down," Sara pleaded. "We want a pleasant family day. Remember?"

"Okay, okay" he said. It galled him to hear such an outright lie, one he had personal knowledge of.

"What's the point of coming home, if you can't unwind?" Sara asked rhetorically.

"Yes, dear."

Barnes went on to compliment Henry Stark's performance. Eventually, a commercial break came. When the program returned, Reese had a new guest.

"We have Hanna Dalton from Salvage And Liberate America, also known as SALA. Welcome to the program."

"Thank you."

"So for the benefit of our audience, please explain what your organization is about."

"We are a grass roots protest and activist group. We are Americans who are sick and tired of the shenanigans that go on in Washington, for instance that shameful Mr. Barnes you had on earlier."

Reese bristled at the insult to a previous guest.

Thank God, Barnes hasn't fooled everyone, David thought.

"Watching that man was like the scene from The Wizard of Oz," Dalton continued. "'Pay no attention to the man behind the curtain.' Do politicians really think we're that stupid?"

"It may be emotionally gratifying to take pot shots at politicians, Ms. Dalton. But what specifics do you have?"

"Here's what I know: Unemployment is on the rise. The top one percent are getting richer. The stock market has dropped, destroying people's retirement savings, provided Kadler Steele wannabes haven't already fleeced them. I mean, why hasn't Corbin Beaumont been put on trial? Why is he still CEO of Kadler Steele? What the hell is going on? And forgive the movie cliché, but 'we're as mad as hell, and we're not going to take it anymore.' What will it take to get their honest and constructive attention?"

"Now, you're speaking at a rally this week, correct?"

"Only briefly. Our main speaker is Jarvis Thayer, founder of SALA. We'll be on the Washington Mall on Tuesday. Jarvis will be speaking at twelve noon." Dalton said. "If President Farnum doesn't like it, he can arrest us like they did in the sixties."

"Are you expecting violence?"

"Of course, not. But we want the politicians to see the pain and anger average Americans are feeling. If they're not going to listen one way, they'll ultimately have to listen another."

"That sounds like a threat," Reese said.

"No, just a prediction if our politicians don't wake up."

CHAPTER 39

By Monday mid-morning, David had returned to Washington. On the train back, he mulled over what he wanted to do about Porter Barnes. With Barnes, Joe Garthwell's awkward request for a political favor, and flying tomatoes, he was not feeling quite as refreshed as he would have hoped.

"Good morning, Congressman," Tyler said, walking out of his office. "I have the next draft of the bill." He handed David a thick folder.

"Is this the final draft?" David asked.

"Until you or someone else says otherwise."

David nodded. "Has Ellen seen this yet?"

"She's reading it now. Should I get her?"

"No. Let her finish reading. Thank you."

David walked into his office and closed the door behind him. He tried to read the text Tyler had assembled, but the unnatural syntax of the legislative copy was unlikely to hold David's attention on his best day. He had to refocus himself several times, but his mind kept returning to Barnes.

Ellen knocked softly on the door.

"Come in."

"I heard you had some tomato trouble on Saturday."

"How did you know about that?"

"Someone in Fred's department does ongoing searches for your name in the media. The incident was mentioned in a couple of the local online newspapers."

"Yes, I guess I didn't show enough outrage. But, I'll be correcting that soon. What time is the House Press Gallery available?"

"Well, it's a little late. All the CART outrage in the media is dissipating. The media has a short attention span. Now, they're focusing more on the earthquake in Chile."

"Don't worry. I'll breathe some more life into the CART story. Just get me the press gallery schedule. Meanwhile, have you read the draft of the bill?"

Ellen nodded. "It was better than I expected. Tyler did a very good job, actually a surprisingly good job. We may have underestimated him."

"And it covers everything we outlined?"

"Yes."

"Okay, send copies over to Carstairs and McCord."

ಚಿ ಚಿ ಚ ಚ

Shortly after lunch, David walked into the House press gallery. The reporters looked up, then at one another. When David walked up to the microphones, the camera operators scrambled to activate their equipment. He waited for them.

"Good afternoon, everyone. I don't ordinarily come down and chat with you. My name is David Grant. I am the Independent Representative from Pennsylvania's 20th District."

One of the reporters chuckled at David's awkward self-introduction. The party leaders who ordinarily stood at these microphones didn't have to explain who they were.

"I assume you are all familiar with Porter Barnes's interview over the weekend, where he claimed he was unaware that citizens' personal Kadler Steele accounts had been frozen by CART. His statement was false."

David looked out at the reporters. He had their full attention now.

"I know this because I personally brought constituent complaints to his attention several days before the news broke. And this was after spending a couple of weeks trying to schedule a meeting with him. Congressman Barnes's response was cavalier and indifferent. Despite my telling him my constituents weren't investing, merely saving, he said, 'your constituents should have invested better.' After which, he proceeded to insult me. Personal insults aside, he showed gross indifference to the plight of average Americans."

"This is the same man who announced yesterday he won't hold hearings into CART's handling of the Kadler Steele affair. It begs the question: Why?"

David was caught off guard by the sudden cacophony of voices yelling out questions. Taking a deep breath, he held up his hands. "One at a time." He pointed to a random reporter.

"Congressman, are you calling for hearings or a special prosecutor?"

"Perhaps those might be in order, but for the time being, I am simply pointing out misinformation that has been disseminated."

"In other words, you're calling Porter Barnes a liar?" Another reporter called out.

"Yes, I suppose I am," David said. "I'm not with a major party, so I'm free to tell the truth. In this case, Congressman Barnes lied about not knowing about the nature of the frozen accounts. What else has he lied about?"

ᛒᚩ ᛥᚩ ᚳᛈ ᚳᚩ

Daniel Narlstrom's legs and back were cramping. He'd lost count of the hours he'd been on the bus. But finally, the coach had arrived in Washington. *Thank God.* He had little sleep, none of it restful.

From the bus station, Narlstrom took a cab to his hotel. Despite the frugality of taking a bus, he chose a nice hotel, the sort he would have stayed in when he was still working for Ariskor. Once he checked in and dragged his luggage into the room, he flopped on the bed. It was infinitely more comfortable than the bus. As he lay there, he realized he could easily drift off to sleep.

Catching himself, Narlstrom abruptly sat up. He had a 10:30 a.m. appointment with Wyatt Wickham, his congressman. He set his alarm, but also arranged for a wake-up call. He double-checked all his papers. He had brought extra copies to leave with Wickham, if necessary. Nothing was to be left to chance. He had to make a good impression.

Then, his eye caught the garment bag on the floor. *My suit.* He quickly unzipped it. The suit had a network of wrinkles from being compressed in the bus's luggage compartment. It reminded Narlstrom of a road map. These wrinkles would have to be eradicated. He started to feel panicky. The room had an iron, but he was afraid he would burn his suit. Jean had purchased a portable steamer years before, but he hadn't brought it with him.

Steam. Humidity. That's what he needed. He hung the trousers and jacket on separate hangers on the bathroom curtain rod and turned on the shower's hot water. Within minutes, the bathroom filled with the humidity he desired. He closed the door, allowing the steam to engulf his suit. No detail could stand in his way.

෨ ෨ ෬ ෬

"My fellow patriots," Ben Glendenning bellowed at the camera. "This is exactly what I have been saying for years. The Democrats are liars. And the Left can't blame their troubles on party politics. Congressman Grant has no party. He's independent confirmation of the aloof, deceitful and uncaring nature of liberal Democrats. You know, for decades the Democrats have been portraying Conservatives as cold-hearted monsters. Who are the cold-hearted ones now? Care to answer that, Porter Barnes?"

෨ ෨ ෬ ෬

"It's obvious this so-called Independent, David Grant," Jessica Dandridge said, "is a pawn of the Right. His alleged conversation with Congressman Barnes conveniently has no witnesses. This marks a new and dishonest tactic for ultra-conservative Republicans, using pretend-moderate puppets. It's either that or Grant's getting some sort of payoff. Or maybe the poor dear just wants some attention."

෨ ෨ ෬ ෬

By that evening, Carstairs and McCord had approved the draft of David's bill. The next morning, David headed to Wyatt Wickham's office.

"Good morning, David," Wickham said, as David walked into the chairman's office.

"Good morning Wyatt. Thanks for seeing me. I have the finalized draft of the energy management bill. I thought I'd deliver it to you personally.

223

Assuming it meets with your approval, when do you think we could have a vote by the sub-committee?"

"Well, I'm afraid, I'm going to have to put the bill on hold."

"Why?"

Wickham sighed. "You attacked Porter Barnes yesterday. It's been all over the news."

"Yes, I know. But that has nothing to do with the bill. I had to tell the truth about Barnes. I didn't attack Democrats in general, or anyone else."

Wickham picked up a piece of paper from his desk. "You said, 'I'm not with a major party, so I'm free to tell the truth.' This implies that those of us in a major party are *not* free to tell the truth."

"You know I didn't mean it that way," David insisted.

"When we first met, I warned you about being a show horse. Don't get me wrong; I have no love for Barnes. Just last year, that S-O-B cost my district a major defense contract. But David, you attacked a key Democrat during a critical moment. You created a media shit storm."

"Wyatt, the man lied. He's Chair of the Banking Committee, and he lied to the country about the one issue people care most about. Barnes knew damn well what was going on with those gateway accounts, if for no other reason than that I alerted him personally. And I'm sure I'm not the only one."

"Look, the bill's not dead. But the Speaker will have my head if he sees me rewarding you with a successful bill right now."

"The bill isn't for me; it's for the country."

"David, I know. I'm not killing it, just delaying it until this storm blows over. If I forward it now, Wilkers would just kill it before it made it to the Floor. He's pretty pissed at you. Keep your head down, and I'll see what we can do."

"How long?"

"I don't know."

"It's ironic." David said. "Barnes lied. I told the truth. But who gets screwed?"

"That's the power of belonging to a party. If you were a Democrat, I could back you up. Maybe it's time you reconsidered your stance on that."

David didn't answer. He felt like he had been punched in the stomach.

Wickham stepped closer. "Don't get too discouraged. Sometimes things just take longer than we expect. Have faith."

"Faith in Washington? I don't know."

David walked out, passing an argument under way in the Wickham's outer office. Some man was angrily demanding to see the Congressman.

"I made the appointment last week," Narlstrom insisted. "And I confirmed it three days ago."

"Unfortunately, we had to cancel it early yesterday," Wickham's secretary said. "We left a message on your voice-mail."

"I've been on a bus for the last two days," Narlstrom snapped.

"I'm sorry, sir, but you should have checked your voice-mail."

"I've come over a thousand miles to see the Congressman, and I'm not leaving."

Wickham came out to see what was going on. Narlstrom recognized him immediately.

"Congressman, we have an appointment," he insisted. "But your secretary now says we don't."

Wickham looked to his secretary.

"You remember, the gentleman with the patent issue," she explained. "Mr. Narlstrom didn't realize we cancelled the meeting."

"It's *Doctor* Narlstrom," he snapped.

"My apologies, Doctor." Wickham said. "Please come in. I have a caucus meeting shortly, so I only have a few minutes." He motioned Narlstrom to a comfortable-looking chair.

"I read your letter and had members of my staff make inquiries with the NSA and the Pentagon. They say your designs are derivative of your defense work at Ariskor, and therefore classified and ineligible for patent protection."

"Of course, they'd said that. They're a bunch of idiots who don't understand thermodynamics. They wouldn't know an exothermic reaction from an endothermic one. But I do." Narlstrom began unrolling schematic plans. "I can show you the difference. See this thermo-coupling design, it's—"

"Doctor," Wickham interrupted, "I'm not qualified to judge the science, certainly not in the time we have."

"Congressman," Narlstrom pleaded. "You're my last hope. I lost my job when Ariskor lost the Cold Vulcan contract. Then, this CART thing locked up all my money."

"The President just unfroze those accounts."

"Did he? Well, I haven't heard anything from the bank," Narlstrom said. "Anyway, I've lost my wife and my house as a result. Damn it, I'm just asking to be able to make a living using my own skills and ideas. But a bunch of ignorant bureaucrats say I can't work in my chosen field because of *national security*, as if making a better industrial insulator would threaten anyone's security."

"I'm sorry. I regret the loss of the Ariskor contract. I fought hard for it. Regrettably, the program cancellation was the result of political infighting."

"Political infighting? Is that worth a man's dignity? A man's livelihood?"

"Of course, not," Wickham said. "I'm sorry, there's nothing I can do. I can't override the Pentagon on technical points I don't understand."

∞ ∞ ∞ ∞

David walked back to his office. He looked out the window at the crowds milling around on the streets. He wondered what was going on.

"Is everything alright, Congressman?" Ellen asked.

"No."

225

"What happened?"

"Apparently, by telling the truth about Porter Barnes, I've offended the Democratic Party. Wickham won't bring the bill to a vote."

"I'm sorry. But on the other hand, you calling Barnes out went over very well with your constituents. Fred told me supportive emails and phone calls have been coming in all morning."

"Great. I'm popular with my constituents, but important legislation has been stalled. Tell me that's not dysfunctional government."

Carol knocked at the door.

"Excuse me, Congressman," she said. "I'm sorry to interrupt. There's a Lieutenant Garcia, from the Capitol Police, here to see you."

"Really?" David asked. "Send him in." He turned to Ellen. "I wonder what the police want."

A stocky man in a police uniform came in. "Good morning, Congressman," Garcia said.

"Hello, Lieutenant. What can I do for you?"

"The Pennsylvania State Police reported there was an assault against you two days ago, at Winton College. Do you have any idea who it may have been?"

"No. Probably a student. It was just a flying tomato near the end of a seminar. I don't think it was personal. He yelled something like 'screw everyone in Washington.' It didn't even hit me."

"Sir, contact is not required for an assault to take place. And we take threats against members of Congress of any kind very seriously, particularly on a day like today."

"Why today?"

"SALA is having a rally today."

"SALA?"

"Salvage And Liberate America. They're a new protest group."

"You think there's a connection between my tomato thrower and these people?"

"We don't know. But we don't want to take any chances. We're advising all members of Congress to not wear their congressional pins when outside of the Capitol complex. I know you might be curious about the rally, but we advise you to avoid it. In fact, since you've recently been in the news, your face might be in someone's short-term memory. That makes you a higher-than-average-risk target."

David looked at Ellen. "Great, another benefit of publicity." He turned back to the Lieutenant. "Has this group been violent?"

"Not really, but there was a shoving incident earlier this morning."

"Well, no demonstrator's going to push me around. That's what Congress is for."

CHAPTER 40

Daniel Narlstrom left Wickham's office. Despite Wickham's sincere regrets, the Congressman provided nothing of value. Narlstrom walked away from the Capitol complex. He was oblivious to the crowds that had developed. He hadn't been in Washington in years, and had no idea this level of crowding was abnormal. As he walked west, he could hear a speech coming from a distant loudspeaker. Yet, it was Wickham's feeble words that rang in his ears. *I'm sorry.*

As he walked closer, the snippets and phrases grew louder.

"The President and the Congress…a disgrace…rigging the game…a great wreck that needs to be salvaged…damaged the economy…breaking the social contract."

Mary Fitzgibbons was speaking. She hadn't expected to address such a large crowd, or to speak at all for that matter. She was just a volunteer, helping with logistics. But Jarvis Thayer, the main speaker, was not ready, or more precisely, missing.

Hanna Dalton was frantically searching through the chaos for Thayer. Finally, she found him behind the canvas backdrop. He was talking—more like flirting—with Tess Cassiere, an actress who had recently joined the movement. Dalton found it odd that Cassiere's manager kept coming around "just to check on her."

"Jarvis, are you ready to go on?" Hanna Dalton demanded.

"What's the rush?" Thayer asked.

"It's noon. Mary's vamping in front of thousands of people because you're not ready."

"Mary's doing great."

"But you're our founder, and you're supposed to go on at noon," Dalton said, guiding Thayer around to the front of the backdrop.

"These people," he said, pointing at the crowd, "aren't going anywhere. What's the difference?"

"The difference is I told everyone in the media you would be speaking at exactly twelve noon. See those cameras?" she said, pointing up at the media platform. "They're why we're here."

"Okay, just give me a minute."

When Thayer was in the zone, his rhetoric was sharp and inspirational. His winning smile and good looks made him quite charismatic. However, Hanna realized certain things were beyond him, such as understanding logistics or punctuality.

"Jarvis?" Dalton called out. "It's time."

He approached the podium and waited for Fitzgibbons to wind up and introduce him.

"My fellow distressed citizens," Fitzgibbons said. "I'd like to introduce the founder of Salvage And Liberate America, Jarvis Thayer."

The crowd erupted in applause.

"I could kill him," Fitzgibbons whispered to Dalton.

"Get in line."

"American brothers. American sisters," Thayer called out to the crowd. "That's what we are, brothers and sisters. Family. Family looks after one another. But our brothers and sisters in the government have lost sight of that.

Where the hell did this brothers-and-sisters crap come from? Where's the fire? Where's the anger we need?"

Dalton could hear the mumbling of the crowd. They weren't disapproving, but they weren't quite entranced. Thayer was capable of much more. Then, the realization came. *Oh my God, he wants to be loved by this crowd.* The last several weeks of rallies and demonstrations had gone to his head. Then, she looked over at Cassiere, who was beaming.

"What the hell is going on?" Fitzgibbons asked.

"Jarvis is getting some from the actress. And apparently she took his balls."

"Over the past few months, talking to people," Thayer continued. "I've learned how you, and those like you, have been treated so unfairly. I want to hear your stories, your stories of hope, your stories of pain. Who wants to testify?"

"Testify?" Mary asked.

"Shit, he's going all Southern revival on us," Dalton muttered. She walked over to the podium and put her hand over the microphone. "What the hell are you doing?"

"We need to give our fellow Americans a voice," Thayer answered.

"Give them *your* voice. This isn't a revival meeting. We need focus, a call-to-action, not a series of impromptu Kumbaya testimonials."

"Trust me, Hanna." Thayer flashed his handsome smile. "Sometimes you have to give power to get power."

She looked out at the crowd. They had gone from pregnant pause to awkward silence.

"Let's start with Tess," he said. "She can get us going."

"What?" Now, Dalton knew why Cassiere and her agent were here. *That vacuous blonde wants a career boost with our publicity.*

Cassiere walked up to the podium with a drop-dead gorgeous smile. "I hate what this government has become," Cassiere screamed. "I hate it. I hate it. I hate it. We have to love each other, and lookout for one another."

Dalton couldn't bear to listen to the rest. *A stupid actress without a script. Brilliant!*

After Cassiere finished her I-hate-it diatribe, another man climbed up to testify. He was a veteran named Harry Branch, who described his experience after he had returned from Iraq. He was more articulate, and more strident, but off the mark relative to the SALA cause.

228

Narlstrom watched all this from the edge of the crowd. He started pushing inward. His arms became the Jaws of Life, separating the people in his drive to climb to that podium. It was like an out-of-body experience, as he walked right up to the platform.

Jarvis looked down at this man in his suit, so out of place from the crowd, where everyone was dressed casually.

"Are you from the government?"

"Hell, no. But, I was blind."

"You have something to say?"

Narlstrom nodded.

"Then testify, my friend," Thayer said, gesturing to the podium.

Narlstrom was dizzy, but determined.

"I was blind. I was comfortable. I was part of the great military industrial complex. I thought life was tough, but that in the end, intelligence, hard work, and persistence could win out. But, the game is fixed. I was blind. I didn't know what the government was putting people through. But now, I realize this is not the government I grew up respecting and honoring. This is not the government that fought the Nazis and the Communists. It is not the government that stood up for civil rights. This is a government that is so isolated from its own people. They're immune to reality."

"Less than an hour ago, I met with my Congressman. That's what you're supposed to do. Right? He had no interest in the problems of real people. All he wanted to do was go to his caucus meeting."

He looked down at his shaking hands, grasping the podium edges for dear life. His knuckles were white.

"This government took away my job. It stole my money. They doggedly destroyed my dreams and self worth. If it wasn't for the government seizing our funds, my dear wife would be alive today. She is dead because of them! This government does not represent the American people. We are just cattle to them! This government is not my government! They couldn't care less. They will make orphans of us all!"

Orphans? Narlstrom looked out at the crowd. *What am I doing here?* Tears started to roll down his face. He stepped back from the podium. *All those faces. What have I done?*

Narlstrom turned right and walked away from the podium, through the crowd, oblivious to those around him, even oblivious to what direction he was traveling. The crowd was silent.

He had denounced his own country in a fit of anger. Yet everything he said was true. *Except maybe the orphans.* He walked as if he were trying to run away from his words and memories.

Narlstrom ran until he couldn't. Suddenly, a body of water was blocking his way. It was the tidal basin. *Should I jump in?* Instead, he fell to his knees and sobbed.

"Sir?" a woman called out. She placed her hand on his shoulder. "Sir, are you alright?"

"No," he said in a low resigned voice. "Did I actually speak in front of all those people? Say all those things?" He recognized her as one of the women from the rally. "I'm sorry. I was so angry."

"I heard what you said. You spoke the truth. I think you touched everyone. Please come back with me."

"No. no." His head was spinning. "I'm so embarrassed."

"It's okay. We can just sit." She motioned over to a nearby park bench. "My name's Hanna."

"I'm…I'm Dan…just Dan."

CHAPTER 41

A few weeks later, an Energy & Power Subcommittee meeting was winding up. As David was packing up his briefcase, Arlo Hudge came over.

"I understand you've put together some kind of energy management bill," Hudge said.

"It's been shelved," David answered, as he dropped the last folder into his case, "at least for the time being."

"That's unfortunate."

"Really? I didn't think it was the type of bill you'd support."

"Don't get me wrong," Hudge said. "I think developing more energy should be our top priority, not tweaking consumption around the edges. But, your bill's harmless."

"If you think it's a waste, why would you support it?"

"It doesn't matter what I think of your bill. It only matters what you think, as in how badly you want it."

David smiled. "And let me guess the price of your support. You want me to vote for the Samu dredging project with full funding?"

"Now you're getting the hang o' things," Hudge said, smiling. "We just merge the two bills, and it'll get outta committee faster than a bull in a cactus patch."

"Let me think it over."

"Fair enough, but Samu's comin' up for a vote pretty soon. Don't wait too long."

⁚ ⁘ ⁓ ⁃

Later, David met Howard Carstairs and Cal McCord for lunch in the Senate Dining Room, which David noted was much nicer than the House cafeteria. The two senators were already seated, waving David over.

"Good afternoon, Howard, Cal."

"Good afternoon," Carstairs said.

"So David, what's new?" McCord asked.

"Well, Arlo Hudge just offered a deal, funding Samu Harbor dredging in exchange for merging it with our energy management bill. What do you think?"

"It's an opening," McCord said. "But, knowing Hudge, he'll probably stick it to you somehow."

"I suspected as much. But after I screwed up going after Barnes, I'm wondering if I have any choice."

"You have to stop beating yourself up about that," Carstairs said. "Barnes is a weasel who needed to be called on the carpet." He looked at

McCord. "I'm sorry; it's true. Everyone in my party agrees on that." He leaned forward and whispered, "So do some Democrats, privately at least."

McCord nodded in uncomfortable agreement.

The waiter came and took their orders.

"I guess I should be more careful about irritating Barnes and his friends."

"He doesn't have friends," Carstairs said, "just people he hasn't pissed off yet."

"If he's so obnoxious and despised, how did he become so powerful?"

"He has one hell of a donor list," McCord explained. "Somehow, he can direct donations to others quite easily."

"So, he buys votes with campaign donations," David concluded. "I knew people did that to get elected, but I guess I was under the naïve assumption that once here, everyone rolled up their sleeves to do some honest work."

"And most do. But nothing's black and white. Can't do the good stuff like your energy bill, unless we get reelected."

"Speaking of the bill, how are things coming on the Senate side? You two haven't said much."

"The Democratic majority is generally favorable to this type of bill," McCord assured him.

"Plus," Carstairs added, "when you add a few RINOs, we have it covered. The Senate is a bit more collegiate and cooperative than the hurly burly of the House."

"Then, why hasn't anything come up for a vote?" David asked.

"Nobody wants to commit until they see a House bill," McCord explained. "Why put in the time unless there's a bill on the other side headed to Conference?"

"And my outburst delayed that. So I guess, that brings us back to Hudge's offer."

"As far as Hudge goes, he might screw us," said Carstairs. "Then again, he might not. It's a gamble."

"Taking that gamble, and adding in the dredging project," David said, "means spending over half a billion dollars for a project that was only supposed to cost 33 million."

Carstairs nodded. "Compromise can be a powerful tool, but an expensive one."

છ છ ભ ભ

Gregory Farnum was finishing his lunch in his private study, just adjacent to the Oval Office. He was reading a DNC brief, when Harris Carver came to the door.

"Mr. President, Amy said you wanted to see me."

"Harris, these SALA people are becoming quite an issue. They're running rallies in all the major cities, especially in states we need to win. We need to change the narrative, lead the charge."

"Did you have anything particular in mind, sir?"

"Well, a good war might do the trick. Who should we invade?"

Carver smiled. "Belgium. I'm getting really sick of their snooty chocolates."

They both laughed.

"But seriously, every time we get ready to launch our education initiative, something comes up to disrupt it. Kadler, CART, etc. Meanwhile, the economy is drifting. The Dow is down over 270 points this morning alone. And, I've gotten a peek at next week's unemployment figures. No one's going to be happy over them either. I can't blame these SALA people too much."

"Harris, we need to do two things at the same time: bolster the economy and launch our education bill. And I'm tired of waiting"

Carver sat down across from Farnum.

"Sir, if we launch the education bill, the Republicans will scream we're neglecting the rest of the country. If we crank up spending to stimulate the economy, they'll wave the tax-and-spend flag."

"We combine them into a strategic investment bill," Farnum explained. "Education is a natural strategic investment."

"I think that'll work, but it'll be a huge spending bill. Your opponents will use the S-word."

"Stimulus? Yeah, I know. But if it's a big train, everyone'll want a ride. Let's build in something for everyone. Find out what each member of Congress wants more than anything else. Then, figure out how to make it a *strategic investment*."

ॐ ॐ ॐ ॐ

Early the next morning, David drove down Route 95 to a hotel in Fredericksburg, Virginia for a Centrist Patriots Party conference. During the breakfast, he made the rounds. Many of the state party leaders and prospective candidates from the party had flown in. David recognized some as volunteers who helped him with his campaign and took the opportunity to thank them again.

After the breakfast, the main event session began. Jason Kennerly stood at the hotel podium beaming. On the screen next to him a projected PowerPoint presentation displaying the Party logo.

David made a note to himself to talk to Jason about initiating more professional graphics.

"Good morning, everyone," Jason greeted them. He proceeded to remind the audience of the origins of the Centrist Patriots Party, concluding with, "The road has been long and grueling. But recently, we have seen some real progress."

233

"I'd like to introduce the most successful candidate the CPP has ever had. He's given the President a piece of his mind." The logo on the screen dissolved to the photograph of David in the Oval Office. "He's put Washington on notice." The image dissolved to a split screen of David at his press conference and an uncomplimentary picture of Porter Barnes. "And never has it been needed more. It is my pleasure to present our friend, Congressman David Grant."

David stepped to the podium. He was met with a standing ovation, which caught him off guard.

"Thank you. Thank you. You've just made me realize I do need to leave Washington more often."

More applause erupted.

"People often ask me what it's like being a Congressman. The answer is I don't know completely. To be truthful, I am fairly isolated. Not having my own party in Congress means I have to live by a slightly different set of rules. But, I'm hoping you can help change that."

"This morning. I met a number of you who are planning to run for the House in the next election. I look forward to the day when you and I stand side by side in the House Chamber. People are quite frustrated. We need to harness that unrest and turn it into constructive action. Many of you saw the SALA rally in Washington a few weeks ago. It was the anguish and raw pain of our citizens laid bare. Yet, there was no action, no proposals, no solutions."

"Find those people in your communities. Recruit them. But first, before all else, listen to them. This may mean embracing the concerns of other third-party candidates. These people have something important to say, too. Just like you, they care enough to run against all the odds." David proceeded to tell of how he convinced Paul Lurtz to halt his candidacy.

The afternoon was spent in breakout sessions. David met a few more prospective congressional candidates. As he spoke with them, he evaluated them on their issues, plans and ability to articulate their ideas. He knew the party couldn't support all of them. A few of them were clearly not candidate material. David would ration his support.

As the meetings were winding up, Jason brought a tall man with thinning hair over.

"David, I'd like you to meet Marshall Vreeland."

"It's a pleasure," David said, reflexively offering his hand.

"It's very good to meet you, Congressman. I'm a big fan."

"Thank you."

"I believe," Vreeland said, "Jason has told you of my intent to run for the presidency."

"Yes, he has. Did he tell you about our House strategy?"

"No."

David tried not to give Jason an annoyed look.

"You know, during the last presidential campaign, each side spent roughly two billion dollars. Whenever someone's going to spend such a tremendous amount of money, I believe they deserve the truth."

"Sure." Vreeland nodded. "And what is that truth?"

"You're not going to win the presidency. Plenty of people think they're the reincarnation of Ross Perot. Even so, remember Perot didn't win a single electoral vote."

"But things change," Vreeland said. "People are angry and frightened. Did you see that SALA rally a few weeks back? And, I must point out you were elected against the odds."

"Yes, I was talking about the SALA rallies earlier. And true, I did win against the odds. However, I was running against a scandal-laden incumbent and a weak challenger. Also, my constituents knew they weren't giving me the nuclear launch codes. If they made a mistake, they knew they could rid themselves of me in two years. I fully expect to face two highly competent challengers next time around."

"You know what I think? I think you like being the biggest fish in this small pond. You don't want the competition."

"You couldn't be more wrong. I know how difficult it is to be the loner in Congress. I need reinforcements. That's why I'm here today."

"What's a better reinforcement than the President of the United States?"

"Except, you're not going to win, thus hurting the credibility of our party. In addition, your campaign will eclipse and dilute the efforts of the House candidates. And then, where will we be?"

"I see the wisdom of what you're trying to do," Vreeland admitted. "Tell you what, I'll back every one of those candidates to the hilt, publicly, financially and any other way I can. But I'll do it on one condition."

"What's that?" David asked.

"You run as my vice-president."

CHAPTER 42

David couldn't believe Vreeland's demand. "Run as your vice-president? Where did that come from?"

"I did some polling," Vreeland explained. "Four percent of likely voters already know who you are."

"I think that's skewed a bit high. Half the people in my own district don't know who I am."

"You made the news when you blasted that guy, Barnes. The fact that you're a sitting congressman would provide the ticket with a certain amount of gravitas."

"No offense. That's not happening."

"Why? Because you disapprove of me?"

"Not at all. This is not personal."

"Then, why?" Vreeland demanded.

"I have two reasons off the top of my head. First, I need to run for reelection in my district. If I'm running for VP, my constituents are not going to take me seriously."

"You can run for both simultaneously. I've seen others do it."

"Sure, major-party incumbents, who are probably safe in gerrymandered districts. I fail on both counts."

"What's your other reason?"

"My wife."

"Your wife?" Vreeland snickered.

"Yes, she wasn't thrilled about me becoming a congressman. Running for VP probably means a divorce. And, I love my wife."

"Wives can be handled."

"I'm not sure what that means, but I respect my wife too much. How long have you been married?"

"Three years."

"Three years?" David found this odd, as he judged Vreeland to be in his fifties. "Do you have an ex-Mrs. Vreeland?"

"Sure, two of 'em."

"You have two ex-wives and you want to run for president? The media will have a field day."

"Hey," Vreeland countered, "Reagan was divorced."

"True, but he only had one ex-wife. And Jane Wyman kept quiet."

"Don't worry. I know how to keep 'em quiet. Don't worry about this small stuff. You know, I'm a man who's used to getting his way."

David smiled. "Then, politics may not be for you."

"Excuse me, Marshall," Jason interrupted, "can you give the Congressman and me a moment?"

Vreeland nodded. Jason and David walked several paces toward the corner of the ballroom.

"Please don't blow this for me," Jason whispered emphatically.

"For you?"

"I mean for the party."

"Jason, we had a strategy. Backing him means throwing that out the window. You know, he'll lose. We need the meager resources of the party behind a few well-chosen candidates in targeted districts."

"Why can't Vreeland be one of them?"

"Sure, he'll create a bigger splash, but it won't make us more effective. He will suck all our resources and attention away from the House candidates."

"But he's not taking resources; he's bringing them. Vreeland's done polling already, something we can't do now on any real scale."

David had to admit the truth of that. "Still, I have a bad feeling about this."

"You've met our candidates. None of them has the resources you had. Vreeland can supplement their fundraising. And as the chair of this party, I want them to have the same shot you did."

"Alright, you win. I just hope this doesn't bite us in the end."

They walked back to Vreeland.

"Here's my counteroffer," David said. "You support our congressional candidates, 'to the hilt,' as you put it. In exchange, I'll advise you, support you, and publicly endorse you within a month of your campaign kick-off."

"Why not right away? Vreeland tilted his head and frowned, "What? You want time to renege?"

David shook his head.

"You want my endorsement to seem sincere, as a result of thoughtful reflection, not as an automatic reaction to being in the same party. Plus, we can time the endorsement for best media advantage. Timing is everything."

"And the VP spot?"

"I wish you well in finding someone. I have to focus on other things."

Vreeland nodded. "Fair enough."

With that, they shook hands. They continued to talk for a while about issues and strategy. Eventually, everyone left the ballroom, except for David and Jason.

"You realize we may have just sold our souls," David said. "I guess we'll see if it was worth it."

ಖ ಖ ಞ ಞ

The next day, David was back in his office, explaining to Fred what had transpired in Fredericksburg.

"So, are you really going to support this Vreeland guy?" Fred asked.

"Sure, but I was vague as to how far I'll go. I just hope he doesn't embarrass us."

"When is he going to announce?"

"I don't know, but I think it's a little early. I certainly don't think he should be the first to announce."

"Well, you don't have to worry about that. Buck Howell just let the world know he wants the Republican nomination earlier this morning."

"Already? Wow, the campaigns grow longer every election cycle."

Just then, Ellen came into David's office.

"I've confirmed your meeting with Arlo Hudge on Thursday. He said he's pleased you've 'come to your senses.' His legislative assistant and Tyler should finish consolidating the bill by Wednesday."

"Good." David said, half-heartedly.

"So Ellen, guru of all things political," Fred said, "in a race between Gregory Farnum, Buck Howell and Marshall Vreeland, who wins?"

"Who's Marshall Vreeland?" she asked.

"The Centrist Party's presidential nominee," Fred said.

"I didn't think you guys were doing that."

"Neither did we," David said. "Anyway, in this environment, who wins?"

"Between those choices, Gregory Farnum."

"I'm surprised." David said. "As a Republican, I thought you'd say Buck Howell."

"Howell is loved by the Christian Right, the NRA and Big Business. But he's too conservative to win against the President. That's unless Farnum is found in bed with a hooker or something like that."

"I don't know," Fred added. "Farnum's approval rating has been dropping."

"But Farnum's smart. I hear he's already working on something big, something to do with his education plan. How can anyone be against education?"

ℬ ℬ ℭ ℭ

The following week, Farnum entered the Cabinet Room, where he had gathered his economic team, along with his Education Secretary and other senior staff members.

"Good morning, everyone."

"Good morning, Mr. President," they all said almost in unison.

"This week, we launch the Strategic Investment Act, which will include key investments in long-term priorities such as education, technology and infrastructure with the goal of establishing an economic foundation for future growth. The GDP numbers have slipped slightly. We have to nip it in the bud. We cannot afford to slip back into a recession."

Amy Greene passed out a thick bound volume to each attendee.

"Most of you have already provided valuable input. Now, we've assembled it into a comprehensive bill. Harris, why don't you take us through it?"

"Certainly, Mr. President."

As Carver explained the major components of the bill, Robert Hingecliff thumbed through the pages as he spoke. He looked over at Martha Addison, the Federal Reserve Chair, who was eying him back.

"When discussing this initiative with members of Congress or the press," Carver continued, "emphasize the strategic pro-growth approach we are taking. No one is to use the terms 'spending,' 'stimulus,' 'pork' or 'shovel-ready.' What we must emphasize are the strategic goals of what's to be accomplished, not the cost."

"Mr. President," Hingecliff said. "It's easy to say don't emphasize cost, but this will be the single largest spending bill in American history. At over 950 billion, it will drastically add to the National Debt. I'm concerned about the cost of this package, as will many members of Congress," Hingecliff warned. "It also will remind many people of Obama's stimulus package, a reminder of the Great Recession. Might it be better to propose a series of smaller bills?"

"No," Farnum said. "We don't have time for a series of budget battles. And don't worry, it's been designed for maximum congressional support."

Everyone nodded.

"In addition," Farnum said, turning to Martha Addison. "We're going to need a full point drop in the interest rate to generate private investment to break the downward spiral in the stock market."

"A full point drop in the interest rate would be rather severe," Addison responded.

"Isn't avoiding a recession enough to warrant it?"

Addison was smart enough to not answer that question directly.

"Mr. President, given the current economic data, the Federal Reserve Governors and I believe one quarter of a point would stimulate the economy sufficiently without leading to an eventual bubble. Half a point at the absolute maximum."

"Great, half a point now," responded the president. "Then, another half point next month."

"I'll discuss it with the governors."

The others were silent. While nominated by the president, the Federal Reserve is independent of the President's executive authority. Given the power they held, Federal Reserve Chairs always chose their words carefully. Without explicitly saying so, Addison had just told the president "hell, no". The meaning was lost on no one.

ᏋᎧ ᏋᎧ ᏓᎧ ᏓᎧ

"I need an hour of the Congressman's time today without interruptions," Fred told Carol.

"That's going to be difficult," she said

"How about lunch?"

"He doesn't have anything scheduled."

239

"Good. Pencil me in for a private lunch. Let's make it out of the office."

"Okay. Done."

"Great." Fred pulled out his cell phone and punched in a number. "Okay, we're on for one o'clock. Meet us at…well…um…Le Chevalier. It's on Pennsylvania Avenue...Okay, see you there."

A couple of hours later, Fred and David were walking down Pennsylvania Avenue.

"Why are we going out to have lunch?" David asked.

"Truth be told, there's someone I want you to talk to."

"Who?"

"That would be telling."

"Did Ellen arrange for Sara to come down again?"

Fred shrugged, then opened the front door to Le Chevalier.

"This is a pretty fancy place just for lunch."

"To be honest, I don't eat out much. This is one of the few Washington restaurants I've been to."

"Okay."

They approached the maître d'. "Table for three under the name Arkin."

"Certainly, sir. Your other guest is already seated."

They started to walk in, but suddenly David stopped and grabbed Fred's arm. "What is Armand Nistle doing here?"

"He has some important information for us," Fred explained. "He's here on behalf of others."

Nistle stood up. "Good afternoon, Congressman."

David responded with silence.

"I realize I'm not your favorite person. And I apologize for my behavior at the debate. Thank you for meeting with me."

"Why don't we sit down?" Fred suggested.

"Okay, but you didn't come down to Washington just to apologize."

"True."

"Why don't we cut to the chase?" David said, trying to not sound irritated.

"Very well. Things at Winton have been changing, and not for the better. Budgets have become very tight."

"When I last spoke with President Danzig, he admitted finances were a critical issue. I suspect it's a situation he inherited from President Vander Waal."

"It's more than cutbacks. The faculty can no longer choose their own textbooks. And some of these new textbooks we're required to use are crap. They're written by schlock authors. And, they're thinner, but cost more. To compensate for the inferior textbooks, we supplemented with extra handouts, but then Danzig imposed copier paper rationing."

"I have no control over President Danzig."

"I know, I know. But listen: In addition, three department heads and a dean were fired in the last three months."

"Okay, the high turnover is unusual. But maybe Danzig needed to clean house. I don't know. Did you really drive all the way down to Washington to whine?"

"These were tenured academics. Danzig had no right!"

"Well, I guess he did. Don't get me wrong; I don't like hearing about these measures, but they're not a crime."

"Fair enough," Nistle said, trying to calm himself down. "Have you ever heard of Parnell Education Corporation?"

David shrugged.

"I have," Fred said. "I taught at one of their schools. Never again."

"They're a proprietary education conglomerate," Nistle continued. "They own beauty schools, electronic gaming schools, culinary schools, and a handful of for-profit colleges. Oh, and by the way, they also own the textbook publisher that our *delightful* new textbooks come from. Anyway, all the people hired to replace the department heads and the dean were from Parnell. When a few of us dug a little deeper, we discovered our beloved president, Charles Danzig, was also a Parnell alumni. He was a director of market development."

"Hey, when I started Simplexia, the first three employees I hired were people I knew at my old employer."

"In addition, we have recently heard the Board of Governors is considering selling the college to—guess who? Parnell Education Corporation. I'm not a lawyer, but there has to be something illegal there. Isn't that a violation of his fiduciary duty to Winton? Conflict of interest?"

"It depends on what he may or may not have done to make Winton's economic situation worse. I now see your legal concern, but I'm still not sure why you're coming to me with this. Why didn't you go to the Pennsylvania Department of Education or the Attorney General?"

"We might still do that," Nistle said. "However, there's more."

CHAPTER 43

"Good morning, everyone," Dana Seagram said. "My assistant, Chelsea, is passing out the briefing pages as I speak. The President will join us in a moment with a statement."

As if on cue, President Farnum walked into the White House Press Room.

"Good morning, everyone. Today, I am sending to Congress a vital piece of legislation, the Strategic Investment Act. Rather than be reactive, we are being proactive about securing America's economic future. We will make investments in technology, infrastructure, and, most importantly, education."

"In the last few decades, we have seen a significant decline in low-skill or semi-skilled jobs. Many of these jobs are being taken by machines. Word processing reduced the demand for secretaries. ATMs reduced the demand for bank tellers. Industrial robots have reduced the demand for assembly line workers. It goes on and on. Therefore, we have two choices. We can throw away our machines and revert to a more inefficient economy, something our global competitors are unlikely to do. Or, we can better train and educate our workers to meet the challenges of tomorrow's economy. With this legislation, I choose the latter. I'll take questions, now."

"Mr. President," the reporter from the *Post* called out, "you indicated education is a cornerstone of this new bill. How exactly will funds be deployed and used for education?"

"Jim, that's a very good question. First, we need to beef up the grants and loans available, lowering the entrance barriers for students. Second, we need to enable them to use those funds to go beyond a bachelor's degree. More and more of today's well-paying jobs require a master's degree, even a doctorate. Third, the how and when of innovation cannot be predicted. We need to allow colleges and universities to be more creative in how they use grants to explore the human potential of their students."

"Isn't this leading to a sort of socialistic universal education program?" asked the reporter from one of the conservative news channels."

"Well, Rita, I was wondering how fast it would take someone from your network to call me a socialist." Farnum looked down at his watch. "I believe that's a land speed record."

The other reporters laughed.

"However, there will be provisions to help those who traditionally have not had access to more advanced education. I believe people have a right to the kind of education that will help them be successful in tomorrow's economy."

"Does the timing of this legislation have anything to do with Governor Howell's announcement to seek the Presidency?" asked the reporter from the *Times*.

"Craig, I'm honestly surprised anyone is announcing their intentions so early. Still, Governor Howell's schedule is of no concern to me. We've been working on this for quite a while. And the election is too far away for me to forego focusing on the job of President."

ဨ ဨ ဢ ဢ

All across the political media spectrum, the pundits commented on the President's announcement.

"This is a shining example of political courage, rarely seen these days." Jessica Dandridge announced. "President Farnum has committed to a future far beyond the next election cycle. It reminds me of Kennedy boldly committing us to landing on the moon. The strategic nature of this landmark legislation is inspiring. I certainly hope this wins him a Profile in Courage Award."

ဨ ဨ ဢ ဢ

"Good evening, Patriots," Glendenning said grimly to the camera. "Forgive me for not being my usual buoyant self. We see the President has finally revealed his true colors. He is trying to institute socialist indoctrination with his so called education program. First, he drove our economy to its knees. Now, he's attempting a takeover of the education system."

"This sounds eerily familiar, with very close parallels to pre-war Germany. Let's see. An economy in shambles. Then, a charismatic leader wants to *educate* the youth of the country. Remember the Hitler Youth!"

"Our democracy is crumbling before our very eyes! This is a warning. How many canaries have to die before we realize the air is being poisoned?"

"He calls education a civil right? Is he honestly comparing getting a degree in basket weaving or video gaming with the right to vote or due process? Since when is it a civil right to receive free services?"

ဨ ဨ ဢ ဢ

The following day, Carol buzzed David on the intercom. "Congressman, I have President Danzig of Winton College for you on line 4."

David frowned. "Thank you, I'll take it." He pressed the button. "Hello, Chuck. How are you?"

"Fine. How are things in Washington?"

"The usual combination of chaos and confusion. So, what can I do for you?"

"I just want to give you a heads-up," Danzig said. "Do you remember Armand Nistle?"

David felt the hairs on the back of his neck stand on end. He certainly hadn't expected Danzig to mention Nistle's name.

"I don't think I could forget him," he said.

"Well, he's become a bit unhinged lately. He's been making a number of wild accusations. He's been spouting all sorts of conspiracy theories."

"What sort of theories?"

"Well, I've had to institute some austerity measures. And I had to let some people go. This has stoked his paranoia. He's been telling people I came to Winton to destroy it. And apparently, he feels you're a part of my grand design for the college's destruction. I don't know if he's dangerous, but if he shows up in Washington, I'd be careful."

"What makes you think he'd come to Washington?"

"Nothing specific, except he mouthed off about how, as he put it, 'cozy' we are. He hasn't made any threats, but given his erratic and angry nature, I'd rather be safe than sorry."

"Well, thanks for the heads-up."

"By the way, did you see the President on TV yesterday? Sounds like he's going to do big things for us."

"Yes, I saw him. Not that I expect him to agree to it, but I've already put in a request to meet with the President to discuss his bill."

"Great. Let me know when you're back home. We should have dinner."

"Sounds nice. Take care."

After hanging up, he called Fred into his office.

"What's up?"

"I just had a very interesting phone conversation with Chuck Danzig. He was calling to warn me about Armand Nistle, saying he was unhinged."

"Really?" Fred said. "That can't be a coincidence. He must know Nistle's been down here."

"Maybe the good professor missed a class to come down here," David suggested.

"No, it's in between semesters," Fred explained. "That's why he came down when he did."

"This seems too much of a coincidence."

"Nistle said he and his colleagues were keeping a low profile."

"According to Danzig, Nistle has been making accusations. One of these guys is trying to play us." David picked up the telephone. "Ellen, could you come in here for a moment?"

Within a few seconds Ellen came in. "What's going on?"

"Do you remember Armand Nistle?"

"The name is familiar," she said.

"He was the Winton professor who ambushed me in the debate."

"Oh, that guy."

"Fred and I had lunch with him yesterday."

Ellen looked incredulous. "Why would you meet with him?"

"He contacted me with an interesting story," Fred said. "I thought David should hear it."

"More like a conspiracy," David added, "about how Chuck Danzig is in bed with Parnell Education Corporation and is trying to undermine Winton for a takeover. He also believes Parnell is politically connected and is trying to manipulate government regulators to make that happen."

"And what was the exact nature of this manipulation?"

"He didn't have a lot of specifics on that."

"Congressman," Ellen said, "has it occurred to you that he's trying to alienate you from one of your biggest supporters?"

"Yes, that was my first thought. But then, less than 24 hours after this private lunch, just a few minutes ago, Chuck Danzig called to tell me Nistle's publicly making wild allegations."

"Well, that fits," she said.

"Perhaps, but something doesn't feel right. If Danzig is laying off faculty members, I think Nistle would want to be discreet, not make trouble. Why would Nistle travel hundreds of miles to meet with someone who already doesn't trust him? And why would Danzig think that he would?"

"Maybe Nistle's a delusional psychopath," Ellen suggested.

"Enough of the maybes," David said. "Fred, I want you to head back to Pennsylvania. Talk to Nistle and more importantly to the faculty members he claims to be speaking for. Be very discreet. Don't meet with anyone on or near campus."

"Sure. Maybe I should also talk to the fired department heads?"

"As long as it's discreet. Chuck Danzig has been very good to me. I don't want to upset him unnecessarily, especially if Nistle's trying to play me. Meanwhile, Ellen, I'd like more information on Parnell Education Corporation. Go deep. I want more than their press releases."

There was a knock on the door. It was Tyler.

"Come in."

"Congressman," Tyler said, smiling. "I have good news. The Speaker's scheduled a full House vote on your bill for Thursday."

"So soon?" Fred asked.

"Apparently, it went to the front of the line, after clearing the committee."

Fred turned to David. "Congratulations, Congressman," he said, "your first bill hits the Floor. We should celebrate."

"But, it still has to pass the Floor vote," David said.

"I spoke with Congressman Hudge's legislative assistant," Tyler explained. "She says there are enough votes to pass. And, Congressman Hudge's office will be working the phones to broaden the margin."

"Great," David said.

Ellen just frowned.

CHAPTER 44

As a cabinet secretary, few beyond the President could command Robert Hingecliff's presence. One of those few was Harris Carver. Hingecliff's secretary told him Carver had called at 7:30 in the morning. Hingecliff was to be in his office at the White House by 8:00. He felt a bit old to be called into the principal's office, but he complied.

"Good morning, Harris," Hingecliff greeted him, as if it was perfectly normal to be in so early.

"Morning, Mr. Secretary," Carver said, with no affection in his voice. He gestured for Hingecliff to be seated. "I understand you made a speech earlier this week on economic policy."

"No," Hingecliff answered. "I don't recall making any speeches in the last month, as a matter of fact."

"Not even at Georgetown University?" Carver pressed.

Hingecliff laughed. "Well, I did give a small talk to my granddaughter's macroeconomics class, as a special favor to her. Hardly a policy speech. It was little more than basic economics. Nothing they couldn't have read in their textbook."

"It seems you made some comments about the President's economic policy."

"Only the preapproved talking points. Anything beyond that, as I said, was basic economics. Besides, it's not like there was any press there."

Carver pulled a thin college newspaper from his briefcase.

"Apparently, one of the students was also a reporter." Carver opened the newspaper and began to read aloud, "Secretary Hingecliff said 'Deficit spending must stop or eventually the American economy will go bankrupt,' The Treasury Secretary went on to further berate President Farnum's economic policy as short-sighted."

"I never said the President's policy was short-sighted."

"What about the rest?"

"Deficit spending? We all know it can't go on indefinitely. Even the President has said that."

"But the words sound like you."

"It's true I have voiced my concerns about the President's current economic plan, but only within the walls of the White House. Don't blow this out of proportion."

"But it was in the newspaper, both in newsprint and online."

"A college newspaper, not exactly *The Washington Post*."

"The student reporter is a straight-A journalism honor student, who's already reposted this story to his own blog."

"Straight A?" Hingecliff asked. "You checked the grades of the student? Are you investigating him?"

"Don't be ridiculous. We live in the age of social media. He brags about it in his blog."

"Harris, this is nothing, unless you make it something. So, what is this really about?"

"We need everyone on the same page. That includes you *and* the Fed Chair."

"Martha Addison? Is that what this is about?"

"Addison, the woman you pushed the President to nominate, is refusing to cooperate."

"You do understand the Fed Chair is not White House Staff or in the Cabinet. It's her responsibility to act independently in the best interest of the economy, as she and the Board determine. On monetary policy, there's none better than Martha Addison."

"But we need her to drop the interest rate."

"And she's agreed."

"But not enough. Persuade her to cooperate, or she won't be re-nominated. And, as for you, message comes out of the Communications Office, nowhere else."

"I've always understood that rule and followed it," Hingecliff said. "Is there anything else?"

"Not for now."

ౙ ౙ ౚ ౚ

Later that morning, Ellen caught David as he came into the office.

"I just heard from Fred. He's headed back to Washington now. He wants to be here in time for the vote."

"Did he learn anything about Winton?"

"According to him, and much to my surprise, everything Nistle told you, checks out. Fred can give you more details when he gets back."

"Did you find anything?"

"Yes. Looking into Danzig's background, I found he did indeed work for Parnell Education Corporation, she said. "Parnell owns about 90 different schools, mostly trade schools, but a few colleges too. They've bought three distressed colleges in the last four years. What's interesting is that Danzig used to be president of one of their beauty schools."

"A beauty school?"

"Yes, but five years ago, he was promoted into their corporate division and became a director of market development. Three years later, he was given one of the small, newly acquired colleges to run. That gave him the college president credentials when the Winton Board of Governors was looking for Vander Waal's replacement."

"Why would the board hire a guy with a résumé that was so thin academically?"

"I don't know, but speaking of boards, here's where it really becomes even more interesting. Parnell has a board member I recognized—Ellis Cornwall. Despite owning 57% of Parnell stock, he's not the chair, and his picture never appears in their annual report."

"Is that the same guy who owns all those newspapers and the Liberty Network?"

"Yes, and he's a big contributor to the Democratic Party. Cornwall is also the largest contributor to the Progressive Institute for Education Excellence, the super-PAC that's been running ads in support of the President's strategic education bill."

"I wondered how they were able to run ads the day after the President announced his bill. They must have had a heads-up somehow."

"And I may know how. Guess who runs the Progressive Institute for Education Excellence? Carl Stavros, the President's former communications director. Very convenient."

"Stavros. I met him at the White House, the day of my photo op with the President." David sat back in his chair, stunned. "This would explain how Danzig knew some of the specifics of the bill."

David pondered how different parts of his life had just collided. He also realized Danzig had been trying to play him longer than he suspected.

ဆ ဆ ဆ ဆ

That afternoon, David tried to push the Winton-Danzig-Parnell-Cornwall connection out of his head as he walked into the House Chamber. Within a few minutes, the acting Speaker called the House to order. After some preliminary business, she called for the vote on HR973, the Hudge-Grant bill.

David didn't see Hudge, as he looked around the chamber. However, with five voting machines and 435 representatives, the odds of spotting any particular member were low. Plus, as a veteran of the House, Hudge would be less sentimental about this vote. He was unlikely to rush in or dally.

David walked up to one of the five voting machines in the chamber. He pulled out his voting card, swiped it, and pressed the button marked "Yea." While he had performed this simple task before, never had it been for a bill he personally sponsored.

He quickly moved out of the way of other members, so they could vote for his bill. He certainly hoped it was *for* the bill. He turned and looked up at the two great portraits of Washington and Lafayette, flanking the Speaker's rostrum. Their contributions had helped establish the United States. And now, David Grant, the son of a Philadelphia firefighter, was making his own small contribution for America's future. The thought gave David butterflies in his stomach.

While most members left the Floor after voting, he sat down. David wanted to be in the chamber when the bill passed. He pulled out his tablet to watch a live feed of the vote tally. At first, the vote was roughly even, with a slight advantage to the yea votes. After a few minutes, the number of nea votes began to climb slightly. He wasn't worried. Hudge had assured him they had enough votes. However, the vote against the legislation continued to climb alarmingly. Then, the critical 218th Nea vote was cast. His first bill had failed.

How was this possible? Had Hudge pulled a fast one after all? David knew better. Hudge wanted the Samu dredging too badly to sabotage the vote. He stood up and walked out. To his surprise, he found Ellen waiting outside the House chamber.

"It failed," he told her. "Hudge said we had the votes."

"I was wondering if something was up," she said. "It moved to the Floor too quickly."

"If the Speaker wanted to kill it, why even allow a vote?"

"I'm not sure what the Speaker's doing," Ellen said. "But, the reason I came over was to alert you. Wilkers has scheduled three more bills for a vote this afternoon and two more this evening."

"What's his rush?" David said, looking back into the chamber.

"I don't know," Ellen said. "And I don't like not knowing."

"Maybe Hudge will have an idea." David walked back onto the Floor. He still didn't see Hudge anywhere. Finally, he approached one of the recording clerks.

"Excuse me, has Congressman Hudge voted yet?"

The clerk looked down at her screen. "Yes," she said.

"How did he vote?"

The clerk gave him an annoyed look.

"It'll be public in a few minutes anyway," David persisted.

She looked down again. "He voted yea."

"Thank you."

David walked to Hudge's office and asked to see him. He found Hudge sitting with a glass of bourbon in his hand, looking out the window.

"I've been expecting you. Would you care for something to drown our sorrows?" he asked, gesturing to the bar.

"So, you know the bill failed?"

"For now."

"You said we had the votes."

"I thought we did, but they just magically evaporated. I've been sitting here trying to figure out what just happened," Hudge said, taking another sip.

"Any conclusions?" David asked.

"Not 'til the Speaker scheduled the additional votes for today. I'm willing to bet they all fail."

"Why do you say that?"

"Every bill scheduled today has significant Republican backing."

"So, Wilkers is trying to stick it to the Republicans?"

"That was my first thought. But, they weren't divisive bills. They're all fairly bipartisan stuff. Then, I realized it was something more."

"Like?"

Hudge took another slow sip of his bourbon, hesitating as if trying to decide whether or not to share his personal revelation.

"Well, you opposed me, but you were honest about it. And in the end, you compromised, so I'll let you in on the grand plan as I see it. The President is sending us his Strategic Bullshit Act. The Democrats always find a fancy name for spending more'n we got. This time it's called 'strategic investment'. But I gotta give the devil his due. Through Wilkers, he's kill'n all our bills first. But we all know the President wants his bill passed. So all we gotta do is amend it with our bills. And it'll sail through Congress like poop through a goose."

David smiled, as he thought the excremental metaphor quite appropriate on more than one level.

"I'll get my Alaskan dredge funding," Hudge continued. "You'll get yer fancy power management thing. I'm will'n to bet they'll let us add almost anything. We should start make'n our Christmas lists."

"What about the Republican concern for fiscal responsibility? You could stand together and hold off adding any bills."

"I appreciate the sentiment, but this trap's too irresistible, far too clever. You ever hear a' game theory?"

"Sure, the Prisoner's Dilemma."

"Exactly, the one who acts noble loses."

"Unless we can convince everyone to act nobly."

"Are you kidding? This is the U.S. House of Representatives. The Dems have the majority. Republicans can only pass legislation with the agreement of some Democrats. It's a perfect trap." Hudge stood up and walked toward his bar. "Yup, a perfect trap," he mumbled to himself. "We should use it when it's our turn." Hudge refilled his drink. "By the way, did you happen to notice the price of the President's bill?"

"About 950 billion," David answered.

"Interesting number, that. We add all our smaller bills to that leviathan, and it'll be over a trillion. That's a trillion with a big, red, capital T. And it won't stand for Texas, but it'll be a helluva lot bigger. If we complain about the size, Farnum'll say it was the Republicans who pushed it over the line."

"If you know about his plan, you can call him on it."

"Well, that's up to the party leadership, Mirreau and the others. Don't worry; they'll make noise, but vote for it all the same, just as long as they get their own pork."

CHAPTER 45

Arlo Hudge was correct. All the subsequent votes failed that day. That weekend, David was fairly depressed. However, he strived to be upbeat for Sara and the children, deciding not to share anything about the bill or Winton with them.

Returning Monday morning, David focused on work for the Intellectual Property Sub-Committee. He and Christa Lemmon were preparing an enhanced patent protection bill most of the morning, but his heart wasn't in it. In the afternoon, Fred briefed him on the details of his trip to meet with Nistle and the other faculty. However, he had no new significant information. David decided to leave the office early, turning off all things Washington in his mind. He headed back to his Georgetown townhouse, which was still fairly empty. He and Sara had decided to put off purchasing much furniture until after his reelection. Selling the townhouse wouldn't be a problem, but disposing of the extra furniture would be a hassle they didn't need.

After discovering his refrigerator was emptier than his townhouse, David decided to go out for dinner. He walked to Rolf's, a German restaurant a few blocks away. The evening walk lifted his mood slightly.

Since moving into the neighborhood, he had enjoyed eating at Rolf's. In addition to the good food, including a particularly excellent strudel, it had the virtue of being devoid of political faces. He wondered if dining in a German restaurant had a bad connotation, even so many decades after the war. Most upscale restaurants in DC fawned over every government official, which he found a bit wearing. Here, he was just an anonymous regular. Accordingly, Rolf's had become his dining sanctuary. So, he was caught off-guard when his sanctuary was suddenly violated.

"Good evening, Congressman."

He looked up to see Robert Hingecliff standing there. David stood up.

"Good evening, Mr. Secretary."

"May I join you for just a moment?" Hingecliff asked. "I promise I won't stay long."

"Certainly," David said, motioning for Hingecliff to sit. "I haven't seen you since Cadillac Mountain."

David recalled how he felt meeting the members of The Circle. It filled him with hope then. Now, hope felt long forgotten.

"I understand your energy bill failed," Hingecliff said. "I was sorry to hear that."

"Thank you. You're very kind."

"It's ironic that most of us who come to Washington, the seat of American power, sometimes feel the most powerless."

"I doubt that's true in your case," David said. "You're a cabinet secretary working for a very popular president...well...at least until recently."

"Yes, the President's drop in popularity is changing the political landscape. That change may have contributed to all the failed bills last week."

"Yes, I've heard the theory that defeating those bills was designed to soften Congress up for the President's strategic education-plus-pork bill."

"That's a very insightful description," Hingecliff admitted. "I recall, in one of your Floor speeches, you were railing against the money wasted by congressional websites."

"You have a good memory. But, I'm guessing that waste will be nothing, compared to what's coming in the Strategic Investment Act."

"That's an understatement."

"I don't think the President will appreciate you saying that."

"No, I don't suppose he would." Hingecliff leaned forward. "When you receive a copy of the bill, I would suggest you look closely at sections 151 and 168."

"Why is that?"

"You're always on the lookout for wasteful spending, aren't you? Isn't that why you initially opposed Hudge's bill?"

"How did you know about that?"

"You're smart enough to figure that out," Hingecliff said with a smile.

"Carstairs or McCord?"

"Both, actually."

"Ah, the Order of the Circle?"

Hingecliff nodded. "But, I'm serious. Check out sections 151 and 168. In any bill, the juicier bits are always near the back. Oh, and by the way, it would be best if you not mention this chance meeting. It wouldn't look good politically for either of us."

"Somehow, I don't think this was a chance meeting."

Hingecliff just shrugged, stood up and said, "Good night, Congressman."

David pulled out his cell phone and moved to the back of the restaurant. He hoped Ellen would still be in the office. Unfortunately, she wasn't. David called her cell phone and left a message on her voicemail.

"Ellen, I want you to obtain a copy of the President's Strategic Investment Act as soon as possible. Check Sections 151 and 168. We're looking for something unusual, probably some wasteful spending."

೮ ೮ ೞ ೞ

At 5:30 the next morning, Ellen sat down in a booth near the back of an all-night diner in a run-down part of Washington. Despite the early hour, the diner had a significant clientele.

"Coffee, Hon?" asked the matronly waitress.

"Sure."

After about ten minutes, a tall blonde woman entered and tentatively approached.

"Good morning, Leslie. I guess you got my message. Thanks for coming."

"I had heard you were back in Washington," Leslie Weaver said, standing a booth away.

"Why don't you sit down? People might stare."

"Yes, we can't have that," she said, sliding into the booth. "Who knows, someone might even take a picture," Weaver said, sarcastically.

Immediately, the waitress trudged over. "Coffee, Hon?"

Weaver nodded.

"So, why did we have to meet so damn early?"

"My new boss, David Grant, wants to see the whole SIA bill."

"He will, when the Speaker releases it."

"No, he needs to see it now."

"That's not possible," Weaver insisted.

"Please, we've both been in Washington too long for that. And you owe me. I kept the secret."

"Ellen, I know you paid a heavy price, but I can't help you. And if you're thinking of blackmailing me, you should know I've already come out of the closet. I have a new girlfriend. And yes, sometimes I have to endure people snickering behind my back, but I don't have to live in secrecy anymore."

"Leslie, I'm not a blackmailer, and you know it. I'm happy your life has come together. But, that doesn't change what I need. If I hadn't done what I did, you would have been the outcast, not me. So I repeat, you owe me."

Leslie shifted uncomfortably. "I'll see what I can do." She started to leave, but then turned back. "You ever hear from Jim or the kids?"

"Just a holiday card."

ಬಿ ಏ ಞ ಛ

When David came into the office the next morning, Ellen wasn't to be found.

"Where's Ellen?" David asked Carol.

"She left a message she would be coming in late," Carol answered. "Is there something I can do for you, Congressman?"

"No, thank you, Carol."

David wondered if Ellen had even listened to his message.

After several hours, she walked into David's office.

"Is this what you had in mind?" Ellen asked, as she wheeled in three thick volumes of documents on a small luggage cart.

"I guess so. Where did you locate it?"

"You don't want to know, plausible deniability and all that. But Section 151 holds a fair amount of pork, completely unrelated to education. What

253

first caught my eye was 26 million dollars allocated for replacing the Hillcrest Road Bridge in a little place called Embler, Pennsylvania. I guess you can call that infrastructure. Did you know anything about that?"

"No," he said. "I'm not an engineer, but I thought the Hillcrest Bridge was in fairly good shape."

"And get this," Ellen said, "it also includes 4.5 million dollars for a solar energy lab at Winton College, an interesting coincidence."

"I didn't put these in, I swear."

"Of course not. But no one will believe you didn't. You're both on the energy committee and a former employee of Winton."

"It's an elegant trap," David concluded. "If I ignore these, they can use them against me, calling me a hypocrite. If I try to pull these provisions, it may hurt me with the voters."

"Who tipped you off?" Ellen asked.

"I'd rather not say. You know, plausible deniability and all that. What about the other section?"

"Section 168? Ah, there you'll find an appropriation for the Voter's Equal Access League, or VEAL. It's a Democratic Party shell. $38 million! VEAL members were big contributors to President Farnum's campaign."

"So, VEAL is the new pork."

"Why didn't your source pass this along to the Republicans?"

"Maybe he has. Although, if the Republicans went public with this, it might look like partisan politics as usual."

"Or maybe," Ellen suggested, "there's a Republican counterpart. Maybe the two sides have an agreement."

"After what Hudge told me, I wouldn't be surprised."

"What do you want to do?" Ellen asked.

"Dig deeper. I want to know what else is in this bill."

"That's a lot of man-hours."

"Get Tyler, Fred, and anyone else we can spare to dig through this. In the meantime, I'm going to try to reconnect with my source."

ဨ ဨ ၧ ၧ

The following morning, Robert Hingecliff was in his office, reviewing the preliminary GDP figures, when his secretary, Maggie, beeped. He hit the speaker-phone button.

"Yes, Maggie."

"Mr. Secretary, Congressman David Grant is on line three for you."

"Tell him I'm in a meeting," Hingcliff answered, but then reconsidered. He wondered if he had misjudged the congressman's ability to understand discretion. "Marge, on second thought, I'll take his call." He pressed the line-three button. "What can I do for you, Congressman?"

"I'm sorry you had to leave the restaurant so early," David said. "The *veal* was excellent. It was a good recommendation, although I found it a bit difficult to chew on."

Hingecliff smiled as he realized David was indeed trying to be discreet while on a speaker phone.

"I'm sorry it was so difficult to swallow."

"I was wondering if you could recommend a good wine to go with it. Perhaps a red?"

Hingecliff appreciated that David was speaking as if the line were tapped, but wondered what the Congressman meant.

"Red doesn't usually go with veal."

"But for balance," David suggested.

Hingecliff then realized what he was asking for. Red was the color associated with the Republicans. The Congressman was looking for Republican pork.

"Hmm, there's a German restaurant I know that might have the answer to that. I'm dining there tomorrow night at eight-thirty. I'll check the menu when I'm there."

"Thank you, that's very kind."

"It was good talking to you, Congressman."

"And to you, Mr. Secretary. Goodbye."

ಐ ಜಿ ೞ ಔ

David arrived at Rolf's early and procured a private table near the back of the restaurant. He saw Hingecliff come in, dressed quite casually and carrying a small white gift bag.

"Good evening, Mr. Secretary,"

"Good evening. Please call me Robert. May I call you David?"

"Certainly."

"Our titles might be overheard and pique someone's interest. So you found the veal on the menu?"

"Yes, $35 million, a bit pricey. My first question is why?"

"Political patronage, of course."

"No, I meant why tell me? Why not the Republicans or the press?"

"I believe you're in the best position to expose all the pork in the bill. It'll be over a trillion dollars. Did you also find the anonymous expenditures for your district?"

"Yes, do you know who put them in?"

"I have no idea, but I'm sure the Speaker does. But you understand why they were put in?"

"A trap for me, should I make waves down the line."

Hingecliff nodded. "Every Democrat and every Republican has or will load it up with their pet projects."

"What makes you think I'm any different?" David asked.

"You campaigned against pork-barrel spending, but unlike most members of Congress, you kept your word."

"Keeping my word may mean this is my first and last term in Congress."

"I can't help you there," Hingecliff said, "at least directly."

"You didn't answer my question. Why did you point me toward Section 151 and VEAL. You work for the 'Big Guy.' Aren't you betraying him?"

As Jack Kennedy famously said, 'Sometimes party asks too much' and I believe that becomes truer every day. Besides, I didn't give you classified military secrets. I merely pointed you in the direction of what will shortly be publicly available information.

"You want me to go up against the President? Go on the Floor and call him out?"

"The thought had occurred to me."

"When I attacked Porter Barnes, I destroyed my chance to get a bill passed."

"There are more important things than getting bills passed. The National Debt is in the trillions. Unless we change course, this country is going to have a crash that will make the Great Depression look like a cake walk. Martha Addison and I have been telling the 'Big Guy' that, but he's running scared. The Kadler Steele-CART situation threw him off. So, he's trying to overcompensate by buying the voters with pork."

Just then, the waiter came and took their orders. Once the waiter was out of earshot, Hingecliff continued.

"Look, David, I'm 67 years old. I came to Washington to improve things. I played the party game, adhered to party loyalty, because I thought I could make a positive difference. But I've seen our government deteriorate into intense tribal warfare. Then, I see you. So idealistic, and not unlike so many before you. But you're different in that you're not playing the party game. That gives you a certain invulnerability."

"Sorry, I don't feel invulnerable. If you want to stop this spending bill, why doesn't the Secretary of the Treasury just stand up publicly and declare it's too much?"

"I could do that. It would be great theater. I'd be forced to resign. It might even stop the bill. It could even throw the next election to the Republicans. Either way, my career would be over."

"So you're saying, better to sacrifice my career than yours?"

"No, you're invulnerable, remember? Did you ever see the film, *Twelve Angry Men*?"

David nodded.

"Early in the film, Juror #8, played by Henry Fonda is outvoted eleven to one. The rest of the jury is shouting him down. He asks for another vote. And to everyone's surprise, another juror votes not guilty, throwing him a lifeline." Hingecliff leaned forward. "I'm throwing you a lifeline of sorts. Or maybe, I'm asking for one from you."

"I'll consider it."

"Before we part, I have a gift for you." Hingecliff placed the small bag on the table.

"What is this?"

"It's a cell phone. I believe criminals call them burner phones, bought with cash, untraceable. You can't call my office again. Nor should you call me on any number associated with me. There's already a number programmed into the phone. It's labeled Dentist."

Hingecliff pulled another phone out of his pocket. "Use only that phone to call this phone. Don't use it to call anyone you know. And if you call me on that phone, don't call from your home or office. It's amazing what the government can do with GPS tracking."

"Excuse me, but this seems a little paranoid."

"Ever since the Patriot Act, the government can find an excuse to monitor anyone."

"You believe someone's tapping your phone?"

"I have no idea. But I had an unpleasant encounter with Harris Carver recently, so I don't want to take any chances. And people think paranoia left Washington with Nixon." Hingecliff gave a dark chuckle. "By the way, if you do decide to take a shot at the President, take a shot at me, too."

"Why?"

"I'm on unsteady ground with Carver, which is tantamount to being on unsteady ground with the President. I'd like to stay close to the President, to either influence him or at least obtain information to help thwart a catastrophe."

"I'll see what I can do," David said.

They finished their dinners, then departed.

As he walked back to his townhouse, David pondered all that Hingecliff had told him. While David didn't completely know whether to trust Hingecliff, the Treasury Secretary did provide him with accurate and verifiable information. But despite Hingecliff's opinion, David knew he was hardly invulnerable.

Suddenly an idea occurred to him. The more he thought about it, the more sense it made. He pulled out his own cell phone and punched in the number.

"Marshall Vreeland, please...Yes, tell him Congressman Grant is calling."

It took a minute or so for Vreeland to come to the telephone.

"Congressman, how are you?" Vreeland asked.

"Just fine," David said. "You still want to run for President?"

"Of course, I do."

"Good. I may have some rocket fuel for your launch."

CHAPTER 46

It took about two weeks to make all the arrangements for Vreeland's announcement. He wanted to use his Zenith Center as the venue. However, David and Jason Kennerly encouraged him to use a less grandiose setting. Vreeland chose a large ballroom in one of his hotels in Denver.

Vreeland was introduced by a friend using the most glowing terms. Once introduced, he stepped up to the podium, grim-faced.

"Good afternoon, my name is Marshall Vreeland."

The audience, mostly his employees, immediately erupted in applause. It forced Vreeland to crack a smile despite his determination to stay solemn.

"Like many Americans," he continued. "I've become distressed by what passes for leadership in this country, whether it's on the Right or the Left. The direction of our country is usually erratic, and often wrong. And now, the President has launched what he calls the Strategic Investment Act. In reality, it's nothing more than a pork-barrel-spending behemoth boondoggle. There's nothing strategic about it."

"I have nothing against a reasonable spending package that stimulates the economy effectively. But why use an atom bomb when a slingshot will do? It's wasteful and extraordinarily messy. When I look through the laundry list of expenditures, I see nothing but pork. Honestly, how is five million dollars for a confectionary museum strategic to America's future? How about two million dollars for prune research?"

"And worst of all is 35 million dollars to some organization called Voters Equal Access League, or VEAL, which on the surface seems to have a laudable mission: helping disenfranchised citizens participate in our democratic process. Yet, VEAL's offices are located in fairly upscale neighborhoods. Sure, equal access, for people named Skip and Buffy. Let's call it what it is, political cronyism with a fancy acronym. VEAL is the new pork."

"And don't think the Republicans are off the hook. There's over 70 billion dollars in farm subsidies. Saving family farms may seem noble, but here's the catch. Most of that's going to large agricultural conglomerates, big corporations that happen to own farms."

"Of course, that bit of corporate welfare is nothing compared to what Wall Street received through CART, probably the brainchild of Wall Street's own Robert Hingecliff. Why are the President, the Treasury Secretary, and Congress throwing away our money?"

"Over the centuries, we've had giants in the White House. We've had statesmen in Congress. Where did they all go? Our country has greatness in it. We put a man on the moon. We beat back tyrants and despots. But now, instead of statesmen, we have a bunch of politicians pimping for special interests!"

"The President and Congress work for you, the American people. If anyone wasted my money like that, I'd fire 'em. In the interest of eradicating this unforgivable negligence and malfeasance, I am announcing my candidacy for the President of the United States."

The hand-picked crowd again exploded in applause.

ಬಿ ಬಿ ಚಿ ಚಿ

After the speech, Vreeland and his entourage took an elevator to the top floor. Jason Kennerly and David were waiting for them in a suite Vreeland had provided.

"So what did you think?" Vreeland asked, smiling.

"Can we be alone?" Jason asked, looking at the crowd filing in.

"Sure," Vreeland turned to his people. "Give us the room guys. Stan, you stay." Stan Erskine was Vreeland's campaign manager.

Once the four of them were alone, Vreeland poured himself a drink. "Can I get anyone anything?"

They all declined.

"So, I heard the networks didn't carry my speech live," Vreeland said.

"C-SPAN did," Erskine said. "The networks will play it tonight, though. That's when it'll count."

"So, what did you think of the speech?"

"It was fantastic, quite inspiring," Erskine said.

"Very strong," Jason added.

Vreeland spied Grant looking down and frowning at some campaign materials on a table.

Vreeland took a few steps in David's direction. "What does Congressman Sourpuss think?"

David looked up. "I think the speech was fine, better than my first political speech."

"So what's the problem?"

"We've been looking through some of your campaign materials." David picked up a sample placard. "Vreeland for a Free Land?" He pointed to another against the wall. "Marshal Your Forces for Vreeland? Who wrote this stuff?"

"Hey," Vreeland interrupted. "My ad agency has done great work for me for over twenty years."

"I'm sure," David said, "selling real estate. But political campaigns require more than pretty architectural photos and square-footage listings. Your brochures read like they're selling condos and office space. You need to sell the benefits of a Vreeland presidency, not your past professional successes. Your slogan needs to be more than a bad pun."

Vreeland shook his head. "You know, Grant, you really are a ballbuster, aren't you? And you don't even think I can win, so why should I listen to you?"

"Maybe you can't win, but you can make one hell of an impression," David insisted. "Your unique power is to bring issues to the forefront, and force the others to deal with them. And if you make a strong showing, you'll have strengthened the party and the centrist cause. And for that we will be eternally grateful." David tossed the placard back on the table. "Maybe I'm wrong, and you can win this thing. Why should you listen to me? I'll always tell you the truth, because—and I mean no offense to Mr. Erskine here—I don't receive a paycheck from you."

"Fair enough," Vreeland said, grudgingly. "What do you recommend next?"

"Two things. You need practice answering questions as if in a press conference or interview. Now that you've announced, the press will start drilling into you. You need to answer tough questions, the kind you don't want to answer, the kind that might get under your skin."

"Well, there's nobody better for getting under the skin than you."

"Okay, I'll write up a list of tough questions to start you off. I'll forward them to Mr. Erskine."

"What's the other thing?" Erskine asked.

"Start conducting polls, and not by anyone connected with your campaign. You want the honest truth, unfiltered."

"You have anyone in mind?"

"No, but my chief of staff will probably know the right people. I'll have her put together a list."

"Thanks," Vreeland said, picking up one of the campaign brochures. "You know, you're a pain in the ass, but I'm glad you're my pain in the ass."

಄ ಇ ಞ ಌ

David took a late flight back to Washington. The next morning, as he was walking to a committee meeting, his coat pocket started to strangely vibrate. He stuck his hand in and realized it was the cell phone Robert Hingecliff had given him. It indicated "Dentist" was calling.

"Hello."

"Good morning. I see you passed the menu onto Mr. Vreeland."

"Was it that obvious?"

"Well, to me it was, especially when he said VEAL is the new pork."

"I hope you don't mind."

"No, not at all," Hingecliff said. "In fact, I think it was a brilliant idea. And I see your Mr. Vreeland also took a shot at me, too. I thank you for that."

"Has it occurred to you how bizarre it is that you're thanking me for a political attack?"

"Yes," Hingecliff chuckled, "Washington is paved with irony, isn't it?"

As David turned, he saw Jack Kripke standing a short distance away, clearly waiting to speak with him. He wondered if he had said anything that would pique Kripke's curiosity.

"I better go. My tooth's feeling much better. Thank you."

"Very good," Hingecliff said. With that, they hung up.

As David put the phone back in his pocket, Kripke approached.

"Good morning, Congressman."

"Good morning, Jack. What can I do for you?"

"Well, we're having a briefing tomorrow night on the education component of the President's bill."

"Really? Sponsored by the Progressive Institute for Education Excellence, by any chance?"

"Yes, Kripke Associates has taken on the PIEE as a client. How did you know?"

"Just a shot in the dark."

"Can we count on the pleasure of your company?"

"Jack, I wouldn't miss it for the world."

"Great. Eight o'clock at Le Chevalier."

David nodded. "See you there."

ஐ ஐ ౧ ౧

After the committee meeting, David returned to his office. Tyler knocked on his open door.

"I've revised the energy amendment," Tyler said, as he handed David the new text.

"Revised? What's the difference between this and our original bill?"

"I removed the Samu funding. I heard Congressman Hudge was going to amend the bill separately. So, I didn't think you'd want him to have redundant funding."

"No. Good thinking. I'll introduce this later today. Thanks. Would you tell Ellen I'd like to see her?"

A minute later, Ellen came in.

"So, how was Denver?" she asked.

"I didn't see much of it. Did you see Vreeland's speech?"

"Yes, very nice. Did he pay you to ghostwrite it for him?"

"Well, I did give him a few lines to use."

"Like VEAL is the new pork?"

David nodded.

"It's all over the news. Too bad it's being attributed to him."

"They're taking Vreeland seriously?"

"The focus is more on what he talked about. The Republican leadership is jumping all over the VEAL thing now. It made Ben Glendenning's day. As to which side has more pork in the bill, it'll be a pissing match."

"Maybe it'll force them to trim the fat in the bill."

"You realize, they may trim your energy amendment," Ellen warned.

"Well, I've come to realize passing our energy bill may be a hard slog after all."

"Getting back to Vreeland, I'd like you to send his campaign manager, Stan Erskine, a list of pollsters you think would be honest and reliable. If you could also come up with a list of tough interview questions for Vreeland, I'd appreciate it. He's too used to the sycophants he's surrounded by. The press'll chew him up and spit him out if he doesn't practice hitting some hardballs."

Ellen stood silently for a moment. "Congressman, I support you in all your congressional duties. You know that. I'll even work hard to get you re-elected. But, I'm still a Republican. I don't work for Vreeland."

"You're loyal to the Republican Party, a party that didn't treat you very well, did it? That's why you were forced to work for the likes of me. Seems like a one-way loyalty to me."

Ellen was silent.

"Look, Vreeland is never going to win the presidency. But he can help us get some information out there without the type of blowback we got after I attacked Barnes. I promise I'll limit what you have to do for his campaign. Okay?"

"Very well." Ellen started to leave, but turned back. "We did find some more pork. There's 40 million for renovating luxury yacht slips and docks. Your Mr. Vreeland could comment on that."

"Thanks, I'm sure he'll appreciate it."

ဆ ဆ ၡ ၢ

The following night, David arrived at Le Chevalier at a quarter after eight. He was immediately shown to a back room, where an open bar was in progress. It was an odd collection of senators and representatives. Most were Democrats, but there were a few Republicans, including Howard Carstairs.

"Good evening, Howard."

"Ah, David. How was Colorado?"

"How did you know I was in Colorado?"

"I heard you passed along some tidbits from our friend, the Dentist."

"Is Dentist his universal code name?"

"Of course, and by the way, you're now IT Support. I'm Barber."

"Not Lobsterman?"

Carstairs smiled. "Don't be a smart aleck. That would be too obvious. By the way, what you did with Vreeland was a smart move. Vreeland fires at the President's bill, but it leaves you free to amend it with our energy bill. Right?"

David smiled. "The thought had crossed my mind. Your office should receive the amendment tomorrow morning."

"You're starting to get the hang of the place."

"I'm not sure I want that."

Carstairs laughed.

Soon, they were all led into another room for dinner.

After steak and red wine, Jack Kripke stood up, knocking his knife against a wine glass to attract everyone's attention.

"Good evening, ladies and gentlemen. Thank you for coming to tonight. I really appreciate it. If no one minds, I thought we'd start our presentation while they served dessert. I'd like to introduce Mr. Carl Stavros, the Executive Director of the Progressive Institute for Education Excellence. Carl and his organization are very committed to the future of education. Carl?"

"Good evening," Stavros said, as he stood up. "It's good to see so many familiar faces. Since I left the White House, I've been able to dedicate myself to the improvement of education in this country, something that's near and dear to my heart. So, when the President came out with his signature education initiative, we became very excited. And then, when we saw the details, we became ecstatic."

"As we analyzed the President's bill, we discovered it boiled down to three main pillars in order to extend college opportunities to Americans who are most underserved by our college and university systems."

"First, it calls for enhancing the ability of students to transfer between colleges, making it easier if the student has to move. A man I know, named Doug, had to choose between completing his degree and moving to another city to keep his job. It was heartbreaking for him. Like many people in his situation, Doug chose to keep his job. Because he was so far into his degree, transferring all his credits was impossible. When his new company had layoffs, he was one of the first to go, because he didn't have a college degree, truly heartbreaking and inexcusable. However, the President's bill guarantees that students can transfer credits between any two colleges. That way, these difficult choices will be eliminated."

"Second, the President's bill empowers colleges to be flexible and creative in how they deliver programs. Much of this will be hybrid and online, crossing national and linguistic borders. By attracting more students from beyond our borders, we will turn our postsecondary educational institutions into a powerhouse industry."

"And third, as the President said, the highest-paying jobs require advanced degrees. Therefore, he's pushing to expand current financial aid programs to cover master's and doctorate programs. In a nutshell, this is the educational component of the President's bill."

Stavros proceeded to present statistics to support the points he had made. Finally, he opened the floor up for questions.

David was the first to stand up. "No offense to you, but why hasn't the White House presented this information to us themselves?"

"I have no idea," Stavros admitted. "Being with what is technically a super-PAC, I can't have any direct communication with the White House."

Others asked questions, but they were fairly innocuous.

David leaned over to Carstairs. "Why aren't your Republican colleagues in the room attacking this? Financing advanced degrees is certainly going to cost a bundle."

"The Republicans here tonight are trying to secure Kripke's campaign contributions. Those who are going to attack Farnum are combing the pork sections of the bill tonight. I have to admit, they're a bit pissed off that Vreeland beat them to the punch." Carstairs changed to a whisper, "Of course, they don't know it was actually you who beat them to it."

"I give my dentist the full credit."

After the presentation, David pulled out his cell phone and called Ellen.

"Ellen, let's forget searching the President's bill for pork. The Republicans will take care of that. I want everyone to take a closer look at the education sections of the bill."

David realized Stavros and Kripke were two new links to be added to the Winton-Danzig-Parnell-Cornwall chain.

CHAPTER 47

The following weekend, David, Fred and Tyler pulled up to the Embler River Inn. They entered the hotel through the back entrance. As they walked in, Armand Nistle greeted them. Fred had phoned ahead to tell him of their imminent arrival.

"Politics, whether national or collegiate, makes for strange bedfellows," Nistle announced. "Doesn't it?"

David shot Fred an amused look.

"The others are already here," Nistle continued, leading them to a small rustic-looking conference room, paneled in walnut. It was the same room David's campaign had used as a private office on election night.

The various professors who Nistle had been working with were gathered around a conference table. One by one, they all introduced themselves,. Finally, everyone settled down into a chair, except David.

"Thank you all for coming. Several weeks ago, Professor Nistle approached me about the situation at Winton. I have no authority over the college. But I suspect there is more than meets the eye. I am going to trust you with a secret. In exchange, I want your help."

"What's this secret?" asked one of the academics at the far end of the table.

"The issues at Winton may be connected to a larger issue. As you may have seen in the news, President Farnum is pushing a new education bill. I believe the two may be connected."

Many of the academics looked at one another in disbelief. How could their local collegiate problems be connected with anything national?

"You realize most of us voted for and supported President Farnum?" called out Jay Eisenberg, a rather rotund man with a gray beard and ponytail.

"Yes. I voted for him, too. But, this is not about him, but rather something that may have been slipped into the bill."

"You say there's a link between what Danzig's doing to us and this bill. What exactly is the connection?"

"I'd rather not say at this time. If I'm wrong, I don't want anyone making false accusations, which would be bad for all of us. Besides, I need you to approach this problem with fresh eyes, unbiased by anything I might say."

"You're the Congressman. Why don't you just go over to the Department of Education and demand some answers?"

"Because, if there's a conspiracy, they're not likely to give me straight answers. If I eventually do something about this, I don't want them to see me coming. That's why we have to keep this under wraps."

"What is it you want us to do?" asked Eisenberg.

David nodded to Tyler, who then started passing out thick binders.

"Dr. Eisenberg, these binders hold the education-related sections of the President's bill. They're now publicly available on a government website, but you would have to wade through all the unrelated pork to find it. I want you to go through the education sections and tell me what's wrong with it. But first, let me tell you what I've been told this bill will do." David then relayed the Stavros presentation to them.

"I can tell you one part of this thing that's crap," Eisenberg said, "this being able to transfer to any college."

"Why is that a problem?" David asked.

Eisenberg smiled at the opportunity to lecture a congressman. "Suppose I'm a student attending…um…Goofball College," he began. "And I take most of my courses at Goofball. Then, I demand a transfer to Harvard or some other Ivy League school. That means I get to slap a Harvard diploma on my Goofball education."

"I can't imagine that would be possible," David said.

"Well, if Parnell is involved, that would be something they'd love," Nistle added.

"Parnell is involved in this?" asked a thin, nervous-looking woman with thick glasses. "When I began teaching, I taught a semester at a Parnell school—worst semester of my career. They actually forbid failing students for any reason. They almost had their accreditation yanked. Congressman, colleges need to be able to maintain their standards. If Parnell is involved with this, then the standards are under attack."

"Then find it in the legislation," David insisted.

"How long do we have?" Eisenberg asked.

"I'm headed back to Washington first thing Monday morning. This room is yours for the weekend. Meals are on me. The President's pushing this legislation hard and fast. Fred and Tyler will be available to work with you. Most of you know Fred Arkin. Tyler Benson, here, is my legislative assistant. He'll be helpful in decoding any legalese."

"If you have your legislative legal eagle, what do you need us for?"

"Tyler can translate the legalese, but I need you to explain the ramifications, like that Goofball-to-Harvard credit transfer thing."

After a few more questions, David excused himself. "Professor Nistle, would you walk me to my car?"

Nistle gave him a surprised look, but complied.

"It's important that everyone keep this meeting under wraps," David explained as they walked down the hall toward the parking lot. "Loose lips sink ships, and all that."

"No problem."

"But that's not why I asked you to walk with me. I just wanted to let you know I'm having dinner with Charles Danzig tonight."

"Playing both sides against the middle?" Nistle asked with a smirk.

"I'm not completely sure what the sides are. But I have to tell you something. Somehow Danzig knew you came down to Washington to see me."

"How?"

"I don't know. I was hoping you could hazard a guess."

Nistle stood there, thinking back. "I didn't tell anyone I was going down, I swear. The only one who knew was Fred Arkin."

"Well, I need to confess that you came down to see me."

"You're gonna hang me out to dry?"

"No. Remember, he already knows. But if I admit it, I may be able to gain some trust. Maybe he'll open up to me. I just wanted to be honest with you. And, I wanted to warn you to be careful."

"Okay, I appreciate that," Nistle said, clearly stunned.

ॐ ॐ ॐ ॐ

David and Chuck Danzig met up at an elegant restaurant just a mile from the campus. It was a stark contrast to the rustic charm of the Embler River Inn.

"So, how's your reelection campaign coming along?" Danzig asked, as they sat down.

David thought it was an odd question considering the next election was well over a year away. Only people like Ellen Langford were talking to him about reelection this early.

"It's a bit early, but fundraising is never-ending."

A waiter came and took their drink order.

"Before we go on," David said, "I have to get something off my chest, something that's been bothering me. A couple of weeks ago, when you called me about Armand Nistle, I have to confess he had already contacted me."

"Really? What did he say?" Danzig asked, with an intently interested expression.

"He ranted about budget cuts, *et cetera*. He practically accused you of being the devil."

"Well, then I suppose that helps me make my decision easier then."

"What decision?"

"To let him go."

David realized he may have miscalculated. "Doesn't he have tenure?"

"The board is considering voiding all tenure."

"Why do that?"

"Winton's financial situation demands it. You know how I said you and Fred Arkin will have positions when you're finished in Washington? That's a promise I want to keep. But if our enrollment keeps declining, even my job might be in jeopardy. Meanwhile, the endowment fund has taken a real hit, thanks to the dropping stock market."

"What can I do?"

"Well, a donation is always welcome," Danzig half-joked. "However, you're in a unique position to help by supporting the President's education bill."

"Is this about the solar energy project? I saw it in the bill."

"Yes, Senator Matthews very kindly put that in for us."

"Really? You could have come to me with that."

"Please don't be hurt. I knew someone in his office."

"Don't worry about my feelings. I'm a big boy," David said.

"Besides Ernie Matthews is on the Senate Education Committee. And, it might have been seen as a conflict of interest for you, since he used to be employed by the college. So it seemed more appropriate for it to come from him."

"That's very thoughtful. But back to Armand Nistle for a moment. Nothing would please me more than having that jerk's ass kicked. But what did they say in *The Godfather*? 'Keep your friends close, and your enemies closer.' Maybe, it's better to keep Nistle on. Once loose, he could become a bigger problem."

Danzig looked down at his wine glass, pondering what David had said. "Perhaps, you're right." Danzig smiled at David. "I appreciate you telling me about this."

₨ ₨ ℛ ℛ

David finally arrived home just before nine o'clock. Sara dutifully hugged and kissed him.

"Hi, how did your meetings go?" Sara asked, as she continued folding some laundry.

"Things are going to get ugly. I'm just not sure exactly how. But I don't want to talk about it. How was your week?"

"Well, I do have some news. Gunther & Cartwright won the bid for a new civic center in Pittsburgh."

"Pittsburgh? Well, congratulations."

Sara gave a taut smile. "Here's the thing," she said, dropping a folded bath towel on the pile. "They want me to manage the preliminary on-site work."

"In Pittsburgh?" David asked, as he attempted to pair some socks. "When?"

"Mid-July into August."

"Wow. What about the kids?"

"That's the problem. I mean, as a 17-year-old, Chris would be all right on his own, as long as we check in on him. He's pretty responsible."

"That leaves Wendy."

"Yeah. The thing is, I don't think it's fair to drop her on the Garthwells for almost half the summer. This isn't just a few overnights."

"True."

"Our careers are growing too big. I don't want us to be those kinds of parents who neglect their children for their careers."

"Me neither," David said. So, what do we do?"

"Wendy had an idea," Sara ventured. "She said she wanted to come down and live with you in Washington. The other night she insisted on watching *Mr. Smith Goes to Washington.*"

"Did she?"

She saw a boy who was acting as a page, helping Jimmy Stewart. She asked if she could be a page. Would that actually be possible?"

"The House doesn't have pages anymore. And she's way too young to be a Senate page, despite what Jimmy Stewart might think," he said, grabbing another pair of socks. "Is there any possibility of taking her with you to Pittsburgh?"

"You can't bring a child onto a construction site. It's too dangerous. Besides, the insurance companies won't allow it."

"I suppose you're right. Well, then Washington it is. I've committed to do some early campaigning for the new Centrist congressional candidates during the summer recess. So, she'll get to do some traveling, too."

"Really? I didn't think you'd agree to this," Sara admitted.

"Well, despite what you may think, I do miss my family," he said, leaning over the laundry to kiss her. "And it might be fun to have Wendy around. I guess the first order of business is to order her a bed for the townhouse."

"And a television."

ༀ ༀ ༀ ༀ

Sunday morning, Narlstrom was laying in bed, warm and comfortable. Out of the window he saw the morning rays coming in the windows. Some called them "God rays." He knew it was simply light rays being diffused and reflected by airborne dust particles engaged in Brownian movement. Yet, it was still comforting. He reached around Hanna's warm body. She was lying with her back to him. He kissed her naked shoulder. She moved her neck. He kissed her shoulder again. She stretched her arm upward, while yawning.

She threw her legs outward off the bed and sat up. He reached out for her hips, trying to coax her back toward him. She turned and smiled.

"Good morning." Then, she leaned over and kissed him. "We have to get going."

"Couldn't we just stay in bed all day?"

"We have to be in Dayton by noon. The rally starts at five."

"Then, why do we have to be there at noon?" he asked. "Prep for the rally is only an hour or two."

"We have to meet up with Harry Branch."

Branch was veteran who had been working hard for the SALA cause in the Western states. He was a former Navy Seal. Narlstrom had met him a couple of times and liked him.

But he liked Hanna more. Narlstrom gave another tug on her hips. She responded by standing up quickly.

"You can make the coffee while I shower." She went into the bathroom and closed the door.

He laid back in bed, listening to the water spray in the shower. *Hanna, my angel.* It had been months since his speech on the Washington Mall. *More like my breakdown.* Yet, it had brought them together. She had comforted him, sitting on that bench across the tidal basin from the Jefferson Memorial. She understood him. Perhaps more importantly, she shared his anger at the government. He was still angry, but she added hope and direction, bringing him into the SALA movement.

Then they became lovers. He was shocked that a beautiful woman, ten years his junior, would be interested in him. He couldn't remember who made that initial tremulous move toward that first kiss. It just happened, as if fated by the universe. He wondered what else was fated by the universe.

ಬ ಬ ಚ ಚ

Early Monday morning, David took the train back to Washington. Fred sat next to him.

"Where's Tyler?" David asked, as the train started its lurching efforts at acceleration.

"He took the train back last night," Fred explained. "I think the professors were getting to him."

"So," David asked, "what did you learn from the Winton Underground?"

"Well, they love free food. You're gonna have one helluva food charge on the bill."

They both laughed.

"They uncovered a lot of education pork, grants and gifts to colleges, none of which they seemed to have any particular problem with. I think they all imagined being the recipients of those goodies. I had to redirect them to focus on the faults in the legislation."

"What recipient doesn't love pork? That's the insidious key to its success."

"Anyway," Fred continued, "Eisenberg was right about what we now call the 'universal credit transfer' clause. Under this legislation, no college or university could refuse the credits of another college. It would tip the balance in favor of lesser quality schools."

"In other words, Parnell Education, selling cheaper college credits, would benefit big time. What else?"

"The financial aid for more advanced degrees; it's more than that though. The bill not only allows for earning an unlimited number of degrees, it includes supplementing income while pursuing those degrees. You know the joke about certain people being professional students? This legislation could make it a literal reality."

"So, people could be supported by the government indefinitely?"

"As long as they are enrolled in a college program or equivalent training program."

"There has to be some limit."

"Only one I could find. No one can start an additional doctoral program until they have completed their dissertation on a previous doctorate. Of course, Parnell doesn't own any universities, so that limitation doesn't affect them."

"Wow." David leaned back against his seat in awe. "This means Parnell and any other school can receive an infinite flow of federal aid as long as they can enroll students."

"This is more than a pork barrel," Fred said. "This could mean the destruction of the American higher education system."

"I think that's a bit extreme."

"Not at all. Degrees from top schools could become worthless. It means endless manipulation of degree programs. It opens the door for a whole range of education scammers. And don't think Parnell is the only one. They'll just be the first one through the door. And all for corporate profit."

"These people have to be stopped."

CHAPTER 48

Once they arrived back in Washington, David called Ellen into his office.

"Good morning," Ellen said. "Tyler told me your Winton brain trust found some interesting things in the President's bill."

"Yes, indeed." David explained about the universal transfer clause and unlimited degrees provision.

"Well, I'm sure the Republicans will support you in attacking this."

"I'm not so sure this is a completely Democratic issue. As we know, corruption frequently crosses party lines. Matthews was the one who put in the solar energy grant for Winton."

"Yes, but the participation of one Republican Senator doesn't make it a bipartisan conspiracy."

"Perhaps." David leaned forward. "There's something Carl Stavros said that struck me odd. I can't get it out of my head. He said something about 'crossing linguistic borders.' Now, ESL is not new, so—"

"ESL, that's English as a Second Language. Right?"

"Exactly," David said. "Helping non-English native speakers deal with English better. It's been embraced by almost every college out there."

"And you don't think this is ESL?"

"I'm not sure. Stavros's words struck me oddly. And after what we've uncovered, I don't trust this legislation, not one part of it. We need to search this bill for whatever he was referring to."

"That's thousands of pages."

"But we have it digitally, don't we? Have someone do a word search for any references to 'language,' 'linguistic borders,' or any similar terms"

"I'll put one of our new staffers on it."

"Good. By the way," David continued, "Wendy is coming to live with me here in Washington this summer."

Ellen turned and closed the door quietly.

"Is there a problem at home?"

David laughed. "No, nothing like that. Sara has a project that will take her out of town for several weeks. That means I may have to have her come into the office. Wendy suggested a job as a page. I know that's not possible."

"Sir, I am not a babysitter," Ellen said warily.

"And I'm not asking you to become one, nor anyone else in this office. I know an office isn't a daycare facility. I've seen people make that mistake. I'm going to look into summer camp activities here in Washington, as well as hiring a companion for her. But Wendy keeps saying she wants to help in the office. I'm just saying that if you think of any small jobs that a ten-year-old can do around the office, I'd welcome them."

ഗ ഇ ൧ ౪

Attendance at the previous day's SALA rally in Dayton had been disappointing. Many of the leadership had gathered to rectify the increasingly downward trend.

"Where the hell's Jarvis Thayer?" Harry Branch demanded. Branch had been leading SALA efforts in the western states. He and Thayer had only spoken on the phone so far.

"He's doing another interview with *Entertainment Express*," someone called out.

"Let me guess, with *the actress*?" Hanna asked.

He nodded.

"What's with this Cassiere character?" Branch asked.

"She's a fame whore," Hanna explained. "She thinks being associated with Jarvis will boost her career."

"Why can't she make a sex tape like the other Hollywood wannabees?"

There were several snickers.

"Then, how would she stand out?" someone called out.

"But wait. Isn't generating press coverage beneficial for SALA?" asked one of the younger and more naïve members of the group.

"The viewers of *Entertainment Express*" Hanna said, in a tone angrier than she wished, "are brain-dead idiots who only care about which celebrity is screwing which other celebrity. How is that beneficial? The number of people showing up to our demonstrations has been going down, and he's bolstering his girlfriend's career."

"We need to do something dramatic," someone else called out.

"Why not some old fashioned flag burning?" a younger member suggested. "It got people's attention in the sixties."

"No!" growled Narlstrom, who had remained silent so far. "I don't hate my country. I just hate the bastards who run it. They are the problem, not the flag, not the principles our nation was built on. It's those fucking bastards in Washington!"

"I'm with Dan on this," Harry Branch announced firmly. "I fought for this country in Iraq and Afghanistan—Special Forces.

No one doubted this. He had the bearing and physique. No one doubted he had seen action of the most extreme kind.

"I'll be damned if I participate in any flag burning. I'm a patriot, not some left-wing long hair from the sixties."

"Hey," the younger members countered, "Those flag burners back in the sixties loved their country, too. They were just expressing it dramatically. That's all."

"No flag burning on my watch," Branch snapped. "Clear?"

"Okay. Everyone calm down," Hanna said, trying to refocus the meeting. "We need to develop a strategy that will get us somewhere constructive."

"Well, there's that Vreeland guy running for president," someone else suggested. "Maybe, we could do something with him?"

"Like he'd be any different!" Narlstrom said. "He's just another money-grubbing businessman, probably just running to stroke his ego. No better than the fame whore in the other room."

"None of this addresses the fact we're losing steam," Hanna said.

Finally, Thayer appeared. "Hey guys, I just had a great interview, really pushed our cause."

Tess Cassiere followed him in, smiling. Everyone just rolled their eyes. Narlstrom and Branch's eyes met. Wordlessly they both acknowledged SALA was going nowhere.

ಬ ಬ ಞ ಞ

The following day, Ellen pulled David aside in the corridor outside a committee room.

"We found the language issue. Very cleverly hidden. Apparently, there's an incentive for non-English-speaking colleges."

David gave her a confused look. "I've never heard of non-English-speaking colleges in the United States."

"There aren't any. To attend an accredited college in the United States, a student must speak, read and write English. This bill eliminates that requirement."

"That's not very practical. How would any student be able to succeed that way?"

"They could if the college taught all their classes in that foreign language."

"We're not talking language schools, right? You know, teaching people to speak French or German?"

"No, this covers accredited, degree-granting institutions. And let's be clear. We're talking about Spanish, the language of our fastest-growing demographic group."

David sighed. "This will rip yet another divide in the country. Why would the President do this?"

"It makes no sense," Ellen agreed. "The Democrats already have the Hispanic vote."

"It's not about the Democrats," David realized out loud. "Remember, Danzig mentioned Ernie Matthews. He's the Republican Senator from my own state."

"This is not about the President. It's about Parnell. I did a little checking. Parnell's colleges have been advertising for bilingual professors in all disciplines. Why would a college math or science professor need to be bilingual?"

"To teach college math or science in Spanish. After this committee meeting, let's get Fred and Tyler together and get them up to speed."

David started into the committee room, but was held back by Ellen's hand on his arm.

"There's something else you need to know."

₧ ₧ ₨ ₨

Approximately two hours later, David, Ellen, Fred and Tyler were sitting around the small conference table in David's office.

"Tyler, we just wanted to review the language of the energy amendment." Ellen picked up a page with a section highlighted in yellow. "First off, I'm a little confused, this sentence here: *Section 114 shall apply to all qualified parties, and shall not be denied based on race, religion, national origin or language spoken, and shall embrace all languages required.*' How does that apply?"

Tyler looked at the text for a moment. "I believe this is to prevent discrimination."

"Why would we need to prevent discrimination in an energy bill?" David asked.

"Well, um, I suppose to protect consumers from being discriminated against by the energy companies."

"Aren't there already laws on the books to prevent that? Has there been a history of energy companies discriminating?"

"Well...uh...you can't be too careful."

"I see. What's in this Section 114?" David pressed.

"I'd have to go back and look."

"Don't bother," Ellen said. "I have it right here. Section 114 applies to the establishment of new curricula in colleges. Why would our energy amendment be referencing the education section?"

"I'm sure there's some error here," Tyler said, starting to perspire.

"You wrote the amendment, which was based on our original bill. The bill, and therefore the amendment, was self-contained. No need for referencing other parts of the bill."

"Well, uh."

"What the hell is going on? Who are you working for?" Ellen demanded.

"Who am I...for you, for the Congressman, I swear!"

"Then, why is my legislative assistant slipping language into this bill that will undermine the American education system?" David asked.

"I wouldn't."

"Does this have anything to do with Jack Kripke?" Fred asked.

Tyler looked horrified. Tears started rolling down his face, which he wiped with his sleeve.

"Mr. Kripke said...he had been a legislative assistant himself once. He was...was trying to help me. I was...struggling with the legislative language."

"You let that sleaze stick his fingers into the Congressman's amendment without consulting anyone?" Fred asked.

"Ellen said the final text was okay."

"I trusted it was the same language that was in the original bill," Ellen said sharply, not letting Tyler shift blame. "I didn't realize you were working for Kripke."

"I wasn't. He was helping me."

"Jack Kripke doesn't help anyone but himself," Ellen snapped.

"Have you told Mr. Kripke about the professors we met with back in Pennsylvania?" David asked.

"No."

"I need an honest answer here."

"I promise. I would never have passed that on to anyone."

"Did you tell anyone about Armand Nistle coming to see me?"

"I didn't even know about that until we went to Embler this past weekend."

"I think that's true," Fred said. "I didn't tell anyone. He couldn't have known."

"Why did you come back to DC early?" David asked.

Tyler laughed. "You're not going to believe it. I had a date. There's this staffer on the energy subcommittee. We've been dating for about a month."

"What's her name?" Ellen demanded.

"Emma, Emma Jacobi."

Ellen wrote down the name.

"Did Jack Kripke ever offer you a job?" she asked.

"No…I mean…he said if and when I ever finished working for the Congressman, he might have a place for me."

"Crap, that's an old lobbyist's trick," Ellen explained. "It's not a direct bribe, but it influences people's decisions just the same."

David remembered Danzig had made a similar offer to him and Fred. Had he been swayed, too, by an old lobbyist's trick?

"I'm sorry, Tyler," Ellen said. "You've been compromised, and therefore can't be trusted. You have to resign." She turned to David. "Don't you agree, Congressman?"

CHAPTER 49

David sat at his desk, reviewing a new piece of intellectual property legislation as best he could. With Tyler Benson gone from his staff, it fell to Ellen to be the primary navigator of legalese. However, David felt a certain sense of negligence about the whole Section 114 incident. He decided he was going to make more of an effort to read and understand the legislative language.

Fred stuck his head in the door. David looked up.

"Good time?" Fred asked.

David shrugged.

"So, what do you want to do about this?" Fred asked, holding up the file on the education bill. "I was thinking you might try to persuade some of the Democrats to take a stand? Cal McCord, Christa Lemmon, maybe even Wyatt Wickham?"

"I can't see any of them going against the President's signature legislation."

"Could give it to Vreeland," Fred suggested.

"No, not this time," David mumbled. "There's no way Vreeland could pretend to know the intimate details of the bill."

"What about the hard-right Republicans? They won't turn down the opportunity."

"True, but when they attack it, it might be dismissed as just more pre-election mudslinging."

"You're trying to protect the Republicans?" Fred asked.

"No, I want this threat to be taken seriously. Besides, I didn't come to Washington to hide behind Vreeland or the Republicans."

"David, if you take on the President of the United States directly, without any party support, you'll be painting a target on your back. If you don't believe me, ask Ellen."

David sighed and looked out his window. "You know, it's already started. Hasn't it?"

"What?"

"Washington-itis. I've been infected. Trying to be so clever and manipulative. Using Vreeland. Thinking about how to use the Republicans." He stood up. "Things shouldn't have to be that complicated."

80 80 03 03

Later that day, Tyler Benson walked into Le Chevalier.

"Ah, Mr. Benson," said the maître'd. "Mr. Kripke is waiting for you. Right this way."

Tyler was surprised the maître'd recognized him. He found Kripke was sitting at a corner booth.

"How are you, Tyler?" Kripke asked cheerfully, without standing up.

"Well, I was asked for my resignation. Apparently, the reference to Section 114 in the energy section tipped the Congressman off to the fact you were supplying me with the legal language."

Kripke motioned for Tyler to sit down. "Did you realize what I was doing?" he asked.

"I may be somewhat inexperienced, but I'm not completely inept. Anyway, you once made me a job offer. Does it still stand?"

"I thought you'd be angry with me. I mean, I did cost you your job, at least indirectly."

"I was at first. But I'm a big boy. I knew the reference to 114 had nothing to do with energy management. I figured it was the price for your help. I look at it as a lesson I needed to learn. Besides, being pissed at you gets me nothing. I'd rather learn how to play the game better."

Jack Kripke smiled. "You're a very wise young man."

଼ ଼ ଼ ଼

David walked to the botanical garden only a short distant from his office. He pulled out the "hotline" as he started to think of it, and pressed the speed-dial button for "Dentist." There was no answer and no option to leave a message. He frowned, put the phone back in his pocket, and started back to the Capitol. After about a minute and a half, the phone started to vibrate. The caller ID read "Dentist."

"Hello."

"I'm sorry I couldn't answer your call," Hingecliff said. "I was finishing up a meeting. What can I do for you?"

"I've made a disturbing discovery. The President's education bill has some pretty nasty stuff in it."

"Tell me."

David proceeded to explain all he had learned.

"You have documentation?"

"It's all in the bill."

"Are you going to be home tonight?"

"I can be. What time?"

"Make it nine o'clock."

At a quarter to nine that evening, the doorbell rang at David's townhouse. He assumed Hingecliff was early. However, when he opened the door, instead of the Treasury Secretary, a thin, young man was standing there.

"Can I help you?" David asked.

"I'm here to sweep the residence for listening devices," the young man said quietly. "Your dentist sent me."

David was caught off guard. He felt for a moment he was dreaming he was in a spy novel.

The young man, sensing David's reluctance, added, "He'll be here in fifteen minutes, but I'll only need ten. May I begin?"

David nodded and stepped aside. As good as his word, the young man was finished in ten minutes.

David was tempted to ask what agency he was with, but decided to remain silent. The man left with no more than a nod. David assumed that meant the place was clean of any bugs.

Several minutes later, Robert Hingecliff arrived.

"Are you my secret contact?"

Hingecliff gave him an odd look.

"Apparently, my place is clear of any listening devices."

Hingecliff chuckled. "Sorry about that. It may seem paranoid. If anyone suspects I'm talking to you, I'll be resigning my position 'for family reasons.' Do you have your documentation?"

"Yes. Everything's on the kitchen table."

Hingecliff looked about as they entered the kitchen. "Ah, the Spartan living of a freshman congressman." He looked back at the boxes in the living room. "Although, I thought you would have been unpacked by now."

"I have. But my daughter, Wendy, is moving in for the summer. So, more boxes."

"Ah."

Hingecliff sat down. David spent the next 45 minutes guiding him through all the details of the legislation.

"My God." Hingecliff sighed, as he pulled off his reading glasses. "Student default rates have escalated in recent years. This'll accelerate the situation into a fiscal disaster. It'll make the mortgage crisis look like a hiccup."

"We've pieced together connections between Ellis Cornwall, Parnell Education, and Jack Kripke. There may also be a connection to the president of the college where I used to teach, but that's not important right now. Kripke worked his dark magic, and manipulated my own legislative assistant into inserting the foreign language clause into my energy amendment. I assume Cornwall and Parnell were big contributors to the President's campaign?"

"Oh, yes," Hingecliff said, shaking his head.

"Do you think the President knew about this?"

"I have no idea."

"Can you talk to the President about it?"

"I'm not the education secretary. I've had nothing to do with the education bill."

David realized Hingecliff had a position to protect. He probably didn't want to expose the Circle either.

"Could you get me a meeting with the President?" David pressed.

"And what would you do in such a meeting? Accuse him of undermining American education? Ask him if he's bought and paid for by Cornwall?"

"I'll simply bring these things to his attention. The one time we met, he asked for my help on the bill. I'll give him a chance to do what's right."

"How much do you plan to reveal?"

"That'll depend on his reaction."

Hingecliff stood up and walked to the window. There was nothing much to see in the townhouse's dark neglected backyard, but it was clear Hingecliff needed a moment to think, to weigh the risks.

"Alright." Hingecliff turned back to David. "You'll have to at least make an attempt at trying to work through channels. Contact the Legislative Affairs office. Ask for a man named Jim Winslow. Present your case to him."

"Will he be helpful?"

"No, quite the opposite. He's a little turd who lives up to the stereotype of the unhelpful bureaucrat. But at least there'll be a record of you attempting to work through channels. Then, I can say, thwarted by Winslow, you ambushed me at some cocktail party, and brought this to my attention."

៨០ ៨០ ៤៩ ៤៩

Hingecliff's plan was successful. Two weeks later, David was escorted through the West Wing, but to Harris Carver's office, not the Oval Office as he expected.

"Good morning, Congressman," Carver said.

"Good morning, Mr. Carver."

"Please, call me Harris. Have a seat. Coffee?"

"No, thank you. I thought I'd be meeting with the President."

"The President did want to speak with you, but there was an emergency security briefing."

"Anything serious?"

"Everything in this building is serious," Carver said. "However, there's nothing to worry about. It just means the President had to ask me to take your meeting. So, I'm told you have certain concerns about the education bill."

"Perhaps I can reschedule with the President?"

"Congressman, I don't have time to put this delicately. You're a first-term congressman, who's not even on the Education Committee. The only reason you're here now is because the President remembered and liked you. But that mild affection only gets you so far. This is the time to make your case."

"Very well." David laid highlighted copies of the key sections of the bill on Carver's desk and proceeded to outline the problems with the bill.

"I wish every Congressman was as clear and succinct as you. You make a very good case." Carver reached for his phone and pressed some buttons. "Could you come into my office for a moment?"

Within a minute, a young man entered, who to David seemed not much older than his son, Chris.

"Congressman," Carver said, "This is Alex Herrera with our legislative affairs office." He looked up at Herrera. "Alex, Congressman Grant has brought to our attention some defects in the education bill." Carver handed Herrera the highlighted copies. "How soon can we have these sections removed?"

"We're expecting to send some minor revisions to the Hill tomorrow. We can easily cut these at the same time."

"Excellent, Alex. Get to it."

Herrera took his cue and left.

"You know, Gregory Farnum is one of the most capable presidents we've ever had," Carver said. "But with a bill this size, it takes people like you and Alex to keep all the gears aligned."

"Maybe you should write small bills."

"Yes, but small bills don't do the serious jobs." Carver stood up, signaling the end of the meeting. "Thank you, Congressman, for bringing this to our attention so quickly."

"Thank you, Mr. Carver, I mean, Harris."

"I'll give the President your regards."

David nodded and left.

Carver picked up the telephone and dialed an outside line.

"Yeah, I just had a meeting with David Grant. He's someone we need to keep an eye on."

CHAPTER 50

As good as Carver's word, changes were made to the legislation, nullifying the sections David Grant indicated.

Jack Kripke was standing at his window watching the raindrops accumulate on the glass panes.

"Tyler?" he called out.

Tyler promptly appeared.

"Have you looked over the revised education bill?" he asked, as Tyler walked in.

"I've just started."

"Check sections 114, 151 and 234."

"Sure. Any particular reason?" Tyler asked.

"Intuition."

Tyler withdrew, but returned within minutes, "Wow, they've all been gutted. How did you know?"

"You play chess, Tyler?" he asked, as he picked up a knight from handcrafted wooden chess set on a corner table.

"Not very often."

"You should. It helps learn perspective. Sometimes you have to sacrifice a rook or a knight, to play a more effective long game."

"You don't seem too upset," Tyler observed.

"Problems are merely opportunities," Kripke said. "At the very least, to bill for more hours."

"So what do you plan on doing?"

"Your grandmaster is still formulating the endgame. Meanwhile, I see that Congresswoman Birnbach had just hired a new legislative assistant. Why don't you go over and make a new friend?"

ဿ ဿ ᘒ ᘒ

The following week, Wendy arrived in Washington. David and Sara helped her settle in at the townhouse. After Sara left for Pittsburgh, David brought Wendy into the office and introduced her to his staff. In his private office, she was introduced to one person in particular.

"Wendy, this is Gretchen Wheeler. She's going to be your companion here in Washington, whenever I can't be with you."

"Very pleased to meet you," Gretchen said. "I think we're going to be great friends."

"You're like my…babysitter?" Wendy asked, sounding somewhat resentful.

"No, not exactly," David interrupted. "We're going to give you and Gretchen a special congressional assignment. We want you two to assess the local facilities here in Washington. That'll include the monuments, the botanical gardens, the National Gallery, the Air & Space Museum, the whole Smithsonian complex. We want a younger person's perspective on what's interesting, and what can be improved."

"Daddy, this sounds like busy work," Wendy complained.

David smiled. "Really?" He walked behind his desk and shuffled through some papers, stalling for time. He wondered when his little girl had grown so smart. Or, had his scheme been so transparent?

"Well, Miss Know-It-All, the Capital has millions of visitors a year. And, those visitors spend money. We want all those people to tell their families, friends and neighbors what a wonderful time they had in the nation's capital, so they'll come and spend more money here too. It's our way of supporting the local economy."

Wendy looked suspicious.

"And we expect you and Gretchen to write a report for us. And if it's good enough, I'll send that report to…the, uh… the Administration."

"To the President?"

"No, I said to the Administration." David realized he was making his ruse a little too elaborate. "Okay, go see Mr. Arkin for the list of places to review. You and Gretchen can work out a schedule. But first, I want a kiss."

Suddenly beaming, Wendy kissed her father on the cheek, and walked out to find Fred.

"Congressman, I want to thank you again for this opportunity," Gretchen said.

"Let's be honest," David said. "Babysitting isn't much of an opportunity. I'm sorry your internship fell through. While you and Wendy are in the office, feel free to ask questions and learn what you can. In fact, we'll be doing some out-of-town traveling. During that time, you can volunteer here in the office. Just talk to Ellen or Fred. And I promise, once you finish at Georgetown, I'll see that you get a proper congressional interview, if not with my office, with someone who's still in office."

"Thank you, Congressman. You've made it an opportunity. And besides, Wendy seems like a very sweet child," Gretchen observed, smiling.

"Yes, but lately she's been getting a bit more willful. Be careful. Her mother tells me she's been bingeing more on sweets lately, leading to sugar highs."

"Well, I better get out there then. I think I saw a bowl of candy out in reception." Gretchen quickly exited as Ellen came in.

"Good morning, Congressman. I hate to bring you bad news," Ellen began.

"What now?"

"We did another scan of the revised education bill. The sections you arranged the White House to remove have been reinserted, but hidden in other unrelated sections of the bill."

"Son-of-a-bitch!" David felt as if he wanted to throw something, but restrained himself. "Did the White House put them back?"

"No, the revisions seem to have gone in piecemeal from different House members, woven into new pork. But it was clearly coordinated. If the White House is behind it, they're covering their tracks very well."

"Either way, Parnell and Kripke are at work."

"The replacement of those sections was extraordinarily quick for something not so public. You think Harris Carver is behind it?"

"I don't know," David said.

"Could have been Herrera, that legislative aid you mentioned, or just another Kripke mole?"

Another mole? Maybe, Hingecliff was right to be so paranoid, David thought.

"So I guess this means I'm going to take on the President of the United States."

"Congressman, we don't know the President's behind this. And besides, if you go at the President directly, without any party support, you'll be painting a target on your back."

"Funny, those were the same words Fred used. Listen, if I'm going to be a one-term congressman, I might as well make this term count."

ᛝ ᛝ ᛞ ᛞ

On Sunday morning at the White House, Dana Seagram and her staff were preparing to monitor the political talk shows. This was fairly light duty, more of a precaution against the unexpected. If no one dropped a bombshell, went "off-message" or made some gaffe, they could all go home and enjoy a relaxing Sunday afternoon.

"Todd, who do we have on this morning's shows?" Seagram asked.

Todd was a fairly new staffer, but quite competent, although not quite as self-confident as one would expect.

"The Education Secretary's on *Face the Nation*," he reported. "Senator Keller's on *Meet the Press*. Congressman Barnes is on *This Week*. And Senator Matthews is doing FOX."

"What about *American Caucus*?"

"They didn't ask for anyone," Todd said.

"That's unusual. What's Dylan Reese covering this morning?"

Todd shrugged.

"You should have found out," Seagram snapped. "Remember that for the future."

Each staff member was assigned a program to watch and report on if something significant was said. Each watched from a different office. Todd was assigned *American Caucus*.

"And the bill is expected to pass with a modicum of bipartisanship." Dylan Reese said, finishing his introduction. "This morning on *American Caucus*, we have Congressman David Grant of Pennsylvania's 20th District with us."

"As votes on the President's signature education bill are being scheduled for as early as this week, you've said not so fast. Why?"

"Two weeks ago, my staff and I uncovered several alarming provisions in the bill including unending financial support for an infinite number of advanced degrees, which will only increase the student loan default rate. Another would allow college programs to be taught entirely in foreign languages. No need to speak, read or write in English. This is only going to lead to an increased societal bifurcation. And a third mandates universal college credit transfers. Think of the worst college in America. This legislation would force Ivy League schools to accept those credits."

Todd suddenly rushed over to Seagram's office. "I think you'll want to see this." He switched her TV screen to *American Caucus*.

"I have discussed this bill with academics," David continued, "who insist it will undermine academic standards. It will enable an unending liability in terms of student loans and grants, and establish foreign language colleges within the United States. In reality, it's a windfall for a number of for-profit schools, some of which are little more than diploma mills. And inevitably, it will cause an explosion in the student default rate."

"Some might say this is a bit alarmist," Reese countered. "I understand you brought this to the attention of the White House. What was their reaction?"

"Harris Carver thanked me for making him aware of it. He ordered the provisions removed by the legislative affairs office, which they were. However, within a few days the provisions popped back up in other parts of the bill."

"Are you accusing Harris Carver or the White House of something?"

"No, I am here to warn the White House and Congress about the dangers of this bill. I am encouraging members of Congress, in the strongest possible terms, to revise this bill, or vote it down. If this bill is allowed to pass as is, it will greatly damage our education system and our country."

"Who the hell is this guy?" Seagram asked.

"David Grant, Independent from Pennsylvania's 20th."

She suddenly remembered Carl Stavros escorting him to the Oval Office the previous January.

"Where's the Education Secretary? We'll have to counter this."

"He's on *Face the Nation*, remember?"

"Can we get word to him?"

"Not while he's on the air."

"Crap."

ജ ജ ය ය

"I warned you, folks" Ben Glendenning bellowed. "I warned you about this power-mad president. The Democrats have always wanted to bankrupt this country, and indoctrinate the youth. This so-called education bill was the scheme to achieve it all. I'm sad to say it wasn't a conservative who yelled out the Emperor had no clothes. It was this man."

A photograph of David appeared on the screen.

"David Grant is a liberal, but without the conviction to formally declare himself a party Democrat. But to be fair—and we are nothing if not fair on this program—sometimes even liberals can't tolerate Farnum's shenanigans. This deceptive bill is so riddled with anti-education provisions, it's traitorous. It's certainly impeachable."

ဢ ဢ ᏣᏍ

"It's so sad," Jessica Dandridge lamented to her audience. "The conservatives are so desperate, they're now attacking education. Education has traditionally been an area both sides could support. True, the right-wingers occasionally go a little nuts about their vouchers. But that's a far cry from what they're doing this time around. They're trying to decimate a perfectly good education bill to score political points with mudslinging. They are willing to sacrifice our children's future for political gain."

"And here's the really pathetic part: They don't have the courage to do it themselves. Cowards, cowards, cowards. They're using Independent David Grant as their puppet, a congressman who is so ineffective, he hasn't authored or passed one piece of legislation. The only thing he's good at is being a right-wing marionette."

ဢ ဢ ᏣᏍ

By Tuesday morning, the inevitable gathering came. Republican leadership from both houses met in the suite of House Minority Leader, Cassandra Mirreau. The Senate Minority Leader and Whip joined their House counterparts. A few up-and-coming Senators were also invited. So was Howard Carstairs, much to Mirreau's annoyance.

"We have to go full bore on this education thing," she announced. "We have to drill a hole in that damned Farnum, a big hole. I mean a really big, nasty hole; the nastier, the better."

"Sympathetic media is already on the warpath," the Minority Whip said. "Did you hear Glendenning last night?"

"Yeah, but it's not enough. We need more noise in the lame-stream media. That means some of our more moderate colleagues will have to step up." She was eyeing Howard Carstairs in particular.

Carstairs nodded.

"What about using Grant?" someone called out. "I mean he uncovered this whole thing."

"He's not a Republican. Don't give him any more exposure than he already has. We want to retake his seat come next election."

"Might I propose drafting an alternative education bill?" Senator Dennis Ogden offered. "We're always accused of being against things. Why don't we go on the offensive and lay out our own strong and comprehensive education plan?"

"Why waste time drafting a bill the Democrats will never pass?"

"Because our past alternative bills have never been substantial, and everyone knows it." Ogden insisted. "Let's really be *for* better education and have a serious plan to back it up."

"It'll take airtime away from the message that *Farnum is corrupt*," Mirreau insisted

After the meeting, Ogden and Carstairs walked together down to the congressional subway to the Senate offices.

"This whole thing is going to change the election," Ogden said, as the train rolled up to the platform.

"Yeah, in only two days," Carstairs agreed, "Buck Howell has jumped eight points. Corey Johnson still has the lead for now, but we could still get that Bible-thumping jackass as our nominee. That's why, Dennis, I think you should run. You're a respected conservative, but not a foot-in-mouth yahoo."

"Nice try, Howard. I just don't have the war chest to survive the primaries."

ဢ ဢ ศ ศ

During the next couple of days, the media was ablaze with accusations and counter-accusations. David noticed while a few of his Republican colleagues privately congratulated him and patted him on the back, none gave him credit publicly, unless forced by a journalist. His Democratic colleagues ignored him. It was particularly hurtful, when Wyatt Wickham and Christa Lemmon cancelled private meetings with him and refused to reschedule.

He had heard about a shake-up in the House leadership. The rumor was that Porter Barnes was going to be the new Majority Whip.

ဢ ဢ ศ ศ

"So, how was the Air & Space Museum?" David asked as Wendy walked into his office.

"It was great, Daddy," Wendy said. "I got to touch a Moon rock."

"Really?"

"Yes, but I had to wait in line. So, I think you and the President should have them put in more Moon rocks, so people don't have to wait in line."

"Me and the President?" David laughed. "Um, well, the President and I have only met once."

Through the door, they heard Carol's voice calling out, "You can't go in there."

Suddenly, the door was thrown open.

"Who the hell do you think you are, you little shit?" bellowed Porter Barnes, "How dare you attack your President?"

David suddenly shoved an upright finger up in Barnes's face. Barnes, confused, took a backstep. David turned to Wendy.

"Excuse me, Wendy, would you step outside for a few minutes while Congressman Barnes and I talk?" David gently closed the door and walked up to Barnes, almost nose-to-nose. Barnes, who was taller by four inches, looked down at him with contempt.

"Don't you ever talk to me like that in front of my daughter," David snapped. "You understand? You do that again, and I will mop the floor with you."

"What?" Barnes asked, incredulously.

"I know your type. You were bigger than most kids growing up, the typical bully. But my father taught me how to deal with bullies. You punch 'em in the nose."

"Are you physically threatening a US Congressman?"

"No, that would be a federal offense. But if I did, no one would believe I threw the first punch, since you're so much bigger than me, especially given your boorish reputation and how you just barged into my office. Now, state your business with civility and get out."

"My business is knocking some sense into you," Barnes growled. "You have a problem with a bill; you go to the Chairman or the Speaker, not to the press. We need workhorses, not show horses. And, you don't attack the President!"

"First, anytime I've gone to the Speaker, he wasn't as rude as you, just more condescending, and completely unresponsive. Second, I didn't attack the President. I warned Carver about the legislation. Then, when that didn't work, I warned the nation. As for horses, I have been a work horse. But, you're too busy screwing people over to notice. Now, get the hell out!"

"I am the Majority Whip, and you…"

"Not of my party. So once again, get the hell out!"

"You'll never get a single piece of legislation passed, not so much as a proclamation that the sky is blue. I destroyed your predecessor. You? I'll grind you into the ground without breaking a sweat."

With that, Barnes walked out into the reception area and spotted Wendy slipping a few pieces of candy into her pocket. She suddenly realized Barnes was there and looked startled and a little frightened.

"Don't worry," he said, smiling kindly. "I won't tell." Barnes walked out and kept smiling all the way down the corridor.

CHAPTER 51

Bob Summers who had just finished the second story of his evening broadcast, was moving onto the third.

"Earlier today," Summers continued, "in a bizarre incident, several individuals entered the Partridge Wax Museum in Cleveland and began pelting an animatronic figure of President Farnum with raw eggs. They then hung a sign on the mannequin with the word 'traitor' written on it. Witnesses claimed throughout the incident the perpetrators yelled 'liar, liar, liar,' before fleeing."

"Several hours later, another group of people attempted a similar stunt in Disney's Hall of Presidents in Orlando. However, security was able to apprehend the perpetrators before they could complete their plan. The individuals in Florida are believed to be a group of copycats."

"With us tonight is political analyst and host of *American Caucus,* Dylan Reese." Summers turned to his owlish colleague. "Dylan, is this just a minor act of vandalism, something forgotten in a local police blotter? Or is it an expression of something more significant?"

"Well, Bob," Reese responded, "this may just be the tip of the iceberg. Polls indicate an unprecedented level of frustration among Americans toward the Federal Government. The Cleveland incident resonated with many people on social media and is believed to have triggered the Florida attempt. The fact that a copycat attack was attempted within hours indicates a certain percentage of the population may be on a hair trigger."

"Dylan, what does this mean, if anything at all, for the politicians in Washington?"

"Well, the President's approval numbers are between 23 and 27 percent, depending on the poll, not a good omen for a president heading into reelection. Congress has an even lower approval rating between five and seven percent. To be candid, most officeholders have individual approval ratings almost as dismal, with the possible exception of David Grant, the new congressman who exposed the corruption in the education bill. But even his numbers aren't that great at 43 percent."

"Does this help the Republicans as we head into the election next year?"

"Not as much as conventional wisdom might suggest. People still remain suspicious of the GOP since President Henderson's failed initiative three years ago to invest Social Security funds in the stock market. And, many blame the Republicans for the Kadler Steele affair. Overall, confidence in government has never been lower."

ဆ ဆ ᘓ ᘓ

289

A few days later, David was sitting on a platform in an Omaha city park. Despite it being a beautiful clear morning, David had not expected such a large crowd. Marshall Vreeland had already begun his speech.

"As you've heard and seen," Vreeland said to the crowd, "there are a lot of accusations going around in Washington lately. With Kadler Steele, CART and this phony education bill, it's a real pile of—" Vreeland suddenly held up his hands. "Oops. My advisors warned me not to use such language to describe what's going on. They think you might be offended by my choice of words. Maybe so. But I think you're really more offended by the actions that evoke such language."

The crowd applauded enthusiastically.

"We haven't had much straight talk out of Washington in a long time. In decades, some people might say. Although recently, one man, surprisingly a member of Congress, has revealed the truth. He pulled the curtain down and exposed the corruption in President Farnum's so-called Education Bill. He spoke up for honesty and integrity, something long forgotten in Washington. Please give a warm Cornhusker welcome to my friend Congressman David Grant!"

David received enormous applause, more than he had ever received in his own campaign. He smiled and waved as he stepped up.

"Thank you, Marshall, for that very eloquent introduction and even more so for that candid assessment of politics in Washington. I think back to when I was elected, almost a year ago, I was very proud. But recently, I haven't been so proud. Our capital is infested with a corps of self-serving operators, so corrosive to our democracy and good government. But occasionally, I have found an individual, here and there, who puts the greater good over personal ambition. Marshall Vreeland is one of those people. Now, some might understandably say there's nothing more personally ambitious than running for president."

Stan Erskine, Vreeland's campaign manager, shifted nervously in his seat.

"However, let's be honest," David continued. "The odds are stacked against him and us. It would be a far more profitable enterprise for Marshall to continue constructing buildings and expand his real estate business. The same could have been said of me, with my old software company. But there is something that tips the balance. It's called patriotism."

"It would have been far more profitable for Washington and Jefferson to continue farming their estates, and for Benjamin Franklin to focus on his printing business and inventing. But they were patriots, and patriots put country before self. And while as a Pennsylvanian I would have loved to have met Benjamin Franklin, I am just as honored to support a Nebraskan patriot named Marshall Vreeland for President of the United States."

The crowd erupted in applause. David looked down at Wendy sitting in the front row and gave her a wink.

Vreeland stood up again and hugged David.

"You were absolutely right about waiting 'til the right time to endorse." Vreeland said as quietly as he could over the cheers. Vreeland turned to continue his speech. As he did so, David sat down next to Erskine.

"You got me nervous there for a minute," Erskine said. "I thought you were going to do a u-turn, talking about personal ambition."

"No, I keep my word," David reassured him.

"By the way, Jason Kennerly just emailed me the new polls. Buck Howell just eclipsed Corey Johnson by two percent. And Farnum's approval rating is down to a 23 percent, his lowest ever. You really are David, the giant killer."

"Don't be too excited. Election Day is over a year away, and Farnum's a very skilled politician."

"Perhaps." Erskine said looking down at his clipboard. "Oh, by the way, we've had a last-minute schedule change. We're going across the Missouri River into Council Bluffs, Iowa, this afternoon. So, you'll need to drop the Nebraskan reference."

"That's going to make for a very long day. Remember, I have my daughter with me."

"Don't worry. Our last stop is back at the hotel. She can go up to bed, while we do the event downstairs."

"Great. With crossing the time zones, she's going to be plenty tired."

"We've also added a small fund-raiser with some of Marshall's local friends and associates. But you can skip that if you like. Maybe, grab some dinner with your daughter."

"Thanks, I think I'll do that."

ॐ ॐ ॐ ॐ

Daniel Narlstrom walked into a local suburban library just outside of Columbus, Ohio.

"Excuse me. Can you tell me where the meeting room is?" he asked the librarian at the reference desk.

"Right over there, just beyond the stacks," she said.

"Thank you."

He slipped in just as the meeting started. Hanna was already there. She smiled at him, but refocused on the meeting quickly.

Although Jarvis Thayer called this a board meeting, there was no official board roster or even any membership criteria. It was more a collection of those willing to show up.

"I'm glad we could all get together." Thayer began. "It's been a while since we'd had a chance to regroup and maybe refine and better coordinate our mission. We need to focus more on using the media and—"

"Jarvis, we've had enough of your crap," Harry Branch called out.

It was obvious by the expression on Thayer's face, that he was forcing himself not to lash out at Branch. Many of the members respected Branch, and Thayer didn't want to lose their support.

"I think we all need to calm down," Thayer said in low voice.

"Why?" Branch asked, standing up. "So you can give another speech? That's all you do. That, and screw the actress. You named this group 'Salvage And Liberate America.' But Jarvis—" Branch leaned over the table. "Liberation doesn't come with just words."

"Well, I was going to get to that. That's why I think we should ally ourselves with Marshall Vreeland, the Independent running for—."

"Are you kidding me? All these guys running for president are a bunch of liars, because there are no consequences for lying. Certainly, they're not afraid of another interview with you and your girlfriend. They're all liars, especially once they become president, from Nixon's 'I am not a crook' to Henderson's 'No American left behind.'"

"Don't forget, 'I did not have sexual relations with that woman,'" the WMDs, and 'You can keep your health insurance.'" someone added.

Branch was visibly annoyed at the one who tried to bolster his argument, shooting the offending supporter a dirty look.

"The point is," Branch continued, "none of them can be trusted until there are consequences."

"This education bill mess gives us a target, a platform," Thayer insisted. "And Tess's very media savvy."

"Really? And what does Tess know about education? Didn't she drop out of community college? Let's get serious."

"What? You think that stunt in the wax museum is the way to go?" Thayer demanded. "Egging a museum dummy?"

"At least, they *did something*. It made the news didn't it? And no one got hurt. And more importantly, it communicated real anger and frustration, unlike your interviews with your D-list girlfriend."

"This is not what we are about. I will not stand for civil disobedience."

"Then, you stand for nothing. When I needed them most, those assholes in Washington betrayed me."

By now, everyone in the group knew Branch's story, how he was betrayed by President Henderson

"And now, Branch said pointedly, "so have you."

Thayer finally broke. "Screw you!" he screamed.

"No, I think Tess is the one you want to screw." Branch walked to the door. "I'm done here."

Thayer was visibly shaken, but quickly composed himself. "Well, I'm sorry to see Harry go, but the mission continues."

"And what mission is that?" Narlstrom asked. People seemed shocked, as he rarely spoke at these meetings. "Harry has a point. As Einstein said, the definition of insanity is doing the same thing over and over, and expecting a different result."

Narlstrom shot Hanna a contrite look, shook his head, and also walked out. He caught up to Branch as he was passing the reference desk.

"Harry?" he called out. "Hold up a moment."

Branch turned and appeared surprised to see him.

"Dan, I like you, but I'm not going back."
"That's alright. Neither am I."

ဟ ဧာ os os

After the appearance in Council Bluffs, the campaign bus dropped David, Wendy and some others at the hotel in Omaha. David decided he and Wendy would take advantage of the buffet offered in the hotel restaurant.

"Daddy, why did you give the same speech five times?" Wendy asked as they walked to the buffet.

"Each time I gave it to a different group of people."

Wendy nodded. David noticed she was filling her plate with chicken and beef. "How about some veggies on that plate, young lady?"

Wendy complied by adding a few string beans and a carrot slice. As they walked back to the table, she asked, "Do you think Mr. Vreeland can really become president?"

"I'm not sure," David admitted.

"Then why are you helping him?"

"Because I believe he can show people there's another way to do things. And I think people need to see that."

Wendy nodded, then speared all her string beans and carrot at once on her fork and shoved them into her mouth, just to get it over with.

"Can we really have all we can eat?" Wendy asked, eyeing the dessert buffet.

"You can have one dessert," David said. "A buffet is not an excuse to stuff your face like a little piggy."

"Daddy, that's not very nice."

David leaned over. "You having a belly ache won't be nice either."

Once they finished their entrees, Wendy chose a very large piece of chocolate cake. However, David spied a small cookie hidden beneath it, but decided to let it go. They finished dinner and walked back to their room.

"Okay, I have to go downstairs and give one more speech. I think you should put on your pajamas and brush your teeth. Then you can read your book or watch some TV. Under no condition are you to open the door for anyone. Understand?"

"Yes, Daddy."

"Good," He kissed her and went down to meet Stan Erskine.

Spying him at the end of the bar, David walked up. "So, how was the fundraiser?" he asked.

"Great, but we're running a little late. Marshall won't be here for another 15 minutes. In the meantime, let me buy you a drink."

"No thanks. It's been a long day. And I should keep a clear head. Besides, you have more important things to do than babysit me."

"Well, I also wanted to take a moment and thank you for your support of Marshall. I know our first meeting didn't go so well. I wasn't thrilled have you part of the team. But I have to admit your long distance coaching and advice has made a difference."

"Well, he's doing some important work. Running for president gives him an important platform, one I certainly don't have."

"Still, I wanted to show you my appreciation. Sure I can't buy you that drink?"

"No, besides you have work to do."

"Okay, I'll see you in fifteen," Erskine said as he headed out.

"If you won't let him buy you a drink, maybe you'll let me," came a woman's voice from behind him. David turned to find a very attractive brunette in a formal, burgundy-velvet dress, clearly designed to emphasize a deep cleavage.

"You're David Grant, aren't you?"

"Yes, and you are?"

"I'm Lorraine Van Deusen." She put out her hand in a way that almost suggested she was expecting it to be kissed. "I was one of the donors at Marshall Vreeland's fundraiser. I was quite put out that you didn't show up," she said in a way that suggested it was David's responsibility to make it up to her.

"I was told I wasn't needed," David explained, as he leaned against the bar.

"Well, I've been following your exploits. You're the real power behind the Centrist Patriots Party. In fact, I was thinking I'd like to make a donation to your campaign."

"Well, thank you. That would be greatly appreciated."

"I'm very interested in the future of this whole centrist movement. Maybe we could talk about it? I could come up to your room later."

David started to blush. He had never been propositioned like this before. "I'm afraid I'm traveling with my daughter."

Van Deusen laid her key on the bar. "We could use my room."

David smiled awkwardly. "That's very kind. But we have an early flight."

Suddenly, there was a burst of applause from the lobby.

"Ah, I think Marshall's here. That's my cue. Have a good evening, Ms. Van Deusen."

"Room 151, if you change your mind," she called out as he was walking away. He smiled back politely, if not awkwardly.

David and Vreeland repeated their respective performances. By the end of the night, David was dead tired as he walked back to his guestroom. He could see the light still on beneath the door. He slipped his keycard into the lock and entered. There was an odd and complete silence, yet the bed was still made up. The bathroom door was open revealing an empty room.

"Wendy?"

David frantically searched the small guestroom. A hole opened in the pit of his stomach. Wendy was gone.

CHAPTER 52

David was frantic. His mind raced. Earlier in the day, Wendy had expressed an interest in using the swimming pool, so he ran down the hall to the pool area. Visions of his daughter floating in the water face down flashed through his head. The pool area was empty except for an older couple chatting. He then bolted to the lobby and rushed up to the front desk.

"Excuse me. Have you seen a young girl, blond hair, about so high?" he asked holding up his hand to approximate Wendy's height.

"I'm afraid not, sir. Is there a problem?" asked the young man with a gold plastic badge identifying him as Reuben.

"She's disappeared from our room."

Reuben seemed unsure how to react. "Sir...I mean...would you like me to call the police?"

"I...I don't know. She's just missing from our room." David was afraid he might be overreacting, but on the other hand, if she had been taken, every second could matter.

Then, he had a thought. "I'll get back to you."

David ran into the ballroom where some stragglers from the rally were still milling around. One of them waved to draw his attention. David pretended to not see him. Wendy was nowhere to be seen. Then, he ran back to the restaurant. His heart was about to burst as he found Wendy sitting at a table gorging herself on some chocolates and a large éclair. His fear turned to relief, then to anger. He walked up to her, red-faced.

"What are you doing here?" he asked in a low, but stern, voice.

She was startled with eyes wide and the guilty look of being caught.

"A man said they put out some more desserts."

"What man? It doesn't matter." He grabbed her hand and dragged her back toward the guestroom. "I told you to not leave the room! Do you know how scared I was?"

"You said to not open the door for anyone and I didn't."

"Don't get smart with me!"

Suddenly, as they got back to the guestroom door, she jerked back, wrenching herself free of David's grasp.

"I'm a big girl now, and I'm going back to the dining room," she said defiantly, and started to walk away.

David was stunned by his daughter's disobedience. "No, you're not," he snapped. David grabbed her arm and pulled her back. "Stop this now!"

She struggled. With his right hand he slipped the keycard into the slot, and then dragged Wendy into the room with his left. Once inside, he grabbed both of her upper arms, and knelt down in front of her. "If you want to travel with me, you can't act like this. You scared me to death."

Wendy's eyes filled with tears. "I'm sorry," she cried, and then fell on the bed sobbing.

He slowly stood up, wondering what had happened to his sweet little girl. He let her cry it out for a few minutes. "Wendy, I want you to go into the bathroom, brush your teeth, and change into your pajamas."

Wendy complied. After finishing her nighttime routine, she climbed under the covers. They said their goodnights. David turned down the lights, walked into the bathroom, and closed the door behind him. He sat on the counter for a few minutes, listening to make sure Wendy wasn't making a getaway.

He finally pulled out his cell phone and dialed Sara.

"Hi," she answered.

"Hi yourself," he said.

"How's the campaign going?"

"It's going."

"What's wrong?"

"Well, Wendy's not too happy right now. We had a bit of an incident. She left the room while I was in the ballroom speaking. She snuck back into the restaurant for the dessert buffet. She was on a real sugar high. I think that and being overtired, turned her into a defiant little monster."

"Oh my."

"I don't think I can bring her on campaign trips anymore."

"Well, the summer's nearly over. Maybe the Garthwells can help."

"No, I'll just cut back on my campaign appearances until the school year starts. Besides, it's still early in the campaign, and I can't hold Vreeland's hand all the time. So, how are things going in Pittsburgh?"

"Actually, very well."

David and Sara continued talking for a while before hanging up. When he walked out of the bathroom, Wendy was sound asleep. She was once again his little angel.

ଥ ଥ ଓଷ ଓଷ

Once back in Washington, David and Wendy returned to their local routines. Everyone in the office was warned about Wendy's sweet tooth. Carol's candy dish disappeared from the front desk. Once sweets were removed from her diet, Wendy remained calm, obedient, and adorable to all. She and Gretchen Wheeler returned to their mission of visiting and reporting on Washington tourist attractions.

A few days later, Fred was editing a press release written by one of the summer interns when Carol came in, ashen-faced.

"Carol, what is it?" he asked.

"Mr. Arkin, there's a man on line 3. He's asking about charges that the Congressman is a pedophile."

"What? Who is this guy?"

She held a note in her trembling hand.

"He says he's Stuart Rithauser of the Rithauser Report."

"Never heard of him." Fred said, as he picked up the telephone.

"Hello, this is Fred Arkin. How may I help you?"

"Yes, sir. My name's Stuart Rithauser of the Rithauser Report. I was wondering if you would like to respond to the charges that Congressman David Grant is a pedophile?"

"Who exactly is making that charge?"

"I can't reveal my sources."

"Oh, I see, an anonymous source making libelous statements. I have no intention of responding to a phantom accuser."

"We have hard evidence," Rithauser replied.

"What evidence?"

"I'm just calling to provide the Congressman an opportunity to comment."

"Mr. Rithauser, I have no intention of commenting on anything until you can give me some specifics."

"Then, I take it you're making no comment." Rithauser hung up before Fred could answer.

Fred quickly did a search for the Rithauser Report. He couldn't believe what he was reading.

"Shit!"

Fred brushed past Carol, heading for Ellen's office. "Quick, I need you in the Congressman's office." He didn't wait for a response.

He rushed into David's office. "David, I hate to tell you this, but there's a report on the Internet accusing you of being a pedophile."

"What the hell are you talking about?" David demanded.

"And they have a video," Fred said.

"What?"

Fred called up the page on his tablet. "It looks like you dragging a young girl into a hotel room."

"That was Wendy and I in Omaha last week. She was on a sugar high during the trip. I told you about that."

"But when they link this footage to an off-the-record accusation of child molestation," Fred said, "it looks completely different."

David felt like there was a hole ripping through his stomach. He could feel his blood pressure rising in his temples. "I'll sue that bastard. I'll sue him for libel."

"He's using the word 'alleged' to cover himself, citing an anonymous bystander as a source. This is obviously a smear campaign," Fred concluded.

"You think?" Ellen snapped sarcastically, as she walked in watching the video clip on her own tablet. "It's one of the nastiest I've seen."

"On the other hand, it's not even a real news site," Fred said dismissively, "just a partisan blog."

"If this Rithauser was able to acquire security camera footage," Ellen said, "he's more than a snarky blogger. It means he has some resources behind him, and he's gunning for the Congressman."

Suddenly the telephones started ringing.

Carol came in again, shaking even more. "It's CPN and the *Liberty* network. They're calling about that...that thing." Carol couldn't make eye contact with David. She quickly withdrew.

My God, she thinks I'm guilty, David thought.

"Rithauser must have notified the media outlets," Ellen concluded.

"We have to give a response," Fred insisted.

"All we have to tell them," David said, "is that the girl was my daughter misbehaving."

"This is a smear campaign," Ellen insisted. "They'll just say you molested Wendy. We'll need something more that a denial to fight back."

"What happened to innocent until proven guilty?"

"Congressman, you're not actually that naïve. They, whoever they are, know that already. And, they'll have a response. For instance, they might demand an interview will Wendy."

"I don't want Wendy to even hear about this," David insisted.

"That's what they're probably hoping. We need to know more."

"But the media is calling now," Fred reminded them.

"Put all the interns on the phones," Ellen instructed. "Others will be calling. The standard response is 'The allegations are ridiculous, libelous, and unworthy of further response.' Fred, impress on each of them, they are to say nothing more than that."

"Is stonewalling the answer?" Fred asked.

"Until we can find out more," Ellen shot back.

"Wendy," David suddenly called out. He pulled out his cell phone and called Gretchen Wheeler.

"Yes, Gretchen. Where are you and Wendy?" he asked, trying to force himself to sound calm.

"We're in the National Gallery," she replied.

"Okay, I want you to take Wendy back to the townhouse."

Ellen started waving her hands. "They'll be staking out your place."

"Hold on, Gretchen." He placed the phone against his chest. "Well. We can't keep her in the National Gallery forever, and she can't come here. The place will be swarming with reporters."

"Maybe a hotel?" Ellen suggested.

"No, a hotel got us into this mess," David said, and then put the phone back to his ear. "Gretchen, are you still there?"

"Yes, sir."

"I want you to listen to me very carefully. And don't react. I don't want to upset Wendy. Do you understand?"

"Yes, sir," she said calmly.

"Good. I know it might be an imposition, but can you keep Wendy at your place tonight? I would appreciate it as a great favor."

"That's not a problem, sir. We can just stop by your house and pick up some things."

"No, don't do that. If you need anything for Wendy, buy it. I'll reimburse you."

"Sir?" Gretchen lowered her voice. "Can you tell me what's going on?"

David sighed. "Someone is making a very nasty, but false, accusation against me. I don't want Wendy to hear it. It involves her. So please keep her away from any newspapers or news programs. And keep her off the Internet."

"I see."

"Gretchen, I'm entrusting you with my little girl at a time when it couldn't be more critical."

"Don't worry, Congressman. I won't fail you."

"Thank you, Gretchen. I'll talk to you soon." He put away his phone and turned back to Ellen. "If my townhouse is being watched, I can't go back there either."

"No. In fact, I'm willing to bet that if you leave this office, there'll be a fleet of microphones and cameras shoved in your direction."

David pondered his situation. He pulled out the burner phone Hingecliff had given him. The rule was to never call from the office or home because of GPS tracking. Perhaps this was the time to break the rule? Or was it a time when the rule was more important than ever? David recalled the man who came and swept his townhouse for bugs. And now, he was trapped in his own office. Reporters would indeed be swarming the Capitol complex.

"Ellen, I want you to take this cell phone outside the building and dial 'Dentist' on the speed dial list."

"I doubt you suddenly developed a sudden need for a root canal."

"I wish. Tell the man who answers you're calling on my behalf. Tell him I need his help."

"Who would I be calling?"

"I can't tell you. It's a condition of his assistance. Don't ask him his name. You're not the only one in Washington who has developed contacts."

"Is this the same person who arranged your meeting with Harris Carver?"

"It doesn't matter."

"What can I tell him?"

"Anything he asks. I trust him completely. Will you do this?"

"Of course, Congressman."

Ellen returned to her office to collect her purse.

She closed her eyes and murmured to herself, "I can't believe this is happening again."

†j ɢɣ

Ellen walked a few blocks from the Cannon Building and dialed "Dentist."

"Hello, David. I thought you might be calling," said the voice on the phone.

"This isn't David Grant, but I'm calling on his behalf."

"Who is this?" Hingecliff asked.

"I'm the Congressman's Chief-of-Staff. He would have called himself, but apparently he's not supposed to use this burner phone in the office."

There was a long pause.

"You're Ellen Langford, correct?"

"Yes."

"Do you know who I am?"

"Not a clue. But the Congressman said you might be able to help."

"I'm not sure what I can do," Hingecliff said.

"And since I have no idea who you are," Ellen said, "I can't tell you that either."

"Maybe you should begin by telling me what isn't being reported in the news."

Ellen reported all she knew from David's account of events. "Can you help the Congressman?" she asked.

"Bring the burner phone back to the office. Tell him he should expect a call," Hingecliff instructed her. "By the way, Ms. Langford, do you find it ironic that you're the one trying to save your boss from a scandal?"

"Yes, that had occurred to me. I just hope you can be his guardian angel. I certainly know I could have used one."

"You have that all wrong. When it came to Shannon Hawthorne, *you* were the guardian angel."

"How do you know? Who are you?"

"Quickly, you better return to the office." Then, Hingecliff hung up.

CHAPTER 53

Ellen returned to the office with David's burner phone. "I spoke to your dentist. He said he'd call back. Apparently, it's okay to call this phone here, but not call out. What, is he on an NSA watch list or something?"

"He's an old-time Washingtonian and extremely cautious," David answered. "I expect he keeps a lot of secrets."

"He certainly does," Ellen mumbled.

"What do you mean?" David asked.

"Nothing."

Suddenly, the burner phone began to vibrate.

"Hello," David answered.

"So, David," Hingecliff said, "you've gotten yourself into a bit of a pickle."

"Yes, and I have no idea how to battle this sort of thing. A straight-out denial is pointless, since a guilty man would also deny it. And these days, if the polls are to be believed, members of Congress don't have much credibility. If I reveal the girl in the video is my daughter, the press will just hunt her and make a worse insinuation."

"True, unless you can wrap this episode up quickly and put a bow on it. By the way, where is your daughter?" Hingecliff asked.

"Safe, but not at my house."

"Good."

"Any ideas?"

"Having all the facts might help. I know someone who might be able to do that. I've taken the liberty of alerting him. His name is Gabriel Farley. He's a private investigator who's very good at getting to the bottom of these sorts of things. He's ready to fly to Omaha immediately. You'll have to compensate him for his services, but I didn't think that would be a problem. He'll be calling you on this phone to confirm."

"Thanks."

Farley called within a few minutes. David gave him the go-ahead.

The next call was the most difficult. David had to explain the situation to Sara. He cleared the room and called to give her the awkward news.

"I can't believe this," Sara said. "I don't want Wendy involved in this."

"Neither do I."

"I should fly down."

"I wouldn't."

"Why?"

David didn't want to reveal what he was thinking. If the perpetrators were as diabolical as he feared, Sara might be under surveillance, or soon would be if she showed up in Washington. Her coming to Washington might make things worse, even lead certain people to Wendy. He now understood how Robert Hingecliff could be so paranoid.

"I think we can clear this up in a day or two," David said. He certainly hoped so.

ଽଠ ଽଠ ଔ ଔ

Ben Stajek drained the last swig of vodka from his glass, feeling quite content over a job well done. Then, his phone rang.

"Hello?"

"Stajek?"

"Yeah."

"What the hell have you done?" Jack Kripke demanded over the telephone. "The plan was to get Grant into bed with a hooker!"

"Hey, Jenny tried to get him into the sack," Stajek said. "She gave it her best shot."

"Who's Jenny?"

"The hooker. We called her Lorraine Van Deusen. Sounded more like a rich contributor," Stajek bragged. "But Grant was too much of a boy scout. So instead of packing it in, we improvised, tried a Hail Mary. And it paid off with some interesting footage. I added what the spin doctors call a narrative and sent it to Rithauser."

"A Hail Mary? That wasn't your call. The plan was to obtain video, so we could put pressure on him. If we ever went public, people were supposed to dismiss him as another Anthony Weiner. Now, this could go sideways quite easily."

"Don't worry. Besides, if you still want to blackmail him, we'll just try a different hooker next time. Maybe Jenny wasn't his type."

"And you don't think Grant'll be on his guard from now on? I thought you were smarter than that. Don't go near him again. We'll just have to bide our time." With that, Kripke hung up.

Stajek was no longer feeling so content. But he poured himself another glass of vodka anyway.

ଽଠ ଽଠ ଔ ଔ

"Well, I suppose by now you've seen the latest example of liberal debauchery," Glendenning bellowed, "Congressman David Grant dragging that poor girl into some motel somewhere for God-knows-what. This is exactly the extreme decadence the Liberals have been driving us toward. But they'll just say we're being *intolerant*. Damn straight, America. Do you want to tolerate this kind of perversion? Do you want this to be the norm? Do you want to have to lock up your daughters to protect them from perverts like David Grant?"

"This is exactly why conservatives have to take back Congress and the presidency! We need God-fearing people with moral fiber in Washington. People like Buck Howell, not these degenerate Liberals."

"My fellow patriots, we've just glimpsed the Godless, liberal, anything-goes future people like Farnum and Grant envision for our country." Glendenning's eyes teared up on cue. The lump in his throat was ready to go. "It makes me so angry to see these liberal sociopaths and psychopaths try to destroy the country I love so much."

ℛ ℛ ℞ ℞

While the partisan propaganda machines on both sides went forward unrestrained, most of the established news media were being somewhat cautious in how they reported the story. However, they were digging furiously. Every exit of the Capitol complex was under media surveillance. In addition, reporters had informants everywhere. Many junior staffers were more than willing to curry favor with journalists in exchange for some future benefit. David was effectively trapped in his office, unless he was willing to walk straight into a news camera.

He tried sleeping on the couch in his office, but had little success. After hours of tossing and turning, he took a chance and slipped down to the House gym in the middle of the night for a shower. Once he returned to the office, he felt even more claustrophobic. So he went up to the roof of the Cannon Building before dawn.

Being already on the top floor or attic, it was a short way to the roof. The early morning breeze felt good. Surprisingly, he found some lawn chairs there in the early pre-dawn light. They were tied to an exhaust vent. He untied them, wiped the morning dew, and sat, waiting for sunrise. He recalled Howard Carstairs treating him to the sunrise on Cadillac Mountain. That dawn had given him hope. This one gave him nothing but despair and dread.

His cell phone rang. It was Fred.

"Where are you?" Fred asked. "You're not in the office."

"I'm up on the roof."

"The roof? You're not thinking of—"

"No, no, I just needed some air."

"I'll be right up." Within minutes, Fred joined him. "I didn't know you could just walk up here."

"Normally, you can't. But the Architect of the Capitol gave me a key, and I left the door open. I'm not the only one who has access. Congressman Garson grills ribs up here sometimes," David explained, pointing to a barbeque grill chained to a roof vent. "He's never invited me, but I hear his ribs are to die for." David sighed. "So what more do we know?"

"No one's indicated they know the video is from Omaha yet. That should give your investigator a clear field. What was his name?"

"Gabe Farley."

Fred pulled up another lawn chair. "David, I know you don't want to have Wendy involved, but you know it's inevitable. Someone will put it together eventually. The thing, I suppose, is to develop a plan for how and when it happens."

"You sound more like Ellen every day."

"Is that a compliment or an insult?"

They both laughed.

"We should go down before the early birds fill the halls," Fred suggested. "I'll take point."

࿄ ࿄ ࿃ ࿃

The day had been as excruciating as the night. That evening, Fred came into David's office with a pizza. "Hungry? I have meatball and mushroom, your favorite."

"Actually, my favorite is balsamic chicken, but meatball and mushroom is good too."

Fred opened the pizza box on the coffee table and offered David a paper plate.

"How's Wendy doing?" Fred asked.

"I spoke to Gretchen earlier," David explained, as he pushed the blanket to the side on the couch and sat down. "Wendy was getting cabin fever. So they went on a field trip to the aquarium up to Baltimore, hopefully outside the media net."

"Well, no one's guessed who she is yet, at least publicly."

"Yet. But whoever's behind this knows, but hasn't leaked it yet. Anything at all breaking on the news front?"

"Not much." Fred said. "Although your favorite ex-employee has just resurfaced."

"Tyler?"

"No, Darren Sagamore."

"Crap. What BS is he pushing?"

"Nothing substantial. Apparently, you were 'overly attentive' to the children during company picnics, that kind of garbage. However, the mainstream news is holding off saying anything too damning."

"Innuendos and white lies. They're building up a nice patina of guilt."

"But I know you're going to hit back hard, the same way you did in the election."

"Thanks."

After a while, Fred walked out of David's office to find Ellen waiting.

"How's he doing?" Ellen asked.

"As well as can be expected," Fred answered, "which means I think he could crack at any moment. I certainly would."

"Did you tell him about Sagamore?"

"Yeah, I didn't feel I could withhold that. But there's something else I didn't have the heart to tell him."

304

"What's that?"

"Apparently, the Capitol Domes have a new song." Fred hesitated, not wanting to say it out loud. "It's called *Kiddy-Fiddler on the Roof*."

"What?"

"I don't have the exact lyrics, but I'm told it's pretty nasty."

"That's not right."

"I know."

"No," Ellen said, "I mean, I was with the Domes for years. The best comedy comes from truth. We never performed mean-spirited skits, certainly nothing based on unsubstantiated charges. Excuse me."

Ellen went to her office and dialed a number from memory. "Brooke Osborne, please....yes, I'll hold."

"Ellen," Osborne answered. "I guess I should have been expecting your call."

"Damn right. You want to explain *Kiddy-Fiddler on the Roof*? Since when is child molestation a joke?"

"It's not."

"Okay, since when did the Domes do parodies based on unsubstantiated charges?"

"Hey, calm down. I didn't vote for the song. You know how the Domes work. All the pieces are voted on. Majority rules."

"Who suggested this one? Let me guess, someone from Porter Barnes' office?"

"No, it was Alan Traeger. You remember him?"

"Yeah, he worked for Sheldon Lannier."

"Well, after Lannier lost to your guy, he joined Senator Matthews' staff. He just traded one Pennsylvania Republican for another."

"When did Traeger submit the lyrics?"

"The day the news broke. Being so timely got a bunch of the newer members really excited. They just performed it earlier tonight."

"That's extraordinarily quick."

"Creativity doesn't go by a schedule."

"No, but sometimes a frame-up does. What are the exact lyrics?"

"Hold on, let me pull them up on my computer...Okay, here they are. Just remember, I didn't write them. It's obviously sung to the melody of *Fiddler of the Roof*. It goes:

Kiddy-fiddler on the roof
This is not just a spoof
Oh yes, I have the proof
I swear I tell the truth

"Wait, he actually wrote there was proof?"

"Proof he was on the roof," Osborne explained. "There's a photograph of your congressman on the roof of some building. It's projected on the stage wall during the song. Anyway, here's the rest of it:"

His name is David Grant.
If he's guilty, tell you I can't
Not one more centrist rant
From Congressman David Grant

Will he jump? Will he stump?
Bump, bump, bump, bump,
bump, bump, bump, bump,

A major, major goof
Posing on the roof
Is he innocent, or just
a kiddy-fiddler on the roof?

"Can you get the song pulled from the line up?" Ellen asked. "I remember the Domes being a way to relieve the stress on the Hill, not add to it. Besides I know for a fact, David Grant is not a pedophile. And there is proof forthcoming."

"It's already been pulled. It wasn't exactly a hit with the audience."

"Thanks, Brooke."

"You know, Ellen, if you ever want to return, we could always use a good mezzo-soprano."

"Thanks. I'm a bit busy right now."

Ellen realized her Congressman was under surveillance. *How far does this go?*

೮೦ ಕಿ ಲಿ ೮ಿ

David's burner phone began to vibrate. It was Gabe Farley.

"Hello, Congressman."

"Mr. Farley, what do you have for me?"

"Plenty. First, let's start with Lorraine Van Deusen. There's no one living in Omaha by that name. The nearest Lorraine Van Deusen lives outside of Des Moine, Iowa, but she's 96 years old and living in a nursing home."

It hadn't occurred to David that Van Duesen was part of this.

"I've spoken to a Lieutenant Saunders with the Omaha Police Department," Farley continued. "She's been very cooperative. I suggest you call her. I'll text you her number. Also, I'm sending you some digital still and video files. Now, you might want to write down what I'm about to tell you."

About thirty minutes later, David emerged from his office.

"Fred, I want you to arrange for the House Press Gallery for late tomorrow morning," David announced. "I'm calling a press conference."

CHAPTER 54

Most of David's staff worked late into the night, preparing for the press conference. Fred and David worked out the best use of the digital files Farley had sent. They made additional phone calls to Omaha. Meanwhile, Ellen reached out to certain members of Congress.

An intern was sent to David's townhouse to retrieve fresh clothes. Unfortunately, a photographer caught him with a deer-in-headlights expression and flooded the Internet with the picture. Thankfully, the intern refused to answer any questions. The incident created just enough impact for the morning news broadcasts to make jokes about it. Some compared David to "Where's Waldo?" This was juxtaposed with the photograph of David on the roof of the Cannon Building. This led to heightened interest in the early-morning announcement that a press conference was just hours away. Speculation on whether or not David Grant would resign was rampant.

At 8:00 AM, Congressman Grant's office received its first visitor, Lieutenant Marilyn Saunders of the Omaha Police Department. She was a slightly plump, stern looking woman.

David greeted her personally. "Welcome to Washington, Lieutenant. Did you fly in this morning?"

"No," Saunders answered. "I caught the last flight out of Omaha last night."

"I'm sorry for that inconvenience. Obviously I'd prefer if you didn't need to come."

"When I saw the footage on the news, I never dreamed this case would be in our jurisdiction. Your investigator, Mr. Farley, handed over a fair amount of evidence. My colleagues are checking it out. So far, so good. But as I said on the phone, I still have to confirm everything with an interview with your daughter."

"I understand."

"So where is your daughter?"

"She's in my chief-of-staff's office. It'll give us complete privacy."

"No." Saunders said. "The alleged perpetrator can't be present during an interview, especially in the case of a related minor. However, another parent may be present. Is your wife available?"

"No, she's in Pittsburgh. But perhaps my assistant Gretchen Wheeler could stand in?"

"That's fine. I have to say you're being very cooperative, especially considering you haven't even been accused, technically."

"Yes, I have. For a public figure, public insinuations are just as bad as a legal indictment. There's a not-so-quiet whisper campaign against me, and I want my name cleared. But more than that, I want to preserve my daughter's childhood. I don't want it marred by this sort of filth."

"If you're innocent, you—and she—have nothing to worry about. I've been doing this type of work for a long time, too long. Don't worry. I'll be sensitive."

"Thank you."

Lieutenant Saunders was introduced to Gretchen. Then, they both went into Ellen's office and closed the door behind them. David stared at that door with great anxiety. While Saunders seemed trustworthy, he wondered if a question might trigger some curiosity in Wendy about what was going on. At that point, he realized his ability to trust anyone was becoming more and more strained.

He needed to focus elsewhere. David turned to Ellen. "Any luck with the members?"

"Carstairs and McCord will stand by you. But none of the others will meet with me, but some are sending staffers, probably just out of curiosity."

"Well, I never had much hope on that front," David admitted. "Courage is not plentiful in Congress. And they have little to gain in supporting me."

"I'll meet the staffers in the conference room downstairs. Hopefully, we'll get some support before the press conference."

"I guess that'll have to do. See you on the tail end of this thing. Good luck."

"Good luck to you," Ellen said, as she walked out to her meeting.

ঐ ৯৩ ৫৪ ৫৪

A few minutes before 11:00 AM, David, Fred and others from the office went down to the House Press Gallery. The reporters were waiting in the press gallery.

"Before you go out there," Fred said, "you should know C-SPAN just rearranged its schedule. They're going to carry you live."

"I guess that's good." David surmised.

"Unless you say something screwy."

David smiled nervously. "You know, Fred, you really stink as a motivational coach."

"What do you expect? I'm a history nerd." Then, Fred grabbed David by the shoulders. "Now, go out and nail those bastards to the wall."

David laughed. "That's better." He took a cleansing breath and walked into the House Press Gallery, straight to the podium. Cameras clicked furiously.

"Good morning, everyone," David began. "As you know, there have been some veiled and not-so-veiled accusations about me in the last 48 hours. I will address those in a statement and then take any and all questions. However, first, I would like you to meet someone, but I ask that you show some discretion and hold any questions until after my statement. Again, I will stay until all your questions are answered." David turned and gave the cue.

Suddenly, there was another flurry of picture-taking. Gretchen Wheeler escorted Wendy to a few feet from the podium. Wendy was wearing the same outfit she wore in the Omaha video, so there would be no doubt of who she was.

"Ladies and gentlemen, I'd like to introduce my daughter, Wendy, who some of you may have noticed visiting the Capitol this summer. She and her companion Ms. Wheeler have been touring the local exhibits and attractions. Wendy is leaving Washington today, but I just wanted to introduce her before she left."

Wendy grinned widely and waved to the reporters.

"We just wanted to say goodbye, Daddy," Wendy said sweetly.

David bent over and hugged her. Shutters started clicking again in a crescendo.

"I'll miss you," he said to Wendy. "Have a good trip home. See you on Saturday."

"Bye, Daddy."

She began walking away as one of the reporters suddenly called out Wendy's name.

"I said, 'wait until after my statement.'" He noticed one of the older journalists had elbowed his offending colleague. David held up his finger until Wendy left the room.

"Now, just in case anyone missed it, let's take a look at the video clip that everyone has been so excited about."

Fred and the intern wheeled over a large plasma screen on a display stand. David pressed a button on the remote control to play the now-familiar video clip.

Most of the reporters were astonished that an embattled politician would play the same footage that was providing so much controversy.

"For the record, this footage was taken on the night of August 9th at the Gatsby Hotel in Omaha, Nebraska. I'm sure you'll be able to confirm this independently, as I was campaigning for Marshall Vreeland on that day. My daughter accompanied me on the trip."

David turned to the screen and played the footage a second time.

"Honestly, I was amazed at the high quality of this footage, HD I believe. I'm told it might have originally been something called 5K resolution. I thought security footage was supposed to be blurry and grainy. What makes it truly surprising is the Gatsby Hotel has no security cameras in its hallways whatsoever, only a handful covering the lobby, parking lots and swimming pool area. As you'll see in a moment, the quality of those cameras doesn't approach what we see here."

"So the burning question is where did this footage come from? I certainly don't recall anyone standing in the hallway with a video camera. In fact, you'll notice there is no camera movement whatsoever, so the camera must have been locked down, either on a tripod or a bracket attached to the wall or ceiling. And I would have noticed a tripod with a video camera, and there was none."

"As it turns out, there is physical evidence that suggests a camera was installed in the hallway. Scratch marks were found on the drop ceiling supports at a location that would coincide with where the camera would have been."

David clicked his remote control again, bringing up a close-up photograph of metal scratches on the video screen.

"These marks were likely the result of a clamp used to mount the camera. Similar scratch marks were found at the other end of the hallway, indicating a second camera was mounted there. But obviously, the first camera provided a more dramatic angle."

"Further investigation suggests an additional camera was set up inside my hotel room." David clicked through a series of photographs shot by Gabriel Farley showing his hotel room, each one progressing closer to a hole in the ceiling tile. The following photographs showed the tile removed, revealing similar clamp scratches.

"If there's a photograph or footage of any real wrongdoing, I ask you, where is it?"

David paused for effect.

"So now, let's go over the timeline of the evening. At about 7:30 PM, my daughter and I had dinner in the hotel's restaurant which offered a buffet. The dessert buffet particularly intrigued my daughter, who has developed quite a sweet tooth."

The reporters laughed. David hadn't expected that, but welcomed it. Some were now on his side, at least for the moment.

"We returned to the room at approximately eight o'clock, after which I headed to the main ball room to deliver some brief remarks at a rally for Marshall Vreeland."

"Mr. Vreeland was delayed arriving at the hotel. While waiting, I was approached by a woman claiming to be a campaign contributor, using the name of Lorraine Van Deusen. According to the Vreeland campaign, no such contributor by that name exists. Ms. Van Duesen, or whatever her name is, suggested we return to my room after the rally. I politely declined, citing my daughter's presence. She then suggested going to her room. Again, I declined. Instead, I proceeded to give my speech in support of Marshall Vreeland. When I returned to my room afterward, my daughter, Wendy, was missing. In a panic most parents can relate to, I searched the hotel."

David clicked the remote control again. Hotel surveillance footage, not nearly as sharp, appeared on the plasma screen.

"Ah, now this looks more like *bona fide* surveillance footage. There I am, searching the pool area." He clicked again. "Here, I am running to the front desk. Eventually, I found Wendy in the restaurant, gobbling down some high-sugar desserts. And then," David continued, as he clicked back to the original footage, "here I am returning to my room with Wendy, who by then was overtired and suffering from a sugar high. My daughter usually is quite sweet, as you saw a few minutes ago. To see her act like that was painful enough the first time. To see video of it repeatedly on the Internet, linked to such a reprehensible accusation, is unbearable. Now, why would anyone do such a thing?"

David paused, trying to hold his emotions in check. A reporter raised his hand, unsure if David had finished or not.

"Missing from this timeline," he continued, "was an anonymous phone call placed to my room while my daughter was there alone. Wendy reported it was simply a man telling her that more desserts had been added to the dessert buffet, and inviting her to return to the restaurant."

"Someone went to a lot of trouble to obtain some rather uncomfortable footage. Dirty politics has always been around, but I think many will agree, this crosses every line. To take advantage of my daughter. To lure her out of our room, to manufacture such a hideous lie is beyond reprehensible. It's criminal. Please note: Not one person has made a direct accusation against me. A video clip posted online with innuendo and conjecture may create doubt and web traffic, but it does nothing to further the truth, raise political discourse or help our country. I'll take questions now."

David pointed to a reporter up front.

"If you're innocent,' the reporter asked, "will you be making your daughter available?"

"To the media? No. Given her age and the sensitive nature of these innuendos, I'd like to protect her. I think you can understand why I wouldn't want her exposed to this. In my place, would you expose your own child to such a trial? However, Wendy has been questioned by an Omaha police detective."

"When did that occur?" another reporter blurted out without being called on.

"At about 8:15 this morning. The interview was conducted by Lieutenant Marilyn Saunders of the Omaha Police Department."

"Were you present?"

"No. Lieutenant Saunders preferred I not be there during the interview. I believe this is standard police procedure. And from a police perspective, I can understand it."

David called on another reporter.

"Congressman, you've provided new footage and an account of the old footage. Do you have anything else to verify your story?"

"I would suggest asking my accuser, Mr. Rithauser, if he has anything substantial to verify his story. However, to answer your question, the Omaha police are investigating and have access to everything I have. I'm sure they will make a statement as soon as they can. When I spoke to Lieutenant Saunders, after she interviewed my daughter, she seemed to be more interested in how the video clip was obtained than any allegations against me."

The elbowing older reporter finally spoke up. "Congressman, do you believe that this incident had anything to do with your exposure of the defects in the President's education legislation?"

"If by 'incident,' you mean the surreptitious recording of my family and the gross insinuation of pedophilia. I'd say yes. There may be special interest groups who might benefit from discrediting me."

"Which special interest groups are you referring to?"

"Well, unlike Mr. Rithauser and his so-called Rithauser Report, I don't make unsupportable accusations, direct, alleged or whatever weasel word he cares to use."

The cameras suddenly started clicking again, but they weren't pointing at him. David looking behind him to see Howard Carstairs and Cal McCord approaching.

"We don't mean to interrupt your press conference," Carstairs said. "We just wanted to show our support for a libeled colleague."

Carstairs and McCord didn't surprise David nearly as much as those who followed next: Wyatt Wickham, Christa Lemmon, Helen Parno and Arlo Hudge. Each made a brief statement of support. The last was Arlo Hudge.

"Congressman Grant and I don't agree on a lot," Hudge said, "but we agree on one thing. This hideous and libelous attack was beyond all decency. To manipulate an innocent little girl like this is beyond all propriety. It's downright evil. Family is supposed to be sacrosanct. If Attorney General Warrenburg doesn't call for a special prosecutor, then Congress should launch its own investigation."

Sitting in his K-Street office, watching the press conference live, Jack Kripke suddenly threw a coffee mug at the wall. "Stajek, you idiot!"

„ „ ‛ ‛

For the next day, the media devoured this story of conspiracy. The Gatsby Hotel was deluged with journalists. All wanted access to the room the Grants stayed in on August 9th. However, they were all denied by order of the Omaha Police, who still considered the room a potential crime scene.

"But which crime?" they all asked.

The day after David's press conference, the Omaha Police Department released a statement that there was no evidence of any crime or inappropriate activity by David Grant. However, they were still investigating possible illegal surveillance crimes by parties unknown.

„ „ ‛ ‛

Friday night, David arrived at his house in Embler. He had never been so relieved to come home. Despite the light banter over dinner there was some undercurrent of tension. It wasn't just Sara. David wondered what was going on.

312

Finally Chris spoke. "Dad, I have some news you might not like."

"Really? Maybe now is not the time."

Chris looked to his mother. Sara gave him the nod to continue.

"No. It's been put off long enough. I've decided I'm not going to engineering school."

David burst out laughing.

Everyone else was startled by his reaction.

"Sorry. I was expecting you to say something else."

Sara gave him an annoyed look.

"Like what?" Chris asked.

"Never mind." David dropped on to the couch. "Tell me what you're thinking is."

"I want to be a chef."

"Really? But I thought you really were keen on engineering?"

"I just love cooking more."

"You can always cook. You could invite your fellow engineers over to dinner."

"Dad?" Chris blurted out, expressing his annoyance.

"I have nothing against being a cook. Lord knows your grandfather was a great one. But this country is going to be in great need of engineers."

"Can you stop being a congressman for one second?" Chris snarled.

"Hey, don't talk to your father like that," Sara warned.

"I'm sorry, Dad," Chris said

"Chris, all I meant was that there will be a huge demand for engineers, which would be an advantage for anyone who has those skills." David sighed and paused for moment. "That being said, if you're sure you really want this…well, it's your life. Just remember cooking everyday is a lot tougher than cooking occasionally for your family and friends."

"I'm sure."

"So, have you thought about where you might go to school?"

"I'm thinking Johnson & Wales, or maybe Culinary Institute of America."

"Ah yes, the other CIA." David exhaled. "Well, I guess we have some campus tours to make."

The rest of the evening was quite pleasant. After dinner, Chris went out with his friends, visibly happier than before dinner. Wendy and Sara cleaned up the table with David.

After Wendy went to bed, Sara signaled for David to come into the bedroom. She closed the door behind them.

"We need to talk," she said.

"Okay."

Sara seemed more nervous than Chris had been.

"David, you've been down in Washington only—what? Eight months?—and you're already involved in a scandal."

"Which scandal are you talking about? The one where the President's people tried to rip apart our education system? Or the one where they accused me of being a pedophile?"

"Is this a joke to you?" she snapped.

"No, it's anything but a joke. Those bastards tried to use Wendy. This last week has been hell. I will never forgive them. And if I can hunt them down, I will."

"Enough of this!" Sara cried. "I want you to quit Congress. I've never asked this sort of thing of you, but this is insane."

"If I quit, it'll look like I have something to hide or am guilty. And it'll embolden them to do this sort of thing to someone else."

"Fine. Then, just don't run again."

"There again, they've won. And then, they'll do something like this again to anyone who stands up against them. I think it was Edmund Burke who said 'All that is necessary for the triumph of evil is that good men do nothing.'"

"I don't give a damn about Edmund Burke or good and evil. I care about protecting our children."

"So do I."

"Really? Then, why did you parade Wendy around in your press conference?"

"So, everyone would know there's nothing to hide. So they'd stop pursuing her. Notice I didn't let any reporters ask her questions."

"Except they weren't pursuing her until you brought her to that damn press conference. Do you know a reporter showed up at the house yesterday? I had to ask Peggy Garthwell to run interference."

"Why didn't you tell me?"

"It all happened so fast."

"Sara, you know I didn't mean for any of this to happen."

"I know." She sighed. "But there's no way Wendy's going back to Washington, *ever*. I have one more week to go in Pittsburgh. I'll ask the Garthwells to watch her."

"But if there are any reporters still skulking around Embler, they could ambush her. How about if you take Wendy with you to Pittsburgh?"

"I can't bring a child unto a construction site. I've told you that."

"Then take Gretchen Wheeler with you. You met her. She's great with Wendy."

"Well, I suppose so."

"Sara, we'll get through this. Look, there are about six or seven people who look like good candidates for the House. If I can get them elected, and the next time around, things are still bad, I promise I won't run for a third term."

"How do you define bad?"

"I'll leave it to you to define it. You can give me the thumbs-up or thumbs-down."

"You mean it."

"Yes, absolutely."

"You honestly think you can be reelected for a second term?"

"Strangely, these scandals have bolstered my popularity."

"That's one hell of a cost."

"No argument here."

Suddenly, the phone rang.

Sara answered. "Yes, may I ask who's calling?...I'll see if he's available." She put her hand over the receiver as she turned back to David. "It's Armand Nistle. He says it's urgent."

What the hell is Nistle calling about?

CHAPTER 55

The following Monday evening, members of the Winton College Board of Governors walked solemnly into the boardroom, a room paneled in well aged mahogany. The room had been designed by Reginald Winton himself, who wanted to emulate the feeling of an Ivy League institution. It was one of the few rooms to remain unchanged in the 84 years since Reginald Winton reigned over the school. No one other than the Board of Governors was allowed to use the room, something many felt was a waste.

Along the side wall, there was a table filled with platters of sandwiches, salads and cookies, less impressive than the board's usual cuisine for these meetings. The downgrade in faire reflected the school's condition.

"Good evening, everyone," Chairwoman Eleanor Galloway, called out to the board members. "I hereby call this meeting to order. For obvious reasons, we only have one agenda item tonight. I would like to suspend the reading of the minutes. Would someone like to make a motion?"

One of the board members made the motion. It was seconded. The vote was taken and the motion carried. Given the importance of this meeting, no one wanted to waste much time on procedural minutia.

"President Danzig, you have the floor."

"Thank you, Mrs. Galloway. At our last board meeting, Mr. Andrews gave us a thorough account of the college's finances. I'm sad to report there hasn't been much improvement. We were hoping the President's education bill would help us out, but that was not to be. I feel I've let the College down, but I am determined to not let this college fail. Accordingly, I've opened up discussions with Parnell Education. They are very interested in acquiring a quality institution with a strong academic reputation, such as Winton. In exchange, the college will receive an infusion of funding and be able to access Parnell's resources and expertise."

"Has it really come to that?" one of the board members asked. "Isn't there some other way? Couldn't we sell off some assets?"

"Selling off assets would be a temporary fix and make us less attractive to Parnell or any other potential buyer," Danzig said,

"Actually, partnering with Parnell seems like the perfect solution," another board member said. "Parnell is a very efficient organization. Winton could use some of that efficiency."

The receptionist pushed her head through the conference room door. Everyone focused on the surprise intruder into this grave meeting.

"Excuse me, President Danzig. There's a Congressman Grant here to see the Board."

"Really? Tell him, this is not a good time. We're in the middle of a critical meeting."

"Excuse me, President Danzig." Galloway said. "When a congressman shows up in a time of crisis, maybe we should let him in and hear what he has to say." *Nistle was right after all*, she thought.

"With all due respect," Danzig continued, "this is an internal matter. College business, not some governmental issue. Besides, let's be honest, the Congressman betrayed this college. He said he was going to support us and the education bill, and instead undermined it."

"Still, he is here, and I'd like to hear what he has to say." Galloway turned to the receptionist. "Send the Congressman in."

"Madame Chairwoman," Danzig snapped. "The Parnell offer is on the table."

"Then, I make motion we suspend the Parnell discussion until we hear what Congressman Grant has to say."

"Seconded."

"All those in favor?" Galloway asked.

Nine board members raised their hands.

"Those opposed? The motion carries."

Danzig glared at Galloway. "Send the Congressman in," he said in a tone that failed to hide his resentment.

"Good evening," David greeted them, as he walked in. He looked around at the fine paneling, such a contrast to the adjunct dungeon he was familiar with. "I apologize for interrupting your meeting, but I understand you're considering a buyout offer from Parnell Education Corporation. Before you vote on this, I thought it my duty to make you aware of certain facts. I assume you know President Danzig's connection to Parnell."

"Excuse me, Congressman," said one of the board members. "We're all aware of Chuck Danzig's résumé."

David looked into a folder he carried in with him. "You must be Arnold Spetzler. You should know, Mr. Spetzler. You reported directly to Chuck Danzig when you were at Parnell, didn't you? In fact, of the 15 board members, four of you are former Parnell employees, all of whom joined the board in the last three years, not including Chuck Danzig himself."

"It's not that incredible," Spetzler countered. "It's just a matter of networking, Besides, didn't you sell your firm to a company you used to work for?"

"Ah, someone has done their homework. Yes, I did. But that was different. Simplexia was my company to sell. And I didn't cook the books to make it happen."

"Cook the books?" another member asked. "What do you mean?"

"Chuck Danzig has raised tuition, yet offered such discounts—or scholarships—effectively lowering tuition, and revenues. The higher published tuition rate scares away price-sensitive families. And through the scholarships, he's reduced the revenue value of those students who aren't price-sensitive. His financial manipulation has been very clever. By driving down the financial health of the college, he's made it much easier for Parnell to acquire Winton."

"That's quite an accusation. Can you prove it?" asked an elderly man at the far end of the conference table.

"A proper audit and financial analysis will. However, I would have it done by someone who has no previous affiliation with Parnell Education."

"How dare you?" Danzig yelled. "You come in here and put your politician's spin on a plan that could save this college. I thought we were friends."

"I thought we were too. Then, I realized you were far more of a politician than I was. You were playing me from the very beginning. It was all part of a Parnell conspiracy to acquire Winton."

"You can't prove any of that. You're just slandering me."

David stepped forward. "I know what it is to be slandered. I would never do that to another human being. But it doesn't really matter. Ellis Cornwall is going to be under investigation."

"Who is Ellis Cornwall?" another board member asked.

"The true power behind Parnell. So if you allow Parnell to take over, Winton College will be tainted by a brewing scandal. Again, I'm sorry to intrude on your meeting, but I care about the future of Winton and I felt you needed to know this." He turned to Galloway. "If you need the names of some excellent auditors and investigators, I'll be glad to provide some."

"Thank you, Congressman." Galloway said.

"Well, I'll let you get back to your meeting. Good night." With that, David left quietly.

"Given these charges," Galloway said, "I believe it is our fiduciary duty to take Congressman Grant's advice and investigate."

"Parnell won't wait," Danzig snapped. "They're looking at other schools. Our financial situation requires quick action."

"Then, we will investigate quickly. I move we adjourn."

After the board dispersed. Danzig pulled out his mobile phone and punched in a number.

"Yes, I need to speak with Ellis Cornwall."

፠ ፠ ፨ ፨

The following morning, Jessica Dandridge was editing her opening remarks for that night's program. Her assistant stuck his head in her office door.

"Jessica, there's a call for you," the assistant said with a certain nervous reverence. "It's Mr. Cornwall," he added, as if God himself was calling.

"I'll take it here," she replied, smiling at her assistant's timidity. "Good afternoon, Ellis."

"Mornin' Jessica," Cornwall said. "How's the smartest and prettiest woman on American television?"

"Always wary of what a silver-tongued devil is about to ask."

"Honey, I don't *ask*. You know that."

"So what's up?"

"I was wondering, what are you going to talk about on your program tonight?"

"Well, I have some new material on Buck Howell. There are some questionable donations from…"

"Yes, yes, that can wait. What are you going to say about Grant?"

"You mean the one with the daughter? It looks like he was set up. I've talked to several people. His story seems to check out."

"I don't give a crap. He may not have an elephant tattooed on his ass, but he's the enemy just the same. Did you notice, how at Grant's press conference, that Neanderthal, Hudge, called for a special persecutor?"

"Yes."

"People only call for special prosecutors when they're aiming for the President. We have to protect the President at all costs."

"And I'm dedicated to that with all my heart and soul. But Ellis, there are still such things as slander and libel."

"And that, my dear, is what I pay a battalion of lawyers for."

"I'm not sure I like making an innocent ten-year-old girl the center of something so ugly and most probably false."

"Damn it, Jessica, we are in a war for the soul of this country. Those right-wing, Bible-thump'n yahoos trying to pull this country back to the middle ages. Besides, that Grant is a weasel no matter how you slice it. So in war, yes, there are casualties, and sometimes collateral damage. But that is the nature of war. You know that."

"Ellis, I just think Grant's story holds up and there's going to be a backlash against anyone who attacks him. I've seen the instant polls. People believe him."

"We don't follow public opinion. We *make* public opinion."

"I'm just thinking of the reputation of the program, of the network."

Dandridge could hear Cornwall's slow burn over the telephone. She had never opposed him before. She wasn't sure she was going to survive this call.

"Jessie, honey, I don't like compromising, *ever*. But just this once, because I love you so, if you don't want to deal with this on your own show, fine. Go on Dreeves. Do it there."

"*Dreeves Peeves*? You're kidding me?" She couldn't stand Joe Dreeves, who hosted Liberty's late night show. In Dandridge's mind, Dreeves acted as if he was the reincarnation of Johnny Carson, but mistakenly believed snark was a sufficient substitute for wit.

"Jessie, I'm giving you a choice. Do it on your show or Dreeves's."

୏ ୏ ୒ ୓

"We have some great guests on *Dreeves Peeves* tonight," Joe Dreeves announced. "First up, Liberty's own opinionatrix, Jessica Dandridge." The audience responded enthusiastically to the applause sign. "Jessica said she couldn't come on without her whip, so we invited House Whip Porter Barnes."

Dreeves proceeded with a lackluster monolog, but gave it a pretense of humor. After the commercial break, he brought Dandridge on. They went through the ritualistic hugging and kissing, but Dandridge was quick to sit down on the couch.

"Jessica," Dreeves began, "I really enjoy all your books, but I have to say my favorite is *101 Things You Can Do with a Dead Republican.* In fact, I bought ten copies."

"Thank you. Why so many?"

"Well in my mind, that makes 1010 things I can do with a dead Republican. You just can't do enough to the Republicans."

Dandridge just smiled, as the audience obeyed the laugh sign.

"So what do you think of this David Grant mess?" Dreeves began.

"Well, I think it's just that, a mess," Dandridge agreed. "Listen, I want to be fair. I don't know what went on in that hotel room in Omaha, probably nothing that bad. But what father leaves a young girl alone in a hotel room, while he's going to the bar to meet a hooker or a campaign contributor or whomever?"

"So the real question is who was receiving money. Grant? Or a hooker?"

Again, the audience obeyed the laugh sign. Dandridge's face was stone. Dreeves and Dandridge moved on to talking about the upcoming presidential campaign, particularly taking time to bash Republican frontrunner, Buck Howell.

"Anyway, my next guest is House Majority Whip, Porter Barnes."

Barnes lumbered onto the set. He and Dandridge hugged in a way that was slightly more genuine than she had with Dreeves. Dandridge moved down the couch to make way for Barnes.

"So, you two are old friends. How many times have you been on Jessica's show?"

"A few times. I've lost count."

"We were just discussing the whole—what do we call it? Wendy-gate situation?"

Dandridge winced at the term Dreeves had just coined.

"Well, I've met Wendy Grant," Barnes said, "and she seemed like a very nice young lady. Congressman Grant had been keeping her very close at the Capitol. I never thought it unusual, but clearly I may have been wrong. The claim that this sweet little girl was suddenly overcome by a sugar-high, turning her into a raging monster, I find it a little fantastic. When I saw that video, I saw fear in that little girl. That's the true nature of Wendygate."

"Could we please not use that term?" Dandridge interrupted. "We have to remember there's a little girl who may or may not have been abused. Let's not add to the trauma."

Both Dreeves and Barnes were caught off guard by this, but Barnes recovered quickly.

"Jessica's quite right. We need to protect children, something the Right has never had much interest in. Certainly, David Grant should never have abandoned his daughter in a hotel room, regardless of whatever else he may or may not have done.

CHAPTER 56

Since the first week David arrived in Washington, he had been invited to an endless stream of cocktail parties around the DC area. Most were cordial opportunities for lobbyists to sell their positions, the political equivalent of the old Tupperware party. So, he generally avoided them. The number of invitations only increased as the winter holidays approached.

However, when David received an invitation from retired General Zeke Collier, he was slightly more inclined to accept. He hadn't seen the general since Cadillac Mountain. When he read the handwritten notation, *Remove all batteries from mobile phones before arriving*, he decided this was one gathering he would definitely attend.

As he pulled up to Collier's house, he was met by a very familiar valet, the same man who scanned his townhouse for bugs.

"Good evening, Congressman. Don't worry. I'll take good care of your car. I trust your batteries have been removed?"

"What? Oh, yes. I'll take care of that right now. Thank you."

The valet took the keys and drove off. David wondered what exactly was going on. He wondered if the mysterious valet had performed the same security sweep tonight. Or maybe, he was moonlighting. *Or maybe he's bugging the cars?* David tried to put that thought out of his mind, but given the recent events in Omaha, that was difficult.

He walked into the front door and was met promptly by General Collier.

"Congressman, I'm so glad you could make it."

"Me too. Thank you for inviting me."

"I'm sorry to see you've been taking so much fire recently," the general said.

"Well, it seems to have died down. And I suppose that comes with the territory."

"No," Collier said sternly. "There are weapons you don't use. We refrained from using poison gas after World War I, and nukes after World War II. Certain weapons you just don't use. In political war, that goes for attacking one's family, especially the way they went after your innocent little girl. I'm glad you survived that war."

"Unfortunately, I think it was only a skirmish, a battle at best. The bigger war continues."

"Amen," Collier said. "I hope you'll stick around later. I think you'll find a few old friends back in the dining room, or wherever they've migrated to."

David started to mingle. Among the attendees were other members of Congress, military brass, and the odd ambassador. Several people walked up to him to express their support. Finally, he found Howard Carstairs.

"David, how are you?" Carstairs asked. "Has the Omaha thing finally died out?"

"Pretty much, although it's still cited in discussions of political woes and corruption, along with Kadler Steele, CART and the education bill."

"Yeah, Farnum's gonna get his ass kicked come Election Day. Too bad. He had a lot of potential."

"I'm surprised to hear you say that. I would've thought as a Republican you'd be happy with Farnum weakening."

"I might have, except that poor excuse for a candidate, Howell, is probably going to be our nominee."

"But there's a pretty broad field of Republicans."

"And they'll all go up and down in the polls, but Howell will be there in the end because he's the best financed and the biggest yahoo in the party. Everyone at CPAC practically had an orgasm when he came on stage. The only one who received a bigger reception was that idiot, Ben Glendenning. So what does that tell you? I tried to convince Dennis Ogden to run, but he was too smart for that."

"But Howell's so far to the right. Won't that give Farnum an advantage in the general election?"

"Well, it's almost a year 'til Election Day. Anything can happen. And who knows what your Mr. Vreeland might do?"

"We both know Vreeland can't win," David said.

"Yet you're campaigning for him."

"In exchange for his support in other areas."

"You mean his contributions to the Centrist House candidates?"

"Yeah, I guess you can say I finally sold my soul."

Carstairs laughed. "Yes, but did you get a good price for it?"

Now, it was David's turn to laugh.

As the party wound down, most of the attendees departed, leaving only members of the Circle and a few others. David noticed Martha Addison, the Federal Reserve Chair. He wondered if she were a Circle member, too. His question was soon answered.

Zeke Collier walked into the middle of his living room.

"Good evening, everyone. It's rare everybody in our little group is able to gather all together like this. And thank you for enduring the cover of a cocktail party. Before we begin, there's a bit of housekeeping we need to attend to. Mr. Black?"

The man who had been attending to cars, walked in, no longer dressed as a valet, but wearing an expensive looking suit. He looked perfectly at home as a guest.

"Thank you, General. Each of you, at one time or another, was provided with a burner phone. Hopefully, you all followed the request to remove the battery. I ask that you now place your phones and batteries in this box."

Collier was the first to comply. Addison, McCord, Carstairs and the others followed suite, as did David. However, he noticed one man standing in the corner, unmoving. David wondered whether the man was being defiant, or had just not been given a phone. Then, David realized someone was missing. *Where's Hingecliff?*

"As we head into the election," Mr. Black continued, "there will be increased temptations to conduct opposition research and dirty operations. As we saw in Congressman Grant's case, it can be quite intrusive."

There were grumbles of agreement and nods in David's direction.

"As the election cycle goes into full swing," Mr. Black, continued "it would be prudent to expect greater monitoring, both legal and illegal. Therefore, caution should be exercised in communicating in all aspects of our lives, especially with one another."

Just then Robert Hingecliff walked in. "My apologies." He looked at the box in the middle of the room. "I see we've already started," he added, as he dropped his phone and battery into the box. "Didn't mean to interrupt."

"No problem, Mr. Secretary," Mr. Black said. "I had just finished."

"Robert, why don't you introduce your guest?" Collier said.

"Certainly, I'd like you all to meet Kevin O'Hara, the U.S. Attorney for the Southern District of New York. You may have heard of him because of his work on the Kadler Steele case. Now he has a little problem." Hingecliff gestured to O'Hara. "Kevin?"

O'Hara, the man David had wondered about, stepped forward.

"Thank you for inviting me to your gathering tonight."

David realized this was probably O'Hara's first contact with the Circle, his version of Cadillac Mountain.

"Well over a year ago," O'Hara continued, "a corporate vice-president at Kadler Steele, named Erin Korelev came to my office. Everyone knows what came from that meeting. She sacrificed not only her job, but her career. No financial services company will hire her now. Since then, I've been able to get a few minor convictions of low-to-mid level employees. But Corbin Beaumont eludes us, which is ridiculous, since we have a recording of Beaumont admitting to a full understanding of illegal Kadler Steele activities. We obtained this with the kind assistance of then-Commerce Secretary, Robert Hingecliff."

O'Hara nodded appreciatively in Hingecliff's direction.

"Despite this, I've not been able to move forward with a prosecution of Beaumont."

"What's been the hold-up?" Martha Addison asked.

"My superiors in the Justice Department have been requiring additional briefs, requesting more information, and creating a bunch of other bureaucratic delays. Individually, none of them is particularly extraordinary. However, the sheer volume is like nothing I've ever seen."

"You could go public," David suggested.

"That would end my career. But if it would guarantee Corbin Beaumont's conviction, I'd do it in a heartbeat. Meanwhile, my direct superiors are waving a promotion under my nose, one that would take me off the Kadler case. Clearly, certain people are already thinking of how to remove me. Whenever I've expressed concerns, I'm told to not rock the boat in an election year. And the election year hasn't even started."

"There's also been pressure from Wall Street," Senator McCord added. "I'm on the Financial Services Committee. Plenty of lobbyists are expressing concern over the possibility Beaumont might be prosecuted."

"But wasn't Kadler Steele prohibited from lobbying under the conditions of CART?" General Collier asked.

"It's not Kadler," McCord explained. "The other Wall Street firms are worried that if Beaumont is convicted, it would set a precedent. That scares the shit out of them, or at least their CEOs."

"Perhaps," Hingecliff ventured, "a non-aligned third party could take up the cause."

"Why do I feel Robert is talking about me?" David asked.

Everyone chuckled.

"Or perhaps your friend, Mr. Vreeland?" Hingecliff suggested.

"I might be able to speak to him."

"Excellent. And perhaps some of our Republican colleagues might also speak out."

"Now, he's talking about me," Carstairs blurted out.

Again, the room laughed. The discussion continued for another hour. David learned quite a bit more about what was happening in Washington.

"Well, the hour grows late." Collier announced. "In accordance with the season, Mr. Black has a gift for everyone."

Everyone turned toward Black, who was bringing in a tray of identically wrapped packages. The red wrapping paper and bows looked quite festive.

"New burner phones?" Carstairs asked.

"So much for the surprise," Collier chuckled. "Happy Holidays, everyone."

The party broke up fairly quickly. David said his good-byes, but waited to speak to O'Hara.

"Congressman, thank you for your support," O'Hara said.

"Don't mention it. Beaumont and his kind deserve punishment after what they've done to this country. You mentioned you might be promoted out of New York."

"Yes, as a way of sidelining me."

"If that comes to pass, maybe there's someone else worth investigating."

"Anything to do with a false allegation of pedophilia?"

"Only tangentially. The Omaha smear was the tip of the iceberg. Interested?"

"Very much so."

ಬಿ ಬಿ ಲ ಲ

In the following weeks, Marshall Vreeland did bring up the question of Beaumont's prosecution or lack thereof. So did Howard Carstairs. However, they made little impression on the American public, who had grown used to scandalous charges, countercharges, excuses and rationalizations. Members of Congress were uncharacteristically quiet, including the Republicans. It was apparent the lobbyists had already built a siege wall made of campaign donations.

As the New Year began, the primaries opened up and campaigning intensified. Each Republican presidential candidate took turns surging in the polls as each asserted he or she was the only one conservative enough to lead the country back to prosperity, strength, trustworthiness, or whichever buzzword was polling best that week.

As Howard Carstairs predicted, Governor Howell held the lead in the polls. By April, Buck Howell of Oklahoma collected enough electoral votes to earn the Republican nomination. Now the full Republican ire could be redirected toward Gregory Farnum.

Through the summer conventions, the polls put Howell on average ten to fifteen points ahead of the President.

In August, Farnum briefly surged ahead as he aggressively addressed some saber-rattling from North Korea. However, the conservative chorus accused him of posturing, despite the fact he did exactly what the hawks had prescribed. The momentary lead evaporated as September began. Shortly thereafter, Republicans raised questions about the President's sexuality, citing the Farnums had no children. Accordingly, Mrs. Farnum began making more campaign appearances, dropping hints, subtle and not-so-subtle, about her husband's virility. In the end, she confessed the reason they had no children. She made infertility awareness her new cause. Then, Republicans accused her of faking infertility. Some such as Glendenning demanded her medical paperwork. However, the public was generally sympathetic to Mrs. Farnum.

Despite this, few believed the Howell juggernaut could be stopped. People would frequently bandy about the phrase, "President Howell." That was until the beginning of October.

ॐ ॐ ॐ ॐ

"We have some interesting new video from the campaign trail," Jessica Dandridge announced. "It's so self-explanatory, I'm not going to set it up except to tell you it's Buck Howell obviously talking to his kind of people."

From the angle of the video clip, it appeared as if the camera must have been sitting on a serving table. A tray of cookies was visible in the foreground. Howell could be seen in profile, facing his audience. The surroundings suggested the venue was a private home.

An older woman's voice from off-camera complained, "What I am tired of is seeing America being eaten away by all these Hispanics or Latinos or whatever they want to call themselves these days. If they want to come into America, they should come legally, and not try to change our American way of life. And they should learn to speak English!"

Howell smiled. "I can sympathize. I went by the drive-through window of a restaurant a few months ago. Everything on the menu was chipotle-this and habanera-that. But the worst thing was I could barely understand what the woman trying to take my order was saying. It was quite frustrating. They should change the name of the restaurant to SpicDonald's."

This comment received some laughter.

"And Farnum wanted to educate our college students in that language? So, you're absolutely right. It's a cultural war, a war we must win."

The clip ended, and the program returned to Dandridge.

"I'm just amazed at the racism. Here we are in the 21st century, and a man who wants to be President of the United States is campaigning like it's the 1950s. What more can I say?"

Dandridge smiled in her signature way that assured her audience there was plenty.

"Let's see. Howell's an evolution denier. He's a climate-change denier. But you know, I think he's got at least one more denial left in him."

ᛞ ᛥ ᚳ ᚽ

"Welcome again to another edition of *Dreeves Peeves*." Joe Dreves said, opening his monolog. "Well, as everyone has heard Governor Buck Howell is taking a break from campaigning for sensitivity training or some other strategic voodoo."

"However, in place of campaigning, the Governor has moved into merchandising. And we want to help, because the Republicans can use all the help they can get." Dreeves held up a doll.

"Introducing the new Buck Howell doll, complete with synthetic hair and hidden messages." Dreeves pulled the string out from the back of the doll, which proceeded to play the recorded message: "Don't worry. The Rapture will take care of global warming." He pulled the string again. "Oooo-kla-homa, where the wind comes sweeping up your [bleep]." He pulled again. "At least we're not Texas."

"And finally," Dreeves said, pulling the string one last time.

"I'm hungry. Where's the nearest SpicDonald's?"

"Call now for your Bucky Howell doll. Qualities are limited."

"Excuse me, Joe," a voice from off-stage called out. "I think you meant *quantities* are limited."

"No, I got it right the first time," Dreeves said, grinning to the camera. "The Buck stops here. In fact, he can go Buck himself."

CHAPTER 57

The last few weeks before the election were becoming quite intense. The charges and counter-charges were more negative and extreme every day. David was exhausted, splitting his time between his own campaign, stumping for a half-dozen Centrist candidates, and advising Marshall Vreeland from afar.

David was headed to Oregon to campaign for Kate Garner, a promising candidate from Hood River, when he received the distress call from Jason Kennerly, requesting his help. David adjusted his flight plans to include a one-day stopover in Denver. Jason picked him up at the airport.

"How was your flight?" he asked.

"It was a flight," David said in a weary tone.

"I really appreciate you altering your schedule to help Marshall out with the debate prep."

"No sweat. What seems to be the problem?"

"I'm not sure. But Marshall doesn't seem to come across as well as he could. He sounds weak."

"Alright, I'll see what I can do. But we're going to have a strategy meeting first, right?"

"Absolutely."

"Outside of debate prep, how's the campaign going?"

"I think you'll be pleasantly surprised. Vreeland's organization has evolved. Stan McKenzie has built a much more professional operation. We've all learned a lot. But now, we may have hit pay dirt."

"How so?"

"After Howell's gaffe, his lead just dissolved. And those voters are flowing Marshall's way."

"Yeah, but how many?"

"Reach into my bag in the back. Pull out the orange folder. It has all the latest polling."

David reached over the seat and retrieved the folder of spreadsheets from Jason's bag. The shift in the polls was more than he expected. However, it still wasn't enough to win the race.

"The undecideds could actually help him win several states," Jason explained.

"I think that's extremely optimistic. In the end, most of the undecideds will return to the security of the major parties. Most voters aren't ready to entrust the presidency to a third party. Right now, they may be just expressing their disgust for the other two guys. That's why we need to move more resources behind the House candidates."

As much as David repeated this idea, he knew he wouldn't win this argument until Vreeland lost the election. By then it would be too late. But there was always the next election cycle. They arrived at Vreeland's hotel, most of which had been converted into his campaign headquarters. Within a few minutes the strategy meeting began.

"The true battleground states," Stan Erskine explained, "are Ohio, Pennsylvania, Colorado, Virginia, and yes, Florida, Florida, Florida. They have the highest number of undecided voters."

"Just because they're undecided, doesn't mean they'll break for Marshall," David called out.

"What? You think we should concentrate on California and Texas?" Erskine asked, with some annoyance in his voice.

"Of course not," David said, leaning forward. "Winning even one entire state will be difficult. However, there are two states that aren't winner-take-all. Nebraska and Maine award their electoral vote by congressional district. All the other electoral votes are based on a state-wide popular vote. "

"I'm not sure I follow you."

"If you concentrate all your efforts on Nebraska and Maine, you can do what no third-party presidential candidate has done in recent times: *Capture actual electoral votes!* According to the data Jason showed me, Nebraska, with its five electoral votes, is tracking slightly in Howell's favor. Maine has four, and is leaning toward the President. Obviously, Marshall's tracking better in Nebraska, since he was born there."

"Dumping everything into just two states is insane," Erskine fired back angrily.

"Now, everyone calm down," Vreeland called out. No one had noticed him entering the room.

"David wants us to abandon everything for Maine and Nebraska. That means—"

"I heard what he said from outside the door. So here's the plan. Load up for Nebraska, Maine, Virginia, Ohio, Colorado, Pennsylvania, and some place called Florida, Florida, Florida."

Everyone laughed, relieving the tension.

"Anyone have any objections?" Vreeland looked to David. He nodded no.

After lunch, the team moved to another room set up with three podiums. Jason played the part of the questioner. He didn't know the people playing Farnum and Howell, but they weren't doing their jobs. Neither was the Jason Kennerly for that matter. David saw the problem immediately.

"Stop."

"What's the matter?" Jason asked.

"You're all softballing this. You need to ask tougher questions. And you two," David said, pointing at Vreeland's mock opponents. "You need to answer the question more like they would. Stop acting like weak parodies of those candidates. You need to attack Marshall. Make him feel the pressure. Farnum and Howell won't pull their punches. Neither can you."

"Marshall?" Jason asked.

"The Congressman's right," Vreeland agreed. "Let me have it with both barrels, guys." He nodded gratefully at David. The mock debate continued for another two hours, then stopped for a critique. Everyone agreed there had been significant improvement in Vreeland's responses. They broke for dinner, and would resume in the evening.

"Marshall, I'm sorry," David said. "I need to head out. Before I go, I want to give you something." David pulled a dollar bill out of his pocket.

"What is this, a campaign contribution?" Vreeland asked, smiling at the pathetic looking dollar bill.

"In a way, but it's not a financial one. I've been holding onto this idea for over a year, never quite sure how to use it. But now, I'm giving it to you." David pointed down at the red stamp that read "Where's George?"

৪০ ৪০ ৫৪ ৫৪

After a couple of days of campaigning, David stopped by Howard Carstairs' office.

"How goes the campaigns?" Carstairs asked.

"I'll probably win my race. I'm hopeful about the other Centrists. Marshall Vreeland? Well, anything could happen. Would I be able to convince you to come out in support of Vreeland?"

Carstairs laughed. "An endorsement?"

"If you came out for Vreeland, it would mean an awful lot. I know what you think of Buck Howell."

"True, but if I go against my party's nominee, I'll be a complete pariah. I've already been marginalized as a RINO."

"You could join our party? We'd make you an instant party elder."

Carstairs laughed again, shaking his head no.

"Alright, I had to give it a try. Instead, can you tell me what the important issues are in Maine? It's become an important state to us."

"Maine? We only have four electoral votes."

"It's a key state in Vreeland's strategy."

Carstairs looked at David quizzically, then smiled.

"Vreeland's or yours? I saw Vreeland's intensified campaigning in Nebraska. Didn't think much of it, since that's where he's from originally. But now, I know what you're up to. It's a long shot in a long game."

"It's the only shot."

"Okay, I can give you some local intelligence, you know, what the local issues and hot buttons are, more important, what land mines to avoid. Don't piss off the lobstermen, etc. How's that?"

"Thanks. That would be great."

"It'll be interesting to see how your game turns out. You could turn out to be the most dangerous man in Washington, you know that?"

৪০ ৪০ ৫৪ ৫৪

Two days later, the presidential debate was about to begin. Each candidate was allowed no more than 60 supporters in the audience. This way no candidate would have an advantage. David Grant and Fred Arkin were among Vreeland's quota. The remaining seats were filled with news media and Secret Service agents.

"Good evening," Dylan Reese announced, "and welcome to St. Louis and this evening's presidential debate. Each of the candidates has agreed to the debate rules. We ask that the audience withhold all applause until the end of the evening, so we can have more time for a meaningful and civil discourse among our candidates. Before we begin with questions, each candidate will have 90 seconds for an opening statement. Mr. President?"

"Thank you, Dylan. Being president is not an easy task, because it's a sacred trust. Everyone thinks they can do this job, but few know what it really entails. It's not a shoot-from-the-hip kind of job." Farnum gave a nod in Vreeland's direction. "Decisions in one area affect another. Simplistic solutions don't exist," he added, looking at Howell, "But simplistic mistakes do. Sound bites may work for campaigning, but they're useless for governing."

"The presidency isn't a dictatorship, where a snap of the finger solves all. It requires the negotiation of complex issues among many diverse stakeholders. Government is where we as a people come together for all, not just for the wealthy."

"For years, the Republicans have brought little beyond strident hard-right demands and political division. We must once again become the *United* States of America, not the warring factions of self interest. And that is my goal."

"Thank you, Mr. President," Reese said, turning to the opposing podium. "Governor Howell?"

"Mr. Reese, I just wanted to thank you for your participation and support of our democratic process tonight." Howell turned to the camera. "For years, the Democrats have overreached and tried to control every facet of our lives from healthcare to education, turning us into a nanny state. What have we gotten for it? A crippling National Debt, a prolonged recession, a bafflingly complex and burdensome tax code, not to mention a complete loss of faith in the Federal Government."

"Despite how the Liberals would like to paint me, I don't want to deny people welfare checks. I want them not to need those checks in the first place. That's the true meaning of 'yes, we can.' There has been a war on hard work."

"I believe this country has lost its connection with what made it great. Immigrants came from far-off lands to our shores to build a better life, not to apply for handouts. I believe rugged individualism is the key to American exceptionalism. I want the Federal Government out of our lives, so *everyone* can reach their potential."

"Thank you, Governor. Mr. Vreeland?"

331

"I mean no personal disrespect to the President or the Governor, but what a bunch of hot air. And the American people know it. Carefully crafted words are not a substitute for straight talk or honest and fair decision-making."

"But some politicians have forgotten that. And that's why every politician's approval rating it so low. Yes, Mr. President, problems are complex. But there are a core set of values that can always guide us. And by values, I mean honesty, courage, common sense, not political expediency."

"The Governor says he wants the Federal Government out of our lives, except when it comes to things like farm subsidies, corporate subsidies, and religion or faith-based initiatives. He's especially interested in subsidizing religion. I have to ask, what happened to the separation of church and state? Each of these men is so beholden to special interests and lobbyists, I honestly can't see anything improving with either of them in office."

"Well, he certainly came out swinging," Fred commented to David.

"Thank you, gentlemen." Reese said. "I'll start now with our first question. Mr. President, a major issue during your presidency has been education. Your education bill, which has been described with words such behemoth, gargantuan, and leviathan, still has not been able to pass in Congress, despite having a majority in both the House and Senate. How will you pursue the pledge of improving education, if you are given a second term?"

Farnum broke into his best telegenic smile. "Well, Dylan, the bill has been blocked by short-sighted Republicans, using the weapon of the Senate filibuster to block passage. I've said this before; to compete in the global economy we need highly educated workers. And that's why I made it my top priority. However, the Republicans don't seem to comprehend how important education is to our future."

"I noticed he didn't answer the question," Fred murmured.

"If he did, then he might be held accountable." David whispered back

"Governor Howell," Reese continued, "would you care to respond?"

"I agree education is important to our country's future. But the President's bill was a monstrous waste of money, driven by a socialist agenda. He focused on colleges, an area that would benefit his patrons, people like Ellis Cornwall. This bill would have provided Mr. Cornwall and his cronies with a significant return on investment. The President's corruption aside, we need to focus on the basics, things like, math, science, and oh yes, *English.*"

"I can't believe he went back to the issue that got him into so much trouble," David mumbled."

"Mr. Vreeland?" Reese said.

"Education is not something the Federal Government does particularly well. The key to good education is quality teachers, higher standards and smaller classrooms, not huge pork-laden legislation. I find these men talking about math and science a little bit like theater of the absurd. Look at the President's budget. You'll see it shows a complete disregard of mathematical principles, such as simple addition and subtraction. He said in a statement last week, his budget came closer to being balanced than any in a decade. That's not saying much. But he can say it only because his giant education-and-pork bill failed. Well, that crosses off math."

Vreeland turned toward Howell. "Then, to hear the Governor talk about science is even more absurd. Buck Howell doesn't believe in global warming or evolution. I have to ask, what is his idea of science? Alchemy? Astrology?"

Some of the audience burst out laughing.

"Can we really entrust our children's education to either of these men?"

The next few questions pertained to foreign policy, an area where the President was stronger. But eventually, the questions returned to domestic issues.

"Governor Howell," Reese said, "The National Debt increased to over 34 trillion dollars this summer. What would you do, if anything, to address the debt?"

"Well Dylan, we need to cut national expenditures, especially in many of the President's liberal giveaway programs, the pork he set aside for his campaign contributors is just something we can't afford. Our economy needs to be light and nimble, able to pivot on a dime. Our businesses need to be relieved of the heavy tax burdens, so they can invest in needed technologies, open new markets and employ more of our citizens."

"Mr. President?"

"Dylan, I'm sure you noticed the Governor didn't answer your question. He mentions investing in new technologies. But as companies invest in technology, they tend to employ fewer workers. So again, advanced education for high-tech jobs is vital to achieving full employment. And we need to invest in infrastructure and private-public sector partnerships."

"Mr. Vreeland?"

"Mr. Reese, I'm sure you noticed the President didn't answer your question either. You know, we've heard variations of these same two answers for several decades. Tax more and spend less. Each makes sense. Yet neither of the two sides has balanced a budget, because politically it's more expedient to spend more and tax less. Neither of them can think outside their respective boxes."

"That's very well to say," Reese said, "but what would you actually do?"

Vreeland smiled as he pulled something out of his pocket.

"See this dollar bill? It's traveled quite a bit. There's a website that has tracked this bill as it circulated through the economy. It's visited Oregon, Georgia, New Jersey and probably a few other states. Think of how far and wide our currency travels. And of how many hands it passes through. Now imagine if the government sold advertising space on the back of those bills. It would circulate through the population for years. No one would throw it out. How much would Madison Avenue pay for that kind of advertising power?

Now, there's a truly new idea, and it wouldn't increase taxes or reduce spending. That's thinking outside the box!"

"That's a very unorthodox idea," Reese observed. "Governor Howell, would you care to comment?"

"Defacing our currency is unacceptable. It's like defacing the flag. Thoroughly un-American. And while I am a supporter of free enterprise and capitalism, this is a sacrilege."

"Mr. President, would you like to comment?"

"I have to admit I'm not in love with this idea. Unlike Governor Howell, I don't believe our currency is so sacred. I reserve the word, sacrilege, for more important things than money. If we could put certain safeguards in place, I might be willing to consider such a proposal."

"What the President means," Vreeland blurted out, "is he hasn't done a focus group on it. So much for leadership!"

"Mr. Vreeland, please confine your comments to answering the questions," Reese warned. "But, I have to ask how would you respond to the Governor's objection?"

"Do I like the idea of selling advertising space on the back of our currency? Of course not, but the two major parties have pushed us to a point where there's going to be some pain. This is a less painful alternative, certainly less painful than what the two major parties will bring down on our heads. Dealing with these inevitable problems will take out-of-the-box thinking. They just recycle and repackage old ideas, and then kick the can down the road."

"Is that the same dollar that's been sitting in your desk?" Fred whispered.

David nodded yes.

"Maybe you two should have worked out a lip-sync arrangement."

David smiled. Just then, his burner phone vibrated. It was a text message from Cal McCord. As he read the message, a pit opened in his stomach.

CHAPTER 58

Two days later, David received the call from Emily Carstairs. He dropped everything and raced to George Washington University Hospital. As he headed into the critical care unit, he saw Emily Carstairs talking to a nurse. As the nurse finished and walked away, Emily spotted him and waved him forward.

"Hi, Emily. How is he?"

"He's still paralyzed on his left side. He can talk, but with difficulty."

"How are *you* doing?"

"Okay, under the circumstances."

"Is there anything I can do?"

"No, there's nothing. The people here at the hospital have been wonderful."

"I see your family's here," David said, noticing a young man who looked strikingly like Howard, along with a woman he guessed was a daughter-in-law. "I don't want to intrude."

"No, Howard asked for you. After two days of doctors and doting family, he wants to talk shop with someone, you know, to take his mind off things. Cal McCord was here earlier, but had to leave."

David walked into Carstairs' room. The droop in the side of his face was quite evident. The old senator gave a crooked smile, valiant and heartbreaking at the same time.

"You're looking better than I expected," David lied.

"Bullll-shhhit,…yer-ra…such…a…pol-it…tish…shhhun."

"Now, Howard, you're just being nasty."

Carstairs' chuckle sounded surprisingly normal.

"Tell…me….Is…yer…big…pa…plan…wor…kinggg?"

"I don't know. The polls are all over the place. Anyone could win."

"You…will…winnnn."

David talked for some time, filling his friend in on the latest inside news. But after a while, he saw Carstairs was tiring.

"Howard, I've got to go. But I want to thank you for all you've done for me. You better get well soon. We still have a lot to do."

The ailing senator smiled and gave a thumbs-up.

൝ ൭ ൫ ൫

As Election Day became imminent, all the candidates departed for their respective states and districts for last-minute campaigning. On Election Day, each was televised entering and leaving the voting booth, usually uttering some clever one-liner.

Again, David's organization rented out the Embler River Inn. That evening, all his campaign staff, volunteers and supporters enjoyed plenty of food, as the news reports poured forth on three large plasma screens in the ballroom.

"Good evening," said Bob Summers, kicking off the broadcast. "Welcome to our coverage of one of the most contentious presidential elections in recent history. It's a unique combination of a close race, a disgruntled electorate, and a strong third-party candidate. With us tonight is Chief Political Analyst, Dylan Reese." Summers turned to Reese. "Dylan, we've each covered at least half a dozen presidential elections. Have you ever seen an election quite like this?"

"No, Bob. The forces you just described are creating a perfect storm for election chaos. So what the final outcome will be, no one can predict with any degree of confidence."

"Is there a possibility that by the end of the night, none of the candidates will have enough electoral votes to win?"

"That is a distinct possibility. As you know, we don't directly elect the president. It's done through the Electoral College. Each state has a number of electors committed to vote for a given candidate. The overall number of electors is 538. So the magic number to win is 270 electoral votes."

"But this year," Summers interrupted, "it isn't that simple, is it?"

"No, because if Marshall Vreeland earns just one electoral vote, we might have a deadlocked Electoral College, depending on the number Farnum and Howell receive. And if some compromise isn't reached during the Electoral College voting, it could throw the election into the House of Representatives."

"Well if that happens," Summers interrupted again, "then President Farnum will certainly be reelected since the Democrats hold the House."

"Yes," Reese agreed, "provided the Democrats hold the House, which we do expect. However, there is a strong possibility the Republicans might gain control of the Senate, which selects the vice-president. Theoretically, we could end up with a Democratic president and a Republican vice-president."

"That would be one for the books," Summers said.

ଇଠ ଇଠ ଔଷ ଔଷ

Again, David's campaign set up its war room in the hotel's conference room. At one end, Ellen was coordinating all the information for David's campaign. At the other, Fred was monitoring information about Vreeland's campaign and those of the six Centrist candidates. To Ellen's annoyance, David seemed more interested in Fred's end of the room. But he also seemed distracted by something else.

As the evening turned late, Ellen walked over to David.

"I know you're a bit busy, sir. I just thought you'd like to know, you've just been reelected to Congress. The local news just called the election in your favor. McMann and Yendrick will be making their concession speeches in a few minutes."

"Great," David said reflexively. "Have you seen any data on Maine?"

"Excuse me," Ellen said, slightly annoyed. "Um, no. Sir, you need to make your own speech in a few minutes."

"I'm sorry," he said, refocusing on the news Ellen brought him. "I'm a little distracted. Ellen, thank you. Again, I couldn't have done this without you, and I know it."

"My pleasure, sir."

"Have you seen Sara?"

"Right here," Sara said from behind him. She was holding two Champagne flutes.

"I'll let the press know you'll give your speech in 20 minutes." Ellen said. "Okay?"

David nodded his approval.

Sara handed him one of the glasses. "Here's to your last campaign," Sara said, raising a glass. "Thank God."

David said nothing for a moment, grim-faced. "I just received word. Howard Carstairs died late last night."

"I'm so sorry," Sara said, regretting her previous remark. "He was a very nice man. I know you liked him very much. I feel awful for Emily. Is there anything I can do?"

"Yes, there is. However, it has nothing to do with Howard, or my campaign, for that matter. It will require your special talents, and there's not much time."

Sara looked at him quizzically.

ဆ ဆ ର ର

It was two in the morning. Summers and Reese had been on the air for more hours than expected. They could have been relieved by their on-camera colleagues, but neither was going to forego broadcasting the election story of the century.

"And now," Summers announced, "we can finally call the state of Hawaii with its four electoral votes for President Farnum." This brings the President up to 266 electoral votes, with Governor Howell holding 265, both short of the required 270. This leaves only the two states, Nebraska and Maine, neither of which are winner-take-all. Dylan, why don't you take us through the electoral math there?"

"Well Bob, there are nine electoral votes in play. It's safe to say at least two of Maine's will go to the President, and three of Nebraska's will go to Howell. That leaves four crucial votes in play. However, these are both states where Marshall Vreeland has surged in the polls in the last weeks. Election officials in both states are being very cautious, counting the votes very carefully. That's why it's taking so long. Everyone remembers Florida in 2000. No one wants a repeat of that drama."

"But if Vreeland receives enough votes, this could be worse. It could be a constitutional crisis."

"Not really. It'll be dramatic certainly, but the Constitution does have a path to resolve such a stalemate, should that come to pass. Providing no electors switch their vote, the election will be thrown into the House of Representatives."

ဆာ ၾ ၾ

"How are we coming along with the House races?" David asked.

"Well, Dern in Missouri has lost for sure," Fred lamented. "Garner in Oregon is looking strong. Lee in Florida, not so much. Spinelli and Yost also look good. Brooks could go either way. So it looks like you'll have at least three, maybe four, new playmates in Congress come January."

"Great."

"Excuse me, Congressman," one of the volunteers called out. We've got news on Maine and Nebraska."

They all turned to the television.

"Well, it's official," Summers announced. "The final electoral count is Farnum 269, Howell 268, and Vreeland four. Barring defection, none of the candidates has enough to win in the Electoral College. So, the election will likely be thrown into the House of Representatives, where the Democrats have retained control. The Senate, however, has been reclaimed by the Republicans."

David turned to Fred. "Find me the telephone numbers for Vreeland's electors in Maine and Nebraska." David then walked outside into the parking lot. He pulled out his burner phone and selected "Blacksmith" in the menu.

Mr. Black answered the call.

"I'm sorry for calling so late, but I need your advice. I need four people to disappear for a few days. I mean go completely off the grid, invisible to anyone searching. Nothing illegal. Can you help me?"

ဆာ ၾ ၾ

Howard Carstairs' funeral was set for Thursday after Election Day. David and Sara flew up to Maine the night before and stayed in a local hotel. While Sara was upstairs in their room changing, David unexpectedly came across Marcus Finn in the lobby. He shouldn't have been surprised given that Finn and Carstairs had been close.

"How are you, Congressman?" David asked.

"Please. You're the congressman now. Why don't you just call me Marcus? And I'll call you David."

David nodded. "It's a sad day. Howard Carstairs was a great American and a good friend."

"Yes, he was," Finn agreed. "Too bad his funeral is going to be turned into a side show."

"What do you mean?"

"I spoke with Emily earlier. The President's coming, which means a huge Secret Service detail, as well as media coverage."

"Why would Farnum come? He wouldn't even return Howard's calls when he was alive."

"I know. But the President told Emily he couldn't pass up honoring such a great senator. He said, 'Howard was the epitome of bipartisanship.'"

"You think he's trying to sway some of the Republican members of the Electoral College?"

"Your guess is as good as mine. But I can't see any Republican electors budging. Only the most loyal and die-hard Republicans are asked to be electors. No RINOs allowed. No one on either side is going to switch."

"I suppose not."

"By the way, how's my girl Ellen doing?"

"Your *girl* is doing fine. She's been a godsend. I'm surprised she hasn't given up on me."

"No, she doesn't give up," Finn said with pride in his voice. "She'll drive you mad, but she'll never give up on you. She's loyal to a fault."

"Congressman Grant," another voice called out.

David turned and was shocked to see Joe Dreeves standing there, grinning and offering his hand. David was tempted to spit in the man's face. Dreeves has continued the Omaha smear longer than anyone.

"I just wanted to meet you and say hello," Dreeves said.

"What the hell are you doing here?" David asked angrily. "You're not doing a show about Howard Carstairs's funeral, are you?"

"Oh no, of course not," Dreeves said in a tone of sincere reassurance. "That would be tacky and offensive."

"That's never stopped you before," David said.

Dreeves gave an understanding smile. "Congressman, you misunderstand me. I'm a Maine resident. I was born here and still have a house in Bangor. Howard Carstairs was my senator. I'm here to show my respect. I promise there'll be no cheap shots."

"I should hope not," snapped Finn.

"Congressman," Dreeves said, addressing David, "I'd love to have you on my show some time."

"Why, so you can accuse me of being a pedophile to my face?"

"That was over a year ago," Dreeves said in defensive tone. "And I realize I was wrong and have some fences to mend."

"Keep your distance, from us and the Carstairs family."

David and Finn walked away immediately. Once in front of the elevator, a thought occurred to David. *Why would he need to mend fences?*

৪০ ৪০ ৫৪ ৫৪

The next morning the simple memorial service went forward. The President insisted on being one of the pallbearers, joining Howard's son,

339

David, Cal McCord, and two of Carstairs' local friends. The irony was felt by all present. A Democratic president, whose presidency was in peril, was helping to bury a Republican. The late-night comedians would have a field day.

The local minister gave a short, but touching, sermon. Farnum also made some brief remarks, as did Maine's Governor Shelly Montag. She had just been reelected, a fact that had been overshadowed by the presidential election drama. David noticed Joe Dreeves being very chatty with Montag, both before and after the ceremony. David supposed Dreeves was trying to woo her as a guest, but he had an odd feeling there was more to it.

David turned to Cal McCord, who was standing next to him. "Do you know what the deal is with Dreeves and Governor Montag?"

"Just a supporter. I think Howard mentioned Dreeves campaigned for her. He didn't think much of either of them."

David was caught off guard when Harris Carver walked up to him. "Congressman, Senator, are you both heading back to Washington?"

They both said yes.

"Good. The President would like to offer you a ride back on Air Force One."

"I'm afraid I'm going to have to decline," David said. "I already have a flight booked."

McCord put his hand on David's shoulder. "No one turns down a ride on Air Force One," he whispered.

"Honey," Sara interrupted. "I can cash in your ticket. We were going on separate flights anyway. Besides, how often are you asked on Air Force One?"

"What about the package?" David asked.

"I called your office," she said in a whisper. "Ellen said it arrived this morning."

"Thank you." He turned back to Carver. "Very well. Tell the President I'd be honored."

340

CHAPTER 59

Like most guests, David was impressed with the luxury of Air Force One. It was much more comfortable and spacious than any commercial flight. The food was certainly better. And now, David could tell friends he had flown on Air Force One. But he knew there would be a price. An Air Force sergeant approached David.

"Excuse me, Congressman Grant?"

"Yes."

"The President was wondering, if you could spare a moment to speak with him?"

David was amused by the so politely phrased question. As if anyone on Air Force One would claim to be too busy to speak with the President of the United States.

"Certainly," he said.

The sergeant escorted David past the Secret Service alcove to the President's onboard office. An agent opened the door. The President stood up and motioned him toward a chair.

"Good afternoon, Mr. President."

"David, I'm sorry about Howard Carstairs. I understand you two were close."

"Yes, sir. He was good man."

Farnum nodded in agreement. "By the way, congratulations on being reelected."

"Thank you, Mr. President."

"The second campaign is the critical one. Once the voters become accustomed to you, you have the advantage of name recognition. Unfortunately, *my status* is still in limbo."

David realized now why Farnum had come to the funeral. It was to have this conversation. The President was fishing.

"I wouldn't think so, sir. The Electoral College will vote. Assuming no one violates their pledge, it'll be thrown into the Democrat-majority House. And you'll be sworn in on January 20th. Fairly straight forward, I would think."

The President smiled. "Things are rarely straight forward in Washington. But you're probably right. Anyway, I have been thinking about my second term. My first was bogged down in...well you know as well as I do." Farnum leaned forward. "I'd like you to join my administration."

"I beg your pardon?"

"You've had no party support. Somebody threw some of the nastiest mud I've ever seen at you. Despite that, you were reelected and helped three new Centrists get elected to boot. I don't have to be a genius to recognize you're a very talented man. I want you on my team."

"I'm very flattered, sir."

"You know, I'll keep my stars in the Cabinet, Warrenburg, Hingecliff and some others. But it's always wise to bring in some fresh thinking. I'm told you put together a very thoughtful energy bill. Maybe you're the man I need to lead the Department of Energy."

David was not expecting anything like this.

"Also," Farnum continued, "you were right on top of the education bill. Very diligent. Maybe as Secretary of Education, you can help us get it right this time."

David smiled, and despite his better judgment, asked, "Won't Ellis Cornwall object?"

Farnum couldn't hide a grimace. "Cornwall is not a part of this administration. I've just run my last campaign. It's down to business now."

"Legacy time?"

"For lack of a better phrase."

"Mr. President, I will be glad to work with you on any bill you choose, energy, education or otherwise. But I have to decline your offer of a cabinet position."

Farnum tried to conceal his surprise. "May I ask why?"

"I would, like all other members of the Cabinet, serve at the pleasure of the president. And *not serve* at his displeasure."

"You think I'd fire you after you resigned from the House to join my administration? That would be a PR nightmare."

"I also have other reasons, some personal, others political. As I said, I'll be glad to work with the White House on any bill, but only as a member of the House."

"Is there nothing I can offer to entice you to join my administration?"

"No, sir."

"Strange. No one comes into my office without wanting something from me."

"In this case, I came in because you invited me. Of course, there are many things I want. But sacrificing my independence is too high a price."

Farnum frowned, clearly displeased. "Thank you for your candor."

"Thank you, Mr. President."

Harris Carver walked in after David left. "How did it go with Grant?"

"He turned down all offers. I practically offered him *carte blanche*. There was nothing to make him jump. Maybe we overestimated his ambition."

"Sir, I don't think so. All four of Vreeland's electors have disappeared. Their cars are still in their driveways. Their cell phones are in their homes. But they're gone, completely off the grid. Not even any credit card activity."

"Any chatter at the RNC?"

"They're looking for the electors as well."

"Maybe it's not Grant. Perhaps Vreeland is making a deal with Howell."

"No, we've got people monitoring Vreeland. Nothing."

ಬ ಬ ಧ ಧ

Early the next morning, David Grant walked into the office of the Speaker of the House with seven other people in tow. He was also carrying a large orange cardboard tube.

"Oh, we weren't expecting so many of you," the Speaker's secretary said. "Why don't you wait in the Speaker's conference room? He'll be with you in a moment."

"Thank you," David said. He motioned the small group into the side room.

After waiting a few minutes, Everett Wilkers walked into the conference room, followed by Porter Barnes.

"So Grant, what's so important, I had to come in on a Saturday?" Wilkers demanded. "And why did you have to bring your staff?"

"Oh, these people aren't my staff," David said. "Let me introduce Liz Spinelli, Craig Yost, and Kate Garner. They were elected to the House earlier this week. They'll be joining us in January."

"Well, Congratulations," he said, looking at the incoming representatives. "Normally, we don't meet with new members until the orientations which will start in a few weeks."

"Well, there was an urgent matter that needs to be attended to, our status."

"Don't worry. We'll make sure everyone gets an appropriate committee assignment."

"No," David said.

"Excuse me?" Wilkers asked in an annoyed tone.

"There are four of us now."

"Yes, four Independents. Believe me, I've been paying attention."

"No. Four Centrists. We're all of the same party."

"There are only two major parties," Barnes interrupted. "Everyone else is considered an Independent. Those are the House rules."

"But the Speaker can rewrite the rules."

"What exactly are you looking for?" Wilkers asked.

"We want full minority party status, just like the Republicans."

Barnes snorted.

"And why would I do that?" Wilkers asked, looking condescendingly over his half-rim glasses.

"Because," David answered, "I brought you a gift of great value."

Wilkers eyed the orange tube lying on the conference table. "And what would that be?"

"The opportunity to choose the next President of the United States."

Barnes and Wilkers looked at each other.

"The next president will be Gregory Farnum. Even with your four additional votes, the Republicans won't be able to overcome the Democratic majority, especially as the House vote for president will be by state, not individual representative."

"That only matters if the vote comes to the House. Let me introduce a few other people. This is John Siglor, Anna Dominguez, Gary Weitz, and Janet Dale. John and Anna are from Nebraska. Gary and Janet are from Maine. And they are such good and loyal Centrist party members, they were asked to be electors for the Electoral College."

The color drained from Wilkers face.

Barnes started to speak. "You son of a…"

Wilkers grabbed his arm to stop him.

"Well, it's very nice to meet you all," The Speaker said slowly. "I don't know what Congressman Grant has told you all, but in the Electoral College, you are bound to vote for Mr. Vreeland."

"Actually, they're not," David countered. "It's unusual, but not illegal to change their vote."

Wilkers kept his focus on the electors. "In that case, you all would be what are termed *faithless* electors. And while there have been faithless electors before, none have ever changed the outcome of a federal election. It would be a betrayal of—"

"Betrayal?" Janet Dale cried out. "That's rich, really rich, you hypocritical bastard. You and the Republicans play your smoke-and-mirror games, spending all our tax money on your campaign contributors. You think we're all stupid. You only care about power. Don't you dare lecture us about betrayal.

"Let's all calm down," David said.

"I joined the Centrist party," Dale continued, "because there was finally an alternative to you lot. Give Mr. Grant what he wants, or I swear, I'll change my vote to that hillbilly Howell."

"Here, here," said one of the other electors.

Wilkers took a deep breath. "What do you want?" he asked in a low voice.

"We want the same amenities for our leader as the Minority Leader currently has," David explained. "That includes a leadership suite, a private jet, equivalent salaries for the Leader and a Minority Whip, and the ability to assign members to any and all committees."

"By your leader, you mean you."

"Our membership hasn't voted, and won't be able to vote until they're sworn in."

The Speaker smiled at that.

"A private jet will cost between five and ten million," Barnes snarled. "I thought you were always complaining about the deficit."

"Oh, we're willing to share a jet with Leader Mirreau," David assured them.

"She's not going to like that," Wilkers said.

"At least there's a small silver lining," Barnes muttered.

"Well," Wilkers continued, "we don't have room for a leadership suite within the Capitol building."

"Actually," David said, as he reached for the orange tube, "that's not completely true." He opened the end of the tube and pulled out a roll of architectural plans. "It won't be as grand as your office, but it'll give our party leadership an appropriate home base."

"Where did you get these?" Wilkers asked, pointing to the plans.

"My wife is an architect specializing in public buildings. You know, civic centers, courthouses, that sort of thing. She jumped at the chance at redesigning part of the Capitol. And she did it for free. So, that doesn't add to the deficit one bit."

"This is ridiculous," Barnes complained. "The four of you are still less than one percent of the House. It would give you disproportionate power. Your numbers don't warrant this."

"You're saying it's not proportional," David countered. "Well, the Electoral College isn't proportional either."

"Alright," Wilkers interrupted. "We'll announce it at the beginning of the new session."

"No, you'll announce it before the Electoral College meets, including the new construction."

"How do I know," Wilkers asked, motioning to the electors, "that they won't switch to Howell anyway?"

"You don't. But you have to ask which do you fear most, a legitimate, but small, third party, or Buck Howell as President? Plus, *President* Howell will have a Republican Senate to work with." David walked over to a telephone in the corner of the room and picked up the receiver. "Perhaps you should call the President and ask which he prefers."

"Okay," Wilkers said, "but now I have a condition. Your electors have to change their votes to Farnum. That way, I don't have to deal with this mess on the House Floor in January."

"So faithless electors are acceptable, as long as they switch to Farnum?" Janet Dale snapped.

David smiled, and then looked to the four electors. They exchanged nods. He turned back to Wilkers and Barnes. "Two will remain faithful to Vreeland. Two others will switch to Farnum giving him the 270 electoral votes and the presidency."

"Why hold out on the other two?" Wilkers asked.

"Because Marshall Vreeland earned them. He deserves his due in the history books. Plus, it'll look more natural if some of the electors hold out. So, do we have a deal?"

CHAPTER 60

Wilkers announced the change in the rules that would allow for a second minority party. Preliminary construction had begun on what was being called the Second Minority Leader's Office. As the Republican Leader, Cassandra Mirreau's title would be changed to First Minority Leader. While no Centrist Party vote could happen until January, all the incoming representatives agreed; David Grant would be elected Second Minority Leader.

Shortly after, the Electoral College ballots were counted, giving President Farnum the critical 270 votes and a second term. The next day, David was standing in the gutted space, trying to imagine the completed suite.

"So, how does it look?" Ellen asked.

"It looks like a beginning. I was thinking your office would be over there. And you wouldn't have to share it with any pesky legislative assistants. What do you think?"

"That works," she agreed. "Congressman, we've been so busy the last few weeks, we haven't had much time to talk. Can I ask you a question?"

"Sure."

"When did you decide on this master plan of yours? You know, using Vreeland to hold the presidency hostage? And why didn't you tell me about it until the last minute?"

"Initially, I supported Vreeland quite reluctantly, and only because he agreed to support the Centrist candidates. But as we closed in on Election Day, I started to see how the electoral math was lining up. Why didn't I tell you when I first saw this long-shot opportunity? You would have thought me crazy."

"Are you so sure of that?"

"Yes, because I thought it was crazy. I'm sorry I didn't share my thinking."

"Is it because I'm still a Republican?"

"No. Your loyalty is unquestioned. So much so, I'm going to tell you a secret: I don't think I'll be running for office again."

"Why?" Ellen asked with a rare shocked expression on her face. "You've just made congressional history. They're building you this office."

"After the Omaha incident, I promised Sara I wouldn't run for a third term unless she agreed. On Election Night, she pointedly toasted my 'last campaign.' She might change her mind, but I wouldn't bet on it. I honestly can't blame her. And believe me, I love my wife far more than this place."

"That's why you wouldn't accept a cabinet post," she realized out load.

"Partly."

"You can't let anyone else know this. They'll tack the lame duck sign on you as fast as they can."

"Don't worry about that. I haven't even told Fred yet."

"Why are you telling me this two years ahead of time?"

"Because you deserve the truth. You'll have a position with me as long as you want. I know you have baggage with the Republicans. I don't know if that's been resolved, or ever will be. Although if you change your party affiliation to Centrist, I'm sure I could convince the next Second Minority Leader to keep you on."

Ellen shook her head. "You're a very strange man. You've just made a huge political coup, yet you're willing to walk away."

David just shrugged. "Sorry for the bad news."

"While we're on the topic of bad news, I have some for you. The governor of Maine has appointed Howard Carstairs' replacement."

"Well, that was inevitable."

"It's Joe Dreeves."

"What?" Now it was David's turn to be shocked. "That miserable excuse for a human being?" David picked up a scrap of 2x4 off a makeshift table and threw is across the room. "That's why he was chatting up Montag at the funeral. Howard Carstairs was a true statesman, a patriot. And he's replaced by a snarky bozo!"

Suddenly a Capitol policeman came running in, reacting to the crashing noise.

"It's alright," David called out. "Just an accident. My fault."

℘ ℘ ℃ ℃

Progress on the new suite went slowly. David suspected the Speaker was deliberately delaying construction. However, he did receive a more pleasant surprise, an invitation to be seated on the platform, behind the President, on Inauguration Day. However when the day came, he discovered his seat was as far from the podium as one could be. It was unlikely any photograph of the day would include him, except as a dot in the background.

After the swearing-in, they all attended an inaugural lunch inside the Capitol building. The members milled about before sitting down.

"David," Wyatt Wickham called out, "although I suppose I should call you Leader."

"From you, I prefer David."

"I have a quick question. Will you be continuing to serve on the Energy Committee?"

"I was planning on it."

"You obviously no longer need my approval, but with your new responsibilities, I wasn't sure. I also heard you're taking a seat on the Budget Committee."

"True, but I'd still like to push through our energy bill."

"Polaron's CEO is still pretty pissed at you for the grilling you gave him way back when. Their lobbyist is trying to kill it."

"Yeah, I know. Polaron's Super-PAC was a big contributor to my Republican opponent this past fall."

"And now Arlo Hudge is going to be the ranking Republican on the committee. Doesn't bode well for your bill."

"Strange, such huge resistance to such a small bill."

Suddenly Wickham looked over David's shoulder. "Mr. President," he said. "Congratulations."

David turned around to find Farnum directly behind.

"Yes, congratulations," he added.

"Thank you, gentlemen," Farnum answered. After some small talk, Harris Carver walked up and asked to speak to Wyatt Wickham in private. It was a not-so-subtle way for Farnum to speak to David privately.

"I understand you'll be giving the Centrist response to the State of the Union."

"Yes, but no need to worry, Mr. President. Most of America will be fast asleep by the time I get on the air after the Republicans."

"Actually, one of our pollsters determined about 28 percent of Americans watching, nod off before a President finishes speaking."

They both chuckled at that.

"I was very impressed that you turned down my offer of a Cabinet position. No one's ever done that to me."

"It was nothing personal, sir."

"No, I understand. Everett Wilkers told me about your meeting. Very impressive maneuvering. I'd like you on my team, now more than ever."

"But you've already filled all your Cabinet posts."

"Yes, but with a thinner majority in the House, an alliance would be profitable for both of us."

"Even now, with the Republicans controlling the Senate?"

"Ah, but with the addition of Joe Dreeves, the Republican majority is also thinner."

"No offense, Mr. President. And please forgive my indelicacy, but Dreeves is a turd."

The President smiled. "When you're president, you have to deal with a great many turds. My point is now both houses of Congress are run by razor thin majorities. So, I need to work more closely with those on that razor's edge. I look forward to working with you."

℘ ℘ ℘ ℘

Two weeks later, Hanna Dalton walked toward the Tidal Basin across from the Jefferson Memorial. Even though it had been a warm winter and the sun was shining, there was still a chill in the air so early in the morning. A man was standing in the cold sunlight with his back to her.

"Daniel?"

Narlstrom turned around. "Hello, Hanna. It's been a long time."

"Over a year," Dalton agreed.

"Thank you for coming." Narlstrom smiled. However, it was a smile taut with pain. "You look good."

"It's good to see you. What have you been up to?"

He sighed, not answering the question. "I'm sorry. I thought it best to stay away."

"When you left that last SALA meeting," Dalton said, "I didn't think you'd be walking out on me."

"I didn't mean to. I loved you, but our relationship was more powered by the passion of our work. It just felt wrong to continue and split your allegiance."

"So, why did you call after all this time?"

"I'm going away."

"Excuse me? You call after a year to tell me you're going away?"

"I wanted to tell you I'm sorry. And to thank you for saving my life. You did it right here."

"Yes, I remember," she said, looking at the park bench where they sat. "I could never forget. So, what's this all about?"

"You know, how everyone asks 'what's the meaning of life?' Well, I've found my purpose."

"And what direction is that purpose taking you?"

"New York."

"New York?"

"I've done everything I can do here."

"Done what? What the hell are you talking about, Dan?"

"It's all here," he said, handing her a small box. "Just put this in your pocket. In a few days, when you're less angry with me, open it."

"What is it?"

"That would be telling. Just do me one more favor?"

"What?"

"Kiss me goodbye. One last kiss."

She pulled him toward her. It was a kiss that neither wanted to end. But the inevitable end came.

"I have to catch my flight. Be well."

He walked toward a waiting car. Hanna noticed the driver looked like Harry Branch.

ଔ ଔ ଓ ଓ

Later that day, Skip Parker walked into the network control room in New York. He had been assigned directing duties for the State of the Union. His working relationship with Bob Summers and Dylan Reese had always been good, so he expected a smooth program.

He reviewed the camera list. Summers and Reese would be sitting in a Washington law office, which had a large window with a view of the Capitol.

349

The law office allowed the network to use it for Inaugurations and State of the Union addresses. The other cameras were the government ones in the House chamber, usually used by C-SPAN. There would be additional cameras for the Republican and Centrist responses, as well as exterior cameras.

"Who's loading the Chyron?" Parker called out. This was for the text identifications that would appear in the lower third of the screen."

"New kid, Abrams," someone answered.

Abrams came running in, having heard his name.

"You Abrams?"

"Yes, sir."

"Are all the lower thirds loaded?"

"Yes, sir."

"Any typos?"

"No, sir."

"Let's see."

Parker winced at the first one.

"*Gregory Farnum, President of the United States*? Kid, do you think anyone watching the State of the Union won't know who the president is?"

Rookie.

బి బి ಇ ಆ

The President and Harris Carver were in the Oval Office finalizing last-minute details.

"The First Lady and all the special guests are already heading to the Capitol," Carver reported. "They go up to the balcony ten minutes before you enter."

"Good. We'd better be going. Jill never likes to be kept waiting," the President joked.

Amy Greene stuck her head through the door.

"Yes, Amy?"

"Mr. President, Secretary Hingecliff is here."

"Send him in."

Hingecliff entered immediately. "Good evening, Mr. President."

"Robert. Good to see you. Thanks for being the stay-behind this time."

"My honor, Mr. President. I expect you'll hit it out of the park tonight."

"With a 31-percent approval, I'm not so sure."

"I have confidence in you, sir. Legacies are built on accomplishment, not polls."

"Thank you, Robert. I better get going."

"Good luck, sir."

Farnum walked out, but Carver stayed behind.

"Mr. Secretary, a word."

"Of course."

"It's recently come to my attention that you've been communicating covertly with people outside the party, people like the late Howard Carstairs and David Grant."

"I communicate with a great many people. It's how we learn things and stay informed."

"Yes, I agree. But then why all the burner phones?"

Hingecliff's face went pale. He realized there was nothing to be gained with denial. "How did you learn about the phones?" he asked.

"When we went searching for the missing electors right after the election, some of our people used more creative methods. The technical details are unimportant."

"What do you want?"

"Your resignation?"

Hingecliff was surprised, considering the warm reception Farnum had just given him. "Does the President know about this?"

"No. I'd prefer to not tell him. But I will, if I need to. He likes and respects you. If he knew someone so close betrayed him, he might become paranoid. And we don't need a paranoid president. We've had enough of those."

"So you're paranoid on his behalf?"

"Part of my job description."

"I had nothing to do with the Electoral College incident," Hingecliff insisted.

"I didn't think so. Your burner was unused the first weeks of November. But in the course of the search, it was discovered your phone was very active around the time of David Grant's Omaha problem."

"We threw away all those phones."

"Yeah," Carver said, "it's amazing what those cyber-analysts can figure out. I don't know how they do it."

"I understand the President is now seeking to build a better relationship with Leader Grant. I can be helpful there."

"He doesn't need you to build relationships," Carver snapped. "Your loyalty can't be conditional. It must be absolute."

"I've always given the President the best advice I could."

"Maybe. But I have to protect the President from any and all *possible* threats. Or leaks. It's nothing personal."

Carver headed toward the door, but stopped to look back.

"I believe you had a minor heart attack ten years ago. You can cite that, saying you're leaving for health reasons. You have a new grandchild I understand. So, you can use that old chestnut, 'to spend more time with your family,' whatever you like. Just tell the President before the end of the week. You could even tell him tonight when he returns."

ဆ ဆ ၈ ၈

David and Ellen were standing in his still-incomplete offices. David was preparing to give his first national address from what looked like and was a construction site to show the progress the Centrist party was making. In addition, he hoped the unfinished framing would embarrass the Speaker into speeding up construction. The video camera and teleprompter had already been set up. Kate Garner, the new representative from Oregon, had just arrived. She and the other new representatives would be standing behind him during the address.

"Have you done a run-through with the teleprompter yet?" Ellen asked.

"We'll do that in a moment, when the technicians come back," David said. "Is Fred down in Statuary Hall?"

"Yes, he's with Spinelli and Yost. They're giving pre-address interviews for various local news programs. Then, they'll grab seats in the balcony for the President's speech."

"Just make sure they get up here before we start. We don't know how long Ogden is going to speak. I want all our representatives to be on-camera with me."

Ellen left for Statuary Hall, the large gallery outside the House chamber. Meanwhile, the cameraman, teleprompter operator and sound technician walked in.

"We're ready for a run-through and sound check," said one of the technicians.

David stood on his mark, took a cleansing breath and began reading from the teleprompter.

೮೦ ೮೦ ೧೪ ೦೪

It was a few seconds before nine o'clock.

"Stand by to roll the intro," Skip Parker called out. "Bob, stand by."

"Good to go," Summers said, acknowledging the director's voice in his earpiece.

"Standby Intro. Standby Camera 1." The clock turned to 9:00 PM. "Roll intro."

An elaborate 3D graphic sequence played with stars, stripes and the Capitol morphing into the words "State of the Union."

"Take Camera 1."

"Good evening." Summers said to the camera. "In a few moments, President Gregory Farnum will make his way into the House chamber to deliver his fifth State of Union address, his first after winning reelection—"

೮೦ ೮೦ ೧೪ ೦೪

David finished his practice run.

"I think you nailed it," Kate Garner exclaimed.

"I thought it was very good, too," a voice from behind them said.

They turned to see Harris Carver standing there with an overcoat draped over his arm.

"Good evening," said David. "I thought you'd be headed to the Floor with the President."

"I did that for the President's first State of the Union. Since then, I prefer to watch it on TV, the same way most Americans do. May I?" he asked, gesturing to the large plasma screen on the wall. "Don't worry, I'll be gone by the time you're set to go."

David walked over to Carver.

"Why here?" David asked, gesturing toward the unplastered wallboard. "I'm sure the Democratic cloakroom would be much more comfortable."

"I just wanted to stop by and let you know the President is dropping an *ad lib* comment into his speech, favorably acknowledging the arrival of the Centrist party."

"Really?"

"See for yourself," Carver said, nodding toward the screen. "You might want to reciprocate."

Garner turned up the volume on the plasma screen. Bob Summer's reassuring tones were caught mid-sentence.

"...door opened. Here now, we see the Sergeant-at-Arms."

"Mr. Speaker!" the Sergeant-at-Arms called out, "The President of the United States!"

The obligatory standing ovation erupted in the chamber. Farnum worked his way down the center aisle, stopping to shake hands with various leaders and other prominent legislators.

"It's a very enthusiastic crowd tonight. There we see the President literally reaching across the aisle to shake the hand of Minority Leader Cassandra Mirreau. I don't think she was expecting that."

"Up front, we see seven members of the Supreme Court. As you all know, Justice Seymour Chester is on a respirator, not expected to live much longer. Also absent is Justice Catherine Sisk. She apparently was not feeling well tonight, although we're told it's nothing serious. We also see the Joint Chiefs. Of course, the cabinet is there in full, except of course for one of the cabinet secretaries, who traditionally remains behind at the White House. This year, Treasury Secretary Robert Hingecliff is performing that role."

Robert Hingecliff pondered the irony of the anchorman's words, "performing that role." There was really nothing to perform. His duty consisted of sitting in the Oval Office watching the State of the Union on television. And if Carver had his way, this would be his last time in the Oval Office."

Finally, the President reached the podium and handed the Vice-President and the Speaker each a copy of his speech. After the Speaker introduced the President which triggered another standing ovation, the audience settled down for the President to speak.

"Good evening. Tonight America stands at a crossroads. Through vigorous action, we are beginning to come out of a recession that has dampened our spirit and sapped our strength. But, there is a new wind blowing…"

"Anyone want to do an over/under on the cliché tally? I count four so far." Garner asked.

David looked over at Carver. "Yeah, but he carries them off well. I'm glad I'm not speaking directly after him. Luckily, Ogden's not quite as good. I just hope—"

David never completed the sentence.

CHAPTER 61

Robert Hingecliff watched President Farnum begin his speech. Suddenly the television went blank.

After a few seconds, Bob Summers returned to the screen. "We apologize," Summers said. "We seem to have lost our feed from inside the House chamber."

Across the nation, television viewers switched channels to find one that still carried the President's speech, but to no avail.

Frantically, Skip Parker's technical director was trying to find a camera that still had an incoming signal. The only two had a signal. The first was from the Rotunda balcony and showed only some marble columns. The second, from the Centrist office, didn't seem to make sense.

"What the hell? It looks like someone leaning against the side of a cave wall."

"It's on its side." Everyone tilted their heads. They all realized it was a body lying on the floor among debris.

"Holy crap! Pull up the exterior shot. Take Camera 7."

Summers, not knowing what was going on, started summarizing the advance copy of the President's speech as filler until the signal could be restored.

"Take Camera 1," Parker snapped. "Camera 7, zoom in on the Capitol."

The cameraman smoothly zoomed in on the dome.

"Now pan right!"

The cameraman obeyed.

"Damn it, we need to be higher. Can we get an aerial?" he called out.

"No helicopters allowed. Restricted airspace," someone called from behind him.

"Bob's higher," someone suggested.

"Take Camera 7."

Parker hit the button to speak into the anchorman's ear. "Bob, you're not on camera. Keep talking, but move your chair camera-left." On the Camera 1 preview monitor, he could see Summers awkwardly shifting while trying to sound calm.

"Camera 1, zoom through the window to the Capitol Building, to the right of the dome." Nothing.

"Wrong side. Camera 1, Go to the left. Pan to the other side of the Dome."

The cameraman obeyed.

"What the hell is that?" someone mumbled.

They saw a reddish-yellow light hitting the misting rain. "Holy Crap! There's a hole in the roof. It's a fire!"

Summers stopped speaking and turned around. He started to describe the scene to the audience.

"There's movement on Camera 9!" someone yelled.

"That's the new Centrist office."

"Cut to Camera 9!" ordered the director.

ॐ ॐ ॐ ॐ

Lying on the floor, David was aware of only two things: his headache and the heat. *Why is it so hot?* Why did he have a headache? *What was Kate saying? Something about clichés.*

He lifted up his head. His nose filled with the smell of burnt wood and plaster. He heard something that sounded like muffled sirens. He coughed. His face was wet. He tried to wipe the dampness from his forehead. Looking at the red fluid on his hand. *Red paint?' The workers hadn't started painting yet.* He looked over at Garner. She was on the ground too.

"Kate?" She didn't answer. He pulled himself over to her. "Kate, wake up!"

He reached for her wrist. There was no pulse. This snapped him out of his daze. "Kate!" he cried. He leaned over her and put his hands on her sternum to administer CPR. As he began the compressions, his mind raced back to a class he had sponsored at Simplexia for his employees. *How many compressions did the instructor say? Thirty or sixty?* He couldn't remember.

"Help! Is there anyone in here?" he yelled. He looked down. "This woman needs a medic!" There was a pool of blood forming beneath Garner. It was expanding rhythmically with every compression. He turned her over to find a large piece of splintered lumber impaled in her back. He let her down gently. He looked around to see the teleprompter operator beneath his equipment. David check his pulse. There was none. The cameraman and sound technician were nowhere to be seen.

"Is there anyone here?"

There was a groan. David followed the sound. Suddenly, he remembered Harris Carver. Pulling a section of wallboard away, he found Carver lying beneath a diagonal timber that used to be part of a column.

"Harris?"

Carver's eyes started to flutter, then squint against the airborne dust. "What happened? An earthquake?"

"I'm not sure. Are you hurt? I mean, does anything feel broken?"

"I don't think so," Carver said, not completely sure. "Just got the wind knocked out of me."

"Let me get you out from under this timber. I don't think it's too secure."

The word 'secure' rang in Carver's ears. "The President? Where's the President?" he asked in a panic. Suddenly, infused with adrenalin, Harris Carver pulled himself up. He stumbled and fell against the wall. Carver cried out in pain.

"What is it?"

"My ankle. I think it's broken or sprained. We need to find the President. Did the Secret Service get him out?"

"I don't know." David pulled Carver's arm over his shoulders to help support his weight. They headed for the exit. David pulled open the door, only to be hit with a wave of heat. The sirens became markedly louder in the marble hallway. The leaning column fell behind them, as unbearable heat and smoke blew into the room.

David suddenly remembered something his father taught him. "Drop to the ground," he commanded. "Heat and smoke rises."

ಬಿ ಜಿ ಚ್ಞ ಚ್ಬ

Sara Grant was in a panic. The anchorman had just reported that there had been an explosion in the Capitol Building. The only pictures they could show were of the exterior of the building.

"Mom, what's happening?" Wendy cried.

Sara tried to call David's cell phone. There was no answer. He had told her he would turn it off before his speech. She tried not to panic for Wendy's sake.

ಬಿ ಜಿ ಚ್ಞ ಚ್ಬ

The two men crawled their way to the House chamber, but the closer they moved, the more intense the heat. David felt a heavy hand on his shoulder. He turned to see a crouching, but burly, firefighter wearing a respiratory pack.

"Go out this way," his voice boomed, as he pointed down the hall they came.

"We have to find the President," Carver yelled.

"Go out this way, now!" the fireman repeated.

"I'm the Chief of Staff. I need   "

Two other rescue workers grabbed Carver and Grant, pulling them down the hall to the outside. As the rescuers brought them out into the night air, it felt like they entered a freezer. It wasn't that cold, but emerging from a 120 degree environment made it feel like one. Paramedics ran up to them with oxygen masks.

Suddenly, a Secret Service agent from the President's detail ran up to them.

"Where's the President?" Carver asked.

"Headed to the White House. Mr. Carver, I have orders to bring you and any other staff back to the White House, ASAP."

Carver gave a sigh of relief, as David and the agent helped Carver to a vehicle.

He turned back to David.

"What about you?"

"I'm good. Go," David insisted. "Whatever this is, the President will need you."

As the car sped away, David turned and looked back to the Capitol building. He looked up, surprised to see the dome intact. He was sure an earthquake would have toppled, or at least cracked it. He looked around to see if he could find any of his fellow legislators.

The first responders had already set up triage areas. Ambulances were arriving. Then a strange thing occurred to him. No other buildings were being focused on. Only the Capitol. This was no earthquake.

ᘒ ᘒ ᘕ ᘕ

Robert Hingecliff opened the door to the outer office. He wasn't going to watch this disaster passively. Amy Greene was standing in front of the plasma screen, switching between channels.

"Do we know anything more than what the media has?"

Amy nodded no. Her eyes were moist as the various commentators were speculating on what had happened.

"One network claimed the President is dead. Another said he's been whisked back to the White House." Given the President's absence, they were inclined to believe the former.

Hingecliff was determined to get better information than the chaotic reporting on the television networks. He marched out of into the hall, searching for someone who knew *something*. Before he could get three steps, a squad of Secret Service agents arrived.

"Mr. Secretary, I'm Special Agent Bartolli. Given this evening's events, I need you to return to the Oval Office."

It was clear to Hingecliff, this was not a suggestion. He dutifully complied.

"What do we know so far?" he asked as they walked back.

"That there was an explosion in or around the House chamber," Bartolli said.

"Damn it man, I got that much from the networks!"

"My superiors are assessing the situation. I've been ordered to secure you until the line of succession is clear." Hingecliff felt his chest tighten.

"Then, the President is dead?"

"Probably, but there's been no confirmation."

"My god!" Hingecliff sat down in disbelief. "Bomb? Missile? What was it?" The room was spinning. He looked back to the television. "How is this possible?" he breathed.

Agent Bartolli jerked his hand to his ear. He nodded.

"What is it?" Hingecliff demanded.

"Chief of Staff Carver," the agent reported, "has returned to the White House."

"Maybe he'll know something." Hingecliff felt as if he was going to vomit.

ᘒ ᘒ ᘕ ᘕ

"Where's the President?" Carver demanded as he emerged from the car. An agent met him with crutches. Apparently, someone radioed his condition ahead.

"I'm Special Agent Ross," he said, handing the crutches to Carver. "I've been ordered to escort you to the Situation Room."

"Let's go."

They descended to the Situation Room. They were met by an Army general and a Navy commander.

"Mr. Carver, I'm Commander Martino, please sit down for a moment."

"I need to see the President," Carver insisted.

"Mr. Carver, we are now operating under Code Purple protocols," the general explained.

"What?"

"I'm a doctor," explained the commander. "I need to examine you."

"My ankle can wait. I'm fine."

"Sir, you need to cooperate," said Agent Ross.

Carver was surprised to hear an agent speak to him in such a way.

"Mr. Carver," Martino asked, "did you lose consciousness in the explosion in the Capitol Building?"

"I don't know…if so, just for a minute."

"How do you know it was just for a minute?"

Carver shrugged.

"Please look at the general." The doctor held a flashlight, whipping it in and out of his eyes, which Carver found very annoying in his agitated state. Martino then pressed his fingers on various parts of his skull and neck. "Does anything hurt when I press it?"

"No"

"Any headache at all?"

"I didn't notice until you mentioned it."

"I'd like you to count down from 100 by seven."

Carver complied. "93…86…um…79…72…65…58…51…."

"He's cleared." Martino said, turning back to Carver. "You still may have a minor concussion. You should be checked in the morning."

"Okay, let's go," ordered the general.

A corporal opened the door to the Sit-Room. Inside were various generals, admirals and others, almost none of whom Carver recognized. *Of course, all the Joint Chiefs are dead.* The only people he recognized were Thad Randall, the CIA Director, and Trevor Yardley of the NSA.

"Where's the President?" Carver demanded.

"We believe President Farnum is dead in the House chamber," Yardley reported.

"The agent who picked me up said the President was heading back to the White House!"

"Under Code Purple protocols, all agents are instructed to say that outside of a secure environment," said another man whom Carver realized was the Director of the Secret Service.

"What the hell is Code Purple?"

"The protocols for handling an attack on the Capitol during the State of the Union."

Carver vaguely remembered a briefing on Code Purple he and the President had received a couple years before. The probability of such an attack was so unlikely, he didn't retain the details.

"At 21:07 hours there was an explosion in the House chamber," Yardley explained. "There was no indication of an incoming projectile."

"How do you know?"

"Admiral Westerick?"

"Show 21:06 hours from Sat-3," ordered the admiral.

A large plasma screen came to life. It showed an infrared satellite view of the Capitol Building. There was a time counter in the corner. It changed to 21:07. Twelve seconds later a huge white circular blob flared over where the House chamber was.

"At 21:08 hours, Code Purple was declared. The city was sealed; all street traffic and trains were frozen in place. Rescue services dispatched. All air traffic has been grounded or diverted away from DC. All cellular service cut."

Carver didn't hear the last part. He was fixated on the infrared image. "Can you show what's happening now?"

The admiral nodded. The image switched to a live version. Ambulances and people outside the Capitol Building could now be seen.

"Are there still explosions going on?"

"No."

"Then, what's that white glob above the House chamber?"

"That's the ongoing fire."

"Oh god! It's an inferno."

"Yes sir, it's unlikely there are any survivors. However, most would have been killed instantaneously by the explosion."

"Any indication on who did this?" he demanded.

"It's too early to tell," said the CIA Director. "We are working on an intelligence assessment now."

"Our main concern right now is line of succession," Yardley added. "Secretary Hingecliff is upstairs in the Oval Office. The question is, is anyone ahead of him still alive?"

Carver mentally ran down the line: *Vice-President, Speaker of the House, Senate President Pro tempore, Secretaries of State and Defense.* Harris Carver picked up the phone. It felt like it weighed ten pounds.

"Amy, call Justice Sisk. I know she's under the weather, but ask her to come to the White House....Yes, send a car for her....No, don't mention this to anyone else. Thank you."

Carver sighed. "I suppose we should go upstairs and brief the new president."

CHAPTER 62

Hingecliff waited impatiently in the Oval Office with the ramrod straight Agent Bartolli. He pondered the curved walls that had witnessed so much history. How many tears had been shed because of decisions made in this office, the bridge on the ship of state? Many people fantasize about becoming President of the United States, some for the power and prestige. Others imagined how they would do things differently. Robert Hingecliff had done so himself. The fantasy was too irresistible. However, now that it might actually come to pass, he prayed it wouldn't. If Farnum were dead, he hoped someone else in line would be alive and ready to take the reins. Of course, if not, he would not shirk the duty. Men like Hingecliff didn't run from responsibility, but the presidency was one hell of a responsibility. He got up and headed to the outer office.

"Mr. Secretary, we need you to stay here," Bartolli insisted.

"I was just going to ask young Amy for an antacid."

"We'll get one for you, sir." Bartolli signaled to the other agent, who left in search of one.

"Agent Bartolli, has any new information come through that infernal earpiece of yours?"

"Mr. Carver is heading up to our location now, sir."

"Hopefully, he'll have some answers, or better yet, some good news."

Within a minute, Carver entered the Oval Office on his crutches.

"My God, Harris," Hingecliff exclaimed. "Are you okay?" There was no trace of animosity from their earlier conflict.

"This is nothing. I'm lucky to be alive." It was the first time Carver had even considered his own fate and how close he had come to death.

"So, is this what I think it is?" Hingecliff asked.

"The Capitol is an inferno. I've just seen the satellite images. It would be beyond a miracle if anyone in the House chamber survived. Even if they did survive...well...it wouldn't be pretty."

"Am I next in line?" he asked reluctantly.

"I'm afraid so. We have people on site with the fire teams, but it will be impossible to identify all of the bodies."

"Dear God in heaven." Hingecliff muttered, as his stomach tightened. *Where was that antacid?*

୫୦ ୫୦ ଔ ଔ

David was helping carry the wounded to the squad of ambulances that showed up. It struck him odd that none of the people he saw were fellow legislators, only support staff or building personnel. Perhaps, members of Congress had been evacuated from the other side of the building.

He saw someone being wheeled out of the building on a gurney. As the gurney got closer, he realized it was Fred Arkin. His face was burned, but his features were recognizable.

"Fred, it's David." But he was unconscious. "Which hospital are you taking him to?" he asked the first responder.

"I don't know," the paramedic answered. "Dispatch will tell us in a moment,"

"Can I ride with him?"

Before the paramedic could answer, a Capitol policeman stepped forward. "Congressman, the Secret Service needs you."

"Me?"

"All members of Congress, sir." The policeman guided David over to a Secret Service agent standing by a car, as David looked back at Fred's gurney being lifted into the ambulance."

"We have two now," the agent said into his wrist microphone. He opened the car door without any introduction and motioned Grant into the back seat.

Another man, whose face was smudged with soot, was already in the backseat. The smell of burnt wood permeated the car.

"Senator Ogden?"

"Grant. Thank God."

"Do you know what happened?"

"I'm not sure. I think a bomb or missile or something hit the House chamber or Statuary Hall."

Ellen was in Statuary Hall.

He looked at Dennis Ogden, who was as shaken as he was. "Where were you?" David asked.

"Prepping for my response on the Rotunda balcony. The shockwave damn near knocked me over the edge."

Out the window, David spotted a news crew. He wondered what all this looked like to the television audience. He suddenly realized Sara was probably in a panic. What had she seen? Did she think he was dead? He pulled out his cell phone, turned it on and hit the speed dial button. A bizarre screech came out.

Must be broken.

"Mine doesn't work either," said Ogden. "Either the attack damaged a cell tower, or they've cut service as part of a citywide lock-down."

David pulled out his burner phone, but it didn't work either.

"I think everyone in the chamber is dead," Ogden said quietly.

David felt a numbness beyond the cold.

"Wait, an agent said the President was back at the White House," David said.

"I don't see how that's possible," Ogden countered.

There was a profound silence as each man pondered the horror of what had just happened, and all the friends and colleagues they had just lost.

After several blocks had passed, Ogden finally spoke. "Most of the line of succession must have been wiped out. I guess whichever cabinet secretary they left behind is now president. I can't remember which one it was."

"Robert Hingecliff," David answered.

"Hingecliff?"

"He's a good man. We could do a lot worse." The irony of that statement hung in the air. How could anything be worse, given what these two men had just witnessed?

ᚥ ᚥ ᚲ ᚲ

Justice Catherine Sisk had been asleep when her husband woke her to tell her the White House was calling. Her husband Peter knew why they were calling without being told. He had been watching the State of the Union and the subsequent news chaos. Catherine had wanted to stay up, but Peter had convinced her it would be better to sleep.

"Cathy, Cathy," he said softly while gently rubbing her arm.

"What?" she said groggily.

"You need to get up."

"What? You told me I needed to sleep," she snarled from under the covers. Peter knew there was no easy way to tell her.

"Cathy, the President's dead." Catherine's eyes shot wide open.

"What?"

"They want you to swear in the new president."

"Why don't they get the Chief?" she said, pulling herself up.

"I guess he's not available."

She looked at him strangely. Even if the Chief Justice wasn't available, there were certainly other justices more senior than her to call. Technically, a justice was not required. It was just tradition. Her head was throbbing.

"Get dressed," Peter prompted. "They're sending a car for you."

Her adrenaline started. She got dressed quickly. As she did so, Peter explained what he knew about the Capitol explosion from the news reports. She looked awful as she saw herself in the mirror.

"Did they say who was being sworn in?" she asked as she tried to fix her bed-headed hair. Luckily Catherine wore her hair in a simple style that did not require much primping.

"No, they didn't say," Peter answered. "The news media is speculating the Secretary of Treasury." Catherine quickly applied some make-up just to make herself look less sickly. Suddenly, they heard the squeal of car brakes outside. She rushed outside in the night air, which just made her feel more miserable. As soon as she got into the Secret Service car, it sped off.

"We're going the wrong way," Sisk complained.

"No, Ma'am, Washington has been sealed off. We're going another way." Suddenly, the car veered onto a park field where her son used to play baseball. She saw a large helicopter shining in the moonlight in the outfield.

363

She and the Secret Service agent boarded the helicopter. She had never flown on one before. And in her present condition, she was starting to feel airsick.

"Ma'am," said a young Marine, "you have a call from the White House." He offered a headset. She placed the heavy contraption on her head.

"Hello?" she called out.

"Madame Justice?" rang the voice in the headset.

"Yes."

"This is Harris Carver, White House Chief of Staff."

"Mr. Carver, what's going on?"

"We are at Code Purple. Do you know what that is?"

"No, but I get the idea," she replied. "Who is the new president?"

"Robert Hingecliff."

"I presume since you're calling me from my sick bed, the rest of the Supreme Court has also been killed."

"Yes, Madam Justice. I'm terribly sorry."

Her eyes welled up. All her colleagues and friends on the court were now dead. Within twenty minutes, the helicopter landed on the White House helipad. It would have arrived quicker, but the Code Purple protocols required the helicopter to stay in a holding pattern before approaching the White House airspace.

ဏ ဏ ၆၃ ၆၃

The car carrying David and Dennis Ogden pulled up to an opaque canopy at the West Wing entrance. To David, the heavy canopy material strangely reminded him of Kevlar. They were met by Commander Martino just inside the door.

"Gentlemen, given you've just been in a blast area, I need to give you a cursory neurological check."

"I'm fine," David said dismissively.

"Sir, you have a rather nasty gash on your head. We are operating under Code Purple, which requires you to be examined." David had no idea what Code Purple was, but he nodded his consent anyway. The Naval physician repeated the same exam he had given Harris Carver earlier. Martino instructed a medic to clean Grant's wound while he checked Senator Ogden.

The commander turned to Agent Ross. "They're cleared."

"Gentlemen, follow me, please," Ross said.

As they were moved down the hall, they were joined by another agent escorting a woman. David recognized her as a Republican from the House, but couldn't recall her name. She radiated the same burnt smell. They were all brought into the Roosevelt Room.

Joe Dreeves was standing at the end of the conference table arguing with another senator. What was odd was that Dreeves's suit was clean and crisp, unlike everyone else's filthy and scorched clothes. David recognized the other senator as Grace Wilcox, a Democrat.

"Dreeves, where were you?" demanded Ogden.

"In a TV studio. I was going to provide commentary on the President's speech." Dreeves sounded a little embarrassed as if he had been missing in action during a big battle.

"I was entering Statuary Hall," Wilcox explained. "If I had been five seconds earlier, I'm sure I'd be dead." Her hair was singed. She also had a scar on her cheek along with the now-familiar burnt scent.

David realized Ellen, Spinnelli and Yost must be dead. Having crawled out of the Capitol himself, he could easily imagine what that inferno was like.

Harris Carver came in. Someone had supplied him with a cane to replace the awkward crutches. Some aides had followed him in. Carver looked pale. To David, he seemed paler than he had been outside the Capitol Building.

"First, I suppose I should confirm that President Farnum is indeed dead." he said as if each word caused him physical pain. "As are the Vice President, the Speaker and the others in the line of succession."

"Who did this?" asked the Republican congresswoman.

"We don't know yet, but there are people down in the Situation Room working on that. In this room, what we need to do is address the line of presidential succession."

"Hasn't Robert Hingecliff been sworn in yet?" David asked.

Carver seemed to grow paler if that were possible.

"No," he said. "Robert Hingecliff died of a heart attack fifteen minutes ago."

CHAPTER 63

"Apparently, the stress of what happened tonight was too much for Hingecliff's heart," Carver explained. "He collapsed in the Oval Office."

It was as if another explosion has ripped through them, particularly David. To him, Robert Hingecliff was the one small, bright light at the end of this very dark tunnel. And now that tunnel had collapsed completely. He felt like all the air had been sucked out of the room. David never cared for that metaphor, but tonight it felt devastatingly accurate.

"If the Treasury Secretary is dead," Grace Wilcox asked, "who's next in line?".

"No one," said a heavyset man behind Carver. "I'm Taylor Whitcomb, White House Chief Counsel." He sat down at the table between Carver and Grant. "No succession provision has ever been made beyond the cabinet level. That's why one cabinet member always stays behind during the State of the Union."

"Just one? That sounds pretty irresponsible," Dreeves blurted out.

Most looked at Dreeves in disbelief.

"In the entire history of the Republic," Dennis Ogden explained, "no one has ever succeeded to the presidency from below vice president. The probability of the entire line of succession being killed is the longest odds one can imagine."

"But occasionally, the most improbable actually happens," Wilcox mumbled.

"But the odds of Hingecliff having a heart attack, too?" Odgen added. "Inconceivable."

"He did have a heart condition," David said, remembering Hingecliff referring to his cardiologist one night at Rolf's.

"Fine, but what do we do?" asked the Republican Representative. David finally remembered her name as Angela Barone.

"What's the procedure?" she asked.

"There isn't one," answered Whitcomb. "Of course, Justice Sisk may think differently."

"Justice Sisk? She survived?" asked David.

"She was sick, so she didn't attend the State of the Union," Carver explained. "She's on her way here, expecting to swear in Robert Hingecliff. She should be here momentarily."

Within a few minutes, Sisk was escorted into the Roosevelt Room.

"We're sorry to bring you out tonight, Madam Justice," Carver apologized. "Please have a seat."

"Is what I've been told about Mr. Hingecliff true?" Justice Sisk asked. "Beyond any doubt?"

"Yes, Madame Justice," answered Carver. "And that is why we need your guidance."

"My guidance?" she asked as she lowered herself into a chair at the end of the table.

"As to what to do next."

"Look," Dreeves interrupted, "we've been through constitutional crises before. The country survived. I mean, we survived Watergate."

"Senator," she said, "despite the insistence of some *commentators*, Watergate was not a constitutional crisis. Neither was the recent election, despite some irregularities. Sometimes certain politicians have failed to follow the Constitution. However, the failing was not in the Constitution. Tonight is different. Nothing in that revered document, or in any other law, covers this situation."

"Isn't there at least something in the Constitution to guide us?" Carver asked.

"Only its spirit. The Presidency, the Congress and the Supreme Court, for the moment, appear to be completely paralyzed. We are in a legal oblivion."

"There has to be *some* legal rationale for selecting the next president," Barone said.

"Perhaps seniority?" David suggested.

"True, the President *Pro Tempore* is based on seniority," observed Ogden.

"That's a matter of custom, not law," warned Sisk, who was trying to get her head around this situation. "Whatever criterion is used, it should be a reasonable extension of current law."

"Failing that, we could cut cards for it," Dreeves suggested sarcastically.

Senator Wilcox leaned over to Dreeves and whispered, "This is a critical and historic moment. Don't embarrass yourself."

"Too late," David murmured.

Despite the stupidity of Joe Dreeves's comment, it drove home the point that the next President of the United States was probably sitting at this table.

"Are there any other members of Congress still alive?" asked Angela Barone.

Carver turned, as an aide handed him a list.

"Representatives Olsen and Roundtree are in surgery. We have no idea of the prognosis for either one. We've located three other representatives who were back in their districts and a fourth was on vacation."

"However, none of them would come close to the line of succession. All of them were freshman members of Congress," commented Whitcomb.

"Seniority," explained Sisk, "is not a very good criterion as Senators Wilcox and Ogden have equal seniority, Besides seniority has never been the legal basis of determination, only position." Then she turned to David. "Congressman Grant, aren't you minority leader of your party in the House?"

"Um, yes."

"You're kidding!" spat Dreeves. "He's an independent! The head of a Mickey Mouse party." Dreeves was completely unaware that he just contradicted himself.

"The Speaker of the House recognized the Centrist Party in the House," Sisk stated. "Was the Congressman not going to address the nation in that capacity?"

"But that was as a *minority* leader," David interjected.

"True," Sisk agreed. "But as the majority leaders are dead, it could be argued that succession might then proceed to minority leaders. As the Republican or First Minority Leader is dead, the presidency would go to the Second Minority Leader."

"Majority leaders are first though, right?" Wilcox asked. "Why can't we simply elect a majority leader?"

"Which majority? From the House of Representatives or the Senate? And who would vote? There is no quorum in either chamber."

"Well, we have a majority in the Senate," Dreeves observed.

"As I remember, the Republicans have the majority," answered Ogden.

"No longer," Dreeves snapped. Wilcox shot Dreeves a horrified look.

"You cold bastard!" yelled Ogden. "We all lost a great many friends and colleagues tonight!"

Dreeves realized he had gone too far. "I'm sorry. I know sometimes I'm an ass. But like you, I'm just trying to find a solution."

"The problem is the transfer of the presidency is considered instantaneous," Sisk explained. "Once President Farnum died, Robert Hingecliff became president. And once Robert Hingecliff died, the office transferred to the next president. The presidency doesn't skip a heartbeat. Voting retroactively will easily be challenged in court."

"Listen, I don't particularly have a problem with seniority in this situation," David interrupted. "But no matter what method or criterion is used, everyone in this room must agree and support the new president in his or her legitimacy."

"I agree with the Congressman," Whitcomb said. "I guarantee every constitutional law professor will voice a different opinion whatever is decided here tonight."

Dana Seagram, the Press Secretary, came in and whispered into Harris Carver's ear.

"We need to decide quickly," announced Carver. "Someone has leaked Hingecliff's death to the press. The press room is in pandemonium. The public will know in minutes, if not seconds that the United States is without a president."

"So will our enemies," said Ogden. "This would be a moment ripe for an attack."

"Always the hawk," Dreeves chided him.

"There's already been an attack," Carver announced.

"What?" everyone exclaimed.

"There was an attack in New York. Nobody was killed as far as we know. For the moment, let's allow others to handle that. We need to focus on the line of succession. Madame Justice, we need a decision."

"Let me be clear. I can't give you an official legal decision, as we are not in a court of law. But as I see it, there are three options: The first is to elect a majority leader or President *Pro Tempore*. However, there's a paradox and doubt about which party has the majority, which would be problematic. In addition, it would be a retroactive election and without a quorum. It would be like Representatives Barone and Grant alone electing a new Speaker of the House."

"The second option is to use seniority as the criterion. In that case, either Senator Odgen or Senator Wilcox will need to resign. Even if one were willing to do so, there is still the retroactive issue."

"I believe the strongest option is to succeed to the remaining congressional leadership position. There are no retroactive issues. And it is based on succession according to position, rather than seniority, which again currently has no legal precedent."

"Can I ask a question?" asked Dreeves sheepishly.

Everyone was bracing for another inappropriate comment.

"What about the Chief of Staff? To be quite honest, he is the most experienced among us."

"Chief of Staff is a completely unelected position," Carver insisted.

"So are cabinet members." David countered.

"But they're at least confirmed by the Senate," Barone countered.

"No," Harris Carver insisted. "Let's take that off the table. If I assumed the presidency, it would be seen as a coup. It must be an elected official or at least someone confirmed by the Senate."

To David, this was a nightmare just getting worse. He was hoping either Grace Wilcox or Dennis Ogden would suddenly stand up and resign, allowing the other Senator to assume the presidency under seniority. Instead they were lost in thought, presumably doing their own political calculus. He noticed Harris Carver writing something, handing it to an aide and asking to have it typed up. He turned back to the silent room.

"Well?" Carver asked.

"Congressman Grant holds a legitimate leadership position, publicly acknowledged by the Speaker and the House rules." Senator Wilcox stated. "He should be our next president."

"David Grant is our next president," agreed Senator Ogden.

"I concur," said Angela Barone. They looked to Joe Dreeves.

"I suppose so," he mumbled.

The aide returned quickly with a typed document. Carver handed it to the Chief Counsel, who read it carefully.

"I'm sure Justice Sisk would agree it has no legal weight," responded Whitcomb.

"It's not for court. It'll be for public consumption at some point." He then handed it to David.

It read: "We, the undersigned, in sober deliberation of the urgency and seriousness of the line of succession to the Presidency of the United States, hereby endorse the ascension of David Grant to the office of the President of the United States by virtue of his position as the only surviving Minority Leader in the US House of Representatives. While there is no specific provision beyond the recognized Line of Succession, this crisis requires this action be taken and endorsed."

"We all need to sign this," Carver insisted.

Everyone but David and Justice Sisk signed the paper. Grant's signature would have been too self-serving. Justice Sisk claimed she might have to rule on this at some point. Everyone understood.

"Madame Justice, would you administer the oath?"

"That's why I came," she said sadly.

"We should do this in the Oval Office. I think everyone should be present as witnesses."

"Mr. President?" David's neck snapped in a split second of hope, but then realized Carver was addressing him.

"Yes, I'd like a moment with Justice Sisk."

"I'll set up in the Oval." They all filed out.

Once they left, David turned to Catherine Sisk. "Is there no other way?"

She turned and looked up at the painting of Franklin Roosevelt. "The country has just been pushed off a cliff. You're the only parachute I could find. I'm sorry."

There were tears in her eyes. David wondered whether the tears were for him, her dead colleagues or the whole country. It didn't matter.

"Do you have a Bible?" she asked, as she dried her eyes.

"Yes…um…back in Pennsylvania." David suddenly remembered Sara. He would have to call her immediately. He didn't know what the media had reported, but she probably thought he was dead.

"It's alright," Catherine Sisk said. "I brought my family Bible. But if you prefer another one, I'm sure Mr. Carver can find one."

"No, I would be honored. But first, I need to call my wife." He picked up the telephone on the credenza and attempted to obtain an outside line, but to no avail.

Harris Carver returned. "Are you ready?"

"Hell, no." He immediately regretted his response. "How do you get an outside line?"

"You can't, at least from that phone. Code Purple. All but certain secure and select lines have been blocked. Amy will be able to get you an open line." They marched across the hall into the Oval Office to his awaiting "electors."

"Amy, we need an outside line for Congressman…I mean…President Grant to call his wife."

Dana Seagram marched up to them. "Actually, we need to do the Oath immediately. There are all sorts of wild speculation across the networks, and it's getting worse by the minute, real Armageddon stuff. We need to make an announcement and get a picture of the Oath out there."

The White House photographer entered as if on cue. David realized that with all of them in their dirty, torn and/or scorched clothing, it would be a dramatic picture, rivaling the famous picture of Lyndon Johnson taking the Oath on Air Force One in Dallas. David felt sick.

"Are you ready?" Catherine Sisk whispered.

"It doesn't matter," he whispered back.

"Please repeat after me," she directed. "I, David Michael Grant, do solemnly swear that I will faithfully execute the office of President of the United States, and will to the best of my ability, preserve, protect and defend the Constitution of the United States."

"I won't shake your hand, as I'm probably infectious, and you need to stay healthy. But know I'll be praying for you, Mr. President."

"Thank you, Madam Justice."

Carver walked up. "Mr. President, we have a briefing for you down in the Situation Room."

౸ ౷ ౷ ౹

Dana Seagram stepped into the White House press room. She was immediately bombarded by a cacophony of indistinguishable questions. She held up her hand, and the volume subsided.

"I have a brief statement," she announced, "after which, I will take a few questions."

The reporters settled down somewhat.

"As you all know, there was an explosion in the House chamber during President Farnum's State of the Union address earlier this evening. President Farnum was killed, along with the Vice President, Speaker of the House, the Joint Chiefs, seven members of the Supreme Court, over 500 members of Congress and all but one member of the Cabinet. Secretary of the Treasury Robert Hingecliff, who remained behind here at the White House, was to be sworn in. Unfortunately, Secretary Hingecliff died of a heart attack at 10:14 PM. Commander Harold Martino, the Naval physician assigned to the White House, believes this was due to a pre-existing heart condition, exacerbated by the stress of this evening's traumatic events."

A second cacophony of questions erupted.

"Let me finish. Then, I'll answer questions." She looked down at the hastily scribbled notes. "All available surviving members of Congress, as well as Associate Justice Catherine Sisk, were brought to the White House for consultation on the Line of Succession. After serious discussion, it was determined that Congressman David Grant by virtue of his minority leadership position in the House is next in line to the presidency."

There were more whispers and murmurs of disbelief and confusion. Seagram raised the volume of her voice to compensate.

"President Grant was sworn in by Justice Catherine Sisk in the Oval Office at 10:47, approximately ten minutes ago. We will have photographs of the swearing-in for you shortly. President Grant is being briefed in the Situation Room as we speak. I'll now take questions."

"How is Congressman Grant considered in any way in the line of succession?" asked the reporter from *The New York Times*.

"Admittedly, the official line of succession was exhausted. The remaining members of Congress met in consultation with the White House Counsel Taylor Whitcomb and Associate Justice Catherine Sisk. It was agreed that David Grant's status as Second Minority Leader in the House of Representatives provided the best legal rationale for succession."

"Weren't there more senior members of Congress who could have assumed the presidency?" blurted out the reporter from CBS.

"Seniority was deemed a legally unsupportable criterion."

"Which members of Congress were in this meeting?" asked the *Washington Post* reporter.

"Senators Grace Wilcox, Dennis Odgen and Joseph Dreeves, as well as Representative Angela Barone."

"Will David Grant address the nation tonight?" asked the reporter from FOX.

"Obviously there are enormous demands on *President* Grant's time tonight. He's currently receiving a security briefing in the Situation Room. I'll keep you advised. Thank you." With that, Seagram left the podium.

"Isn't this really a coup d'état?" someone called out.

Ordinarily she would not have responded to a question called out after she left the podium. However, as the entire country was probably watching live, she couldn't let that question hang out there. Every news anchor would comment and speculate on it. She returned to the podium.

"Who asked that question?" she demanded.

"Stuart Rithauser, *The Rithauser Report*."

Seagram couldn't believe this blogger had received White House credentials.

"Well, Mr. Rithauser, tonight Gregory Farnum, a man I worked for and admired, was murdered along with most of Congress and the Supreme Court. I want vengeance on those who did this. But I can damn well tell you David Grant wasn't the one responsible. President Grant is a man who stepped up tonight, when his country needed him. If you can resurrect someone in the line of succession, I think no one would be happier than David Grant."

"Are you saying David Grant doesn't want to be president?"

That was a question she could leave hanging, especially as she had no idea on how to answer it. She left the room, wondering why she would so vehemently defend a man she hardly knew.

ഌ ഌ ഏ ഏ

David had been escorted down to the Situation Room. The Marine guard opened the door.

"Good evening," Carver called out. He saw something was wrong. Ordinarily, all military officers would snap to attention when a president entered the room. They were instead huddled in the corner talking with a civilian.

"Excuse me. Isn't it protocol to come to attention when the President enters the room?" asked Carver.

The generals and admirals looked distinctly uncomfortable. The civilian among them stepped forward.

"Mr. Carver, I'm Bennett Yang, Pentagon Chief Counsel. The problem is the legitimacy of Mr. Grant's claim on the presidency. If any of these officers accept orders from him, they could be court marshaled for treason."

"What?" yelled Carver. "Have you been paying attention tonight? President Farnum is dead! And so is every member of the line of succession."

"Are you absolutely sure?" Yang asked. "Have you recovered all the bodies? The fire in the House chamber is still being put out. Besides even if that is so, what legitimate claim does Congressman Grant have on the presidency?"

CHAPTER 64

Not ten minutes into his presidency, David's authority was already being challenged.

"Excuse me," interrupted David. "I understand the concerns of the generals. This is a difficult time for all of us. I didn't come down here tonight to launch an invasion or use the nuclear launch codes. I'm just here for a briefing."

"I don't believe you have the appropriate security clearance," Yang persisted.

Carver opened his mouth to speak, but David held up his hand.

"Well, if I am the President, I'm pretty sure clearance is automatic. If I'm merely a Minority Leader in the House, I can assign members of my party to committees. If that's the case, I hereby assign myself to the House Intelligence Committee. So, your ass is covered."

"I'm not sure," answered Yang, "If these officers—"

"Excuse me, Mr. Yang," Admiral Westerick interrupted. "I stand ready to brief this man whichever position he holds. We should proceed."

Westerick nodded to the generals. Everyone seemed to relax slightly. They began reviewing the information on the Capitol attack, which was almost identical to what was presented to Harris Carver earlier.

"Given that we don't yet know who the perpetrator is, we are now at Defense Condition 3." The Admiral explained what DefCon3 meant in terms of military bases, ships at seas, embassies, satellites and other defensive assets. It was quite an education for David.

"Just so I understand, you went to DefCon3 without the President's authorization?" David asked.

"It was automatic, once Code Purple was invoked. President Farnum signed off on it, as did President Henderson before him."

"I'm not criticizing anyone, but isn't that pretty risky? Could any of our enemies misinterpret this?"

"We've communicated to our allies and other important governments," a woman on the other side of the table answered. "This is not a prelude to any military action, only a precaution to any who would seek to exploit our crisis."

"I'm sorry," David said, "you are?"

"Wilma Pasternack, Deputy Secretary of State."

"And no one's claimed credit? Not even in the Middle East?"

"No, not yet," Pasternack answered. "Most of that part of the world is still asleep. We've only had some minor reactive chatter."

"What about the attack in New York I heard about earlier?"

FBI Director Bensinger stepped forward. "Within minutes of the Capitol explosion, someone fired a rocket-propelled grenade or RPG at the New

York Stock Exchange. However, no one was killed, and the building is still standing with only superficial damage. We believe the New York attack was probably symbolic."

"So they could place a bomb inside the Capitol during its most secure day, but couldn't put one inside the stock exchange?" David suggested. "I'm not a security expert, but this doesn't make sense. It seems too asymmetrical."

"I agree, Mr. President. There's no doubt the attack on the Capitol was designed to kill as many key personnel as possible. However in the exchange building, there were only a couple of security guards at the time. Plus, RPGs are not an effective way to destroy a stone building that size."

"Could the New York attack be an impromptu one? Someone was watching television and decided to add to the chaos?"

"It's possible," Bensinger said. "We have been tracking a record number of protest groups. Or, it could have been a terrorist cell trying to take advantage of the chaos. We'll find out when we capture the perpetrator."

Someone came in and handed the Director a sheet of paper.

"According to this report," Bensinger said, "the exchange floor is intact with only some broken windows. Technicians are being called in to assess any possible damage to the trading systems."

"We should close the exchanges for tomorrow," Carver said.

"I agree," said David. "Let's do it." He turned back to the others. "What else?"

"We'll have more in a few hours," Westerick added.

As David stood up, all the officers snapped to attention. It felt very strange.

"Thank you, gentlemen."

"Thank you, Mr. President," Westerick said.

As they ascended from the Situation Room, David asked "Are the generals going to be a problem?"

"I don't think so," replied Carver. "I think they wanted to follow you all along, but they're just more sensitive to chain of command issues. I'll have Whitcomb rip Yang a new one. Hopefully that will straighten him out."

When they had returned to the main level, they were met by Dana Seagram.

"Harris, um, Mr. President, I just gave the press briefing announcing—"

"Yes, how did it go?" asked Carver.

"As expected, until I started to leave. Some troll named Rithauser asked if this was a coup d'état.

"Rithauser?" David exclaimed. "What the hell is he doing here?"

"We've been rotating some bloggers through the Press corps. Letting him in was an obvious mistake." Carver turned back to Seagram. "Revoke his credentials."

"No problem," she said, "but the point is: Everyone already has footage of him asking me about a coup. I snapped at him and rebutted his claim, but it was still the last thing in the live feed."

"Damn."

"Mr. President," Seagram continued. "I'm having the television camera moved into the Oval Office. You need to address the nation tonight. Reassure them that you are indeed the legitimate President. I've called the speechwriters in to work on language now. Mr. President, may I announce that you will address the nation?" David looked to Carver.

"I concur," echoed Carver. "It makes sense."

"It's so late. Will anyone still be up to watch?"

"I expect the whole world is watching. Besides, it's still early on the West Coast."

"I suppose it was inevitable." David nodded yes.

"Thank you, Mr. President." Seagram turned and headed for the press room.

"Harris, I *need* to call my wife. I tried before, but this Code Purple thing."

"This way, sir."

They cut through the Oval Office to Amy Greene's desk.

"Amy, the President needs to call his wife immediately." He turned. "You can take it in the President's—I mean, your private office."

ဢ ဢ ၛ ၛ

Agent Bartolli walked into the Secret Service Command Center. He found the Director of the Secret Service looking at the myriad video monitors.

"Good evening, Director," Bartolli said. "Are you taking charge?" Since the agent in charge of the president's detail was killed in the Capitol, he assumed that's why the Director was present.

"No, I was just across the hall for the President's first security briefing. Besides, I haven't worked the White House detail since the Bush years. But I have good reports on you though. You stepped up, tonight."

"A lot of people stepped up."

"Especially that poor Congressman from Pennsylvania."

"Yes, sir."

"*Special Agent-in-Charge* Bartolli," the Director addressed him, thus promoting him. "Tonight was the Secret Service's greatest failure. Do better."

"Yes, sir."

"By the way, what's his codename?"

"President Grant wasn't in the line of succession," Bartolli explained, "so he doesn't have one. I was thinking we might use Ulysses."

The Director looked at the live video feed from inside the Capitol, showing the smoke and flames. "He actually climbed out of that hellhole?" He sighed. "No, not Ulysses. *Phoenix*."

"Very well, sir. *Phoenix* is in his private office."

376

Phoenix in the Middle of the Road

The President's private office was a small room directly off the Oval Office. David entered and saw all Gregory Farnum's personal photographs and memorabilia. The phone rang. David picked up the receiver to hear Amy's voice. "Mr. President, I have the First Lady on the line. Here she is." He was caught off guard by Sara's new title. Then, he heard a click.

"Sara?"

"David, thank God you're alive. I thought you were dead. Are you okay?"

"A little scorched around the edges." David instantly regretted his glibness. "Ellen and the new Centrist members are all dead. Fred is alive, but badly burned."

"Oh, my God."

They just listened to one another's breathing for a moment, taking in the grief. Finally Sara spoke.

"There are all sorts of crazy stories on the TV. You're not going to believe this. One story has you becoming the new president. Isn't that crazy?"

"I took the Oath of Office a few minutes ago. I tried to call you, but I couldn't get through. I'll be addressing the nation in a few minutes."

"What? How could this happen? I mean, you being president?"

"Everyone in the line of succession was dead."

"I know, but aren't there others?"

"Apparently, being a Minority Leader made the difference." David took a deep breath. "I didn't really have any choice."

"What the—?"

"Sara, what's going on? What's the matter?"

"There's some commotion out front, police cars. Someone's ringing the door bell. I better go answer it."

"OK, I'll talk to you later."

"Sara...I love you."

"I love you, too. Be safe."

Sara opened the door. It was Mayor Tom Burke and Sam, the Embler police chief.

"Good evening, Sara," Burke said.

"Good evening, Tom, Sam."

"Have you spoken to David?" Gurnsley asked.

"Yes, I was just on the phone with him."

"Thank God. I was afraid he might have been hurt in that dreadful explosion down in Washington." Sara noticed two Pennsylvania State Trooper cars pull up.

"What's going on?"

"Well, it's the damnedest thing," Gurnsley explained. "I got a call from the Secret Service down in Washington. They asked me to provide you and your family with as much security as I can muster. They wouldn't tell me

377

why. But I assume it has something to do with that horrible blast. Do you know what's going on?"

"I think my husband has just become President of the United States."

They were all dumbstruck at this realization.

৪ৣ ৪ৣ ৵ ৻ৡ

"We've just received confirmation," Bob Summers reported, his voice slightly hoarse, "the new president, David Grant will address the country tonight. Meanwhile, candlelight vigils have popped up all over the country. Churches have opened for impromptu prayer services. People are gathering in crowds everywhere."

"We have Paula Gonzalez, reporting from in front of St. Patrick's Cathedral here in New York. Paula?"

"Thanks, Bob. St. Patrick's Cathedral is packed. All the people you're seeing behind me are those who wouldn't fit into the cathedral. Police are conducting crowd control, but things are still peaceful. One of those people is Billy O'Keeffe." Gonzalez turned to a tall, middle-age, blond man standing next to her. "How did you learn of the attack in Washington?"

"I was watch'n the game. Then, the news cuts in, say'n the President and all Congress was killed. I couldn't believe it. And then, there's an explosion down on Wall Street. It's like 9-11 all over again. I just hope this time we wipe out them bastard towelheads."

"There's no confirmation of who did this."

"Come on, we know," insisted O'Keeffe. "We all know who did this. And this time, we better finish the job."

"Bob, back to you," Gonzalez said, with a shocked look on her face.

৪ৣ ৪ৣ ৵ ৻ৡ

As David came out of the private office into the Oval, he found it filled with technicians and video equipment. Carver and Seagram were talking.

"Mr. President," Seagram said, "we're ready for a rehearsal with the teleprompter."

"Where's the speech?"

"On the teleprompter."

"Don't I get to see a hard copy?"

"Given the time we have," Carver said, "I thought best to load it straight into the prompter."

David sat down behind the Resolute Desk, the one he and Farnum had their picture taken in front of just two years earlier.

"Good evening. As you have all heard by now, President Farnum and several hundred top officials and legislators were killed at the State of the Union address in a vicious terrorist attack. Only a few survived the blast. Those who killed our beloved President will pay. As I have not been elected, I swear to not only uphold the constitution, but to continue President Farnuim's policies."

David squinted in disgust.

"No, I'm not reading this."

"We can make any adjustments you like," Carver said.

"Mr. President," Seagram said, "we're scheduled to go live in less than five minutes."

"Then reschedule."

"What? Given the   "

"Do it."

"I am not making a blind commitment to follow all of Farnum's policies. Harris, are you saying I can't make a decision except by trying to guess what Gregory Farnum would do? Is this some Democratic Party maneuver?"

Carver stepped closer.

"No, sir," Carver replied in a low voice. "I just believe making that kind of commitment would dull any charges of a coup, the kind Rithauser made. If the incoming president commits to following the same policies, no one can accuse you of trying to take advantage of this crisis. In reality, no one would really know exactly what decision he would have made, so you have flexibility."

"Let's all take a breath. This is how mistakes are made."

"Send in the speechwriters, and we'll cobble something together." David desperately missed Fred Arkin, who had always been very helpful with speechwriting.

Over the next 15 minutes they reworked President Grant's first address to the nation. It was a lot more difficult than he expected. Farnum's speechwriters were shell-shocked and were trying to write a eulogy to their beloved president, while David needed to reassure the country he was in control. He needed to be the comforter-in-chief.

ଽଠ ଽଠ ଽ ଽ

"There were concerns over the delay in President David Grant's first address to the nation," Bob Summers announced. "Given all the horror and chaos of this evening, many people wondered if this delay was a signal that something else had gone wrong. Press Secretary Dana Seagram has assured everyone in the press room, this is not the case, but 'merely the new administration getting their act together.' President Grant will indeed deliver an address from the Oval Office."

ଽଠ ଽଠ ଽ ଽ

David again sat behind the Resolute Desk.

"I think we need some make-up to cover up that gash," observed Harris Carver.

"I think we should let people see the gash," suggested Seagram. "It's authentic."

"I think I've had enough make-up already," David complained. "When do I begin?"

"In about 20 seconds, Mr. President," said the video technician.

David took a few cleansing breaths. It seemed like an eternity.

"Five, four, three," The technician called out, followed by hand signals for two and one. David began his first speech as President of the United States.

"Good evening. As you have all learned by now, President Farnum and several hundred top legislators and officials were killed at the State of the Union earlier this evening. Only a few, such as myself, survived the blast. As a result, I have reluctantly assumed the presidency."

"Most of you don't know me, or at least not very well. But to allies and enemies alike, know that our government still stands, and our republic endures. We have lost many good people tonight, but America has a deep bench. Although bombs may explode, our values and ideals are indestructible, and so, they will carry us through."

"To those who perpetrated this brutal massacre, know that American righteousness will prevail. You had better run and hide, because all of our resources are now committed to bringing you to justice."

"To the American people, I ask for your prayers, for those who died, and for those who must pick-up the mantel of government, and for our country's future."

"No one knows where the next days and weeks will take us. We only know they hold great challenge. But America is strong and will endure as long as we remain united and determined. Tonight, we lost a dedicated president and Congress. As we go forward, I will try to honor them with equal dedication.

God bless you, God bless America, and good night."

"And…we're out," announced the technician.

"Not exactly a Gettysburg address," David mumbled.

"Actually," Seagram said. "It was good, quite good, Mr. President."

"Mr. President, I think you need to get some sleep," Carver suggested.

"I need to know what's going on."

"It's nearly midnight. You need to be fresh when the calls come in."

"What calls?"

"Foreign leaders will be calling, expressing their condolences. And you'll need to convey yours."

"Convey *my* condolences?"

"Yes, 78 foreign ambassadors attended the State of the Union. And the foreign leaders'll also be trying to get a measure of you. But don't worry; we'll prep you for that in the morning."

"Maybe you're right. I'll need someone to drive me to my townhouse." At that point, a tall man stepped forward.

"Mr. President, I'm Special Agent-in-Charge Bartolli. We're still operating under Code Purple. I'm afraid we can't let you leave the White House just yet."

"When will this Code Purple end?"

"Well, it's a difficult question to answer, but the FBI Director anticipates the city will be unsealed within the next few hours." David was pretty sure that as President he could override this. But he thought it best to leave it in the hands of the professionals.

"I know this sounds petty, but I'm going to need a change of clothes."

"Not at all, sir. If you give me your keys, we'll have agents bring your clothes and other belongings here." David was too tired to argue. He pulled his keys out of his pocket, pulled the house key off the ring, and handed it to Bartolli. He wondered if and when he would ever use the other keys again.

"Good night, sir." Carver said. "We'll have a fuller briefing for you in the morning."

"Good night, Harris. You should get some sleep too."

"Yes, sir."

Amy Greene escorted David up to the residence level. "Mr. President, this is Darius Jackson, the residence manager. He'll take care of you this evening."

Darius Jackson looked like he was going to break down in tears.

"Good evening, Mr. President," he said in a brave voice.

"Good evening."

"We haven't had time yet to remove the Farnums' possessions."

"Don't worry. A cot would be fine."

"I took the liberty of having the Lincoln Bedroom prepared for you, sir," Jackson said, guiding him into the room. "Normally, the president doesn't sleep here, but given—"

"It's fine, more than fine."

"Can I get you anything, sir?" David looked at his watery eyes.

Tears everywhere, David thought.

"No. How long have you worked at the White House?"

"Seventeen years. I became Residence Manager during the Henderson administration, but mostly with the Farnums. They were a fine couple."

"Yes, they were." David didn't know why he said that. He had never met the late Mrs. Farnum. The attempt at small talk was awkward for both of them.

"Good night, Mr. President."

"Good night, Darius."

Jackson slipped out silently. For the first time since this ordeal began, David Grant was alone, with not even Sara to speak to. He pulled off his clothes and headed for the four-poster bed. He discovered pajamas laid out with the presidential seal on them. He didn't know why, but the sight of the presidential seal on pajamas made him chuckle as he crawled into bed. His laughter turned to silent weeping, a pure emotional release. He thought of the tears in Catherine Sisk's and Darius Jackson's eyes. As he drifted off, he wondered how many others were crying silently into their pillow tonight.

CHAPTER 61

David woke up, not completely sure of his surroundings. As he looked up at the bedside clock, which read 5:18, it all came flooding back. The nightmare was real

He stood up and turned on the lamp. Lying on a chair, he found a white terrycloth robe with the presidential seal on it. It didn't seem quite so amusing this morning. He looked around but couldn't find his clothes. He felt panic swelling in side him. *Someone's taken my clothes.* It was like one of those mortifying dreams, to be in the White House in his underwear. He quickly pulled on the robe. As he did so, he wondered if this had been Greg Farnum's robe. Then he caught sight of his clothes under the bed. He must have kicked them underneath. Picking them up, the smoky stench filled his nostrils, sharply reminding him of escaping the Capitol ordeal.

He went to the door and slowly opened it a crack. In the wide hall, he spied clothing racks.

"Good morning, Mr. President," said Darius Jackson, startling him.

"Have you been here all night?" he asked.

"On and off, sir. The Secret Service delivered your clothes. I didn't want to disturb you, so we set them up out here. I'll have them put away once you're dressed. This is Maurice," Jackson said, introducing the young man across the hall. "He'll be your valet."

"I've never had a valet. Maurice, I guess you'll have to educate me."

Maurice smiled awkwardly and nodded. "Yes, Mr. President."

"The shower is down the hall," Jackson continued. "I'll arrange for breakfast. Is there anything in particular you'd like to eat?"

"No, whatever you have." David felt a strong need to get dressed as quickly as possible.

Out of the corner of his eye, he saw one of the Secret Service agents talking into his wrist microphone. He wasn't sure, but thought he heard him whisper "Phoenix is awake," but convinced himself he must have misheard.

David quickly showered and dressed. Despite the small buffet, David only had coffee and a few forks full of scrambled egg. He quickly headed down toward the West Wing. In the main hall, David spied the official presidential portrait of Gerald Ford. He stopped to look at it and wished Ford were alive to advise him. *At least Ford had an idea of what might be coming.* Suddenly he heard a click. He turned and stared at the White House photographer.

"Good morning, Mr. President. Sorry, I didn't mean to disturb you."

"No," David answered. "Not at all."

David would have ordinarily stopped and talked to the man, but there would be time for that later. He turned back to the photographer. "Which is the quickest way back to the West Wing."

"The most direct route is outside, along the Colonnade," he said, pointing to the left.

As he made his way, David could hear the camera clicks behind him, documenting his first morning as President.

As he walked along the West Colonnade, he peered into the Press Room, feeling a bit like a peeping tom. A handful of reporters were dozing, slumped in chairs. He reentered the West Wing through the entrance between the Press Office and the Cabinet Room. Everyone was still wearing the same clothes as the night before. No one had gone home. Despite having only four hours sleep, he felt somewhat refreshed, especially when he looked at the people who had been there all night.

He came to Dana Seagram's office. She had her back to the door, watching her briefing from the night before on a large plasma screen.

Seagram sighed.

"You did a good job last night," David said, startling Seagram.

She jumped up. "Good morning, Mr. President."

"Relax."

She nodded and lowered herself back into her chair.

"Have you gotten any sleep?"

"No," she answered. "Well, a couple cat naps."

"Good. I know it's going to be a busy day, but try to get some sleep, even if it's only 20 minutes."

"Yes, sir," she said.

David wasn't sure he believed her. "What has the media been reporting?"

"Mostly showing file footage of the President, um, I mean President Farnum, aerial footage of the Capitol, my briefing and your address. They're cycling until something new happens. Later, I'm guessing there'll be legal analysis of the line of succession, although that may be delayed as they bring bodies out of the Capitol. Apparently, the fire has finally been put out."

Over Dana Seagram's shoulder David saw the slightest glimmer of dawn out the window. He suddenly craved daylight. He had been in darkness too long.

"Okay, keep me apprised of any developments. I'm a little turned around. Which way to Harris Carver's office?"

"Down past the Oval and then to the left."

As he followed the hall, he noticed black ribbons on a few of the office doors. He realized these were for the staffers who died the night before. Reminders of death were going to be everywhere. At the end of the hall, he found Carver's office.

"Morning," he said.

"Good morning, Mr. President." Carver started to stand.

"Sit. You look awful. I presume you didn't get any sleep."

"No."

"Do we know anything more?"

"The fire at the Capitol is out. The FBI is examining the forensics. About thirty bodies have been identified, including the President, Vice President and Speaker. Congressman Olsen died in surgery early this morning, but Congresswoman Roundtree is expected to survive."

"On another front, Secret Service details have been dispatched to protect your family, both in Pennsylvania, and at your son's college. Unfortunately, your son was not too cooperative. Since the agents weren't familiar with the campus, he was able to give them the slip."

"What?"

"The Secret Service believes he's just hiding."

"Sorry about that. I have his cell phone number. I'll call him and straighten him out. So, what's the schedule for today? I suppose a press conference is called for."

"No offense, Mr. President, but I don't think you're ready for a press conference."

"I've done press conferences before."

"Yes, and quite well as a third-party congressman. However, the White House Press Room has the most aggressive reporters anywhere. In our current situation, they can come at you from any direction."

"No offense taken, but I can't hide."

"All right, Mr. President. What's your plan for the Middle East? Immigration? The upcoming World Trade Organization meeting? Russia?"

"I don't think anyone will be asking about those things today."

"Perhaps not, but they'll try to trip you up in a number of other ways. Catching a president unprepared is what they live for."

"But the public needs to be reassured."

"Sir, you did an excellent job of that with last night's address. And we can build on that by issuing photographs of you meeting with a range of people, the generals, deputy secretaries, and so forth. You'll be seen taking charge. Don't worry, they'll be reassured. Dana will see to it."

"But am I really in charge?"

"You are, Mr. President. But you're also, through no fault of your own, the least prepared president we've ever had. There was no transition. Usually a president has months of briefings before taking office. Vice Presidents do nothing but prepare. I know this is impossibly difficult. But I will help you as best I can."

"Thank you, Harris. I do appreciate that."

"Here's the schedule I propose: first, another security briefing. You're going to need a lot of them. Also, we need to send you over to Bethesda for a full medical workup."

"I had a physical seven or eight months ago. I passed with flying colors. Yeah, I need to lose a few pounds, but that's it."

"I guarantee your last physical wasn't as thorough as a presidential one. Plus the doctors need a baseline. That's something else that would have occurred during a transition."

"At a time like this," David said, "I shouldn't be tending to myself."

"Mr. President, your health is now a national security issue. If you think we had line-of-succession issues last night, imagine the nightmare if something happened to you. Plus, a report of a clean bill of health will reassure the nation, especially after Robert Hingecliff's heart attack."

"Okay, on one condition. You have Commander Martino or another doctor look at your ankle."

Carver pulled his bandaged leg up onto the desk. "Done."

"Okay, when's the security briefing?"

"Whenever you're ready, Mr. President."

"Let me make a few calls."

David spoke with Amy for a few minutes, then headed to his private office. All of Farnum's personal effects had been removed. *At least this part of the government was efficient*, he thought. Thanks to Amy, he had now learned how to dial direct numbers from within the White House. He dialed Chris's number.

"Hello," answered a drowsy Chris.

"Chris?"

"Dad, are you all right? I tried to call you after those goons woke me up. Are you really the new president?"

"Yes, unfortunately. And those men are not goons. They are dedicated agents assigned to protect you."

"Yeah, but they woke me up like storm troopers. They ruined the whole night."

"I personally know about 600 people who had a much worst night."

"Man, I'm sorry," Chris said, realizing the inappropriateness of his comment.

"Where are you?"

"I crashed at Chad's place."

David knew Chad was one of Chris's college buddies.

"What's the address?"

Chris gave his father the address.

"Stay there. The Secret Service will arrive shortly to bring you here to the White House."

"Can Chad come, too?"

"Uh, not just yet. We all need to get our bearings first." There was an awkward pause. "Chris?"

"Yeah."

"I'm sorry to put you through this."

"Don't worry. I'll hold tight 'til the Secret Service comes."

"Thanks. See you soon."

David hung up and dialed his home.

"Hello," Sara answered.

"Good morning. Did I wake you?"

"Yeah, but it's okay. I wasn't sleeping very well as it was."

"Sorry."

"It's okay,"

"How's Wendy doing?"

"She's scared."

"Me, too."

"David, how does this work?"

"How do you mean?"

"I mean…are you going to stay president? If so, what happens to us?"

"I don't know. I guess you'll come down to the White House."

"You mean as First Lady?"

"I guess so."

"David, I have a job. I'm right in the middle of the Kelvin Civic Center redesign. I told you a long time ago I wasn't going to be one of those political wives. You said you wouldn't run again, but you found a way around that. This is selling Simplexia all over again."

"No, it's not," David insisted. "I had no choice."

"Really? Last night, I watched that woman, um…Seagram, during a press conference, say there were a bunch of senators in that meeting. Couldn't one of them have become president?"

"Sara, don't you think I would have allowed someone else to do this if I could have? Right now the government's an eggshell, easily cracked. I swear to you, I really had no choice."

"Okay, okay, I believe you. I need to get showered before I go down for breakfast." Sara normally ate breakfast first. "I hate having the Secret Service here."

"They're in the house?"

"Just downstairs."

"By the way, I spoke to Chris."

"Good. I tried to call him last night, but no answer. Is the Secret Service going to protect him, too?"

"Yes, but he'd already given them the slip. He went to Chad's place. The Secret Service is headed there now. They'll bring him down here."

"So far I'm not having much confidence in this Secret Service of yours."

"Mine? I guess it is mine now. Anyway, it's a mess however we look at it. And I have to clean it up."

"All right, I have to get going. We'll talk later. By the way, what's your new presidential phone number?"

"I don't know," he said. It hadn't occurred to him. "I'm sure the agents will have it. I love you."

"I know. I may be upset, but I do love you….Mr. President," she added awkwardly.

"Bye."

ᛒᛒᚳᚳ

The rest of David's morning consisted of several briefings. The first was one on the current security situation. This was followed by another with the Deputy Secretary of State, an orientation on the defense protocols, and finally, the infamous nuclear launch codes. Photographs were taken of each briefing for Dana Seagram to share with the press. He then took condolence calls from several foreign heads of state. Luckily, he was able to keep all the calls short.

After lunch, he headed to Bethesda Naval Hospital. It was David's first ride in the presidential limo. He was amazed at how thick the walls and doors of the limo were. Riding along, he felt like he was in a vault on wheels. In essence, he was. In front of him was a bank of phones and video screens. He supposed at some point he would receive a briefing on those too. The ride to Bethesda was short. The roads had been cleared. No gridlock for the presidential limousine.

At Bethesda, he was greeted by a team of doctors, including Commander Martino from the night before. He was ushered into a special suite, which Admiral Hynes explained was used exclusively for the president. David never knew there were admirals who were also doctors.

The medical team conducted a thorough examination. Hynes explained that usually an incoming president would have this examination before assuming office, confirming what Carver had said, so there was a baseline for the future. The tests included the usual physical exam, an EKG, a cardio-stress test, several blood tests, an EEG, a lung capacity test that left him feeling winded, and the dreaded presidential prostate exam.

"You're in pretty good shape, Mr. President," declared Hynes. "Unless you have some objection, Commander Martino will check on you every week. He'll take your blood pressure and other vitals, just as a precaution."

"Does this mean you found something?"

"No sir, not at all. It's a national security protocol."

"Well, thank you, Admiral."

"No, Mr. President. Thank you." There was an extra emphasis in Hynes's voice that indicated he really meant it.

ᛒᛒᚳᚳ

"Mr. Carver, I have Ed Leems from the DNC on the phone," his secretary announced. "He called several times last night and this morning."

"Thanks, I got it." He picked up the receiver. "Good morning, Ed,"

"Harris, are you alright?"

"I'm fine. Twisted my ankle, but I'll be okay."

"I have to ask: How the hell did David Grant end up President of the United States?"

"I thought that had been explained pretty clearly on TV."

"But you were in the meeting," Leems persisted. "Couldn't you do something?"

"Like what?"

"Work it so Grace Wilcox became president."

"Ogden had equal seniority."

"Harris, you're too skilled an operator to let that get in your way."

"Justice Sisk made the case. It was important we have a bulletproof consensus."

"Grant has only been in Congress little more than two years. Besides this whole Centrist thing has me spooked. He's the enemy of the two-party system. He's damn near said so. We have no idea what he'll do."

"Obviously, no one wanted this situation, including Grant. But look on the bright side. There's no way he can win the next election. It'll be a wide-open contest in three years.

"You don't think a Grant presidency will energize the Centrist Party?"

"I can't see them being a match for us or the Republicans. In the meantime, I'm trying to guide him toward the path set by Farnum."

"Harris, I hope you know what you're doing."

ಬ ಜ ಞ ಚ

"As David returned to the limo, he asked one of the Secret Service agents about the telephones and video screens. Apparently, the phones were direct lines. The first was to Amy Greene's desk, the second to the situation room and the third was an open line. One of the video screens was a video feed from the situation room, but the other was a regular broadcast television.

Once the limousine was on its way, he picked up the third handset and punched in the number of his congressional office.

"Pennsylvania, 20th Congressional District," answered Carol. "How may I help you?"

David thought this odd. Usually she answered "Congressman Grant's office." Then, he realized he was no longer the 20th District's Congressman.

"Hello, Carol. It's David Grant."

"Oh my God," she squealed. "It's the Congressman, I mean the President," she yelled to someone else in the office. This was followed by an awkward pause.

"David?" said another voice.

"Ellen?"

"Yes…um…Mr. President."

"My God, you're alive. I thought you were dead."

"No one's more surprised than me," she said.

"How? Almost everyone in Statuary Hall was killed."

"Ever hear of the ladies room?"

David chuckled.

"I tried to reach you at the White House, Ellen said, "but no one would connect me. I even went to the gate, but no one would let me in."

"Well, go back now. I'll call ahead."

"Where are you now?"

"Returning from Bethesda Naval Hospital."

"Bethesda? Is everything okay?"

"Much better, now that I've heard your voice."

David picked up the first receiver,

"This is the President." David suddenly realized this was the first time he had referred to himself by that title.

"Yes, Mr. President," Amy Greene replied.

"A woman named Ellen Langford will be coming to the White House. Please make sure she's escorted to the Oval Office."

"Yes, Mr. President."

80 80 03 03

Colonel Frank Grisby and thousands of others had been assigned to various interagency task forces investigating the Capitol bombing. Grisby didn't think he had much to contribute. His background was weapon systems. Until three years earlier, he had been a weapons procurement officer at the Pentagon.

When a procurement officer is assigned to evaluate a weapons system, the job is less about evaluation and more about successfully bringing the weapon through development and congressional approval. Unfortunately, he had failed his role in the "Iron Triangle," the alliance of the Pentagon, Congress and defense industry, also known as the military industrial complex. While the system he was assigned was technologically feasible, it was politically suboptimal, meaning it was opposed by a more powerful member of Congress, specifically, the late Porter Barnes.

Since then, Grisby had bounced around from assignment to assignment. The Capitol bombing provided an opportunity for an old general and mentor to recall him to the Pentagon. It was an opportunity he wasn't quite sure he wanted. However, this duty could not be refused.

Grisby read through the preliminary FBI reports. He was reviewing the metallurgical data on fragments found in the House chamber, when unexpectedly familiar data jumped out in a flash. He had seen this odd combination of alloys only once before. Could it be a coincidence? The more he read the report, the less a coincidence seemed likely. He snapped up the telephone.

"Captain, bring me the full chemical residue report." If he found certain chemical traces, it would confirm the impossible. The young captain returned with the forensics file. Grisby grabbed the file and ran through the list of trace compounds. He couldn't believe it.

Cold Vulcan had come back from the dead.

CHAPTER 66

Amy Greene escorted Ellen to the waiting room outside the Oval Office. "The President's in a meeting, He should be up soon."

"Up from the Situation Room?"

"I'm not at liberty to discuss the President's schedule," Amy said.

"Of course, I apologize."

Just then, Harris Carver walked in. "Amy, have you received the list of surviving ambassadors?"

"The State Department is revising it," she answered. "They expect to have a finalized version to us by 2:30. Also, Prime Minister McCabe has requested another phone call with the President."

"Yes, him and everyone else. Ask Deputy Secretary Pasternack to return the call on the President's behalf." Carver turned to see Ellen. "I'm sorry, you are?"

"Ellen Langford. I'm here to see the President."

"I'm afraid the President's schedule is packed."

"Mr. Carver," Amy interrupted. "The President called and asked me to escort Ms. Langford to the Oval Office."

"Of course," Carver said, turning back to Ellen. "I apologize. As you can imagine, things are very intense here today. If the President requested it, then I suppose you should wait in the actual Oval Office." He cordially ushered her in, still hobbling along with a cane.

Ellen sensed his distress was more than physical.

"I know what it's like to have a boss die on you," Ellen said. "I was working for Senator Shannon Hawthorne when her plane went down. You work for years promoting and protecting them. It's almost like having a spouse die."

"I appreciate that. I really do," Carver said, "but this is a bit worse."

"I know," she said awkwardly.

"If you'll excuse me, I also have a packed schedule."

"Of course." After Carver limped out, Ellen took in the details of the room, such as the bronze bust of Lincoln and the Resolute Desk. She was surprised by how high the ceiling of the Oval Office was.

As David walked in, he saw Ellen standing there, looking up, almost transfixed by the point where the wall met the ceiling. He walked quietly up beside her and then looked up at the ceiling, too.

"You know, when I worked in the corporate world, I desperately wanted a corner office. When I didn't earn it fast enough, I started my own company. Now, I have an office with no corners. Ironic, isn't it?" He turned and hugged her tightly. "I am *so* glad to see you."

"My," Ellen said, "does every visitor receive a presidential bear hug?"

He finally released her and stood back. "You're not a visitor," David said. "You work here now. But first, tell me what happened. The ladies room?"

"I believe you men refer to it as the call of nature. Farnum had already begun speaking. Spinelli and Yost headed back into the House Chamber. So, I went to the rest room, then I heard and felt a huge explosion, and was stuck in there for over an hour. The door frame got warped by the blast. But eventually a firefighter rescued me." Ellen noticed the gash on David's forehead. "But I think you have a far more interesting story."

"Yeah." David retold his account of the last 24 hours, of climbing out of the Capitol and the pivotal meeting in the Roosevelt Room.

"Have you had any word," she asked tentatively, "on what happened to Fred?"

"He's alive. I saw him loaded onto an ambulance."

"Thank God."

"He has some severe burns and still hasn't regained consciousness. One nice thing about being President, you can demand reports on just about anything."

"I met your Mr. Carver."

"Ah, yes. My presidential chaperone."

"Do you trust him?"

David was silent for a moment. "When it comes to keeping the country in one piece, yes. After this crisis passes, I'm not sure. Last night, he tried to get me to pledge publicly to follow all of Farnum's policies. He gave a plausible rationale. So far, he's been indispensible. But I still need another opinion in the room."

"What about your guardian angel?"

"Guardian angel?"

"You know," Ellen said, "the one on your burner phone's speed dial."

David sighed. "I'm afraid he's also dead. In fact, I believe he died in this very room."

It took Ellen a moment to process this. "You mean Hingecliff? The Treasury Secretary?"

David nodded yes.

"Oh God, what are the odds of that?"

"In the last day, I've learned *odds* provide nothing but a false sense of security." David straightened himself, adding a determination to his posture. "Anyway, most of the people I depended on are either dead or incapacitated. So I need you badly. And I want to bring some other people in, too."

They walked to the outer office.

"Amy, I'd like you to contact General Zeke Collier and former Congressman Marcus Finn. Please invite them to meet with me at their earliest convenience."

"Sir, when do you want them here?"

"At their earliest convenience," David repeated. He sensed Amy wanted to say something, but was holding back. "What is it, Amy?"

"Sir, I mean no disrespect, but you're the President now. People arrive at *your* convenience."

"I guess I need to get used to that. Thank you, Amy. If there's anything else you think I need to know, please speak up."

"Yes, sir."

"Ask the General and Congressman Finn to join me for dinner. Also, Ms. Langford will be joining the White House staff. Please arrange for an office here in the West Wing and whatever human resource paperwork is required."

"Yes, sir. What will her title be? Special Assistant?"

"No, Senior Advisor."

"Thank you, Mr. President."

ᔒ ᔒ ᘓ ᘓ

Less than an hour later, Chris arrived at the White House. Over the objections of the Secret Service, David met his car out front.

"Dad," Chris called out.

They hugged. *Presidential bear hugs for everyone.*

"Mr. President," the agent said, "we should move inside as quickly as possible."

David and Chris complied.

"What's your name?" David asked the agent.

"I'm Special Agent Randall Elgin."

"Agent Elgin, did my son apologize for being so uncooperative last night?"

"Yes, sir, he did."

"Very well, Agent Elgin, thank you for delivering him safely."

"Thank you, Mr. President."

At that moment, Carver appeared. "Mr. President, I apologize. I don't mean to interrupt a family reunion, but the Deputy Secretary is waiting in the Oval for you."

"Thanks. Tell her I'll be right in."

"Yes, Mr. President."

"Oh, Harris."

He turned back. "Yes, sir."

"After this briefing, I want you to go home. You need to get off that ankle and grab some sleep."

"Yes, Mr. President," Carver said. But clearly, he was not pleased with this order.

David turned back to Chris, who was in awe of what he just witnessed.

"As you can imagine, things are a bit hectic. I'll see you for dinner. Oh wait, I'm sorry. I'm having dinner with some other people."

"It's cool, Dad. I know you got some serious stuff to handle. Just point me to the kitchen and I'll be good."

David chuckled. "The trouble is I have no idea where that is. I know, I'll have Darius Jackson get you settled. Then you can tell the President where everything is."

By 7:30, David had completed another several rounds of security briefings. He felt the volume of information was beginning to exceed his ability to absorb it. The experience was worse than cramming for a giant exam. *But this exam might be a killer.*

Finally, it was time for dinner. Ellen conducted Collier and Finn into the dining room. He was pleased to see them.

"Gentlemen, thank you for coming. I don't know if you two have ever met."

"Oh, we've met," Finn said, with a smile.

"Marcus," Collier said, "was one of the founding members of the Circle."

"He was?" David smiled. "Somehow, I'm not surprised. Anyway thanks for coming. Let's sit down. I'm a bit exhausted."

"I'm not surprised after what you went through last night."

"Actually, it's all the security briefings that have really done me in. Middle East, Russia, NATO, nuclear protocols, Africa, China, North Korea. I'm sure there are some I'm forgetting."

"No one can absorb that much information in such a short time," Collier agreed.

"But I have to be ready should something happen."

"Mr. President," Collier said, "if something happens, your people will brief you on the relevant issues at the time. I'm not saying remain ignorant, but it's a matter of balance. As a former Chair of the Joint Chiefs, I can tell you many details of today's briefings will be obsolete by next week."

"Thanks, I needed to hear that."

"Mr. President, is there any news on who bombed the Capitol?" Finn asked.

"Not yet, but thousands of agents are working on it."

"To slip a bomb inside the House Chamber, it's just inconceivable."

"One thing I'm learning is I have to compartmentalize. The military and all our three-lettered agencies will find the bastards. Until they uncover something, I need to focus on figuring out how to be a good president."

"Well, you should call on those who truly understand it, the former presidents," Finn suggested. "I suspect the President's Club may be a valuable resource."

"I haven't had a chance with all these briefings, but I think I'll do that. Thank you."

"Even so," Collier said, "none of them had to face what you're facing."

"But they can still provide good advice," David answered.

"No argument there, sir," Collier continued, "But if you'll permit me to be frank, I think you have a golden opportunity. For the moment, you are the most powerful president we've ever had."

"Really? How so?"

"I don't mean to sound crass, but without a Congress, you are a *de facto* dictator. Now, I'm not suggesting you start a war or do anything extreme. But clearly, executive orders will have to be issued beyond their usual scope."

"I must respectfully disagree with the general," Finn countered. "Your presidency sits on a fragile pedestal, being elevated from beyond the line of succession and all that."

"Well, I do have a Supreme Court justice backing me up."

"But a new Congress can still impeach you, once reconstituted."

"How long before it's reconstituted?" Collier asked.

David had spoken with Taylor Whitcomb earlier about this very subject. "The House will require special elections," David explained. "Usually, that can take months. The senators for most states can be nominated by their governors. Even in those states that require elections, the state legislators might change the law for this emergency. Theoretically, the Senate could have a quorum within days, but that's not too likely."

"Regardless of how they came to office," Finn said, "most presidents are primarily known for just one big thing. For Obama, it was healthcare. Bush, the War on Terror, Johnson, Civil Rights."

"What about Roosevelt?" Collier asked. "He pulled us out of the Great Depression *and* led us in World War II. That's *two* big things."

"Yes," Finn admitted, "but FDR had over three terms. That'll never happen again. The point is, Mr. President, you're going to have one shot at a legacy achievement. So the question is, what will that be? Or more specifically, what *can* it be, given both parties may be opposed to you. You won't have a majority party to back you up."

"Sir," Collier interrupted, "that's why you need to act before Congress returns."

"To do what?" Ellen asked.

"Something that's popular with the people," Collier said, "but Congress would make difficult."

"Also," Finn added, "it would have to be something Congress would be unlikely to overturn once they do assemble."

"Isn't there a danger of overreaching?" Ellen warned.

"Each of you is quite right," David responded, "but—"

Suddenly, Harris Carver opened the door and entered.

"Excuse me, Mr. President, I'm sorry to interrupt."

"Harris, I told you to go home for the night," David said. "You need some rest."

"We have one more security briefing."

"Harris, I think I've had enough briefings for one day."

"May I speak with you privately, sir?"

David stood up with a weary look on his face and followed Carver, but only to the doorway.

"They believe," he whispered, "they now know who was behind the attack,"

"Who?"

"Everyone's downstairs in the Sit Room, ready to brief you."

CHAPTER 67

"It's no secret," Ben Glendenning announced, "I wasn't a big fan of Gregory Farnum, God rest his soul. But he was our president, no matter how he manipulated the Electoral College to get himself reelected. So I won't speak ill of him."

"Given the horrendous events of last night, we must now rely on the Three G's: God, Guns and Gold. Yes, we must pray. Pray that the good Lord sees us through this darkness. And yes, unfortunately, we must have our guns at the ready, because we still don't know who has decapitated our government. Regardless of who the villains are, we must be ready for any coming chaos. Will survival necessities, such as food, water, gasoline and other commodities, become scarce? Will there be battles for these commodities? I don't know. Will our currency stand? Again, I don't know. That's why I'm invested deeply in gold. And so should you, my fellow patriots. Our new president has closed the stock market because he knows what will happen. The bottom is about to fall out of the market."

"I hate to *see* it. I hate to *say* it. But I am a patriot and therefore must tell the truth. To not warn you would be the act of a coward."

The camera zoomed in slowly for the close-up.

"I swear I love my country. I love it with all my heart." On cue, the tear came out of his eye and down his cheek.

"So we must be prepared to defend it and ourselves." Glendenning barely seemed able his utter his words. "We'll be back in a moment."

The first commercial in the break was for a precious metals dealer.

ಬಿ ಬಿ ಚಿ ಚಿ

As David and Carver entered the Situation Room, everyone stood at attention. Admiral Westerick was the first to speak.

"Good evening, Mr. President, we've reassessed our initial assumptions about the Capitol attack. We now believe it was a missile, not a planted bomb."

"A missile?" David said. "But you said the radar showed nothing. No heat signature either."

"Sir, this is Colonel Frank Grisby from the investigational task force. It was his findings that changed our minds."

A square-jawed Marine officer with slightly graying hair stepped forward.

"Mr. President, I believe this attack utilized stealth missile technology from a shelved weapons project codenamed *Cold Vulcan*. As you know, anti-radar stealth technology has existed for decades. However, a missile always has a heat signature. The Cold Vulcan project at Ariskor Defense developed what's called an endothermic sheath to shield objects from thermal detection. I was the Pentagon procurement officer assigned to Cold Vulcan."

"Admiral," David asked, "without this endothermic sheath thing, would a missile have been able to hit the Capitol."

"Extremely unlikely, sir," the Admiral answered. "Our anti-missile defenses around Washington were at maximum alert last night."

"Could some foreign power or terrorist group have developed or stolen this technology?" Carver asked.

"We don't believe so, sir," answered Trevor Yardley, the National Security Advisor. "The technology was too sophisticated for a terrorist group. And it was still classified."

"That doesn't mean a foreign government couldn't have developed similar tech," Carver suggested.

"Sir," Grisby said, "the metallurgical composition of the endothermic sheath fragments found at the Capitol matches the Cold Vulcan specifications exactly. Even though the project was shelved, and despite its detractors, the technology was sound and ready to proceed. It was just denied funding."

"Well," David said, "that's one hell of a proof of concept."

"We believe the man behind the attack," FBI Director Bensinger said, as a photograph appeared on the screen, "was Dr. Daniel Narlstrom, former director of the Cold Vulcan project."

David looked at this innocuous-looking, middle-aged man on the screen. Narlstrom looked quite different from how David envisioned the perpetrator of the worst terror attack against the U.S. Government.

"Narlstrom," Bensinger continued, "was laid off from Ariskor after the project was shelved."

"Colonel Grisby," David asked, "did you know this man?"

"Yes, sir."

"Did he strike you as someone who had a grudge against his country?"

"No, Mr. President, at least not when I knew him."

"Gentlemen, what makes you think it's this Narlstrom, and not someone else assigned to the project?" David asked.

"We have a video," Bensinger said, "of Narlstrom at a SALA rally from over a year and half ago." The FBI Director clicked a button. The clip showed a large crowd on the Washington Mall. The camera zoomed in on the stage area. A man pushed through the mob and was allowed up to the podium. An obviously distraught Narlstrom began to address the crowd:

"I was blind. I was comfortable. I was part of the grand military industrial complex. I thought life was tough, but that in the end, intelligence, hard work, and persistence could win out. But, the game is fixed. I was so blind. I didn't know what the government was putting people through. But now, I realize this is not the government I grew up respecting and honoring. This is not the government that fought the Nazis and the Communists. It is not the government that stood up for civil rights. This is a government that is so isolated from its own people. They're immunized from reality."

"I lost my job, my life's work, and *thanks to CART*, my money, my wife and ultimately, my self-respect. Less than an hour ago, I met with my congressman. That's what you're supposed to do when you have a problem with the government. Right? He had no interest in the problems of real people. All he wanted to do was go to his caucus meeting."

The video clip ended there.

"That day, Dr. Narlstrom joined SALA. Several months later, he and another member left the organization's leadership over some sort of dispute. The other man was former Captain Harold Branch, Special Forces.

Branch's military portrait flashed on the screen. Branch looked like he could have been related to Grisby.

"What's Branch's story?"

"He was an Iraq War veteran, served several tours of duty. His last op was the raid against ISIL outside of Al Bukamal, Syria. What happened was—"

"Even I know what a mess that was," David said, trying to avoid a long cover-your-ass session. David thought how ironic that Zeke Collier, the general who President Henderson made a scapegoat for Al Bukamal, was sitting just upstairs.

"Branch was captured and tortured. President Henderson refused to authorize the rescue op, but eventually Branch escaped and swam across the Euphrates River."

"Not exactly our finest hour," David lamented. "Alright, we have two men with grudges against the government. But it's still circumstantial. How do you know it's actually Narlstrom and Branch?"

"We are currently interviewing a former SALA associate of theirs, a Ms. Hanna Dalton. She said Narlstrom contacted her on the morning of the State of the Union. Dalton said Narlstrom was speaking strangely and cryptically. Then she saw him get into a car with Branch. Narlstrom told her he was going to New York."

"The RPG attack on Wall Street?"

"Possibly," Bensinger said. "Now that we know who we're looking for, we have Federal agents and the NYPD scouring Manhattan."

"That's assuming they're still in New York."

"We're setting up a nationwide manhunt, but the RPG attack seems too amateurish for Branch. If he wanted to take down the stock exchange, he wouldn't have been that incompetent."

"Regardless, we better keep the exchanges closed at least one more day," David said.

Carver nodded. "Yes, sir."

David turned back to Bensinger. "Which congressman?"

"Excuse me, sir?"

"In that clip, Narlstrom said he met with his congressman. Which one?"

"I don't know, sir," Bensinger said.

Colonel Grisby stepped forward again. "Sir, that would have been Congressman Wyatt Wickham. Wickham was the primary advocate in

Congress for Cold Vulcan. Both Ariskor Defense and Narlstrom were in his district." Grisby opened his mouth to say something else, but closed it instead.

"What?" David asked. "You were going to say something."

"It doesn't matter at this point, sir, but Porter Barnes was the one who sidelined Cold Vulcan. I understand it was a political grudge against Wickham."

"My God, are you telling me congressional politics was the cause of our worst terrorist attack?"

Carver suddenly shot David an odd look.

"No, Mr. President," Grisby said, sensing he had crossed a line. "Narlstrom and Branch alone are responsible."

"There's a difference between cause and responsibility. Very well," David said, as he stood up. Everyone else stood in response. "Find Narlstrom and Branch. Keep me informed."

80 80 03 03

David and Carver returned to the main level.

"I'm not sure" David said, "whether I'm relieved or terrified that this was domestic terrorism."

"I know what you mean, sir." Carver said.

"Have you read the list, yet?"

"Which list, sir?"

"The list of the bodies they've identified. It's haunting. Cal McCord, Wyatt Wickham, Christa Lemmon, Arlo Hudge, even that pain-in-the-ass, Porter Barnes. So many people I knew." David sighed. "I understand it's traditional to declare 30 days of mourning when a president dies."

"Yes, sir."

"I think, in this case, 90 days would be more appropriate. We also need to plan some special memorial service."

"Yes, sir." Carver said, flatly.

David could see the exhaustion in Carver's face."

"Harris, are you okay?"

"Yes, sir. Fine, sir."

"I want you to go home *now* and get some sleep. You need it. You're not doing anyone any good unless you stay healthy."

"Yes, sir." Carver smiled weakly. "Good night, Mr. President."

"Good night, Harris."

Carver walked back to his office. Karen, his secretary, was gathering her things to go home.

"Karen, why is it so warm in here?"

She had a puzzled look on her face. "It doesn't feel warm to me."

"Call maintenance."

Karen could see beads of perspiration moving down the side of his face.

"Where's the President?" he asked.

399

"I thought he was with you in the SitRoom."

"No, we separated."

Karen picked up her phone. "This is Mr. Carver's office. What is POTUS's current location?...Thank you." She hung up. "The President's in the Oval."

Without saying a word, Carver turned and headed for the Oval Office. He burst through the door, startling David and Ellen.

"Why is it so hot in here?" he demanded. "Where's the President?"

David and Ellen looked at one another.

"I'm right here, Harris," David said. "What's going on?"

"Where is he?" Carver shouted. "My God, he's burning up!"

"Harris, what's the matter with you?" David demanded.

"We've got to find him!" Carver yelled. "It's my fault. We've got to save him!" He limped another step, but tripped over one of the chairs.

David lunged to catch him, but was only able to soften Carver's fall onto the carpeting.

"It's not my fault," Carver sobbed. "Barnes demanded that Cold Vulcan be killed."

David turned to Ellen. "Go get Martino."

"Who's Martino?" she asked.

"Naval doctor. Just ask Amy."

Ellen hurried out, passing Dana Seagram coming in.

"What happened?" Seagram asked.

"He fell."

"Barnes, Wickham," Carver wailed. "CART, Narlstrom, it's all my fault."

"How?"

Tears were streaming down his cheek. Harris Carver was the last man David ever expected to shed a tear, much less break down in hysterics. Martino came rushing in, followed by Ellen and a squad of agents."

"Are you okay, Mr. President?" Martino asked.

"It's not me. Harris has collapsed."

"Let's move him to the couch," Martino said.

David went to assist, but one of the agents pushed past. "I've got this, Mr. President." They easily lifted him up onto the sofa. Martino pulled out a stethoscope and other instruments from his bag.

"Mr. President, can you tell me what happened?" the doctor asked.

"He came walking in rambling about how hot it was. He was looking for and trying to save the President. I think he was talking about Farnum."

"When he fell, did he hit his head?"

"No, I was able catch him in time."

Martino continued to examine Carver.

David turned to the agents. "Maybe we should give them some space." They all filed out.

"Congressman," Carver called out at David. "We've got to go the other way. We've got to save the President!"

400

At that point, Martino gave him a sedative.

"The man always was wound too tight," Seagram said. She turned to David. "Mr. President, we can't let this become public. It sounds like Post Traumatic Stress Disorder."

"I'm not sure I follow."

Seagram took a breath. "The most experienced man in the White House just collapsed with what may be PTSD. It's going to add to the country's hysteria."

"Hysteria?"

"There's a lot of isolated end-of-the-world panic out there in the chatter sphere. Not most people, but just enough to make the news. Add this to it, and who knows?"

"Are you suggesting a cover-up?"

"Not that he collapsed, just the PTSD part. I'm not a doctor, but maybe it has to do with a concussion from the Capitol attack, an attack in which he and you climbed out of together. The next question will be: Does the President also have PTSD?"

"No, I don't."

"How would you know? How can anyone be certain?"

"Damn it, the man needs help," David snapped. "And he is going to get it."

"We can send him to a private clinic," Ellen suggested.

"Once he goes to a clinic," Seagram said, "it'll be swarmed by reporters. Orderlies and nurses will be offered bribes."

"Bethesda," David blurted out. "We'll send him to the presidential medical suite. Reporters won't be able to swarm there."

"I'm not sure that will completely do it," Seagram said.

"Why?"

"Mr. President, let me be blunt. Every administration has leaks, but I expect yours will have more than its share. With the exception of Ms. Langford, General Collier and Congressman Finn, everyone here is a Farnum Democrat. Some of the staff think of you as a usurper. No one necessarily blames you, but there is little personal loyalty to you. You're going to have a very leak-prone administration, at least for a while."

"I appreciate your candor. Are you going to leak it?"

"Of course not, sir."

"Good. What about the Secret Service agents?"

"They're the most tight-lipped people I know, at least until they retire. I also assume Commander Martino is prevented by HIPA from revealing information about his patient."

"He's also military, so he'll follow orders."

"Okay," David said, "prepare a statement for the press. Nothing false, just vague enough."

"Thank you, Mr. President." Seagram walked out of the door.

He turned to Ellen. "I guess I'll need a new Chief-of-Staff."

David returned to Collier and Finn to thank them for coming and apologized for interrupting their dinner. He explained the evening's events and asked them to return in the morning, essentially drafting them into his administration. Eventually everyone departed. So David headed up to the residence. After walking around the residence level, he found his new valet.

"Maurice, I've looked everywhere. Have you seen my son, Chris? This place is so big."

"Yes, Mr. President, it's a big house. It'll be easy to lose your family here." Maurice said. He suddenly had an embarrassed look on his face. "I'm sorry…I mean…I think I saw him up in the solarium."

"Thank you, Maurice."

David walked up the stairs, despite there being an elevator. Chris was, as Maurice said, in the solarium. Chris was looking out at the night sky. The Washington Monument rose prominently above the night skyline.

"So, did you ever find the kitchen?"

Chris jumped, startled. "Dad, I didn't see you coming. Yeah, I found the kitchen. It wasn't as big as I expected. But I'm used to the kitchens at the Institute. The head chef made me the most amazing pizza. She's also pretty cute."

"Not one day at the White House and you're already flirting with the help."

"No, it's not like that. She's an alum of the Culinary Institute. She actually knows some of my professors."

"You said, 'she was pretty cute.' Let's not get too comfortable here. I don't know how long we're going to be here. And we don't need a family scandal."

"Dad, come on. All we did is talk, nothing more. And what do you mean; you don't know how long we're going to be here?"

"I'm here under very fragile circumstances. All I'm saying is tread carefully."

"Okay. By the way, I spoke to Mom."

"Damn, I was going to call her."

"Well, she and Wendy will be here tomorrow."

"They will?"

"Excuse me, Mr. President," a Secret Service agent said. "Mr. Yardley from the NSA is here to speak with you."

"Send him in." He turned to Chris. "Could you excuse us?"

"Is there going to be a lot of this?" Chris asked.

"I don't know. Still my first day."

Yardley stepped into the solarium as Chris left.

"Good evening, Mr. President, I'm sorry to disturb your privacy."

David motioned him to a chair. "What's up?"

"Sir, it's come to my attention that Harris Carver is no longer able to perform his duties."

"Yes, I guess there's no hiding anything from the NSA," David joked.

Yardley smiled politely, but it was obvious he was not amused. "Are you considering Ellen Langford as his replacement?"

"Yes, why?"

"I'm afraid," Yardley said, "Ms. Langford may pose a serious national security risk."

CHAPTER 68

"Ellen Lanford, a security risk?" David exclaimed. "How so?"

"Sir, I'm not sure if you're aware of her sexual orientation."

"You're kidding me," David said, rolling his eyes. "You're not honestly that homophobic, are you?"

"Not in the least, Mr. President. My own brother is gay."

"Then what's the problem?"

"The problem is Ms. Langford is not *openly* gay, which means someone might be able to use that information as leverage to compromise her."

"You think she would betray me? Quite the contrary, she's never been anything but loyal."

"Mr. President, while I generally deal in facts, I must also analyze probabilities. Even the slimmest of possibilities can crystallize into reality. For instance, what was the probability a second-term congressman would be elevated to the presidency? What is the probability someone would try to use knowledge of Ms. Langford's sexuality as leverage to obtain a presidential favor or sensitive information? The latter is more likely than the former."

David knew he had much to learn about being president. But one thing he knew already was the presidency came with a unique set of rules. Something he might have dismissed as a congressman might be a real problem as president. He picked up the phone.

"Ellen would you come up to the Residence? I'm in the solarium."

Within three minutes she walked in. David introduced her to Yardley.

"Ever since I've known you," David began, "you've had a personal secret, 'baggage' you called it when I first interviewed you. I learned what it was quite a while ago."

"Excuse me, sir," Ellen said, "but I don't think you did."

"You're a lesbian," David said flatly. "And I couldn't care less."

Ellen seemed unsurprised by the charge. "No, Mr. President, I'm not."

"There's a photograph," Yardley insisted.

Ellen shot him a look. "Yes, I know the photograph you're talking about."

"What photograph?" David asked.

"I'm not a lesbian," Ellen said, "but Shannon Hawthorne, the senator I used to work for, was. I learned of a photographer named Skidmore who was stalking her. A committee staffer named Leslie Weaver and the Senator were having a secret rendezvous at a cabin in Virginia. I don't know how, but Skidmore got wind of it. The Senator's cell phone was turned off, so I drove out to the cabin to warn them. I arrived before Hawthorne, just in time to see the scum paparazzo in the bushes with his lens pointed toward a picture window. I could also see the Senator's car approaching. So, I charged in and hugged Weaver to throw him off the scent and warn her. Before I could explain what was going on, Weaver misread my intentions and kissed me unexpectedly. So Skidmore got his picture, only with me, instead of the Senator. Fortunately, two staffers having an affair wasn't quite the same level of sensationalism."

Ellen sat down, weary.

"That's a very convoluted story," Yardley observed.

"Yes, I know. That's one reason I don't tell it." Ellen turned back to David. "Coming so close to being exposed shook the Senator up pretty badly. She was from a very red state. If outed, the Religious Right would have crucified her. And despite her indiscretion with Weaver, she loved her husband, Jim. Plus, she had two kids. She didn't want them hurt. Two days later, Hawthorne was headed home to when her plane went down."

"Did her husband ever find out?" David asked.

"I don't know," Ellen said. "Certainly not from me. After the special election, the new senator wanted nothing to do with me. He told me he had his own people. But I quickly found out the photo had been passed around. No Republican was going to take a chance on me. Luckily, I found a very decent man from Pennsylvania who decided to run for the House."

"Well, Mr. Yardley," David said. "I guess that settles that."

"Quite the contrary, Mr. President, it's worse. However noble, it's still a story Ms. Langford's hiding. She could still be compromised."

"This is a woman who threw herself on a political grenade for her boss. Do you think she would do anything less for her president?"

"I suppose not." It was obvious Yardley was still uncomfortable, but he realized this was a battle he wouldn't win. "Thank you, Mr. President."

Yardley withdrew.

"I have to say, Ellen, I'm more impressed with you than ever."

"Mr. President," she said, "maybe Yardley is right in a sense. The photograph and the whole Weaver affair might be dredged up to mar your presidency. It could be used to create a distraction when you need it least."

"Go home. Get some sleep. I've already lost one chief of staff to sleep deprivation. See you early in the AM."

ဢ ဢ ଷ ଷ

David began the next morning with a 7:00 AM security briefing. Unfortunately, there wasn't much additional information on Narlstrom and Branch, although there had been some progress. David asked Zeke Collier to join them. Many of the generals knew him and trusted the old warrior. Afterwards, he called Ellen and Dana Seagram into his office.

"Dana, what's the media chatter about this morning?"

"Much is the same as yesterday, sir. Except we now have a final tally of 639 dead in the Capitol. The final body was removed from the Capitol early this morning."

"Have they identified the final body?"

"Yes, sir. Christa Lemmon of—"

405

"Florida," David said, followed by a sigh. He had to refocus himself back into the moment. "Any blowback on the Carver news?"

"Not really, sir. The fact that he had been seen walking around on a cane helped the credibility of a physical ailment. Plus, the press is more focused on Congresswoman Roundtree who's being released from the hospital this morning."

"Mr. President, you should give Roundtree a call," Ellen suggested.

"I agree," Seagram said. "Also, bringing in General Collier has been received well. He's always been popular with the media."

"Good." David said. "After we're done here, Ellen has a personal story to tell you. You don't have to do anything about it for now. I just don't want you to be blindsided should it come up."

Ellen nodded in agreement.

"Yesterday," David continued, "Harris discouraged me from giving a press conference. He felt the press corps might try to snare me with some sucker-punch questions."

"Sir, it's a possibility," Seagram answered. "But I think the press and the American public are eager to learn about their new President. They want to see the man who stepped up during this crisis."

"And for better or worse, they deserve nothing less," David agreed.

"Sir," Seagram said, "may I suggest surprising the Press Room? Just walk in. It might keep them a little off balance."

⁎ ⁎ ⁎ ⁎

"Good morning, everyone" Seagram said, walking into the Press Room.

"Dana," one of the reporters blurted out, "when is the President going to address the nation again?"

Seagram smiled. "Well, Curtis, funny you should ask about that." She looked across the Press Room, watching as everyone settled down. "Ladies and gentlemen, the President of the United States."

David walked in and strode over to the podium. All the reporters quickly stood up, shocked by David's unexpected appearance. Some quickly pulled on jackets, while others straightened ties.

"Good morning," David began. "I'd like to begin my first press conference with a moment of silence for those who perished in the Capitol attack."

David bowed his head. The moment of silence also gave the networks just enough time to interrupt their programming to cut to the press conference.

"Thank you. I am announcing a 90-day period of national mourning for President Farnum and the 638 others who died in the Capitol attack. All U.S. flags around the world are to be flown at half staff for that duration in remembrance of those who died in public service for their country."

"Now I know you have many questions. Please understand I've only been in the job for less than two days. If you want to play stump-the-president, I suppose you can, if you must." He looked down at the most senior correspondent sitting in the front row. "I believe traditionally the first question is yours."

"Yes, Mr. President. Do you know yet who is behind the February 3rd attack?"

"As it is an ongoing investigation, I'm going to say very little. However, I can assure you and the American people, the agencies of the US Government are focused and aggressively closing in on the perpetrators."

"Can you tell us if the terrorists are foreign or domestic?"

"It appears most likely to be domestic, which is obviously quite a shock to everyone."

David pointed to the next reporter.

"Mr. President, beyond apprehending the bombers, you face a range of issues that confronted President Farnum and are now sitting on your desk. What is your top priority?"

"My top priority? Reassembling the Federal government including the Congress and the Supreme Court."

"Sir," one of the wire service correspondents began, "you will have the unprecedented opportunity to appoint seven, possibly eight, Supreme Court Justices. You could pack the Court."

"Is that what you're suggesting I do?"

Everyone chuckled a little bit, but not too much.

"My approach to government has always been a pragmatic one, based on what will benefit the most people without hurting others. I am not a particularly ideological guy. Ideology often leads to narrow, polarizing decisions. In looking for nominees, I will seek men and women who reflect that philosophy. Even so, I'm sure that will lead to a diversity of nominees and legal opinions."

David cued the next reporter in the row.

"Mr. President," began a blonde woman from the Conservative Patriots Network. "Given you were neither elected nor nominated, how long do you believe you will continue as president?"

David looked oddly at the young journalist.

"There's no mechanism in the Constitution for presidential special elections. It is my duty to continue for what would have been the duration of President Farnum's term, just as, say, Harry Truman did for FDR."

"But Mr. President," the reporter shot back, "Truman was the same party as Roosevelt."

"Neither the line of succession nor the Constitution recognizes party, only position."

"But the Constitution doesn't officially recognize you either."

"Is this a debate?" David asked.

Again, there were some stifled chuckles.

"Given the horrific circumstances of February 3rd," David continued, "we had to improvise. I had the support of everyone in the room, three senators, one congresswoman, the White House Counsel and a Supreme

Court Justice." David deliberately omitted any reference to Carver. "I believe the press office has already released the document signed by everyone in the room that night."

David pointed to the next reporter, who turned out to be from the Liberty Network.

"Mr. President, given the manner in which you came to office, some have suggested you pledge to restrict yourself to being a caretaker president. How do you respond to that?"

"Some have suggested? Like who?" David asked. "Your editorial board perhaps? Well, I'm not completely sure what the definition of a caretaker president is. I am perfectly aware I have nothing close to a mandate. My first priority is to stabilize the government and to facilitate its full restoration. If you consider that caretaking, so be it."

"A quick follow-up, sir. It's been noted your wife does not live in Washington and rarely visits the capital, particularly within the last year."

David was surprised anyone would be monitoring his wife's comings and goings. "And your question is?"

"Will your wife be acting as First Lady?"

"Well, she *is* First Lady. How she will handle any duties has yet to be determined."

"When will she be coming to the White House?"

"She'll be arriving later today." David turned to acknowledge the *Post* reporter next.

"Mr. President, there is the matter of the budget. Without a viable Congress, a budget cannot pass. As a Congressman, you were particularly critical of wasteful spending. How do you plan to address that? Will you take this as an opportunity to implement cuts using executive orders?"

"Rest assured, there will be no shutdown of the government. The budget process will still be a congressional one. Any executive orders in regard to the budget will be kept to an absolute minimum. There are relatively easy things we can do to alleviate budget problems in the interim. Right now, finding the terrorists and restoring the government are our highest priorities. Thank you for your time, ladies and gentlemen."

"Thank you, Mr. President."

Once back in the Oval Office, he asked Seagram, "So, how did I do?"

"You certainly held you own, sir. May I ask why you were so combative with the Liberty reporter?"

"Let me ask you a question, how is it the Liberty Network knows so much about how often my wife visits Washington?"

"I have no idea, sir."

"That was Ellis Cornwall sending me a message."

"Ellis Cornwall?"

"Yes, I spoke up against the excesses of Farnum's education bill. I also blocked Parnell Education's takeover of Winton College."

"You've lost me, sir."

"So you really don't know?"

Seagram shrugged.

"Ellis Cornwall doesn't just own the Liberty Network; he's the largest shareholder in Parnell, the largest for-profit education company in the United States. And now, a major thorn in his side has become President of the United States. I also believe Cornwall may have been behind the Omaha incident with my daughter."

"You mean the one that alleged you were a pedophile?"

"And apparently, that bastard is still watching my family."

ಔ ಔ ಞ ಞ

That afternoon, David and Chris waited just inside the front door. The Secret Service was now more insistent that he not step out into the open air, even though the streets of Washington had become the most secure area in the world within the last 48 hours.

"Daddy!" Wendy yelled out with delight as she came through the door. She ran and grabbed him tightly around the neck.

More bear hugs. "I missed you, Pumpkin."

"I missed you, Daddy," she said, with tears in her eyes. She hugged him even tighter.

David spied Sara walking in behind Wendy. She hugged Chris, and then gave David a polite kiss on the cheek.

"So, welcome to the White House," David said, trying to sound upbeat.

"Yes, a most elegant prison," Sara murmured.

"Why don't we go upstairs to the Residence? Chris, how about giving your sister the full tour first."

"Sure, Dad." He turned to Wendy. "Let's go do some exploring. They've got a movie theater and bowling alley downstairs."

Once the children were out of earshot, David asked, "What's with Wendy's tears?"

"You don't know? She was afraid you had died in the explosion. Even after she knew you were alive, she couldn't sleep that first night."

"Oh, God. Let's go upstairs."

Once they arrived in the Residence, they settled in the parlor. But Sara was pacing back and forth.

"I'm not a fan of your Secret Service," she began. "For the sake of security, they insisted on setting up metal detectors at Gunther & Cartwright, if I was going to continue working there. Ted Cartwright wasn't too pleased with that idea. So I guess I'm on indefinite unpaid leave."

"Ted has no right to do that."

"I don't blame Ted," Sara said, finally sitting down. "And don't even get me going on what they wanted to do at Wendy's school. This is like you selling Simplexia all over again, only so much worse."

"That's not fair."

"Damn it, David. I don't want to be First Lady! You're now the national champion of democracy. But when the hell do I get a vote?"

"I didn't want to be President."

"Really? Then why did you agree to it?"

"I told you, I didn't have any choice."

"There's always a choice."

"Yes, I suppose I could have let the country fall into anarchy."

"Shit, get over yourself," Sara snapped. "There were other people in that room, all more experienced than you. One of them could have become president."

"Like who? The two equally senior senators, neither of whom would have had a legally defensible presidency. Maybe Harris Carver, the man who collapsed in my arms last night from PTSD."

"What?"

"Or better yet, how about that idiot, Joe Dreves, who wanted to *cut cards* for the presidency? The very same man who persisted pushing the Omaha story after everyone else dropped it? Would you want him to be president? Yes, it was a quick decision, certainly a painful one for us, but one that had to be made."

David walked away and slumped into a chair at the far end of the room. "I'm sorry. I didn't mean to yell."

But he wasn't sorry, at least not completely. His frustration had been building. He needed to release his pent-up anger, but he did regret Sara was the recipient. He leaned forward, his head in his hands.

Sara suddenly regretted her own outburst. She walked over to him and sat on the arm of the chair. She rubbed his back and kissed the top of his head. "I'm sorry. The trouble is I married a good man, a man far better than me."

"That's not true," he said, leaning back and taking her hand. "I was selfish when I ran for Congress. And I was arrogant to think I could change Washington."

They looked into each others eyes.

"Maybe," Sara admitted. "But now, *Mr. President*, you have the power to do something about that."

David chuckled. "You sound like Zeke Collier."

"Who's he?"

"General Zeke Collier. He's another good man. He's been helping me."

Suddenly, there was a knock at the door. It was Maurice.

"Excuse me, Mr. President, Mrs. Grant. Sir, FBI Director Bensinger is here to see you."

"Alright, send him in," David said.

Maurice left to retrieve Bensinger.

"I'm sorry," David said. "This will be about the attack. We have a suspect."

Bensinger arrived. "Mr. President, Mrs. Grant, I'm sorry to interrupt.

"No problem. What's the story?"

Bensinger hesitated, looking at Sara.

"Oh, I guess this is something else I need get used to." Sara excused herself and walked out.

Bensinger looked apologetic. "We found Narlstrom's workshop. We now have reason to believe there may be a second missile."

CHAPTER 69

Once again, David met with his national security team down in the Situation Room.

"As I explained upstairs," Bensinger began, "we found Narlstrom's workshop in an abandoned warehouse owned by a company called Coburn Trucking. The owner, Saul Coburn, a friend of Narlstrom's, claims he was using the space primarily for storage and some amateur woodworking. We sent a full forensics team there. They found evidence that three missiles were constructed. Admittedly, the one might have been a prototype for testing. But we're concerned another is pointed at a target somewhere."

"The stock exchange?" David ventured.

"Then why not fire the missile that night?" the FBI Director asked.

"I don't know," David admitted. "I'm just guessing. If the stock exchange isn't the target, then what is?"

"Maybe" Zeke Collier suggested, "Narlstrom lied when he told that Dalton woman he was going to New York."

"We have surveillance video of Narlstrom and Branch at the airport," Bensinger explained. "They definitely went to New York."

"If they were in New York," Collier asked, "how could they have fired the missile here in Washington? There must be others."

"Possibly," Bensinger said. "However, in Narlstrom's workshop, our team found components that could be used to construct a timer or even a remote control."

"If his missile is undetectable," Admiral Westerick said, "it could be aimed anywhere, even the White House."

David thought immediately of his family upstairs.

"If they were going to attack the White House," Collier concluded, "they would have the same night. There's been too much security added since."

David felt reassured by the old general's logic.

"Okay, New York is the likely target," David agreed, "but if not the stock exchange, where? The Empire State Building? Yankee Stadium?"

"Unfortunately, there are a wide range of strategic targets. Bridges and any large venues would all be vulnerable," Bensinger said. "The NYPD anti-terrorism unit is on high alert. Every inch of the city is under surveillance."

Then David had a realization. "Besides the US Government, who else does Narlstrom have a grudge against? Kadler Steele."

৪০ ৪০ ৫৪ ৫৪

Daniel Narlstrom was getting anxious, cramped into his box for so long. He was waiting for Branch's next text message. It finally came. He pulled the phone out of his pocket. The text message read:

PACKAGE STILL HOME. NO SIGN OF MOVING. YOUR CALL.

Damn. Whoever the copycat bomber was who attacked the stock exchange had spooked Corbin Beaumont. He was now staying away from his Kadler Steele office. The Capitol part of their plan had worked magnificently. But Phase Two was now wobbly. Time for the contingency plan.

He pushed off the box, his personal prison for nearly a day. The box had been made to look like an air conditioning unit, fairly inconspicuous on this Manhattan rooftop. It had the added advantage of being lined with endothermic sheathing to evade thermal scanning.

He stood up, then stumbled and fell, hitting his knees on the hard roofing and then falling over. He regained his balance and stood up. He picked up his dropped phone and typed his text response:

TIME TO GO?

Within less than a minute came Branch's reply:

AGREED. DIVIDE AND CONQUER.

Narlstrom shoved the phone in his pocket and walked across the roof to a second fake air conditioner. He pushed it over, revealing the missile launcher, a year's worth of work.

He whispered to the small missile, "Your sister did so well. Now, it's your time to shine."

He powered up the circuits and started to go down through the checklist. He decided to make a slight adjustment to the trajectory. The wind was stronger from the north than he originally anticipated. Branch had been indispensable in teaching him artillery techniques. He would have preferred to use GPS, but that might have exposed them.

୫୦ ୫୦ ୧୫ ୧୫

Harry Branch wore his best suit. It was his only suit. *Pinstripe camouflage.* He had previously scouted Corbin Beaumont's house and neighborhood. He knew Beaumont's routine. However, since the unexpected RPG attack against the stock exchange, Beaumont had hidden inside his luxurious house. *Cowering weasel.*

"Captain Branch?" someone suddenly called out.

Branch's heart skipped a beat. *Had they been compromised?* He turned to see a tall man also in a suit. Suddenly, the approaching man broke into a huge smile.

"I thought it was you," the man said, quite pleased to see Branch.

"Oscar?" Branch laughed. "Sergeant, I didn't recognize you out of fatigues. What are you doing here?"

"Got myself a security gig. How about you?"

"Same here."

"Corbin Beaumont, by any chance?" Oscar asked.

"How'd you guess?"

"Man's been so damn jittery. After three years of death threats, he suddenly hires a bunch of extra security to protect his skinny ass. Which firm are you with?"

℘ ℘ ℭ ℭ

Dressed in khakis and a teal golf shirt, Corbin Beaumont hung up the phone in his study, He was frustrated the SEC wouldn't make a decision on when to reopen the exchange. *Our new president doesn't seem to understand the importance of financial markets.* He decided to find his wife, Amanda, and take advantage of his stay-at-home time. As he walked into the main hall, he saw one of the new security guards.

"Who are you?" Beaumont asked. "Where's Oscar?"

"Oscar's been incapacitated," Branch said, pulling out an old 45-caliber automatic, aiming it straight at Beaumont's chest. "I was going to kill him, but I decided to not make him pay for your sins. Although he will need some physical therapy."

Beaumont took a nervous step backwards. "My sins?"

"Yes, primarily the callous disregard for the American people."

"You don't understand. I had a duty to my stockholders."

"Duty? Don't you dare speak to me about duty!" Branch stepped closer. "What about your duty to your fellow human beings, huh? Know all those people who trusted you with their savings and retirement funds."

Branch tried to calm himself down.

"Speaking of your beloved stockholders, how are they doing? I mean how's that all-important stock price, huh?" Branch taunted him. "Down how many points? I'd say you failed your duty on that front as well."

"I have cash in the house," Beaumont blurted out.

"What?"

"I have cash you can take with you. You haven't killed anyone yet. Theft and assault are far lesser crimes. And that's only if you're caught."

Branch laughed.

"It's all about money with you people. You have loyalty to nothing but your bank accounts. And you believe everyone else must see the world the same way. I bled for my country. I almost died for it," Branch added, punctuating with a shake of his gun. "But you people, all born with silver spoons up your asses, you just see the rest us as investors or consumers, or just plain marks to be duped. On your knees, shithead," Branch commanded.

"What?"

"You heard me," he said, pointing his pistol toward the floor.

Beaumont hands were trembling as he lowered himself to the floor. Branch could see he was about to start crying. As much as he despised the man, he wasn't about to endure those kind of theatrics.

"Goodbye, you miserable worm."

Then the shot rang out.

Narlstrom readied the firing sequence. It was much simpler than the one he aimed at the Capitol building. It didn't require remote control or a timer. This time he'd be able to witness the justice served up first hand.

"Freeze!" yelled a voice from behind him. "FBI."

Narlstrom turned slowly to see five men aiming weapons at him. Rather than the panic he would have expected, he felt an amazing sense of calm. He knew he had always been a merchant of death, but only at the furthest distance, contributing to weapons of mass destruction used beyond his personal horizon. He always wondered if he would ever have the kind of nerve Harry Branch had, to confront an enemy face to face. Did he have the nerve? Now, he would find out.

"Drop your weapons," he said, "or I'll launch this missile."

Hesitation appeared in the lead agent's face, but not for long.

As the bullet ripped into his abdomen, Narlstrom fell to his knees.

Pain. Narlstrom had never felt such incredible physical pain. He looked up at the lead agent who was now standing over him. Even through the intense pain, the calm stayed with him.

"Why not a head shot?" he asked. Branch told him that's how they would do it.

"That would have meant aiming higher," the agent answered. "I might have missed and stuck someone in the building across the street. But if you'd really like a head shot now, I'd be willing to oblige."

Narlstrom turned to view the building the agent referred to.

He suddenly started rolling toward it. As he flung himself over the edge, plummeting toward the street below, he had one thought. *Jean, here I come.*

୫୭ ୫୭ ୧୬ ୧୬

Several hours later, reporters gathered in the East Room of the White House. Unlike David's previous press conference, this one was well announced. All networks transmitted live as David walked down the red-carpeted Main Hall toward the podium.

"Good evening, my fellow Americans. I am here to announce the two perpetrators of the February 3rd Capitol attack are now dead."

"One of them was a Dr. Daniel Narlstrom, an unemployed engineer, laid off from a defense contractor. The second was a former special operations officer, Captain Harold Branch."

"Daniel Narlstrom was shot in New York by an FBI agent, who cornered him on a rooftop in the financial district. Narlstrom intended to fire a second missile at the Kadler Steele headquarters. Meanwhile, his co-conspirator, Harold Branch, was shot in the home of Corbin Beaumont, CEO of Kadler Steele. Branch was shot by Mr. Beaumont's wife, Amanda, in defense of her husband."

"While the investigation will continue, the general consensus is that this was a two-man operation, both of whom are now dead. I am deeply grateful to all of the members of the various agencies and departments that pursued this investigation. This terrorist threat is now over."

"I'll take questions now."

୬୦ ୧୬ ୫ ୫

Over the next few days, the media cycle swirled around the events in New York and New Jersey. Many delved into the backgrounds and motivations of Narlstrom and Branch. Others focused on the 363-point drop in the reopened stock market. The most sensational programs focused on Amanda Beaumont, the former fashion model who shot America's most wanted terrorist with a .22 caliber pistol. One tabloid referred to the Texan as "gun smok'n hot." The NRA quickly tried to make her their new poster girl.

୬୦ ୧୬ ୫ ୫

Zeke Collier had been summoned to the Oval Office.

"Good morning, Mr. President."

"Good morning, Zeke." David said waving Collier to the sofa.

"What can I do for you this morning, Mr. President?"

"I have a job offer for you." David motioned for him to sit down on the sofa.

"For you, sir, I'd be proud to put the uniform on again."

David smiled. "No, this job doesn't require a uniform. In fact, it's prohibited."

Collier looked puzzled.

"I'd like to nominate you as my Vice President."

The surprise was quite evident on the general's face. "That's quite unexpected, Mr. President. Are you sure, sir? I've never held elected office. I'm not exactly the most politically experienced person."

"I think you're more experienced than you claim. Besides, people trust you. I don't want you for political reasons. You're loyal without being a yes man. And if something happens to me, we'll need a respected and responsible leader. Whoever my VP is will have a higher than normal probability of becoming president."

"How do you figure that, sir?"

"People have accepted me as president for now. But as soon as I do something even slightly unpopular or beyond their view of a caretaker president, some partisan ass will be calling for my impeachment. And given how I came into office, it might be hard to fight."

"Sir, we've already lost one president. I don't believe the American people want a revolving door on the Oval Office. I can't imagine such a thing."

"Given what we've been through, I've started to imagine the unimaginable. So, before you accept, understand that you might actually become the President of the United States. So, think carefully before you answer."

CHAPTER 70

Like the rest of the country, David was relieved to have justice served. No one else seemed to be involved with the Narlstrom-Branch conspiracy. The RPG attack was an attack of opportunity by an unrelated group. Those perpetrators were quickly apprehended by the NYPD. While David's personal nightmare was not over, at least the panic could subside and the healing could begin. It allowed him to focus on reconstructing the government.

The following morning, David decided to personally call the governors and discuss the restoration of Congress. Ninth on his call list was Oklahoma Governor Buck Howell.

"Good morning, Governor."

"Good morning, Mr. President. Congratulations on nabbing Narlstrom and Branch."

"Thank you. We owe a lot to our law enfocement agencies."

"Amen to that. How can I help you, this morning?"

"I'm touching base with all the governors to discuss restoring Congress."

"Well, I'm certainly doing my part. Later today, I plan to announce an accelerated primary and election schedule for Oklahoma congressional districts."

"I appreciate that, Governor. That's great news," David said. "What about Senate appointments?"

"I'm narrowing down the candidates now. I expect to make a decision by early next week."

"Good. I'd like to ask a favor in that regard."

"If I can, sir."

"One of the factors that contributed to Narlstrom and Branch's actions was the political polarization in Washington."

"I'm not sure I quite agree with you on that, Mr. President. From where I sit, it seemed clear that Democratic Party shenanigans denied Narlstrom his money and livelihood."

David realized he should have anticipated Howell's partisan bias.

"Well, at the very least, the political polarization has prevented Congress from moving forward."

"Mr. President, I know your time is valuable. Why don't you tell me what you're looking for?"

"Very well. I'd like to ask you to appoint senators who are not so partisan, perhaps a bit moderate. I'm confident you won't appoint any liberals, but I'd ask that you not appoint anyone too conservative either."

"Mr. President, I appreciate what you're asking. I really do. But what guarantee do I have that some liberal governors won't appoint the most left-wing wackado they can?"

"I'm making the same request of all the governors, left or right."

"That's just the thing. It's merely a request. We can't take the chance that the country might crash to the left. But don't worry, Mr. President. I'll send you some top-notch people."

"Governor, we have a unique opportunity here. I was really hoping for some cooperation in reducing the hyper-partisanship and gridlock."

"Sometimes gridlock is preferable to more disastrous outcomes."

David just sighed and realized he would get nowhere with the conservative governor.

"Well, I thank you for at least accelerating the election schedule."

"Before we hang up, Mr. President, I have a personal question."

"Yes?"

"Do I have you to thank for saving my life?"

"I'm not sure I follow you."

"It occurs to me, if I had won the election, I would be the dead president, not Gregory Farnum. Now, I'm not accusing anyone of doing anything illegal, 'cause all is fair in love, war, politics, and all that. However, I've heard rumors you nudged the Electoral College in Farnum's favor. So, do I have you to thank for saving my life? If so, I'm quite grateful."

David realized the cleverness of the way Howell was asking the question, but he wasn't going to fall for the Governor's trap.

"It's true I pressured Everett Wilkers into giving the Centrist party minority status in the House, but I would never defy the electoral will of the American people. Gregory Farnum received more votes than you. And those four Centrist electors weren't going to vote for you, no matter what I did."

"Fair enough, Mr. President. I'm not certain on how much you and I will agree on in the future, but I appreciate the load you have taken on. And I thank you."

"Thank you, Governor."

David slumped back in his chair. Almost immediately, Ellen walked in.

"Governor Markowitz is next on the list," she said.

"This may be a waste of time. I've spoken to nine governors so far, but each one gave essentially the same answer. Moderation seems to be in neither party's interest."

ॐ ॐ ॐ ॐ

Fred Arkin slowly woke up in a haze. He stared at the ceiling and realized it was not his own. As he raised his left hand, he saw it was bandaged. He suddenly realized the ceiling was that of a hospital room. He felt the bandages on the side of his face. *What happened? How did I get here?*

Later that day, Sara peeked through the door to the Oval Office.

"Good afternoon, Mr. President," she said with a smile. "I have a special visitor for you." Sara walked in, followed by Reverend Margaret Garthwell.

"Peggy," David said, "you're a sight for sore eyes." Grinning, he stood up and walked over to his pastor and friend. Another presidential bear hug ensued.

"Well, I'll leave you two," Sara said. "I want to make sure Wendy and Nancy don't get into any trouble."

"Nancy's here, too?"

"I thought Wendy could use some familiar company," Garthwell said, "given the sudden change in her environment."

David felt a deep sense of gratitude. "That was extremely thoughtful, Peggy."

"Anyway," Sara said, "the girls are down in the bowling alley. I'll see you two later."

David invited Garthwell to sit down.

"So, how are you holding up, Mr. President? My, it's so strange to call you that."

"Yeah, welcome to my weird new world," as he sat on the other end of the sofa.

"You know, God spared you for a reason. Back in Embler, we had a special prayer service for you, just to stack the deck in your favor."

David smiled. "Thank you. I can use all the prayers I can get."

"So, you didn't answer my question. How have you been?"

"Between you and me, it's been pretty rough. I could never have imagined this. All those people I worked with now dead. A man collapsed in my arms, right here in this room, just three feet from where you're sitting."

"Oh, my."

"But enough about me. Tell me about the outside world. How are people holding up? What are they saying?"

"You mean what are they saying about you? Obviously the people of Embler know you. They trust you. But when I travel beyond our town, people are just worried. You're a stranger to them. I guess they just need to get to know you like we do."

Then there was an awkward silence. David noticed Garthwell's hand was trembling slightly. The expression on her face faded as if a mask were evaporating.

"What is it?"

She hesitated, then sighed. "I have a letter for you."

"From who?"

She sighed again. "The Interfaith Council of Bishops."

David suddenly became wary. "Do you know what's in this letter?"

"I haven't read it," she said, as she pulled an envelope from her purse. "But I know the gist of it."

"And that is?"

"They want you to appoint only pro-life nominees to the Supreme Court. They see this as a unique opportunity to overturn *Roe v. Wade*."

David stood up and walked across the room away from Garthwell, as if to put distance between them. "They see an opportunity, huh?" He paused and turned back toward her. "Do you have any idea what that would do to this country? An unelected, unconfirmed president packs the court with ultra-conservatives. That would rip this country apart. And let's say *Roe v. Wade* were overturned. That wouldn't really reduce the number of abortions by very many. The back alleys will be open for business."

David felt a flash of anger at his pastor and friend.

"How did it come about that you are the carrier of this letter? Did you volunteer?"

"No," she said, in a defensive tone. "I was approached by our bishop, who was approached by the Interfaith Council. I balked, but my bishop said if I didn't do this, he would move me to the least desirable church he could find. He suggested it might be a high-crime neighborhood in the inner city. Maybe I could live with that, but I couldn't inflict that on Joe and Nancy. I'm sorry. He also insisted I do what I can to personally persuade you."

"Wow. The forces of partisanship move quickly. What happens if I don't accept this letter of theirs?"

"They'll announce it to the media. I'm not a political expert. I guess they might denounce you as a pro-choice liberal, intolerant of Christian values."

"That sounds like the Interfaith Council alright. But, I meant what happens to you?"

"I don't know."

"And if I accept the letter?"

"I guess they'll report it and whatever your response is. David, I promise I'll only share whatever you tell me to."

"Give me the letter," David said, holding his hand out.

"Are you sure?" she asked.

David nodded.

"I want you and Nancy to stay for dinner. In fact, Wendy wouldn't forgive us, if we didn't have you stay overnight. They can have a slumber party. I'll give you a response before you leave."

He asked Amy to find an escort to take Garthwell to the bowling alley and then asked Ellen to come in. David explained to Ellen what had just transpired.

"Last year, they tried to use Wendy against me. Now, they're trying to use my friend and pastor against me."

"I don't think they're connected," Ellen said.

"No, that's the problem. They don't have to be connected."

420

"To be honest, now that Narlstrom and Branch are dead, every group will be concerned about the Supreme Court nominees. Some of the more Liberal websites are saying you're only a legitimate president if you appoint liberal judges."

"Yes, I guess there's no shortage of groups trying to push their agenda over the needs of the country. And there's no limit to how low they'll go."

"Do you feel Reverend Garthwell really betrayed you?"

"No, she's a pawn, a victim of her association with me."

"Then let's give her the power to fight back."

"How?" David asked.

"Put her in the spotlight."

𝔅𝔒 𝔒𝔒 ℭ𝔒 ℭ𝔒

About hour later, David walked into the solarium. Wendy and Nancy were off exploring the seemingly endless rooms of the White House. Sara and Peggy were talking. From their demeanor, he could tell it wasn't light banter.

"I told Sara about the letter," Garthwell blurted out. "I'm ashamed. I should have been stronger."

"It's okay. It's the cesspool of politics." David sat down on a chair across from the two women. "Peggy, I've read the letter and I've thought about your position. As you may know, in two days, we're having the funeral service for President Farnum. What hasn't been released for security reasons is that there will be a second memorial ceremony in the House Chamber."

David leaned forward. "Peggy, I'd like you to lead us in prayer in the Chamber. They'll be media coverage. With 15 minutes of fame, the bishop may find it harder to stick it to you. If you accept, you'll have two days to prepare the most important sermon of your life."

𝔅𝔒 𝔒𝔒 ℭ𝔒 ℭ𝔒

One of the first things a president is required to do when entering office is to establish a funeral plan should he pass away. This plan is maintained and updated periodically, even after the president leaves office. In the last few decades, almost all of the presidential funeral plans included a casket being carried along Pennsylvania Avenue on the same caisson that bore Abraham Lincoln and John Kennedy. This was usually followed by lying in state in the Rotunda as visitors passed by. Farnum's funeral service followed these traditions.

Once this phase was complete and President Farnum's body was on its way to his home state, the second ceremony began. As the participants entered the Chamber, they realized the House of Representatives was no longer a legislative meeting room. It was a blackened cavern. Despite having all the loose debris removed and the atmosphere specially filtered to remove any toxins, the air still smelled of burnt wood, as if someone had just put out a large campfire. This smell would haunt David for years to come.

421

Despite seeing photographs and trying to mentally prepare himself, it was still a shock. David looked around the room, which once had been so familiar. He imagined seeing the large portrait of Lafayette on the side wall, which was now no more than ashes.

David placed a memorial wreath on a stand where the well of the chamber had once been. Others had suggested a serviceman perform the actual physical task, but David insisted on doing it himself.

Peggy Garthwell began the service with a prayer, followed by a short but stirring sermon. Despite security objections, all three senators and five representatives attended. Justice Sisk, having now recovered from the flu, also attended. David then stepped to the microphone.

"Today, we grieve deeply, more deeply than we could ever have imagined. We mourn not just those we lost. We mourn what we've taken for granted. We will mourn beyond today into a multitude of tomorrows. This is a time we look inside ourselves and discover what we are made of. The question is what will we find? Strength comes from being tested. It can be no other way."

"This is not just a meeting room where a legislature met. This room, along with the Senate Chamber, are the expressions and instruments of our democracy and freedom. All nations must be governed. But instead of kings or dictators, our Founding Fathers chose the people as final arbiters of disagreement. The people chose those who sat in this chamber, and they will again."

"As deeply as we mourn them, and as hard as it might be to admit, the men and women who died here were not irreplaceable, but rather an indispensible link in a historic chain, stretching from our Founding Fathers into an unknowable, but optimistic, future. And I doubt those who died here would want it any other way. We will never forget, *because* we will endure."

He stepped back, bowed his head, and then pulled Sara aside. "Look around," he whispered.

"I know it's awful," Sara agreed.

"That's not what I mean. Look with your architect eyes. How long would it take to rebuild and restore the Chamber?"

"It's hard to say."

"Could it be done in two months?"

"That would be really difficult."

"Maybe three? Could *you* do it in three months?"

"Me?"

"You're certainly qualified. You designed the Centrist offices. You know the bones of this building."

"Can you do that? What about the separation of the branches of government?"

David nodded. "I think so. I've decided what I want to do with my presidency. It'll be difficult, just like rebuilding this chamber. It'll be like jumping out of a plane, not completely confident the parachute will open. But I have to do it. And I need you with me."

CHAPTER 71

At the end of the memorial ceremony, David invited Grace Wilcox and Dennis Ogden back to the White House. The two senators seemed surprised, but welcomed the opportunity to meet with the President.

Once they arrived at the White House, they were escorted into the Oval Office and offered coffee.

"The ceremony was simple, yet very touching, Mr. President," Wilcox said.

"Yes, very dignified," Ogden agreed.

"Thank you," David said.

There was an awkward silence, not borne of conflict, but of the emotional time they had been through. David gestured them to sit.

"I've spoken with a number of the governors," David finally said. "We expect the first new senators to be announced within a few days. I'm assuming you two will be the Majority and Minority Leaders. Obviously, we have no idea which of you will be which, perhaps not even until the last senator is appointed. I hope we can all work well together, regardless of which way it turns out. Even without a quorum, there's no reason the Judiciary Committee can't start having hearings."

"You mean to confirm a vice president?" Ogden said.

"Yes."

"May I ask who you have in mind?" Wilcox asked.

"Zeke Collier."

The two senators looked at each other.

"I don't think he'll have any trouble being confirmed," Wilcox said.

"I agree. He's a sturdy choice," Ogden added. "Of course, then comes the issue of the Supreme Court."

The elephant in the room had been revealed.

"That's where I'd like your assistance. I know Supreme Court nominees receive the highest amount of scrutiny, even more than vice president. Hearings for seven nominees could take months and months, if we follow the usual process.

"The usual process?" Ogden asked. "Mr. President, I appreciate your position, especially as we are partly responsible for putting you in it. However, the risk of packing the court is too great. All nominees will have to be carefully vetted."

"But what if you two were the ones to pack the court?"

"I'm not sure I follow," Wilcox said.

"I'd like you two to submit names for consideration, three potential nominees for each seat, which means 21 potential nominees overall. From those 21, I'll choose seven. I want to nominate three centrist justices, along with two liberals and two conservatives."

"What if we don't agree?" Ogden asked, "I mean with one another, on the specific nominees?"

David smiled. "I suggest good faith negotiation and compromise. I know it's an old-fashioned idea, but I thought we could give it a try."

"That's very generous, Mr. President. I'm certainly open to that approach."

"Me, too." Wilcox added.

"Excellent. There was one other thing. In exchange, I want to ask your support on another matter. Even with special elections, I expect we won't have a full Congress for two to three months. Obviously, a quorum would be achieved before then. However, I'd like the Architect of the Capitol appointed immediately, with the mission of restoring the House Chamber before then. In this case, it makes perfect sense to have a real architect running things."

"We have a number of candidates," Wilcox said.

"Actually, I have just one," David said

"Who?"

"Her name is Sara Grant."

"Your wife?" Ogden asked, frowning.

"She's completely qualified, and she'll work *pro bono*," David insisted. "She's a Senior Architect at a firm that does this type of work. Becoming First Lady against her will has forced her to go on an unexpected, unpaid leave. Her world has been turned upside down. Once the chamber is restored, she could step down, unless the congressional leadership prefers she stay."

Wilcox and Ogden looked at each other, puzzled.

"Think of it this way," David continued. "You'll have a hand in choosing seven Supreme Court Justices who'll serve for life. And I choose one congressional administrator, who may step down after a few months. Seems like a pretty good deal to me."

"No offense, Mr. President," Ogden said. "This seems like an incredible waste of your political capital. What's the catch?"

"None. We create a balanced Supreme Court. My wife has something to do, worthy of her talents. The House Chamber is restored. It's a win-win for all of us. See how easy things are when cooperation replaces partisanship?"

ৰু ৰ ৫৪ ৫৪

David had a similar meeting with the surviving representatives of the House. A few days later, Sara Grant was appointed Architect of the Capital. She immediately transformed the East Wing into an *ad hoc* architectural firm. She engaged the services of Gunther & Cartwright, as well as other firms, *pro bono*. Each donated their services in exchange for being able to claim they helped rebuild the House Chamber.

While Sara was busy in the East Wing, David was twice as busy in the West Wing. The few current members of Congress were frequently invited for cocktails or dinner. Some referred to it as President Grant's charm offensive. As each new Senator was appointed, David invited him or her to the Oval Office, just as Gregory Farnum had done with him years before. Each visitor was made to seem of special interest to the President.

Once a couple of dozen senators were sworn in, hearings began to confirm Zeke Collier as the next Vice President of the United States. The hearing went quite smoothly and lasted less than two days, partly because of Collier's reputation and popularity, but also few of the new senators had the experience to rigorously interrogate a legend. Once the Senate had a quorum, Collier was confirmed.

In an East Room ceremony, Zeke Collier was sworn in, followed by a modest reception. At the end of the event, David pulled Sara aside.

"Say, Mrs. Grant, what do say we blow this pop stand?"

She laughed. "Are you feeling okay?" she asked, smiling at her husband's buoyant demeanor.

"Better than I've felt in days. I want to take you out to dinner."

"Out? As in *out* out?"

"Yes, there's a nice restaurant called *Le Chevalier*. I've only been there once, but I thought we could eat there tonight."

"Really?" Sara asked in a skeptical tone. "What about the Secret Service?"

"They can get their own dinner."

"I mean isn't that a tremendous security risk."

"Oh that?" he chuckled. "Haven't you heard? I have a Vice President now. Once again, there's a proper line of succession. So tonight, it's you and me. Okay, you, me, and a Secret Service detail."

ೞ ೱ) ೦ ೞ

For the first time since the memorial service, the Presidential limousine rolled down Pennsylvania Avenue. However, no presidential seal adorned the side. No motorcycles led the way. This was as discreet as a motorcade could be. However, streets were still cordoned off at the precise moment to allow the motorcade to pass.

Despite the seemingly impromptu nature of this excursion, it had been well planned. The Secret Service had been posted in the restaurant's kitchen, monitoring deliveries all day. The reservations for that night were recorded and screened. No sudden new, last-minute reservations were allowed. This was not as much of an imposition as it would sound. Given the state of morale in Washington, reservations had been off anyway. The fact there were 639 fewer prominent customers in Washington didn't help business either.

The staff at *Le Chevalier* was told the Secret Service was securing the restaurant for a visiting foreign dignitary. A prime minister was alluded to.

However, the owner of *Le Chevalier* was a Washington veteran and guessed the true identity of the "dignitary."

The maître'd was only told their true identity moments before David and Sara's arrival.

"Good evening, Mr. President, Mrs. Grant," the seasoned maître'd said. "We've prepared a special table for you."

As they walked through the dining room, one of the few diners stood up and started to clap. The other diners followed her example.

David was shocked. He had never had a standing ovation before. This was his first time in an even slightly public place since becoming President. He was grateful it wasn't boos and hisses.

"Thank you," he called out.

Sara whispered, "Shouldn't you go over and shake some hands? Isn't that what politicians are supposed to do?"

David gave her an embarrassed look.

"Go ahead," she said, smiling.

၈ဝ ၈ဝ ၐ ၏

Tyler Benson walked quickly along Pennsylvania Avenue toward *Le Chevalier*. As he approached, a tall Secret Service agent blocked his way.

"Please, I need to give this note to the President."

"What makes you think the President is here?" Agent Ross asked.

"The Secret Service has a unique presence," Tyler lied. "It's urgent the President get this note. You can give it to him yourself."

"Sir, we don't pass notes to the President from unknown parties."

"I'm not unknown. I used to work for David Grant when he was a congressman. You don't want to give him the note? Fine. Then, you read it," Tyler said, shoving the note into the agent's face.

Agent Ross's eyes widened slightly as he read the brief note. He turned to the agent next to him. "Detain this man."

Ross quickly headed inside the restaurant. He approached the table as quickly as he could without arousing attention.

"Excuse me, Mr. President," Ross began. "I deeply apologize for interrupting your evening. This note was given to me by a gentleman outside," he said, as he passed the note to David. "I believed it prudent to take the message seriously."

He read the note and frowned.

"What is it?" Sara asked.

"Um." He looked up at Agent Ross. Then, he looked back to Sara. "National security." He looked back to Ross. "Is the man still outside?"

"Yes, sir."

"Do you have a piece of paper?"

Agent Ross checked his pockets. "Just a card."

"That'll do."

Ross pulled a business card out of his pocket and handed it to him. David scribbled a note on the back and handed it to Ross. "Give this note to the gentleman."

"Yes, sir."

He turned back to Sara. "So tell me how the House renovation is going?"

Sara wasn't sure what had just transpired, but decided not to pursue it.

"Well, we've had a break," she explained. "While the chamber walls were completely charred, there was little in the way of major structural damage, outside of the ceiling where the missile came through. The Architect's staff has been very helpful. They have kept excellent records on the materials used. We're finalizing the materials order this week."

"I've also commissioned some preliminary concept development for a large memorial plaque, something artistic yet tasteful."

"Good."

"We should go," Sara said.

"What? Why?" David stammered. "You haven't finished your meal."

"You're pre-occupied. You're waiting politely, but you're really chomping at the bit to attend to whatever that note was about."

൝ ൝ ൮ ൮

For the last few days Fred Arkin had been floating in and out of a fog-like consciousness. He remembered being told he had been in an accident. The new nurse came in. Another *ghost in the fog*. She was younger than the other ghosts.

"Oh, I didn't know you were awake." The nurse seemed slightly nervous. "It's time to change your bandages," she said, reaching for the pain pump.

The fog maker. "No, don't," he commanded. "Don't touch it."

"Mr. Arkin, you've been in a lot of pain."

"Change the bandages, but I want to see. Get me a mirror," Fred insisted.

The nurse reluctantly retrieved a small shaving mirror. Although not pretty, the burns were not as severe as he had expected. Though burned, he still recognized the face in the mirror as his own.

"What happened?"

"You don't know? I'm new to the burn unit. They needed the extra help with all the additional patients. I'm not sure it's my place—."

"Just tell me," he snapped.

"There was a terrible explosion at the Capitol. So many people died, the President, all the others. The burn unit is completely full."

Fred's mind reeled. *My God. David? Ellen? The new representatives?*

"Who else died?" he asked.

The nurse explained as she changed the bandages. His face and arm stung as she treated the burnt skin, but the news was more painful.

"If the Vice President and the Speaker are dead, who's the new president?"

"Someone I never heard before, some guy named Grant, you know like Ulysses S."

"David Grant is President?"

"Yes," she said as she finished the last bandage.

A bizarre chill engulfed him. "Where are my clothes?" he asked, as he struggled to stand up. He was far weaker than he expected. Fred walked to the closet with difficulty and pulled it open to find it empty.

"Mr. Arkin, you're in no shape—" she protested.

"Where are my clothes?" he insisted loudly.

"They were likely cut off in the emergency room. Now, Mr. Arkin—."

"Where's a phone?"

ஐ ஐ ෬ ෬

David and Sara were sitting in back of the limousine, returning to the White House. "I'm sorry about our big night out," David said. "That note was really unexpected."

"What was that? Are we being invaded or something?" Sara asked.

"Invaded? Hmm, you might say that." David just realized how that sounded, given he was now President. "No, no one's invading us, but I think I just figured out how Chuck Danzig at Winton knew about Armand Nistle visiting me here in Washington."

He picked up the phone that connected to Amy Greene's desk.

"Amy?...I'm glad I caught you before you went home. I have just one thing I'd like you to do before leaving. Call US Attorney Kevin O'Hara. Have him in my office at ten o'clock tomorrow morning."

CHAPTER 72

Fred's cell phone turned out to be damaged. He couldn't access the numbers on his speed dial list. He tried to call the 20th District office, but there was nothing but a recorded message. *Everyone's probably moved over to the White House.* After calling around, he was finally able to reach an acquaintance on the energy committee, a staffer named Tim.

Fred arranged for Tim to bring some clothes to the hospital early the next morning. Tim, like most congressional personnel, had little to do these days. He filled Fred in on what had been happening from the perspective of a congressional staffer. Many on the Hill had come to refer to their workplace as the "Ghost Capitol" due to the lack of bosses or activity.

Quickly, Fred checked himself out of the hospital against doctor's orders. Even Tim tried to talk him out of it. After he went home to his apartment, showered and changed into more suitable clothes, he called a cab.

The driver looked nervously in the rearview mirror as he eyed this man with bandages on half his face.

Trying to sound normal, Fred asked the cabbie, "So, what do you think of this new President?"

"I don't know, but he nabbed them terrorists in just a few days. Took us ten years to get bin Laden. Right? What about you? Think he's gonna be a good president?"

"Actually," Fred said, "I do."

ຄ ຄ ແ ຕ

Tyler Benson showed up at the White House gate early. He decided to walk around the perimeter of the grounds until his appointment. When his appointment time came closer, he stepped up to the gatehouse and nervously gave his name to the uniformed guard, who looked down at a computer screen.

"Yes, Mr. Benson," the guard said, checking his visitors list, "we've been expecting you. Please step through the gate and we'll have an escort take you in."

After a series of security checkpoints, Tyler was surprised to be taken straight to the Oval Office.

"Tyler, it's good to see you," David said warmly. "Thank you for stopping by, both this morning and last night." He gestured toward another man. "I'd like you to meet US Attorney Kevin O'Hara." David turned to O'Hara. "Tyler was my legislative assistant in Congress, but he's been working for Kripke Associates for over a year now. And I believe he has some information he wants to share."

They sat down on the sofa.

Tyler took a small cleansing breath. "Are you familiar with *Le Chevalier?*"

"The restaurant? Yes," O'Hara said, "I've eaten there several times."

"Through a series of shell companies, Jack Kripke owns *Le Chevalier.* He pretends to be a friend of the owner whom he wants to help out by driving business there. He passes out discount cards to Capitol Hill staffers and others. I've recently discovered he's been electronically monitoring and recording the private dinner conversations of various guests, specifically lawmakers and their staffs."

"Mr. President," O'Hara asked, "did you know about this?"

"I only learned about it last night when Tyler sent me a note warning me while my wife and I were dining there."

"Let me get this straight," O'Hara said. "Jack Kripke, one of the most influential lobbyists in DC, was bugging the President of the United States?"

"I assume so," Tyler answered. "I have no direct evidence, but Kripke has been eavesdropping on senators, representatives and staffers for years. The restaurant is practically one giant microphone. If he had the chance, why would he forego doing the same to the new President?"

O'Hara turned back to David. "Mr. President, did you and your wife discuss anything particularly sensitive last night?"

"Thanks to Tyler's actions, nothing so sensitive it couldn't become public. I believe Kripke is connected to a large network of individuals who have been manipulating the Federal government for a long time. I spoke to you about this last year at Zeke Collier's party."

"Mr. President, this is an unbelievable revelation," O'Hara said. "I'm counting the potential felonies in my head, but we must proceed carefully. There may be national security information involved, depending on who he recorded. Then, there's the question of whether Kripke has ever blackmailed any of these lawmakers."

"I hadn't even thought of that," David admitted.

"I don't know that he has," Tyler added. "I think he just uses the information to make decisions about who to support."

"I suggest," O'Hara said, "Mr. Benson and I should have some long private conversations."

"Very well." David said. "I'll leave it in your hands, but keep me advised."

ဆ ဆ ભ ભ

After another security briefing, David moved on to a legislative planning session. Just as noon arrived, he finished explaining the strategy and intent of his first bill to Zeke Collier, Marcus Finn, Ellen Langford, Dana Seagram and Taylor Whitcomb. "As you can guess, this will be a shock to everyone."

"Mr. President," Seagram said, "That's an understatement. Make no mistake, this will trigger a firestorm."

David smiled and nodded his head. "If it didn't, a previous president would have done it. Do you want to talk me out of it?"

"No, sir," she said. "However, might it be better to initiate this bill closer to the end of your presidency, after you've built up some political capital?"

"Even I know a president has less power at the end of his term," David said. "The time is now."

"Mr. President," Whitcomb inquired, "why are you cutting out the Office of Legislative Affairs?"

"Well," David said, "as Dana previously pointed out, this may be a very leak-prone White House. You're the President's lawyer, so I assume you're bound by client-attorney confidentiality, but I can't say the same about Legislative Affairs."

"We'll need to keep this under wraps," Ellen added, looking at the others. "No one outside of this room can know until the President is ready to announce it. Legislative Affairs will be brought in as soon as the announcement is made."

"What do you think, Marcus?" David asked the retired congressman, who had been sitting, thinking quietly.

"It's risky," Finn said, shaking his head. "It's dangerous." Then he leaned forward and smiled. "And I want to be a part of it. How can I help, Mr. President?"

"The best way might be for you to go home—"

"Go home?"

"Yes, and run for Congress again. We could use someone on our side on the Hill. How do you stand with the Wisconsin Republicans?"

Finn exhaled in despair. "I'm afraid that's a burned bridge for this old RINO. The state chair hates my guts."

"That's a shame," David said, disappointed.

"But," Finn said in an exploratory tone, "I could run as a Centrist. Hell, who's going to oppose me in the primary?"

David smiled. "Well, I think I can guarantee a presidential endorsement, maybe even a campaign stop or two."

"Can you loan me my old chief of staff?" Finn said, looking over at Ellen.

"Afraid not. I need her here."

Amy peeked through the Oval Office door. "Excuse me, Mr. President."

"Yes, Amy."

"I'm sorry to disturb you, but the Secret Service called from the side gate. There's a man at the gate demanding to see you."

"There are always people at the gate," David said. He was surprised Amy, a White House veteran, would interrupt a meeting for this sort of thing.

"I recognized the name, sir," Amy explained. "He claims to be the man in the hospital, the one you had me check on, Fred Arkin. The guard said he's wearing bandages."

ဆ ဆ ဆ ဆ

A few minutes later, Fred Arkin had been brought into the Oval Office. Despite having seen Fred on the gurney on the night of the Capitol attack, David was shocked at his current appearance.

"Fred, you should be in the hospital. What the hell are you doing here?"

Fred turned and looked around at the furnishings.

"I see you finally moved out of that cramped attic office in the Cannon building," Fred joked. "I like the new digs." However, Fred could see the serious expression on David's face. "*Mister President*, you've got something big planned. And I want to be part of it. I just thought I'd stop by and tell you, whatever you need, I'm yours to command."

David wanted to hug his old friend, but with his burns, he decided it would be a bad idea.

"The President commands you to sit down. You look like you're going to collapse."

"I sit when the President sits. I learned that at some protocol seminar last year."

"The President is sitting," David said, as he guided Fred to the sofa. "Sit."

Fred sighed. "Well, just a moment to catch my breath."

David was impressed with how brave Fred seemed. "How do you feel?"

"Ready to go. Whatever you need."

"Rule number one in this White House," David said, "Never bullshit the President. I'm serious."

Fred sighed again. "Yes, I have some pain. But I can't sit in that damn hospital while you're fighting the good fight. That…that would kill me."

"What makes you think I'm fighting any kind of fight?"

"Now, who's bullshitting? You're David Grant. You were the lowliest of congressmen, but you kicked their asses when needed. You beat those bastards at their own game. You created the position of Second Minority Leader." Fred coughed, and had to take a breath. He looked David straight in the eye. "And I helped. Now, you're in the driver's seat." Fred leaned forward, wincing as he did so. "So what's the plan?"

ဆ ဆ ဆ ဆ

The following day, Jason Kennerly walked into the bar at a small hotel a few blocks from the White House. He immediately spotted Ellen.

"Ellen, it's good to see you," he said, as he sat down at her booth. "How's David doing?"

"The *President* is well."

"I'm curious. Why aren't we meeting at the White House?" Jason asked, obviously disappointed.

"There's a visitor registry at the White House. The President is going to be under a lot of scrutiny in the coming months. He wants to be seen as being as non-partisan as possible. A visit from the Chair of the Centrist Patriot Party might contradict that. However, he wants me to impress upon you the importance of getting Centrist candidates elected in the upcoming special elections."

"Easier said than done. Our best people were wiped out. I liked the line in the President's speech about having 'a deep bench,' but that doesn't apply to the Centrist Party."

"But there were other candidates."

"Yeah, the ones who lost back in November. The only one who might have a chance is Serena Brooks from Washington State. She almost won back in November. But that's it."

"Well, good news. My old boss, Marcus Finn, will be running as a Centrist in Wisconsin. He has the best chance of winning because of name recognition in his state. But he'll need financing. Is Marshall Vreeland still excited about Centrist politics?"

"I don't know. Marshall was pretty upset about losing, despite David repeatedly warning him he wasn't going to win."

"Well, tell Vreeland his President needs him. Ask him if he could financially support them."

"Okay, fine. Serena Brooks and this Marcus Flynn. That's two. *Maybe*."

"Marcus *Finn*," Ellen corrected him. "Reach out to the other centrist parties, like the Modern Whigs, the Reform Party, and any others you can think of. Maybe they have some candidates."

"Those guys never wanted to talk to us very much."

"Well, you have the President of the United States in your party now. I think they'll be somewhat interested in what you have to say. See what viable candidates they have. Maybe suggest a merger. The President worked his butt off last time. He needs reinforcements, because this time, he's putting it all on the line."

"What do you mean, *all on the line*?"

༄ ༄ ༄ ༄

The following month seemed a blur in Washington. In another East Room ceremony, seven new Supreme Court Justices were sworn in. David publicly praised Senators Ogden and Wilcox for their hard work in facilitating the process.

As the new senators were selected and sworn in, the Senate returned to Democratic control. However, as the special elections proceeded, it was clear the House of Representatives was going Republican. Angela Barone became the new Speaker of the House. Six centrist candidates were elected, all running under the new banner of the United Centrist Coalition, including Marcus Finn, who became the new Second Minority Leader.

Meanwhile, Sara and her army of architects, contractors and craftsmen worked day and night to complete the reconstruction of the House Chamber. Everything had to be in place and ready for May 3rd.

433

"Good evening, I'm Bob Summers. Tonight, May 3rd, is exactly three months since the Capitol Attack. President David Grant, who almost literally rose out of the ashes of that disaster, will address Congress for the first time tonight. Technically this is not a State of the Union speech, but it does bear the solemnity of one, especially as the official period of mourning ends at midnight."

"This will be the first speech given in the House Chamber since that horrible night. Although some finishing touches are still to be completed, the Chamber has been functionally restored under the supervision of Sara Grant, a woman who bears the dual titles of First Lady and Architect of the Capitol. The consensus is Mrs. Grant has performed a monumental task in cutting through the red tape and restoring the House Chamber and surrounding rooms in an incredibly short period of time."

"Joining us tonight is Washington Bureau Chief Dylan Reese. Dylan, a lot has happened in the last three months. How would you describe this unsettled period?"

"Well Bob, we all remember the initial shock. President Grant didn't simply rise from the ashes, he walked into a constitutional crisis. Since then, the government has existed in a bizarre limbo."

"This lack of certainty revolved around three things. First was the legitimacy of David Grant's presidency, given he was never in the line of succession. For days there was niggling unease about whether a congressional leader or cabinet secretary, someone higher in the line of succession, would be discovered unconscious in a hospital somewhere. That never happened."

"The second concern was over how David Grant might use his presidency, especially given the complete collapse of the other two branches of government. According to many accounts, he has been painfully aware of this and therefore has issued a minimum of executive orders. He worked closely with Senators Wilcox and Ogden, now the Majority and Minority Leaders, to reconstruct a balanced Supreme Court. Everyone seems to give him high marks for not overreaching."

"The third concern is what kind of president will he become? Many suspect the caretaker phase is over, and he's now ready to begin his presidency in full, tonight. This concern has been exacerbated by the fact that the press did not receive the usual advanced copy of the President's speech."

"Excuse me, Dylan," Summers interrupted, "We have word that the President has arrived."

The video feed cut to the wide shot of the House chamber and then to the entrance to the House Floor.

"Here we see Daryl McClennon," Summers announced, "the new Congressional Sergeant at Arms."

"Mr. Speaker," McClennon called out, "The President of the United States!"

CHAPTER 73

David walked through the applauding Congress, shaking hands with those who had waited for hours in an aisle seat for a fleeting photo opportunity with the new President. *The relentless pursuit of optics.*

David knew all too well the standing ovation was perfunctory. It was protocol, not necessarily any personal affection for him.

The Presidency had been a surreal experience. Although David had spoken in the House Chamber before, it had usually been only for the benefit of a handful of representatives and a C-SPAN camera. But doing so as President was a new level of surrealism. The presidential butterflies fluttered.

Despite this, he walked confidently up to the central podium and shook hands with Vice President Collier and Speaker Barone. David turned to the applauding audience and held up his hands to tamp down the applause. *And now to jump out of the plane without a parachute.*

"Good evening, my fellow Americans, Mr. Vice President, Madame Speaker, members of Congress and honored guests. Tonight marks the end of the official period of mourning for all those who lost their lives on this very spot on February 3rd, although, let's be honest, unofficial mourning will continue for quite some time. Three months ago, two men attempted to topple our republic. But you cannot destroy our republic as long as the people's determination and love of freedom endures."

Another standing ovation erupted.

"I'd like to take a moment to thank someone without whom we might not be able to gather here tonight: my wife, Sara Grant. I asked Sara to take on the monumental task of rebuilding this room and the adjacent damaged areas. Sara wasn't sure she could do it. But she did it." David looked up at his wife in the gallery. "Sara, I am so proud of you."

Another ovation erupted as everyone stood and looked up at Sara.

"Sara is the only woman I know who, with such grace and poise, could upstage the President of the United States at a congressional address."

The room laughed.

David and Sara stared at each other with great pride in one another. He was now ready to jump out of the airplane. Sara was his parachute. He waited for the audience to settle down.

"You have questions about me, an unelected, unconfirmed president. And so you should. What will my policies be? What road will I lead the country along? These questions are normal and cause a bit of anxiety. But they shouldn't. They shouldn't because our most powerful guide should not be a president's personal will, but rather the Constitution."

"Our Constitution begins with the most important words that separate us from tyranny. Those words are 'We the People.' *We...the...People!* Not we the lobbyists. Not we the corporations. Not we the unions. Not we the moneyed special interest groups. And *certainly not* we the super-PACs."

"However, in pursuit of political advantage, many have forgotten that. The people have been de-prioritized, supplanted by political factions and parties. That…ends…tonight."

"For my first piece of legislation, I offer to Congress and the American people the Democracy Restoration Act. For too long, we have allowed powerful lobbying groups to dominate lawmaking and hold elections hostage for individual advantage over the general welfare."

"Don't misunderstand me. Lobbying is the right of every individual and group that peaceably assembles for a redress of grievances. Our First Amendment guarantees it. And I would have it no other way."

"However, despite the 2010 *Citizens United* Supreme Court decision, campaign contributions are not exactly free speech. They're more accurately described as a form of bribery. Oh yes, it's been all or mostly legal, and that makes the corruption that much more insidious. The cleverness of lawyers, lobbyists and politicians has drowned out the voice of the people."

"How is it that 90 percent of Americans want a balanced budget, and yet pork-barrel spending continues to explode?

"How is it that 90 percent of Americans, including members of the NRA, favor universal background checks for gun purchases, yet no lawmaker dares to put forth such legislation?"

"How is it that most Americans want a cleaner energy policy, yet oil companies continue to receive tax breaks and subsidies? The list goes on and on."

"The answer is the same in each case: *moneyed special interest groups*. How can we tackle the tough and complex issues, when the decision process is polluted with bribery and manipulation?"

"At least a third of a legislator's time is devoted, not to the people's business, but to campaign fundraising. The People pay our salaries. And I think they deserve our full-time attention, not just two thirds. The rationalization for the excessive fundraising has been the enormous cost of running for political office. Yet, how absurd is this in the age of the Internet, social media and other ubiquitous media channels? It should cost less, not more. But it doesn't, because it's a financial arms race, super-PAC versus super-PAC. Let's have the courage to fix this."

"Under the Democracy Restoration Act, no organization of *any* type will be allowed to donate to the campaign of any candidate, thus subverting an election. The ability of individuals to donate to an election campaign will be limited to $5000. Organizations will still be free to express themselves publicly on issues, but may not endorse or oppose a candidate in their advertising, explicitly or suggestively."

"But embers of Congress, be warned. Tomorrow morning, every lobbyist will be calling, promising or threatening all sorts of things to persuade you to vote against this bill. Voting for this legislation will require courage."

"Courage is not about confidence in your likely success. Courage is about confidence in the righteousness of your position. So I say to you, have courage."

"If our Congress cannot be free, how can our people? The People's Voice must be restored."

හ හ ශ ශ

Early the next morning. Jack Kripke was in his office, watching the morning news, while writing on his laptop.

"Last night during the State of the Union," the morning newscaster proclaimed, "political observers witnessed a seismic event."

No one in Congress was commenting publicly. Kripke was disturbed by the radio silence. *What happened to the loyal opposition?* By his reckoning, there should have been a double helping.

"President Grant effectively declared war on K-Street," the co-anchor added.

"No shit," Kripke muttered, as he tried to focus on writing talking points. The telephone rang. His secretary wasn't in yet. Kripke assumed it was probably a reporter looking for a comment. He ignored it.

Soon after, his secretary arrived. "Good morning, Jack."

"Thanks for coming in early, Alice. It's gonna be a day."

The telephone rang again.

"Kripke & Associates," Alice answered. "How may I help you? ...I'll see if he's in yet. Please hold."

"Jack," his secretary interrupted, "I have Mr. Cornwall on line one."

"Thank you, Alice."

Kripke hesitated. Ellis Cornwall almost never called him directly. He picked up the receiver.

"Good morning, Mr. Cornwall."

"Really? You really think it's a *good* morning? I assume you saw the President's speech last night."

"Of course, I did. I'm writing up talking points to counter him now."

"Talking points? There's only one point, one strategy. Tar and feather that bastard in the White House. He has got to go!"

"Ellis, I've been spending the last three months building relationships with all the new members of Congress with a special eye toward promoting a new education bill."

"My God, you're a shit-for-brains."

Kripke had never heard Cornwall swear before.

"To hell with the education bill. The goal is to get Grant impeached!"

Suddenly Kripke heard Alice yell out, "You can't go in there."

He was in shock as two FBI agents pushed through the doorway.

"Jack Kripke, we have a warrant for your arrest," the lead agent informed him, as he took the receiver from Kripke's hand and placed handcuffs on his wrists.

"What the hell is this about?" he demanded, as Kevin O'Hara stepped through the door.

"We're also executing a search warrant for *Le Chevalier*," O'Hara said. "I sure hope there's nothing there that would incriminate you."

The color drained out of Kripke's face.

"By the way, I wonder if any of your clients are foreign," O'Hara said with satisfied smile. "I really hope so, because I've never had the opportunity to try an espionage case before."

O'Hara turned to the agent. "Please read Mr. Kripke his rights."

ଓ ଓ ଔ ଔ

Ed Leems called an emergency meeting of the Democratic National Committee and other leading Democrats.

"The President is trying to turn everything upside down," Leems complained, as he waited for the last members to arrive. "To commemorate the attack, that bastard set off another bomb."

"Easy, Ed," said one of the committee members.

"Don't worry. It's unconstitutional," the DNC Treasurer assured him. "Don't forget *Citizens United*. The Supreme Court ruled that money is an expression of free speech. Even if this thing passes—and it won't—the bill will be shot down in court."

This just made Leems angrier. "Are you an idiot? Have you failed to notice the President just packed the Court?"

"Didn't he delegate that to Grace Wilcox?"

"Yeah, and to that GOP turd, Ogden. Speaking of which, where the hell is Wilcox?"

Clay, the head researcher, walked in with a pile of thick folders.

"It's about time, Clay," Leems snapped. "Have you gotten anything on these new Justices?"

"Yeah, we've been up all night." Clay said, as he dropped the folders on the conference table. "At various times, five of the seven have made public statements opposing the *Citizens United* decision. The other two have never publicly commented."

"But I'm willing to bet Grant asked each nominee about *Citizens United*," one of the committee members said.

"You think?" Leems asked sarcastically. "That bastard packed the court. I know it!" He noticed Grace Wilcox walking in at the moment. "And you helped!"

"Hey, easy," the treasurer said.

"And good morning to you, Ed," Wilcox said, throwing her coat on the back of a chair. "Yes, apparently President Grant had a litmus test we didn't realize."

"You have to kill this legislation," Leems demanded. "Democracy Restoration Act indeed. What hubris! As Majority Leader you can prevent this bill from ever coming to a vote."

"Actually, I sort of like the idea of not having to spend so much time fundraising and—"

"You can't be serious!" Leems spat. "You know the Republicans can outspend us."

"Yeah, through super-PACs," Wilcox countered. "Ed, have you looked at the polling? Before last night, Grant had an 83 percent approval rating. After last night, I'm sure it's going higher. Do you remember what Congress's approval rating was back in November? Three percent! Maybe we should take the hint. Grant has given us a chance to make politics a noble profession again."

"Great, delusions of nobility!"

"Ed," pleaded the treasurer, "chill out, or your blood pressure's gonna pop your head right off."

"Okay, okay" Leems said, raising his hands, trying to calm himself down. He turned back to Wilcox. "Listen, I understand it was important to support the President in a national crisis. But now, it's back to business."

"You mean business as usual," Wilcox said.

"Listen, you could have saved us this entire nightmare. In fact, you could have been President, if you had the balls to grab for it."

Wilcox bristled at Leems's words. "May I remind you, you're speaking to the Senate Majority Leader."

"Sure, you're Majority Leader, not because you really earned it. You just didn't happen to die like everybody else. If you want the support to stay Majority Leader, you had better toe the line...*Senator*."

"You know, Ed, I think you've been in this job too long. You've forgotten there's a difference between governing and electioneering. But if all you care about is elections, take solace in this: Four years from now, Grant won't get a second term because he doesn't have the political infrastructure."

Leems laughed. "We dismissed Grant three years ago as a rank amateur. Not only did he get himself elected, he later got three others elected. Now there are *six* Centrists in the House, infecting Congress like a damn virus! Who knows how many next time around? His party almost cost us the presidential election last November. Grant leveraged that into becoming Second Minority Leader. And now, his party is merging with other third parties. This plague is mutating!"

"Republicans *and* Centrists," another committee member called out. "We can't fight a two-front war,"

"Why does it always have to be war? David Grant is a decent man," Wilcox insisted. "At least he's not one of those GOP yahoos."

"Funny you should mention our Republican brethren. I spoke with Russell Beacham over at the RNC earlier. In a rare case of bipartisanship, we agree we have common ground in opposing this bill."

"Oh, great. You won't support a moderate president," Wilcox said with disgust, "but you're jumping into bed with the GOP?"

"Grant is no moderate. He's a radical centrist. Oh, and by the way," Leems added, "in regard to your 'difference between governing and electioneering' crack, don't forget, if you don't win your next election, you won't be governing."

⚭ ⚭ ⚮ ⚮

"My fellow patriots," Ben Glendenning called out, "after last night's display, we should be at Defcon 10! That insidious snake who wormed his way into the White House in our most vulnerable hour has finally shown his deadly colors. His proposed bill is tantamount to scraping the First Amendment."

"How dare he quote the Constitution in loving terms as he tries to stomp all over it? Campaign donations are an expression of our political will, our democracy, which he hates so much."

"I am a patriot. And I won't stand for being driven down the road toward tyranny, especially by such a manipulative pretender. He wasn't elected. Who the hell is he to try to subjugate our civil rights?"

"He should be impeached. There, I've said it. And if he won't go, the military should remove him. Why? He wasn't elected!"

"I love this country too much to stay silent," he added. Once again, the camera moved closer for the tear-up.

"We'll be back after these messages."

⚭ ⚭ ⚮ ⚮

"Tonight," Jessica Dandridge announced, "we have as our guest Senator Joe Dreeves, a Liberty Network alumnus." She turned to Dreeves. "Senator, welcome home."

"Thank you, Jessica. It's good to be here."

"Three months ago, you were in 'The Room,' as they say, when David Grant was selected as President, right?"

"Yes, I was," Dreeves said with pride in his voice. "I may have been the only one who wasn't mentally impaired that night."

"Mentally impaired?"

"I don't mean to be insulting. It's just that Grant, Barone, Wilcox and Ogden, all climbed out of the Capitol. I know the White House doctor was very concerned about concussions."

"Well, what about Justice Sisk? She wasn't in the Capitol when the missile hit."

"That's because she had a serious case of the flu. She was barely conscious. At the time, I was against Grant being selected, but I was overruled by a group of people who—let's be honest here—were thoroughly shell shocked, but there was no one I could appeal to. And from last night's performance, we see their selection was deeply flawed."

"In essence," Dandridge added, "this man is trying to undercut the First Amendment. Right? The Supreme Court already ruled that campaign donations are free speech."

"Absolutely," Dreeves agreed, "In the modern world, this is how it's done. This man was not elected. How dare he decide to rewrite the Constitution?"

"Wasn't there anyone else that night?"

"Oh yes, I forgot to mention Harris Carver. I understand he's been diagnosed with PTSD. By the way, why can't anyone find him anywhere? It's like he's been whisked off to some black site."

ಬಿ ಬಿ ಲಿ ಲಿ

Within 24 hours of David's speech, a website had been erected with the domain address, ImpeachGrant.org. Social media was filled with anti-Grant propaganda. Tweets included:

"Grant is the front man for the Illuminati."

"Grant to lead new combined Neo-Nazi-Communist party."

"Grant is creating a constitutional amendment to protect pedophiles."

"David Grant poisoned Robert Hingecliff to become President."

"President Grant plans to impose martial law."

"Grant is the secret grandchild of Hitler and Eva Braun."

ಬಿ ಬಿ ಲಿ ಲಿ

The following morning, David stepped into the White House Press Room.

"Good morning, everyone."

The press corps had been anticipating this moment and quickly settled down. David immediately called on the senior correspondent.

"Mr. President, there are a number of commentators who have equated your proposed legislation to damaging the First Amendment. How do you respond to those charges?"

"I think as a veteran of political journalism, you know that's not true. Look at who are making these charges? People like Ben Glendenning? Mr. Patriot? Let me remind you what a patriot is. A patriot is someone who sacrifices for his or her country, or at least risks something of personal importance. What has Mr. Glendenning ever sacrificed? He's made millions from his barn-burning rhetoric. Patriotism is not shedding a tear for the camera. That's just theatrics. I don't doubt he loves his country. Why not? It's made him quite rich."

David pointed to the next reporter.

"Mr. President," the *Post* reporter said, "Senator Dreeves has made the accusation that those who selected you were mentally or emotionally impaired at the time. What was your assessment?"

"Yes, I've heard about Senator Dreeves's comments. On the night of February 3rd, everyone in the room was in shock. If they weren't, I'd be worried. But everyone was focused and serious, except possibly for him. The only thing Senator Dreeves contributed to the discussion was a suggestion that we cut cards for the presidency."

"The question of where Harris Carver is was also raised."

"Harris was injured. He's recuperating at Bethesda Naval Hospital. I ask that you respect his privacy."

"There are increased calls from both the Left and the Right for you to step down. Some have already suggested impeachment. How do you react to that?"

"By the Left and Right, you mean those who are heavily invested and earn their money from the partisan warfare?"

David held up his hands to delay another question.

"Okay, maybe they're right."

An uncharacteristic silence filled the room. The reporters weren't quite sure what they had just heard.

"How can I operate effectively," David continued, "if every time I make a difficult decision they threaten impeachment because of how I came to become President? The more hysterical and irresponsible individuals will paint me as a dictator. So here's the deal. I'll defer to the American people. If people really want me out, then I'll make it easy for them. What tyrant does that?"

"Congress has to do just two simple things. First," he said, holding up his index finger, "they need to pass the Democracy Restoration Act in full without any alterations. Then, if they want, they can pass a resolution calling for my resignation. No impeachment hearings will be necessary. If they do those two things," David added, holding up two fingers, "I will resign the presidency."

CHAPTER 74

"Mr. President," one reporter finally asked, "are you honestly saying you would resign the presidency?"

"I can't have Congress or others throwing in my face the fact I wasn't elected every time they don't like something I propose," David answered. "In fact, come to think of it, I insist on such a congressional vote. The American people need to be confident of the President's status, one way or the other."

"Mr. President, what if Congress votes against a continuation of your presidency, but doesn't pass your bill?"

"My price for leaving quietly is Congress passing the Democracy Restoration Act."

"Isn't this just a bluff?" one of the younger reporters called out.

"I didn't nominate a lightweight for Vice President," David said. "This is no bluff."

જ જ છ છ

When David returned to the Oval Office, he was surprised to find Sara waiting there. He was having difficulty translating her expression.

"I just heard. Is what the staff told me true? David, would you really resign the presidency?"

"Yes," David admitted, "if that's what it takes to pass the bill. Besides, it would get us back to Embler. You could resume your job at Gunther & Cartwright without any further First Lady complications."

David looked at the shock in Sara's face.

"Uh-oh," David said. "I did it again, didn't I? Let me guess. Simplexia all over again?"

Sara shook her head no. "I'm sorry I've been such a bitch about you becoming president."

She slumped into a chair.

"What?" David didn't expect this reaction. "No, you had every right to be upset at being forced into this. Three months ago, I did what I had to do. I don't apologize for it. But if I can pass this bill, I can leave the Presidency knowing I've left the country better than I found it."

She stood up and put her hands on his face, caressing it lovingly.

"You're wrong, Mr. President. The country won't be better off, not without you."

David started to say something, but Sara put her finger to his lips

"David Grant, I love you. I would hate to be the reason you did this. You're a good man, probably the best that's ever inhabited this office."

"I don't know." David smiled. "Lincoln? Roosevelt? The competition is pretty tough."

443

"So are you."

⁝ ⁝ ⁞ ⁞

"This morning on *American Caucus*," Dylan Reese announced, "we have with us White House Spokesman Fred Arkin."

The camera cut to Fred, who was seated to the right of Reese. This forced the scarred side of his face away from the camera when looking at Reese.

"Mr. Arkin was the Communications Director for *Congressman* David Grant," Reese continued. "He is a survivor of the February 3rd attack on the Capitol. Since leaving the hospital, he has become a Senior Advisor to the President." Reese turned to Fred. "Welcome to the program."

"Thank you, Dylan, for having me."

"First, I have to ask how are you feeling? You were unconscious for quite a while after the bombing."

"I wasn't in a coma," Fred assured him. "The doctors kept me sedated to reduce my pain, but I'm feeling fine now. Thank you."

"You suffered significant burns. Have you fully recovered?"

"Well, as you can see," Fred said, turning his head to provide the camera with a better view of the burned side, "my appearance is a bit like Two-Face from Batman. Sort of a metaphor for politics, don't you think?"

Reese's eyes widened, not expecting that kind of response.

"Are you planning to have cosmetic surgery?"

"I will have some 'work done,' as they say in Hollywood. But for now, I need to serve the President and country. Until then, I'll look in the mirror every morning and see a reminder of the ongoing war for the soul of this country."

"I'm not sure I follow."

"These burns," Fred said, again turning the left side of his face to the camera, "are the scars caused by indifference."

"You mean Narlstrom and Branch's indifference?"

"It goes way beyond them. Ask yourself, what drove them to that point?"

"You're not honestly trying to blame others, are you?"

"Branch and Narlstrom were the direct cause. My anger at them will never die. But every cause, in turn, has another cause. We have to ask ourselves, what would drive two previously patriotic citizens to turn on their government? Branch earned a Purple Heart and numerous other commendations. But after he was wounded, he was cast aside by the government and allowed to be victimized by a corporation that cared only about profit. He should have been protected."

"Daniel Narlstrom worked in the defense industry as an engineer. He lost his job because of congressional infighting. His personal accounts were frozen because of CART. His patents were nullified without proper review. The government wasn't simply indifferent. It was downright callous."

"It sounds like you're excusing these men," Reese observed.

"No, not at all," Fred said. "Understanding is not excusing. Failing to try to understand is just cowardly or lazy."

"Let's turn to the President's proposed legislation." Reese said. "Some have contended the President's bill could be viewed as restricting First Amendment rights. How do you react to that?"

"Quite the opposite. The People's voice has been drowned out by campaign money. Those who oppose the Democracy Restoration Act are on the side of moneyed special interests. It comes down to this: Do we want democracy or oligarchy? The Middle Class is already under enormous pressure to stay afloat. Over the last several decades, most campaign finance reform has been gutted. We finally have a President who's willing to stand up to the super-PACs."

"There are those who will argue," Reese said, "the bill is designed to weaken the two major parties, and that would be a huge benefit to the United Centrist Coalition, which is merging into a single party. Isn't this just a way to provide the Centrists with a political advantage?"

"How is it to David Grant's advantage to offer his resignation to his political rivals? You realize what this means for him? The only other President ever to resign was Nixon. David Grant will share that distinction with Richard Nixon. What president wants that? But David Grant is a patriot. He is willing to sacrifice his presidency for the betterment of our country."

℘ ℘ ℘ ℘

Monday morning, Grace Wilcox and Dennis Ogden arrived at Angela Barone's office.

"Good morning, Madame Speaker," Wilcox said.

"Leader Wilcox. Leader Ogden. Please make yourselves comfortable," Barone said, sounding a bit harried. She handed a briefing book to an assistant. "Please make sure all the Deputy Whips read every line of their respective budgets."

The assistant departed.

"I envy you in the Senate," Barone said. "You've had a two-month jump on us, getting fully organized. Pardon our appearance. We still haven't replaced all the furniture."

"I didn't realize the fire extended to your office," Ogden said.

"It didn't, but there was plenty of smoke damage." Barone collapsed into her chair. "So, I guess we're here to talk about the President's bill. I suppose you saw the performance by Grant's crispy critter?"

There was an awkward silence.

"I'm sorry, that was inappropriate," Barone said. "Mr. Arkin's pain should not be—"

"It's all right." Wilcox said, "Arkin's scar-fest made quite an impact on a great many people."

"Every representative I've spoken to has reported broad constituent support for the President's bill."

"The story's the same in the Senate," Ogden said.

"The public loves it." Wilcox admitted. "Understandably, the lobbyists are going ballistic, and therefore so is our party chair."

"If we don't pass this bill," Ogden admitted, "there might be riots."

"The President has played his hand brilliantly," Wilcox said, "whether he knows it or not. Offering his resignation, that's an original move. I have to admit, I don't yet know how to make all the maneuvers to counter it. I guess I shouldn't admit that."

"Let's be honest." Barone said, "We all received unexpected promotions. It would have probably taken me another 20 years to become Speaker, if at all."

"Yes," Wilcox said, "I had a meeting at the DNC last week where that was rubbed in my face. I was told my primary qualification was not dying."

"I heard a somewhat similar tune over at the RNC," Ogden said.

"Yeah, I heard Leems and Beacham have a hot line of sorts."

"To be honest," Barone admitted. "I wouldn't mind this legislation being passed. I just don't want to be the one to pass it. We'll all be targets within our own parties."

"The President's put his ass on the line," Ogden said. "I feel cowardly not to do likewise."

"Anyone who votes against it will be in a weakened position, come the midterms. That may be less of a problem for you two, but it's a killer for us in the House with our two-year election cycle."

"We could delay," Wilcox suggested.

"No," Ogden said. "Grant has already put the presidency in play. The markets dropped again after Grant announced he might resign. This uncertainty also presents problems in foreign relations. How can we negotiate with allies or enemies when no one knows which man will be president?"

"I like him personally," Barone said, "but you're right. The uncertainty has to be resolved, one way or another."

"So we vote for his bill," Wilcox asked, "then respectfully show him the door?"

"If he's willing to throw his presidency away so easily," Barone said "then maybe he doesn't deserve the job."

"Giving Grant the boot will not be popular with the public," Ogden added.

"I've spoken with a great many House members," Barone said. "They also like Grant. Hell, the President has met with almost all of them personally."

"We can fashion the resolution," Ogden explained, "to read something like this: *David Grant legitimately succeeded to the presidency in a crisis. However, given the unusual nature of his succession, the Congress prefers that the President step down in favor of the confirmed Vice President.* No vitriol. No insult. We can argue that as an unelected president, he would never carry the credibility of an elected one."

"Collier wasn't elected either," Barone countered.

"But at least he was confirmed by the Senate, just like Gerald Ford," Ogden said. "We thank him as a caretaker president, then vote him some nice, fat post-presidential benefits."

"You realize this is all bullshit." Wilcox said. "We could just as easily confirm him with a resolution. The people have already accepted him."

"Yes, but that wouldn't get the parties off our backs." Ogden said. "Grant himself has given us this out."

ෆ ෆ ය ಚ

"Good afternoon," Bob Summers announced in an unusual midday broadcast. "The House of Representatives passed the Democracy Restoration Act yesterday afternoon. And a few minutes ago, the Senate has just passed their version. This is historic legislation. The moment it was passed, a coalition of lobbying groups immediately announced they will fight this law in court. However, legal and political analysts believe such a challenge will be unlikely to succeed, especially as seven of the justices in the Supreme Court were appointed by President Grant. With us again is Dylan Reese. Dylan, now comes the next vote, which will reveal if President Grant will pay the price of this victory."

"You're exactly right, Bob," Reese said. "We can't underestimate the importance of the Democracy Restoration Act. However, it is emotionally overshadowed by the resolution to ask the President to step down. The House version passed last night by the slimmest of margins. Now, the Senate will shortly take up the vote on their version, which is identical to the House bill. This means no conference committee reconciliation will be needed should the Senate pass it."

"Of course," Summers added, "this is a non-binding resolution. The President is not legally required to resign."

"True, it would be difficult for him not to, given his public promise to do so, if the resolution is passed. But my sources say the Senate will pass the resolution. Then, the Senate and House leaders will come to the White House this afternoon, where President Grant will sign the Democracy Restoration Act into law. He'll give a short speech and then resign, after which Zeke Collier will immediately be sworn in."

ෆ ෆ ය ಚ

"The House vote was pretty close last night." Ellen said. "I've been making some calls. I think we can swing a couple of senators."

"No, let the Congress exert its will. I just won the most important vote of my presidency."

"You mean the only vote of your presidency," Ellen responded, unable to hide her disapproval.

"True. But this afternoon, I will sign the Democracy Restoration Act into law. That makes it a great day."

447

"Congress asks for your resignation, and it's a great day. I guess you don't really want to be president."

"Ellen, it's not that I don't want to be president. I just didn't earn it. But if I can restore faith in the government, that's a legacy I can relish."

"We could have done great things."

"We have." David said, taking Ellen's hands in his. "And you will continue to do great things. Zeke Collier is going to need your help. By the way, where is Zeke anyway?"

"The Secret Service reported he left the residence at the Naval Observatory about an hour ago."

"Really?" David looked at his watch. "Would you go and find him?"

Ellen left as Sara appeared.

"Hey, you." Sara said, "How are you doing?"

"Great. The DRA just passed the Senate vote."

"I don't mean the legislation. I mean my husband. You're about to lose your job."

"Dear, I'm an emotion-repressing machine, in other words, a man. We're not in touch with our feelings."

Sara caressed his cheek.

"You know, Grant, you're full of it."

David took her hand in his and kissed her palm.

"Congress is giving me something magnificent. Yes, it's going to cost me something that was never mine to begin with. Yes, I'll probably be moody for a few days. But this bill is worth it."

They hugged for a long time. Finally, David pulled away. "There's something I have to do."

"What? Launch some nukes while you still have the chance?" she joked.

"Hmm, that's an idea," David chuckled. "No, I have to write a letter."

"To whom?"

"Zeke Collier."

"Can't you just talk to him? You'll see him in a little while."

"It's a tradition."

"Then, I'll leave you to it."

"No, stay."

"Okay." She sat down on the sofa and watched her husband sit down behind the Resolute Desk. She wished she had a camera at that moment.

David pulled out a pen and a sheet of White House stationary and began to write:

Dear President Collier,

In this letter, it is traditional to give advice to the incoming President, but given the short tenure of my own presidency, I feel woefully inadequate. I would never dare to advise you on courage, integrity or perseverance. You have all these qualities.

Ellen burst in before David could completely gather his thoughts for the next paragraph.

"We found Collier," she said. "He's just outside the Senate Chamber."

"Has the Senate finished voting on the resolution?"

"No, they haven't even started, and apparently Collier is demanding to speak."

"What?"

୫୦ ୫୦ ୦୫ ୦୫

"Mr. Vice President," Grace Wilcox said, "this is highly irregular."

"Senator," Collier said, "according to the Constitution, in addition to being first in the line of succession, I am also President of the Senate."

"So you can break a tie vote. No vice president has actually presided since John Adams."

"That's because Thomas Jefferson was a slacker."

"Sir," Wilcox insisted, "I know how the Senate will vote. There will be no tie to break. I don't think it would be good for your presidency to have your image associated with this vote."

"Let me worry about my image," the old general said. Collier walked through the door, onto the Floor and toward the presiding officer's desk. All the senators were stunned by his presence. Joe Dreeves, the senator presiding over this session—the only senator who wanted to preside over this particular vote—looked at Collier, dumbfounded.

"Senator, you're relieved," Collier said.

Dreeves looked to Wilcox, who nodded for him to vacate the desk.

"Clerk of the Senate," Collier ordered, "call for a quorum."

She did so. The senators not already there arrived quickly from the nearby cloakrooms. Collier picked up the gavel and banged it a few times.

"Ladies and gentlemen of the Senate, you have just passed vital and monumental legislation." Collier announced. "I congratulate you on your courage. You should be very proud. I know President Grant could not be happier."

"As I look at the schedule, I see you will next vote on a resolution to ask for the President's resignation."

"In his speech, the President spoke of patriotism. He was right. A true patriot is someone who risks and sacrifices. He has risked his personal honor for the greater good. He is willing to sacrifice the highest office in the land and endure the personal humiliation of resigning for us."

"I will not serve with any pleasure, knowing a better man was needlessly sacrificed. David Grant is the President we have all yearned for, an honest man and a courageous statesman. He is willing to fall on his sword for us! You know what is right. Confirm he is the President, not the one we deserve, but the one we need." Collier looked down with a pained expression on his face. He was barely able to speak. "I hereby call for the vote on Senate Resolution 39."

The clerk looked to Wilcox. The Senator nodded.

"Voting on Senate Resolution 39 will be open for thirty minutes," the clerk announced.

૬૦ ૬૦ ૭૨ ૭૩

David watched this on C-SPAN in the Press Office. He and Sara stood with Ellen, Fred, and others.

"Why would he do such a thing?" David whispered.

"Because he's like you," Sara said. "He loves his country more than the presidency."

They watched the vote count on the screen. The tension was excruciating. No one was voting. Finally, after several minutes, the first vote tallied. It was a "yea" vote for the resolution.

"A 'yea' means they want David to stay?" Sara asked.

"No," Ellen said, "Yea means they want him to resign,"

"Oh."

The next vote, a minute later, was a nay. Several more minutes passed.

"What are they waiting for?" Dana Seagram asked.

"They're reconsidering," Fred said. "Collier got to them."

Additional nay votes started to appear. Within another ten minutes the outcome was clear. David turned to his wife.

"I'm sorry, Sara. I thought we'd be going home."

"I'm not. Those senators aren't as stupid as you thought. They confirmed what I've always known: David Grant is a man of honor and integrity. I guess deep down that's something they'd like to see more of."

Epilogue

Upon hearing of the result of the Senate vote, Speaker Barone immediately called an emergency session of the House of Representatives to vote on a new resolution affirming David's presidency. That afternoon, David signed the Democracy Restoration Act into law. A broad coalition of lobbyists who would ordinarily be opposed to one another immediately united and challenged the law in court. However, the Supreme Court ruled the Democracy Restoration Act was constitutional, reversing the Court on the previous *Citizens United* decision.

Under the supervision of Attorney General Kevin O'Hara, Jack Kripke and many of his associates were tried on numerous felonies. Tyler Benson proved to be a reliable prosecution witness. In an effort to reduce his sentence, Kripke testified against others, including Carl Stavros and Ellis Cornwall.

Meanwhile, Corbin Beaumont became the first Wall Street CEO successfully convicted under the Sarbanes Oxley Act. His wife, "gun-smoking hot" Amanda divorced him, moved back to Texas, and eventually appeared in a short-lived reality TV series.

David Grant completed Gregory Farnum's term, facing many more challenges. He was successful with some, less so with others.

David did run for President in the next presidential election with the full support of the First Lady. However, Harris Carver and Grace Wilcox had been correct in saying David could not win. However, Carver would never know how right he was. He committed suicide several months after being released from Bethesda Naval Hospital.

His presidential run was the first election David had failed to win. The combined forces of Democratic and Republican parties were too much for the nascent United Centrist Party. Although David lost, the election was not without extraordinary consequence. Being a significant three-way race, the election was once again thrown into the House of Representatives. Having two presidential elections in a row fail to be decided by the electorate triggered the demand for a new constitutional amendment to abolish the Electoral College.

Upon completing the Oath of Office on Inauguration Day, David's successor publicly thanked him for his service to the country in its time of need.

In that same election cycle, Joe Dreeves lost his Senate seat. The people of Maine decided wholeheartedly to decline his further services. Dreeves returned to late night television, although with the demise of the Liberty network, his remaining media career was short. The Dreevism, "We could cut cards for it," became an Internet meme and general comment, suggesting a lack of seriousness. His last public appearance was in the same reality show that co-starred Amanda Beaumont.

Former Winton College President, Charles Danzig was convicted of financial malfeasance for the purpose of paving the way for a takeover by Parnell Education Corporation. The college was able to begin its financial recovery by selling land at the edge of its property for the establishment of the David M. Grant Presidential Library. As expected, the library was designed by Gunther & Cartwright's Senior Architect, Sara Grant. Although not the largest presidential library, it did win several architectural awards.

Under the supervision of its director, Ellen Langford, the library thrived. David established the Annual Conference for Trans-Partisan Government. The library became a robust center for those wishing to foster a better and more ethical government. It also served as a Mecca for Centrist candidates. A frequent guest speaker at the library was the head of the Political Science department at Winton College, Professor Fred Arkin.

In the coming years, the total number of United Centrist Party members elected to Congress slowly increased, eventually depriving any party a majority in the House of Representatives. During this period Congress yielded some of the most streamlined budgets in modern history.

Looking back on the Grant Presidency, many historians regarded it as a bizarre fluke of history. Others claimed, given the level of corruption and public distress that had developed, it or something even more radical was inevitable. Academics would continue this debate for decades.

Near the end of his life, when asked of his proudest moment, David Grant never cited a single day in political office. Instead, he recalled the day almost 44 years after his own painful swearing-in, when he attended the inauguration of the first duly elected Centrist president.

By then, he walked with a cane. His hair had turned white. The incoming president had asked David to provide the Bible for the ceremony, specifically the one bequeathed to him by the late Justice Catherine Sisk. David's normally clear and sharp eyes became understandably misty as the incoming president placed her hand on the old Bible.

"I, Wendy Grant Austin, do solemnly swear that I will faithfully execute the Office of President of the United States, and will to the best of my ability, preserve, protect and defend the Constitution of the United States."

ABOUT THE AUTHOR

J.R. Bale has always tried to explore the themes in his stories from an unusual perspective, whether it was politics in *Phoenix in the Middle of the Road* or consciousness in *Cognition Chronicles*. In his pursuit of diverse perspectives, he has traveled to over a dozen countries across four continents. He even applied to NASA's space program. When not writing books, he is a marketing consultant and college professor.

J.R. is also the founder of Page Bound Success, a cooperative marketing group for authors. You can learn more about him at www.jrbale.com.

A NOTE FROM THE AUTHOR

I hope you enjoyed this book. If so, I ask a small favor, not simply for me, but for all authors. If you appreciate a book, any book, please write an online review. The best place for your comment is Amazon, the largest bookseller in the world. Another important site is goodreads.com. It doesn't need to be extravagant. Just let people know you liked the book.

In a world of marketing algorithms, a personal endorsement carries a lot of weight. It's a way of thanking and encouraging authors. It is a random act of kindness, and the world needs more of those.